BETWEEN
THE
SHADOW
AND THE
FLAME

GEOFFREY LEE HODGE

BETWEEN THE SHADOW AND THE FLAME
A Penumbra Invictus book

First Printing: March, 2012

Copyright © 2012 by Geoffrey Lee Hodge

Library of Congress Control Number: 2012907192

ISBN-13: 978-0985180201
ISBN-10: 098518020X

PENUMBRA
INVICTUS

PART I

Fire and Shadows
The First Questions

CHAPTER ONE

WAKING IN DARKNESS

In the beginning there was nothing. Not even darkness. As awareness grew, the nothingness slowly gave way to sensation. It was sensation without context—darkness and cold, but relative to nothing. And fear—a driving primordial fear. Feet pounded mechanically, unconsciously, in a steady rhythm against a firmament below, over and over, until suddenly it was not there. Reeling, tumbling, scrambling up, running on. There was no object of fear, no thought—only the raw emotion and a will to flee. Out of the darkness shapes took form, contrasted against a faint backdrop of light. Tall strips of blackness materialized and raced past, or loomed ahead to be followed by a dull pain and a sudden, jolting change of direction.

The black columns gradually resolved into objects that could be avoided—trees, firmly rooted in the earth. A dim light filtered through them from above, illuminating a rolling forest floor that dropped away periodically into small depressions. The feet now raced along over obstacles and between trees. Hands thrust out to protect against the slashing branches, head ducking and weaving behind them.

Time passed and eventually fear was joined by a new sensation. It started as a curious distraction but grew steadily stronger until it became a burning and hammering from within that filled all perception. Lungs gasped for air, and the rhythm of the feet slowed and stopped as the urge for flight was finally consumed by this internal fire. He became aware of his body, the pulsing of his heart in his chest, the cold air filling his lungs with each gulping breath, and now, consciously, the chill of fear that crept along his spine. As he recovered his breath and the fear subsided, pain took over. He could feel it everywhere. His hands and knees were torn, his ankle throbbed, his face burned. He put his hands to his face and his fingertips ran across welts and scratches sticky with blood. One shoulder was wracked with what should have been incredible pain, but inexplicably, although he was aware of all these injuries, they did not cause him to suffer. It was as if he were in a dream, or just waking, his nerves still numbed from slumber.

Panting, he sank to his knees and strained his eyes into the darkness. The ground was covered with an intricate web of fallen needles, and he examined them with wonder. They lay beneath him, layer upon layer, covering the ground and rolling away from him in all directions like a vast ocean. Picking up a single thin needle, he examined it briefly before it snapped between his trembling fingers. He watched the pieces fall back to earth to rejoin the multitude. How many where there? Could such a number even be comprehended? He scanned again along the sea of needles until his eyes, caught by the roots of a tree, were drawn upwards along the length of its massive trunk to the branches high above him. Through distant gaps in the canopy, dim shafts of light filtered down from a shrouded moon. His warm breath burst out into the night air in gusts of mist, swirling in the moonlight. Transfixed, he watched as the coils of vapor twisted away from him and faded into nothingness. He was filled with a sense of awe at the complexity of their dance, the vastness of the wilderness, the infinity of the darkness. He did not know where he was or how he came to be there. He was lost, adrift on this narrow raft of moonlight in the darkness, small and alone.

For some time he remained on his knees, watching his breath play out into the night, struggling to remember. Why was he here? What was he running from? What happened before? Nothing. There was no before. He was tired, exhausted. Exhaustion must have dulled the pain, he realized. Dulled his memory. Give it time. Rest. Try again later.

A shiver of fear returned to him. No! He pulled himself to his feet. Rest now and you may never get back up, he told himself. Got to keep moving. He dragged himself up and willed himself to move forward, one foot and then the other until they fell back into their own rhythm, plodding once again unconsciously against the earth. With his body thus set in motion, he returned to the questions. Vague memories and impressions swirled about, just out of reach, mixed with dreamlike images of shapes looming out of the darkness. What was real? Why was he here? No answer came.

As he wound his way between trees and under branches, he kept looking back over his shoulder. He recalled nothing, and yet somehow knew that everything was wrong. Something had been chasing him. He was certain that this was true although it was a feeling more than a memory. How long ago? How far away? Time and space had no meaning in this place. It was impossible to tell. His pace quickened and his senses sharpened. He became aware of the smallest noises—a cracking sound off in the distance, rustling in the branches above him. Shadows seemed to keep pace with him, flitting between the trees, always on the edge of his vision but never directly seen. A new worry scratched around the edges of his mind, but he shut it out and pushed himself into a jog as if to outrun it. Unrelenting, it took physical form in his gut, churning there for a while before spreading on a wave of nausea to his chest, where it seemed to squeeze the air from his lungs. Then it burst as a fully formed thought into his head. The forest was haunted. He could feel it, ancient and evil, watching him through a thousand hidden eyes. The logical part of his mind told him that this was just irrational paranoia— nothing more than fear of the dark—but this knowledge only helped a little. He could not shake the lingering apprehension.

It was then that he first thought that it might truly all be a dream. He willed himself to wake. In his thoughts he shouted a desperate appeal to some higher consciousness to take notice and save him from this nightmare. There was no answer. Everything seemed so absurd, yet too real to dismiss. He could not picture what it would be like to awaken, but the possibility that he might be saved, that the nightmare might end, gave him some small comfort. Nonetheless, he worried that it would be dangerous to rest and pressed on, realizing that movement, in itself, was not enough. He needed a plan. Pushing his anxiety aside, he forced himself to clear his mind and think. What were the facts? He was lost. He needed to know where to go. Again his mind groped unsuccessfully for memories. He fought back a wave of frustration and anger. The past was a blind alley. He would need to look for his solutions in the physical world. A vantage point was what he needed. Some place where he could look out and get his bearings.

With a purpose now established, his spirits lifted. He hoped that whatever pursued him was long behind, but realized with a liberating fatalism, that in his current condition he could do little more than just keep moving anyway. And so he walked, swinging his head from side to side, amused by the odd sensation it produced. When his vision shifted from right to left, the movement of his head seemed to lag slightly behind it, out of phase.

Whenever there was a choice he followed the path that took him higher. Eventually the terrain began to slope steeply upwards, in places so steep that he could only continue by using his hands to pull himself along. His body was tired beyond all sensation, and now the maybe-dream worked in his favor. He continued to climb, knowing that he was pushing his body farther than it could go, doing what could not be done. When his feet slipped he used the branches to haul himself upward, sometimes moving quickly, sometimes struggling to make any progress at all, but always moving. Gradually the earth yielded to rock, the trees thinned, and finally the slope tapered off enough that he was able to stand firmly on his two feet again and walk to the summit.

He allowed himself a short rest to catch his breath, braced against a small pine tree, before looking out from his hard-earned vantage point. Were it not for their trembling, he would not have been able to feel his legs at all, yet he still did not dare to sit down to rest for fear that he would never get back up. When the trembling subsided, and the throbbing returned to his ankle, he located a large opening in the tree line and shambled toward it. Looking back for the first time over the distance he had climbed, he saw the tops of dark trees dropping sharply away into a valley far below. In the distance he thought he could make out the pale outline of a taller peak. The moon was high overhead, identifiable only as a luminous patch in the otherwise dark gray of the night sky. It was the only light.

Undaunted, he turned and navigated through the branches and toppled trees until he came to the other side of the summit. Again he looked out beyond the cover of the trees. On this side the mountain dropped away more gradually until it disappeared into shadows far below. His eyes scanned the darkness. It was unbroken except for what little moonlight escaped the cloud cover. Panic gripped him once again. He had hoped to see a light somewhere—a city in the distance, a car moving along a highway, a house, a campfire, anything. Now from the summit of this mountain he could see all around him and there was nothing but the moon and the vast darkness.

He stood for a while, unable to think, staring into the black of night. It stretched out in all directions as far as he could see, broken only by the tops of trees or distant peaks barely discernable in the scant moonlight. It was eerie, he thought. Unnatural. The irony of this idea caught him by surprise and he broke into a momentary fit of silent, hysterical laughter. Unnatural? It was perfectly natural. This absolute darkness was a natural state. What he had hoped to see—even expected to see—was unnatural. He was looking for artificial light that signaled humanity somewhere in the natural darkness. There was none to be seen.

For a time he wrestled with himself. He had achieved his goal and reached a vantage point, but it had not shown him where to go. He considered sitting down or even lying down and sleeping. Perhaps upon falling asleep the dream would end and he would wake up in a better place, he thought, but without much conviction. Perhaps he would wake up still on the mountaintop but refreshed, able to remember, able to think of something. Perhaps he would not wake up at all. The last possibility bothered him less than it should have.

Unsure of what drove him, he launched himself into motion, scrambling down from the summit in a new direction. The decision was made. Now the mountain worked in his favor and he found himself straining to hold back gravity, grabbing at handholds to slow his descent and keep his feet beneath him. As he clambered down the slope, pulling himself over the fallen tree trunks and branches that attempted to block his way, the uneasy feeling returned to him. There *was* something wrong with the forest. As with his memory, it was maddeningly just out of reach, but this time he did not dismiss it or surrender his thoughts to superstition. He continued to sift through his impressions as he picked his way down the mountainside, and at last touched upon something.

The forest was empty. There was no one single thing that disturbed him, but instead the absence of many things. Save for the rattling of branches in the wind, there was no noise. No owls, no small animals scurrying away in the darkness, no planes overhead. This in itself would not have seemed odd, but the trees too seemed empty. The leaves had fallen, and though that should not have seemed significant, it did. Then he realized that even the evergreens seemed bare. He did not know what this meant, but a shiver returned to his spine, no longer attributable to superstition.

Doggedly he continued onward until the slope faded into a hillside and the sky began to lighten. It was very faint at first—almost imperceptible—not so much light as a slight fading in the intensity of the darkness. A great feeling of relief swept through him and he felt, however irrational, as though the light of day would show him the things he had failed to find in the darkness, bringing answers to all his questions.

It was the first true light of morning when he emerged from the woods.

At the top of a tall slope, too steep to support the growth of anything but brush and the occasional scrub pine, he stood and surveyed the area below. In the pale morning light he could see the small shapes of cars scattered along a country highway. His eyes quickly traced the road across rolling hills to the horizon, but were drawn back almost instantly to the cars strung out along the road.

None of them were moving.

CHAPTER TWO

GOLDEN AFTERNOON

Not a single cloud marred the perfect cobalt sky. Sophia admired it absently, wishing she were elsewhere. The party was wonderful for people who liked such things. It was a golden afternoon on the last weekend of summer and the house, a small mansion really, was a beautiful structure of faux-stone built in a Greek revival style and reflecting the sunlight in whitewashed glory. A large patio ran the width of the house along the back, and a lawn set with small walking gardens sloped gently down to a pool ringed with Doric columns, where a strip of carefully manicured grass guarded the deck of the pool from an encroaching meadow that surrounded the house in all directions. In the distance a dark line of forest separated the yellow expanse of waist high grass and scrub from the blue expanse of sky. On the patio, servers moved among the knots of people offering drinks and hors d'oeuvres from silver serving trays. Sophia observed them from a distance, replaying the psychoanalysis she had performed on herself many times before.

Growing up in an age of political correctness, none of Sophia's schoolmates had given her any trouble specifically because she was Chinese, but that fact had been catalogued subconsciously among a list of features that served to separate her from her peers. In those days she was short and chunky, her moon face covered with acne and hidden behind glasses with lenses the size of tea saucers, her hair in ridiculous pigtails. Her physical appearance might have been sufficient to provoke the merciless teasing she received, but her sins had been compounded by her academic performance, sealing her fate. Not only was Sophia exceptionally bright, but she was also so studious that any time she failed to raise her hand to answer a question it caused a pandemic of whispering to ripple through the classroom. Predictably the social elite made her the butt of their jokes. The few students who did not jump on this bandwagon avoided her for fear that they would make targets of themselves by mere association, so Sophia spent her formative years sitting alone at lunch and walking home by herself, more comfortable with her thoughts than with other people.

Aware that she had been pigeonholed as the hard working Asian, she did nothing to change public opinion. If anything, she played into the stereotype. Even at this early age she was wise enough to realize that the problem did not lie with her. Instead she determined that the strange behavior of her classmates was some quirk of human nature, and she became increasingly interested in understanding why people acted the way they did. She enjoyed observing them, from a distance.

In college and the years following, a slow transformation had taken place. Whether it was a new lifestyle or a late metabolic change, her acne cleared and her excess weight gradually melted away. Now, just past her third decade of life, Sophia was a successful professional in an image-conscious field and actively watched her figure. Over time her glasses shrank and then, after laser surgery a few years ago, disappeared altogether. Although she would never be a supermodel, Sophia was attractive in a natural way that seemed as comfortable in workday business suits as it was in the old tee shirts and blue jeans of the weekend. She still preferred to be alone, although she could be very good with people when she needed to be. As the result of many years of clinical observation, she understood people much better than most of her colleagues did, a fact which had helped her to rise very quickly in the ad agency where she worked. Now, after years of studying humans, they had accepted her as one of their own and she could walk among them, like Jane Goodall among her chimps. Occasionally she even identified with them.

But not today.

Having had her fill of both food and people earlier in the afternoon, Sophia had made her way down to the pool where she stood apart from the crowd, next to a small table, using the platter of fruit it held as an alibi. She had just broken off a cluster of grapes when she noticed one of the guests heading down the slope toward the pool. In her antisocial frame of mind, she hoped that he would head toward one of the other grazing stations, but that was not the case. Instead he walked directly toward her and made some pretense of examining the pile of fruit as he greeted her.

She gave him a thin smile and a nod of acknowledgement in return.

"Beautiful day, isn't it?"

"Uh-huh." Sophia sighed inwardly. Clearly she was not going to escape a conversation.

"You've been standing over here for a while," he said. "Is anything wrong?"

"No."

She was trying to strike a delicate balance between being polite and giving the man the signal that she was not in the mood for chatting, but the answer came out a little more terse than she had intended. "Thanks, though," she added hastily. "I guess I'm just all talked out."

He failed to take the hint.

"I know what you mean. It's tough making conversation with a bunch of people you don't know," he replied, studying her face. "Are you sure there's nothing wrong?"

Sophia briefly debated which of several possible responses to give him. There was no one else within earshot and he was not a coworker or a client, so she decided to take his question at face value and give him an uncensored answer.

"It's just that everyone's having the same conversations over and over again, and they're all depressing," she told him. "It's either the epidemic in India and China spreading to Europe and how soon will it show up here, or the war and whether or not we should get involved or whether we'll get dragged into it anyway, and I know that they're important topics, but I've had the same conversation every day when I come in to work, and when I go to lunch, and with just about everybody at this party. Nobody knows anything new. Nobody has anything useful to say. Just the same old bad news, opinions and speculation rehashed again and again. And the few people that aren't talking about the depressing news stories are talking about trivial things like sports or celebrity gossip."

The man regarded her with an expression somewhere between surprise and amusement, and there was an awkward silence. Then they both spoke at once.

"I thought you were all talked out."

"Well, that was therapeutic," she said at almost the same time.

"Tell you what," the man said, "I'll make you a deal. If you'll indulge me with a little small talk for a minute or two we can talk about whatever you like afterwards."

She had to give him credit for his effort. He watched her expectantly with a smile that suggested a genuine love of life—the kind of expression that was contagious. Sophia smiled in spite of herself. He was handsome, with Mediterranean features and dark soulful eyes. Sophia snuck a quick glance at his ring finger, which was unadorned. She guessed him to be about ten years her elder. He had an athletic build and his broad moustache and goatee, both peppered with gray, were framed by black hair that cascaded almost to his shoulders in loose waves, conjuring to Sophia's mind an image of the Three Musketeers. She pictured him in a cape and a wide-brimmed hat with an ostrich plume and nearly laughed aloud.

"Okay, I accept."

"Great. Let me start by introducing myself," he said, extending his hand. "I'm Newman Theophiles. I'm a friend of Nico. Well, actually, my friend works with Nico and he dragged me along in case there wasn't anyone else here he knew. I haven't seen him since we walked through the door."

"Nice to meet you, Newman. Sophia Xiao," she replied, shaking his hand. "Nico's wife owns the ad agency where I work."

"Really? Are you a graphic artist?"

"No, I'm a client rep. Sort of a project manager and a liaison between the project team and the client."

"That sounds like an interesting job. How did you get into it?"

Sophia thought he sounded a little overly enthusiastic and suspected that he would have been happier if she were an artist, but her mood had shifted sufficiently that she was flattered rather than annoyed by his effort.

"I was always pretty good at telling what the clients wanted. I got a little more authority with each big project and basically just worked my way up. I've been there almost twelve years."

"Twelve years?" Newman had guessed her to be no more than thirty and was clearly surprised.

"Yeah, I started there right out of college. I majored in philosophy, so I suppose I was lucky to find a job at all," she replied. "It's a great group of people and most days I actually enjoy my job. It is a bit ironic though. I went to school on a quest to find the truth and now I just create it."

"That's very…um… philosophical," Newman remarked, pausing briefly to laugh at his own joke. "I don't know that much about philosophy. I remember reading some Socrates in school and learning that he was the first philosopher, but that's about it."

"Socrates was pretty important, but he certainly wasn't the first philosopher."

"Really?"

"Yes, really." Sophia confirmed. "The first questions in philosophy were much simpler than the ones Socrates tried to address. Many people consider Thales to be the first philosopher, because he was concerned with what made up the world around him. He came to the conclusion that everything was reducible to a single element, which is a pretty amazing conclusion for somebody in those days if you think about it."

"What did he think it was?"

"Water."

"Water? Why water?" asked Newman.

"It's not that far off the mark," Sophia replied. "Water's essential for life. It covers most of our planet, and Thales could have seen it as a solid, liquid and gas, which accounts for all the states of matter. But then Heraclitus staked out the opposite side and raised one of the grandest debates in the history of philosophy."

Sophia stopped herself from continuing, but Newman looked genuinely interested.

"Opposite side?" he repeated. "What was the first side?"

"Well, in trying to find the basic element that makes up everything, Thales was assuming that there was some immutable basic element. Heraclitus argued that the nature of reality is contradiction and change. He raised the question of whether it's meaningful to talk about anything in concrete terms. First, he pointed out that opposites are often united. The path up the mountain is the same as the path down the mountain, and the young Heraclitus is the same person as the old Heraclitus, even though they're obviously different. Contradictions are inherent and everything is in flux. He said, 'You can't step into the same river twice.' That's probably his most famous saying."

"Sure you can," Newman insisted.

"In a way, you really can't," said Sophia, "because the river is constantly changing. It won't be the same river the next time you put your foot into it. Some of the old water will have flowed out to the sea. Some new water will have flowed in from the mountains. The current will have carried old things away and carried new things to you. It's a good analogy for time because everything changes over time. How can there be an absolute truth when everything is constantly in flux?"

Newman did not seem impressed by this argument.

"Change is just a property of real things," he said, "but that doesn't make the things themselves any less real. And you *can* actually put your foot in the same river twice. The river has the same banks and starts and ends in the same place. If you pull your foot out and put it back the water will still be there and the water will still be wet. It can be distinguished from other rivers in other places by its location, and they can be compared to each other. How could you even talk about rivers if there wasn't some absolute reality of what a river is?"

Sophia smiled. Newman's response was more passionate than she had expected and she could tell that he was genuinely engaged in thinking about these ideas. She decided to challenge him further.

"It's all a matter of perspective and perception really," she said. "If you're far enough away it may not seem like the river's changing, but if you get close enough that you can see the current it will. And that's true of anything. If you look closely enough you'll always find change."

"But even when things change is there any question that they're real? You can't say that something isn't real just because it changes. Either it exists or it doesn't."

"True, but it's not quite as easy as that."

Sophia thought for a moment, and then picked an apple from a platter of fruit on the table beside her.

"What's this?" she asked, holding it up.

"An apple."

Sophia handed the apple to Newman.

"Take a bite out of it," she instructed.

Newman gave her a puzzled look for a moment, but took a bite.

"Now what is it?" she asked.

"An apple with a bite taken out of it?" he replied through a mouthful of apple.

"But is it an apple?"

"Yes, of course."

"And if you take another bite, will it still be an apple?"

"Yes," said Newman, a bit more hesitantly.

"What if you keep taking bites out of it until there's nothing left but the core? Would you still call it an apple?

"I'd call it an apple core."

"But would you call it an *apple*?" As Newman considered this, Sophia continued, "If you came into the house and saw it sitting on the table, would you call it an apple?"

"No," Newman conceded. "I'd call it an apple core, but I wouldn't call it an apple."

"Right, so at what point did it stop being an apple? If you want to define the fundamental nature of apples, how can you do that when you can't even determine what is an apple and what's not?"

"Isn't that just a language problem? The Inuits supposedly have something like thirty different words for snow. If we cared enough about half-eaten apples, we could have thirty words to describe apples with more and more bites taken out of them."

"True, language is part of the problem," Sophia conceded, "but you have to realize that you have the benefit of more than two thousand years of assimilated knowledge that Heraclitus didn't have, and even at that it's not such a simple question."

"Sorry, I didn't mean to jump ahead," Newman said with a laugh. "How did the ancient Greeks respond to Heraclitus?"

"Are you sure I'm not boring you? I love this stuff and I'll talk your ear off if you give me half a chance."

No, it's very interesting. Honestly. Much better than sports or celebrity gossip."

Newman cast a meaningful glance over his shoulder as he said this and Sophia chuckled.

"Okay, well, in arguing that everything is change, what Heraclitus really did was issue a challenge that if anyone wanted to talk about the fundamental nature of reality, they'd have to account for change. Parmenides countered the idea that everything is change and nothing is fundamental in an interesting way, along the same lines of reasoning you were using. He said, 'That which it is possible to think is identical with that which can be,' and he argued that it doesn't make sense to think that something comes from nothing, or that something can become nothing, so therefore the universe must be eternal. Although parts of the universe may shift around, Parmenides pictured it as one eternal, interconnected whole and thought that change was an illusion of the senses."

"Right," said Newman, his voice slightly triumphant. "Like the principle from physics that matter is neither created nor destroyed."

"Yes, exactly, which means there must be something permanent and fundamental. And if you think that Parmenides anticipated modern physics consider that Leucippus and Democritus took his theory one step further and proposed that everything is made up of fundamental particles which are neither created nor destroyed, and which are too small to be seen and too small to be broken down any further. They said all that exists are space and these basic particles—nothing else. These particles come together in different patterns to form the variety of physical things that we observe in the world. Care to guess what they called their particles?"

"They sound like atoms."

"Right again. The word *atom*, along with the general concept, goes back to the ancient Greek philosophers. See, I thought you said you didn't know anything about pre-Socratic philosophy."

"So if these philosophers were discussing important topics like the nature of change and reality and they even anticipated modern physics, why is Socrates so much more famous?"

"It's probably due to several different things," Sophia said. "It's a long story."

"I'm not going anywhere," Newman replied, and for emphasis he straddled the stone bench nearby and sat down with his back up against a column.

Sophia laughed. "Are you just humoring me? I seem to be doing most of the talking here."

"No, I'm really interested. Don't worry, I'll take my turn, but I am dying to know why Socrates is so much more famous. Besides, you're a good storyteller."

"If you say so," Sophia replied, trying to stifle the smile that his blatant flattery threatened to bring out. "I suppose the biggest reason Socrates is so famous is Plato. Plato was his student and recorded the conversations Socrates had with other philosophers of the day. In fact, as far as we know Socrates didn't ever record any of his own ideas. He was more concerned with demonstrating the lack of wisdom of other philosophers. He sought out people who thought themselves to be wise and engaged them in debate. His approach to these debates is another reason for his fame. He used a dialectic style that has become known as the Socratic Method. He'd typically engage his opponents in conversation by asking a few harmless questions on the pretext that he wanted to learn from their wisdom. Then he'd ask an important question like, 'What is Justice?' or 'Can Virtue be taught?' that would force his opponent to commit to a specific answer. For the remainder of the discussion, Socrates would keep asking leading questions until his opponent was either forced to contradict his original premise or at least substantially redefine it. Socrates didn't really offer his own answers to these questions, and if anyone asked him for his theories he liked to say that he was only wise enough to know that he didn't know anything. Of course, the last big reason Socrates is so well remembered is his dramatic death."

"Wasn't he forced to drink poison hemlock?" Newman recalled.

"Yes. He was sentenced to death at least. But actually he could easily have escaped into exile, and when the sentence was handed down, that's probably what most people expected him to do, even those who sentenced him. It was his belief in the law and his principles that kept him in Athens, and he willingly chose to drink the hemlock. The fact that he chose to die rather than act against his principles ensured that he'd be remembered throughout the ages."

"But why was he sentenced to death in the first place?" asked Newman.

"Socrates lived in Athens at a time when the sophists were the dominant school of philosophy. Protagoras was one of the best known and eldest members of this school which held that it wasn't possible to find a universal truth. It was Protagoras who said, 'Man is the measure of all things,' by which he meant that everything is relative. The sophists were teachers to the Athens elite, and since they didn't believe in anything absolute, they taught their students rhetoric and emphasized skills necessary to compete and persuade and be successful in the world. Socrates tried to demonstrate that things like Truth, Justice and Virtue were universals that transcended any examples that the sophists could give and maintained that the fact that they couldn't be fully described or attained didn't mean that they were relative. In doing this he made many of the powerful citizens of Athens look bad, and taught the young men of the city to question things. It was believed that he was corrupting the youth, and he was eventually charged with not believing in the gods of the city. These were probably just trumped-up charges made because he had angered too many influential people. Socrates likened his role in Athenian society to that of a gadfly stinging a horse. Eventually the gadfly got swatted."

Newman nodded and fidgeted with the gold chain around his neck. "That's a familiar story, isn't it?"

"Yes, I suppose so." Sophia replied, eyeing the chain. The end was tucked inside his shirt, but she had no doubt that it held a crucifix.

CHAPTER THREE

THE STILL OF THE MORNING

The first rays of morning light broke over the horizon and a young man stood at the top of a steep hill. Bits of leaves and bark peppered his spiky blond hair. His shirt and pants were torn and caked with dirt and the left shoulder and breast of his light jacket were stained dark with blood. The young man noticed none of this. His eyes were fixed on the highway below him where the cars all sat motionless. The eerie feeling he had in the forest came back to him, amplified a thousand fold by the facts that lay below him in the light of day and his mind spun, trying to make sense of what he was seeing.

Without thinking, he launched himself down the embankment. It was too steep to climb and his feet slid out from under him, sending a shower of loose stones clattering downward, breaking the absolute silence of the morning. Arms and legs splayed out to keep himself upright, he slid, clutching at what handholds he could find to control his descent. When he finally came to rest on a slight outcropping partway down, he hesitated only for a second before pushing off into a slide again.

Once at the bottom, he scrambled across the drainage ditch and pulled himself over the guardrail onto the blacktop. The nearest car was several hundred yards away, and he broke into a loping jog, slowing as he neared it, partly out of fatigue and partly out of apprehension. A set of skid marks veered toward a section of the metal guardrail that bore a long streak of green paint, before angling obliquely away again. The man observed this as he cautiously approached the car where it had apparently stopped after the grazing collision. He peered through the back window as he drew closer, looking for a shape in the driver's seat. The morning light was still weak and the highway was a shadowed valley, making it difficult to tell for certain, but he did not think anyone was inside the car. He let out a small sigh of relief, and circled around to the driver's side door, his heart pounding so hard that he could hear its rhythm hissing inside his ears. Looking through the window, he could see the pale outline of the passenger window, unobstructed by any human form, but the dark tint on the windows prevented him from seeing inside.

Upon closer examination, he realized that the tint was actually a fine black powder, which covered not only the window, but the entire car. Running a finger along the hood uncovered a green several shades brighter than the car had originally appeared. He looked at his blackened finger then held it to his nose. It was soot. This realization triggered another one—he had been smelling a faint odor of smoke since some time before dawn without registering it.

While he was thinking about the significance of the soot, he absentmindedly pulled on the door handle, but the door was locked. Why would someone abandon their car in the middle of the road, then bother to lock the door? He allowed himself the luxury of being distracted by this mystery for the moment and walked around the front of the car to the other side. A scrape and dent along the front fender and passenger's door showed the point of impact with the guardrail. It was long and wide, but not very deep and certainly not serious enough to make the car undriveable. The passenger door too was locked. He wiped the soot from the window and looked in. As he expected, there were no keys in the ignition, and it had been shifted into park. He scowled at the car, baffled. The best explanation he could think of was that the engine had suddenly quit and the driver had abandoned the car with the intention of coming back for it later. Obviously that had not happened.

It had been several hours since he had tried to remember anything about the past, but now something tugged at his memory—a fact from long ago. The car, dead on the highway, but the driver well enough to lock the doors and take the keys with him. Other cars, also abandoned. Soot. There was something in the back of his mind—a scrap of knowledge that might explain it all. He stopped thinking. It was something he did not want to know.

He ran again. Jogging along the highway a fresh panic gripped him. He kept moving to keep himself from thinking, but his mind raced along as well, heedless of his wishes.

"Hello? Hello?" he called. "Can anybody hear me?"

There was no answer except the muffled echo of his own voice in the distance.

A forest fire would explain the soot and maybe force people to abandon their cars, he told himself, but he knew he did not believe it before he could even finish the thought. He threw it out as an alternative, a distraction, to keep himself from completing the thought that was forming against his will. He kept running, hobbling as fast as his twisted ankle could manage, until he reached a pickup truck at the bottom of a small hill and collapsed against the tailgate. It was covered with the same black film.

Still panting, he pulled himself along the bed of the truck to the driver's door and tried the handle. The door opened, and he stepped up toward the cab. Again, no one inside. Again, no keys. There was a fast food bag on the passenger seat and a matching cup in the drink holder, along with an open soda can. Looking at the can he realized how thirsty he was. But not that thirsty, he told himself. Not yet.

The truck had been abandoned at a low point in the rolling highway, and the road continued up a woefully long shallow hill until it eventually disappeared around a bend. The last burst of panicked running had drained him of all remaining energy. The bench seat tempted him to lie down and take a nap, but he recalled his decision during the night to keep moving. Nothing had changed. Clearly there was nobody around to find him here if he stopped. This fact became his motivation to press on, pacing himself, setting one weary foot in front of the other, his body on autopilot once more. His only thought was to get somewhere, to find someone, before he could go no further. He stubbornly refused to let his mind think of anything else.

Nearing the top of the hill what seemed like hours later, he came to another car. This one had been heading in the opposite direction and seemed to have continued in a straight line rather than following the curve of the road. It had gone off the pavement in a spot where there was no guardrail and canted sideways into the drainage ditch. He continued walking; only looking through the windows as he passed by to confirm that it was empty.

Hidden behind the trees along the edge of the road, the sun was fully up, its orange morning light mixing with the thick clouds overhead, giving them a queer brownish tinge. It was an ugly, depressing color, and he searched for something else to focus his attention on. Ahead where the road flattened out, a large tree had fallen, partially obstructing the highway. It seemed to have tumbled down a naked slope, bringing its shallow roots with it. He was able to skirt around it on the far shoulder of the road, but as he did, he noticed several more trees and large branches that had fallen in the forest. He was immediately convinced that this was significant, and fought to repress the logical portion of his brain before it could go any further. He managed to keep himself calm and focused until a short while later when he spotted a large splash of yellow through a strip of woods up on the hillside ahead of him. Although obscured by the trees, it was the right size and shape to be a house.

The man broke into a run.

About a hundred yards later the forest ended abruptly where it had been cleared away for a development. He continued a few more staggering steps until the entire neighborhood came into view, and then collapsed to his knees, burying his head in his hands. He was at the foot of what had been a small residential development set on a broad, shallow hill overlooking the highway. The houses had all been destroyed.

The yellow house he had spotted through the woods had collapsed inward on itself. Only the two side walls remained standing, like gigantic bookends for a jumble of wreckage. The other houses were in various states of ruin. The best ones were missing roofs and windows with portions of the walls intact, the worst had been reduced to piles of rubble on their foundations. In the yards, small trees had been snapped off near the ground and some of the large trees had been partially uprooted. Shingles and papers and glass and other debris littered the ground everywhere across the hill and up into the woods beyond.

Eventually he forced himself to stand up again. Holding out little hope of finding someone alive amidst all this devastation, the young man walked through the streets calling out nonetheless. From the lawn of a home at the very top of the rise he looked out across the highway at the rolling hills and roadways beyond, and what might be the gray shape of a city through the haze in the distance. Nowhere did he see any motion or any sign of life.

Unable to travel any further, he headed for the car in the driveway. It was an old convertible sports car, but the cloth roof had been ripped open from the back and now lay across the hood, still attached to the top of the windshield by some sturdy buckles. He opened the door and sat down, fumbling beneath the seat until the back collapsed behind him. He used the last of his energy to sit up and pull the roof back over the car. Almost like a blanket, he thought, as consciousness slipped away.

CHAPTER FOUR

FORM AND FUNCTION

Holding up the apple, Newman considered the nature of change for a moment before taking another bite.

"So how did Socrates demonstrate that all of these seemingly relative things were universals? I thought he only asked questions."

"For the most part that's true," Sophia confirmed, "but some of his questions were in the form of statements that he asked his opponent to agree or disagree with, and if you read enough of these dialogues you can see some common themes to his questions. Even though he didn't offer answers to the great questions he posed, he definitely had his own ideas. His dialogue with Meno is a good example. He asks Meno to define Virtue and Meno, who is fairly powerful and successful, answers that virtue for a man is being able to conduct public affairs to benefit himself and his friends and harm his enemies, and that virtue for a woman is managing the house well, and that there's yet a different definition of virtue for children. Socrates leads him through a series of questions and examples that basically ask Meno how he can say Virtue is one thing if it is many different things for different people. Later he uses Meno's servant to demonstrate how there can be something universal that's knowable without teaching."

Sophia bent down and fished around in a basin of ice water until she found a soda she wanted. Then she sat down on the bench next to Newman.

"Socrates and Plato were both heavily influenced by Pythagoras," she continued.

"The mathematician? From the Pythagorean theorem?"

"Yes. Pythagoras lived a hundred or so years before Socrates and he and his followers were more than just mathematicians. For them, mathematics was something that was semi-divine because it seemed to describe so many things in nature, like musical harmonies for example, yet it transcended any specific examples and could be expressed and understood in universal principles."

"Sounds like just the thing to prove to the sophists that there's something that's not relative."

"Exactly," Sophia agreed. "And that's just what Socrates did with Meno's servant. Because he's a servant he's presumably not educated in geometry, but Socrates shows him by example the relationship between the length of the side of a square or the diagonal through the square to its area, then demonstrates that the servant can understand these as universal principles by asking him to apply them to a square of a different size. Socrates believed that there must be universal principles of Justice and Virtue to govern the actions of people as well. It was Plato who helped to turn these ideas into a full-fledged philosophy. Plato not only recorded the ideas of Socrates—he built on them and organized them into a philosophical framework. Most scholars believe that Plato also colored the dialogues, probably more and more over time, with his own thought, so it's sometimes hard to tell which ideas were actually those of Socrates and which were Plato's. From the way you reacted to Heraclitus, I bet you'd like Plato."

"It sounds like it so far," said Newman. "I certainly don't like the sound of the sophists."

"Plato drew on the ideas of Parmenides as well as Socrates, and shared a reverence of mathematics with Pythagoras. In the philosophy he developed there are two levels of reality—the physical world that we live in and a transcendent spiritual world, which is composed of perfect Forms."

Sophia stopped to take a drink.

"What are these Forms?" asked Newman. "And how does the spiritual world relate to the physical world?"

"According to Plato, the spiritual world is a transcendent world of universal Truths. The Forms are perfection, and things in the physical world are imperfect reflections of them."

Newman looked confused. Sophia started to say something, but then stopped and dug in her pocket. She handed Newman a pen and a paper napkin.

"Draw a right triangle," she told him.

He looked puzzled, but set the napkin on the bench and drew a triangle on it.

"Is that a right triangle?" she asked when he was done.

He looked at it again, still puzzled. "Yes."

"What's the definition of a triangle?"

"A figure with three sides?" he said tentatively.

"And what makes a triangle a right triangle?"

"Is it too simplistic to say a right angle?"

"No, that's fine. A right triangle is a triangle that contains a right angle. Okay, and what are the sides of a triangle made up of?"

Newman shook his head in confusion, clearly failing to understand what she was getting at.

"In a triangle, what is it that connects one point to another point?"

"A line? I guess technically it's a line segment," he amended.

"What's a line segment?"

"The shortest distance between two points," Newman responded quickly.

Sophia gave him a mischievous smile. "So is that a right triangle?" she asked again, pointing to the figure on the napkin.

"Yes," Newman said, this time a bit more emphatically, but he gave her a wary look.

"Are you sure that angle is exactly ninety degrees?"

Newman examined his drawing but did not reply.

"And what about these sides? See how this one bumps out a bit here? It doesn't look like the straightest distance between two points. Besides, aren't points infinitely small? That means line segments should be infinitely thin."

"But it would be impossible…" Newman started, then paused. "I see. It's impossible to draw a perfect right triangle because it's an ideal. The best I could ever hope to do is draw a crude approximation of a right triangle. So the ideal right triangle would be like one of Plato's Forms?"

"Exactly," Sophia said. "And Plato applied this same reasoning to things like Justice and Virtue. He believed that they existed in the transcendental world, and it should be our goal to try to understand them the way we understand the principles of mathematics, even if it's impossible to find perfect examples of them here in the material world."

"So why did people think that those ideas were corrupting the youth? It sounds like a pretty noble philosophy to me."

"Socrates believed that people were just misled," explained Sophia. "In fact, he went so far as to say that no one willingly chooses to do evil. The only reason people do evil is that they mistakenly think it's good. He felt as sorry for the perpetrator of a crime as he did for the victim because to Socrates, the perpetrator was so far astray on the wrong path. Plato would certainly have believed that most people don't try to seek the transcendental ideals because they're misled, and the sophists with their relativism were guilty of doing a lot of the misleading. Are you familiar with the Allegory of the Cave?"

"It sounds familiar, but I have to confess that I don't really remember it."

"It's one of the most famous ideas in all of the history of philosophy. I wouldn't be surprised if you ran into it somewhere along the line. It's from Plato's great work *The Republic* and explains his view of the Forms, the transcendent world and their relationship to the material world and our perception. Imagine that a group of prisoners has been chained up in a large cave facing the same wall of the cave for their entire lives such that they can't turn their heads to look anywhere else, even at each other. Behind them there's a large wall, like a castle rampart. People can walk along the top of the wall. Beyond the top of this wall there's a fire. As the people travel along the rampart, the fire casts their shadows over the heads of the prisoners and onto the cave wall in front of them and the voices of the people on the rampart echo about the cave such that the voices seem to be coming from the direction of the cave wall. Anything that was carried across the top of the parapet would project a shadow onto the wall. The prisoners, having never seen any real people or objects, would assume that the shadows were the extent of the real world. They'd theorize about their properties and study them in great detail, never realizing that they were just fleeting images of something more permanent and well defined."

Newman nodded vigorously. "Yes, yes. So Plato believed that the material world was like the shadows, and we get so caught up in the material world that we forget to look beyond it for something more important."

"Right," Sophia said. "Now imagine that one of the prisoners manages somehow to escape. He stumbles through the darkness until he finds his way out of the cave, into the world outside. What do you think his reaction would be?"

"He'd be amazed."

"Eventually he'd be amazed," Sophia allowed, "but first he'd be stunned and bewildered. His eyes wouldn't be accustomed to the sunlight and they'd be blinded. He'd be dazzled by colors and see things beyond his wildest imagination."

Newman nodded his agreement.

"Now imagine that this freed prisoner, after getting a glimpse of the outside world, turns back to free his fellow prisoners."

Sophia paused to let Newman picture the scenario.

"He'd have to lead them through the darkness, wouldn't he?" Newman suggested. "And help them when they were first blinded by the sunlight."

"Yes," Sophia said, "if he was lucky. But imagine that you were one of these other prisoners, not the one that escaped. This guy comes to you and tells you about this amazing world and bright light, and how everything you have ever seen or believed in is just an illusion."

"I might think he was crazy," Newman suggested.

"That's how Plato explained why people might not listen to Socrates and be more inclined to listen to other philosophers, such as the sophists, who emphasized the material world. In his view the sophists and their followers were too caught up in the shadows to look for the universal truths behind them. The other thing that's important about Plato's philosophy is that it helped reconcile all the various philosophical arguments that had gone before."

"How so?"

"Many of the pre-Socratic philosophers offered opinions on the nature of the world, but didn't seem to have any sort of framework to back them up. Some argued about various properties of materials, others, like Heraclitus and the sophists, argued that because of change it wasn't meaningful to speak of universal truths at all. Plato synthesized the two views with his philosophy of a changing, temporary material world that's a reflection of a perfect, eternal spiritual world."

"You were right," said Newman, "I do like Plato. Now I can appreciate why Plato and Socrates are so famous."

"Yes," Sophia agreed. "Probably the only ancient Greek philosopher to have as much of an impact on Western thought as Plato was his student, Aristotle."

"Now that's a name I definitely recognize. Are you going to tell me about Aristotle next?"

"If you want, sure. But first I think you should tell me a little bit about yourself," Sophia said. Although she was enjoying the conversation, she was beginning to feel like a lecturer. "What do you do for a living?"

"As little as possible," Newman said stroking his goatee.

Sophia gave a polite laugh and continued to look at him expectantly.

"I'm still trying to figure that out I guess," he said. "Right now I have a part time job in a music store and play some gigs in the evenings. Before that I worked for a moving company, I was a waiter for a while, a truck driver for an auto parts store and I was almost a priest."

"Really? A priest?"

"Yeah. I was sort of a problem kid until my older brother and a Jesuit priest turned me around. It was the priest who helped me take a look at my life and find some meaning beyond just living day to day. I was so impressed by what this guy did for me that I actually went into seminary for almost a year."

"What happened?"

"They didn't think I was ready and encouraged me to go out into the world and live a little before I made any commitment. So that's what I did."

"I can see why you like Plato then. Have you ever thought about going back?"

"I did at times. But I don't think I'm really cut out for it. Hey," he said, "that reminds me, are you familiar with the Union of Faith?"

Sophia shook her head.

"How about Asha Zendik?"

"I recognize his name from the news, but no, not really. Is the Union of Faith his organization?"

"Yes. I've been going to their meetings for a while now," Newman said, and fished in his pocket. "I know it's short notice, but they're having a retreat in Maine next weekend." He pulled a small piece of paper out of his pocket, unfolded it and handed it to Sophia. It was a plain tri-fold pamphlet, printed on light green paper. She scanned it as Newman continued.

"It's by invitation only," he said. "I think you'd really enjoy it." Then, sensing her reticence he quickly added, "You can bring someone with you if you'd like."

"I don't know, Newman," Sophia replied. "I'm not a terribly religious person."

"You don't need to be. That's the whole idea. All you need to believe is that there's something out there that's greater than us. We get people from all different religious groups, and a lot of people who don't belong to any organized religion. I bet they'd love to hear you explain the Allegory of the Cave."

Something on the flyer caught Sophia's eye.

"I don't know, 'the false gods of science and technology'? That sounds a bit extreme," she said, reading from the pamphlet and shaking her head. "Maybe I should tell you about Aristotle before you invite me to this thing."

"The flyers are a little sensationalistic," Newman apologized, "but the Union isn't really as radical as that makes them look. They just think humanity is on the wrong track, kind of like Plato thought about the sophists. And Asha Zendik is a terrific speaker. This is actually part of a worldwide event, and he's coming back from Russia just to be there for the afternoon. If nothing else, you should come just for the day to hear him. Who knows, you might hear something that'll make you see things in a different light."

Sophia looked thoughtful and mumbled something to herself. Then to Newman she explained, "Socrates always said that the unexamined life is not worth living." She held up the flyer. "I'll think about it, okay?"

"Sure, I didn't mean that to sound like a sales pitch. Here," he said, reaching for the flyer. Sophia handed it to him. He wrote something on it and handed it back to her along with her pen.

"If you're interested, give me a call. If not, maybe we can get together some other time."

"I'd like that," Sophia said.

They were both silent for a moment, searching for something to say.

"Maybe you should tell me about Aristotle," Newman suggested.

"Okay, but I don't think you'll like him as much as Plato," warned Sophia. "Since Aristotle was Plato's student, he was well versed in Plato's concept of the spiritual and material worlds, but although Aristotle recognized Plato's genius, he disagreed with Plato's conclusion that there was a separate spiritual world containing ideal forms. Aristotle felt that once you start talking about things that you can't observe you were wandering onto shaky ground, so he proposed a different theory to explain the nature of things and the reason that things change. Aristotle's father was a physician and Aristotle himself was a devoted naturalist. From his observations of nature and living things, he determined that there must be several factors that cause a thing to be what it is. The first factor he called the material cause, and it was both an acknowledgement and a refinement of the materialist philosophies of people like Democritus. Aristotle said that material does influence the nature of a thing. For example, you can make a sculpture out of stone, but you can't make a sculpture out of water."

"What about ice sculptures?" Newman quipped. Sophia rolled her eyes and continued.

"The point is that stone can hold the form of the statue, but liquid can't. So material certainly has an impact on the nature of a thing. It's necessary, but not sufficient. In response to materialists like Democritus who thought that material and space was all that existed, Aristotle replied, 'If the art of shipbuilding were in the wood, we would have ships by nature.' Obviously ships don't just spring up from piles of wood, so there must be something more than just material involved. So he introduced a second factor, which he called the efficient cause. The efficient cause is that which shapes the material. For the sculpture it would be the artist's chisel, or for a ship, the shipwright's tools. Next there's the formal cause, which is like the design or image. It's the design of the ship or the picture of the finished sculpture that the sculptor has in his mind when he first starts to chip at the block of stone. And last but not least there's the final cause. This is the reason for it all—the reason that the sculptor set out to make a sculpture in the first place, or the shipwright to build a boat. The purpose of the boat is to sail, so this would be its final cause. The purpose of the sculpture might be to please the eye."

"That all makes sense for man-made things," Newman said, "but how does that apply to nature?"

"Good question. The example I have often heard is this one—consider an acorn growing into an oak tree. The wood and leaves and bark would be the material cause. The external forces like the sunlight, rainwater, nourishment from the soil would be the efficient cause. And in this case, the formal cause and the final cause are the same. The fully grown oak tree is the formal cause, and the purpose of the tree is just to be a tree."

"But where do the formal and final causes come from?" Newman asked.

"Aristotle believed that they were inherent in living things. That concept, called hylomorphism from the Greek words for matter and form, says that the form provides matter with its characteristics—both its potential and the driving force to move toward that potential. Of course he didn't know about DNA and genetics, but in a very general sense he anticipated those discoveries."

Sophia was going to continue, but she was interrupted when one of the guests approached the pool gesturing to Newman.

"Sorry, that's my ride," Newman told her. "I've got to go. You'll have to tell me more about Aristotle some other time." He paused as he turned away and pointed at the flyer in her hand. "Give me a call some time. And let me know if you're interested in this weekend."

Sophia found herself smiling as she watched him jogging across the lawn to catch up with his friend. Shortly afterward she said her goodbyes and went home herself.

CHAPTER FIVE

WINDS OF CHANGE

Evening was descending on her neighborhood as Sophia returned home from shopping on the weekend after the cookout. Although she had been tempted to go to the event in Maine with Newman, it was a little too far from home and he and his group were just a little too unknown. She had intended to call him to make her excuses and maybe set up some time to get together once he got back, but the week had been so busy that she never found the time to do it. Now on the first day of the retreat, Sophia was feeling a bit guilty as she pulled into her driveway under the long shadows of her house and took the groceries out of the trunk.

With a lucrative career and no family or friends to fill her days she had both the time and money to invest in her house. It was a small colonial, but more than large enough for her solitary needs. The neighborhood was a quiet professional community and her house stood near the top of a wide flat rise overlooking more rolling hills. These were dotted with houses and networked with roads and power lines, but even in the most developed areas there were enough trees still standing to give the overall impression of the forest that had once covered the hills completely. In the distance Sophia could see the gray concentration of shapes and dim skyline of the city of Albany.

In the few years that she had lived in this house Sophia had done a great deal of cosmetic work, refinishing and wallpapering most of the interior, and repainting the ugly brown exterior with a pale blue that offset the brick entryway. Upon buying her first house she had also taken up gardening. Flower boxes hung from each of the lower windows, and an ambitious vegetable garden occupied most of the western side of the house. Reasoning that gardening was more enjoyable than mowing, Sophia had converted the entire side yard into a garden. She found it relaxing to unwind out among the vegetables, pulling weeds and tending to the plants.

As nice as the scenery was out her front window she preferred the view from the back, up the hill where the woods were untouched. Often she would sit on the deck in the back and revel in the bright green of the leaves in the summer sunlight. Now in the fading orange light they had lost some of their brilliance, but retained a somber beauty. She lingered outside for a moment, admiring the scene before balancing one bag on her knee and unlocking the door.

Once inside, Sophia set the bags on the stove, put some new food in the cat dish, and went about putting away her groceries. The kitchen area was small, so she had recently annexed the stairwell to the basement by erecting shelves along the wall inside the door. This space now served as a small pantry. The next project on her list was to hang a recently purchased cast iron pot rack over the kitchen counter. In the short time it took to put away the groceries, the sun had set significantly and it looked more like night than day out the living room window. Sophia switched on the video and her wall lit up with a slowly morphing swirl of muted colors. She touched the screen and chose "music" from a list of options, then narrowed it to a random selection of upbeat music from the nineties. She watched the wallscreen for a moment, intrigued as the computer generated image of something like a genie in plate armor flew through octagonal passageways to a strong synthesizer beat. The scene quickly gave way to air cars in a futuristic cityscape as a male voice began singing in Latin.

Satisfied with her selection, Sophia returned to the kitchen to prepare dinner. She was watching her frozen dinner spin slowly in the microwave and listening to the soulful female vocals that had just joined the song in the next room when suddenly the power went out. It was immediately clear from the intensity of the darkness that the streetlights had gone out as well, and Sophia carefully made her way back into the living room to look at the rest of the neighborhood. All the other houses were dark, and there was no light visible from the distant hillsides either. Sighing and shaking her head, Sophia went back to the kitchen once more, and rummaged through the drawers in the nearly complete darkness until she found a box of utility candles and some matches. She lit one of the candles and dripped some wax into a coffee mug to use as a makeshift candle-holder.

For a while Sophia tried reading by candlelight, until her stomach reminded her that she had not yet eaten dinner. Returning to the kitchen, she rooted around in the cabinets, eventually pulling out a can of tuna. Only after she had set out a plate, mixing bowl, bread, cheese and mayonnaise did she realize that her electric can opener was unlikely to be of any use without power. Already committed to the idea of a tuna salad sandwich, she went down to the basement to retrieve a can opener from her camping supplies.

Just as she was starting back up, the doorway at the top of the stairs was illuminated with a flash of brilliant white light. Reflexively, she tensed in anticipation of the thunderclap that should follow, but it was several seconds before she heard a distant low rumbling, and instead of fading, it seemed to grow louder. It was accompanied by a hiss of wind that increased rapidly in pitch and volume to a shriek. The house was slammed with such force that Sophia could feel the foundation tremble. An explosion of glass heralded a great gale that roared through the rooms upstairs. Above her she could hear furniture scraping across the floor and the clatter of shattered glass and debris. A split second later, with a horrific groan, the walls gave out and Sophia watched, frozen in place, as the doorway at the top of the stairs collapsed sideways and disappeared beneath a pile of rubble.

CHAPTER SIX

LOST OR FOUND

Bright light met his eyes the first time he opened them, blinding him momentarily. It was full daylight, although still overcast, yet he had the impression that it had been a sound which had awakened him. Fighting to keep his eyes open, he listened carefully for any noise. After concentrating for a few minutes, he leaned back into the seat to continue listening from a more comfortable position.

When he woke the second time, it was with a certainty that he had heard something. He awoke more quickly this time, physically and mentally improved from the sleep. His neck, shoulder and ankle still throbbed, but the pain was manageable, and the leaden weariness in his limbs had subsided. His heartbeat, pounding in his chest, told him that he had been startled out of sleep, but he did not know how long he had slept or what exactly he had heard. Again he focused his attention and listened for the sound. All was quiet. He pushed the convertible top away, raising his head cautiously to look around. His eyes scanned the devastation with fresh horror and dismay, but found nothing moving and nothing to account for the sound. Giving up, he settled back into the seat and closed his eyes.

Then he heard it.

He had almost fallen asleep again, but this time he heard it clearly and snapped back to consciousness. It was a dull and distant clanging sound. He sat up, but before he could locate the sound it stopped again. Unsure of what might be out there, he was reluctant to abandon the security of the car to investigate, but the even and deliberate sound raised his hopes of finding people. He sat, motionless and listening, for several minutes before hearing it again.

The sound was like metal striking metal. Clang-clang-clang.

It was coming from in front of the car. Clang. Clang. Clang. Slower now. The house before him or off in the woods? It was too soft to judge the distance well.

Clang-clang-clang. Fast again.

The sound had stopped and he was still not sure where it had come from. The pattern was important. He was still foggy from fatigue, but knew he was missing something. Fast, slow, fast. What did it mean? Then he realized—not fast and slow—short and long. S-O-S. It was a call for help.

He climbed out of the car and scrambled over to the wreckage of the house yelling, "Hello, Hello! Is someone in there?" There was no reply. He walked around the ruined structure, surveying the damage, trying to assess whether the sound had truly been coming from inside. The house was completely demolished. The front had apparently been an actual brick wall that had buckled inward and the upper floor and side walls had collapsed on top of it. It would be a miracle if anyone had survived in there.

In the back yard the roof of the house lay upside down where the trees at the forest edge had stopped its flight. It was intact, held together by the rafters and braces which now faced the sky, as if a giant had lifted off the top of a doll house and set it aside. Under the edge of the roof the man spotted a handle and pulled out a garden trowel. He took it around to the front yard, to the spigot he had seen sticking out of the concrete foundation, and banged five times on the spigot as hard as he dared. A moment later, five clangs answered back from underneath the rubble. Someone was definitely inside.

Ripping excitedly at a few boards and shards of plaster, ignoring the fresh pain this caused in his left shoulder, he worked to clear away the rubble. After a few minutes of pulling out chunks of debris and throwing them on the lawn he stopped, realizing the enormity of the task. Even knowing exactly what spot he was trying to reach it would take him many hours to clear away the rubble enough to make a path and he was not sure how much daylight he had left. Briefly he entertained the idea of trying to find help, but realized that there was no guarantee of finding someone else more quickly than he could get through the rubble himself. He decided that without knowing how long the person had been trapped or what their condition was, it was more risky to leave them than to try to dig them out on his own. With the decision made, he looked again at the remains of the house to determine where to start.

While he was thinking, he went over and clanged on 'the spigot again just to let whoever it was know that he was still out there. There was an immediate reply. He tried to determine where the sound was coming from, but it was difficult to pinpoint, and he knew that sound traveling through pipes, which was what the clanging sounded like, could be deceptive.

There was a garage, what was left of it, in front of the car, and he decided to spend some time searching through this smaller pile of rubble in the hopes of finding something to help. Eventually his efforts paid off, and he retrieved a hatchet, which allowed him to chop apart some of the larger beams and chunks of wall that he would have been otherwise unable to move. While he was chopping he heard a new sound. It was a thumping sound, and it seemed to be coming, unfortunately, from near the center of the wreckage. It had its own pattern. Thump. Thump, thump. Thump. Then a pause of several seconds, then it repeated. With the ax still in his hand he returned to the spigot and banged out the same pattern in reply. Then he returned to work.

After several hours he had cleared away a respectable path, and was making good progress toward the center of the house. It was growing late in the afternoon, and the sun was still obscured by thick clouds. Although it was unseasonably cold, he was sweating profusely from exertion. Already tired from his ordeal in the woods, his arms and back and legs were now spent from hours of hauling big chunks of rubble out of the pile. After pulling away a large section of the upper floor to reveal a black leather recliner that was still largely undamaged, he finished excavating the area and sat down to take a break. He chuckled inwardly at the thought of what he must look like—unshaven, dressed in torn and bloodstained clothes, sitting in a luxurious black leather recliner in the middle of a pile of rubble. It would make a good poster, he thought, or a good ad campaign for something. Homeowner's insurance maybe.

He laughed out loud. The first laugh released a cascade of hysterical laughter and soon he was doubled over out of breath sitting on the leather armchair laughing in fits. He stopped when he heard the thumping sound again, fairly close this time. Maybe only an hour or two away now. Then he heard a voice—a woman's voice.

"What's so funny up there?"

He was so happy to hear another voice and to have someone to talk to that without thinking he replied, "It's sort of a visual thing." He had not expected anyone to be able to hear him and she had caught him by surprise. Now, looking around at the destruction, he felt guilty for laughing and stupid for this automatic reply.

"I'll have you out soon," he added quickly. "Are you okay down there? Are you hurt?"

"Yes, I'm okay," the woman's voice replied, "Maybe a little dehydrated, but that's all. I can't wait to get out of here. I'm so glad you found me. I was beginning to wonder if…"

Struggling to his feet, the man set to work again. He was starting to get the familiar feeling of numbness, and threw himself into the work, partly out of inspiration at having someone to talk to but mainly to assure that he was able to finish. The voice continued.

"It's so nice just to hear someone else's voice," she said. "It's like being in solitary confinement down here." There was a pause. "I guess I was really lucky though. From what I saw I'm probably better off down here. What happened up there? How bad is it?"

Looking around at the house, at the neighborhood, he was unable to find the words. After a long pause he said, "Bad," and the conversation ended there.

He continued clearing rubble for a while in silence until he heard the thumping again right near his feet.

"It sounds like you're right above me," came the voice. "You must be almost there."

"Get back if you can," he replied. "I think this is going to do it."

With that warning, he pulled on a large fragment of wall. Small bits of debris rattled loose, and it sounded like some fell down many feet, clattering into the basement.

"Yes! That's it! Keep going!"

Twisting and pulling, he heaved against one of the beams. Finally it broke free, sending a shower of wreckage down into the gap it uncovered, and an overpowering stench of refuse met his nostrils, like the smell of a summer camp latrine. A set of stairs led down into the hole.

From the darkness a woman emerged, squinting and blinking, into the daylight. He studied her, the physical form that went with the voice. She was a bit shorter than he had expected, and younger, although he guessed her to be a few years older than he was. She had long black hair, dark eyes and facial features that suggested Asian ancestry, and a natural, down to earth beauty that survived her disheveled appearance. She appeared worn and haggard, but otherwise well.

He offered a hand as she stepped over the last bits of rubble into the space he had cleared.

"Are you okay?" he asked.

She nodded slightly. "Yes. Fine." Her eyes were beginning to adjust to the light and she looked around her. "Thank you," she said absentmindedly as she looked around her. Then, more emphatically, "Thank you."

He stepped aside and watched her silently as she surveyed the scene of the disaster, first her house, then the neighborhood, then out across the distant hills.

"Oh my God," she whispered.

The man nodded and after a short silence asked quietly, "What happened?"

The woman shook her head, turned her palms up and shrugged helplessly and shook her head again.

"I don't know," she finally managed to say.

It occurred to the man that he should be disappointed that she could not shed any light on what had happened, but he was so glad to have found someone else that he was overcome with relief and joy. This feeling hit him in an almost tangible wave, leaving him light-headed with his pulse pounding in his ears.

"You mean you don't know either?"

He shook his head. The same sensation of moving in slow motion that he had experienced in the night returned and he realized that it was probably only adrenaline which kept him on his feet.

"I'm not even entirely sure where I am," he said.

The woman pulled her eyes away from the wreckage and looked at him. "This is Woodgate." She pointed toward the horizon and added, "Albany is just up the highway that way. On a clear day you can see it from here."

A large highway ran in the direction she pointed and he traced it until it faded from view. Beyond the haze that shrouded the horizon there seemed to be a darker area that might be a city, but it was impossible to see details. When he looked back, she was still looking at him.

"Is anybody else...?" she motioned at the ruins of the neighborhood and her voice faltered.

He shook his head.

"I don't think so. You're the only person I've heard."

At this news she appeared to be physically weakened and cast about for a place to sit down.

"This was my house," she said, looking around her. Her eyes and hand stopped at the recliner. "Have a seat. Make yourself at home."

The man gave a feeble laugh, more out of sympathy than humor. The woman laughed too, laughing until her laughter turned into sobbing. She turned to face the hills and crouched down, back to him.

"I can't believe this happened. I can't believe it's all gone. Everything." She spoke in a half-whisper, her voice catching on the words. "Do you want to hear something really stupid?"

When he did not respond, the woman turned around and locked her eyes onto his. Tears streamed down her cheeks. He shook his head and shrugged helplessly.

"All I can think about is my cat. My neighbors are probably all dead, and who knows who else, and all I can think about is my cat. Isn't that crazy? Isn't that stupid?"

She turned away again.

He walked over and crouched down behind her, putting his hand on her shoulder. Her face was turned away, but he felt her shoulder heaving as she fought to gain control of her tears. He tried to think of something comforting to say, some way to let her know that he understood, that he sympathized, that she was not crazy, but language seemed insufficient to the task, and before any words came to him he realized that he too was crying. For some time they said nothing, she weeping quietly, he blinking in an effort to dry his eyes without moving.

Abruptly, the woman stopped crying and stood up.

"I'm sorry," she said, wiping her eyes and dusting off her pants. "You have no idea how glad I am to see you. You probably saved my life. I'm not sure how long I was trapped down there, but it was days. I was beginning to think nobody was ever going to find me." She put out her hand. "I'm Sophia," she said.

"Hyle," he replied automatically, pausing briefly. Earlier he had been unable to recall anything about his past. At least he knew his name. "And you have no idea how grateful I am to see you. You're the first person I've seen since..." His voice trailed off.

Sophia opened her mouth to pursue this half-statement, but stopped when she looked closely at him for the first time. Tall and thin, he was wearing a lightweight jacket, a pale blue dress shirt and tan pants that were all torn and dirty. His dirty blond hair was cropped short and hazel eyes met her gaze from an unshaven face that was unnaturally pale and bloodied with dozens of small cuts.

"Oh, look at you!" she exclaimed. "You look horrible."

Her eyes darted from his face and fixed on his shoulder. She gasped.

"You look like you've been shot!"

This caught Hyle by surprise, but it had a ring of truth to it. He looked down at his sore shoulder. Most of the fabric around his left shoulder and breast was stained darker than the rest of his jacket and might fit the description of a dried blood stain. Inside that darkened area was a smaller glistening patch, and within that, a little hole. Suddenly his shoulder began to throb. He felt a surge of dizziness and swayed on his feet. Sophia caught him by the other shoulder to steady him.

"We have to get you to a hospital," she said.

Slinging his good arm across her shoulders, she put her arm around his waist and led him carefully out of the debris to her car. Pulling the roof out of the way, she helped him into the passenger seat. Then she unbuckled the roof, tossed it aside and jumped into the driver's seat.

"It's a lucky thing I still had these in my pocket," she said, pulling out a set of keys. She selected one of the keys and put it in the ignition.

"It works!" Hyle's voice conveyed his surprise when the engine turned over.

Sophia looked at him, puzzled. "It just had the roof blown off. The rest of it looks fine."

They were quiet for a while as she backed the car out of the driveway and drove slowly along the road, moving from side to side to avoid the scattered debris. At length Hyle spoke again.

"What happened here?" he asked. "How did you get trapped in the basement?"

"It was just lucky. I was down there getting something. I was just coming back up when I saw this blinding flash of light upstairs, then a few seconds later the house was blown over. There must have been some kind of huge explosion, but I don't know what could have caused it." She shook her head in disbelief. "It was just lucky for me that the power went out or I would have been upstairs when it happened."

Hyle leaned forward anxiously. "The power went out before the explosion?"

"Yes. A while before. I don't think it was related." She paused, suddenly unsure.

"How long before?"

Sophia thought for a moment, replaying her activities between the time the power had gone out and the time she had gone into the basement.

"Maybe an hour or so. Why?"

"I passed some cars on the road on my way here…"

She looked at him quizzically.

"They looked fine. They weren't damaged, but they'd been abandoned."

"What does that mean?"

Hyle shook his head despondently. It seemed to move a split second too late, out of phase. Looking at the demolished houses, the thought he had been shutting out had returned again. He was tired—both physically exhausted and emotionally drained—and considered all the information as if he were detached from it, watching a movie, a different person from the frightened man who faced the mystery of the cars alone. What had then been suppressed as an unsubstantiated fear now seemed like a real possibility.

"EMP," he said. When she did not seem to understand he explained, "Electromagnetic pulse. It's a field that's generated by a nuclear explosion. It's supposed to be able to burn out circuits and knock out power."

"Are you saying that someone attacked us with a nuclear weapon?"

"It seems like the best explanation," Hyle replied with a shrug.

Sophia could not quite bring herself to consider this theory. It was as though accepting an explanation would somehow make everything more real, and she was not ready to accept any of it.

"But that can't be. Why? I mean, we weren't even involved in the war. Why would somebody attack us? And…And wouldn't there have been something on the news? An emergency broadcast or something? There was no warning at all."

"I don't know why. But the power may have been knocked out to prevent any warning. During the cold war both U.S. and soviet military doctrine called for a high altitude burst to generate EMP and disrupt communications as the first step in a nuclear war."

"You mean you think we were attacked twice?"

Hyle shrugged, and his shoulder throbbed.

Sophia was silent for a moment.

"But why Albany?" Sophia persisted. "Why would someone target Albany? And twice? Wouldn't they—whoever it was—have attacked New York or Washington D.C. first?"

Maybe they did, Hyle thought, but he said nothing.

"I don't know why," he repeated, "but the first attack may well have been far away from Albany. The EMP effects of a single bomb can cover thousands of miles."

The conversation ended, Hyle exhausted, Sophia overwhelmed. Hyle closed his eyes and began to drift into a warm, peaceful sleep.

"Hey! Wake up. Don't go to sleep."

Navigating through the obstacles on the residential streets, occasionally cutting across yards when the road was blocked, Sophia made her way out to the small highway that paralleled the interstate to the city. She tried to keep Hyle talking as she drove, absent-mindedly asking him questions while she focused on the road.

As they drew closer to the city they passed neighborhoods where trees and houses had been flattened, cars overturned. Several times they had to turn around and look for another route when the road before them was blocked. The sun was low in the sky, and the scent of smoke thick, as the tall shapes of buildings grew near. Finally they crested a small hill and got their first good look at the city.

The husks of a few broken buildings were all that remained of the skyline, and a handful of smaller buildings still stood, largely intact. Everywhere else was empty space. Block after block had been smashed to flat, black rubble. It appeared that a fire had raged through the city reducing everything but a few bits of concrete and steel to ash. Plumes of smoke still rose from invisible fires smoldering beneath the ruins and a fine dust clung to the air creating a brown fog over the desolate patch of earth that used to be a city.

CHAPTER SEVEN

BAD TO WORSE

Even though the city had been destroyed, Sophia continued traveling toward it, stunned and not sure what else to do. She drove slowly through the outskirts, past the burnt out shells of cars and ruined buildings. Many of the cars had been moved to the sides of the street, and she realized that this must have been done by people some time after the blast, even though there were no signs of those people now. She was also relieved that there were no dead or wounded in sight, although occasionally a stench carried by the wind reminded her of what she could not see.

Eventually they came to the remains of a large building near the edge of the city. It caught her attention immediately because it had been covered with papers and was surrounded by makeshift signs. Leaving the engine running, she got out of the car and approached the wall. The signs were messages, and the papers posted on the wall were messages too, hundreds of them. Bouquets of withered flowers and extinguished candle stubs lay at the base of the building below the papers. As high as one could reach, the wall had been covered with notes and photographs from survivors letting people know where they could be found or looking for lost friends and relatives. Several of the notes mentioned Parklawn Hospital in Rosemount. Armed with this information, Sophia returned to the car and turned changed course for Rosemount.

Beyond the outskirts of the city the damage started to decrease again. There they found the large squat edifice of Parklawn Hospital flanked by a series of apartment buildings and stores. The storefront windows had all been smashed. Whether this was from the blast or the work of vandals was unclear, but the contents of the stores had been removed. Aside from the evidence of looting, there were no other signs of life.

Now that it was close to nightfall the lack of artificial light became obvious. There was not a single light to be seen—no streetlights or traffic lights, no lights in the windows of any store or apartment, no headlights of cars. To see such a large expanse of architecture with no electric light drove home the extent of the destruction. The hospital itself was a sturdy old stone building, well preserved from the damage, but it was dark as well. Many of its windows remained intact, others boarded with plywood. The large parking lot beside the hospital was a sea of tents.

Bothering to find a parallel space beside the curb, Sophia parked the car just down the street from the hospital, and then circled around to help Hyle get out. His eyes were opened, but most of his shirt had become one large wet stain. He had not spoken in a while and Sophia was gripped with a momentary panic that he had died right there beside her. Grabbing him gently by the shoulders, she tried to sit him up, and although he was groggy, he eventually did sit up under his own power, open his door, and step out. Leaning back against the car to hold himself up and looking around first, he took a few shaky steps toward the hospital and braced himself against a streetlight. Sophia rummaged for something in her glove box, and then caught up to him, helping him the rest of the way up the sidewalk to the main entrance of the hospital. They went through the revolving door and into total darkness.

"Hello? Is anyone here?" Sophia called. Then turning to Hyle she whispered, "Come on, let's go in further and look for someone."

There was a scraping sound, and a small flame burst from the lighter in Sophia's hand. With one arm around Hyle and the other holding the lighter, she made her way down the main entrance hall, pushing through a set of double doors into an intersecting hall.

Just inside the hallway, a dark object lay on the floor. With a muffled yelp, Sophia shuffled backwards and the light went out. There was a frantic scraping and the flame reappeared. At their feet lay the body of a young woman, a nurse or doctor judging from the lab coat thrown unfastened over her dark clothes and the clipboard that lay nearby. Sophia looked away and guided Hyle further down the hall. Not much farther along was another body. This one was an older woman, presumably a patient, with one arm and part of her face bandaged. And just beyond that was another.

Rushing Hyle down the hall, she looked behind them nervously until they reached the emergency room. In the dim light of the small flame the room appeared at first glance to be full of people awaiting treatment. Most of the chairs were occupied and still more people sat or lay on the floor. None were moving. With a gasp Sophia pushed Hyle back into motion. Behind the triage desk a corridor opened into curtained bays on either side. There in gurneys were the worst of the patients, many disfigured and most extensively bandaged. Other figures lay on the floor beside them and in the hallway. Gruesome images popped out of the shadows into the flickering light as they hurried by. Sophia tried not to look.

By all indications the hospital had been in full operation when disaster struck a second time. Near them in one of the bays a man lay face down. Hyle pulled them toward the figure. A large, almost round stain surrounded a small hole in the back of the lab coat.

"He's been shot," Sophia hissed. "What's going on here?"

Hyle did not respond. His mind seemed to be moving sluggishly and he could do nothing but stare.

"Let's get out of here," Sophia whispered, pulling him along.

Continuing down the corridor, stepping over bodies, Sophia dragged Hyle along as quickly as she thought he could go. They turned a corner and followed signs for the cafeteria and east parking lot. The cafeteria was much the same as the hallways. People appeared to be in the middle of their normal activities, sitting at tables, eating meals, when they were struck down. Sophia headed straight for the doors that led outside, but again Hyle pulled her back. The light from the flame glinted on some small objects off to one side of the doorway. Hyle bent down, scooping up a handful of them with a metallic sound and holding his hand open in front of the lighter to show Sophia. They were shell casings.

"Bullets?" she asked.

Hyle nodded. "Casings. Lots of them. Looks like someone had an automatic weapon in here."

He felt a wave of fear wash over him, and with it enough energy to refocus his senses. Leading Sophia further into the cafeteria, he picked up something else from the floor and showed her a large empty cylinder made out of dull metal.

"What is that?"

"Gas canister," he whispered. "At least that's what I think it is. I thought I saw one in the emergency room too. We should get out of here fast."

Sophia agreed silently, and they both exited the cafeteria into the parking lot, looking around, fearful that they might see someone moving, but the tent complex was no different than the hospital. Rows and rows of beds and hospital equipment were laid out beneath the tents, with motionless bodies in each gurney, and more bodies scattered along the aisles between them. They skirted their way along the edge of the building, back out toward the main street where they had left the car.

When someone did move, neither of them noticed until it was too late.

They were nearing the outer edge of the tents, when a figure stepped out of the shadows and slid in behind the two. A hand clamped over Sophia's mouth and another around her wrist, yanking her hand downward, sending the lighter clattering to the ground and plunging them into darkness.

A deep voice behind them whispered, "Be quiet! I won't hurt you."

Even though Hyle had been on the lookout for anyone moving, he was caught completely by surprise. Aware of a movement near Sophia's face, he had been just turning to look when suddenly the light shifted as the lighter fell and went out. By the time he began to react, the voice was speaking again.

"That light will get you killed," it hissed.

Sophia, who had also been taken by surprise, regained her wits enough to consider these words. They sounded like a warning rather than a threat and she relaxed slightly.

"I will let go now. Be quiet if you want to live."

Sophia nodded her agreement, and the hands released her mouth and wrist.

Only then did Hyle recover from the paralysis of surprise enough to act, and his action came without thought or planning.

"Get away from her!" he said in a low voice as he turned to face their assailant.

He saw, when he turned, a large figure standing motionless, just out of arm's reach. There was not enough light to make out more than a dark silhouette, but the person seemed to be at least as tall as he was, towering over Sophia, whose dim outline was just visible beside him.

Ignoring Hyle, the figure addressed Sophia, still whispering. "We can get medical help, but not here. Follow me."

The silhouette turned and walked back along the wall under the tents.

Fumbling on the ground where she had heard the lighter fall, Sophia located it and then took Hyle around the waist again.

"Come on," she whispered.

Hyle was not sure that it was a good idea, but he did not resist.

The stranger led them to the back of the parking lot where the tents stretched from the wall of the hospital across the lot to the building on the other side. Leaving the scant light of the tents, they descended a short flight of concrete stairs into a darker stairwell below ground, Hyle leaning on the metal rail and Sophia feeling her way along the wall. There was a rattle, then the sound of a door being opened. An arm reached around their shoulders and guided them through a doorway. A moment later the door thudded closed behind them. It was completely dark. The cool, stagnant air held a thick musty odor.

A red light appeared at their feet. The small beam of red penlight motioned from their feet toward a set of wooden stairs before them.

"What—" Sophia started, but was immediately cut off.

"Shhhh."

The beam waved insistently toward the stairs. Reaching out to place one hand on the railing, Sophia obliged, guiding Hyle up, step by step. She could hear footsteps behind them, and the red beam preceded her feet up the stairs, lighting her way. Just at the top it disappeared.

She emerged into the kitchen of a small restaurant.

Hyle drew a long breath. "I need to rest."

"No," the figure whispered. "Follow me. You can rest soon."

He pushed past and led them through a narrow seating area decorated with pieces of ornate metalwork and mosaics which glinted in the diffuse moonlight that filtered through the remains of a large front window. They did not venture too near the window, instead crossing over to an adjacent seating area and heading for the rear of the building again. Following a narrow hallway back into darkness before emerging into a back alley, the figure led them quickly past back doors and dumpsters reeking of putrid garbage, stopping finally at the last door before the alley opened out onto a street. He motioned them inside, stepping in after them and closing the door.

They stood in a drug store, near the pharmacy counter in the back of the building. The peg hooks along the walls and the aisles of metal shelves were bare, stripped of all merchandise. When their guide circled around in front of them, Hyle tried to get a look at him, but the man's back was to the light from the window, and he was wearing a sweatshirt with the hood pulled forward, concealing his face in deep shadows. Hyle did not entirely trust this mysterious person, but grudgingly admitted to himself that he was in no shape to do anything but follow where Sophia and this stranger led. His head was swirling and it was an effort just to remain standing.

"Wait here. I will get your car. Do not move until you see it out that window," the silhouette instructed, motioning toward the front of the store, "then come quickly."

No, Hyle thought. We're lucky to have a car that still works. If we give him the keys, we may never see him or the car again. He thought this, but did not say it because speaking required too much energy. His heart rate accelerated, but this time, instead of a burst of energy it made him feel weaker. To his surprise, their guide disappeared again into the alley without asking for the keys.

For a long time the two stood there in silence, Hyle leaning on Sophia for support, both watching the window and alert for whatever else might happen. Eventually Sophia broke the silence.

"How are you doing, Hyle?" she whispered.

He stared back at her blankly, his eyes narrowing slightly.

She waited.

"Hyle?" she whispered again urgently.

"I think…" he began. "I think I need to lie down."

"Hang in there. I'm sure he'll be here soon."

Hyle nodded weakly, and stared out the window again. Time crawled by. His peripheral vision darkened. Through his remaining tunnel vision he finally saw the car roll into view. The lights were off, and it moved slowly and silently. There was something not quite right about the scene, and he was still trying to identify what it was when the man in the dark sweatshirt came into view. He was walking beside the small car, leaning forward against the open driver's door, pushing the vehicle along the road.

The man helped Sophia escort Hyle to the passenger seat and whispered some quick instructions to her. She climbed into the driver's seat, and the man perched on the trunk of the car with his legs between the two seats.

"As soon as you start the engine, get us out fast. Take a right up there and keep going. Do not stop for anything."

Nodding, Sophia switched on the lights and turned the key in the ignition. The engine rumbled to life. She shifted quickly and the car sped away from the pharmacy, careening around the corner at the end of the street. As soon as they rounded the corner onto the broad main street, the man instructed her to shut the lights off, and a after a few streets, to turn again.

Several blocks later he said, "Good. We are safe now."

These were the last words Hyle heard.

"Safe from what?" Sophia asked, speaking in a loud voice, but still not quite daring to yell over the wind. She did not take her eyes from the road. She was traveling fast with no lights, and the city streets, though partially cleared, were still filled with obstacles.

"The death squads."

"What?"

"There are people out looking for survivors. Like you. Killing them. Death squads."

They turned and traveled a few blocks and then turned again, never staying too long on any road, never running into a dead end, their path leading them further out of the city into the suburbs.

Sophia thought about what the man had said. Already overwhelmed, her mind could not quite grasp the idea.

"Is that what happened at the hospital?"

"Yes. It is not safe to go out. Especially places like that where people gather."

"Why were you there?" Sophia asked.

"To save you."

Sophia could not tell whether or not this was meant as a joke. Between watching the road, the darkness and his position behind her, she was not able to see his face to judge his expression. He wore a dark hooded sweatshirt and she could just make out the word *Colgate* in white block letters across the chest. Inside the hood, shadows concealed his face such that she could only see the whites of his eyes and the occasional flash of his white teeth. Before she could pursue the issue, he had changed the topic.

"This was on your floor," he said, handing her the pamphlet Newman had given her.

"That's where I was supposed to be when the bomb went off."

"Then who would have saved him?" the stranger asked, gesturing toward Hyle. "You should still go," he told her. "It will be safe, but do not split up. You need each other now."

"It's too late," Sophia replied. "That started last weekend."

"They will still be there. Just ask for the man who invited you."

"How do you know—"

"Everyone has to be invited, yes?"

"Were you invited?"

"No, no. Not me."

Sophia thought she heard a muffled laugh before he pointed out a sign in the distance, and told her to turn there.

"They will take care of you here, but leave as soon he is able. Before tomorrow evening."

The sign was barely visible as a silhouette against the dimly luminescent clouds. Dark letters on a large white sign marked the entrance to the Forum department store parking lot. Sophia barely had time to register his words as she sped across a wide parking lot to the front doors of the giant building. Before she had even finished putting the car into park, they were surrounded by men with rifles.

CHAPTER EIGHT

THE FORUM

Garbled voices buzzing in the distance, light, warmth—all of these sensations seemed out of place, and even before he opened his eyes, Hyle was struggling to remember where he was and what had happened. As he forced himself to wake up and look around, memories came back to him, one triggering the next in lightning succession. First was the strong impression of darkness, cold, isolation and danger. Then he remembered the hospital, the stranger, Sophia and her home, and the destruction everywhere, but he could remember nothing of his current surroundings except a vague memory of waking before and hearing many voices in low conversation. And the smell of food. The memory of that smell shook the remaining sleep from his mind and gave him the energy to turn his head and look around.

There was a ceiling, high and wide above him, with dark racks of fluorescent lights hanging from painted steel beams. Blankets covered him and there was something soft beneath him, but he could feel the hard surface of the floor through it. Daylight flooded in from a nearby window at the entrance. Two men stood there, and he realized with a start that they both held rifles. Back to him, they were looking out the window. He surveyed them briefly. Neither of them spoke or turned away from their watch, so he turned his head the other way, toward the sound of voices, but here his view was blocked by some odd structures that he finally identified as a row of checkout counters. An old man sat on the end of one of the nearby counters, looking out of the window. He turned and looked down at Hyle.

"Oho, you're awake," he said with a crooked smile. "Stay right there. There's some-body who wants to see you."

The man slid down off the counter and disappeared behind it. Concerned about what might be coming, Hyle tried to sit up to take stock of his surroundings, but the effort took more energy than he realized. Light-headed and with his vision fading, he propped himself up on his elbows until the fog of dizziness began to lift again. He had managed to pull himself up to a sitting position when Sophia appeared behind one of the counters and hurried toward him.

She knelt down beside him and reached out to hug him, then with a quick glance at his chest, clasped his arm in both hands instead.

"I'm so glad to see you sitting up," she said. "And smiling. You slept through the whole day. How are you feeling?"

Hyle's chest felt tight and throbbed with pain. "A little weak, but not bad."

"When we brought you in here you had lost so much blood..." her voice trailed off. "I thought you were dead," she confided, her voice fading to a whisper.

"I was only mostly dead."

"Well, I'm glad," Sophia replied, forcing a laugh. "After digging me out of my house and saving me, I would have felt awfully guilty if you hadn't recovered."

"I guess this makes us even then."

Sophia nodded, and they were both silent. Eventually she said, "You must be hungry. Do you think you can walk? If not, I can bring you some food. We just had dinner."

Once Hyle decided that he could try to walk, Sophia, who had not let go of his arm, stood and helped him to his feet. Now that he could see over the checkout counters it was clear that they were in a large department store. Like the shops near the hospital, the merchandise was gone from the aisles, and many of the shelves and clothing racks had been removed or pushed to the side to make room on the floor. To the rear of the store, in one corner, clothing racks had been lined up and draped with sheets to make a few semi-private sleeping areas, and in the other back corner a makeshift dining room had been assembled from various dining room, patio and picnic tables. Several dozen people sat at these tables, engaged in conversation. A small group of children played on the floor nearby.

Sophia led him past the tables to the side door of the building where a couple of women sat at a small table with a large stew pot on it. One of the women got up as they approached.

"Your friend is awake now, is he?"

"Yes, and hungry," Sophia replied, and then addressing Hyle she explained, "This is Helen. She's our resident chef. One of the men shot a wild turkey today and she made a nice stew out of it."

"It's a little cold now, I'm afraid," Helen said, smiling at Sophia's compliment. She reached into the pot, pulling out a ladle full of stew and pouring it into a bowl for him.

Hyle took the stew gratefully, but then a thought struck him. Helen regarded him staring at the stew.

"What's the matter?" she asked.

"Where did you get the water for this?"

"Out of the creek beside the building," she replied, gesturing over her shoulder.

"But it could be contaminated with fallout…"

"Don't worry," she reassured him, "We boil everything before we serve it."

Hyle shook his head. "That'll kill germs, but it won't do anything about radiation." He felt a wave of nausea as he considered the possibility that all of these people had been drinking contaminated water. The woman's expression was grim, but she shrugged.

"It's all we've got. Radiation or dehydration—take your pick. If you don't want it, leave it here. Somebody else will have it."

"Oh…I…" Hyle felt suddenly awkward. He nodded in a gesture that was both apologetic and sympathetic. "Thank you," he said, almost in a whisper, and turned away with his bowl.

Sophia took him by the good arm and guided him toward one of the tables.

"There's someone I want you to meet," she told him as they walked. An older man and woman sat there, watching him approach.

"Hyle, this is Alexander and his wife Roxana. Alexander is the one who bandaged you up when we brought you in. He's also leading the effort to go out and find other groups of refugees like the folks here and unite them. They've already ventured as far west as Ithaca and Syracuse."

"You're lucky to be alive, young man," Alexander said. "You had lost some blood, but it looks like the bullet passed clean through you without hitting anything too important."

"Thank you," Hyle said. "Are you a doctor?"

"No, no," Alexander laughed. "Got some basic first aid in the service is all. But I saw plenty of people shot up in my day, and you're a lucky man. That was a close call. What happened?"

After thinking for a second Hyle shook his head. "I don't know."

"It was probably a death squad," Alexander ventured.

Sophia saw the look of incomprehension on Hyle's face and came to his defense.

"Hyle knows even less about what happened than I do. And he's still recovering," she said, meeting his eyes sympathetically. "Alexander and Roxana have been filling me in on everything that has happened in the last couple weeks. You were right. There was a nuclear attack, and it wasn't just Albany."

"Not hardly," said Alexander. "It was everywhere."

Hyle's eyes narrowed. "Everywhere? What do you mean everywhere?"

"I mean everywhere. New York, Boston, Chicago, L.A., London, Moscow, Beijing—just about any city you can name. You'd have to go pretty far down the list to care about nuking Albany."

With this introduction Alexander began to recount the story of a global nuclear war which had evidently caught most of the world by surprise. Roxana interjected tidbits of knowledge or rumor here and there, and as passersby heard the topic of conversation they stopped, listening and nodding in solemn agreement until they were compelled to jump in to share conflicting bits of information or propose alternate theories. Soon there was a small knot of people gathered around the table with side discussions and a few heated arguments. Hyle was interested in learning all he could, but he did not miss his opportunity to use the distraction of a particularly passionate debate to shuffle his untouched bowl of stew into the mix of dirty dishes on the table.

Sophia, who had been in Hyle's position the night before, was still struggling to accept what she had heard. Intellectually she knew that there was no reason to doubt it, but the scale of the calamity, the improbability of it, had left her in a comfortable state of denial. She watched Hyle closely for his reaction as he listened.

Although there was a lot of contradictory information, a common theme of consensus ran through some of the stories. Tensions were high because of the war overseas, and it looked as though several of the major world powers were on the verge of being pulled into the conflict. In addition to the well-established mobilization of U.S. troops to overseas bases, the United States was rumored to have dispatched Special Forces and military advisors to the region several weeks before the first nuclear strike, but had not officially entered the war. Aside from one man who claimed to have heard something like an air raid siren just a few minutes beforehand, there was no indication that an attack was coming. In the following days, most people had heard similar reports of widespread global attacks, and they agreed that communications had gone out altogether with a second wave of attacks, five days after the first, while Sophia was still trapped in her cellar.

That was where the consensus ended. Even the simple question of who had launched the first attack could not be agreed upon. One theory implicated Russia, another pointed to one of the new nuclear powers, and there was even a claim that the first missiles had been fired from within U.S. borders. At first the Pentagon had denied that there had been any launches from inside the United States. Later there were mixed reports either confirming counterstrikes without any detail or vague sketches of terrorist action. The government was in chaos. Rumors disagreed on whether the president had been killed or trapped overseas.

Estimates of casualties ran from fifty to eighty percent of the population. There was no rescue effort. There were no emergency crews—only pockets of people here and there trying to help each other. Even while communications were working, attempts to set up emergency centers had been thwarted by the so-called death squads. Some said that these were nothing more than bands of looters or vigilantes, but others insisted that there had been a military coup or an invasion. Alexander vehemently supported the latter view, along with the theory that the "Mumbai Plague" was actually a biological weapon designed to soften U.S. resistance to invasion.

Eyes moving from one speaker to the next, occasionally narrowing or widening, but otherwise showing no expression, Hyle listened quietly. Sophia thought that perhaps he too was too overwhelmed to truly absorb what he was hearing. And there was so much information! Everyone had a story to tell, a fact to share, an opinion to offer. It was as though the discussion itself was a cleansing ritual which required each participant to contribute every scrap of information they could share. There were so many different conflicting facts, stories and opinions that it was difficult to make sense of any of it, even the second time around. Sophia fully understood why he could only sit and listen dumbly. But he surprised her. Not only did he begin asking questions, he pursued each thread of the story relentlessly, challenging sources, double checking facts and interrogating everyone until there was no more information to be learned before turning to the next thread.

First he tried to establish how much was really known about the extent of the attacks, going back over the list of cities and countries that people had mentioned and separating news reports from second hand information and rumor. He also asked about a few places that Sophia did not remember anyone mentioning, checking sources in the same way. Even when the information cited was from a dependable news agency, he would ask whether it had been reported as established fact or an unconfirmed report. Sophia became aware of an odd emotion as she watched him, a mix of admiration and something else. Maybe it was a strange sort of pride that she was with him—this man who had, within such a short time of meeting all of these people, completely taken over the discussion of something he was still learning.

At last the questions ended. "If this is all true, this is much more than just a war," Hyle concluded.

"It's the apocalypse," said a woman with a bandage over both eyes.

"Thanks for telling us the obvious," a heavyset man said under his breath at the same time. The left side of his face was red and blistered while the other side looked perfectly normal.

Hyle turned to him. "What do you think happened then?"

"It's pretty clear to me. It's the old cold war military doctrine. Mutually assured destruction. I don't know what started it, but we nuked the Russians and they nuked us. Simple as that."

"Ah," said Hyle, feigning enlightenment. "Then maybe you can also explain why either Russia or the U.S. would also attack such a wide range of countries which have no involvement in the war whatsoever?"

The man was silent.

"No? Then maybe you can explain why, even though several reliable means of communication seem to have survived the first round of attacks, there's no clear story that the Russians attacked us, even though we should have been able to track their missiles for twenty minutes before they landed?"

Again the man was silent.

"Or maybe you can tell us why all the attacks seem to have focused on population centers rather than military targets? That's not cold war military doctrine, is it?"

The man glared at Hyle.

"Well, what do you think happened then?"

"I don't know," Hyle admitted. "But I think it's more than just a war. It sounds like it was a concerted effort to wipe out as many people as possible."

This comment sparked a flurry of conversation, and talk turned once more to speculation about the Mumbai Plague, death squads and military coups. Hyle was content to listen again while people shared their theories. When the crowd had thinned and only a few people remained, a man approached the table and made eye contact with Hyle. He was a short gentleman of dark complexion with large ears and a warm smile. Tufts of white hair covered his temples and sprouted from his ears. While Alexander finished his current point, the man waited politely for Sophia to introduce him.

"Hyle, this is Mr. Arwani. He was the store manager. I told him how you saved me from being trapped in my house."

Mr. Arwani put out his hand, and they exchanged greetings.

"I am happy to see that you're feeling better. We were all quite worried about you, but you look like you have made a speedy recovery. Perhaps you'd like to change out of those clothes. We don't have much food left, but we have plenty of clothes. I can show you the wash room too if you'd like to freshen up first."

Hyle looked down at his clothes. They were riddled with small rips and besmirched with a variety of stains that read like a travelogue of his past several days—soil ground into his knees and elbows from his flight through the woods, soot from the stalled cars, gray dirt and white plaster dust from Sophia's house, dried blood from his gunshot wound and through everything the lingering odor of wood smoke. The scent of wood smoke unexpectedly triggered the image of a cabin in the woods where he had been working, and suddenly facts and images, people and places, came flooding back, filling in the gaps in his memory.

"Are you okay?" asked Sophia, clasping his arm in both her hands again. "You look like you just saw a ghost."

"Huh? Oh, yes. I'm fine," Hyle replied absently, taking a mental inventory of his rediscovered memories. Then he saw Mr. Arwani waiting patiently for a response to his offer. "Yes, I'd like to wash up and get some new clothes. Thank you."

Stopping frequently to introduce him to people, answer questions or give instructions, Mr. Arwani led the way across the store. He was like the mayor of a small village taking a stroll through town. As they walked he explained that he had been working when the power went out.

"At first we didn't suspect anything. We had to close our registers and people waited in line for a while. But then people started coming in from the parking lot saying that their cars would not start and their cell phones were not working. Soon it was a panic. Nobody knew what was happening, but we knew something was wrong. Then there was a flash. It was so bright that the poor people in the parking lot who were looking the wrong way were blinded. Burned their eyes," he said, shaking his head sympathetically. "Since then quite a few people left to try to make their way home, but we have almost a hundred people who stayed or found their way here, like you and your lady friend. Ah, here we are. Pick out anything you need here and the washroom is right down that little hallway."

"Thank you, Mr. Arwani," Hyle said and felt his back pocket. "I'm afraid I can't..."

"No, no, no. Money is the last thing any of us needs," said Mr. Arwani, putting his hands up and shaking his head. He gave Hyle a friendly smile tinged with sadness.

After looking through the racks of clothes, Hyle picked out a pair of durable looking tan cargo pants and a heavy blue and green plaid shirt and headed down the hallway to the men's room. The door was wedged open, allowing in just enough daylight to see himself in the mirror. His face looked no better than his clothes. It was riddled with scratches and partially concealed by a several day growth of beard. Dried blood, bits of leaves, plaster dust and black soot were mixed into his dirtier than usual dirty blond hair. Even in the dim light he could tell that he was quite pale, except for the dark circles under his eyes.

He was momentarily surprised when he turned on the faucet and nothing came out. Then he registered the significance of the large yellow camping cooler on the other sink. It had been set atop a wire shelf stolen from a barbeque grill such that the tap at the bottom hung over the side of the sink toward him. He soaked the blood stain with a little water from the cooler, carefully peeling away the cloth. The shirt had been slit from the collar to the edge of the sleeve and a large patch of gauze had been taped to his shoulder. He pulled the shirt over his head and examined the dressing. It was saturated with blood and something oily that he assumed was an antiseptic. He started to pull at one end of the tape where it was beginning to irritate his arm pit, but then decided against removing the bandage. Just at the limit of his reach his fingertips he felt the edge of a similar dressing on the back side of his shoulder.

On top of the large square trash barrel by the door Hyle found a pile of clean towels, an open pack of disposable razors and various other toiletries. He shaved, and to the best of his ability, washed his hair in the sink, one cupful of water at a time. When this was done he changed into the new shirt and pants, smiling at his reflection and pausing for a moment to appreciate the feel of clean warm clothes.

CHAPTER NINE

THE PAST REMEMBERED

In the dining area most of the adults were still engaged in conversation, although their voices were lower. Light was fading and some of the children had gone to sleep. With help from the half-burned man and a few of the older children, Helen was bussing dishes and sorting them into plastic storage bins. Pointing him toward the side door, out through the garden shop, she informed Hyle that Sophia had volunteered to clean up after dinner and had taken a bin of dishes out to the stream to wash. Hyle doubled back quickly to grab a hunting jacket and went to help her.

The evening sky was overcast and suffused with an eerie orange glow that reminded him of smoke enveloping the light of a campfire. It was unseasonably cold, and he was glad to have gone back for a coat. Just outside the side door was a vast field of waist-high grass that extended behind the building in one direction and all the way to the street in the other. It was separated from the store and parking lot by a small buffer zone of mown grass that was still less than a foot high. Hyle could not see the stream, but a well-trodden path led straight away from the door through the tall grass. At the other end of the path he found the stream and Sophia. She was loading dishes into a plastic bin when she spotted him.

"Well, you clean up nicely," she said, with a gentle smile.

He realized that she must have also washed and changed some time while he slept. The jeans, white blouse and sweater vest she had chosen all fit her snugly, and she had pulled her hair back, the overall result being a much more feminine look.

"Thanks. You look, uh, very nice yourself," Hyle said. He hoped she could not see his cheeks in the fading light.

"Don't look so surprised," she said, grinning. Hyle was trying to think of what to say next and just beginning to feel awkward when she stood up and added, "I was just headed back."

Hyle offered to take the bin full of dishes, but Sophia refused, telling him that he needed to take it easy. He followed her back along the path to the store, but hung back as they passed through the garden shop.

Sophia had already half filled the bin with more dirty dishes when Hyle emerged from the garden shop pushing a large wheelbarrow. He parked it by one of the tables and began loading dishes into it, to a mixture of good natured laughter and praise.

"Oh, that's so very clever of you," one woman gushed. "And we've been walking back and forth to the stream all this time."

"If necessity is the mother of invention, laziness must be the father," Hyle replied as he continued clearing dishes into the wheelbarrow, careful not to move his wounded shoulder too quickly. When he came to his own table he realized with a twinge of guilt that his bowl was the only one with any food left in it. He cleared it away furtively and quickly put another bowl on top of it.

With a full load of dishes, they set off down the path to the stream, Sophia adding her praise for his creativity as they walked. Hyle carefully piloted the wheelbarrow down the gentle slope to the edge of the water. The stream was wide, shallow and slow moving, the bottom covered with smooth pale rocks.

"Now for my second efficiency initiative," he announced, and dumped the contents of the wheelbarrow into the stream.

"Are you always this innovative?" asked Sophia.

"Innovative? This is how I do my dishes at home. I always soak them first," he told her, "one wheelbarrow full at a time."

Laughing, they both set about washing dishes, each enjoying the company of the other for a while in silence as they fished one object at a time from the cold stream, rinsing and toweling each one off before placing it back in the wheelbarrow. They were both in good spirits as they worked, but as the sunlight faded, a darkness grew again in Sophia's thoughts.

"Do you think it really is true?" she asked suddenly. "Are there even enough nuclear weapons to do what they were saying in there?"

Hyle nodded slowly. "Yes, there were. Back at the end of the nineties, during the disarmament talks, the U.S had around six thousand nuclear weapons and Russia probably had roughly the same number. The targets after disarmament were still a couple thousand each. If you used five for every state in the union that would still be only two hundred and fifty. And these were much more powerful than the ones that ended World War II—most of them more than fifty times more powerful."

"How do you know so much about this?" Sophia asked. "I mean, you seemed to be as confused as I was when you dug me out of my house, and now you sound like an expert."

"I'm a science writer. That's what I do... did for a living. The trauma must have blanked my memory, but I just pieced together how it was that I stumbled across your house."

Sophia finished drying a bowl and placed it in the bin, then set down the towel to give Hyle her full attention.

"I was writing a book. I rented a cabin in the Catskills for the summer. This place was very primitive—no electricity, no running water. I know, pretty ironic for a science and technology writer, but it was really isolated and it let me focus on my reading. I had a lot of research to plow through before I could start writing. Every week or so I'd jump into the car and go into town to stock up on supplies. This one night, just as I was coming off the dirt road onto the highway, a couple guys flagged me down from the side of the road. They had the hood up on their truck, and I thought maybe I could give them a lift. One of them came up to my window to talk to me. While I was watching him, his friend got in next to me on the passenger side. Then the guy outside pulled a gun on me and told me to get out."

"Oh my God. And he shot you?"

"Not right then." Hyle hesitated. "I did something pretty stupid," he confessed. "Out of habit I shut off the engine and took the keys with me. I guess I still didn't quite understand what was going on, but neither did they. I was out of the car and backing away toward the woods when they realized that the engine wasn't running. The guy with the gun started yelling, 'Give us the keys! Give us the keys!' but I froze. I should have just given him the keys, but I was trying to think of something to say to him. I couldn't come up with anything fast enough, so he shot me. That unfroze me. I bolted into the woods. They chased me for a while, and shot at me a couple more times, but it was just getting dark and it was hard to see in the woods so I lost them pretty quickly. I found a little depression behind a big fallen tree and hid there. I think I must have passed out. Sometime later in the night I climbed up a mountain to see if I could see the lights of a town, but it was dark in every direction. It was daylight again by the time I found the road that led up to your house. I was taking a nap in your car when I heard you banging on the pipes. The rest is history."

Sophia looked appalled.

"I can't believe that someone was willing to kill you just for your car."

"Neither could I. But now that I know they had just survived a nuclear war, I suppose they might have been a bit desperate."

They were silent for a moment. Sophia found herself thinking about the horrible things that people might be doing to each other around the world and decided to end that line of thinking.

"I bet Alexander will be disappointed to learn that it wasn't one of those death squads that shot you."

"Yeah," Hyle paused thoughtfully. "I'm not sure what to think of all that. Obviously people are capable of doing some pretty crazy things, but the hospital…"

"The guy who brought us here said that was the work of a death squad. I think he even used that same term."

"Where is he? I forgot all about him. I didn't see him at dinner."

"No," Sophia replied, "he disappeared right after he brought us here. Nobody even remembers seeing him because they were so busy getting you into the store and bandaged."

"Is your car still here?"

Sophia laughed lightly, but then her expression grew suddenly serious.

"I'm sorry. I'm sure it must be hard to trust people after everything you've just gone through. Yes, my car is still here." She filled Hyle in on the trip from the hospital to the store and the crowd of people who had rushed out to help him. It was clear that she had seen a much kinder side of human nature than he had recently, but she also remembered the stranger's warning.

"Do you… do you have anyone who will be looking for you?" she asked quietly.

Hyle shook his head. "Not really. My parents passed away years ago, and I was too wrapped up in my career to have time for anyone new. You?"

"No. That's why I was so glad when you found me. Before I even knew how bad things were I was wondering if anyone at work would worry about me enough to come by and check on me. I'm not sure what I'm going to do now." Sophia waited briefly to see if Hyle would suggest anything. When he did not, she decided to press on. "I was thinking that maybe we should head up to Maine."

"Maine? Why would you want to go to Maine of all places?"

In order to avoid awkward questions, Sophia tried to explain the Union of Faith, her invitation to the retreat, and the logic of finding a safe haven, without specifically mentioning either Newman or the stranger. She felt that Hyle might jump to the wrong conclusion about her relationship with Newman and knew that she could not explain why she trusted the advice of the stranger. Hyle seemed to be familiar with Zendik and his organization, but not necessarily in a favorable way.

"They sounded very tolerant of all different ideas," she said, trying to anticipate his objections. "And besides, I think a little more faith and spirituality is exactly what people need right now. It's hard to explain, but I really think it's the right thing to do."

Without looking up, Hyle reached down into the stream and started scrubbing a handful of spoons.

"I don't know," he said slowly. "Let me sleep on it. I'm a bit of a skeptic when it comes to spirituality, and too much of a cynic to believe in the pure intentions of a televangelist."

"A cynic and a skeptic? I had you pegged as a stoic."

Hyle looked at her blankly, confused by the apparent non-sequitur. Sophia laughed.

"Sorry. That was a joke. A bad philosophy joke."

"I don't get it."

"That's why it was a bad joke."

"Then if you explain it to me it'll be a good joke," Hyle suggested.

Sophia chuckled again.

"They're all schools of philosophy. The Cynics, the Skeptics and the Stoics. And the Epicureans too for that matter. It's kind of funny—interesting, I mean—that these four schools of philosophy all came about around the same time and all turned into English words, but none of them quite mean what they originally meant."

Grateful for a change of topic, Sophia paused to gauge Hyle's interest and decided that it was sufficient for her to continue.

"Alexander the Great had conquered most of the civilized world. He had his own link to philosophy since Alexander was tutored by Aristotle, who was a student of Plato, who in turn was a student of Socrates. Anyway, Alexander had turned the world upside down and the power of the Greek city-states had been overthrown. It was a stressful and uncertain age, and these four philosophies evolved to address the question of how to best live in such times."

"A philosophy designed for stressful times sounds good right about now," Hyle commented. "But what did the Stoics believe in if it wasn't being stoic?"

"They were stoic by our modern definition of the word, but it was more than just keeping a stiff upper lip," Sophia clarified. "There was a whole philosophy which justified their behavior. The Stoics believed that logic was supreme, even in nature. They didn't believe in a supernatural or eternal world, but they did believe in a natural law and a natural order of things. For them God was more or less the logic of nature, rather than something existing outside of nature. The Stoics thought that everything happened for a reason, so there was no use fighting against personal tragedies. The best thing to do was to accept things gracefully, with dignity, and if emotions got in the way of this they were to be conquered with logic."

"Alexander the Great must have loved this philosophy."

Sophia gave him a perplexed look.

"If the basic message is to accept things the way they are, they must have been model citizens," Hyle explained. "You know, don't rock the boat. Don't challenge authority."

"Oh, I see. I suppose there may be something to that. Even though the school was founded in Greece by Zeno—"

"No," she said, seeing the look of recognition on Hyle's face and anticipating his question, "The Zeno you probably know is Zeno of Elea, from the famous paradox. He was much earlier. It was Zeno of Citium who founded Stoicism. Anyway, most of the greatest Stoic writers were Romans who came just after Alexander the Great—Seneca, Marcus Aurelius, Epictetus. And it's true that Marcus Aurelius was an emperor, but I don't think Stoicism was propagated to keep people in line. I think the concept of a natural order just fit well with the very orderly nature of Roman society. Epictetus was a slave after all. And it wasn't so much that they tried to avoid all conflict—Stoics were often actively involved in politics—they just thought it was futile to be in conflict with the order of the natural world."

"I suppose I can get behind that," Hyle said. "What about the Skeptics? Were they skeptical?"

"Well, sort of. The Skeptics were skeptical, but in a broader sense. Nowadays being skeptical just means that you're less likely than most people to take something on faith, without some kind of evidence. The Skeptics of ancient Greece questioned everything, even the basic assumptions about the nature of the world. Pyrrho probably brought skepticism back from India during the conquests of Alexander the Great in the third century BC, and his followers helped develop it into a philosophy. Arcesilaus developed the idea that nothing could be absolutely known or refuted and summarized this with the saying, 'Nothing is certain, not even that.' Skeptics would often be able to argue both sides of a question equally forcefully to demonstrate this principle, but they also had some logical arguments for their philosophy. Timon of Phlius made the observation that every logical argument starts with assumptions, which in turn must be proven. They're always in the form of *if* A equals B then B equals C, but then you have to prove that A really does equal B, and to do that you need to start with another assumption and so on—an infinite regress. Ultimately, about five hundred years later, Sextus Empiricus tied many of these ideas together into a milder form of skepticism which also incorporates many elements of modern empiricism."

"Milder than what?" asked Hyle. "It sounded pretty logical to me."

"There was a story about Pyrrho that he was supposedly so sincere about questioning everything that he'd stick his hand in a fire to see if it really burned and his pupils had to travel around with him to keep him out of trouble."

"Okay, I'm not that much of a skeptic," Hyle conceded. "What about the Cynics?"

"The Cynics questioned social conventions in the same way that the Skeptics questioned the nature of things. They rejected things like wealth, titles, private property, marriage and other social norms. The most famous figure in that school, Diogenes, took this philosophy to the extreme. He's said to have lived outside Athens in a funeral urn, sometimes not bothering to wear clothes or cook his meat. Because of the way he lived, people referred to him as the dog, *kynos* in Greek. That's where the word cynic comes from. He became so famous that Alexander the Great supposedly traveled to visit him at his urn. The story goes that when Alexander asked if he could do anything for Diogenes, Diogenes told him, 'Yes, you can stand out of my light,' which has a great double meaning if you think about it."

Hyle laughed briefly. "I guess I'm not that much of a cynic either, but I do appreciate cynical humor. How about the Epicureans?"

"Epicurus had a very practical, almost scientific basis for his philosophy. He believed the theory of an earlier philosopher Democritus, who said that everything was made up of basic particles that combine in different ways to make up material objects, and eventually break apart again. Epicurus believed that this applied to people too, so his followers held that there was nothing after death, nothing immortal, and focused on how to minimize fear and pain and enjoy life."

"So what did they do, just have parties all the time?"

"Not exactly. They did believe in a life of physical pleasures—good food, good wine, good conversation with friends, things like that—but they also believed that doing anything to excess caused problems, so they taught moderation as a way to avoid conflict and pain. And while most Greeks were out trying to achieve fame and glory or serve the state, the Epicureans were happiest living a quiet life, removed from all the inevitable conflicts of active society."

"So they were more the types to sip a pina colada on the beach than have a wild party?"

"I suppose so, but there was a very well-developed philosophy about the nature of the world that led them to that lifestyle. The word *epicurean* nowadays captures the essence of that belief in material pleasures, but loses all of the philosophy behind it, just like stoic, cynic and skeptic."

"There are pieces of each of those that appeal to me," Hyle said. "Do you subscribe to any one more than another?"

Sophia gave him a distant smile. "I identify with different ones at different times. The Epicurean way sounds particularly good to me right now. Imagine finding a place far away from the conflicts of the world with a few other decent people who just want to live a good quiet life."

"You mean like this place in Maine?"

"Saw right through that, didn't you?" Sophia's smile turned into a sheepish grin. She was in the process of formulating a convincing argument when her thoughts were interrupted by a gunshot.

CHAPTER TEN

SUDDEN DEPARTURE

Night was creeping in from the east, preceded by the murky twilight that covered the parking lot. When they turned in the direction of the sound, the first thing that struck Sophia and Hyle was how dark it had gotten behind them. Already it was too dark to make out details, and colors were distinguishable only as shades of gray. In the lot, just visible above the field of brown grass, a group of men had taken up position behind a Humvee. They looked like soldiers, wearing camouflage fatigues and combat boots, although their heads were bare. They were armed with assault rifles. A truck, painted in the same flat army camouflage, was just pulling into the lot behind them. As men piled out of the truck, several short bursts of automatic weapon fire issued from the Humvee. In the store front glass shattered.

Sophia started to climb the bank for a better view, but Hyle grabbed her arm and pulled her back down.

"Wait," he said, and even as he spoke several men broke from behind the vehicles and dashed to the wall beside the entrance. Others, working in pairs, fanned out across the parking lot, keeping low behind the cover of parked cars. Sophia tried to pull away from him up the bank.

"We have to help them! Let me go!"

Hyle grabbed her by the waist and pulled her down, yelling over the gunfire.

"No! There are only two lives we can save right now—yours and mine." He held on as she pulled away and tried to push his hands off her arms. "What are you planning to do—run up and kick them in the shins? Those are automatic weapons. You'd be dead before you even got to the pavement."

Accepting the feeling of helplessness was devastating, but Sophia knew he was right. She absentmindedly cooperated as he helped her to put on his jacket. Hyle had reasoned that it was more important to use the hunter's camouflage to cover the white sleeves of Sophia's blouse than his dark flannel shirt.

Occasional shotgun blasts and long barrages of automatic weapon fire from the store answered the spitting bursts of the assault rifles. There were shrieks of pain and panic from inside the building. Sophia made no further attempt to leave the stream bank, but stood up, not wishing to see, but unable to keep herself from watching. Most of the men were now gone from sight, but a few were still outside, circling around the store. A small contingent kept watch on the parking lot. The gunfire and screaming continued for several excruciating seconds, the assault rifles now unanswered. Hyle cursed under his breath.

"Those two soldiers by the side of the store, where did they go?" he hissed.

He scanned along the side of the building finding nothing, but his eyes caught a movement in the tall grass between the stream and the parking lot, and he snapped his head over to look. In the long shadows of the fading light he was unable to see what had drawn his attention. There was no motion now, but after several seconds his eyes fixed on a furrow in the otherwise undisturbed field. From the parking lot it extended halfway across the expanse of grass in a straight line directly toward them.

"Oh crap, let's get out of here."

Grabbing Sophia's hand, he led her up the opposite bank of the stream, keeping low, through more tall grass and a narrow stand of trees, into another parking lot. It was a car dealership. Orderly lines of vehicles stretched in all directions, and floodlight poles adorned with tattered strings of pennants rose along the border of the road like a row of dark trees with willowy branches waving in the breeze. A large showroom occupied the center of the lot, its glass front miraculously intact. Looking back, Hyle and Sophia saw two men in fatigues running toward them from the far side of the stream, and accelerated through the cars, weaving toward the showroom.

When they reached the front doors, Hyle pulled on one side while Sophia tried the other. Locked. They saw that the soldiers had not yet emerged from the trees and raced around the far side of the building, looking back over their shoulders. Hyle hoped that they had made it around the corner of the building unseen, buying them a little time, but there was no way to tell. He wished that it were just a little darker.

Around the corner their path was blocked by an adjoining building set back from the showroom. A row of broad windowless overhead doors confronted them. In the corner next to the showroom was a personnel door with a small dark window. Their eyes found it almost instantly.

It too was locked.

In anger and desperation Hyle twisted the doorknob with both hands and slammed his shoulder into the door, but it refused to yield. Listening and trying to estimate how many seconds they might have before their pursuers rounded the corner, he scanned around for a better place to hide. Finding no good options, he decided to risk making some noise and smashed one of the small panes of glass with his elbow. He reached through and opened the door, following Sophia closely as he pushed her in, pulling the door closed quickly behind them. Relocking the door, he cast about in the blackness, waiting for his eyes to adjust. Sophia's breath came in short panicked gasps from the darkness beside him. He was able to discern the outline of a large tool cabinet nearby and had his hands on it, ready to push it over to the door, when he thought he heard voices.

A light flickered outside the door and the knob rattled.

Hyle ducked behind the cabinet and Sophia fell in quietly behind him, clinging close to his back. A beam of light appeared, streaming in through the window and searching the wall opposite the door. It moved back and forth along the wall as an arm reached through the window and unlocked the door.

The light retreated.

Silence.

Hyle fought to stifle the sound of his own heavy breathing. His heart hammered in his chest, sending blood surging into his ears, and he strained to hear any sound outside, but all was silent. Several long seconds passed.

Suddenly the door burst open and again the beam of light flashed in, this time swinging rapidly back and forth through the bays in a frenetic dance of scattered light and shadows. From their hiding place behind the tool drawers, the bright flashes of light in the darkness brought back to Sophia memories of fearful nights as a child, clutching stuffed animals for comfort as lightning split the night sky outside her bedroom window. In a familiar helpless gesture, she squeezed Hyle and closed her eyes, left with only the desperate hope that it would all soon go away.

There was a quick shuffle of feet inside the door, only a few paces away on the other side of the cabinet. A second light stabilized on the far end of the garage. The beam, just above them, cast a long shadow over the narrow space where Hyle and Sophia were crouched. It moved steadily along the walls, revealing a dark hatchback in a service bay next to them, stopping at each window, searching beneath it, then moving on to the minivan on the lift in the next bay and on both sides of that until it had covered the entire area.

A circle of light bobbled up and down randomly on the back wall and there was a brief exchange of whispering, no more than ten feet away. Then the beam swung quickly back toward the cabinet and the silence was ripped by a blast of automatic gunfire. A tire exploded next to their hiding place and a car window erupted in a shower of glass. Hyle felt Sophia's fingers dig into his sides as his body tensed, but neither of them made a sound. Silence again.

Nobody moved. Hyle heard only the sound of his breathing and wondered whether it was loud enough for the soldiers to hear. His leg, twisted beneath him in an awkward crouch, felt like it was on fire. He ignored it as well as he could, focusing on his breathing and trying to make it steady and ever quieter.

There was a slight rustle. One of the lights fixed on the space between the front of the hatchback and the tool chest. A footstep scuffed closer on the concrete floor, and the angle of the light broadened toward them. Then another gentle footstep. The end of an assault weapon appeared a few feet away, the source of light affixed to it just beyond sight.

Outside an engine started nearby. It was a deep unmuffled rumble, like a big motorcycle or a hot rod. It revved several times, then tires squealed and the sound of the engine receded quickly. The gun barrel disappeared, the light flashed away, and after a few rapid footsteps the door was thrown wide open with a slam as the soldiers ran out.

Hyle and Sophia did not dare to move for a long time. When Hyle did finally move, it was to quietly adjust his sore leg and slowly raise his head above the cabinet to watch and listen for several more minutes. Once he was convinced they were alone, he felt for Sophia's hand and helped her to stand.

For several seconds the two stood there, squeezing each other's hands and looking at each other in a silent exchange of relief and fear. Finally Sophia put her hand on Hyle's ear.

"I think I saw some keys behind that counter," she whispered, and pointed to the back corner of the garage, opposite the door.

"I'll watch at the door while you get them," he whispered back, trying to keep his voice from sounding as tremulous as hers had.

The door had bounced almost closed again. Hyle pushed it gently shut and crouched behind it, watching through one of the lower window panes. He avoided the broken one, as if the intact glass would offer him some protection. The sound of the engine had long faded and there was no sign of the two men, so he motioned to Sophia that it was safe. With her eyes adjusting again to the scant light, she moved around the service counter and removed the four sets of keys from their hooks. While Hyle continued to watch at the door, she skirted around the bullet-ridden hatchback in the first bay, past the raised minivan in the second bay, and fumbled at the door of the third car. It was a large white sedan, and Hyle could see Sophia's torso clearly silhouetted against it in the space between the roof of the hatchback and the bottom of the lift. He heard the faint clatter of keys followed shortly by a muffled click. Sophia's head appeared in the gap and she waved him over.

"It's open," she hissed.

"Good. Let me in, then try to start it."

Before she could protest, he moved quickly around to the passenger side. Sophia quietly lifted the latch, opened the door and slid in. Hyle slid in beside her, leaving his door open. She put the key in the ignition.

"Now?" she whispered.

"Yes. No, wait. I'll go get ready to open the overhead door first. Give me three seconds." He climbed back out and went to the bay door. Although it was an automatic door, he found a chain that would open it manually. There was a small lever that slid through the railing to lock the door. Not realizing that it was spring loaded, he put one hand on the chain and slowly tugged on the handle.

The lever jumped out of his grip and settled with a clang so loud that it sounded like the railing had been struck with a hammer. His heart leapt. The impact rippled through the lifting springs of the door and they vibrated with a tinny high-pitched echo like lasers in a low budget science fiction movie. Hyle waited by the door ready to pull the chain as soon as the engine turned over. When he could not wait any longer he ran to the door and stuck his head in.

"It won't start?" he hissed

"No. I heard—"

"Shhhhhh! They're coming back! Get down!"

Hyle ducked below the roof of the car as the light returned to the doorway, bouncing up and down and growing rapidly stronger.

"Get out! This way."

Sophia crawled across the seat and slid onto the floor as the personnel door opened again. Hyle eased the car door shut just as a beam of light swept quickly through the garage. He motioned Sophia to the rear wheel, and she moved over and crouched behind it. He moved in behind her and held his hand out in front of her. She understood.

Slowly and deliberately she handed him the remaining three keys as the light played through the windows of the white sedan above them. The light retreated momentarily then reappeared along the ground below the vehicle. Hyle pulled his feet in tight. The beam crept along the floor on one side of the wheel, flickered out and reappeared on the other, inches away from his foot. As soon as it moved away, Hyle duckwalked quietly to their last hope, an ancient Jeep wagon manufactured in the days before they were marketed as trendy sport utility vehicles. The second key worked in the door.

While the light was focused on the jumble of cabinets, tool chests and work benches along the rear wall, Hyle risked popping his head up for a quick look. Both men were inside. One was standing near the doorway and seemed to be splitting his time between the parking lot and the garage. The other had moved to the rear wall and was heading for the front end of the hatchback in the first bay. Searching inside the car as he moved, aiming the light on his assault rifle through the windshield, he circled slowly around it as Hyle watched from the darkness. Without warning, the soldier snapped his rifle in Hyle's direction. The action caught Hyle by surprise and he began to duck only after the beam of light had found its new target, which was fortunately still two bays away.

As the soldier searched the pit below the minivan, Hyle slid down against the Jeep, biting back the startled gasp that almost managed to escape his mouth, and trying to collect his wits. They were searching much more thoroughly this time and Hyle knew it would not be possible to hide. The soldier at the door had a clear view along the front wall of the garage and the other one was moving along the back wall, drawing closer as he searched. The front wall was the lesser risk. Hyle caught Sophia's eye and motioned her toward the front of the building, around the back of the old Jeep to the other side.

She moved quickly, bent over double. Although she made no sound and moved in relative darkness, the soldier by the doorway swung his light up along the front wall where she crossed. The light illuminated the overhead doors, the underside of the minivan, the rear of the white sedan and an empty space behind the Jeep. The second soldier turned his light to the same area, but his view was largely blocked by the minivan. It bounced up and down as he moved out from behind the lift to get a better vantage point.

Before the soldier had a clear line of sight, Hyle lobbed the two useless sets of keys across the garage. They hit the wall behind the counter and clattered to the floor. The momentary distraction was successful. Both lights moved to track the sound and the soldier by the door squeezed off several bursts at the counter, advancing toward it as he fired. Sophia seized the opportunity to open her door and slide in. Hyle knew what she had done immediately. The dome light went on inside the Jeep. Hyle threw open his door and reached for the ignition even before putting his foot inside. The starter turned over reluctantly as the two lights snapped around again. For a few fractions of a second that seemed like eternity, it was unclear whether the car would start, but the starter did catch and Hyle slammed the transmission into reverse, stomping on the accelerator.

The combination of one car on a lift and another on the ground prevented the soldiers from getting a good line of sight, but they opened fire anyway. Glass shattered in the white sedan, and the closest soldier sprinted around the end of the minivan. He had a clear shot only for a second as the Jeep lurched backwards.

"Hold on," Hyle yelled. Bullets ricocheted off of steel and a hole erupted in the windshield, surrounded by a spiderweb of cracked glass, just as the Jeep slammed into the overhead door. The door slowed them only briefly. Fragments of the wood panels somersaulted in the air around them and rained down, bouncing off the hood and roof as the truck slammed to a stop with a metallic crunch against a car behind them. Without hesitation Hyle thrust it into drive, cut the wheel hard and raced along between rows of cars. One of the soldiers was able to get out and squeeze off a few more bursts before Hyle cut the wheel again and sped down another lane, putting parked cars between them and the garage.

The dealership was out of sight and several miles down the road before either of them was able to speak. Sophia broke the silence, but her voice was barely more than a whisper.

"I'm still shaking. I don't think I have ever been so scared in my entire life."

"Me too."

"But you've been shot at before. I've never—"

"I didn't see that coming. This was worse. Much, much worse."

The talking helped. Hyle, who had tremors in his arms and legs, felt himself beginning to relax.

"I think we're safe now," he said.

They agreed to keep driving for a while to put some more distance behind them and the car dealership. Many hours later and several towns away, where the suburbs slowly gave way to country, the incident was far enough behind them that they felt comfortable stopping, and pulled over at an isolated convenience store, hoping to find some food. They lost their appetites as soon as they opened the door. Immediately they were assailed by the stench of rotting food and sour milk. In the illumination of the headlights they could see dark masses in the deli cooler and milk spattered on the doors of the refrigerators in front of cartons that had split open. But spoilage seemed to be the only damage. They saw no signs of looting or vandalism and realized with surprise that they had walked in through an unlocked front door. Sophia took some comfort from this until Hyle speculated that people might be afraid to come out even for looting and recommended they make the most of it while it lasted.

The store provided everything they could have reasonably hoped to find. A flashlight and batteries allowed Hyle to turn off the headlights and park the car around the side of the building, beside a van and well concealed from the street. Although he thought it unlikely that anyone was searching for them, he felt better taking the extra precaution. A can opener enabled them to have something more substantive than candy bars and potato chips for dinner. Despite the odor Hyle, who had passed up his stew, ate greedily from cans of ravioli and tuna fish.

Exhausted from their panicked flight, they decided to sleep before making any further plans. To be safe, Sophia locked the front door, hoping the sound of breaking glass would provide sufficient warning should someone come, then went into the back room where they slept on a stack of broken down cardboard boxes.

When Sophia woke the next day, the sun was already high in an overcast sky. The back room did not receive much light from the front window and Hyle was still asleep. After eating a few handfuls of dry breakfast cereal and washing them down with a bottle of warm iced tea from the cooler, Sophia busied herself with searching the store more thoroughly and setting aside things that might be useful to take with them on the road. Looting, she reasoned, was taking advantage of a lapse in social order and usually for personal gain, as opposed to something that was a matter of survival during wartime. Even though she believed in this distinction, it was not entirely sufficient to quell the vague discomfort that seemed to come from somewhere other than her mind. She made a silent pledge that for this and whatever else she might take in the days ahead she would try to pay back her debt to society.

Eventually Hyle got up. He sat on the floor and looked over her discoveries as he ate a package of cream-filled chocolate cupcakes.

"It looks like you have everything we need for a long trip except a towel," he said playfully.

Sophia did not respond. She was absorbed in a road atlas. She had been flipping pages, but then stopped about halfway through the book and examined one of the pages thoroughly, running her finger up and down and tracing along highways. Upside down, Hyle tried to make out the page.

"Is that Maine?" he asked.

"Yes, actually."

"So you're still set on going there?"

"Are you kidding? After last night?" she replied. "We have to get away from here. I mean very far away. If everything we heard is true, all the cities will be like this. I don't think I can stand to see anything like that again," she said, her voice dropping to a whisper. She looked away, out the window and took a few deep breaths. "You know, if we are able to find them, we wouldn't have to stay if you didn't like it. And if we don't find them, at least we'll be far away from the cities."

"Okay," Hyle conceded. "I suppose we can give it a shot. But I don't think we should go now. We should only travel after dark to decrease the chance of being spotted by anyone."

Sophia agreed with this strategy and they spent the afternoon preparing to travel. She tried to convince Hyle to abandon the Jeep, but he seemed to have an irrational attachment to the vehicle. Her argument that they would need something faster in case they were pursued did not sway him, even after she pointed out a sleek Nissan sports car a few spaces away.

"I doubt that it'll start," he said. "Besides, we need something that can take a beating. We're more likely to run into something on the road than get into a high-speed chase."

"What about gas? This thing probably uses twice as much as a smaller car," she reasoned.

"It's a fair trade for cargo space, and there should be plenty of cars on the way to siphon gas from."

"But why was it in the shop? What if the wheels fall off?" Sophia persisted.

Hyle sighed.

"If you want to try to start the Nissan, be my guest, but I know this will get us there," he said, thumping the dented hood of the Jeep.

After searching for keys to a couple of the faster looking cars, Sophia gave up on the idea of taking something other than the Jeep and grudgingly loaded it with food and beverages, the flashlight and can opener, lighters, batteries, oil, coolant, tire sealant and miscellaneous supplies. Over the course of the afternoon her discomfort with taking things from the store faded, and within a few hours the back was packed almost to capacity with cans, bottles, boxes and other assorted items.

Meanwhile Hyle was preparing the truck itself. His first project was to fill the gas tank. On the side of the building there was a compressed air machine for filling tires and he pulled off the hose from this, using it to siphon gas from the other vehicles in the parking lot, eventually filling the gas tank and all three of the spare gas cans. He then scoured the store for a screwdriver. After a fruitless search he ended up using a pointed can opener to try to remove the plastic covers from the tail lights. He wanted to eliminate any lights except the headlights, to decrease the chance of being spotted on the road. He considered just smashing them, but could not bring himself to do it. He also reasoned that the less damage the vehicle had, the less attention it would attract during the day, just in case anyone was still looking for them.

The Jeep was old enough to have solid metal bumpers. One end of the rear bumper had been dented in and folded up against the body, but aside from that and a few bullet holes in the tailgate, the back end of the vehicle had survived their escape undamaged. After a long and frustrating effort, Hyle was finally able to get the screws out and take the cover off. He removed all the bulbs, replaced the cover and repeated the process with the other tail light. He then taped down the door switches so that the dome light would not come on when the door was opened, and covered the bullet holes in the tailgate with small patches of duct tape. While he was taping over the hole in the windshield he discovered a deep gouge in the frame on the driver's side of the windshield and his heart raced as he realized that they had literally dodged, not just one bullet, but two.

Once Sophia finished loading the truck she turned her attention back to the road atlas. Newman had mentioned the name of a town near the retreat site and she had been struggling without success to remember it. She searched the map, town by town, hoping to see a name that sounded familiar. Her search did not reveal the town, but she was reminded that Newman had said it was a few hours north of Bangor. There was not much in the northern part of the state. One interstate highway ran north from Bangor then turned east, leading to Houlton on the eastern border with Canada. A single smaller highway ran straight north, unevenly bisecting the northern half of the state. Although the smaller portion to the east of this highway had many roads and towns, the vast area to the west was covered only sparsely with unpaved roads. She shared this information with Hyle when he finally came back inside.

They decided to avoid major towns and highways and plotted a course north and east through Vermont, then east across northern New Hampshire and southern Maine, ultimately meeting up with the interstate about an hour north of Bangor. All they could think to do once they got there was see if they could find someone who might have heard about the retreat. It was not much of a plan, Hyle pointed out, but they were both happy to have something to focus on nonetheless.

A thick haze, tinged brown like smog, clung low in the sky and obscured the sun. Twilight came early. They set out once it was dark and drove with the lights off. The entire night sky was faintly luminescent under the filtered moonlight and it was only possible to make out objects a dozen or so yards ahead. The convenience store was on a stretch of road in an unsettled area, so they made reasonable progress at first, but soon the road took them back into a populated area and their hopes of reaching Maine in one night of travel evaporated. It was extremely slow going. Stalled cars frequently blocked the way, forcing them to turn back and try other routes, and these and other obstacles made traveling at even moderate speeds very dangerous without lights. As they left Albany behind and crossed, unknowingly, into Vermont the towns became smaller and farther apart.

Occasionally they passed a house with a soft light flickering inside, but this was rare and only served to remind them of how otherwise dark everything was. A few times early in the night they saw headlights on the road ahead. Each time they were far enough away that they were able to pull over, shut off the motor, and lie down in their seats until the engine sounds had passed by and faded away. At one point Hyle thought he saw a single light trailing them at a distance. It was impossible to tell if it was a motorcycle or a car with a light out, and it disappeared as they rounded a curve. He checked the rear view mirror frequently as they came out of the curve, waiting for it to reappear. When it failed to do so, Hyle decided that he must have been mistaken about the motion and convinced himself that he had seen light from a house. An hour later it appeared again. This time Sophia confirmed that it was moving behind them. When the fields around them gave way to woods again they decided to pull over, and ducked down in their seats to wait for it to go by. Several minutes passed. There had not been any other paved roads for several miles, only a few dirt roads leading to farmhouses, and yet no sound of an engine approached. Hyle and Sophia exchanged looks of surprise and growing concern. When Hyle poked his head up to look around, the light was gone. After a few more minutes, he started the engine and continued driving.

Less than a mile away a tree lay across the road. Fearful of an ambush, Hyle brought the Jeep to a stop several dozen yards away and checked the rear view mirror again. Sophia too turned to look behind them and they both looked nervously into the woods on either side of the road. The tree was a poor choice for a roadblock. It was a large evergreen, and although it was a foot thick near the base there were almost no branches on the lower part of the trunk. After another careful look in all directions, Hyle guided the Jeep up to the naked end of the tree trunk and crawled carefully over it.

When they were speeding away, safely on the other side of the tree, Hyle made sure to point out how difficult the feat would have been in a car. In reply Sophia expressed her thankfulness that the wheels had stayed on. From the combination of nerves and fatigue, they spoke very little after that, focusing their attention on the world outside the windows as it rolled by.

CHAPTER ELEVEN

SOME ENCHANTED EVENING

Night seemed to crawl slowly along, matching their pace through the countryside. After several hours of driving without seeing any more lights, Hyle decided to risk putting on the headlights, and they covered ground much more quickly. The increased sense of danger and the novelty of being able to read road signs kept them awake for a while, but after a few more hours the rumble of the engine and the drone of the road under the tires lulled Sophia to sleep. Soon after, on a long stretch of road through the Green Mountains, Hyle suddenly became aware that he was drifting toward the guardrail. The jolt of adrenaline helped him to realize how tired he was, and he began looking for a good place to stop.

Just past the access road to a ski area Hyle spotted a small semicircle of cabins extending back into the woods. There were no cars visible, and as the headlights of the Jeep swept over the large first cabin that served as the main office, Hyle could make out a sign that said, "Closed for the Season." He drove around the end of the last cabin, parked behind it, sat there for a moment debating whether to wake Sophia or let her keep sleeping, and then climbed quietly out of the Jeep and pressed his face against the back window of the cabin. Sophia stirred when he came back for the flashlight but did not wake. When Hyle finally did wake her, she was very unhappy with his decision to let her keep sleeping while he went off alone and made him promise never to do it again.

Hyle did promise, and also vowed to make it up to her.

"I got us a luxury suite," he said as he led her around to the front of the cabin. He pushed open the door and stood aside to let her see. A candle fluttered in a small Mason jar filling the space with a comfortable orange light. The main room held a queen-size bed and a narrow dresser, leaving just enough space to walk between them. On the dresser was a small, battered television set accompanied by something covered with a bath towel.

"Wow, you sure know how to treat a girl."

"Wait until you see the extravagant dinner I have planned. What did you do with the can opener, by the way?"

He guided her to the foot of the bed, across from the dresser and pulled away the towel to reveal a wooden tray with cans of food, and plastic cups, bowls and utensils.

"Plastic," he said, "but better than eating with our fingers. Go ahead and pick something. I'll be right back."

He disappeared into the bathroom briefly while Sophia moved the tray onto the bed and picked one of the cans.

"Uh-oh," she said, when she saw him leaning against the wall and noticed his expression. "What else have you got back there?"

Triumphantly, Hyle produced something from behind his back and held it out for her.

"Oooh, a box of wine. This is a high class establishment."

He laughed. "I see ze lady has shozen ze ravioli. An excellant shoice. May I suzhest a gallon of our finest white wine to go wiss your meal?"

"Are we celebrating something?" Sophia asked.

"How about being alive?"

"I'll drink to that."

After pouring some wine into the two plastic cups, Hyle sat down beside the tray.

"To being alive," he said, holding out his cup.

She tapped her cup against his and they drank. They quietly enjoyed their dinner of cold canned pasta and warm wine for a few minutes before Sophia spoke again.

"So what did you do before all this happened? I mean, what does a science writer do?"

"Write mostly. About science," he said. "No, really that's about all there is to it. I've done a lot of magazine and newspaper articles, written a couple of book chapters."

"But what do you write about?"

"Whatever's interesting. Sometimes I'm contracted to do a story on a specific subject, but often it's a topic that I hear of that I want to learn more about or tell other people about. Sometimes it's medicine, sometimes computer technology. Often people get interested in a topic because of something in the news—like last year after that European commission reléased their report on global warming, all the papers and news magazines wanted articles on global warming. For a couple days, anyway. The Nobel Prizes are always good for a couple stories too."

"Did you travel a lot? You live in New York City, right?" When she saw his surprise she explained, "You told me when I was driving you to the hospital. I think you were a little out of it."

"Oh. Yes, I did live in the City, and no, I didn't really travel that much. I went to some technology shows and traveled for a few interviews, but I was able to do most of my work by phone or online."

"It sounds like you like your work."

"Liked my work," he corrected with a meaningful look at his wine cup. "Yes. It gave me a chance to learn about lots of different things. Kept me interested. I've never been able to decide what I want to be when I grew up. In college I switched majors from biology to computer science to physics. I started off teaching high school physics for a couple years on a program where you teach while you work on your certificate, but it wasn't for me."

"How long ago was that?"

"A few years ago. Why?"

Sophia saw Hyle's eyes narrow slightly as they had when he was first learning about the nuclear attacks. She gave a casual shrug.

"I don't know. Just curious."

How about you? What did you do, before?" Hyle asked.

"I'm... I was," Sophia corrected, "a project manager at an ad agency. I fell into it right out of school. I've never really done anything else."

"Did you like it?"

"I guess so. I was pretty good at telling what people would like." She paused thoughtfully. "There were a lot of meetings with clients and the big ad agencies though. Too much image and glamour for me really."

"I'm sure you left them all in the dust, even if you didn't like it that much."

"Thank you, that's very sweet, but completely wrong. I don't do glamour well. Once I tried to dye my hair. I was going for a chestnut or auburn color, but it came out orange. Can you imagine me with orange hair? I dyed it black again, but what a fiasco."

"Why would you want to dye your hair? It looks...very nice the way it is." He had almost said "beautiful" but caught himself and then immediately wondered if he should have said it.

Sophia met his eyes and smiled sweetly. "It's a girl thing, you wouldn't understand. I have had this same straight black hair ever since I was a child. I wanted something that was a statement of my personality, not my genetics."

"I guess I'm just not a glamorous kind of guy."

"That's a good thing," Sophia said.

She moved the tray of empty cans and used plasticware to the dresser, retaining her cup for him to refill. The conversation meandered from careers to college to childhood and back, Sophia confessing her isolated grade school years and Hyle claiming that he had been a 'proud and socially integrated geek,' but living a rather mundane life. Eventually they both ran out of things to say at the same time and there was a long pause until Hyle offered to pour some more wine.

"To being alive?" Sophia proposed tentatively, holding out her cup.

"To Epicureanism," he replied, tapping her cup, "and to being alive."

"To people who wander out of the woods, dig you out of your house and keep you from getting yourself shot, and to being alive," she countered.

"To people who drag you around unconscious to find help and to cars that start when you really need them."

"Oh, I knew you'd have to say something about that truck," Sophia said, and punched him playfully in the shoulder. There was another short silence and Sophia's playful expression turned pensive before she spoke again.

"You know, we really have been very lucky," she said. "It almost feels like someone has been watching over us."

"Too bad they weren't watching over us before someone decided to start a nuclear war."

"Maybe. But if there had to be a nuclear war, we really were pretty lucky to have found each other when we did." Sophia leaned against him and put her arm around his shoulder. He could feel the pressure of her arm against his back and its warmth radiated through him. It was more wonderful than anything he could remember. He slid his arm around her waist, pulling her closer, and she leaned her head on his shoulder.

"My uncle used to say that everything happens for a reason," she said quietly. "I know you probably don't believe that. It's funny, I've only been with you for a couple of days, but I feel like I know you so well. Sometimes I almost feel like I can tell what you're thinking."

"And you haven't slapped me yet?"

Sophia chuckled and slapped him on the chest, then rested her head on his shoulder again. They sat quietly for some time, Sophia drifting off into thought and Hyle aware of every minute movement of her arm and head and the press of her body against his side.

"Have you ever felt sometimes like everything is all just a dream?" Sophia asked at length. "That's how I feel right now."

"That's because you're drunk," he replied softly.

"Oh, are you ever serious?"

"Not if I can help it, but I have been known to slip up on occasion."

"Well, maybe those plashtic cups were a little bigger than I thought, but I am shtill in full posheshion of my faculties," she said, intentionally slurring her speech.

They both laughed softly and fell back into silence. For Hyle it became an increasingly awkward and difficult silence. This was one of those special moments, he knew, when something could happen. He wanted to turn toward her and kiss her, but he could not bring himself to move. He realized with wry amusement that it was very much like being in a dream, but not the kind that Sophia had in mind. This was more like a lucid dream. His mind was racing, seeing the opportunity for what it was and knowing that it would not last, yet he felt somehow disconnected from his body, like an outside observer, unable to translate thought into action, or like first waking in the morning, when the drowsy warmth of bed occupies all sensation and cannot be violated with movement. Reluctantly he conceded to himself that he was going to let the moment pass. After some time, Sophia spoke again.

"I feel very safe here with you," she said, and the moment passed. Hyle's conscious thoughts faded into a vague regret and then melted away altogether into the gentle rhythm of her breathing.

They sat there in the flickering candlelight for a long time without moving or speaking until at last Sophia yawned.

"I'm sorry," she said, "but I think I'm tired. I'm going to go to bed now."

She kicked off her shoes and climbed back onto the bed. Hyle grabbed the bedspread and threw one of the pillows on the floor, but Sophia protested.

"Do you think I'd really make you sleep on the floor after everything we have been through? I think you're at least entitled to half the bed. I won't promise you'll get to keep half the covers though."

A strange sensation woke Hyle. Disoriented, he looked toward the window and saw a border of daylight around the curtains. Then he smiled and let himself slip away again into the warm comfort of the bed with Sophia's arm draped across his chest. The next time he woke, the light was in the wrong place. The window was dark, and a soft light danced against the curtains from a candle behind him. He rolled over to find Sophia lying next to him, propped up on one elbow.

"Good morning," she said, "or evening again actually."

"Good morning."

"Did you sleep well?"

"Yes," he said drowsily. Then, realizing how terse he sounded, added, "It was nice to sleep in a real bed again. And you left me half the covers."

She was watching him intently and he could tell she wanted to say something.

"Can I ask you a question?" she asked.

He nodded, trying not to let his anxiousness show.

"Last night—or this morning, I mean—how come you didn't try anything with me?"

The directness of her question caught his sleepy mind off guard. He only managed to blink at her in response.

"I thought you were hitting on me, but then you didn't do anything. I just wondered why."

"I wish I knew myself," said Hyle, and shook his head in a display of disappointment that was only half in jest.

She chuckled. "I think you're just too much of a gentleman."

"It's a common misconception," he said.

"It's not a misconception," Sophia insisted, and kissed him on the cheek. Then, before he could react, she rolled out of bed and disappeared into the bathroom with the candle.

CHAPTER TWELVE

THE ROAD TO MAINE

In the evening they set off once again under the cover of a moon obscured by clouds. Sophia had volunteered to take a turn behind the wheel and Hyle, freed from the need to focus on the road, stared into the sky. He realized with a jolt of insight that it was not mere clouds that darkened the skies, but dust thrown violently into the air by the atomic bombs mixed with smoke from the fires they had caused. Along with this dust cloud layer came the colder temperatures he had noticed—the so-called nuclear winter theorized by some doomsday scientists. Not only did this realization confirm the magnitude of the calamity, it also meant that a sunny day and a blue sky now seemed as distant as a hot shower, a nice meal or a secure home. He decided not to share his revelation with Sophia.

They traveled with the lights on. The road was clear of cars, stalled or moving, and Hyle plotted their progress on the map each time they passed a useful road sign. When he attempted to estimate how long it might take them to reach the interstate in Maine, Hyle discovered that neither of them had a watch, and that they had no way to tell time.

"If you hadn't insisted on taking this truck we could have taken something modern enough to have a clock," Sophia teased.

"If it started," Hyle countered seriously. "I think the old cars like this one, and like your old sports car for that matter, are more likely to have survived the EMP than more recent models, specifically because of all the sophisticated electronics the new ones have."

"How does that work, EMP?"

"It's kind of like an electromagnetic shock wave that's caused by a nuclear explosion. Gamma rays from the nuclear reaction collide with air molecules and knock electrons free. The electrons all flow away from the blast, creating a current, and if the explosion is high enough they flow down and get trapped in, and accelerated by, earth's magnetic field. When this shockwave hits electronic circuits it essentially overloads them in the same way that a lightning strike blows out your home electronics. It can fry circuits whether or not they're in use, but they're more susceptible if they are in use. That's why so many cars were abandoned in the middle of the road."

"And you think just one bomb could really cover the entire country?"

"It's possible it could have been just one. I remember reading a report about one of the tests the U.S. did with nuclear weapons in the Pacific in the 1950s. The one high altitude detonation in that test knocked out power, cars and radio stations in Hawaii, over a thousand miles away. Why?"

"I was just thinking about how it all started. Do you believe that it could have been a terrorist act?"

"I don't know. I wish we could learn more about it. Maybe there was some act of terrorism or sabotage involved, but it's extremely difficult to obtain and move nuclear weapons, even in some of the more turbulent countries, if only because all the major world powers have their spies on the lookout for that type of thing. Maybe terrorists could have gotten a hold of one warhead to launch that first air burst, if that's what you're thinking. That would cause a lot of confusion, but there are pretty sophisticated systems in place for tracking incoming missiles and making sure nothing is launched accidentally or at the wrong target. It would take more—at least it should take a lot more—than a single air burst to start a war."

"What about the Mumbai Plague?"

"Being a biological warfare agent you mean? It seems plausible. It has all the right characteristics if you want to wipe out lots of people indiscriminately. What puzzles me about that is that a military doesn't want to wipe people out indiscriminately. They'd be more likely to use something that's not fatal but incapacitates the enemy, or if it were a lethal agent it would have to be something that would burn out quickly."

"What does that mean?"

"It means kill everyone so quickly that they don't have a chance to spread it to unintended targets."

Sophia shuddered. "Oh, it's horrible to even think that way."

"I'm not advocating the use of biological weapons," replied Hyle with a shrug, "just trying to figure out what happened."

The conversation ended there. They drove in silence for a while, following the rural highway through farmland and woods, past a stretch of isolated businesses—a gas station, a strip mall, a supermarket—into a small town. Old buildings of brick and stone squatted close to the street, reflecting light from shattered glass in every window frame of every first floor shop. At the edge of the headlights, between the cars parked intermittently at the meters along the curb, a pair of figures sped up the sidewalk and darted around a corner. Sophia accelerated cautiously. Bracing herself against some unknown danger ahead, she strained to see into the darkness, but could make out nothing as they passed through the intersection where the people had disappeared.

A few minutes later, as the town gave way once again to solitary businesses and houses, Sophia got the impression of a light appearing beside them as they passed by.

"What was that?"

As if in answer to her question, the cabin of the Jeep was flooded with an intense light from behind them. Turning in his seat, Hyle stared backwards into a pair of bright headlights and watched as the lights kept pace a few dozen yards behind.

"I don't like this," Sophia said in an overly calm voice.

"Keep driving. Just don't let them pull alongside us."

As they drove, Hyle tried to make out any details of the vehicle behind them, but the lights were too bright.

"He's got his high beams on. I don't know—"

Suddenly the lights flared even brighter as a rack of floodlights lit the cabin, joined by the unmistakable flashing blue of a police cruiser and a brief blast from its siren. Squinting into the rearview, Sophia took her foot off the accelerator and started drifting toward the shoulder.

"What are you doing? Let's get out of here!"

"We're being pulled over."

"I can see that. Let's go."

"No, I'm going to stop."

"Are you out of your mind?"

"No, this is a police officer."

"Or some punks who stole a cruiser."

Sophia brought the Jeep to a stop. While they continued to argue, a figure stepped out of the cruiser.

"We have to try to restore social order. If we—"

She interrupted herself to throw the car into gear. Gravel sprayed and tires squealed back onto the pavement as the car shot forward.

"He's got a gun!"

"Of course he—"

"Out! He already had it out!"

In her rear view she could see the figure, framed against the flashing lights, scrambling back to the car.

"He's coming after us. What do we do?"

"We lose him."

"But that's the police. That would make us criminals."

"I'd rather be a live criminal than a law-abiding corpse," Hyle argued. "Look, we're screwed either way. If this guy isn't a cop and he already had a gun out, he's going to shoot us before we have a chance to find out. And if he really is a cop, what's he going to do, give us a speeding ticket? I mean, technically, we're in a stolen car and we've been looting every shop we've come to along the way. Do you think he really cares about a traffic violation? Why would he be pulling us over? He should be out trying to stop the death squads. And if he's not a cop he's probably going to kill us. Why would he be pulling us over? Just keep driving!"

"Maybe he's trying to warn us about something. Or maybe there's a martial law—a curfew in the state and we're out past it." Sophia did not slow down as she presented these possibilities.

He was quite sure that there was no argument that would convince him to stop, but this was a more plausible explanation than Hyle had expected. He paused to consider it.

"We don't need to be warned about anything, we're paranoid enough already. And as far as martial law, if he can't catch us, who cares? And if he does we can plead ignorance."

By this time the cruiser had caught up to them again, easily trailing them at a moderate speed. Sophia thought for a moment, and then convinced by Hyle's logic, stepped on the gas, expertly weaving around an abandoned pickup truck that appeared suddenly in the headlights. The cruiser followed, matching their speed. As the suburbs gave way to countryside, the road straightened and Sophia accelerated once again until the truck began to shake. Understanding that their current speed would give her mere fractions of a second to swerve if something appeared in the road ahead, she focused intently on the shadows at the farthest edge of the headlights, not daring to even glance in the rear view mirror.

The cruiser roared up behind them, closing the gap to a few car lengths, as if the driver wanted to let them know that both he and his vehicle were prepared for a high-speed chase. Then it dropped back to follow at a safe distance, waiting for them to make a mistake.

"He's too fast. We can't outrun him," Hyle said.

"If I had my sports car we could, but no, you had to have your big slow antique truck."

"You might as well slow down again and buy us some time," replied Hyle, ignoring the jibe.

Sophia eased off on the gas and loosened her grip on the steering wheel. Lights still flashing, the cruiser continued to pace them at a safe distance. The pursuit stretched out over several miles, Sophia concentrating on the road and Hyle scanning the darkness, looking for an opportunity. Opportunity came in the form of a railroad overpass. The slope up to it was blocked by small trees on one side, but the other side was covered only with light brush.

At Hyle's instruction, Sophia slammed on the brakes just before the overpass and swept across the road to the opposite side where the grade was clear. The nose of the Jeep ground into the earth, plowing bushes up from the hillside as it took the sharp upward angle and began climbing. The wheels spat out a spray of dirt and debris as the four wheel drive dug into the hillside and pulled the vehicle to the top.

The cruiser swerved across the road, but pulled up short of the embankment, clearly unable to handle the steep grade. It turned back onto the highway and crossed under the bridge but found no easier ascent. Sophia pulled the truck up onto the tracks and turned to follow the rails. They watched as the flashing lights disappeared out of sight behind the hill. Only when the blue pulsing reflected in the trees became too distant to see did they let themselves relax.

"Try that in a sports car," said Hyle.

"Hmph. I hate it when men gloat."

For a long time they had no alternative but to follow the rails along the narrow path through the woods. Steep hills rose, sometimes on both sides of the track, sometimes on one side with a steep drop on the other. Occasionally the land opened out into flat clearings where the dim shape of farmhouses and silos could be seen in the distance. Finally, in one such stretch of farmland, the tracks crossed a small dirt road, which led them to a larger road and eventually to the outskirts of a town. From the signs of the businesses they passed they were able to deduce the name of the settlement, but after a fruitless search for the area on their map, they decided to continue on in the hopes of finding other clues to their location. Even after getting a route number from a road sign and entering a second town they were unable to determine their position and decided to pull over in order to examine the map more carefully. It was only when Sophia decided to flip the pages of the road atlas that they were able to find their landmarks in the map of New Hampshire. Their entry into the state had been farther south than intended, but they were pleasantly surprised to see that the railway journey had been generally beneficial. With their location determined, they plotted a new course, and a few hours later they were skirting along the northern edge of the White Mountains, east toward Maine.

Both travelers were more conversational than they had been the previous night, and Sophia held up well against the fatigue of driving, so it was the growing light along the horizon ahead that induced them to look for a place to sleep. It was difficult to find a place that met all of their criteria—isolated, preferably set back from the road with a place to hide the car, with no signs of being occupied and nothing that might attract looters. They pulled into the driveway of a lone house, separated from the road by a strip of woods. There was no car in the driveway and no garage to hide one, but after a brief discussion they realized that, short of seeing a light inside a window, it would be difficult to tell whether or not a place was occupied, and at this hour, people would be asleep, with their houses dark. Still uncomfortable with the idea of breaking into someone's house, Sophia decided that they should continue the search, and a short while later they pulled into the parking lot of a small building. It was a single story structure that had been built in the style of a house, or perhaps had been a house that was subsequently converted for business use. A wooden sign, green with gold lettering below the image of a golden crown, read Karlings Optometry, and a matching green awning hung over the front door. Sophia followed the access road slowly around to the back and stopped the car.

Behind the building the ground sloped away and a set of concrete steps led up to a solid back door. They parked beneath a spreading oak tree and got out. Picking up a thick branch from the ground, Hyle headed for one of the windows and stopped beneath the sill, which was just above eye level. Sophia hurried around the car to catch up with him.

"What are you doing?" she demanded in a whisper.

"I'm going to break the window. If you give me a little boost I can crawl through and let you in."

Their exchange was interrupted by the sound of an engine out on the road. Instinctively they moved closer to the back of the building and waited for it to pass. A low rumble and very loud, like a car that had lost its muffler, passed by slowly, eventually fading in the distance and returning them to silence. Hyle turned his attention back to the window.

"Boost me up," he said.

"I think you should knock first."

Hyle was going to argue that they had picked the place because it was a business and that there were no cars around. Knocking was a waste of time, and even a bit foolish, but he did not see much harm in it either. Sophia sensed his hesitation.

"I'd just really feel better if you did," she urged.

With a shrug, Hyle turned from the window, mounted the stairs and rapped on the door. He jumped and nearly fell backwards down the stairs when a voice shouted from inside.

"Get out of here! Get off my property!"

Momentarily stunned, Hyle stood there on the first step, gripping the railing in one hand and the large stick in the other.

"I've got a loaded shotgun in here and I'll blow you both to Kingdom Come!" the voice yelled again.

He backed down the steps and walked briskly toward the Jeep, looking back over his shoulder.

"Come on, let's go," he said to Sophia, who had not moved since the voice had first spoken.

"Wait a minute," she replied.

"Come on," Hyle said more urgently. "You were right. Let's go find another place."

Ignoring him, Sophia walked toward the door instead. She had heard something in the voice that Hyle had not. There was an undercurrent of fear—the same type of fear that she had experienced herself in the past few days.

"We don't mean any harm," she said to the door. "We don't have any weapons."

"Then what are you doing here?" the voice demanded.

"We're traveling to northern Maine. We've been driving all night and we were just looking for a place to sleep for the day."

"And you think you can just break in wherever you want?" The trace of fear was gone, replaced by skepticism and indignation.

"No, no. We were just looking for a safe place," Sophia explained. Her voice was calm and level. "We have had some scary run-ins on the way and we were just looking for some place that nobody would bother with. We thought that if we found a business that didn't have any food or valuables, like an optometry shop—"

The door swung open and Sophia found herself looking up into the eyes of an older woman, along the twin barrels of a shotgun. The woman's hair, pulled back behind her head, was dark with wide streaks of steel gray that matched the steel of her eyes. She wore a black and green plaid pair of men's flannel pajamas and an incongruous pair of fuzzy yellow slippers. The woman watched Sophia suspiciously, slowly scanning her clothes and empty hands before focusing again on her face. She then turned her attention, along with the shotgun, toward Hyle. Suddenly conscious of what he was holding, Hyle tossed the stick carefully aside and held his hands out in front of him in preparation to raise them over his head. The woman scrutinized him and the Jeep, then relaxed her grip on the shotgun, letting the barrel drop slightly.

"Fine," she said, addressing Sophia, "I believe you."

"If you could suggest some place else we could try..." Sophia suggested hopefully.

As she spoke the woman addressed a heavy sigh to the universe.

"Oh, all right, you might as well come in. Come on now, I can't afford to be heating the outdoors."

Sophia exchanged glances with Hyle, then with a little shrug turned and stepped around the woman into the building. With one eye on the shotgun, Hyle hurried up the steps after her, trying not to look threatening.

"Thank you," he said quietly as he passed through the door.

They entered into a small foyer that served as a mud room. Winter coats and light jackets hung on a row of hooks on a short wall across from several pairs of boots under a rough carved wooden bench. A snow shovel and ax leaned in the corner by the door. The woman closed the door and introduced herself as Julia, going on to explain that her husband's examining room and office occupied only the front of the house and they lived in the back. After replying with their own introductions, Hyle and Sophia tried to express their gratitude, but Julia brushed their thanks aside.

"I can't feed you," she said. "We don't have much food, but we do have a bed. Are you... together?" she asked, pausing to look from one to the other.

Hyle opened his mouth, but then realized that he was not sure how to answer.

"Yes," Sophia said.

"Good, then you can sleep together in here," Julia told them, starting down the hall that led toward the front of the building and pointing to a door with the shotgun. "Just let me get some fresh sheets."

Sophia started to protest, but Julia silenced her and disappeared around the corner. Hyle and Sophia waited, looking around the room and exchanging silent looks. The bedroom was as large as the entire cabin had been. A single large bed occupied the center of the far wall, flanked by nightstands. In one corner stood a small roll top desk and chair, and along the walls two dressers, topped with lace runners, were set with a careful arrangement of jewelry boxes, framed photographs and a wind-up alarm clock. Their host reappeared with a pile of sheets and, to Hyle's relief, without the shotgun, and the two women started stripping the bed while he stood awkwardly in the corner, trying to stay out of the way. Julia caught him looking at one of the photographs, an image of two boys, about high school age, posing in baseball uniforms.

"My boys. Of course they're a bit older now," she said with a strained laugh. "Dennis, that's the younger one, he does computer graphics for the movie business out in Hollywood. Anthony is a surgeon down in Boston."

She turned back to making the bed, straightening and smoothing the blanket and meticulously boxing the corners without looking up. Sophia gave Hyle a helpless look of empathy.

"We have some food out in the truck. We'd be happy to share some with you if you're low on food," she offered.

Julia looked up. Her lips tightened momentarily, but then relaxed.

"Yes, I suppose that would be nice."

When Sophia returned from the back of the Jeep with an armful of supplies, Julia showed her down a short hallway to the kitchen where they piled the items on a small table. They all shared a meal of miniature sandwiches made from tins of deviled ham, cheese spread from a spray can and assorted crackers, while Julia asked them about their journey. Any news from beyond her town was of great interest, so Hyle and Sophia took turns giving her the details of the events that had brought them to her door. Her particular interest in the hospital and the attack on the department store was explained when she revealed that her husband had gone out the day before in search of medicine and more food, but then she quickly changed the topic. In return for their information, Julia was unable to tell them much to help with their journey other than to confirm that they were a little less than two hours from Bangor if the roads were still clear. The retreat in Maine and the Union of Faith were both unfamiliar to her. Well after they had answered all of her questions about the trip and stopped bothering to politely stifle their yawns, Julia dismissed them from the conversation and told them to go get some sleep.

The aroma of food cooking woke Sophia and she realized that it was something she had not smelled for several days. Daylight still filtered in through the blinds, but the hands of the old alarm clock on the dresser told her that it was late afternoon. She nudged Hyle awake so that they could go find their host, but first Hyle insisted on taking a quick detour to the front of the house to peek into the optometrist's examining room. Once his curiosity was satisfied he accompanied Sophia into the kitchen and then, guided by the smell of wood smoke and food, into the adjoining living room. There Julia was stooped in front of the fireplace where an iron grate stood over a low fire.

"Ah, good morning," she said jokingly as they came in. "Did you sleep well?"

"Yes, very well, thank you," Sophia replied, and Hyle nodded vigorously in agreement.

"Since you shared your dinner this morning, I thought I'd cook you some breakfast for dinner. I've got some water heating for oatmeal and scrambled eggs here," she explained, gesturing toward a pot and small skillet on the grate. "I hope you don't mind, I put a little hot sauce in them to give them some kick."

She told Sophia where to find things in the kitchen and sent her off to set the table, then asked Hyle to bring in the pot of boiling water while she followed with the eggs. Once they were seated, their host produced a container of instant oats from the cupboards, and an apple, which she chopped into small pieces for the oatmeal.

While Julia was bustling around the kitchen preparing their food, Sophia noticed Hyle looking at the pot of steaming water.

"Is the water safe to drink?" she asked on his behalf.

Julia stopped, as if confused by the question. Then after a moment's consideration, replied, "Yes, we have a well. When the power went out Leo rigged this up so we could still get water out of it."

She pointed to the kitchen sink, where pieces of garden hose and a large quantity of duct tape had been used to splice a hand pump to the faucet. Hyle was grateful, both for Sophia's question and for the answer. They ate the meal slowly, feeling the warmth and savoring the flavor of the food. While they ate, Julia told them how her town had fared in the disaster. The winds after the first attack had been favorable, and the fallout was low. Although she knew of some people who were showing signs of radiation poisoning, most houses still had well water and word had spread quickly to stay indoors and eat only packaged or well-washed food. She was less optimistic about the future. Already several people had been shot in conflicts over looting or trespassing and she feared that the worst was yet to come. People were just now starting to come out of their houses to check on friends and family or find food and supplies, she told them, but the shootings had everyone on edge.

As they ate and talked and helped clear away the dishes, the hazy sky turned from light gray to an unnatural deep red-brown. Comforted by Julia's relatively good news about the town, the two travelers decided to depart before dark, and their host met them by the back door and handed Sophia a two-liter soda bottle that had been re-filled with water.

"You never know when you'll be able to find good water," she said. "Be careful. Good luck."

"Goodbye. Thank you," Hyle said.

Sophia added her thanks to Hyle's and lingered as he headed down the steps.

"I hope your husband makes it back safely," she added tenderly.

"He will. You don't need to worry about that," Julia said. She gave Sophia a taut smile and her eyes narrowed fiercely, but Sophia could not help noticing the mist that was beginning to form as she turned away.

The trip this night was short and uneventful. As the redness spread across the sky and the eastern horizon darkened to purple, they stopped in the parking lot of a strip mall to refill the gas tank. Hyle emptied their gas cans into their tank and then fed the air pump hose into one of the parked cars to siphon some gas. He was puzzled at first when he could not get the siphon started. Sophia looked on as he tried pulling the hose up and down to make sure the end had not curled up above the liquid level inside the tank.

"I think it's empty," he said finally, pulling the hose back out. He tried the next car, and the one next to that with similar results. "Someone has already been here," he concluded. "Let's go try down there."

The other end of the lot proved to be luckier, and once Hyle got the siphon going he filled the empty gas cans while Sophia shuttled between, filling the Jeep and returning the empty containers to him to be refilled. With a full tank of gas, they set off again, Hyle driving and Sophia tracking their progress. As they crested a shallow hill, they could see in the distance a point of light moving slowly along the horizon ahead of them. A short while later they crossed under the interstate and over the Penobscot River to meet up with a state highway. It was still early in the evening and they turned north on this road, paralleling the interstate in the hopes of finding a place where they could inquire about the retreat. On the far side of a small town they spotted a dim light on a hill and followed a maze of side roads and a dirt drive up to an old farmhouse.

All their efforts to reach the farmhouse were rewarded with only a brief conversation through the front door. The suspicious farmer inside told them he had not heard of any such retreat and that they had best try elsewhere. It was not until the next town that they saw another lighted house, but the window quickly went dark as the Jeep approached the house. No amount of knocking provoked a response from inside, so reluctantly they gave up and moved on. In the third town along the way, after two more conversations through closed doors, they finally received some useful information. At first they got the same response that they had heard several times before, but as they were turning to get back in the Jeep there was a muffled conversation behind the door and the unseen occupant of the house called out after them to try asking at a place called Danny's.

The directions were good, and a very short drive brought them back across the Penobscot to Route 116. As they drove north, something by the side of the road caught Sophia's attention. Scanning back along the shoulder, she thought she saw the silhouette of a large man astride a motorcycle, but a second later the spot disappeared from view behind some bushes. She watched the road behind them for several minutes, but saw nothing more.

A few miles up the road they encountered an odd sight. A light was visible at the side of the road from some distance away. As they drew closer, they could see an old style country store, complete with a front porch which was illuminated by a hanging light. Under the flickering glow of an oil lantern sat an old man, reading a book. He looked up and watched them from his seat as they pulled into the empty parking lot and crunched slowly to a stop.

"Good evening," he said calmly as they stepped up onto the porch. "What can I do for you?"

Sophia stepped up beside Hyle and told the man about their search for the retreat.

"A little late, ain't ya?" he asked.

"So you've heard of it?" Sophia asked excitedly.

"Yup. Had some folks stop in here a week ago Thursday asking how far it was to Madauros Village and saying that they were going up to that Union of Faith that you were asking about."

"Madauros Village? Yes! That sounds right! That's got to be it! Where exactly is Madauros Village?"

"Don't know. Never been there," he said, and paused to smile at Sophia's expression of dismay. "But I did help some of your friends with their directions. Quite a ways up there up Route 11 if I recall correctly."

"Just a minute," Sophia said and jumped off the porch to grab the road atlas from the Jeep. She stepped back up already running her finger up and down a thin red line in the top portion of the page. "We thought it might be up here," she said, addressing Hyle and the man, but I don't see it on the map.

"Yup. We do that sometimes to keep the tourists away."

He moved in to get a closer look over Sophia's shoulder. "Well, I wouldn't worry too much about it," he advised after examining the book. "According to that map, this town isn't here either."

Hyle looked significantly up and down the highway. "We didn't really see any town on the way here."

The man nodded thoughtfully. "I suppose that's why we're not on the map then."

Hyle was not sure whether or not he was joking.

"Do you need anything for the rest of your trip? You're welcome to come in and look around," the man offered. He unhooked the lantern and held it up to light the interior of the store while he held the door open for them.

Inside the store looked almost normal. The food shelves still had a sparse collection of canned and boxed goods on them. One corner, dedicated to tourist items, looked untouched. Shelves held guide books and histories, natural products and souvenirs. Plastic bags on peg hooks nearby held a variety of "authentic" items, and stuffed bears, moose and lobsters of various sizes peered out from a rack of wooden baskets. The coolers that once held soda now held an assortment of clothing, mainly jackets and boots and a few blankets. The lockable ice cooler had been turned into a make-shift gun cabinet. Hyle stopped and examined the collection of firearms and ammunition inside.

"People are willing to trade quite a bit for food these days," the man explained. "And some people have more rifles than they need. Right now everyone wants food, but I expect come winter that guns, warm clothing and medicine will be more important."

"Aren't you afraid someone will decide to use their gun on you instead of trading it?" Hyle asked.

"Wouldn't be much of a life if I spent it thinking that way." Noting Hyle's dubious expression the man continued, "My sister in-law bought a real nice sofa just after she got married. It was so precious that she never took off the plastic cover that come on it 'cause she was afraid of it getting wrecked. Anybody who came to visit her had to sit on that damn plastic wrap."

Hyle waited for the man to continue but he was finished. Sophia smiled quietly to herself.

After some negotiation, they ended up trading one of their gas cans, including the gas, for a pack of D batteries, a lighter, a hibachi and a small bag of charcoal. Then they were back on the road, headed for the interstate, Route 11 and Madauros Village.

CHAPTER THIRTEEN

MADAUROS VILLAGE

Northern Maine was devoid of all signs of life, and nearly all signs of human tres-
pass, aside from the road they travelled and an occasional road sign along the way. A
small sign nailed to a telephone pole on Route 11 was the only indication that they were
near Madauros Village. The black letters were barely visible against the weathered gray
wood which, deep in the grain, still held small strips of the original white paint. It was
fortunate that Sophia caught the words at all as they went by, and it was understandable
that she did not notice the shape of the sign, taking it instead to be a marker for the
town line. It was only after driving for some time through the unspoiled woods that they
decided to go back for a second look, discovering then that it was an arrow pointing
them down a narrow paved road that they had overlooked.

A half hour later they traversed a small concrete bridge and arrived in Madauros
Village. The focal point of the settlement, surrounded by a cluster of a few dozen
buildings, was a grassy triangular common described by two dirt roads that intersected at
the apex, and the paved road which formed the base. Several old colonial homes
bordered the green along the unpaved roads, and an official looking whitewashed
building with a flagpole occupied the small side of the triangle adjacent to the paved
road. There was no sign of the retreat, so they continued past the common and a few
more houses that lined the road until the yards gave way to fields.

A farmhouse sat far back from the road behind an immense field of blueberry bushes
which continued along the left hand side of the road long after the farm was out of
sight. On the right hand side were several smaller farms. A combination of hayfields,
fallow fields and crops surrounded these farmhouses and a number of paths diverged
from the road into the fields. Some appeared to be well-worn dirt roads, others barely
discernible as parallel depressions in the ground where the bushes did not grow as high.
Eventually the pavement ended.

At the edge of the woods Hyle brought the Jeep to a stop. The road continued on
unpaved and a forest loomed up ahead, just visible at the edge of the high beams. Sophia
uttered a sound of shocked annoyance.

"I don't get it," she said. "It's supposed to be here."

"There are a lot of little side roads," Hyle reassured her. "Maybe they were set up in a
field way back off the road. We can ask around tomorrow."

Sophia agreed with this idea and they pulled ahead into the woods just off the road to
take a nap until daylight.

They were awakened by an irregular tapping on the roof that quickly became insistent.
It took a moment for them to collect their senses enough to realize that the windshield
was being spattered with large drops of water from the branches above. It was well into
morning when they woke, in part because the typical brownish haze that covered the sky

had been replaced by dark rolling storm clouds, such that little light filtered in through the canopy. Emerging from the woods, the Jeep was plunged into a blinding downpour. Visibility was too poor to search the town from inside the vehicle and there was no question of getting out, so Hyle shut off the engine again and they dozed intermittently until the rain let up.

Eventually the storm tapered off to a light rain and wisps of mist curled up from the fields. They drove back to the common and parked in front of the white building. Broad concrete steps spanning the width of the facade led up to dark green double doors. A narrow strip of grass in which a barren flagpole stood, separated the steps from the street. Through the glass of the doors all was dark, but Hyle and Sophia thought it a fitting place to start a systematic investigation of the town nonetheless. They were not surprised when rapping on the doors brought no response. Nor were they surprised when there was no answer at the first few houses nearby, but their suspicions grew as they continued moving door to door, and they would have been surprised to hear anything by the time they reached the last house on the common.

"Where is everyone?" Sophia asked in a half whisper.

Hyle shook his head, equally baffled. Avoiding puddles, he stepped carefully across the muddy road and onto the grass of the common.

"Hello? Is anyone here?" he shouted.

Sophia ran up next to him. "What are you doing?" she hissed.

"Trying to find out if anybody's here?" The hint of annoyance in his voice disappeared when he looked at her face. "Why, what's wrong?"

"Doesn't it seem strange that nobody's here? This place is too far away to have been attacked. Nothing's been damaged."

"Maybe they're all at the retreat?"

"Maybe they're all hiding from something. I just don't think you should be yelling until we know what's going on."

Hyle grudgingly conceded. "Still, we'll have to keep checking houses until we find somebody or something that gives us some clue about this mystery retreat."

They decided to check the big farmhouse by the blueberry fields next. The original portion of the house, sided with broad white clapboards, was much larger than the old colonials by the common. A large green shingled addition, windowless on the first floor, extended from the back, almost doubling the living space. The front of the house and the side facing the paved road were surrounded by a sagging farmer's porch. The dirt road that served as a driveway continued on past the house and barn, disappearing into the mist of a small valley before reappearing again as a gap in the hazy island of blueberry bushes on a distant hilltop.

Knocking on the front door yielded the expected silence, so they made their way around the porch, looking in the windows, and then extended their search to the grounds. A heavy pickup truck was parked between the house and barn. It was unlocked and held a few receipts and a grocery list, but no clues to the whereabouts of its owner or the retreat. The barn too was unlocked and housed a tractor and a variety of tools. The small shed behind it turned out to be a smokehouse. It was empty, but the aroma of smoked meat was still strong. Hyle's stomach growled loudly enough for Sophia to start at the sound.

Hyle wanted to force his way into the house through one of the windows, but Sophia convinced him to wait until they had checked all the other houses first. Traveling in a rough circle around the town, they repeated the process of knocking on doors, peering in windows, crawling into vehicles and searching yards, until they came once again to the blueberry fields and the four smaller farms that stood across from them. These they checked hastily as the light was fading and found nothing.

Thorough exploration had confirmed their early suspicions that nobody remained in town, unless perhaps they wished to stay out of sight and were well hidden. There had been no signs of human activity and no indication of where everyone had gone.

"I'm going to try to get in through that window," Hyle announced as they reached the back of the last farmhouse. "We might as well stay here for the night."

"You want to stay out here?" Sophia asked, in a tone clearly indicating that she did not.

"Sure, why not?"

"Don't you think we should stay closer to the center of town?"

Hyle looked at her blankly and shrugged.

"I don't see what difference it makes. We're here now."

"It's just…" Sophia herself struggled to understand why she felt it would be better to be near the common. "I don't know. Maybe it's just that it would feel more secure with more houses around. It's pretty isolated out here."

"Deserted houses wouldn't make me feel any more secure," Hyle replied doubtfully, "but if you really want to, we can drive back there again."

Sophia tried to find a better rationale for moving back up the road, but could not think of anything that made sense. She shook her head.

"No. This is fine, I guess."

Using the butt of their flashlight, Hyle broke the glass of the back door while Sophia held the screen door open. With Sophia close behind, he stepped inside and swept the flashlight beam around the room. Cabinets and a small stove and refrigerator defined the kitchen area at one end of the room while the other held a round table and a couple chairs. The linoleum tiles, white with black diamonds, reminded Hyle of the home he had grown up in. The kitchen opened into a dining room to one side. Ahead a hallway ran through the house to the front door, flanked on the right by the balusters and railing of stairs leading up to the second floor. They crossed through the kitchen to the dining room and skirted around the table.

"Hello," Hyle called softly as he exited the dining room through another arch. "Is anybody here?"

The only reply was the squeak of the wide pine floorboards. From the dining room they entered a carpeted living room in the front of the house and then the foyer they had seen from the kitchen. Across the foyer, the last room on the first floor held an old picture tube television set, well-worn armchairs and a sofa, and shelves made of wide boards and cinder blocks, which held boxes of board games. In the midst of searching the room with the flashlight Hyle froze, thinking he had heard something, and listened intently for the sound to repeat. Sophia moved up beside him, trying to determine what was so interesting about the part of the shelves illuminated in the flashlight beam. Not wishing to worry her, Hyle gave a shrug and finished examining the room.

Out in the foyer, Hyle stopped to listen again, a little more certain that there had been a noise, but again he heard nothing. With the lower floor fully explored, he headed for the second floor, stepping quietly on the carpet runner which covered the center of the stairs. Just as he reached the top step, there was a dull thud and some shuffling in one of the rooms. Three closed doors surrounded a small landing at the top of the stairs. He looked back to see if Sophia had heard the noise. She edged up closer to him and pointed at the door on the right. Hyle nodded, gestured silently up the stairs, then back toward the front door, and gave Sophia a questioning look. She thought for a moment, and then pointed determinedly at the upstairs door. Hyle nodded again. His heart was pounding. All concentration that was not focused on the door was channeled into maintaining a façade of calmness and keeping the flashlight beam steady.

"Hello," he called out. "Is anyone there?"

There was no sound from the room.

He stepped up onto the landing on one side of the door, knocked quickly and pulled his hand away.

Still nothing.

Listening for any more sounds, he put his hand on the doorknob and turned it slowly and quietly. Sophia stepped up a few more stairs and looked around the corner. Hyle flung the door opened and aimed the flashlight into the room while his lower body retreated back around the door frame.

He looked into a children's bedroom. Against the far wall a single bed and a bunk bed were separated by small desk. Hyle stepped into the room and looked around. Short bookshelves piled with cascading stacks of books lined the walls, and he had to step carefully to avoid the toys scattered around the floor.

Looking toward the window he noticed something that set his heart pounding.

He motioned for Sophia. She came up quietly beside him and watched as he pointed out what he had seen. Kneeling on the bed by the window, Hyle looked across the top of the garage, cautiously poking his head out to search in all directions. There was a screen in the window, but it was ripped in several places and the bottom corner had been torn away from the frame. It was a short drop to the roof, providing easy access for anyone who wanted to get in and out that way. Sophia kept an eye on the window while Hyle finished searching the room thoroughly, looking in the closets behind the hanging clothes, under the beds and behind the door.

"Nobody's in here," he reported in a hushed voice.

Sophia shut and latched the window and they moved to the next door, looking back over their shoulders frequently. The center door opened into a bathroom, and the last door led to another bedroom. The windows were closed in both rooms, but Hyle checked the shower and under the king-size bed anyway.

"Whoever or whatever it was, it's gone now," he said quietly.

"Maybe it's just wind blowing through the open window," Sophia suggested hopefully.

Just as she finished speaking there was a sudden mad scraping from that direction. They both looked at each other. It sounded like a frantic, furious scratching of something hard against the glass of the windowpane. Hyle stepped across the landing and aimed the flashlight at the window.

A pair of luminous eyes stared back at him fleetingly then disappeared.

"It was only an animal," he said, with audible relief.

Sophia, who had also seen the eyes, was already on the bed opening the window. Hyle was going to object, but instead walked around behind her and pointed the light out the window across the top of the garage. A cat scurried down the roof into the shadows.

"Don't, you're scaring her," Sophia said, and then called to the cat, rubbing her fingers and making kissing sounds. Hyle trained the flashlight on the foot of the bed and waited while Sophia kept patiently calling the cat, reporting on its progress as it came slowly closer. After several minutes she had coaxed it to the other side of the window where it watched them with equal patience for a while before finally deciding to push its way through the screen to sniff Sophia's hand. She gave the cat a moment to smell her then rubbed the top of its head. Immediately the cat burst into explosive purring and threw itself headfirst at any part of Sophia it could reach.

"Poor thing must live here," she concluded. "I bet she wants to know where everyone went too."

Hyle laughed. "It probably knows, but won't tell us. You know how cats are."

Sophia shot him a mock glare on behalf of the cat and scooped it up in her arms.

"She must be starving. Let's see if we can find her some food downstairs."

"After that, maybe we can feed the humans too," Hyle suggested.

Down in the kitchen the cat fared better than the humans. The cabinets had been selectively emptied. They found an open bag of flour and a bottle of vinegar in one, boxes of tea in another, and spices and a few other cooking supplies in the rest. The refrigerator, which Hyle opened cautiously, was completely empty as was the small freezer above it.

"All the useful food is gone," he observed. "Either they went to look for more food or they packed it up for a trip."

Meanwhile Sophia had found a plastic bucket of cat food under the sink. She pulled it out and set it on the counter, careful to interpose herself between the container and the cat who was watching Hyle from one corner of the kitchen. The bottom of the bucket scraped the counter slightly as she set it down and the cat snapped her head around, raced over to Sophia and began pacing back and forth and weaving between her feet, looking up at her and meowing insistently.

"At least somebody gets to eat," Hyle said as Sophia dropped some handfuls of food onto the floor.

Hyle set up the hibachi on the steps of the back door and used one of the pots he had seen in the kitchen to boil some water while Sophia found bowls and utensils. They had a dinner of dairyless macaroni and cheese at the small kitchen table. The cat curled up by Sophia's feet, making a point to lay part of its body over her toes.

"I wish we had some milk or butter," Hyle said apologetically, between forkfuls of bright orange pasta. "But I was getting pretty sick of canned tomato sauce pasta. Hopefully we'll find some food in one of the other houses."

"Do you really think we'll find anything in those houses to let us know where the Union of Faith was set up?"

"Maybe," Hyle replied, but he did not sound very hopeful. "Or at least where everyone in town went. They may be connected."

"Then we should keep trying to find the retreat. They have to be around here somewhere."

"I don't know, Sophia. We've looked through the town pretty well and not even seen one sign of the retreat. You said this was a pretty big event, right?"

"Yes. They were supposed to be busing people in from all over the eastern U.S."

"Then shouldn't there be some signs somewhere? I'm not sure they're here."

"No, this is the right place," insisted Sophia. "I recognized the name as soon as I heard it. And where would they go? I'm sure some people tried to get home, but somebody must still be around."

"But the townspeople have vanished too," Hyle reminded her. "It can't be coincidence that they're all gone."

"I know, I know, but I'm not going to come all this way just to give up on finding this retreat."

"I never said anything about giving up," Hyle replied. "I'm just not sure what to do next. I was hoping that something in one of the houses would give us a clue, and maybe we could find some food too."

Sophia shook her head doubtfully.

"There are still a lot of roads leading out of town that we haven't checked." Hyle opened his mouth to object, but Sophia knew what he was going to say. "Maybe the signs fell down. Or maybe someone took them down because they didn't want to attract people to the town. I don't know. But maybe they're in some cabins off in the woods down one of those roads."

"It would have to be a lot of cabins for thousands of people. But okay," he added quickly, "tomorrow we'll check out some of those roads."

They continued talking for a while, trading theories and speculating about what they might find down the roads the next day until they were tired. The rain had started again and the gentle patter on the window of the master bedroom swiftly lulled them to sleep.

In the middle of the night something disturbed Hyle. The cat was moving at the foot of the bed, but that did not seem to be the cause. As he woke more fully he became aware of a soft rumbling sound, straining his ears to pinpoint it while he tried to identify it. It broke the silence in a distinctly mechanical artificial way. The cat opened its mouth in an impossibly wide yawn, stretched its paws out and curled up again.

Hyle leapt out of bed.

"An engine! Wake up Sophia! There's an engine," he called, rushing to the window. He pulled it opened and stared into the darkness and rain. It was definitely the sound of a motor. He confirmed this for himself even as the low throbbing grew softer and soon faded beneath the hiss of falling rain.

Sophia listened sleepily as he explained that he had heard a large engine, maybe a truck, very nearby, and then she yawned and like the cat, curled up and went back to sleep.

«« »»

The next morning Hyle and Sophia discussed which roads to explore first, deciding on the one that continued the path of the paved street, since it appeared to be wide and well traveled. The road took them deep into a forest of tall pine trees and after a few hours ended on the shore of a lake, where a wide slope had been graded and covered with gravel to make a small area for parking and launching boats. The opposite side of the lake was visible in the distance and the gravel slope they stood on was the only man-made disturbance in the otherwise natural shore. When searching the tall grass on both sides of the parking area failed to turn up another road, they turned back and returned to town, past a distressing number of side trails.

The next road turned out to be more interesting. This one led through the blueberry fields, past the farmhouse and barn. The rain had stopped and the mist of the previous day had long dissipated. As they climbed out of the small valley and reached the top of the hill, an unexpected panorama of colors greeted their eyes. Over a few smaller hills and beyond the edge of the field of bushes were cars, hundreds of them, parked in orderly rows.

"I can't believe it! It was right here under our noses all the time!" Sophia exclaimed with equal parts outrage and euphoria. "It looks like the mall at Christmastime. How could we have missed it?"

The road descended into the middle of the vast sea of vehicles and they followed it past row after row until it dead-ended at the solid line of cars which marked the end of the field and the beginning of the forest. They turned and followed the perimeter of the parking field, and Sophia's joy gave way once again to discouragement as they began to realize that there was no obvious route out other than the way they had come in. At her insistence they walked into the woods in several directions until the cars were barely visible behind them, but they found nothing. As a consolation they cruised up and down the rows of cars, stopping periodically to look inside. Several of them had the same green pamphlet that Newman had given to Sophia, but nothing else of interest. Hyle bothered to count the cars in one row and revised his estimate to several thousand.

Reluctantly they left the field and returned to the farmhouse as the gray sky darkened into black. After dinner they sat by the back windows in the near darkness talking. Sophia was frustrated by the knowledge that they were so close to finding the retreat and yet unsuccessful. Hyle was consoling her, pointing out that there were only so many roads to check and it was just a matter of time, when he stopped speaking in mid sentence.

Sophia heard it too. The low thrumming of an engine.

"Come on, let's go!" Hyle cried, jumping from his chair for the kitchen door.

A moment later they were speeding along the road toward the center of town.

CHAPTER FOURTEEN

CITY IN THE WILDERNESS

Gunning the engine and travelling as fast as possible, they arrived at the town common within a few minutes of hearing the rumbling sound of the motor nearby. All was quiet when they got there. Desperately they scanned all around looking for the lights of a vehicle, Hyle shutting off the engine and opening his door to listen, but the only discernable sound was the gentle rustling of leaves in the breeze and the periodic thump of the rope against the flagpole.

"I guess we should have stayed up here," Hyle admitted, trying to stifle the irritation in his tone.

Sophia sighed. "There's always tomorrow. At least it seems to go by every night."

Hyle was staring absently up the road toward the highway.

"Let's not give up just yet," he said slowly. He shifted his gaze toward the common and regarded it for a moment through narrowed eyes.

"It sounded like the same thing as last night," he continued. "Something big. A truck. Or a bus maybe. It never sounded any closer than this, and we got onto our road pretty fast, so we can rule out that way."

He turned the key in the ignition again, cut the wheel sharply and accelerated straight across the grass of the common. At the edge of the grass he jumped out to investigate the spot where the two dirt roads intersected under the wash of the headlights.

"There are deep tire tracks that go straight through," he announced excitedly and slid in behind the wheel again and put the Jeep in gear.

The road led them out of town past more fields. They had to stop at the first fork to check for tracks again. Once again Hyle found a fresh tire track bearing off down one of the roads. This time it struck him that it was a single track, far too thin for a heavy vehicle. He jumped back into the seat, but did not put the Jeep into gear. Sophia looked at him questioningly.

"I think it's a motorcycle," he told her.

Sophia recalled the silhouette she had seen down the road from Danny's store and the single light that had trailed them through Vermont. Reading her look of trepidation, Hyle shook his head helplessly.

"It's the only clue we've got," he said. Sophia could only shrug. Hyle was torn himself, but speaking the words out loud seemed to give them more power. He decided to continue the pursuit.

Stopping frequently at first, they checked for tracks at every fork or side road, speeding along in between these points to make up for lost time. Soon the fields ended and the road wound its way over and between hills which grew more and more heavily wooded. There were few forks beyond the fields, but it was also more difficult to discern tracks. They made their best guesses, and Hyle drove as quickly as he dared, headlights bouncing wildly between the road and the overhanging branches of the trees which began to close in around them. At one point Hyle slowed to point out some of the low hanging branches that choked the path. The broken ends of branches dangled along the side of the road ahead.

"Something has come through here recently," Hyle said confidently.

Soon there was only one road. It slowly climbed upward, twisting through the hills, which gradually grew into small mountains. As they skirted around the crest of one steep rise and the trees thinned, Sophia shouted excitedly. In a valley ahead of them a distant point of light flickered as it moved slowly beneath the forest canopy. The road turned and plunged them back into the forest, but the brief glimpse of moving light was all the encouragement they needed.

A long time later they crested another hill and Hyle stepped on the brakes.

"Holy cow," he exclaimed under his breath. "Look at that."

Far below them hundreds of lights twinkled in the darkness. Sophia was reminded of the stars that had filled the night sky before clouds of dust had permanently obscured them. She gasped and gripped Hyle's arm.

"It's like finding Shangri-La," she whispered and leaned against him.

He shifted into park and he put his arm around her shoulders. They sat in silence for several moments looking down at the lights.

"Now what?" Hyle asked quietly. Seeing the collection of lights in the distance and knowing that they had reached the end of their search, regret was beginning to gnaw at the back of his mind.

"Now we go there and try to find Newman."

Hyle almost suggested coming back in the daylight, but decided to say nothing. Only a week earlier, lost and alone in the woods, he had searched for a view like this in hopes of finding his way. Now he felt as though he was losing it.

Sophia seemed to read his thoughts. She put her hand on his knee and gave him a reassuring squeeze.

"We'll stick together no matter what, okay?"

He nodded, drew a deep breath and put the Jeep into gear again.

The drive took much longer than either of them had expected. Their ascent had been so gradual that they did not realize how high they had climbed or how far away the valley actually was. Slowly descending, the road wound its way back and forth along the mountain sides, until eventually the trees thinned and the grade flattened as they reached the valley floor. A dark form began to take shape against the backdrop of the dim moonlight.

Ahead of them a wide black band curved away as far as they could see in both directions until it merged with the darkness. The road led straight toward it, between two taller shapes which, as they approached, resolved into towers. Hyle slowed the Jeep to a crawl as they rolled up to an enormous gate in what the high beams showed to be a tall smooth wall topped with two lookout towers. It was reminiscent of the entrance to a walled medieval town.

"This is more than just a few cabins in the woods," Hyle observed with a tinge of concern.

"Yes," Sophia agreed slowly. "He did say they expected thousands of people, but—"

She stopped speaking because something had suddenly appeared out of the shadows in front of the gate, crossing through the headlights into the shadows on the driver's side of the car. In the diffuse reflected light they could make out the figure of a stocky man walking toward them. He wore a cap and a jacket with thin epaulettes that appeared to be part of a uniform. As the man approached the car he switched on a flashlight and aimed it into the window. Hyle scowled into the glare and put the window down.

"I'm afraid you're not allowed to bring vehicles in here."

It was not the friendly greeting that Hyle had expected, and he was annoyed at being forced to stare into the flashlight, but he answered in the most respectful tone he could muster.

"Okay, where do we park?"

"You were supposed to park back in the town," said the voice behind the light.

"Oh, we must have missed the signs," Hyle replied. Sophia elbowed him subtly. When there was no immediate response he added, "I'm sure you don't expect us to go back and walk all the way here."

There was a short silence, just long enough to make them wonder if that was indeed what they were expected to do. Then the guard spoke again in an irritated and officious voice.

"What is the nature of your business here?"

"We're selling vacuum cleaners," said Hyle.

Sophia elbowed him again harder, concealing the maneuver as she leaned over toward the window.

"Don't mind him," she said. "We're here for the Union of Faith retreat."

The light shifted to her face for a moment, then tipped down, so that they could finally see the guard's face.

"Were you invited?"

"Yes," Sophia told him, "by Newman Theophiles."

The guard considered this but did not seem impressed.

"I was supposed to come with him last Saturday," she continued. "I couldn't make it then, and it took me a bit longer to get here than I thought."

"What is your name?"

"Sophia Xiao"

"And you?"

"Hyle."

"Wait right here," he said and switched off the flashlight.

"Are you sure we won't be blocking traffic?" Hyle muttered under his breath as soon as the guard was just out of earshot. "What is the nature of your business?" he mimicked in a tone of complete contempt. "Great, we drive around for days after a nuclear war trying to find this place out here in the middle of east cowflop and the first person we meet is a rent-a-cop with an attitude."

He took a few deep breaths then turned to Sophia.

"They don't seem to be too keen on visitors, do they? And what's the story with this wall?"

"I don't know."

"It must be at least twenty feet high. And they have lookout towers on top. Do you think they're expecting a lot of people to find their way here from town with no signs? They must be worried about something."

"I don't know," Sophia repeated and shrugged helplessly.

Time passed. They discussed the mysterious aspects of the place for a while—the remote location, the lack of signs, the requirement to park cars so far away, and the wall—until there was little left to say. As the thoughts and questions gave way to increasing periods of silence and the excitement of reaching their goal faded, they began to realize how late it was.

Sophia closed her eyes.

"If we're going to sleep in the car, I'm not going to do it here," Hyle said softly.

Nodding her agreement, Sophia opened her eyes sleepily.

"What do you think they'd do if I rammed the gate? Do you think they have any of those spikes that shred your tires?"

Sophia opened her eyes wide in a horrified expression and opened her mouth to speak. Hyle laughed.

"I'm just kidding," he assured her. "But we should do something. It's been a really long time. Do you think I should honk the horn or go pound on the door, or should we just leave and come back in the morning?"

"Let's give them a little while longer."

They waited.

Some time later, after almost leaving several times and agreeing to wait just a few more minutes, their patience was rewarded as three figures emerged from the gate. The first one was the guard, appearing in the headlights as suddenly as he had the first time. After him a second figure could be seen emerging from a dark opening in one of the doors of the gate, the third following a few seconds behind and bearing a lantern. As they neared the car, Sophia recognized the second figure as Newman, looking all the more like a Musketeer in what appeared to be a dark traveler's cloak and robe. The third was an older man, also in a robe, this one white trimmed with maroon and draped with a maroon cowl. He was tall and thin, though far from frail. His face was lined but held such an expression of youthful vitality that it was hard to reconcile with his graying hair. It was the third man who addressed them.

"Welcome. You must have had quite a trip," he said in a voice that conveyed both friendship and authority as he approached Hyle's window. "Sorry to keep you waiting like this." Then he turned and said something quietly to Newman, who moved to look into the car.

"Sophia!" he said happily as he stuck his head in the window. "I'm so glad you made it." He shook his head in disbelief. "Yes," he said to the first speaker. "That's my friend Sophia and her friend. I'll vouch for them."

The man in the white robes smiled.

"You can't take your car in, I'm afraid," he said, "but if you'll come with me, Joshua will take care of it for you."

The guard glowered back impassively, as Hyle looked at him with suspicion.

"Don't worry," the man assured him, "he will bring it back when you are ready to leave."

Hyle looked questioningly at Sophia, who answered with a barely perceptible shrug and then opened her door. Following her lead, Hyle stepped out on his side, still uncertain.

"Do I have to tip him?" Hyle asked, shooting a look at the guard and then glancing back at the Jeep with its staved-in rear bumper and bullet holes. He flipped the keys to the guard. "Don't scratch it."

The old man smiled indulgently.

"I am Magister David Delacroix," he said, extending his hand to Hyle as Newman caught Sophia in an embrace that lifted her off her feet. The title was unfamiliar to Hyle. The way Delacroix said it left little doubt that it was a significant office, yet he said it without any trace of self-importance. Newman traded places with the magister and the four exchanged greetings and introductions in the glow of the headlights as the guard climbed in behind the wheel.

"Hey, we still have things in there," Hyle said, turning to look when he heard the door close behind him.

"You won't need those things," Magister Delacroix told him. "We'll take care of everything you need."

Before he could object, Hyle found himself watching the Jeep backing away up the road, leaving a plume of mud in the receding headlights. He was struck with a sickening fear that everything was slipping out of control—a feeling that solidified into a knot in his stomach when he looked back and saw Newman listening raptly to Sophia with his hand resting on her shoulder. He heard nothing of what Delacroix said to him as they walked toward the gate.

Except for the seams that showed the construction to be of poured concrete, the walls had every appearance of those surrounding a medieval city. The massive doors across the entrance were made from thick planks of wood, bound together with wide straps of metal. The gate was taller than it was wide, and easily wide enough for two cars to pass through side by side. This close to the doors, Hyle realized that ramming them would most likely have done little more than crumple the front end of the vehicle.

"Watch your head," the magister cautioned as he gestured them through a small door set inside one of the enormous doors of the gate. Although there would have been plenty of room for a standard sized door, the doorway that opened before them was a narrow arch, so short that even Sophia had to tuck her head slightly and Hyle, the tallest of the group, had to nearly double over. Delacroix held the lantern by the opening as they passed through and followed after them, closing the door. His voice from the darkness behind them swelled with unmistakable pride.

"Welcome to the City of Asher."

PART II

Lux Aeterna
The City of God

CHAPTER FIFTEEN

A NEW BEGINNING

The view as they stepped through the door was impressive, even in the darkness. A vast sea of small wooden houses, punctuated by a few larger structures, rose and fell on gentle hills as far as the eye could see. Inside a few of the houses a warm yellow light flickered, thin serpentine lines streaming from their chimneys, gray against a near-black sky. The air was heavy with the smell of woodsmoke. Several houses had lanterns hung by the front door, casting light on the spider web of footpaths that ran among them. A wide road led from the gate up a long shallow rise until the lanterns that lit the way had diminished to barely perceptible points of light.

The old man led Hyle and Sophia up the road, watching as they surveyed the buildings.

"Amazing, isn't it?" he said softly.

The two newcomers nodded as they continued to look around.

"How many houses do you have here?" Hyle inquired, his voice equally subdued, in part by his awe at the size and tranquility of the city spread out before them.

"Fifteen hundred," Delacroix replied with more than a touch of pride. "Designed to house twelve thousand people."

"Twelve thousand? Wouldn't it have been easier to rent a convention hall for a week?" Hyle asked, only half joking.

Delacroix laughed. "Less expensive perhaps, but you get what you pay for, as the saying goes. It would have been difficult to find a convention hall for so many people and we wanted to build something away from the influences of the outside world in order to immerse people in a community of faith."

"Then your organization owns this place?"

"Yes. The Union purchased the land from a paper company a few years ago and built this sanctuary for our retreats."

"How many people are here now?"

"Over eleven thousand."

For several seconds the only sound was the soft rhythm of packed earth grinding beneath their feet. Then a thought struck Sophia suddenly.

"Does everyone know what happened out there?"

"Yes, of course," Newman assured her somberly, his voice dropping to a whisper. "We heard the night it happened."

"But you have eleven thousand people who stayed anyway?" Sophia asked, her voice revealing her amazement.

"What was there to go back to?" said Delacroix over his shoulder. "Most people came here with their families and loved ones. A few did leave of course, but we were very particular about who we invited to be a part of the Asher family. The truly faithful understood that, even if it did mean leaving people behind, they had been chosen to be here. Just as you two were."

Hyle glanced back at Sophia uncomfortably. He turned back to Delacroix and opened his mouth, but it was several long seconds before he could bring himself to speak.

"I'm not sure that's true in my case. Sophia was invited, but I just came along with her."

The old man studied Hyle with fresh interest. The eyes that surveyed him were gentle, yet intelligent and sharp.

"That's all right Hyle. Newman tells me he invited Sophia and her friend, so you were invited."

"But Sophia didn't even know me then," Hyle persisted.

The magister smiled. It was a smile of patient wisdom tinted with amusement.

"You were chosen nonetheless. Everyone was invited by word of mouth and only a fraction of those invited made the trip to join us. Everything happens for a purpose, Hyle, even if that purpose is not revealed to us. You are here for a reason. You and Sophia."

Hyle began to say something, but Delacroix held up a finger and continued.

"Let me tell you something more. I told you we have over eleven thousand people here now in a city designed for twelve thousand. When the Prophet put out the call for people to be gathered, we had no idea how many people would come. Much like Noah before the great flood, we built this city to the specifications given to us by the Prophet, and the people came to fill it. I don't doubt that more travelers like you will find us and soon our number will be twelve thousand."

"Sorry," Sophia interrupted, "but who is the Prophet?"

"Asha Zendik," answered Newman, and then turning to Hyle explained, "Zendik is the leader of the Union of Faith. He arranged this retreat and several others like it. Some people called him the Prophet before, but since the nuclear attacks occurred while all the faithful were gathered in his retreats, that's what most people are calling him now."

As the road continued to rise, a large building took shape in the darkness ahead. The exact size was difficult to make out at first, but it was considerably taller than the one story houses and quite broad. The roof curved in a gradual downward arc from the apex in the center to a narrow tower on either side, giving the impression of a wide pointed dome.

"That's Unity Hall, where we meet," Delacroix explained as they approached. "We have prayer services here every night and throughout the weekend. It's not big enough to hold everyone, but there are plenty of unity meetings in the cabins as well. Newman leads one. That will be a good way for you to get to know some of the people here. I'm sure he would be happy to have you join his group."

"Of course," Newman agreed enthusiastically. "It would be my pleasure."

As they continued along the road, which began to rise a bit more steeply, the dark structure ahead continued to grow, always seeming to be just a few hundred feet away. When at last they reached it, the peak of the roof towered several stories above them. The road widened into a gravel lawn before the base of broad steps which led up to the front doors. A pair of tall double doors stood in a pointed arch in the center of the building, flanked by two more pairs of doors, smaller but still quite large. Above the doors was a rose window of stained glass. As they continued around the huge structure it became clear that it was the center of the settlement. Roads similar to the one they had just walked led away from the building in several directions, like the spokes of a great wheel.

Delacroix led them around to the back of the building where a cottage stood nearby, the only other structure in any direction for a considerable distance. It was a little larger than the houses that filled the rest of the city, and rather than the board and batten construction of the houses, the walls of the cottage were made of stone and brick. The tiny windows, painted wood door and thick thatched roof completed the illusion that the dwelling had been lifted from the English countryside. A lantern hung on an iron hook, lighting their way to the front door. The magister opened the door and ushered them inside, following after them.

The room they entered was rustic and comfortable, serving as both a common area and a kitchen. In the center was a simple round table surrounded by chairs. Across the room a fire blazed on the hearth, bathing them with warmth and illuminating the room with a rich pleasant light. Much of the opposite wall was brick, with several brick ovens above the fireplace, cabinets filling the recess to one side of the chimney and a small counter and tiny sink set in an alcove to the other.

"Nathan, we have company," the magister called. "Put on some tea, would you?"

A young man who had been crouched by the fire stopped prodding the logs, resting the poker against the wall. He hung a teapot on the spigot over the sink and began working the hand pump while Delacroix circled around the table toward one of the four doors and opened it to reveal a small office.

Inside the office Delacroix asked them all to sit while he lit some oil lamps and then took his place on the other side of a large desk. Despite the small size of the room, in the flickering light of the flames the office had the feel of a study in an old world mansion. The walls, paneled in dark wood, were covered with maps, paintings and photographs in thick frames. One of the large paintings behind the desk was a portrait that Sophia recognized as Zendik—now the Prophet evidently—and a series of small photographs arranged around it showed him shaking hands with various foreign dignitaries. There was also a pencil sketch of the city, as viewed from a distant hilltop. The ramparts, she noticed, were much less prominent in the artist's conception. A large bookshelf filled most of one wall, and the elegant desk, with its gently curving sides and intricately carved legs, dominated the center of the room. The seat and arms of the wooden chairs were padded with leather which creaked softly as they sat.

"Once again, Sophia and Hyle, I would like to welcome you to our city," said Delacroix, and went on to ask them about the events that had brought them to Asher.

His voice was friendly and sincere and yet carried with it the self-assurance of authority. In the relatively bright light of the oil lamps Sophia studied his face as he spoke. His eyes were a piercing blue, almost intimidating in the intensity of their gaze at times, but offset by cheerful crow's feet at their corners and bushy white arches above them. His thinning gray and white hair, which seemed to grow in all directions at once, was cropped short in an apparent attempt to compensate for the futility of combing it. He was well spoken and charismatic, and reminded Sophia simultaneously of a kindly grandfather and one of her favorite old professors.

Hyle did not speak much and Sophia found herself telling most of the story, beginning with the cookout, her conversation with Newman, and her narrow decision not to attend the retreat. She went on to tell about being trapped in her house, being excavated by Hyle, the discovery that he had been shot and the horrific scene they had encountered at the hospital.

"The world has gone mad," the old man lamented quietly, shaking his head.

Sophia told them about the stranger who had told her about the death squads and led them to safety.

"Yes, we have heard that there are bands of looters and bandits wandering about unchecked," the magister said. "It's lucky that you made it to us safely. This stranger didn't come with you?"

"No, he disappeared soon after he helped us," Sophia said, going on to explain that the stranger had brought them to a group of survivors in a department store, and the people there had cleaned and treated Hyle's wounds, probably saving his life. She then recounted the story of the attack on the store and their narrow escape from the car dealership. When the magister said something about looters and bandits for the second time, Hyle who had been interjecting occasionally to add details to Sophia's story, decided to correct the misunderstanding.

"These were not just looters," he said. "This was a military unit."

"I'm sure it must have looked that way," the old man replied sympathetically.

"It didn't just look that way. It was a lot of men with automatic weapons and military vehicles. And training—these guys knew what they were doing."

"A lot of people in this country have large gun collections and know how to use them," the magister asserted calmly. "I'm sure that some people would consider a department store full of supplies a prize worth assembling a small group of people to capture."

Hyle was silent for a moment, stewing in his frustration with the old man for his unwillingness to accept their account of what they had seen. He was saved from a confrontation by a knock on the door. Nathan entered bearing a steaming kettle and four mugs. When he had finished pouring tea for all but Hyle, who declined, Sophia continued the story of their travels through New Hampshire to Madauros Village and the motorcycle that had led them to the city.

Delacroix's eyes widened when Sophia mentioned the motorcycle.

"Did you see it come to the city?" the magister asked curiously.

They had lost sight of it long before reaching the city, Sophia admitted, but had seen the lights of the city from the mountain road and had been able to follow it.

"Right to the front gates," Hyle added. He was sure the motorcycle must have also come to the city since they had seen no other roads after losing it and he was intrigued by the old man's apparent surprise.

"Yes, that was very fortunate," the magister agreed absently, saying nothing more about it. "And so here you are. As you can see, we lead a fairly simple life here. Newman has found you some space near his house, and we will get you settled in there shortly. I'm sure you must be tired from your travels, but before I can let you sleep I must converse with you about life here in Asher."

Hyle braced himself, certain he was about to receive either a lecture or a sales pitch.

"This is a wonderful community," the magister began. "We are diverse in our individual beliefs, but united in our faith in a single Creator who watches over us and brings purpose to our lives. Some know Him as God, some as Allah or Adonai, and others know Him in yet different ways. Some are still struggling to find their own way to know Him. But these differences are less important than our common ground. It's our common faith that will keep us together even while the word outside falls apart. Here we learn to help one another and trust one another. There are no locks in Asher and there is no crime."

Delacroix paused to offer more tea, filling Sophia's mug, and then pulled open a desk drawer, taking out several objects.

"We also have very little illness and we mean to keep it that way. If you want to stay you must take this," the old man said, placing a small white plastic bottle in front of Sophia and another in front of Hyle.

"I suggest that you take one of these too, but it's not mandatory." He poured several pills out of an amber bottle and placed one in front of each guest. "The pills are iodine to help prevent radiation poisoning," he explained. "The squeeze bottles are a nasal vaccine against the Mumbai Plague. Put it in your nose and while you're inhaling steadily, give the bottle a sharp squeeze. You'll hear a little snap of glass breaking if you do it right."

Sophia took the iodine tablet with a sip of tea and unwrapped the seal of the bottle. Out of the corner of her eye she caught Hyle watching her, making no move toward doing the same. Newman must have also noticed his trepidation.

"I've had both. They're safe," Newman assured him.

"The vaccine is required if you want to stay, even for the night," Delacroix added. "We can't risk exposing anyone in this community."

Hyle was going to point out that if they had been exposed to the Mumbai Plague, taking a vaccine now would be too late, but he had the sense this argument was unlikely to make any difference. Sophia inhaled and crushed the bottle. Grudgingly, Hyle followed suit.

"If you two wish to stay, as I hope you will," the magister continued, "you must do so as active members of our community. Our faith and our will shall be tested over the coming months, perhaps years, and we cannot afford to have spectators. If you choose to stay, you will both be expected to work. The work here is not glamorous, but we each serve God in our own small way. Whatever life you had in the old world must be left outside the city walls. We have investment bankers tilling our fields and cardiac surgeons wielding hand tools to help build our new school. You will also be expected to participate in our evening discussions and prayers. If you choose not to stay you may leave any time you wish, but you cannot come back."

"Ever?" Sophia asked.

"I'm afraid not," Delacroix replied solemnly. A heavy silence followed. The magister's penetrating blue eyes shifted between Hyle and Sophia. Only when he looked away and poured himself some tea was the trance broken.

"So the people who want to stay here are stuck here their entire lives?" Hyle persisted.

Delacroix smiled tolerantly at his choice of words.

"The rest of our lives may not be very long, Hyle. The final Judgment Day is near at hand. The nuclear holocaust was merely the first step that will lead us to the final battle. Until that time we cannot allow anyone to leave if they wish to remain a part of this community."

Hyle looked at Sophia. Delacroix watched the silent exchange between them.

"You don't need to make up your minds now," he added. "Stay, work, converse and you will know in your heart soon enough what is right. Newman is an excellent discussion master—he will help you to find clarity. And if he cannot help you with your questions, you can ask me anything at any time. My door is always open to you."

The magister rose and Newman rose immediately after him, as if on ceremony, leading Hyle and Sophia out of the office.

There is one more thing I must ask of you," Delacroix said, pausing with his hand on the door latch. "Please keep what you saw at the hospital and the department store between us. Many people here have left loved ones behind out there."

Sophia nodded sympathetically. Hyle said nothing, his face impassive.

"Newman will lead you to your beds and help you get settled in," the old man told them as he opened the door, "and he will have work assignments for you tomorrow. Goodnight. Sleep well."

Magister Delacroix stood in the doorway holding the lantern high to light their path as Sophia and Hyle followed Newman around the corner of Unity hall and down one of the roads. Nathan stepped into the doorway behind the old man as he watched the three figures fade into the darkness.

"Are they the ones?" Nathan asked, his voice heavy with concern.

"Yes, Nathan," Magister Delacroix answered, "I believe they are."

CHAPTER SIXTEEN

UNITY MEETING

Hiking down a long side road and along a maze of small footpaths, Newman led them through the darkened village to his house. A lantern hung outside, and Newman took it inside with him. The house was an almost exact replica of the magister's cabin except that embers glowed in the fireplace where a roaring fire had been.

A young woman sat by the fireplace. She rose to meet them when they came in. Newman introduced her as Phoebe and explained that Sophia would be sharing a room with her. After her offer to make tea was declined, Phoebe offered to help them with their things, but did not seem surprised to hear that they had nothing with them. She showed Sophia their room, through one of the side doors while Hyle looked curiously over their shoulders. Like the main room of the cabin, the bedroom was simple, with just space enough for two narrow beds on high platforms. Drawers underneath the platform provided the only storage, and under the window a wide shelf held a hand mirror and brush, a journal and pen and a few other miscellaneous items, serving as both a dresser and writing desk. The small stool tucked under the shelf was the only other piece of furniture.

"Hyle, we found a place for you in the house right next door," Newman said as soon as Sophia and Phoebe had reemerged.

Sophia looked quickly at Hyle. His lips were tight, but he said nothing.

"Isn't there any way he can stay here?" she asked. "Or we could stay together somewhere else maybe?"

Newman shook his head doubtfully.

"Most houses are pretty full. The only bed here is in Phoebe's room, and it was fortunate to find another open bed right next door." Newman looked from Sophia to Hyle and back again and sighed. "We can try asking around tomorrow, but this is probably the best we can do."

Although he concealed it well, guilt gnawed at Newman as he spoke. What he said was true, but only part of the truth. He knew he could not tell them the real reason the magister wanted them to be separated, but it did not make the secrecy any easier for him.

"Take good care of her," Hyle told Phoebe. He turned to Sophia. "I'll see you in the morning, I guess," he said, and Sophia gave him a parting hug.

«« »»

A distant bell woke Sophia in the morning. The bedroom was empty when she woke, and a gray light poured in through the window. Emerging from her room, she was greeted cheerfully by the other residents of her house—Newman, Phoebe and a family of four—who were all seated around the large circular table in the center of the room. At their invitation she sat down to a breakfast of oatmeal where she was introduced to

Rachel and Joel, the parents of two young children who took turns questioning her about the journey that had brought her to Asher. Sophia was telling them about Danny's store when Hyle arrived. She smiled and greeted him, but was immediately distracted by more questions about her travels. He listened quietly as she recounted their escape from the police cruiser and their experiences in the small towns along the way.

"I'm surprised you saw that many people," Rachel commented over her shoulder, en route to the kitchen counter with a set of dirty dishes. "The Prophet said that everyone would be killed either by the plagues or the nuclear holocaust."

"They may still be," Newman pointed out. "The Prophet said they'd be killed, but he didn't say that it would happen immediately. Many people who survived will starve or die of disease, especially during the winter."

"We didn't see that many people," said Sophia sadly. She knew that Newman was right, but at the same time the calmness of his assessment bothered her. "There are a lot of innocent people out there. Good people who had their lives ruined and lost families. You're lucky to be here. It's hard to describe how devastating it is to see."

Newman gave a grim, sympathetic smile.

"I know. It must have been pretty horrible, but the good people out there have nothing to fear from death," he told her, emphasizing the word *good*.

"Besides," the woman by the counter interjected, "the truly faithful will find their way here. That's what the Prophet told us."

"What did the Prophet tell you about the truly faithful that don't live anywhere near New England?" Hyle asked pointedly.

The casual way people were talking about the death, violence and destruction he had witnessed firsthand triggered an unexpected surge of anger and he was surprised at how acerbic his question sounded. He tried to amend it quickly with another question that sounded more curious than caustic, but he did not want his original question to go unanswered.

"I'm sure there are faithful people in Europe, for example. Where are they supposed to go?"

"You're right, Hyle," Newman said evenly. "The Union has built eleven other cities like this all over the world. Most people should be able to reach one of them."

He started to say something else, but the sustained tolling of a bell interrupted him. The crowd of people dispersed from the table.

"That's the call to work," Newman said and quickly explained to Sophia and Hyle that the bells not only tolled on the hour to mark time, but also announced the call to work in the morning and the call to prayer in the evening.

"I'm sorry I'm not able to bring you to your work assignment myself, Hyle, but one of my duties as proctor is to round up all the children in my canton and bring them to school. I have asked John to bring you along with him."

As if he had been waiting just off stage for his cue, John appeared in the doorway. He was a huge man, a few inches taller than Hyle and several times as wide. His head was covered with a thick mop of sandy hair which somewhere halfway down his face transformed into a great bushy red beard leaving only a small mask of skin visible around his eyes. John had a booming voice that ended all conversation when he spoke, but it was offset by such a pleasant disposition than nobody seemed to mind. When Hyle got his first good look at his roommate during breakfast, he was reminded of an old fashioned portrait of Father Christmas, perhaps crossed with a sheepdog.

"Sophia, you'll stay here and help Phoebe and Rachel out with the housework," Newman said. "Hyle, you'll go with John to help with food distribution, but maybe John can give you both a quick tour of Asher before you go to work."

John led them through a rabbit warren of pathways and houses, across a main road and back onto more paths. The sun was low in the sky, casting an orange glow over the city through the haze that drifted down from the mountains. The houses and roads, so quiet when they arrived in the city at night, had sprung to life in the daylight. Men and women of all ages flooded the roads and paths now, some hurrying with single minded intent, others walking casually in groups and chatting. Most people were dressed in unremarkable casual clothing, but every now and then Hyle saw someone in a robe or a hooded travel cloak. It was like being at a medieval faire or a historical recreation where a large number of tourists and customers mixed with a small number of actors in historical garb. They worked their way past an old woman in a black robe who had stopped in the middle of the road. While a group of children, from preschoolers to teenagers, hovered around her in the street, the woman shouted back for two young boys who had evidently been distracted by something along the bank of the stream, which percolated along beside the road through a narrow rocky bed.

As they walked John described aspects of life in the city in a stream of consciousness monologue which he interrupted occasionally to point out landmarks. He had nothing but the highest praise for Magister Delacroix, who as the highest ranking member of the Union in the city, served both as spiritual leader and monarch of the realm. He was less complimentary about the food.

"I wish the portions were just a little bigger," he grumbled. "I think that's why they put me in the same house with two small boys." He laughed, patting his considerable mid-section for emphasis. "And I miss eating meat, but what can you do? Maybe after the Judgment Day there will be a big juicy steak waiting for me in Heaven. At least Ruthie is a good cook."

Ruth, in John's words, lived in the luxury suite of the cabin, a double sized room on the opposite side of the common room from theirs, made to accommodate families. Her job was to stay at home to do the cooking, cleaning and other household chores. Her youngest son Matthew, a toddler, stayed home with her while Mark, who was a few years older, had gone to school with Newman.

"Ruthie is a single mother," John said lowering his voice as if it were a dark secret that somehow explained everything that needed to be known about the woman. "She's a real sweetheart though. Works hard and never has a bad word to say about anyone. Leah is pretty nice too. Judith, well, she's okay. She may give you a little attitude every now and then, but don't let her get to you." He paused for a moment and added, "I'm not sure about the two of them."

"What do you mean?" asked Sophia.

John slowed his pace and leaned in closer.

"I'm not sure they like men, if you know what I mean," he said conspiratorially. "Of course I'm not casting any stones. Doesn't matter to me anyway. I took a vow of celibacy, you know."

"Celibacy?"

"Oh don't worry," John said quickly, mistaking Hyle's surprise for concern. "You don't have to do it. It's not a requirement or anything. I just figured if I'm going to come all the way up here to try to get closer with the Lord, I'd better not have any distractions."

As they walked, John recounted his entire life history, from his childhood on a family farm in Iowa to the recent bitter divorce from his wife of almost twenty years. It was the divorce and the months of depression and drinking that followed that had led John to the Union of Faith and Magister Delacroix.

"He helped me turn my life around and give it new meaning. Now I'm living in service of the Lord, and nothing can bother me because I know Jesus loves me," John said, then added with a wink, "even if nobody else gives a rat's ass about me."

The tour ended when they reached the distribution center, a typical warehouse constructed of prefab plastic sheets embedded in a metal frame, but enormous against the backdrop of the small cabins of the city. John offered to escort Sophia back to her house, but she assured him that she could find her own way. Several men stood in a circle just inside the overhead door, talking and glancing frequently over at the newcomers, so Sophia limited her farewell to a wave and wishes for a good day. She hurried back along the roads and paths and made it back to her house just after another sustained tolling of the bell.

"You're late for your first day of work," Phoebe teased as Sophia came through the door. "Come with me. We'll start in the garden."

They spent the morning tending to a sizeable side garden planted with a variety of vegetables and herbs. Phoebe was pleased to learn that Sophia had an aptitude for gardening. "I can kill a plant just by looking at it, but I'm even worse at cooking," she confided. "That's why Rachel does the cooking and housekeeping. She actually enjoys that stuff. Gardening's okay, but I think you'll like our project this afternoon better."

Much as John had, Phoebe told Sophia the story of her life as they worked. Born and raised in a small town in Ohio she had been desperate to get out of the house after high school and had moved in with her boyfriend. It was her boyfriend who had introduced her to the Union of Faith, but after almost a year together they broke up and he moved out, leaving her to pay the rent by herself. She had been working double shifts as a waitress for the last year and dreaming of finding the time to earn a nursing degree. Although Sophia liked her well enough and felt a bit guilty coming to the conclusion, she decided that if Phoebe were to succeed in life it would be on the basis of her personality and appearance rather than her intellect. Sophia was content to let her do most of the talking, a role which Phoebe seemed more than capable of filling, and the day passed quickly.

Not long after the bell tolled five, Newman returned from his rounds and shortly after that Joel came in from the fields. They were finishing a dinner of dumplings and gravy when Hyle arrived.

"How was your day?" Sophia asked. "I got to learn how to spin wool and see how they make clothes," she continued before he had a chance to answer. "I'm learning how to make a cloak. Phoebe showed me most of the process today. It's really fascinating. I got to wash the fleece, comb it and spin it into thread on that big spinning wheel. And tomorrow I'm going to learn how to weave on the loom and do the dyeing. It really makes you appreciate what we were taking for granted every time we bought a piece of clothing off the rack."

"Somehow I can't see you as a spinster," Hyle said.

"Actually she's a very quick learner," Phoebe interjected, missing the joke entirely.

Sophia laughed and asked Hyle about his day again, this time giving him an opportunity to answer. There was not much to tell, he said, but went on to describe his day distributing food. He had been paired up with a young man named Reuben and together they pushed a handcart from house to house dropping off food and other staples until it was empty and then returning to the warehouse to restock it. To Hyle's great amusement, he seemed to intimidate Reuben, so he had spent most of the day working in silence. Although less enthusiastic than Sophia, he realized as he described his day that it had been satisfying. For the first time since waking up lost in the forest he felt secure and his sore feet and weary limbs were constant reminders of what he had accomplished through his manual labor. The day had been positive, he decided as he spoke. There were some things that bothered him about the city, but he decided to save that for a conversation later when he could speak to Sophia alone.

People began to arrive as they talked, and the residents folded the legs under the table and rolled it into a narrow closet between the bedrooms to make more space in the central room. The spinning wheel had been cleared away before dinner. A fire was lit and two lanterns were hung outside the door, one with clear glass to provide light once it grew dark and the other with blue glass, Phoebe explained, to let people know that there was a unity meeting being held there. The room was already quite crowded when the chiming of the bell announced the call to prayer. By the time it tolled seven o'clock, the floor was packed to absolute capacity. Most people sat on the floor, some of them on cushions or folded blankets. Those who had come early sat on the few chairs or the small storage benches that lined the walls and several of the residents leaned against their doorways or sat on their stools.

As the bell rang in the hour, Newman appeared from his room carrying some papers and took a seat in the empty chair near the fireplace. The assembled crowd gave him an enthusiastic round of applause as he entered the room. He shook his head, looking slightly embarrassed and gestured for them to stop as he sat down.

"Thank you for the warm welcome and welcome to our house," he said as the applause reluctantly faded away. He led the assembly through a short prayer, asking for blessings for the people of Asher and guidance to show them the right path in their daily work. After the prayer he raised his head and surveyed the room.

"I recognize most of you from other nights. Is there anyone new here tonight?"

A few hands went up and Newman asked them to introduce themselves and tell everyone if there was anything in particular they were interested in conversing about. He then informed the room that two people had found their way to the city from the outside.

"One of them, I'm proud to say, I invited myself. I think it shows a lot of courage and determination for them to have made it here, so please make them feel welcome." He motioned to Sophia. "Maybe you could tell everyone what it was that made you decide to make the difficult trip up here."

Sophia nodded and turned to face the room. Hyle strained to hear every word above the background noise, interested to hear what she would say.

"I'm Sophia Xiao," she managed to say before several people interrupted to welcome her to the city. She smiled and mumbled her thanks quietly, looking thoughtful all the while. "I'm not sure what brought me here exactly. With everything that has happened and people making such a mess of the world, I guess I just wanted to find something beyond just the world of people to put my faith in. I suppose what I'd like to discuss is what it is that all of the different faiths here have in common."

She gave Hyle a look that was a subtle equivalent of a shrug and the crowd turned their attention to him.

"My name is Hyle, and I'm just here to listen," he said quietly and turned away before the wishes of welcome began.

"We'll let you get away with that for a couple of nights," Newman said lightly. After a few more people offered topics or asked questions, he continued, saying, "I'd like to converse with you about Sophia's topic. Not just because I invited her, but because her question really gets to the core of why we're all here. How is it that we can all have come from different Christian sects or non-Christian faiths, and still have so much in common? What is it really that we share?"

A spirited discussion ensued. At first Sophia's full attention was not on the conversation. She was more interested in watching Newman in action. He led the discussion masterfully, encouraging people to contribute, letting them speak freely and do the majority of the talking, yet stepping in to ask a leading question or draw a parallel when a participant's points became contentious, paraphrasing and summing up when they became too confusing or long-winded, and always steering the conversation back to the points he was trying to develop. She was every bit as impressed with his skill as a discussion leader as she had been with Hyle the night he first learned the details of the nuclear attacks.

Although Sophia originally had some reservations about the unity meeting and had attended out of equal parts curiosity and obligation, she was surprised to find herself engaged by the developing story. Newman started by asking for examples from the Old Testament of stories that illustrated a faithful relationship with God. More specifically he was interested in examples from the first five books—known to people variously as the Five Books of Moses, the Pentateuch, or the Torah—explaining that this body of scripture formed the basis of Jewish law and religious doctrine.

People began to shout out answers and Newman sifted the chaos, recognizing them one by one to share their ideas. The freeing of the Israelites from Egypt, the anger of Moses upon discovering the Israelites worshiping the golden calf, the last speech of Moses to his people, and the willingness of Abraham to sacrifice his only son Isaac were among the examples offered. Newman probed each of these examples, and then tied them together, making the case that the original understanding of faith was obedience.

"A recurring theme in the Old Testament is that those who respect and obey God are rewarded and those who do not are punished," Newman concluded. "Obedience to God isn't an abstract idea in these stories, is it? It's achieved by adhering to a very concrete set of laws, including the Commandments given to Moses, and in some extreme cases—like Job's suffering or Abraham's willingness to sacrifice Isaac—by proving that obedience to God comes before all else. Obedience is demonstrated by action—by doing specific things that God wishes and refusing to do other specific things that He has forbidden. Now what about the New Testament?"

Again there was a flurry of conversation and Newman was barely able to keep order as participants offered observations and examples of ways the New Testament differed from the Old Testament. Several people pointed to Jesus dying for the sins of humanity as the central theme of the New Testament.

When Newman asked why this was important, he received a variety of responses having to do with original sin and salvation, but he seemed to find what he was looking for when one woman in the back offered her suggestion.

"It was the supreme demonstration of His love for us."

"So if a recurring theme of the Old Testament is obedience inspired by fear and respect, what is the recurring theme of the New Testament?" he asked.

"Love," answered many people, almost in unison.

"Now if Jesus' sacrifice is a demonstration of His love for us, what according to the spirit of the New Testament, should our relationship be to God?"

Once more many people answered, "Love."

"But why?" Newman challenged.

There was a momentary silence. Sophia looked around the room expectantly and saw that several people had been taken by surprise by the question, apparently realizing that something which at first glance appeared so obvious was difficult to express clearly.

A few people attempted explanations involving the teachings of Jesus, but even as they spoke they seemed to realize they were not quite able to put into words what they wanted to say.

"We should love God because He sacrificed his Son for us, just like Abraham was willing to do with Isaac," Rachel suggested. "Except this was God making the sacrifice for us, even though we didn't deserve it. It was the ultimate act of devotion to us, so how could we feel anything but love back?"

"Well said," Newman agreed. Then turning to Sophia he said, "We haven't quite answered your question yet, but we're getting there."

He turned to the room again and asked, "What are some phrases that come to mind to describe someone faithful?"

One of the participants, seeing where Newman was headed, suggested "God-fearing" and "God-loving."

"Right,' said Newman. "And everyone who is faithful to God probably is a mix of the two—God-fearing and God-loving. We fear and love other things. That's part of life, but this is different, right? God speaks to Moses out of the burning bush and Job out of a whirlwind. When Jonah tries to avoid God's will the tempest catches him and he cannot escape. If you truly understand God's infinite power, your fear will transcend any other fear you can experience, just as if you understand God's love for us, your love for God will transcend any other love. In both cases there's a sense of being overwhelmed by something so great that it can't be fully comprehended. That's something that the truly faithful share."

The room was silent again while people considered this idea.

Then someone asked "Does that mean that loving God is more important than obedience?"

Newman took a deep breath.

"That's difficult to answer quickly, but I think ultimately the answer is yes."

There was some scattered whispering and quiet laughter in the room.

"Don't think you're off the hook," Newman told the room, grinning. "Think of it this way. Imagine being a child. You might decide to obey your parents because you know they'll be angry if you misbehave and they might punish you. But you may equally well decide to obey them just because you love them and want to make them happy or because you trust that what they want for you really is best for you. It's just two aspects of the same relationship."

"So what does Paul mean in Galatians when he says that we're not justified by the works of the law but by faith in Jesus Christ?" asked a man sitting on one of the storage benches. He was a distinctive man, with a long serious face and large ears. After watching him for a moment after he asked the question, Sophia got the impression that he already knew the answer. She wondered if he was leading up to something, or whether this was a test of some sort.

"To really understand that you need to take it in its historical context," replied Newman. "God had made a covenant with Abraham and the people of Israel. Anyone born into the tribe of Israel was born into this covenant, circumcised according to the law of the covenant, and lived by the Jewish laws. After Jesus was crucified, those who believed in His resurrection included Jews and non-Jews—the gentiles Paul refers to in his letter to the Galatians. Paul was trying to solve the problem of how the gentiles could be justified by God—in other words, how could someone who wasn't born into the tribe of Israel become righteous in the eyes of God. Remember, at that time there were no Christians technically. Jesus and His disciples were Jews, and so was Paul who came a little later. What Paul is arguing in that passage is that gentiles don't have to become Jews and be justified according to the works of the law of the covenant. They can become justified, or righteous, by faith alone."

As Newman was speaking, the bell tolled eight o'clock.

"Of course this laid part of the theological groundwork that helped Christianity to become a separate religion. It also had some other significant theological repercussions, but we'll have to pick that up tomorrow."

Around the room people stood up, stretching stiff legs, putting on coats and cloaks and saying their goodbyes to one another. Many made their way over to Sophia and Hyle to greet them and welcome them to Asher. Meanwhile the residents rolled the table in and restored the common room to its former order while Newman moved to the doorway and shook hands with everyone as they left.

CHAPTER SEVENTEEN

PROPHECY AND DINOSAURS

Eventually the last of the guests filed out of the common room and Newman closed the door. One visitor remained. She was a short rotund woman with a perpetual warm smile. With her thick gray hair pulled back in a bun, Sophia could not decide whether she looked more like a Norman Rockwell grandmother or a Russian babushka doll.

"Sophia, Hyle," Newman said as he walked the woman over to them, "I'd like you to meet Deborah. Deborah is one of the people who convinced me to come here. She actually told me that I'd be caught in some type of catastrophe if I stayed in Albany."

"I have a gift," the woman said modestly.

"I didn't believe her, of course," Newman added, "but fortunately she persuaded me to come anyway or I might not be alive today."

"Most people don't believe," Deborah said, her eyes sparkling with a mischievous energy. "Hyle doesn't. Do you Mr. Wissen?"

He had been ready to agree until she mentioned his last name. Since he had only given his first name when he introduced himself to the unity meeting, he was momentarily thrown.

"Don't look so worried. Yes, there is a logical explanation," she reassured him. "I remember you from a science show you hosted on television."

Again Hyle was surprised. He was thinking of ways she might have heard his last name since his arrival in the city and had already partially forgotten the time, only a few weeks earlier, when he had lived in what now seemed to be a completely different world. The memory of the show, many years earlier, seemed more like remembering a dream than any actual experience.

Deborah watched him with a penetrating stare and an amused smile as he thought.

"Ah, so you were the other viewer," Hyle joked, regaining his composure. Turning to Sophia and Newman he explained, "We only made four shows before the series was cancelled. I don't meet too many people who actually saw it."

"That's too bad," Deborah said. "It was a good show. Not that I understood all those crazy theories you were trying to explain, but then I guess you don't have to understand something for it to be true."

She watched Hyle closely. When he did not respond immediately she continued.

"Let's see what we can see about your future," she said, sitting down at the table and indicating a chair next to her.

Hyle tried to politely refuse, but before he got many words out Sophia began cajoling him while Newman watched expectantly.

"Humor a crazy old woman, Hyle, and play along," Deborah said.

He rolled his eyes and laughed.

"Okay, okay, you've badgered me into it," he told everyone and sat down at the table. He laid his hand on the table in front of Deborah, palm up.

She took his hand, turned it over and held out her free hand for his other one.

"I need both of your hands dear."

"I don't mean to tell you your business," Hyle said, matching her mischievous smile, "but isn't it the other side of the hand you're supposed to be looking at?"

"No, I'm not a palm reader. I just need to concentrate."

"Don't you need a crystal ball, or some tarot cards, or sheep entrails or something?"

Deborah's face exhibited an amused exasperation.

"You're a real intellectual hard-ass, aren't you?" she replied, smiling wider than ever. She turned to Newman. "Here's my first prediction. He's going to drive you crazy."

Sophia and Newman both laughed, and Hyle chuckled despite his efforts to stay somewhat serious. He gave his other hand to Deborah, who held both hands lightly and stared into his eyes.

"While I do your reading, don't speak," she instructed. "Nod if you want to agree with something, or shake your head if you disagree. Do you understand?"

Hyle nodded.

The smile dropped from her face and her eyes lost their sparkle, looking distant instead, as if she were listening intently to hear a far away sound. Sophia thought she looked older, more like an ancient wise-woman and less like a kindly grandmother.

"Let me see," she said to herself, staring into his eyes. She spoke slowly, pausing between each sentence. "You're an intelligent man. You pride yourself on your intelligence and your logic. But you're also very sensitive. Much more than you let other people know."

"I thought you were going to predict my future," Hyle protested.

Deborah blinked and scowled briefly.

"Did I say you were intelligent?" The amused smile returned to her face. "The future begins in the present dear. Now, close your mouth and open your mind," she told him, in a tone that a teacher would use to admonish her favorite student.

She focused on his eyes again, holding his hands gently and fading back into concentration.

"You pride yourself on your rationality," she said softly, "You use your sarcasm and humor as a shield to protect you. They keep you safe from ideas and situations that make you uncomfortable."

Hyle did not nod, but it was clear from his face that she had struck a chord. For a moment she looked as if she were going to continue, but she changed topics.

"You're driven by a great need to understand. You need to know how everything works and why everything happens the way it does."

Hyle nodded slightly in agreement.

"That need will push you and pull you away from here on the trail of a mystery."

Her face grew more somber and she leaned forward, looking more intently into Hyle's eyes.

"You'll solve your mystery, in the end," she said at last, "but it'll lead you to a greater mystery. One that you may someday understand but you'll never solve."

Deborah sat back and smiled warmly at Hyle.

"You have big things ahead of you dear," she told him.

From the way she spoke, Hyle got the impression she was done, but being chastised for speaking, he waited until he was sure.

"Thanks," he said at last. "That was interesting."

The old woman smiled at his choice of words.

"I suppose that was the best I could hope to get out of you," she teased.

"What was the mystery you were talking about?" Sophia asked her. "And the greater mystery?"

"I don't know. I'm just the vehicle. The entire future is too overwhelming to grasp completely. Certain things give me an impression, like a brief flash that I can understand by relating it to something I know. All I know is that I sensed a mystery within a mystery. The smaller one will seem most important until he discovers the larger one. I don't know what they are, but he will when the time comes. Unless he writes me off as a crazy old woman, of course." She winked at Sophia. "Come, sit down. Let's have a look at you."

Hyle got up and Sophia took his place at the table. She held her hands out and Deborah took them and stared into her eyes the way she had with Hyle.

"You're also very intelligent, but in a different way. A way that people may not see immediately. You have a way with people. You're very in tune with them."

Sophia nodded.

"That's because you have been blessed with the gift too. You're just not aware of it yet."

Deborah paused and leaned in closer. Sophia could see the old woman's eyes looking straight into her own, yet unfocused, as if she were looking through her at something on the other side of the room.

"In your future, very near, you'll have to make a difficult decision. That choice will lead you on a journey," she continued, then paused for several long seconds and frowned slightly. "On this journey you'll undergo a very difficult transformation. The more you try to find your way, the more lost you will become."

She looked at Sophia with such an expression of sympathy and compassion that Sophia felt her own heart freeze inside her.

"I see pain and suffering ahead for you," she said in barely more than a whisper. "But don't despair. In your darkest hour, remember that in the end you'll pass on to a better place."

Her eyes focused again on Sophia's face and Deborah leaned back.

"You have quite a journey ahead of you child," she said.

"Yes, it sounds like it," Sophia agreed, "but what does it mean?"

"I don't know," said the old woman. "You may be the only one who can tell. You'll know when the time is right for you to know."

"And you could tell all of that just by looking into my eyes?"

"The eyes are the window to the soul, dear. Now if you'll excuse me, I'm weary and need to get along to my bed. It was very nice to meet both of you."

Newman walked Deborah to the door then came and sat at the table with Hyle and Sophia.

"She's a sweet woman," Sophia said.

"Yes, she is," Hyle said, chuckling. "She sure knows how to give a guy a hard time though."

"What do you think she meant about you understanding a mystery without solving it?" Sophia asked him.

"Who knows," he answered dismissively.

"She also said it was a greater mystery," Newman reminded her. "Maybe she was talking about coming to know God."

Hyle gave a contemptuous laugh.

"That fits," Sophia said, ignoring him. "A mystery you could understand without solving. Although it's hard to imagine even understanding God."

"I can't believe you're both taking this so seriously," Hyle said.

"What do you think yours meant?" Newman asked her, also ignoring Hyle.

"I don't know," she said, "but I didn't like the sounds of it. Being lost, a difficult choice, a difficult transformation…"

"Maybe you're a werewolf," Hyle said brightly. "That would be a difficult transformation, and they always seem to be changing back into humans in some place they have never seen before and wondering how they got there."

Sophia sighed. "Really, Hyle."

"What?" he said in mock surprise. "You mean you believe in fortune tellers but not in werewolves? How was I to know?"

"I don't know if I believe it yet," Sophia replied, "but I won't discount it either."

"You don't have to understand something for it to be true," Newman added.

"Besides, Newman says she predicted the nuclear holocaust, and everything she said about me being good with people was right. What she said about you sounded pretty accurate too."

"That's exactly why she said you have 'the gift' too," Hyle shot back. "The gift is being good with people. That's what fortune tellers do. They use clues they see about how people look and how they act to guess things about them. She already knew that I hosted a science show, so guessing that I favor logic and rationality wasn't much of a stretch. That's also why she asked us to nod when she guessed something right—to confirm that she was on the right track. But she was probably good enough to tell just from our facial expressions. She's a sweet woman and very good at what she does, but I don't think she's a psychic."

"Why?" asked Newman cautiously. "Because you think she's not a real psychic or because you think there's no such thing?"

Hyle considered the question carefully.

"Let's put it this way. I've never heard of a psychic predicting something so specifically that it was actually convincing that they could see the future. Psychic predictions are always expressed in vague, symbolic terms like 'you'll go on a difficult journey' or 'you'll discover a great mystery.' And usually you can't remember the exact words, only the general message, so you can adapt it to fit whatever actually happens in the future. Do you remember the exact words she told you before you came up here?"

"I don't think so," Newman admitted. "I'm fairly sure that she used the word catastrophe though."

"But if the nuclear attacks never happened, a catastrophe could have been your car overheating on the Maine turnpike or spraining your ankle walking down the sidewalk in Albany. That's what I mean. You'll make the events fit the prophecy if you believe it."

Newman was thoughtful but did not respond.

"We're not going to resolve this," Sophia said in a voice devoid of her previous excitement. "We'll just have to wait and see what happens."

There was an uncomfortable silence for a moment as Sophia's comment effectively closed the conversation and they all searched for something else to talk about. Newman saved them with a new topic.

"What did you think of your first unity meeting?" he asked his guests.

"I loved it," said Sophia. "I wasn't sure I was going to, but there were some pretty bright people in the crowd, and I thought you did a really good job of pulling out the interesting ideas and leading the discussion."

Newman thanked her for the praise, looking somewhat embarrassed.

"I'd have to agree," said Hyle. "Frankly I wasn't expecting much, but it was more interesting than I thought it would be. If you'd been my Sunday school teacher I might have kept going to church."

"Did you really go to Sunday school?" Newman asked with genuine interest. "What made you stop?"

Hyle shrugged. "It's kind of a long story."

"We're not going anywhere," said Sophia and Newman nodded his agreement.

"Okay. Well, I guess I was maybe eight or ten years old and like most boys that age I was really into dinosaurs. I had read all sorts of books and I could name about a hundred dinosaurs by their Latin genus and species. I could name all the epochs in order—"

He paused, noticing Sophia's look of incomprehension.

"The epochs were the names of the ages. You have probably heard of the Jurassic period, which is when a lot of the most well-known types of dinosaurs lived?"

Sophia nodded.

"I knew the names for all the epochs, Pre-Cambrian, Cambrian, Silurian, and Devonian, through the Jurassic, Triassic and Cretaceous and up to the Pleistocene. Most of the kids in my neighborhood were from pretty religious families, but my parents were not very religious. We went to church on Christmas and Easter, but that was pretty much it. When all of my friends kept talking about Sunday school, I asked my parents to let me go. I went for about a year. In fact, somewhere at home I still have—"

He caught himself, his face growing suddenly somber.

"—had a Bible with my name on it in gold letters for graduating my first year. But the next year I had a run-in with my Sunday school teacher. She was a crotchety old Bible-thumper who believed everything in the Bible literally."

Newman nodded as he listened, sensing what was coming.

"The first year my teacher had been someone who encouraged lots of questions and discussion. More like tonight. So when we were studying Genesis I put up my hand and asked, if God created the world in seven days, then where did evolution fit in? This woman told me that there was no such thing as evolution. When I asked her about the dinosaurs and fossils, she tried to tell me that God had put the bones in the earth and made them appear old. I guess God was just trying to confuse us—I never quite followed her argument. But essentially she handed me a choice between believing in the story of Genesis or believing in evolution and dinosaurs. I hope I don't get struck by lightning for saying this, but it was no contest. Dinosaurs were much cooler than God and having made my choice I never went back to Sunday school."

Sophia chuckled, but Newman shook his head sadly.

"It's too bad that you ran into someone that narrow-minded at so young an age. Hopefully we can convince you that you don't have to choose, because I'm guessing that you still think dinosaurs are cool."

The trio laughed quietly, trying not to disturb the other residents of the house who had already gone to sleep.

"You have a better chance than she did. I'll try to keep an open mind," Hyle promised. "Especially since staying here evidently depends upon how good a job you do."

Sophia knew Hyle well enough to detect the skepticism that he was trying to suppress.

"Believing in God may not be as different from studying dinosaurs as you might think," Newman responded. "You have never seen a dinosaur, have you? Just books about them. And you believed what you read in those books just as many people believe what they read in the Bible. As with all books though, people can interpret what they read differently."

"Yes, but I don't have to just depend blindly on a book," Hyle pointed out. "The dinosaurs left evidence behind like fossils and footprints in the rock. Unfortunately God wasn't kind enough to leave us any fossilized footprints."

"No, although some would argue that he left us the scriptures and the words of the prophets. I know that's not what you're looking for, but you can see God's mark in other ways. Look how incredibly complex and intricately balanced the world is. It offers us everything we need. Earth is the right temperature for our survival, it has plentiful food and water, air for us to breathe. How could this all be an accident?"

"I see your point. The complexity and organization of the world and the fact that it's an ideal environment for us to thrive in seems to suggest a creator," Hyle acknowledged. He thought for a moment. "But couldn't it have evolved this way according to the laws of nature without a creator? Maybe we evolved to be well suited for our environment rather than the environment being created to be well suited for us. All the other parts of nature could similarly adapt to work together in a complex but organized way following the laws of nature."

"But where did the laws of nature come from?" Newman asked.

Hyle reflected on this, realizing that he did not have a satisfying answer. They talked for a little while longer until Sophia began yawning and they all decided to turn in.

CHAPTER EIGHTEEN

FAILURE TO ENGAGE

Sophia was talking with Phoebe on the evening of their second day in Asher when Hyle arrived early for the unity meeting. He had eaten dinner quickly and hurried over to Newman's house in the hopes of catching Sophia alone before people began to arrive. Phoebe gave him an odd smile as he approached the table where they were seated.

"Hyle, what's your favorite color?" she asked.

"Blue," he answered without thinking. The question, "Why?" half-formed on his lips, but he did not ask, suspecting that he would not get an answer.

The two women traded looks and laughed at his confusion and then Sophia quickly changed the topic by asking him about his day. It had been much the same as the day before he told her. His muscles were a little less sore and he was starting to feel comfortable finding his way around the city.

"Not that you can really get lost with a big wall all around us," he added.

He realized quickly that Phoebe was not likely to leave the conversation before more people started to arrive for the unity meeting and Sophia's other housemates were nearby in the kitchen area, making a private conversation impossible even if Phoebe did leave.

"Sophia, could we talk privately for a minute?"

While Hyle was watching Sophia get up from the table, Phoebe grinned and shot her a scandalous look.

"What's the matter?" Sophia asked as soon as they were in her bedroom. Instantly Hyle regretted his request.

"I don't know. Nothing serious. I'm not sure exactly," he paused, trying to decide how to begin. "What do you think of this place?"

As soon as he asked the question, Sophia understood the problem. They had come into Asher together, partners in a long quest to find this city in the wilderness but since their arrival they had not been able to share their uncensored opinions of what they found. She had not been bothered by this fact, Sophia realized, because she had made a new friend in Phoebe, enjoyed learning a craft during the day and found their first unity meeting to be interesting beyond her expectations. Now she realized that this was not the case with Hyle.

"I like it here," she said hesitantly. "Like you said, I feel safe here, and it's nice to put in a good day's work and feel like you accomplished something." She stopped to study his face, but it gave no clue as to his emotion. "How do you like it here?"

"It's great in a lot of ways. The people here are all very nice and I feel safe but—" his voice trailed off.

"Are you uncomfortable with all the religious talk?"

It was a reasonable guess. In addition to the formal discussion about religion at the unity meeting, the piety of the people Hyle encountered throughout the day, at his house, at the warehouse, at the houses on his food distribution route, stood in sharp contrast to his own beliefs, or lack of them. It did make him uncomfortable and self-conscious, but there was something else. He thought for a minute trying to put his finger on it.

"Have you noticed that nobody here has a watch?" he asked suddenly. She had not. "No watches, no cell phones, no radios, nothing."

"This is supposed to be a retreat," Sophia reasoned. "They probably asked people to leave those things at home."

"I can understand leaving phones at home, but watches?" Hyle said doubtfully.

"We could ask Newman," Sophia suggested, but Hyle had already moved on.

"And what about the wall?"

"What about it?" Sophia shrugged.

"Why is it here? We're out in the middle of the wilderness. There's plenty of privacy without it, and it must have been a major construction project to put it up just for a retreat."

"Maybe they wanted to protect the place when they weren't using it," Sophia speculated.

"Who would they be protecting it from? It took us a week to find the place when we were looking for it." Hyle shook his head. "And despite what Delacroix says, they do have locks in Asher. I took a walk last night after you went to sleep and I went past the warehouse. It has a big lock on the door at night."

"Hyle, I think he was being figurative. There are no locks on any of the houses. I don't think he meant there wasn't a single lock anywhere in the entire city. You're getting all worked up about nothing. Are you sure there isn't something else bothering you?"

"I don't know. Doesn't it strike you that everything is just a little too perfect? These people all came here for a one week retreat but now, not only are they all content to hang out here after learning that everything from their lives in the outside world has been destroyed, but they have a perfect little community going where everyone knows their job and there's a system for everything."

He stopped, realizing how excited he was getting and that Sophia did not seem to share his concern. She started to say something about the power of people sharing common values, but she was interrupted by a knock on the door. It was Newman.

"Ah, Sophia, there you are," he said, adding, "Hi, Hyle," when he noticed who she was talking to. "Sophia, could you give me a hand with something?"

"We can talk more later," she said to Hyle.

"I forgot to tell you," Newman said apologetically, lowering his voice. "Only married couples are allowed to close the bedroom doors." His cheeks flushed as he spoke.

«« »»

It was after Sophia's second weekend in Asher that Newman pulled her aside to his room to have a similar private conversation, being careful to leave the door open.

"I'm beginning to worry about Hyle," he told her in a low voice.

"Why?" asked Sophia. Her response was a reflex because Newman's concern had surprised her, but even as she spoke she suspected at least part of the answer. Although there was no clear mandate, it was generally understood that everyone was expected to attend unity meetings each night and to pick one day of the weekend on which to work, attending one of the many services in Unity Hall on their day of rest. Newman had invited them to go to services with him on Sunday afternoon the previous week. Sophia had accepted, but Hyle had not, instead volunteering to work an extra shift. He had done the same this weekend.

"Is it because he skipped the service again yesterday?" Sophia ventured.

"Yes, that's part of it. That and the unity meetings."

"But he's come to every unity meeting since we got here."

"He has," conceded Newman, "but he hasn't really participated."

It was true. Newman went out of his way to moderate the conversations in order to pull in as many viewpoints as possible and persuade people to share their opinions. Although she had been quiet many of the nights, Sophia had also entered into some lively discussions without any need for encouragement. Hyle on the other hand had not said much of anything. His response, "I'm just here to listen," whenever Newman prompted him had become something of a running joke among the group, but the joke was already starting to wear thin.

"I think he's just taking a while to adjust to the environment here," Sophia said. "I told him he should come talk to you, but he didn't want to."

"Why? About what?"

"You have to understand, Newman, we weren't part of the Union of Faith and didn't really know what to expect when we got here. This is a pretty immersive community. I like a lot of it, but it's overwhelming for me at times. I can only imagine how it is for him. Hyle is suspicious by nature. I don't think that a community built on faith is really his cup of tea. It's going to take him a while to acclimate."

"I can understand that," Newman said, "but why doesn't he want to talk to me? It's part of my job as proctor to help people with just those sorts of issues."

"I know, but I think he doesn't want to cause trouble. When he has asked questions at work people seem to get annoyed with him and they don't know the answers anyway. He's convinced that even if you could answer his questions you'll be obligated to give him the party line answer."

"Party line? What exactly is it that he's worried about?"

"A lot of things. Nothing major. A lot of little things."

"Sophia, we need to deal with this before it becomes a bigger problem. Tell me what he's worried about."

Newman watched her expectantly. She knew he was right, but she did not want to betray Hyle's confidence. Moreover, she did not want to paint him in a bad light. Most of his concerns made a certain amount of sense to her, but he did seem to be almost on a crusade to find problems with Asher. Conveying that impression to Newman would certainly be a breach of trust. The issues themselves were not necessarily meant to be secret she reasoned. After all, he had been asking around at work.

"For one, there's the wall," offered Sophia, adding, "It is a pretty high wall. And he noticed that it's patrolled by guards."

"That one is easily addressed," Newman replied. "The wall was built to protect church property. Remember that nobody lives here most of the year. If it seems a bit high, that's to help make it feel like an isolated community. The point of coming here was to leave the outside world behind. It's the same reason that monasteries are often on mountains. As for the guards, you know better than anyone else why we need them. There are bands of looters and maybe worse out there." He watched Sophia to make sure that she seemed satisfied with his response before moving on. "What else have you got?"

"He also noticed that there's no technology here—no radios, mobile phones, not even wrist watches. I pointed out that this started as a retreat and probably people were encouraged not to bring such things, but he said that Magister Delacroix orchestrated some sort of 'technology burning' on the first day."

"You're right, of course,' Newman confirmed. "People were encouraged to leave their electronic gadgets behind before coming. Some did and some didn't. Then, after the nuclear attacks, the magister gave a very impassioned sermon about how our misplaced trust in technology had led us away from the very things we sought to focus on in this retreat. There was a bonfire in front of Unity Hall and he invited people to throw in their gadgets as a symbolic gesture. People not only participated, but they also went back to their houses and spread the word and soon the whole square in front of Unity Hall was packed with people trying to push their way up to the fire to throw something in."

Until she listened to Newman's description of how the event unfolded, Sophia had not realized how much of her own suspicion she had been suppressing. She had imagined an angry mob, as in an old fashioned book burning, but now after listening to Newman, pictured it as a positive and unifying event. Her unconscious concerns about the wall and the guards had also been addressed, and she scrolled through the list of other items Hyle had mentioned, anxious to resolve them for her own benefit as much as for his.

"What about food?" she asked. "The warehouse is still full of food even though people have been here several extra weeks."

"We started rationing food right away, as you can imagine," replied Newman. "Hunting and fishing will help a little until the late crops we planted are ready for harvest."

"I know, but that wasn't the question. Hyle thinks that the supplies in the warehouse aren't disappearing fast enough based on how much food is being distributed. He said that he tried to ask the warehouse foreman about it, but the foreman just told him some story about a lamp and then made him go mop the floor."

Newman laughed and nodded.

"I bet I can guess the story," he said. "The miracle of the lamp is one of the stories about the founding of Hanukkah. The Temple in Jerusalem was the focal point of Jewish worship when it stood, and it still has a place in Jewish prayers. It was first built by King Solomon almost a thousand years BC, but destroyed by the Babylonians four centuries later. The Second Temple was rebuilt soon after, but that was captured and desecrated in the second century BC. When it was recaptured and rededicated a few years later, the story goes that there was only enough sacred oil to burn for one day, but it lasted for eight days until more oil could be provided. That's why the menorah has eight arms—one for each day that the lamp burned and one for each day of Hanukkah, which celebrates the rededication of the Temple."

"That's a beautiful story," Sophia said, "but somehow I don't think that'll be a sufficient answer for why the warehouse is still so full."

"Then maybe he's just not as good at estimating large volumes of food as he thinks," suggested Newman. "In any case, I need you to help me make sure that all his questions and suspicions don't prevent him from integrating into the community here."

Sophia agreed to do this and went to catch Hyle before the unity meeting. On the pretense of showing him the basil which was already starting to sprout in the herb garden, she brought him around the side of the house where they could talk privately.

"I found another lock in Asher," he said, before she had a chance to tell him about her talk with Newman. "There's this large wheel on the back wall of the warehouse, like the kind you'd see on a bank vault, and it's locked so that it can't be turned." He ignored Sophia's sigh and dismissive wave. "I want to figure out what it's for, but it doesn't seem to be connected to anything and nobody seems to know what it does. Or at least they're not telling me."

"Hyle, why do you have to turn everything in to a conspiracy?"

"What? Who said anything about a conspiracy? I was just making an observation."

"All your observations are about things that make you suspicious. I think you're looking at everything in the worst possible light." She filled him in on her conversation with Newman and his face darkened as he listened.

"If I wanted to hear what Newman had to say I would have talked to him myself."

"But you were never going to do that and *I* wanted to hear what he had to say. And you know what? He has some good explanations for the things that are bothering you. I feel a lot better after talking to him."

"Of course he made you feel better. That's his job."

Sophia sighed. The conversation was not going the way she had hoped. In fact, it was not going anywhere. She decided to change topics.

"Hyle, why don't you say anything in the unity meetings?"

"I just don't have anything to say."

"I don't believe that."

Hyle exhaled slowly and debated how honest to be. Sophia waited patiently.

"Okay, the truth is that the questions I want answers to will probably upset people."

"No they won't. The Union of Faith was founded on the idea of tolerating all kinds of beliefs. The whole purpose of these unity meetings is to discuss all sorts of different ideas and find the common ground between them. That's Newman's job—give him a shot. Besides, I think that people are starting to be upset because you don't say anything. They'd probably be happy to know what you're thinking."

Sophia watched his face intently. She could see that he was giving her argument serious consideration, yet he was still hesitant.

"Please," she said. "As a favor to me."

"Let me think about it," he said at last.

She could tell that more pressure would be counterproductive. That was the best she was going to get for the moment.

"Okay, there's something else I wanted to show you," she said. "But you have to come inside."

Once inside, Sophia led him to the threshold of her room and instructed him to close his eyes. He heard Sophia take a few quiet steps, pull open a drawer and take a few more steps back toward him before she told him he could open them again. When he did she stood in front of him holding a long travel cloak with a deep hood.

"This was my first project," she told him proudly. "What do you think?"

He looked at it. The cloth was coarse and irregular. She handed it to him.

"Go ahead, put it on."

She helped him put it on and showed him how to arrange the folds of cloth so that he could reach out of it while keeping everything but his hands protected from the rain. The fabric was thick and the cloak was heavier than it appeared. It fit well and began to get hot almost as soon as he put it on. Upon close examination the seams were uneven in several places, but it appeared to be sturdily made. And it was dark blue.

Hyle thanked Sophia and complimented her on her craftsmanship while she explained what had gone into making it. By the time he had taken the cloak back off and folded it up, he had decided on the question that he would ask.

CHAPTER NINETEEN

FROM OUTSIDE IN— AND UP

In the fading evening light, people filtered into Newman's house, gathering in pairs and small groups and talking in low voices until the start of the unity meeting. By the time Newman emerged from his room, the common room was filled well beyond capacity, with people packed shoulder to shoulder on the floor, standing in the doorways of the side rooms and spilling into the kitchen area on either side of his chair. Taking his seat, Newman made a downward motioned to silence the applause, led the assembly in a brief prayer, and then made his traditional request for questions and topics. He was clearly taken aback when Hyle's hand went up, staring at it for a second without responding.

"I have a question," said Hyle, filling the silence.

The normal background noise of whispering and people shifting in their seats quieted.

"You've been holding out on us," Newman joked. "That's great. What's your question?"

Hyle did not speak for a moment and then drew a deep breath.

"You said in one of the first meetings I attended that the purpose of these meetings is to help us to come to know God in our own way. Most of the meetings, people talk a lot about various passages out of the Bible, or occasionally other religious texts, but it's not clear to me how this helps anyone to know God."

He paused, choosing his words carefully. There was a subtle tone that Sophia, only because she had come to know him well during their travels, was able to detect. She knew that he was asking this question at her request, but she suspected that he also hoped to stir up a little trouble.

"We come to know things through experience," he continued. "We see a fire and we feel hotter as we get closer to it. Maybe we get burned. We see that it burns wood and paper, but not water and through our experience we come to know the nature of fire. I have read about Napoleon Bonaparte and George Washington, but I wouldn't say I have come to know them. Not in the way that I understand fire and not in the way that many people here talk about coming to know God." He looked around the room and saw understanding on some faces, but confusion still on others. "What I mean to say is the Bible, even accepting for the sake of discussion that it's divinely inspired, comes to us in the form of words on paper just like any other book, so you can learn the history of God, but I don't see how you can hope to do anything more."

"Thank you, Hyle," Newman said when he had finished. "That was worth waiting for. It's an excellent question that really gets to the heart of what it means to have faith."

Polling the room, Newman collected responses, keeping each person to a short reply. Although a few people protested the oversimplified assessment of the Bible, several people praised Hyle for contributing and the responses were mostly sympathetic. Newman parsed their ideas into two general categories, one arguing that it is indeed possible to come to know God through a study of the scriptures, and the other claiming that there had to be some type of transforming personal event.

"While the first argument is valid if it works for you, it doesn't work for everyone and doesn't really answer the question," said Newman. "The early church fathers like Augustine, or Saint Augustine for the Catholics among us, wrestled with some very similar issues. I think if we take a look at Augustine and the questions he tried to answer it'll help address Hyle's question."

Newman paused to look for any comments, questions or objections. Seeing none he continued.

"Augustine was born in the middle of the fourth century AD, in the last days of the Roman Empire when there was no single set of Christian beliefs. The Emperor Constantine, after his conversion to Christianity had convened the Council of Nicea in the year 325, just before Augustine's birth, to reach agreement on some of the fundamental precepts of Christianity. Three hundred bishops attended, which gives you an idea of how widespread Christianity had become in three centuries, yet there were still a lot of competing ideas, both in the Christian mainstream and at the fringes, as well as challenges from adherents to the old pagan religions and philosophies. Even though the Nicene Creed established a core set of beliefs, it was arguably Augustine who did more than any other person to work out the core philosophy to support those beliefs."

Newman gestured toward a young man sitting near the back of the room who had raised his hand.

"What did the Nicene Creed say?" he asked.

"The big issue it resolved was the tripartite nature of God," Newman answered. "There had been a debate about whether the Father, Son and Holy Spirit were three different entities or different aspects of the same God. It may seem a subtle point, but it was the difference between polytheism and monotheism. The Nicene Creed established that all three were of one essence, and codified the core beliefs for Christians—at least Western Christians—that Jesus was the Son of God, made flesh by the Spirit through the Virgin Mary and died for our sins at the hands of Pontius Pilot."

"You said 'Western Christians.' Isn't that what all Christians believe?" the same man asked.

"The Nicene Creed did a lot to unite Christian belief, but some competing ideas never quite died out and continued as heresies. The united Church also split again, in part, over some of the language in the Creed. The Eastern Orthodox Churches disagreed with language that said the Holy Spirit proceeded from the Son. They also disagreed with the degree of papal authority. Eventually, centuries after Augustine's lifetime, they split from the Western Catholic Church in the Great Schism of 1054. A lot of different churches came out of both sides of the schism. They're all much more similar in belief than they are different, but Augustine probably had the most influence on the Western Church, especially the Roman Catholic Church."

After making sure that the questions about the Council of Nicea had been answered to everyone's satisfaction, Newman asked the meeting participants what any of them knew about Augustine.

Joel, who had read Augustine's *Confessions* in college, recalled being particularly amused by Augustine's invocation "Lord, make me chaste, but not yet," and the other stories of his human weaknesses. Ignoring an elbow in the ribs from Rachel, who was seated beside him, he expanded on the theme.

"My favorite passage is when he's talking about trying to give up the pleasures of the world to devote his thoughts to God. He describes it as being like the feeling you have when you wake up in the morning. You know you should get out of bed, but it feels so good to sleep that you keep telling yourself 'just a little bit longer' and roll over and go back to sleep."

"Yes, even though Augustine was very spiritual, he was also very human, and understood that about himself," Newman agreed. "He was a product of a materialistic Roman Empire and raised in a culture where success was measured by education and rank. He was, by his own account, a bit of a *bon vivant*, shall we say, with a particular weakness for women and sold on the material measures of success and happiness that this culture taught. Even two millennia later his *Confessions* are worth reading because everyone can identify with them. Anyone else remember anything that struck them about the teachings of Augustine?"

"Didn't he write another book to console the Christians after Rome fell?" Joel asked.

"Yes," confirmed Newman. "More than just a book. *The City of God* was a twenty-two volume work which he wrote after the Visigoths sacked Rome. Many Romans believed that Rome fell as punishment for abandoning the old Roman gods, but Augustine shifted the focus from struggles in the material world, which he symbolized as the City of Man, to the perfect eternal world, symbolized as the City of God. He consoled the Romans with the belief that the City of God would prevail in the end. What else?"

"I remember that he taught that God created time when He created the universe," said Deborah from one of the side benches. "But I don't remember why that was important."

"It was his answer to some pagan challenge about why God chose some arbitrary time to create the universe," Newman explained. "He also taught that God exists outside of time, but that our human mode of existence is the present. The past only exists as memories and the future as possibility or imagination, so the present is where we actually reside. He had some very interesting ideas about the nature of time. Anyone else, back to the idea of coming to know God?"

"He was very introspective, wasn't he?" offered Rachel. "I mean he kind of came to know God on his own."

"Yes. It's true that he was very introspective, although he was also well educated, so he had lots of material to think about. He studied rhetoric which gave him an education that geared him for political success, but during this education he read Cicero, who encouraged the pursuit of philosophy. That's what convinced Augustine that he needed to pursue wisdom. He spent a lot of time with a cult called the Manicheans before discovering some classical philosophy and ultimately turning to Christianity. By the time he came to Christianity, he had traveled a lot and encountered many different ideas. Apparently he was particularly influenced by the philosopher Plotinus. Does anybody know anything about Plotinus?"

When a lone hand went up in the room, Newman chuckled quietly to himself and gave Sophia a knowing look.

"It might be worth taking a bit of a tangent to hear a little about Plotinus. Sophia, do you want to tell us what you know about his philosophy?"

Agreeing happily, Sophia started by noting that while Plotinus may have influenced Augustine, he in turn derived his philosophy largely from Plato, and was the founder of the Neoplatonist tradition of philosophers who emphasized the spiritual aspects of Platonism. She introduced the idea of eternal Platonic Forms in contrast to the material world, which she explained as a poor and transient reflection of the Forms, and then went on to clarify this idea by recounting the Allegory of the Cave.

"Plotinus was the last great classical philosopher," Sophia told the room. "He lived in the third century AD, so about a hundred years before Augustine. He built on Plato's ideas, organizing them into more of a structure. He started with an idea of the intelligible world, similar to Plato's forms, which he called the Divine Intellect. The Forms exist within the Divine Intellect."

She paused and looked at Newman.

"How much detail do you want?" she asked him. "You know I could talk about philosophy all night."

Newman looked around the room. Most people were still watching Sophia intently.

"I know that Plotinus was a big influence on Augustine. Since Augustine was so foundational for western Christian thought, I think it would be worth spending the rest of the night on him if you need it."

"Okay, but I don't think I'll take that long," she replied, turning back to address the room. "The Divine Intellect is like the organizing force behind all the Platonic Forms, but even superior to the Divine Intellect, Plotinus conceived of something he called the One. The One is similar to the Good in Plato, like the sun that lights the real world outside Plato's cave. It's the central thing from which everything else derives. You might think that the One would have to be infinitely complex to give rise to everything in the intelligible world, but Plotinus came to the opposite conclusion. He believed that complex things were inferior. If something can be broken down into parts, either physically or conceptually, it loses its wholeness. If you can define what something is, you can also state what it's not, therefore it's lacking in some way—it's less than being everything. So Plotinus viewed the One as being irreducibly simple, existing outside the confines of the material world, time and space. It's also outside, or above, the Divine Intellect. In a way, it's even above existence.

"From the One at the center of this organized view of reality emanates the Divine Intellect, including within it the Forms. Outside the One and the Divine Intellect is what Plotinus called the World Soul, and beyond that is the material world. The World Soul is the interface between the Divine Intellect and the material world. It's the source of our individual souls, so in that sense we're all connected according to Plotinus, but we spend most of our time outside the level of the World Soul in the material world of physical existence. We exist in the material world, but there's a way for us to reach the intelligible world. Here's the last important aspect of Plotinus—he believed that conceiving and creating were the same. Things that are conceived in, or comprehended by, the Divine Intellect have real existence. So borrowing an idea from Aristotle, he believed that by understanding something, we become one with it."

Sophia stopped to scan the room. More than a few people looked confused.

"Picture it this way," she explained. "Imagine the One in the center of reality, so perfect that it's overflowing with perfection and giving rise to the Forms of the Divine intellect outside the One. Then imagine a crystalline sphere that surrounds the Divine Intellect. This sphere is the World Soul. Outside of the World Soul is the material world. It's like a gradient from the perfect to the imperfect, from the eternal to the ephemeral. Plotinus described it as being like the light from a candle that gradually fades until it disappears into darkness, and of course we're living right on the edge of that darkness, between the shadow and the flame. Now picture that on the crystalline sphere there are countless faces, all looking outward. That's us. Even though we're all united in the World Soul, we're not looking back in that direction, so we don't see that connection. We're looking out toward the material world, away from the World Soul, away from the Divine Intellect and away from the One. The goal of the philosopher, according to Plotinus, is to try to turn inward toward the Divine Intellect and the One. I can see how an early Christian might be very attracted to this idea of how the universe is ordered."

"Thank you, Sophia," Newman said. "Now I have more clarity about how Augustine was influenced by this philosophy."

He turned to address the room again.

"I want to get back to Hyle's original question and how Augustine answered it. He had spent a lot of time with the Manicheans who were materialists. One of the challenges to Christian thinking he had to address was the question of where God resided in the world. If you take a material view of the world, God would have to exist in the physical world, always interacting with things in order to affect them. There were proposals that God resided in everyone and everything, but that led to the question of whether He existed more in some things than in others, and whether He was 'stretched out' and diminished by extending into more things or across space. Similar to the line of thinking that led Plotinus to propose an irreducibly simple One, Augustine took the view that God couldn't be reduced to existence in the material sense. So Augustine would have agreed with you, Hyle, that you can't come to know God through the physical world."

"So you have to find God in your heart? Is that what he said?" Hyle guessed. Again Sophia picked up a carefully suppressed tone of skepticism that went unnoticed by the rest of the participants.

"Yes and no," Newman replied. "Augustine was far too analytical for something so simple, but you aren't that far off. Augustine talked about looking inside to find his soul and looking in and up to find God. He probably got this language from Plotinus, because he saw the material world as being 'out there' in contrast to the soul. Through-out the *Confessions*, he talks about being distracted from God by the material world. He realizes, looking back as a faithful Christian, that all of these things caused him misery, not because they were bad, but because they were not eternal. He didn't think that political success or wealth or even physical pleasures were bad in and of themselves, since all of these things existed within God's creation. But anything that leads you away from the eternal will ultimately cause you grief. For Augustine, sin was trying to find ultimate happiness in something material and the sin brings about its own punishment because none of it will last. In fact, there's a very moving passage he wrote about losing his best friend where he concludes that even something as pure as love between two friends is a distraction from God. The only way to find eternal happiness is in something eternal, namely God."

"That makes sense," Hyle agreed slowly, "but what does it mean to look inside? Isn't that just a more intellectual sounding way of saying look into your heart?"

Sophia had been watching Hyle carefully. His eyes were narrowed as Newman spoke, as if he were analyzing every word, and there was always a suggestion of skepticism, or perhaps something stronger, in the way he spoke. She decided to keep watching to see if Hyle was motivated out of interest or whether he was merely attempting to make things difficult for Newman.

"Remember, I said yes and no," Newman replied. "Obviously there's some element of saying just look inside your heart, but Augustine was also an intellectual. I think that's why he felt so compelled to reconcile Christian thought with classical philosophy. He spent many years with the Manicheans and what ultimately drove him away was that they couldn't answer his questions. For him to be spiritually satisfied he also had to be intellectually satisfied. He clearly embraced the idea from Plato and Plotinus that the material world is imperfect and passing and that it was to something eternal that we should turn our attention if we wished to pursue wisdom. Now the question for him, the same question you're asking, Hyle, was how to find it. He found part of his answer in 1 Corinthians. Does anyone know what it was?"

There were several suggestions. Newman discussed each one, drawing out some relationship to the ideas of Augustine, but asking for more ideas. Finally after giving a more specific clue that it was something Paul had said about Jesus he got the answer he was looking for from a middle aged man with thinning hair and large ears who was sitting in the back of the room. It was a description of Jesus as "the wisdom of God." Sophia recognized him as the man who had asked about a different passage from Paul during her first unity meeting.

"Augustine loved that quote because he was, after all, searching for wisdom," Newman continued. "That was one of the keys for reconciling Christian thinking to the ideas of Plotinus. Augustine thought of God as being like the One of Plotinus, perfect and eternal, not limited by space or time, and the source of all that exists. We're naturally inclined to look away, outside, to the material world. For Augustine, that meant being distracted from God, and Jesus was the way to help us to look inward and up, to try to glimpse God. Jesus was the divine made material, God made flesh and blood, a connection between the imperfect material world and the eternal world that Augustine was searching for."

He paused and thought for a moment, then gave Sophia a significant look before continuing.

"Here's an example to help give you clarity. Imagine that I had a chalk board behind me and I drew a right triangle on it. You'd all recognize it and if I asked you what it was, you'd probably tell me it was a right triangle. But what are the chances that I'd be able to make my angle exactly ninety degrees with no error, not even a thousandth of a degree? What are the chances that my lines would be exactly straight? And even if they were, a line by definition is made up of points which are infinitely small, but any line I could draw would have a measurable thickness. It would also pass away eventually, even if I carved it into stone. Anything we could draw as a right triangle would actually be an imperfect representation of something eternal and perfect. But the imperfect form helps us to understand the perfect one. It's in that moment that we understand the connection between the material world and the eternal one that we glimpse God. For Augustine, Jesus was like the written triangle, the wisdom of God made flesh to show us the way to God, eternal and perfect."

The man with the big ears spoke again.

"Material things aren't the only things that distract people from God. You know what Paul said about philosophy in Colossians."

"Why don't you tell us, Timothy?" Newman replied.

"He said, 'See to it that no one takes you captive by philosophy and empty deceit.' It's faith in Jesus Christ that should be important to a Christian, not trying to make sense of Greek philosophy."

"Augustine certainly would have agreed with you on the first point," Newman replied. "He felt that faith in Jesus was the starting point. From there he built his intellectual understanding of the Christian faith. But it started with faith. Or technically he believed that it was through God's grace that he came to have faith, but either way he didn't believe that it was an intellectual understanding that redeemed you in God's eyes. In fact in several places in the *Confessions* he talks about the dangers of getting too inflated with your own knowledge to see the path to God, saying that in finding this path children may have an easier time than educated men."

"Then why did he spend so much time trying to work in Greek philosophy?" Timothy insisted.

"Because faith and philosophy don't have to be mutually exclusive. But that's just my opinion. Does anyone else want to converse about this?"

One person agreed with Timothy and a couple voiced their support for Newman's position, but no one added much to the discussion until Sophia spoke.

"I think it goes back to what Hyle said at the beginning of the evening. The Bible is a history. It's the story of God and Jesus, but it's like a collection of short stories by different authors. You can get different themes and ideas from each of them. It sounds like what Augustine was trying to do, at a time when there was no unified set of ideas, was to take these stories and understand them in a framework so that he could tell which ideas to believe and which ones not to believe. It really isn't enough for most people to just have faith. Faith may be part of it, but things have to make sense too. Plotinus was an extremely well-known philosopher in his day, so if Augustine drew on him to make sense of Christian thinking, it may have been as much to reconcile faith with rationality as it was to reconcile Christianity with Greek philosophy. Athens produced a culture very rich in intellectual tradition that placed a high value on rationality and Jerusalem produced a culture that placed a high value in its strong faith. The western world is a product of both cultures and Augustine helped to bring them together."

She was looking mainly at Timothy as she spoke, and when she finished he still appeared unconvinced, but several people agreed and complimented her on the observation. There was a little more conversation before the tolling of the evening bell brought the meeting to a close.

As the guests filtered out, chatting with Newman at the door along the way, and the housemates rolled the table back, replaced the chairs and disappeared into their rooms, Phoebe caught Sophia to ask more questions about Plotinus and Plato. Hyle listened quietly while they talked. When Newman was finally able to close the door he made tea for everyone.

"I thought your question tonight was very good," he said as he returned with the teapot. "Did you feel that your question was answered?"

"Better than I expected," Hyle said carefully.

Newman took the reply at face value.

"Do you think you'll contribute again tomorrow night?"

"I don't know. My mode of existence is the present."

Sophia chuckled.

"You finally got him to contribute, Newman. Now leave him alone," she said lightly.

They talked until late in the evening. Eventually Phoebe decided that she was tired, and Sophia rose with her, saying goodnight to the men.

"Goodnight, Sophia. And thanks for the triangle," Newman said.

She ruffled his hair playfully as she circled the table and disappeared into her room. Hyle said goodnight as well and picked his way across the frost-covered grass to his own house. He brought in the lantern that still hung outside for his benefit, put it out and found his way to bed by the dim orange glow of the embers on the hearth.

CHAPTER TWENTY

THE OFFER

Sunrise burned brightly behind the clouds promising a warm day. After breakfast Newman performed his first daily duty of walking around his canton collecting children to bring to school. Already in the pauses when the mountain breezes stopped blowing Newman could feel the warmth on his face. He guided the unruly horde of children across the city, letting the older ones run ahead and escorting the flock of younger ones. Perhaps because of the nice weather, he allowed them all to stop briefly to watch the blacksmith firing his forge before leading them the rest of the way to the cluster of houses that served as a school and assuring that they all went safely inside, each group into the door of the house that corresponded to their age.

Once the children had all been delivered to school, Newman cut across the city until he came to the narrow river and then followed it back toward his neighborhood. A large group of women washing clothes on the opposite bank gave him an enthusiastic greeting when he bade them good morning as he passed by. Soon after that he was back in his canton attending to his other errands for the morning. He visited a cluster of houses where a newly constructed barbeque pit had caused a disagreement among the residents, paid a visit to a boy who had been on antibiotics for the past two days with a high fever, checked in on a housebound elderly couple and made a few social calls.

At eleven bells, he decided to head for Unity Hall so that he could look up a few things in the library before eating lunch with the other proctors. As he approached Unity Hall, Newman was surprised by who he saw coming out of the magister's cottage. Although he was still far away it was impossible to mistake John's large build, even at a considerable distance. John looked briefly toward Newman, then turned and hurried off in the opposite direction.

The magister was typically very busy tending to the governance and spiritual needs of almost twelve thousand people, and while there was no hard and fast rule, people were strongly encouraged to bring problems to their local proctors first. Even then there were several levels of proctor to pass through before a problem needed to be elevated to the magister's attention, so it struck Newman as odd that John should be there and he made a note to talk to him in the evening when he got home.

Not wishing to raise questions among their respective housemates, Newman decided to wait for John that evening on the path that led to their houses. He tried to make the meeting look accidental, occupying himself with the rearrangement of the woodpile behind his house until he caught sight of the large man approaching. John was walking quickly, his eyes fixed to the ground, apparently deep in thought.

"Hi, John. How are you doing?" Newman called out, stepping out onto the path ahead of him.

A strange expression flashed across John's face as he looked up, but it was quickly replaced by a tired smile. They exchanged pleasantries and Newman got the definite sense while they talked that John was uneasy about something. It gave him the perfect opportunity.

"John, is something wrong? Is something bothering you?"

"No. No, everything is fine," the big man said with a forced laugh. "No worries."

"You seem upset about something."

"Me? I do? Probably just hungry. You know, looking forward to getting home and having a good meal."

Newman gave him a long patient look and waited to see if he would say anything more. John shifted uncomfortably, his eyes looking everywhere but Newman's face, but he said nothing.

"John, I know you prefer to go to the unity meetings at Unity Hall, which means that I haven't really had a chance to get to know you that well, but I hope you'd feel comfortable coming to me as your proctor if something was wrong."

John nodded vigorously.

"Yeah, sure I would."

Newman had hoped to convince John to talk to him about whatever problem he was having, or at least to have John explain why he had not felt comfortable coming to him, but things did not seem to be leading in either of those directions. He considered letting John go and trying discretely to find out if Hyle knew of anything that might be bothering John since they shared a room, but he discarded the idea, realizing that Hyle was much less likely to talk about anything than John was.

"How are things going between you and Hyle?"

"Fine," John said quickly. He nodded his head even more vigorously, but his ruddy face went ashen. He looked like an overgrown schoolboy who just got called to the head of the class to empty his pockets.

"John, I saw you coming out of the magister's cottage this afternoon. As your proctor, it's important for me to know if you're having any problems. I just want you to know that you can trust me to keep whatever problem you may be having confidential."

"I do! I do! It's just that—" He cut himself off, looking quite distraught.

"It's just what?"

"I'm not supposed to say anything," John said ruefully.

"John, it's okay. I'm your proctor. You're supposed to be able to tell me anything, remember?"

John scowled in thought for a moment. Newman held his breath, regarding John with the most passive face he could muster.

"Well, it's not a problem really," John said at length. "Magister Delacroix asked me not to say anything to anyone, but since you're my proctor I guess I can tell you. I don't see what the big deal is anyway really. He just asked me to stop by and tell him how Hyle is doing, that's all."

Once John decided to open up he told Newman everything he could remember about his conversations with the magister and seemed much happier for not having to keep the secret on his own. He told Newman that he had been stopping in to see Delacroix daily and reconstructed the magister's questions as accurately as he could remember them. Newman found it curious to learn this since the magister had also asked him almost daily about how Hyle and Sophia were adjusting. Did the magister not trust his assessment? Or did he think that Hyle might be doing or saying things in the security of his own sleeping quarters that only John would know? From what Newman was able to reconstruct from John's information, the magister was interested to know anything he could about Hyle—what questions he asked, where he spent his time, how happy he seemed. It was odd, Newman thought, for the magister to show so much concern for one person. A little later that evening he pulled Phoebe aside and found out that she had also been having daily meetings with Magister Delacroix, giving him her observations about Sophia.

The next afternoon Newman crossed from Unity Hall, where he had just finished eating lunch, to Magister Delacroix's cottage. He had requested a meeting with the magister intending to talk about John and Phoebe, Hyle and Sophia, but he grew increasingly apprehensive with every step he took toward the door of the cottage. He was still not sure exactly what he was going to say when Nathan opened the door and ushered him to the magister's office, closing the door behind him.

"You wanted to see me, Newman?" Delacroix said, looking up from his papers only after he had finished speaking. He did not invite Newman to sit down.

"Yes, Magister. I wanted to talk to you about Sophia and Hyle."

"I see. And?"

Newman paused. He had still not thought of a good way to broach the subject he wished to discuss and the old man did not seem to be in a very good mood. The only light in the room came from the top panel of a narrow window behind the magister's desk. The bottom panel had been covered over for privacy. The light made it difficult to see his face, but Newman could feel Delacroix's blue eyes boring into him, stretching out every second of his silence. He shifted impatiently behind the desk and his chair creaked accentuating the stillness.

"I saw John coming out of your cottage yesterday," Newman said at last. "He says that he has been giving you daily reports on how Hyle is doing."

The old man shook his head.

"I told him not to tell anyone," he sighed, more to himself than to Newman.

"It was my fault, Magister. I thought that he was bothering you with some problem that he didn't feel comfortable talking to me about. I convinced him that as his proctor he should be able to tell me anything."

Now Delacroix was silent. He stared for some time off toward the wall, toward a black and white portrait of the Prophet as if he were communing with it for guidance.

"I understand," he said at length. "As you are his proctor, perhaps I should have told you from the beginning. I am glad you came to converse with me directly about it. Was there anything else?"

There was, but Newman was reluctant to bring it up. He was curious about something else, but his need to know it as proctor was not as clear. Delacroix could tell that something was still occupying him.

"Go ahead, Newman, speak. What is on your mind?"

"Okay. Well, I—I arranged for them to stay in separate houses and work separate jobs as you instructed, but I'm still not sure why that's necessary."

"Do you need to understand in order to do what I have required of you?" asked Delacroix.

Newman looked down.

"No, Magister. Of course not."

"Good."

"It was just my curiosity," he confessed, not lifting his eyes.

"Are you sure that it's just curiosity that's troubling you?"

"No," Newman replied slowly, studying Delacroix's face to try to make out his expression. "It seems that Sophia and Hyle are very important to you for some reason—much more important than I would have expected—and I suppose I'd hoped that as their proctor I might be entrusted to help with whatever concerns you have about them. More than just being someone else who can give you updates."

Again the old man was silent for some time before speaking. His sharp eyes studied Newman carefully.

"Newman, you are relatively new to the Union, but you seem to be a good man. I sense that you are loyal and your intentions are true."

Newman inclined his head modestly and tried to suppress a proud smile. He knew that the magister did not give out praise like that lightly. He had been judged and found worthy.

"What I am about to tell you is known only to a handful of people in Asher. You must keep it just between us, at least for now, until I understand the implications more thoroughly. You must mention it to no one, not even other proctors. Do you understand?"

"Yes, Magister, I understand."

Newman could not bring himself to believe what he heard, but it explained Delacroix's interest in the two new arrivals. The magister watched him patiently, waiting for him to digest the news.

"What can I do to help, Magister?" Newman asked, not entirely sure he wanted to hear the answer.

The old man smiled at this response.

"For one, you can help by keeping an eye on them and keeping them separate as you have been doing. I am still trying to decide if there is anything more to be done. What is your assessment of them, Newman?"

From his evening discussions with Hyle and Sophia, Newman knew that neither of them had attended church before coming to Asher and that Hyle had had a falling out with organized religion at an early age. He was encouraged that Hyle had begun to contribute in the unity meetings and converse openly about his doubts, but he got the impression that Hyle was a skeptic at heart. He shared all of this with the magister.

"Do you think he belongs in a community of faith?"

Something in the way Delacroix asked the question made Newman wonder whether it was meant to assess Hyle or him. He did not like any response he could think of and took a moment to choose his answer carefully.

"I think it's too early to tell for sure."

The magister frowned. Newman could not tell whether he was thinking or if he was unhappy with the assessment.

"And Sophia?"

"Sophia is a much more spiritual person. She's very open-minded. She enjoys contributing at our unity meetings, but she's equally interested to learn what other people believe. I think she'll fit in very well given some time."

Delacroix looked at him sternly.

"It's clear you two have a close relationship. Are you letting that bias your assessment?"

"No, Magister. She has adjusted well to all aspects of life here. She enjoys her work, she participates in our unity meetings and I think she has been a real asset to our discussions. That's not just my opinion—I expect Phoebe must have told you the same thing."

"She has," Delacroix confirmed. "So it's your recommendation that Sophia be allowed to stay?"

"Yes, it is, Magister."

"And if Hyle were not allowed to stay, what do you think she would do?"

"I don't know. It would be a very difficult decision for her, I'm sure. She hasn't known Hyle for very long and has nothing to go back to out there, but they went through a lot together to get here. It would be tough on her to see him go."

"If he is to stay here," Delacroix said, "there must be no question about his faith or his loyalties. I have my doubts about whether that is possible, but we shall see. In the meantime, what can we do to increase the chances that Sophia will stay if Hyle should need to go?"

Newman was uncomfortable with this line of thinking at first. It felt like plotting against Hyle, but he realized that it was not. There was a chance, despite their best efforts, that Hyle would decide to leave and in that case, Newman told himself, it was certainly in Sophia's best interests to stay.

"She seemed to enjoy spinning and weaving at first," Newman said, thinking out loud, "but I think she may be getting bored with it."

"What would she prefer to do? What do you think she would do if she had more free time?"

"Read maybe. She likes philosophy. She said that she used to read it a lot at home. She actually helped me gain some insight into the teachings of Saint Augustine."

"Would she make a good proctor?"

The question took Newman by surprise.

"Yes. Yes, I think she'd make a very good proctor."

Delacroix decided that he was willing to give her that opportunity, but he was not comfortable giving her any authority until, as he called it, "the issue with Hyle," could be resolved. Since Sophia had not had a religious education and was new to the Union of Faith, Delacroix used that as a pretext for invoking a training period during which she would be allowed to study the scriptures, church history and religious philosophy. Newman was pleased with the plan and he was certain that Sophia would be thrilled. He left the magister's office anxious to tell her the news. The rest of the day seemed to crawl along as he marked each bell carefully in order to catch her at the end of work for the day. As soon as the bells tolled to mark the end of work, he summoned her out of the house and led her to a quiet spot along the river bank where they could talk.

CHAPTER TWENTY-ONE

THE FAVORITE FEW

Days began to fall into a comfortable pattern. Hyle finished dinner quickly and crossed the courtyard to Newman's house. He spent his daylight hours at work, evenings at Newman's house and he went back to his own house only to eat and sleep. Originally he had finished dinner quickly because he was uncomfortable with the strangers he had been forced to live with, but as the days went by meals became less difficult. Ruth had gone out of her way to make conversation with him at first and now he felt at ease talking with her and joking and playing with her boys. He walked to work with John each day and enjoyed listening to his stories. Friendship with John was easy because John did not expect Hyle to do any talking. The only uneasy moments were the rare occasions in the common room alone with Leah or Judith and these usually ended quickly with someone retreating to their bedroom to avoid making conversation.

Now Hyle left dinner early, not to avoid his housemates, but because it was the only time he got to spend with Sophia. They did not see each other during the work day and ate dinner apart. The unity meetings took up much of the evening and Newman always stayed up with them afterwards. Although he enjoyed the three-way conversations over tea after the unity meetings, and sometimes even the unity meetings themselves, particularly after contributing, he also needed some time to talk to Sophia alone. Right after dinner, when Newman was busy planning the upcoming meeting, was the only opportunity to do that. On this evening however, when he arrived at Newman's house she was not there.

"Have you seen Sophia?" Hyle asked Phoebe, helping her move chairs to the sides of the room.

"No, she disappeared right after work. She wasn't even at dinner," she said, surveying Hyle's face. "Neither was Newman. Maybe they had some house business to take care of."

Hyle helped Phoebe start a fire and they took their usual places near the front of the room, saving a space for Sophia between them. When the bell tolled, Newman and Sophia were still missing. Since Newman often appeared from his room on the tolling of the hour, the room had grown quiet in anticipation. Over the course of several minutes the silence gave way to a low murmur, then a buzz of conversation. This faded again quickly when the door opened and Newman stepped in. Reaching back through the door, he led Sophia in by the hand, and then picked his way through the assembled crowd to the front of the room as she followed behind. Newman sat down in his vacant chair and Sophia squeezed into the space between Phoebe and Hyle.

"Where have you been?" Hyle whispered urgently as she sat down beside him.

"We went for a walk," she said, obviously flustered. "I guess we lost track of time."

"You missed dinner."

"Newman had some big news to tell me," Sophia said. She was beaming as she quickly told Hyle that she was going to be a proctor. Hyle did not share her excitement. It was already difficult expressing his concerns about the city to her. Making her a proctor would only make matters worse. He forced a smile.

"Congratulations," he managed.

Sophia could tell something was bothering Hyle, but she did not have a chance to pursue it. Newman began to address the room, apologizing for being late. This evening nobody had any questions or suggestions for a discussion topic, so Newman decided to continue their discussion about Augustine from a few nights earlier and see where that led.

"Sophia and I were talking about this on the way here," he said. "We think that Augustine may have been the first person to use the concept of the inner self. Even though he may have been inspired by Plotinus' description of the faces looking out from the crystalline sphere, Augustine made it more personal. When Augustine turned inside it was to escape from the material world and everyone in it and devote his attention to God. It was much more of a one to one relationship than a re-unification with some collective world soul. It wouldn't have made sense to Augustine to try to translate Plotinus directly to Christianity. Even though the One is a good description of God, the idea that the One is in the center would suggest that God is inside all of us. Augustine was careful to describe looking in and then up to find God. Into his own soul, then up, more like coming out of Plato's cave into the real world and looking up to see the sun."

"Why is that such an important distinction?" asked Timothy, who looked more serious than usual. "The Apostles seem to have done just fine without it."

"First of all, it helped him reconcile Christian thinking with classical philosophy. Although that may not be an important goal for every Christian," Newman conceded, "it was for Augustine. Second, it was the key to answering Hyle's question about how we can find God if we can't find him with our senses. And third, I think it helps us to understand things in a way that matches our experience. Our senses—our sight, hearing, touch, smell, taste—are focused on the physical world which goes on mainly outside our bodies. But if you shut all that out, if you go sit in a quiet room and close your eyes, what are you left with? Just your thoughts. These don't come from outside you like the information from your senses does. It seems like a whole separate world, and it's in this world that we can best understand universal forms like the right triangle or focus our attention on God."

"It still sounds to me like trying to think your way into Heaven, and I don't think that's what Jesus preached," Timothy objected.

"If it sounds that way it's because I haven't explained it well enough. Actually Augustine believed that love was the driving force in the world. Love seeks to unite you with the things you love, so it's love of things in the physical world that could get you into trouble. Loving them to excess is sin according to Augustine—greed, gluttony, lust— these are all a result of loving these transient things as if they could make you eternally happy. But that kind of love will only be fulfilled in God because it's directed toward something eternal and perfect that can return eternal and perfect happiness. So love was the driving force, and he believed that it was the will that controls where we direct our love. Augustine may also have been the first person to develop the concept of free will as we currently understand it. He believed that we can choose to turn our love toward God, so it's our free will and God's grace by which we're saved. It may make it easier for people to make that choice if they can benefit from Augustine's thinking. In other words, thinking may not get you to God, but it might put you on the right path."

"I still don't see how loving God has anything to do with universal forms and philosophy," Timothy insisted.

"Remember the triangle? Imagine the first time you understood that there was such a thing as a perfect triangle," Newman said, pausing to think for a moment. "That may be at too young an age. Imagine later in school. You're trying to understand a difficult mathematical concept. You use your brain to work through a bunch of problems and you think about it, wrestle with it, and then suddenly, understanding comes to you in a flash of insight. It's not just stepwise thinking that leads to this understanding, it's something beyond intellect—it's a flash, an inspiration—and it's a wonderful feeling. Unfortunately it lasts only a split second, but for that instant, you have touched the eternal world that Plotinus would call the Divine Intellect. For Augustine, the path to God was that same path, and the promise of eternal happiness offered by loving God was an eternity of that same feeling of revelation that you get when you have a flash of insight. It was impossible to get it while we're alive, he believed, but once we die and free ourselves from the distractions and imperfections of the physical world, we can enter that perfect state and be one with God."

"I have a question," said Hyle with a quick sidelong glance at Sophia, "but it's not directly related to Augustine."

"That's okay," Newman responded. He was relieved to have someone other than Timothy asking a question.

"It has to do with prophecy."

"Okay," Newman said, a little less certainly.

"You led us in a discussion about some of the prophecies in the Bible a few nights ago and I've been thinking about it. If people can make prophecies, does that mean that God, who is perfect, knows the future perfectly?"

"What do you think?" Newman asked, throwing the question out to the meeting participants.

Hyle nodded thoughtfully, smiling slightly as people responded that, of course, God was omniscient. He sharpened the question.

"So does God already know what I'll be doing, say at five o'clock three weeks from tomorrow?"

Again Newman asked people to contribute their thoughts, and he watched Hyle closely. All those who responded answered affirmatively.

"Then how can I have free will?" Hyle asked.

Newman nodded to himself, his suspicions confirmed.

"Just because God knows what you'll choose doesn't mean that you have no free will," responded an old woman sitting in the back of the room next to Deborah. Deborah herself listened impassively.

"But if he knows that I'll eat an apple at five o'clock three weeks from tomorrow, then I can't choose to have a pear or a steak or wait until six o'clock."

"True, but He's not taking away your choices, He just knows what you'll choose to do before you do."

"He may not be taking them away," Hyle persisted, "but they're taken away nonetheless. If God can know with certainty that I'll eat that apple, then I never had any choice at all because that was the only possibility."

The woman patiently tried to explain her argument in other ways, and Hyle rephrased his, neither of them able to make any progress in the debate. While they talked, Newman reached behind himself and removed the tea kettle from the hook by the fireplace. He held it out at arm's length toward Hyle.

"Hyle, if I let go of this handle, what will happen?"

"The teapot will fall."

"How do you know?"

"Because gravity makes things fall," Hyle replied, intrigued by this new line of argument.

Newman lowered his arm and dropped the teapot. It clattered to the floor.

"You have just prophesied the fate of this teapot," Newman announced.

The room erupted in chuckling and quiet laughter. Even Hyle smiled, although he kept his mirth in check.

"Knowledge isn't the same as causation," Newman concluded.

"No, but the teapot didn't have a choice. That's why I could predict its future."

"You could predict its future because you knew about the law of gravity. God knows all the laws of nature since He created them, so He can predict what you'll do."

"Okay," Hyle said, conceding the point for the moment.

"When you talk about being saved and salvation, is that the same thing as being justified and justification?"

"Yes, they mean the same thing."

"Then what about grace?"

"What about grace?" Newman asked suspiciously.

"You said that we're saved by our free will and God's grace."

"That's right. Grace is essentially a gift that God gives us, pardoning us for our sins even though we don't deserve pardon. It's like a governor granting clemency to a death-row inmate."

"Which comes first?"

"You're asking all the tough questions tonight Hyle. That's one that even Augustine had trouble with. Does everyone understand the dilemma?" Newman asked the room. "Saying that free will comes first is saying that God doesn't really control who gets into Heaven. Saying that grace comes first means that ultimately we're not saved through our own free will, because God must give us grace in order for us to turn to Him."

When Newman threw this question open to the room, a lively debate followed with many participants on each side. As always Newman skillfully moderated the discussion to keep tempers in check and draw out the main arguments of both points of view. Finally someone asked what Augustine had decided.

"It was actually a little more complex for Augustine," Newman answered. "He believed, from his reading of Paul, that everything started with faith. Faith caused us to believe, belief caused us to reach out to God, and God gave us grace to help us love Him—since Augustine believed you can't just choose who or what to love. But then the question put to him was whether faith or grace came first. Essentially the same question—does it begin with us or with God? He didn't decide for many years, but eventually he concluded that grace must come first. That's consistent with the Old Testament where God showed favor to the people of Israel."

"Just like us," Hyle exclaimed brightly. When Newman, looking confused, failed to answer, he continued, "The Prophet built this city for the chosen few to survive the nuclear war, right? The magister said we're all here for a reason."

He surveyed the room. Many people were nodding in agreement and most had an expression that indicated that they were pleased with the parallel that had been drawn.

"Of course," Hyle continued in a deliberate, thoughtful manner, "if we believe that we've been chosen to be here, I guess we'd have to come to the same conclusion that Augustine did about free will."

There was a strained silence for several long seconds while everyone contemplated Hyle's statement. Newman shifted in his seat uncomfortably, trying to think of a new topic for discussion. Before he could, Timothy addressed him, breaking the silence.

"This is what comes of spending too much time with philosophers," he said, casting a meaningful look at Sophia, "and not enough time with Jesus. Maybe you should do more looking in and up."

Sophia looked from Newman to Timothy to Hyle. For the first time since she had met him, she could see anger welling up inside Newman although he fought to suppress it. She had been alternately captivated by the arguments of the debate and annoyed with Hyle for stirring up trouble in Newman's meeting. Now, seeing Newman embarrassed in front of the meeting that he loved so much to moderate, her annoyance had won out. She glared at Hyle, but to her surprise, he was already addressing Timothy.

"What do you have against philosophy, Timothy?" he asked rhetorically, intending to continue, but Timothy answered him immediately. His voice was measured and the reply came almost reflexively.

"It leads people away from Jesus."

"Do you really think so? Do you think anyone in here is going to run out and start worshipping the Divine Intellect? Or go start up the church of the right triangle?"

Nervous laughter rippled through the room and was quickly suppressed. Hyle pressed Timothy further.

"Why don't you want people to think? Does God only like stupid people? Is that your point?"

Timothy returned his gaze, his stern face showing no trace of anger.

"No," he answered calmly, "He just doesn't like people who are full of pride with their own intelligence. They usually think they're too smart for God."

Newman broke in and ended the discussion and the meeting, announcing with a touch of humor that there had been enough conversing to last them until the next evening. The room cleared more quickly than usual, and after talking with Newman while he stood at the door, Sophia said a quick goodnight to Hyle and retired to her room. Hyle followed the stream of guests out the door.

CHAPTER TWENTY-TWO

THE WARNING

Instead of tending to the garden in the morning, Sophia accompanied Newman as he made the rounds of their canton, collecting children and walking them to school, before walking her to Unity Hall for her first day as a proctor. Sophia was excited and more than a little nervous as they entered the huge building by a side door and descended a small flight of stairs to a large open room beneath the main assembly hall. A few long tables surrounded by folding chairs were set up in the middle of the room, with many more stacked against the walls in between the many doors. Delacroix stood up from one of the chairs and strode toward them, greeting Sophia warmly and putting her immediately at ease. He introduced her quickly to the dozen or so people assembled around the table and then led her through one of the doors with Newman trailing behind.

The room they entered looked like a larger version of Delacroix's office. Three of the walls consisted of floor to ceiling bookshelves, one of them interrupted by a lone window set high in the wall. The fourth wall was paneled with dark wainscoting, the upper half painted forest green and hung with an eclectic collection of old maps and documents interspersed with photographs of the Prophet, certificates and awards. Several large comfortable leather armchairs were arranged around small tables. The wonderful musty smell of leather and old paper hung in the air.

"Newman tells me you have read quite a bit of philosophy," Delacroix said to Sophia as they entered. "I thought you might like to spend your time here until we give you your formal initiation."

He gave her a brief tour of the library, pointing out the different sections. There were two books that were mandatory to read, he told her. One was a history of the Union of Faith, written by one of its first members. The second was a three-ring binder of the Prophet's sermons and speeches.

"You can read anything you like when you finish those, or if you want to take a break from them. The history can get a bit dry at times," he confided. "Just don't remove any books from the room, and if you are the last one out, put out the lamp."

Delacroix congratulated Sophia and excused himself, leaving her alone with Newman.

"This is amazing," she whispered. "I had no idea you had anything like this here."

Yes," Newman agreed. "Enjoy it while you can. I spent a lot of time here before I became a proctor, but now I spend so much time meeting with people I don't get to read much."

He walked to one of the shelves and pulled down a thick book while Sophia walked around browsing titles. Eventually she sat down with the binder and began flipping through the pages, picking out sermons with topics that sounded interesting. Newman kept her company for a while until he was called away. People came and went throughout the day, sometimes staying only for a few minutes to look up some particular piece of information, sometimes sitting down and reading for hours. More than once Sophia was so absorbed in a book that she did not notice when they entered.

«« »»

A cold steady rain fell from a leaden sky. Along the muddy roads and under his heavy cloak spattered brown with mud, Hyle pushed a large handcart full of food to be distributed, his head full of thoughts that matched the weather. For his own personal reasons he had volunteered to take a new section of the city, covering for someone who was sick. Despite his dark mood he took pains to make polite conversation at each house, conducting an informal poll of where people had originally called home. To make up for time he had to hurry between groups of houses, splashing through puddles and showering himself with the brown water that continuously sprayed from the wheels of the cart. His discomfort only increased his resolve and he jogged faster to reach the last group of houses in time to get back for supper. When he had completed his rounds and returned to the warehouse with his cart he was surprised to see Newman waiting for him.

"Hello, Hyle." His voice was flat and his face grave.

Hyle nodded a greeting as he passed with the cart to put it away, saying nothing until he returned.

"What's up?" he asked.

"The magister wants to talk to you."

"Is that all? The way you look I thought someone had died."

Newman put his hood up and gestured outside, falling in beside Hyle.

"He told me first, since I happened to be there today and I'm your proctor."

For a moment there was no sound but the hiss of falling rain and the wet crunching of their feet as Newman paused to watch Hyle's face.

"He got some complaints about you after last night," he continued. "More than one."

Hyle listened attentively, his eyes narrowing. Again the hiss of rain filled the silence.

"Where you one of them?" he asked finally.

"Me?" Newman asked, so obviously startled that the solemn expression was chased completely from his face. "No. No, if anything I'm also partly to blame. I encourage people to ask questions and converse freely, so I can hardly blame you for doing it."

It was Hyle's turn to be surprised. He had not expected Newman to say yes, but he was unprepared to be exonerated by him.

"Timothy?"

"I can't say. I probably shouldn't have even told you why the magister wants to talk to you," Newman answered.

"I won't say anything."

The dark mass of Unity Hall materialized out of the fluid grayness ahead. They continued around the corner to the cottage that served as the parsonage. Newman rapped quickly on the door then entered, leading Hyle to the office they had met in on the evening he first arrived with Sophia. Nathan was bent over a pot hanging in the fireplace and a rich savory aroma overlay the more identifiable smell of baking bread. The office door was open and Delacroix rose from his desk to meet them at the door.

"Hyle, nice to see you again. It must still be raining out there," he said, eyeing Hyle's cloak as he reached for his hand. He called to the young man at the fireplace.

"Give your cloak to Nathan here and he will hang it up by the fire."

Nathan took the dripping cloak and bore it away, offering to put on some water for tea. The magister motioned toward the office.

"Please go ahead in and sit down," he said, following Hyle inside. "Thank you. I don't think we will need you for this conversation," he added, pausing at the door to address Newman, and then closed the door behind himself.

He circled his desk and sat down in the large leather chair and leaned back.

"It must be pretty miserable to have to be out all day in that weather. Hopefully your cloak will be dry and warm again by the time you have to go back outside."

Hyle's stomach churned. He was not sure if it was hunger triggered by the smell of cooking food or nervous anticipation. He would not have suspected anything from Delacroix's pleasant demeanor, had it not been for Newman's warning. He let the old man run through the small talk, nodding and answering in monosyllables while he waited for the real conversation to begin.

"How do you like it here, Hyle?"

"It's fine."

"Fine? That's an interesting word. Does that mean you like it, or you're not sure yet?"

Hyle shrugged. "I haven't been here that long."

"Nobody has," said Delacroix reflectively. "I have had the opportunity to speak to some of your housemates. They seem to think you are nice enough, although you keep to yourself."

"Is that bad?" Hyle asked.

"Not necessarily. It depends upon what is going on inside your head. Did Newman tell you why I wanted to talk to you?"

Hyle thought for a moment. His initial impulse was to tell Delacroix what he had been told, knowing that Newman might suffer some consequence as a result. He realized with some surprise that it was this more than honesty that motivated him to tell the truth. His thoughts went back to the conversation he had with Newman as they walked over and he felt a sudden twinge of guilt.

"Not exactly," he answered carefully, "but he looked very serious, so I assume it's not just to talk about how I like it here."

"Do you remember the conversation we had the night you arrived, Hyle?"

He did, and it lay before him like a fork in the road. One path led to the discussion Delacroix wanted to have about the importance of faith in the closed community and presumably a warning not to rock the boat. Hyle chose the other path.

"When you said that everything happens for a reason even though it may not be revealed to us?" Hyle suggested innocently.

The magister looked surprised. A reflexive scowl gave way quickly to an amused smile and perhaps a glint of respect.

"Yes, although I was thinking more of the rest of the conversation," he said. "Hyle, we need to converse about your place here in Asher."

"You mean other than staying at John's house and working in food distribution?"

"I think you know what I mean. I mean your place in the community. In a community of faith."

Delacroix searched Hyle's face, staring into his eyes. There was a long silence. Hyle knew that he was expected to speak. It was an old interrogation technique. People are uncomfortable with silence and are more likely to confess when they know it is up to them to break it. He wondered whether Delacroix used it consciously. The friendly chat had ended and Hyle now felt as though he had been called to the principal's office. He was tempted to outwait the old man, convinced he could get the better of him. He knew that this would make the conversation more difficult, he was just not sure how much he cared.

"What about my place in a community of faith?" he asked, compromising.

"A few people in your unity meeting came to me today. They are concerned about you."

Hyle's eyes narrowed.

"Do you mean that they're concerned on my behalf, or concerned because of me?"

Delacroix smiled, again with a look indicating a grudging respect.

"Perhaps both," he said. "Why don't you tell me what you think they should be concerned about?"

"Nothing," Hyle replied. "I think people worry about too much as it is."

"I see," Delacroix said with an indulgent chuckle. "One concern they have is that you were trying to cause trouble. Is that a valid concern?"

"I was just asking questions. You made it pretty clear that we were all expected to participate."

"It sounds like you were also very disrespectful of another person's views."

"Who, Timothy? He stated his opinion and I stated mine. Maybe he's just never had anyone disagree with him before."

"What was it that you disagreed about?"

"He wasn't happy that we were talking about philosophy. He seems to think that any kind of intellectual discussion is going to undermine people's faith."

"And you disagree with that."

"I think that if your beliefs can't stand up to a little intellectual discussion, it's not the discussion that's the problem."

Delacroix considered the statement.

"Faith is a fragile thing for some people and you need to be careful about treading on the beliefs of others nonetheless," he said sternly. "We encourage everyone here to converse about aspects of their faith, but we will not tolerate attacks on anyone's faith."

"I understand," Hyle replied.

"Good," Delacroix said, his tone softening a bit, "Is this type of discussion helping you?"

"With what, exactly?"

"Helping you decide whether you want to stay here in a community of faith."

"Yes." Hyle answered truthfully.

"Good, because you will have to make a final decision soon. Until that time I want you to save your difficult questions for me. I will be happy to converse with you any time you want if you are serious about gaining clarity around questions of faith." He paused, scanning Hyle's face. The magister rose and the friendly smile returned. "I have probably already caused you to miss dinner. I don't wish to keep you any longer."

Hyle got up on this cue, and followed Delacroix to the main room where the smell of cooking food greeted them again. Nathan brought Hyle's cloak, now warm and damp, and Hyle drew it over his shoulders as he walked with Delacroix to the door.

"I hope to see you at one of the services this weekend," Delacroix called after him as Hyle stepped back out into the rain.

The evening bell sounded the call to prayer early in his walk home and by the time Hyle reached his house the warmth of his cloak had long faded, leaving only the faint smell of wood smoke mingled with the odor of damp wool. The house was dark when he arrived, the fire extinguished, so he brought in the lantern and by its flickering light found a pot on the counter left over from dinner. After a quick meal of cold stew by the light of the lantern, he put on his wet cloak and stepped once more out into the court-yard to Newman's house. Halfway across the soggy ground he stopped and turned around.

«« »»

At dinner, Sophia found a receptive audience in her housemates, who listened with interest to her description of the library and to Newman's explanation of the role of proctor that she was being trained to undertake. Her spirits remained high until the opening prayer of the unity meeting when she looked across the faces in the room and realized that Hyle was not among them.

The meeting itself was much less interactive than it had been in previous evenings. Newman asked specifically for passages from the Bible as topics for discussion and although there was a lot of participation, there was little debate. When the meeting ended and Newman had said goodnight to the line of departing guests, he turned to find the table in the common room empty. The door to Sophia and Phoebe's room was closed. Newman was just about to knock when the front door opened and Sophia stood dripping in the doorway.

"Where's Hyle?" she asked him with obvious concern.

Newman froze in thought for a moment and then shrugged and shook his head. Something had seemed out of place during the meeting and now he realized what it was. Tea and conversation after the unity meetings had quickly become a tradition. The previous evening, when Sophia had gone to sleep early, was the first one they had missed. Newman looked slowly around the empty room, trying to remember if he had seen Hyle sitting somewhere in the crowd. Sophia watched him. To her it appeared as if he thought Hyle might be hiding, cleverly camouflaged, somewhere in the room.

"I just checked at his house. He's not there either," she announced. "Have you seen him at all since last night?"

Newman sat down, poured himself some tea and stared at his mug.

"He may not be in a great mood right now."

He was silent for a moment and Sophia waited for him to continue.

"A few people were upset by his comments last night," Newman explained, still staring into his tea. "They complained to the magister and he had a talk with Hyle."

"What did he say?" Sophia demanded.

"I don't know. I just delivered the message to Hyle."

Sophia looked at him severely.

"You know more than that."

"No, not really. But…"

He looked at Sophia and hesitated, unsure of how much he could tell her. Although he did not know what had been said between Hyle and the magister, he could guess at much of the conversation, and there were other more important things that she should know. When he had told her the day before of the magister's decision to make her a proctor, Newman had mentioned nothing about the rest of his conversation. There was one thing he had sworn to keep a secret, but the rest of the conversation was covered only by an understanding of professionalism. The magister expected his proctors to keep the details of their conversations with him private, but use their judgment about how much of the content to pass on.

"I talked to the magister today before he talked to Hyle. And yesterday too when he decided to make you a proctor," Newman told her. "He was concerned about how both of you are adjusting to life here."

"Me? What did he ask about me? And what did you say?"

"He asked me a lot of questions, but essentially he wanted to know how I thought the two of you were settling in. I told him that I thought you were pretty happy," Newman said tentatively, indicating Sophia and watching her for her reaction.

She gave a confirming nod.

"And I said I wasn't sure about Hyle."

Newman paused, still not sure how far to go. Sophia continued to look at him closely.

"There must have been more than that, Newman. I can read you like a book. There's something else you're not telling me."

He stared at his tea and sighed. He looked into the dying fire, shrugged and then looked into his tea again.

"I'm not sure I should be telling you this," Newman said in a low voice, looking at Sophia to make sure she understood that what he was about to say was confidential. "The magister asked me whether I thought Hyle was going to cause trouble and talked to me a lot about the importance of keeping people strong in their faith. I get the impression that if he thinks Hyle is going to cause trouble he'll ask him to leave Asher."

"What did you say?"

"I told him I wasn't sure about Hyle and I thought we should give him a chance before judging him."

"Good—" Sophia started.

"But he also asked me what I thought you'd do if Hyle left the city."

Sophia said nothing, but her expression told Newman clearly that she was unhappy with the thought.

"What would you do?" he asked quietly.

She bit her lip and looked into the fire.

"I don't know," she said at length. "I don't want to leave." She tried to figure it out, but could not even think of how to begin unraveling her feelings. "We'll just have to make sure Hyle doesn't leave. What did you tell Magister Delacroix I'd do?"

"I said I didn't know," Newman answered, "but I hoped you'd stay."

Sophia laid her hand over his and gave him a warm smile.

"So what do you think Magister Delacroix said to Hyle?"

"I'm not sure, but he told me that I should rein in the unity meeting conversations and keep them closer to the Bible. I imagine he had a similar conversation with Hyle to lay out some guidelines about what he considers to be appropriate topics of conversation."

"Ah, that explains why tonight was so different," Sophia said. After thinking for a moment she added suddenly, "I think that's wrong. I'm already not quite sure I like what he said about Hyle. Even if he was causing trouble, all he really did was ask some questions. And now you're not allowed to have any good conversations anymore?"

"He didn't say they couldn't be good," Newman added, forcing a laugh.

"You know what I mean. The last couple nights when we talked about Plotinus and Augustine were the best conversations we have had, at least in my opinion. Not just because they were interesting, but they were helpful for me too. When I was talking about Augustine reconciling Athens and Jerusalem and rationality and faith, I was suggesting that mostly because that's what the conversation did for me."

"I know," Newman replied, smiling wistfully. "I enjoyed those conversations too. I probably learned as much from them as you did."

"Then why does Magister Delacroix want you to stop having them?" Sophia demanded.

"Remember I told you that I almost went into the priesthood? The Jesuit priest who had been such a good influence for me as a kid told me, 'Everyone finds their own path to God in their own way.' The two of us are thinkers. We like to discuss the reasons for things and explore ideas. That's what brought me here in the first place. But there are also people like Timothy. For them it's all about faith, and faith isn't something you get by analyzing facts or constructing rational arguments. In fact, that's the opposite of faith."

"But it shouldn't hurt to have some of those conversations. And if Timothy doesn't like them, why doesn't he go to a different unity meeting?"

"I don't mean to pick on Timothy. I was just using him as an example. Several other people told me on the way out the last few nights that they thought we were getting too far off topic. At least as many told me they enjoyed the conversation. That's the problem. This community is still very new, and we're still figuring out how to live together. The magister is just trying to make sure that no one stirs up trouble unneces- sarily until we all settle in together, and I think he's right to do that. You and I can still have our conversations after the meetings, and things will loosen up again once everyone is used to living together."

Newman and Sophia continued talking about how to best handle differing beliefs within the community until the tea was gone. The fire had faded to embers which cast a deep orange glow across the room by the time Sophia decided she should go to bed. She felt restless and had trouble falling asleep. When sleep did come, she dreamed of working in the vegetable garden at her old home.

CHAPTER TWENTY-THREE

PUREST CONSOLATION

Venturing out on her own the next morning, Sophia headed directly to the library while Newman set out on his morning errands. She threw herself into her reading. Shortly after arriving at the library she had finished the history and the collection of the Prophet's sermons, flipped through his *World Religions A to Z*, and had started to explore the shelves for other things to read, pulling out several volumes and settling into a chair by the window where the light was best for reading. Late in the afternoon she was startled by a voice behind her.

"What are you reading?" Newman asked, leaning over the back of her chair and squinting at the small leather bound book in her hands.

"Oh, this?" She closed the book and looked at the cover as if she did not remember. "It's *The Consolation of Philosophy*," she said tentatively, turning to watch Newman's face for recognition. "By Boethius."

"And why is he consoling philosophy?"

"It's the other way around. Philosophy's consoling him. Boethius held office in the court of the Ostrogoth king Theodoric, in the early sixth century, after the fall of Rome, and got himself into some sort of political trouble. He's condemned to be executed, and this is his conversation with Lady Philosophy," Sophia said, holding up the book, "who comforts him about his fate."

"What does she say?"

Sophia laughed. "It's a long book, but her consolation sounds a lot like Augustine. She tells him that true happiness can only be found in the eternal, through God, not in fame or riches or temporal things, and that things that appear to us to be bad luck or evil are really good, but we're unable to comprehend them for what they are because we as mere humans can't fathom the full range of God's plans. Even though he was considered a pagan, the Consolation was popular reading with Christian thinkers for the next several centuries. So were his other works."

"Why, what else did he write?" asked Newman.

"Boethius was responsible for preserving Aristotle's works on logic—the only works of Aristotle to survive during the Dark Ages. He translated them into Latin, and they had such an effect on philosophy and theology over the next several centuries that some scholars call it the Boethian Era."

"He got a whole era named after him just for doing some translations?"

"It sounds better than the Dark Ages," Sophia suggested with a smile. "But Boethius did more than just translations. He added commentaries and made his own original contributions too. For example, he made a distinction between faith and reason and he applied Aristotelian logic to theological questions in a way that became characteristic of later philosophers and theologians. Aristotle's logic had a major impact on Western thinking. The rest of his works weren't rediscovered in the West for another five hundred years or so."

"What else did he write about besides logic?"

"Aristotle? He wrote on just about any ancient field of study you could name."

Sophia thought for a moment, composing a list in her mind.

"His *Physics* is what gave the field its name and his *De Anima* was the first serious attempt at psychology. His *Metaphysics*, what Aristotle called 'First Philosophy,' was the only philosophy of that age to rival Platonism. The term metaphysics—literally 'after physics' in Greek—was coined because this work came after the *Physics* in one collection of his works. Aristotle also wrote on biology, ethics, politics, poetry and rhetoric. But his works on logic are some of the most famous because of their impact and his methodical approach to learning."

"What was it about his logic that was so revolutionary?"

"We take a lot of it for granted now," Sophia explained, "but Aristotle was really the first great scientist. He believed that the world was ordered according to principles and that by observing what was true 'always or for the most part,' one could discover these principles. Since he believed that there were many different principles at work, he divided his studies to correspond with them into fields we still use today—ethics, politics, biology, physics, psychology, etcetera. His approach to philosophy was very teleological, and breaking things down into categories helped him find the organizing principle for each area."

"What was that word, teleological? What exactly does that mean?"

"I mean he was concerned with the purpose behind each of these fields. *Telos* is Greek for end. Aristotle wanted to explain why things—animals, people, societies—behaved the way they did. To what purpose? To what end? Remember at the cookout when we first met? I told you about Aristotle's four causes—material, efficient, formal and final?"

"Yes. The material cause was the suitability of the material, like wood for a ship, right?"

Sophia nodded and encouraged him to continue.

"The efficient cause was what changed the material, like the shipbuilder's tools. The formal cause was the plan for the ship and the final cause was the purpose, like sailing."

"Right. Aristotle saw change all around him and he explained it with the four causes. The example of shipbuilding, or the acorn growing into an oak tree, applies these causes to an individual item, but this same idea can also be applied to academic areas. If the purpose…"

Sophia stopped and thought for a moment.

"Purpose isn't a great translation of *telos*. It sounds too intentional. *Raison d'etre*? Place in the universe? *Telos* is both the purpose and the definition. Birds fly by nature. That's both what defines them and their purpose. 'Man by nature desires to know,' Aristotle said. We're thinking animals. That's our purpose and our definition according to Aristotle. And he applied the same thinking to academic areas. What is the purpose and definition of a city? That's what the field of politics studies. What is the purpose and definition of living things? That's what the field of biology studies. What is the purpose and definition of all substance, or what we might call reality? That's what the field of metaphysics studies."

"And in addition to all that he developed logic?" Newman said in disbelief.

"Yes. He laid the foundations of logic so solidly that they weren't substantially improved upon for almost two thousand years. He wrote several works on logic—*Categories*, *Prior Analytics* and *Posterior Analytics*, *Sophistic Refutations*. In order to study in each of his fields Aristotle needed to define the subject, so he looked carefully at language and the use of words. He distinguished between demonstration and definition, subject and predicate, necessary and contingent propositions—"

"I have no idea what any of those things mean," Newman said, shaking his head in bewilderment. "Maybe I'm just not very logical."

Sophia laughed.

"The point is that Aristotle was the first to really study language as a tool for discovering and expressing the truth. Other philosophers knew about the importance of defining your terms and such, but Aristotle turned the close examination of language and the exact meaning of words into a whole area of academic study and developed logic into a field. Probably the most formal example of his work was the development of the syllogism."

The word was familiar to Newman, and he tried to remember the exact meaning, stroking his goatee as he thought as if it were a lucky rabbit foot. He drew a blank and shook his head slowly.

"A syllogism is a series of statements with premises that lead to a logical conclusion." Sophia explained. "Socrates is a man. All men are mortal. Therefore Socrates is mortal. Apples are red. Apples are a type of fruit. Therefore some types of fruit are red."

In the adjoining bell tower the huge bell began sounding, marking the end of the work day with a deep tone that resonated through the walls and floor of the library as Sophia finished the last syllogism. She closed her book and Newman waited for her in the doorway as she returned it to the shelf. On the way home, Sophia's elation at spending the day reading expressed itself in a continuous stream of conversation which flowed rapidly through many aspects of Aristotle to an exaltation of philosophy and learning in general, then into appreciation of the library and finally to such an abundance of thanks that Newman was only able to smile, having long ago given up on speaking.

As the bell tolled once again, inside Newman's house people sat and voices quieted. Newman led the assembly through the opening prayer and began the discussion for the evening. Like the previous night the conversation avoided any controversial topics, drawing on themes pulled directly from scripture. Sophia contributed more frequently than usual, trying to ask questions that would generate discussion and Newman was grateful for the help.

Hyle was absent again.

As soon as the meeting had ended, Sophia told Newman that she was going to look for him. She found one of Hyle's housemates in the crowd of people that was coalescing near the door.

"Hi, Judith," Sophia said, trying to sound nonchalant. "Do you know where Hyle is tonight?"

Judith looked thoughtful and slightly puzzled as her eyes swept around the room.

"No," she said slowly, "he was at dinner. He left before call to prayer, earlier than the rest of us—like he always does. I thought he came over here."

She shrugged, unconcerned. Sophia fell in behind her and followed her out into the night.

"Do you mind if I come back with you and wait for him?"

Judith did not mind, and she and Sophia made small talk as they walked across the small expanse of grass that separated their houses. Ruth and her sons, who had also made the short walk from Newman's house, came in right after them. Sophia rekindled the fire while Judith brought in some more wood. They sat and talked for a while as the rest of the house went through their nighttime routines and went to sleep. Eventually Judith fulfilled her social obligation enough to accept when Sophia told her that she did not need to stay up any longer on her account.

Sophia was starting to have trouble keeping her eyes open by the time Hyle appeared and it was clear from his expression that he was surprised to see her. She greeted him enthusiastically but once her initial relief at seeing him unharmed had faded, she became more serious.

"Where have you been the last two nights?" she demanded before he could speak.

"I thought I'd go check out some different meetings," he replied, scowling slightly. "Delacroix had a little talk with me a couple nights ago."

"I know, Newman told me."

Sophia saw a momentary flash of anger in his eyes.

"I was worried about you when you didn't show up last night," she explained quickly. "He was just trying to give me clarity about why you might not want to be at his meeting."

"Well, he was right about that," Hyle said coolly.

"I'm glad you're okay," Sophia said. "Next time, tell me if you're going to skip a meeting so I won't worry about you, all right?"

"Why? You didn't ask my permission before you and Newman skipped dinner and wandered around town together."

"I wasn't—I didn't," Sophia gave a frustrated sigh. "I wasn't suggesting that you need to get my permission. I was just worried, that's all. You're there every night and then suddenly you're not. That's very different from being a few minutes late to one meeting. You should be happy that I was worried about you."

Hyle stared at Sophia for several long seconds. She looked back at him with a look of such genuine concern that he could not help but soften.

"I am," Hyle said. "I just think it's best if I don't go over there for a little while."

Sophia nodded sympathetically.

"Newman does lead a much more interesting meeting than the other ones I've been to so far though," Hyle confessed. "And I missed my tea."

Sophia gave him a hug, and took him by the hand and pulled him toward the door.

"Where are we going?"

"To get you some tea," she said with a playful smile.

"No, I'd rather stay here," Hyle said, and stopped walking. Then he added, "I could put some tea on here if you want to stay though."

She accepted the invitation and sat down at the table while Hyle pumped water into the kettle and set it on a hook over the fire. Sophia asked about the other unity meetings and he summarized as much of the discussion from each night as he could remember, admitting that he had not paid much attention most of the time.

"I have to say that Newman does a much better job of picking interesting topics and leading the conversations. The one I went to tonight was chaotic—everyone talking over one another, and always to agree in a different way. Last night hardly anyone said anything except the woman running the meeting. It was like going to church."

"Our meetings haven't been very interesting the last few nights," Sophia told him.

"Why, because I'm not there upsetting everyone with my questions?"

"No," she answered, laughing and choosing to interpret his sarcasm as humor. "Because Magister Delacroix had a talk with Newman too and told him to manage the conversation better to prevent any conflicts."

Hyle shook his head in disgust.

"They're just pandering to the most closed-minded people. That's what's wrong with this place. It's just a polite form of censorship."

"I know," Sophia agreed, "but Newman believes it's just temporary. This whole community has only been together for a few weeks, so Magister Delacroix is being conservative until everyone learns how to live together. You know that Newman likes everyone to contribute. I don't think your questions were bad, but you did get a little hostile with Timothy at the end of the meeting."

Hyle rolled his eyes in a look of annoyance that clearly said "not you too."

"Look, okay, everyone overreacted about this whole thing," Sophia argued, "but let's get over it and you can help us change things back."

"Maybe," was all he said.

"Will you come to the meeting tomorrow night?" she asked gently.

"Not tomorrow," he answered. "I need a little bit more time away from those people. If I go back tomorrow I'll probably say something even worse and get myself thrown out of the city."

«« »»

Several days passed. During the daylight hours Sophia went to the library. Newman invariably found her there surrounded by books, sometimes with one book open on her lap and several others open on the table in front of her. In the evenings Sophia attended his unity meetings. Although Newman tried to keep the discussions interesting, the meetings began to run dry of good topics and increasingly often covered the same ground they had on previous nights. To compensate Newman spent as much of his time as he could during the day preparing for the evening meetings by reading commentaries on the Bible. He did most of the talking, but the attendees did not seem to mind.

After the meeting each evening Sophia tried to convince Newman to come along with her to visit Hyle, but he insisted that his presence would only make things more difficult. Every evening she tried to coax Hyle into attending Newman's unity meetings again, but Hyle continued saying that he preferred to try out different unity meetings around the city, although he admitted that he had not found any that he liked yet. When Sophia gave him updates on her days in the library and talked excitedly about becoming a proctor, Hyle listened politely and tried to sound encouraging, but she could tell that he was leaving much unsaid.

CHAPTER TWENTY-FOUR

TRIAL BY FIRE

In spite of an appeal from Sophia to attend a weekend service at Unity Hall—specifically the service on Sunday afternoon in which Magister Delacroix himself was to give the homily—Hyle had decided not to go, saying that he was needed at work and adding that he had already had enough of Delacroix's sermons to last him for a while. The magister had not given the homily at the other services Sophia had attended and Newman had made a point to check the schedule to make sure she caught him this weekend.

Applause was already echoing through the closed doors when Newman and Sophia arrived at Unity Hall along with a scattering of other latecomers. They hurried along one of the side aisles and found some seats near the front just as Magister Delacroix called for quiet and began the invocation. It was very similar to the other invocations Sophia had heard and to the opening prayer that Newman led every night. He thanked God for showing them the way to Asher, for helping them to live together in safety and harmony until the final judgment, and for investing in the Prophet the power to perform His miracles on earth and asked God in a number of ways, both general and specific, to guide them to carry out His will.

After this invocation the magister was silent for a moment. Chairs creaked and people shifted, waiting in anticipation of the homily. A baby let out a single shriek which echoed throughout the hall and there was some scattered laughter. Magister Delacroix smiled as he pulled out some bifocals and set them on the end of his nose. Sophia could hear him shuffling papers just before he looked back up at the assembly.

"Today let us think about what it is that is important to us," he said, and the room grew silent. "I thought I'd start by telling you a story about one of the defining moments of my life. Have you experienced one of those moments in your life when something just strikes you? When you get a flash of insight that you carry with you for the rest of your life? Well I had one of those moments when I was nine years old.

"I woke up one night and I knew right away that something was wrong. I could smell smoke and I could hear my mother yelling downstairs to get out of the house. It was on fire. My house was burning down.

"There I was, in my pajamas, in the middle of the night, and I knew that I had to get out fast. I tried to think of what I would grab to take with me. You know how your mind races a million miles a minute? I was a pretty typical boy and my bedroom was filled with just about every kind of thing you could imagine. Toys and books, a couple of trophies, all sorts of things, but pretty quickly I had come down to three things. I had a big yellow crane. It was the ultimate toy, the only thing I had wanted that year for Christmas. It was summertime when my house burned, and this crane was still my favorite toy, so that gives you an idea of how much I liked it."

The crowd chuckled, particularly the parents.

"It was very realistic, and there was a control box you could use to make the claw go up and down and pick things up and make it move around. I was the envy of every kid on the block.

The second thing was my baseball card collection. I had been collecting for a couple years, but I had just gotten to be a really serious collector that summer. In fact, I almost cried the day I went next door to my little sister's room and made the mistake of leaving my album too close to her crib. She ate a couple good cards, but I had spent the rest of the summer doing yard work to earn money to replace them. That and a couple good trades and my collection was better than ever. I knew everything about every card, and I had all their values and information written on little labels in this album.

The third thing was a hat. It was my grandfather's hat. He was a naval officer in World War II, and he always let me play with it when I came over. He left it to me when he died.

So, before I tell you what I did, before I tell you about my revelation, now that you know my story up to this point, I want to ask you, what would you have chosen? If you were me, what one thing would you take out of a burning house? Would anyone like to contribute?"

Scores of hands thrust into the air and dozens more followed hesitantly.

The magister stepped around to the front of the podium and surveyed the audience. He picked a young woman, who then stood up at her seat to speak.

"I'd pick the hat," she said. "Because it was given to you by someone special and it's something that could never be replaced."

The magister smiled and thanked her, and as she sat down the audience burst into a round of applause and hands went back into the air.

An elderly man was chosen to speak next.

"I agree with the young lady. The hat is the only thing that couldn't be replaced. It's a very special thing. It's the kind of thing that could be a family heirloom, and it probably had meaning to your mother or father as well."

He sat down to another round of applause. Delacroix picked several more people before he got a dissenting opinion. It was a young man, perhaps in his early twenties.

"I'm going to disagree. I think the hat would be okay, but you also put a lot of your own hard work into the baseball card collection. That could have a lot of sentimental value to you too. I think that's probably the thing I would have picked. Besides," he joked, "it could have been worth a lot of money someday."

He sat down amid laughter and applause. Several more speakers contributed their opinions, generally agreeing that the toy was the last choice and the hat was the first. Long before the supply of hands had been depleted, the magister returned to the podium to continue his story.

"All right. All right, thank you all for contributing," he said as the buzz of voices quieted. "I'll not keep you in suspense any more. I'll tell you how the story ended."

The magister's tone became more serious.

"My room was already filling with smoke, and all these thoughts were racing around my head. What should I take? What should I take? I ended up taking the hat, for all of the reasons that you already mentioned. It was sentimental. It was the only thing I could not replace. But that was not my revelation. My revelation didn't come until I had run down stairs with my hat and gone outside. When I saw my family all gathered together on the front lawn—that was when I realized that my baby sister slept upstairs in the room right next door to me."

The audience, which had been quiet already, seemed to collectively stop breathing. Delacroix said nothing for a moment, letting people absorb the significance of what he had just said. Only the occasional creak of a chair or rustle of clothing broke the silence.

"Back in my room," Delacroix continued, "I thought I had the biggest choice of my life. But out on the lawn I realized it was no choice at all. My cards, my toys, my grandfather's hat, none of those were anything compared to my little sister. That was my revelation, my defining moment. It was at that moment that I realized how little *things* matter. You can have all the *things* in the world and still not be happy. And I realized at that moment…"

Delacroix's voice stuck in his throat. He stepped back from the podium for a minute before continuing.

"I realized in that moment that all of my things could burn and I would not care as long as I could have my family. So when I saw my dad out there on the lawn, holding my baby sister in his arms, I thanked God with all my heart. I thanked Him for my sister, and I thanked Him for opening my eyes and helping me see what was really important.

"It was a long time before I was able to look at that hat again and feel good about myself, but I was thankful for learning this lesson while I was still young and it was easy for me to change my path, because I have seen people—I think we have all seen people—who get so caught up in the pursuit of things and their concern for things, that they lose people. They lose their spouse, their children, their parents, their friends, and worst of all they lose themselves and they lose sight of God. We sometimes get so caught up in the material world that we forget that there's a spiritual one as well. These things that are passing objects, lumps of plastic, metal, paper or glass, these things are all temporary. We will lose them, break them, or maybe we will die with them, but still they're temporary and they take our attention away from what's eternal, what lies beyond this world.

"And what is it that makes people so attached to these material things?"

He paused and gestured for people to respond. People shouted out their answers. "What is it," he continued, "that makes people want to drive a nicer car, live in a bigger house, to have more and more and more? Yes, I heard it. Somebody said it. Pride. It was my pride that made me think of taking my toy. The one every other kid on the block envied. And looking back I realized that I didn't enjoy playing with it as much when I was by myself. It was when the other kids were around that I really enjoyed it. It was pride that made me want to take my baseball cards. Pride in all the hard work I had done. It is pride that makes people spend half their lives dieting, trying to fit somebody else's image of what they should be. It is pride that makes people unhappy with their jobs because they don't pay enough money or they're not prestigious enough. Pride is what makes us want to be more important than anything around us. It makes us try to be the center of the universe and makes us forget that there is something greater than us. It is pride that makes us focus on ourselves and this world when we should be thinking about God."

"It was our pride as a race that got us where we are today. Look around you in this room. Look at the people sitting next to you. Can you imagine if everyone in the world learned to work together like we do? Live together like we do? Look up to a higher power for guidance and remember our place in the world like we do? Do you believe there would have been a nuclear holocaust? It was our pride that got us where we are today."

After the sermon Delacroix invited people to contribute about whatever was on their mind. This part of the service also reminded Sophia of Newman's unity meetings although it seemed much more formal, in part because of the place people went to contribute. It was an odd arrangement that recalled a British courtroom. Delacroix stood at the lectern a bit off to one side of the dais. Sharing the dais, off the center in the opposite direction, was a small box constructed of waist-high railings with a slightly raised floor. The people that the magister selected from the crowd stepped up onto the dais and into this box to voice their questions or problems.

The magister addressed them all thoroughly, and Sophia was impressed with the insight that he showed in helping people to unravel some of their problems. She noted with some amusement the influence of the Socratic Method on his style.

A woman about Sophia's age was one of those chosen to contribute. She was heavy, and her auburn hair was pulled back in a thick braid, exposing her small round glasses and round face.

"Hi, my name is Sarah," she said. "I guess…" Her voice faded and was soon lost in a chorus of "Speak up! We can't hear you! Speak up"

"Sorry," she said, looking down from the platform. When she looked back up at Delacroix her eyes were glistening.

"I'm sorry. I guess…. I guess I'm just still having trouble finding clarity about everything that happened." The tears she had been holding back burst free. She just stood there and cried for some time while the magister looked on compassionately. People in the audience looked on sympathetically as well, some shouting words of encouragement or support. Others cried themselves. Sophia glanced over at Newman and saw that he fought to keep his own eyes dry as he watched. Finally Delacroix spoke.

"Sarah, in our hearts we know this is all part of God's plan, but sometimes that's very hard for us to see, isn't it?"

Sarah nodded weakly and looked up again, her cheeks streaming with tears.

"It's so unfair," she said.

Delacroix nodded again sympathetically. "It's very hard sometimes to see what God has in mind for us, but I would like to try to help you Sarah. Will you converse with me?"

She said that she would.

"Tell me what is unfair."

"That everyone had to die. So many innocent people. They had done nothing wrong. Why should they have been the ones to die?"

"I understand how you feel Sarah. I think everybody here understands how you feel. We have all lost people who were special to us. Who did you lose Sarah?"

"My whole family."

"I would like to converse about your family. Tell me about them. Did you live at home?"

"Yes."

"Who lived at home with you?"

Between sobs she managed to answer. "My mother, father, my little brother Mark and my big sister Anna. She was going to be married in November and the whole family was so excited and everybody was getting ready and she was so happy."

"Sarah, who are you crying for?"

Sarah stopped crying momentarily and stared at the old man. She opened her mouth to start a reply, but then closed it again and shook her head. Finally she said, "Everyone. My whole family."

"Why?"

"Because it's so unfair. They didn't deserve to die."

"You're crying because it was unfair?" He shook his head. "I don't think that's the heart of it. Who dies Sarah?"

Again she looked confused and could not answer, but the magister was quiet, just looking at her, waiting for her to respond. After an uncomfortable silence, people in the audience began to whisper their answers to themselves, then eventually louder.

"Everyone," she said. "Everyone dies sooner or later." Her tone held a hint of revelation.

"Do they deserve to die?"

"Well, no. Yes. That's not what I meant."

"I know it isn't. What did you mean? What is making you cry?"

"It's unfair that they had to die so soon. Before they should have."

Again the magister shook his head.

"People die all the time. Every night you watched the news you must have heard about people dying. Every time you picked up a newspaper you must have read about people dying. Did it always make you cry?"

She shrugged. Again the magister maintained silence until she replied.

"No. They're not my family."

The magister smiled an understanding smile. "Yes. Now we are getting somewhere. So who are you crying for Sarah?"

"My family?" she said, unsure of herself.

"Is it? Why would you cry for your family and not all the other people who have died over the years?"

"Because I love them," she said. "And I miss them."

"Yes."

There was a long silence while Magister Delacroix stood looking at Sarah and she stood on the platform looking back, knowing that she was supposed to realize something but she was too upset to see it. Here and there in the audience people shook their heads as if they understood.

"Who are you crying for Sarah?"

"Myself?"

"You tell me."

"I was crying for myself, for my loss, not for my family."

"And how do you feel now?"

Sarah wiped her eyes and regained her composure.

"Better. It's still hard, but I guess it helps to know that it was really just me feeling sorry for myself. This is just like what you were saying about wanting things in this life instead of thinking about the next one, isn't it? Thank you. I think I've got clarity now."

She stepped down from the platform into a sea of applause that echoed through the hall.

CHAPTER TWENTY-FIVE

OF PROPHETS

Newman stood in the doorway of the library watching Sophia from a distance before walking over to perch on the arm of a chair nearby. From the single window high in the wall behind her, sunlight angled downward in a tapered shaft, capturing minute particles of dust in midair and illuminating the leather armchair and reader in the soft light of an oil portrait. She was absorbed in a thick book and did not notice him. Several other volumes sat in rough stacks on the arms of her chair and on the coffee table in front of her.

"What are you reading today?" he asked.

He spoke softly but Sophia jumped at the sound of his voice anyway. After taking a minute to let her heart stop racing, she closed her book and responded.

"Al-Farabi," she replied. "With the exception of John Scotus Eriugena I have been reading medieval Islamic philosophy all day."

"I'm not familiar with either of those names," confessed Newman. "Who are they?"

"Eriugena was a ninth century Irish theologian. He believed that if logic leads to the truth it can't conflict with revelation, so he set out to prove the tenets of Christianity with logic. He's also known for his conclusion that if God is unknowable, even God can't know His own nature."

"That's an interesting idea. I'm surprised I haven't heard of him."

"There was a concern though that his efforts would make faith and revelation irrelevant, so they were not well received at the time," explained Sophia. "A century later Berengar of Tours got himself in trouble with the Church trying to apply logic to theology. I think Europe was just not ready for this type of thinking yet. That's why most of the intellectual progress of the Middle Ages occurred in the Arab world. It was the Islamic philosophers who preserved the works of Aristotle while everything but his works on logic were lost to Europe. I'm sure that was at least partly responsible for the impressive achievements of Medieval Islamic society."

Newman remembered learning that the Dark Ages in Europe had been a time of great cultural and intellectual achievement in the Middle East. He tried to remember whether he had learned any details, and Sophia guessed at what he was thinking.

"We do math today using the Arabic number system," she offered by way of example.

He gave a dismissive shrug.

"Try dividing MMXII by XLVIII," Sophia challenged, and paused a moment to let him consider the problem. "The Arabs introduced the concept of zero. They advanced mathematics, astronomy, medicine—"

"Okay, okay, I get the point," Newman conceded.

"—And they became accomplished Aristotelian philosophers." Sophia continued, gesturing to a tall stack of books on the table. "They seem to have gone through the same sort of thing with Aristotle that Augustine did with Plato."

"You mean trying to unite his philosophy with Islam?"

"Yes, exactly. Legend has it that Al-Ma'mun, the Caliph of Baghdad, was visited in a dream by the ghost of Aristotle. After Aristotle's ghost convinced the Caliph that there's no contradiction between reason and faith, Al-Ma'mun established an institution called the House of Wisdom with a staff of translators, a library and an academy. They had translations of many works of Plato and the Neoplatonists and almost all of the works of Aristotle."

"It must have been a lot more difficult to reconcile Aristotle with monotheism than it was for Augustine to do it with Plato," Newman speculated. "You said that Aristotle was much more grounded in observation and materialism than Plato."

"True. The Islamic philosophers mixed in a fair bit of Neoplatonism," Sophia admitted. "But they were still most heavily influenced by Aristotle, and in fact they ran into some of the exact same problems that Augustine did. Around the time Al-Ma'mun founded the House of Wisdom, there was a group called the Mu'tazilites who wanted to know about the unity of God—how could God be one and yet have many attributes?—so they ran into the question of free will in a world set in motion by God."

"Did they come up with a good answer?"

"Actually, another group called the Ash'arites came up with a novel way of addressing free will," Sophia told him. "They believed that everything that happened was directly due to God's will. Even the things we see as natural laws are just a sort of custom or convenience that God could break at any time. They proposed a concept called *kasb* that says that we all must comply with God's will, but we can do it happily or reluctantly and we're judged accordingly."

"That's an interesting solution," Newman said, impressed. "That doesn't come from Aristotle, does it?"

"No, the first real Aristotelian among the Muslim philosophers was Al-Kindi. He was active in Al-Ma'mun's court and advocated the study of philosophy, but thought it was inferior to revelation. We don't seem to have anything of his here," Sophia said, quickly sweeping her eyes over the bookshelves. "Or Al-Razi either."

"Who is Al-Razi?"

"He was a great physician and a second significant Islamic philosopher after Al-Kindi. He tried to defend Plato's ideas against being corrupted by Aristotelianism. You might know him by a different name. His name got Latinized like Ibn Sina and Ibn Rushd. Maybe you know him as Razes?"

Newman did not and shook his head.

"Who are the other two?" he asked.

"Ibn Sina was Latinized to Avicenna and Ibn Rushd was known as Averroes."

"I have heard of Avicenna," Newman confirmed. "Averroes sounds familiar too."

"I'm not surprised. Their works had a major impact on Christian philosophy, although Al-Farabi laid a lot of the groundwork for them."

"Al-Farabi? That's who you were just reading."

"Yes," Sophia confirmed. "Al-Farabi was the second Muslim Aristotelian after Al-Kindi. He wrote around the beginning of the ninth century, just before Avicenna, and produced a lot of political theory. He also developed a theory of how the intellect works, derived from what Aristotle had described in his *De Anima*. But what I found most interesting about Al-Farabi is that he developed this understanding of the intellect in order to investigate the role of the prophet in receiving, understanding and transmitting revelation to society."

"It's not that surprising," Newman said.

Sophia gave him a questioning look.

"How much do you know about Islam?" he asked in response.

"I know has some similarities to Christianity. It's a monotheistic religion centered on the worship of Allah, and that it was founded by the Prophet Muhammad, who's a central figure, similar to how Jesus is central to Christianity."

"How much do you know of the history of Muhammad?"

"Not that much," confessed Sophia.

"To really understand Islam you need to know the story of Muhammad," Newman informed her. He went on to tell her that as an orphan, Muhammad was raised by his grandfather, and later his uncle, in relative poverty. As a young man he led caravans of a wealthy merchant woman named Khadija who offered him her hand in marriage. Even though he was financially successful, around the age of forty he became restless and spent a lot of time in the desert. There he had the revelations that were later collected and organized in the Qur'an. Around the beginning of the seventh century he began preaching this message in Mecca. At that time Mecca was a polytheistic society and drew a lot of trade from pilgrims of various religions. Muhammad's monotheistic message was not well received among some of the powerful merchants, so in the year 622 he and his followers traveled to Medina.

"This journey is called the Hijra, and marks the start of the Islamic calendar," Newman explained. "Muhammad was received much better in Medina. There Muhammad helped unite two warring factions, his followers grew and he led his people, now known as Muslims in conflicts with the pagans in Mecca. Eight years after the Hijra, with the help of some of the nomadic Arabic tribes, Muhammad took Mecca. The pagan idols there were removed and several Arab tribes joined the Muslim federation. Islam continued to be spread by conquest following the death of Muhammad in 632 and within twelve years the Muslims had reached as far east as present-day Iran and as far west as Egypt. For roughly another century the Islamic empire continued to expand, reaching India in the east and Turkey, northern Africa and Spain in the west.

"The Muslims treated the conquered people well, which helped to win them converts," Newman said. "They gave a protected status to Jews and Christians since they were 'people of the book,' as the Muslims called it."

"Really?" Sophia asked, her surprise obvious.

"Yes. Of course they were a sort of second class citizens, which probably encouraged some of them to convert over time, but since the Jews and Christians worshipped the same God, they had a preferred status among the conquered people of the Muslims."

"Why would—" Sophia began slowly, but Newman realized the source of her confusion.

"Not the same God as each other. The same God as the Muslims. Allah isn't a separate god. Allah and God are one and the same. Muslims believe that Jesus was a prophet. They just don't happen to believe he was divine. Same with Moses and Abraham. They're all, in a sense, Islamic prophets."

Sophia shook her head slowly in wonderment.

"I had no idea," she said.

"The people of the book are people who believe in the revelation of the one true God. Islam means 'submission to God,' so by Islamic standards, Jews and Christians are basically on the right track in that respect, but have been misled by distortions and misinterpretations of God's revelations to them. It's that confusion that Muhammad was meant to clear up with new revelations."

"That must be why Al-Farabi was so interested in prophets," Sophia realized aloud. "Not only was Islam started by a prophet, but if he believed that the message of previous prophets had been misunderstood, it makes sense that it would be important to better understand the role of prophets."

"And Muhammad has a much greater role in Islam than just conveying the revelations of the Qur'an," Newman added. "The Qur'an is the revelation of God, or Allah. For Christians, the life and words of Jesus are both wise example and divine revelation. For

Muslims, the Qur'an is the divine revelation of Allah, and the life of Muhammad provides the wise example. His sayings and deeds were preserved in the traditions known as Hadiths, and along with principles from the Qur'an, these form the basis for the Shari'a, or Islamic law. So Muhammad is seen both as a prophet and as a role model."

"That makes sense," Sophia said. "Al-Farabi believed that the duty of the prophet was part interpreter of God's revelations and part social leader. God didn't just pick anyone to be a prophet. A prophet had to be essentially perfect—good health, moral virtue, intellectual perfection and imagination—in order to be able to accept God's message. In his role as social leader the prophet explains God's revelation to the masses. What was interesting to me is that Al-Farabi believed that the truth given through revelation and pursued by philosophy couldn't be comprehended by the masses. He thought that the role of the prophet is to try to explain this complicated truth through metaphors that the average person can understand."

"But metaphors leave a lot of room for distortions and misunderstandings," Newman observed. "That explains how Jesus and Muhammad could both be prophets of the same God and yet have people understand their messages differently."

"Yes, I suppose it is a way to explain differences in religious beliefs," Sophia agreed. "But Al-Farabi also thought it led to some misunderstandings even within his own faith. He didn't believe in an immortal soul, for example, and thought the Islamic concept of an afterlife was essentially to accommodate the masses. On the other hand, he did think that the intellect of some people could survive after death."

"That sounds a bit like Augustine," Newman replied. "He thought the idea of going to Heaven was allegorical too. Remember, his version of the afterlife was more like eternal enlightenment than any kind of journey of the soul to a different place. Did Al-Farabi get that from Aristotle?"

"No, not that idea. If anything he was probably influenced by the Neoplatonists the way Augustine was," explained Sophia. "Aristotle didn't believe in an immortal soul or God in the Christian sense. At Al-Farabi's time though, some excerpts of Plotinus had been mistakenly identified as the theology of Aristotle, so a lot of the theological ideas that Al-Farabi developed were probably influenced by Plotinus and his contemporary, Alexander of Aphrodisias, in addition to Aristotle."

"Really? I can't imagine what ideas Aristotle had that would be compatible with Neoplatonism."

"For one," replied Sophia, "Aristotle thought that everything had to have something to activate it, including our intellectual ability. He believed that the motive force behind everything was ultimately traceable to something he called the Unmoved Mover, which he describes at one point in terms of pure intellect. Drawing from the commentaries of Plotinus and Alexander of Aphrodisias on Aristotle, Al-Farabi connected the dots to create the explanation that God is pure intellect which radiates out in layers until it becomes the agent intellect. The agent intellect ultimately activates the human capacity for thought. It also serves as a source of truth and common understanding that all rational beings can access through their own intellect."

"So Al-Farabi really did derive some original philosophy by merging Aristotle and Plotinus?"

"Yes, definitely. And building on Al-Farabi, Avicenna developed several other ideas in metaphysics that had an impact on later philosophers, like his distinctions between essence and existence, between necessary and possible beings, or his 'flying man' argument."

"Okay, I have to hear this one. What is the flying man argument?"

Sophia laughed.

"I suppose it does sound funny if you don't know what it means. Avicenna believed that being was fundamental. He argued that the first knowledge we have is the knowledge of being. To demonstrate this he used the example of the so-called flying man. Imagine a fully grown man who was suddenly created such that his eyes were covered and he was suspended in space such that he couldn't touch anything, even parts of his own body. Avicenna argues that this man, even though he was deprived of ever having any sensory experience, would still know that he exists, and therefore knowledge of being is the most immediate and fundamental knowledge we can have."

Newman was going to comment on this, but he noticed that he no longer had Sophia's attention. Turning around to follow her gaze, he saw Nathan standing in the doorway.

"Hello, Newman," said the young man. "The magister would like to have a word with you."

CHAPTER TWENTY-SIX

THE END OF GRACE

Entering the magister's cottage, Newman was assailed with the aroma of baking bread and felt his stomach rumble in protest. Nathan gestured him toward the open door of the office and then headed for the kitchen.

"Close the door and have a seat," the old man told him as he entered. Newman took his seat in the familiar leather chair in front of the magister's desk.

"How is Sophia doing?"

"Fine. She loves the library," Newman laughed, relieved that the topic did not seem to be as serious as he had feared. "Every time I go in there she has more books lying around her than I could read in a month."

Delacroix chuckled softly.

"And what did she think of the service?"

"I think she enjoyed it," Newman replied.

"You put me under considerable pressure you know," the old man joked, "telling me that you wanted to bring her specifically to one of my services. I hope I lived up to your expectations."

"It was a very good sermon. And I think she was also quite impressed with the contributing afterwards."

"Thank you, Newman. I am pleased to hear you say that."

The old man paused for a moment and then his tone grew more serious.

"I didn't see Hyle with you. Did you have any luck convincing him to come along?"

"Sophia talked to him, but," Newman shook his head, finishing the thought. Then, noticing the magister's look of concern added, "He volunteered to work both days of the weekend."

"Will he be coming to a service this evening then?"

Newman hesitated.

"I don't think he was planning to, no."

Delacroix gave a long sigh.

"It's admirable that he has volunteered to work an extra shift but please make it clear to him that he must attend a service next weekend."

"Yes, Magister, I will." Newman was a bit surprised that the magister was mandating attendance at a service. It was generally expected that everyone would go to weekend services, but it was not enforced as a rule. Some of his surprise crept into his voice.

"I think it's important," the magister explained, "particularly now that he has stopped coming to your unity meetings."

"He is still going to unity meetings," Newman pointed out. "He's just uncomfortable at my meeting because he knows that some of the people there complained about him."

"Yes, that is unfortunate. When he was at your meeting at least we knew what he was saying. Now I'm afraid he is a bit of a loose cannon. We don't really know where he is going at night and according to John he has been staying out quite late some evenings. Has he been asking you a lot of questions?"

"No," Newman replied, puzzled by the question. Delacroix scowled thoughtfully.

"I would like you to bring him to my service next Sunday afternoon. I assume you and Sophia will be able to attend."

"Yes, Magister, I see no reason that we wouldn't."

Delacroix sighed again. His gaze drifted to some point on the wall over Newman's shoulder.

"I have been doing a great deal of thinking about our friend Hyle. I think he has had enough time to adjust, Newman. His grace period is over—he cannot remain our guest forever. To stay he must become a member of the Union of Faith. Or not. It's time to find out whether he is meant to stay here."

Newman bit his tongue. He thought that it was a particularly bad time to push Hyle into making a decision and searched for the best way to voice his concerns without sounding like he was questioning the magister's judgment.

"I've been giving him some time," he said slowly, "but maybe I should try to get him back into my unity meetings. Or talk to him myself one on one."

"No. I want this to be Hyle's decision. Do not encourage him. If he is not sure that he should be here then I am sure that he should not be. I don't want you to interfere with his decision. Is that clear?"

"Yes, Magister."

"Good. Thank you, Newman. You may go."

CHAPTER TWENTY-SEVEN

SEEKING PROOF

Returning to the library, Newman was happy to find Sophia still there alone. He stopped outside the doorway, trying to decide what, if anything, to tell her about his conversation with the magister. For the moment he resigned himself to saying nothing, but it was more a failure to decide than an actual choice.

"Welcome back," Sophia said as Newman entered the room. He forced a smile and searched the bookshelves absentmindedly. "I hope it wasn't anything serious?"

From her tone he knew that Sophia suspected that his talk with the magister had, in fact, been something serious and Newman knew himself well enough to know that he was not a very good liar.

"I think Hyle is on the verge of being asked to leave Asher."

Sophia was staggered. She shook her head at first in disbelief, then in denial.

"No. We can't let that happen." She locked eyes with Newman. "Why?"

"The magister is still afraid he's going to cause problems, especially since he's not coming to unity meetings anymore."

"But he is," Sophia protested. "He's just trying other ones."

"Are you sure? His roommate says he's been getting back very late some nights."

"Maybe they're on the other side of the city."

"Maybe. But maybe he's doing something else. Besides," Newman added before she could object, "the point is that we don't know what he might be saying in these other meetings. The magister thinks he's a loose cannon. He didn't say he was going to ask Hyle to leave yet, but he did say that he has had enough time to adjust and insisted that he attend the magister's service this weekend. I think that the magister may give him the benefit of hearing one good sermon and then ask him to make a final decision to either join the Union or leave. That's only a guess, but what I can tell you for sure is that Hyle doesn't have much more time."

"But he's not ready to decide yet."

Newman nodded sympathetically. He could hear the anguish in her voice, as if Hyle had already announced that he was leaving.

"Do you think he'll ever be?" Newman asked softly.

"I don't know, but if we have until the weekend, we need to try to help him."

"It's not enough for him to want to stay out of friendship. This is a community of faith, and the magister will see right through any other motivation for staying."

"Then that's what we'll have to work on," Sophia replied. "His problem is that he's too much of a scientist, so we'll just have to prove the existence of God to him."

Newman kept his doubts to himself and helped her shelve her books.

After the unity meeting that evening, once the furniture was moved back and her housemates were preparing for bed, Sophia put on her cloak and went over to talk to

Hyle. Judith let her in and then returned to doing the dishes. It was not much later that the latch rattled and Hyle stepped in with the lantern, earlier than usual.

"Hi, Sophia," he said, no longer surprised to find her waiting for him.

"Don't put the lantern out yet," she told him. "It's a nice evening. I thought maybe we could go for a walk."

"Okay, sure. That would be nice," Hyle agreed, but he studied her face with narrowed eyes.

Soon they were walking aimlessly along the packed earth roads. In the still twilight, smoke streamed from the chimneys of most houses, looking against the pale horizon like a forest of twisted tree trunks merging into a hazy canopy. Lanterns were suspended by many doors to light the way along the road, and a few doors opened as they passed, people stepping out of them bearing more lanterns to be hung. Rich yellow light flickered inside the houses. The crisp smell of the evening air was laced with the passing aroma of cooking food and smoke.

"It's a beautiful night, isn't it?" Sophia ventured.

"Yes," Hyle agreed quietly.

They reached the top of a hill overlooking a part of the city. Unity Hall loomed dark on its own hill to the west. Looking ahead to the south was a valley of houses, distinguishable only by their lights against the darkness. Sophia stopped and stood looking over the view.

"It's so peaceful. I love to come out and look at the lights on nights like this," she said.

Hyle nodded a silent concurrence.

"What would you think about settling down here?" she asked casually.

"I don't know."

He replied with a finality that indicated that he did not intend to think about it anymore. Sophia tried to read between the lines, but he did not say it as if he had reservations. It sounded as though he truly did not know, but there was a subtle edge to his voice, she thought.

"You seem a little—I don't know—restless."

"Hmm, really?" He shrugged.

"Come on, Hyle, talk to me. I like it here and I—I think I'd like to stay, but I want to know what you think."

"If you want to stay, you should."

"But I want to know what you think."

"Why? What does it matter? If you're happy here you should stay. It doesn't matter what I think."

"Hyle, why would you say that? It does matter. It matters to me. Look, I know you're mad at whoever it was that complained about you to Magister Delacroix, but that was only a couple people out of the whole city. You can't go on being upset forever."

"You think that's it?" Hyle asked, turning to look at her hard. He started to say more, but Sophia could almost see him catch the words in his teeth.

"What is it then?" she asked gently.

Hyle sighed and there was a long silence.

"I don't know. Really. The people here are very nice, and if everything we heard is true, this is a better place to be than most places in the world right now. I don't really know what I'd do if I didn't stay here."

"But something is bothering you," Sophia persisted. "You do seem restless to me."

"I guess I still don't feel like I have found my place yet. You knew Newman before you got here. He invited you because he knew you'd enjoy going to these prayer meetings and talking about philosophy and Bible history. I'm not sure I'll ever feel at home with all of it."

Sophia braced herself and asked the question she had been postponing.

"If you had to choose right now whether to leave or stay for good, what would you do?"

Hyle looked down and kicked at a large rock embedded in the road.

"If you were staying?" he asked rhetorically. "I'd stay."

"What if you had never met me and you wandered in here by yourself?"

"I'm not sure."

"If you had to choose, forever."

"I'd probably go. I hate ultimatums," he added with a laugh.

There was a long silence.

"Unfortunately we have been given a real one," Sophia told him. She filled him in on Newman's conversation with Magister Delacroix and the requirement that he attend the magister's service on the coming weekend. His lack of reaction surprised her.

"I thought you'd be upset to have Magister Delacroix make you decide whether or not to stay here."

"Why? His organization built this city and populated it by invitation only. It's only fair that we should have to make the same commitment that everyone else did."

"What if he asks you about your faith?"

"That's a tough question for someone who doesn't really believe in God."

"According to the Union charter, members only need to have faith in 'a higher power,'" Sophia corrected.

"But they mean God. Those are just semantics."

"Maybe, but they might be important semantics. Hyle, would you do me a big favor?"

"What?" he asked suspiciously.

"Come to Newman's meetings—just for the next week—and stay for tea afterwards. Ask all the questions you want one on one. I'm sure he won't mind. Give us a chance to help you get more comfortable with the idea of staying here before the weekend."

"Okay, but I don't think reading me passages from the Bible is going to help much," Hyle warned. "That's what they seem to do at most of these unity meetings. I know that's how a lot of people find their faith, but to me it seems like reading the Bible would only make sense if you already had faith in what it was saying."

"I know. That's not what I was thinking of anyway. What did you think about the discussion we had about Plotinus and Augustine?"

"It was interesting. Probably the most interesting discussion I have heard since we came here, but I don't really buy the premise that there's a separate perfect transcendent world. It was just interesting as an intellectual exercise for me."

"Fair enough. Can I give you another intellectual exercise?"

"Go ahead."

"Augustine would argue that the imperceptibility of God is like the imperceptibility of a perfect triangle. Something can be real without being perceived," Sophia said.

"Fine, but I don't see how that proves the existence of God."

"Would you agree that triangles are real?" Sophia asked him. "You can see them and draw them, so based on the criterion of having to perceive something to believe in it, would you agree that triangles exist?"

"Yes, I suppose so."

"And squares, hexagons and octagons?"

"Yes."

"What about chiliagon?"

"What's a chiliagon?" Hyle asked.

"A thousand-sided figure. It's what Descartes used to illustrate this point."

"Yes, thousand-sided figures too. Even million-sided figures, but what exactly is the point?"

"Could you draw a million-sided figure?"

Hyle thought for a moment.

"It would take a long time," he said at last, "and a really big sheet of paper."

Sophia looked at him skeptically.

"Really, could you ever draw a one million-sided figure that you could actually see as a million-sided figure? It would either look like a circle to you or you'd only be able to see a tiny part of it."

"Okay, I suppose that's true."

"So it's not necessary to perceive something for it to exist."

"That may be so," Hyle allowed, "but proving that something can exist without being perceived doesn't prove that it does. It just allows for the possibility."

"But you agree that it's possible for God to exist without being able to be perceived?"

"Possible, yes."

"So assuming for the moment that God does exist, and that we cannot perceive him, how would we ever know that He exists?"

Hyle thought for a moment.

"Through logic?" he ventured and Sophia smiled triumphantly.

"So we agree that it's possible for God to exist. Now what remains is to demonstrate that it's necessary. Avicenna constructed a logical argument using exactly this distinction. He said that things can be divided into those that are possible and those that are necessary. Things that are possible may or may not exist. Physical things are a good example—things that may come into being and pass out of being again."

Sophia paused to look at Hyle. He nodded.

"Sounds reasonable so far."

"So if something is possible, if it goes from non-existence into existence, could it cause that change itself?"

"No, of course not," Hyle said. "If it doesn't exist yet it can't cause anything."

"Then possible things exist by virtue of something other than themselves?"

"Yes."

"They could exist by virtue of another possible thing?" suggested Sophia.

"Sure."

"Could all possible things exist by virtue only of other possible things?"

Hyle had to think about this. He could see where the argument was headed and knew he did not agree with the conclusion, but he could not find a flaw with the logic. If possible things could not create themselves, there might be a long line of possible things created by other possible things, but ultimately some possible thing must exist by virtue of something eternal.

"No," Hyle said slowly. "There must be something else that causes at least some possible things to exist."

"Avicenna called that thing 'necessary through itself' or in other words necessary for everything else. That was his basis for proving the existence of God."

"That argument only proves that something must exist through itself, which I suppose is another way of describing something eternal," Hyle pointed out. "It doesn't prove anything about the nature of that something."

"It proves something about it. Human beings do not exist eternally or by virtue of ourselves, so whatever this thing is it's superior in that regard."

"I suppose that's fair to say, but it still doesn't follow that it's God."

"If you think Avicenna demonstrated the existence of something eternal, but not God, what would you call it?"

"I don't know. A force maybe?"

"A power?"

"Sure. A power."

"Since it's superior to human beings, would it be fair to call it a 'higher power'?"

Sophia asked, and a smug grin began to spread across her face. Hyle kicked himself for not seeing what was coming. He smiled in spite of himself and his admiration for Sophia grew.

"Yes," he conceded. "A higher power. And maybe that's enough to get me into the Union of Faith on a technicality, but that's not what Delacroix and Newman mean when they talk about God."

"Yes, that's probably true," Sophia agreed, "but let me try one more line of reasoning on you. Does it matter whether God exists or not?"

Hyle gave her a blank look.

"I don't understand what you mean."

"I mean, would there be a difference if God existed versus if He didn't exist."

"Yes, obviously there would."

"In what way?"

"If God does exist, that means he had the power to create the world and has the power to destroy it or change it. If he does not exist then he does not have the power to do anything."

"Would you agree then that if God exists He'd be superior to a non-existent or just conceptual God?"

"Yes, that seems obvious too," Hyle agreed cautiously. "Where are you going with this?"

"Let me ask you a different question now," Sophia said, ignoring Hyle's question for the moment. "Think of the most perfect being you can imagine—that than which a greater being cannot be thought."

Sophia waited.

"Okay. Got it," Hyle said as soon as he realized she was waiting.

"What are you thinking of?"

"God," Hyle answered slowly.

"Then you do believe God exists."

"That's not an intellectual exercise—it's a trick question. I didn't say I believed in God. I just said I was thinking of God because you told me to imagine the most perfect being I could imagine."

"So you're saying that God is the most perfect being that you can imagine, but that doesn't necessarily mean He exists. Do I have that right?"

"Yes," Hyle said emphatically.

"But you also agreed that God existing would be superior to a non-existent God?"

Hyle did not say anything, so Sophia finished the thought for him.

"The most perfect being you can imagine must exist, because to not exist would be less than perfect."

They were silent for a while, Hyle thinking about the logic of the argument and Sophia watching him, trying to mask her amusement. Eventually Hyle spoke.

"There's something wrong with that argument."

"You can thank Anselm of Canterbury for that one. Keep thinking about it. If you can figure out what's wrong with it, let me know what it is."

As they walked blackness overtook the entire sky and a cold breeze began to blow down off the mountains. Sophia huddled in close to Hyle as they circled back toward their houses. By the time they got home, Hyle had still not figured out what was wrong with the argument.

CHAPTER TWENTY-EIGHT

DELACROIX CONVERSES

Even though he was dreading the conversation, Hyle pushed his cart a little faster than usual to make time to answer his summons to Delacroix's cottage before lunch. At least the day was pleasant enough. The air was warm and the sun burned behind the cloud layer, streaking the gray with a tinge of orange, but unable to pierce through. Beyond the city wall the mountains were cast in a pale orange glow, blurring the features of the terrain. Hyle could hear the sounds of construction—the pounding of hammers and the steady rhythm of sawing—emanating from a valley far across the city and echoing back faintly from the sides of the pastel mountains. He returned to the warehouse early and refilled his cart at a leisurely pace until the singsong chime of the small bells marked the half hour and then made his way to Delacroix's cottage.

"Hyle, welcome. It's nice to see you," Delacroix said formally as they both took seats in his office. "Thank you for coming by."

"No problem," Hyle responded as cheerfully as he could manage. "What did you want to see me about? You didn't get any more complaints about me, did you?"

"No, no. Nothing of the sort," the old man said with a dismissive wave of his hand and smiling amiably. It was supposed to be reassuring Hyle knew, but it made him all the more uneasy. "I merely wished to converse with you about how you are adjusting to life in Asher. I understand you've not been going to Newman's unity meetings since we last conversed."

"I did take some time away to try other meetings," Hyle confirmed, "but Sophia has just talked me in to going back. I guess I'm her first hardship case as a new proctor."

The old man's expression hardened briefly, but he smiled again at Hyle's last comment.

"Yes, she has really found her place here it seems. I am sure it helps that she and Newman get on so well together," he added pensively. "They do seem made for each other, don't they?"

At first Hyle said nothing, taking it for a rhetorical question, but Delacroix watched him expectantly. Hyle felt his insides writhe under the weight of the question, but he gave no indication on the surface. There was a long uncomfortable silence before he spoke.

"I'm sure you didn't ask me here to talk about what a nice couple Sophia and Newman make."

"Have you met any young women here for yourself, Hyle?" asked Delacroix, continuing on as if they were still in the midst of a pleasant chat, apparently oblivious to Hyle's statement.

"No."

"I am given to understand that you have volunteered to work both days each weekend you have been with us. Is that correct?"

"Yes. Is that a problem?"

"Everyone is expected to attend one of the weekend services. Although technically there is no city rule saying that you must, most people also appreciate the break from work that they get on a holy day of rest. But for the moment let us not worry about what you are missing. I am more interested to know why you do it."

Again Hyle was silent, hoping that Delacroix did not expect an answer.

"I also understand from your housemates that you are hardly ever there. You say very little at breakfast and dinner, leave right after your meals and stay out until they have all gone to sleep."

"Why do you care so much about how I'm spending my time?"

The old man gave him a sharp look.

"I care about everyone in this city. They are my responsibility."

"But this is a city of more than eleven thousand people. I'm sure you don't interview everyone's housemates just out of idle curiosity," Hyle countered. He could tell even as he spoke that the tone of his objection had crossed a line.

"I will remind you Hyle that you are speaking to the Magister of Asher. For the people here I represent both the will of God and the highest human authority. If you are to stay here you must not only demonstrate your faith in God, but your respect and obedience to authority in all of its forms. Otherwise we here will fare no better than the world outside."

"I apologize if I sounded disrespectful," Hyle said, with some difficulty. "I only meant that it seems that you have taken a disproportionate interest in how I'm spending my time."

Delacroix looked at him. At first it was a penetrating look and Hyle felt that his sincerity was being measured, but then the magister's expression softened slightly and he seemed to be lost in thought.

"You are right, Hyle," he said at last. "The Prophet warned me to keep a close eye on those who came to us after the holocaust. He said that the first new arrivals would have the potential to bring great good to the city or cause great harm to our organization. I have been keeping a close watch on you and Sophia both."

"Have you come to any conclusions?"

There was another long silence as Delacroix considered how much he wanted to say.

"Yes," he answered eventually. "I have concluded that Sophia will be good for us. I've not yet come to any final decision about you, but there are only three options. The first possibility is that you will find your faith and settle in to this community. The second possibility is that you remain uncertain about your faith. Eventually you will realize that you can never fit in here, yet you will be unwilling to leave, always waiting for something to change. If this happens you will either try to change a society that should not and cannot be changed, or you will become resentful of it. Either way you will become harmful to the community. The last option is that you will see this future before it happens and you will leave."

The old man paused briefly to let Hyle consider the validity of his assessment.

"Why do you spend so little time at home, Hyle? Why do you work an extra day every weekend?"

A tense silence followed the questions. Delacroix's eyes burned into Hyle as if he were trying to pull out the answer by force of will. Hyle knew the answer Delacroix wanted to hear and he gave it in the hopes that it would bring the miserable conversation to an end. He gave it detachedly as if solving a mathematical proof posed by a teacher, as if the answer had nothing to do with him, but in the back of his mind Hyle knew that there was more than a little truth to it.

"Because I don't fit in," he answered.

Upon hearing those words Delacroix's unyielding stare was transformed by an expression of paternal sympathy.

"You have a difficult decision to make, Hyle, but I need to know your mind by this weekend. I will be giving the service Sunday afternoon at two bells and I want to see you there. If there is anything you need to ask or feel you need to say in the meantime come talk to me."

When the conversation ended and Delacroix had ushered him to the door, Hyle nearly fled back to the warehouse to the comfort of his supply cart and the relative solitude of the city roads. As he plodded along behind his cart a whirlwind of conflicting thoughts raced around his head.

«« »»

On their way back from the library Sophia and Newman, unaware the Hyle had been summoned to meet with Magister Delacroix earlier that day, were discussing the ultimatum and Sophia's conversation with Hyle the previous evening.

"It went much better than I thought it would," she said. "He was actually very under-standing about having to make up his mind. The problem is that he doesn't believe in God, at least not in the biblical version of God, and he wants to be satisfied that if he joins the Union of Faith officially, that he can do it honestly."

"So what's he going to do? He'll either have to join the Union or leave."

"I know," Sophia said, clearly pained by the fact. "He agreed to come back to your meetings and talk to us afterwards. I think he wants to be able to join the Union, he just wants to do it truthfully and he's looking for something to help convince him. I think we made a little progress last night."

"What did you do?"

Sophia recounted the proofs of Augustine, Avicenna and Anselm.

"I hadn't heard Avicenna's proof before, but I remember Anselm's," Newman said. "What did Hyle think of them?"

"I don't think they convinced him of anything, but it gave him something to think about. I was looking for some other proofs to discuss with him tonight."

"You should check with the Doctor then," Newman told her. "There are a couple shelves of his works in the library."

"The doctor?"

"Thomas Aquinas. He was called the church doctor because he resolved so many of the tough theological issues of his day. A lot of his views were controversial, but eventually they were adopted as official church doctrine. The *Summa Theologica* is his master work, covering just about every major topic in Christian theology, including five proofs for the existence of God. Augustine and Aquinas were the first two things I read when I thought I wanted to become a priest. Of course they were introduced to me as Saint Augustine and Saint Thomas Aquinas. And Saint Anselm, for that matter."

"When I met you, I thought you said you didn't know much of anything about phi-losophy."

"I didn't. Not what you were talking about anyway. Philosophers to me were ancient Greeks who were interested in wisdom. I never really thought of Augustine and Aquinas as philosophers, just theologians."

"That's funny. When I was reading Augustine and Anselm I never really thought of them as theologians, just philosophers. I suppose they were both really," Sophia replied.

They continued their conversation, taking time to enjoy the walk and pausing to admire the evening sun on the distant mountains. When they arrived home they were surprised to find Hyle waiting for them. He asked to speak to them privately and Newman ushered them into his room. As a proctor he enjoyed the privilege of having a small writing desk and a few simple chairs in his room in place of a second bed. He pulled the chairs out into a rough circle and took a seat.

"I had my talk with Delacroix this morning," Hyle said.

"How did it go?" asked Newman, realizing awkwardly as he did that Hyle's presence was already an answer.

"I think he wants me to leave the city."

Sophia protested, but Hyle shook his head adamantly and recounted his conversation, skipping over the part about Newman and Sophia, which he could not bring himself to repeat. He told her everything Delacroix had said about his work schedule and spending little time at his house as well as the three possibilities for his future. When he mentioned the Prophet's warning about new arrivals, Sophia looked over at Newman.

"Did you know anything about that?" she demanded, realizing from the length of the silence that followed that he did. "What did he tell you? Why didn't you say something to us?"

"I couldn't. I'm sorry. The magister told me only under the condition that I not discuss it with anyone, not even other proctors."

"So you have had people spying on us?" Sophia fired back, locking her eyes hard onto Newman's.

"No, just keeping an eye on you until we knew how you were adjusting."

"What's the difference?"

"The magister was just trying to find out how you were doing, that's all."

"You don't have to worry, Sophia," Hyle cut in. "He's decided you're one of the good guys. He even made you a proctor. But he's not just trying to find out how we're doing. He's really worried about this prediction that the Prophet made. That's the other reason he's keeping an eye on us. It's not just for our benefit."

"That's true," Newman admitted. "He is concerned about Zendik's prophecy."

"What exactly is this prophecy?" Sophia asked.

"It was a little unclear when he told me," Newman said. "The magister couldn't remember the exact words, but he was warned that the first new arrivals to Asher would do either great good or great harm to the Union of Faith and determine the outcome of the final battle. He thought it was supposed to be three travelers rather than two though. That's why he kept asking about the motorcycle that you followed."

"And that's why the safest thing for him to do is to split us up," Hyle concluded. "The whole point of our conversation seemed to be to make me aware that I didn't fit in and if I didn't leave it would eventually be bad for me and everyone else. He's already convinced that I'm the one who will lead to the great harm."

"He didn't say that," Sophia objected. "He was just telling you what might happen if you make the decision to stay without believing in it. And you said you're not sure yet, and that's why you were going to give us a week to help you decide. Don't decide yet. You don't have to decide yet."

Hyle reluctantly consented, and left to have dinner saying nothing more.

CHAPTER TWENTY-NINE

WHAT'S IN A NAME

Visitors began to arrive and take their places for the unity meeting and Newman was pleased to see Hyle among the crowd. He wanted to welcome Hyle back to the group, and considered saying something at the start of the meeting, but then thought better of it. The meeting was uneventful. That Newman chose the theme of forgiveness and tolerance for the opening prayer was not lost on Hyle. The following conversation was restrained. Even though most of the attendees participated at some point, asking or answering a question, Newman did the majority of the talking and no one made any attempt to influence the topic of discussion. Hyle said nothing, and his lack of participation was not as obvious as it had been during his first week.

After the meeting several people stopped by to tell Hyle they were happy to see him again before filing out the door, including the one person he least expected. Timothy said little, only "Welcome back" accompanied by a firm handshake. As usual, his face displayed no trace of a smile, but his tone was sincere. Surprised and moved by the gesture, for a moment Hyle continued to shake hands with other guests absentmindedly. As Timothy fell in line with the people filing out the door and stepped out into the night, Hyle watched him go, staring at the back of his head as if trying to peer into his thoughts.

When the house was clear of guests and the residents began to disappear into their rooms, Sophia and Hyle sat down at the table. Newman threw another log on the fire, put the kettle on and joined them.

"I'm very happy to see you back again, Hyle," he said, and sensing immediately from Hyle's reaction that he had heard that phrase more than enough for one evening, Newman quickly added, "Unfortunately, I can't stay for the discussion tonight, but I'm sure Sophia has lots to talk to you about."

Hyle was somewhat surprised, but Sophia shot Newman a look of shock and betrayal. It was only the hint of distress underlying his statement that prevented her from saying something immediately.

"The magister believes that you should make your own decision," Newman explained. "He doesn't feel that it's appropriate for me to influence your thinking in any way. In fact, he forbade me from doing so."

He addressed Hyle, but looked to Sophia as soon as he had finished his explanation and watched her face.

"Isn't that your job though?" Hyle asked. "I push a delivery cart full of food and supplies around the city every day to make sure people have enough to eat and live comfortably. I thought your job was to tend to their spiritual needs."

"Yes, it is," Newman agreed slowly.

He was still struggling to find a good explanation when Sophia chimed in.

"I'm not asking you to convince Hyle to stay when he doesn't want to. We just need you to help answer some theological questions. Then Hyle can make up his own mind."

Newman thought about this. The tea kettle started spitting and Newman jumped out of his seat to take it off the hook and get the mugs. Taking refuge in this activity, he replayed the conversation with the magister in his mind. He remembered being told not to influence Hyle's decision. That did not necessarily preclude him from talking about faith in general, he reasoned. On the other hand, he had the clear impression that the magister had meant for him to stay out of the issue completely. And yet, the point stood—his duty was to help people with matters of faith. He owed obedience to the magister, who had given him that duty, but he had also sworn his faith in a higher power, and part of his duty was to share that faith. Newman was still torn when he returned to the table. Hyle and Sophia were both silent as he poured the steaming water into their mugs. He felt Sophia's eyes searching his face for several long seconds after he sat down, waiting.

"Okay," he said at last. "As long as we're discussing matters of faith and not reasons for leaving or staying in the city."

Hyle nodded his agreement and Sophia smiled a smile of satisfaction mixed with gratitude.

"Was the meeting helpful at all?" Newman asked.

Hyle was quiet a moment, debating how to answer.

"Not really," he said truthfully. "I learned some things, but it didn't make any difference to me in terms of faith. The most helpful meeting was the one I got in trouble for. I guess you did too. I was serious when I asked how you can come to know God when he can't be seen anywhere in this world. Reading from a book, even though it claims to be a holy book, isn't helpful to me. What I know is what I can see and touch and hear."

"Perception isn't everything though," Newman objected. "Sophia told me that she gave you Saint Anselm's proof for the existence of God last night. What did you think of it?"

"It's interesting, but I'm sure that there's something wrong with it. I just can't put my finger on it."

"It's a very logical argument, though, isn't it?" Sophia said.

"Yes, but I'm still convinced that it's not right."

"So are you saying that you're rejecting logic because of something you know in your heart to be true?" Sophia asked mischievously.

"Touché," Hyle acknowledged, smiling. "But I'm not conceding that the logic is correct yet."

"What about any of the other things we have talked about in past meetings, like Augustine and Plotinus?" Newman asked.

"They haven't been too helpful either," Hyle confessed. "Talking about uniting ourselves with some eternal world through our intellect or the physical world being like shadows cast by something eternal are beautiful poetic images, but they don't prove that there actually is any such transcendent world. Really, all of these Platonic forms, like your perfect triangle example are just ideas. I don't see how they have any connection to the physical world. They do have a sort of reality, in that the idea of perfect triangles will exist long after I'm gone, but they exist as concepts. A perfect triangle can't create the earth in seven days or part the Red Sea and lead Moses out of Egypt."

"That's the problem of universals," Sophia said. "Hyle, you have struck on a question that has plagued philosophy since very nearly the beginning."

"The problem of universals?"

"In a way, yes. That's the form the debate took with the Scholastics of the eleventh and twelfth centuries, but it's really part of a larger ontological debate between two schools of thought, each with lots of permutations."

"Ontological?" Hyle interrupted, looking slightly embarrassed. "I have heard the word, but I have to confess that I don't know exactly what it means in this context."

"Ontology is the question of the nature of being and existence. What's real? What really exists?"

"Okay, thanks. So what are the two ontological views?"

"One school of thought believes that things in the physical world are transitory— always changing and passing out of being—and therefore reality must lie in a non-physical eternal world."

"Like Plato and Augustine," Hyle interrupted again.

"Yes. And because their version of reality is non-physical, it tends to be associated with thinking or conceiving. You can trace that belief back to Parmenides, who said, 'That which can be conceived is that which exists.' Socrates and Plato developed this concept into the theory of an eternal world and a transitory physical world—which we have been explaining with the perfect triangle and allegory of the cave. Then we have Plotinus and Augustine who further developed the idea of trying to unite ourselves with the eternal world by seeing it with understanding or love. Even Anselm's ontological proof for the existence of God hinges on Parmenides' idea that that which can be conceived is real. During the age of Scholasticism, this school of thought became known as the realists."

"I think they'd be called something else nowadays," Hyle said, half under his breath.

"They were called realists because they believed that universals had a reality of their own," Sophia explained, acknowledging the joke with only a passing smile.

"What did they mean by universals?" Newman asked. "Is it the same thing as Platonic Forms?"

"Yes, pretty much," Sophia said. "Universals are categories in which individual objects participate. Socrates is an individual man and Plato is an individual man, but 'man' is also a category that they each belong to. The realists held that these universals had their own independent reality."

"What did the un-realists believe?" Hyle asked.

"The nominalists," Sophia corrected. "The nominalists were Scholastics who believed that it was only physical things that had reality. They can trace their roots back to Aristotle. They were exposed to Aristotle's logic through the translations and commentaries of Boethius who was responding to a series of questions raised a few centuries earlier by Plotinus' student Porphyry."

"Got that?" Hyle asked Newman. Sophia smiled patiently as they both finished laughing.

"Porphyry had asked three questions," she continued. "The first was whether universals had real existence. If they did have real existence, he asked whether they had physical existence. If they had non-physical existence he asked whether they existed in conjunction with physical substances or separate from them. It was philosophers like Boethius, who tried to reconcile Plato and Aristotle, that brought the problem of universals to light because that's one area where the two great philosophers had fundamentally different ideas.

"And what did Boethius say?" Newman asked.

"He chose an interpretation of Aristotle that had been suggested by Alexander of Aphrodisias. Boethius said, more or less, that universals exist in conjunction with physical things, but the mind understands them separately from physical things. The realists took Plato's view that universals have independent reality, but the nominalists came to a view even more extremely opposed to realism than Aristotle had been himself. They maintained that universals had no reality whatsoever. For the nominalists, universals existed only in name, as words, and since words are just sounds, there's nothing special or real about universals. They're just words we happen to use for some sets of individual things, nothing more."

"So Juliet Capulet was a nominalist?" Newman asked. "'A rose by any other name would smell as sweet.'"

"Yes, I suppose she was."

"That sounds like a pretty reasonable argument to me," Hyle said. "It sounds much more realistic than realism."

"But if universals were just words and nothing more they wouldn't mean anything at all," Newman objected. "How could we say that an apple and a stop light are both red if the word 'red' has absolutely no reality?"

"Because they both share the property of reflecting red light," answered Hyle. "I don't see why you need to assume some transcendent reality to call them both red."

"Think of it this way," Sophia said. "Suppose that words are just labels as the nominalist would claim. They'd be like names. You could both be named Hyle or you could equally well both be named Newman, or you could be one of each. Those are all possible. But you can't say that an apple is red but a stoplight isn't. Red is clearly more than just a label. There's something universal about it that transcends the individual items, otherwise what basis would there be for saying that apples and stoplights are red but grass isn't? That is a problem with nominalism. Nominalists can only talk meaningfully about individual things."

Both men considered the question.

"I suspect you have an answer," Newman guessed.

"Yes, it was Peter Abelard who struck a compromise between realism and nominalism that helped end the debate for the Scholastics," explained Sophia. "He was well versed in both positions since he studied with Roscelin, the founder of nominalism, then with William of Champeaux, a realist who had studied with Anselm. What Abelard proposed was a theory called conceptualism. According to conceptualism, universals don't have an independent reality in the external world, but they do have a reality in our minds as concepts."

"You're right, Newman," Hyle said. "That does make more sense than nominalism."

They discussed the topic at great length. Sophia explained Aristotle's moderate realism in which the universals were properties, having reality only in association with individual things, but existing independently in our minds as concepts. Abelard's conceptualism was similar to Aristotle's moderate realism, she told them, even though Abelard had not been aware of Aristotle's solution. When there seemed to be nothing else to say on the subject, and all three were beginning to think about turning in for the night, Newman asked something that had been lurking in the back of his mind throughout the discussion.

"I thought the Scholastics, like Anselm and Aquinas, were mainly concerned with theological issues," he said. "Neoplatonic realism seems to fit very nicely with Christian theology, so what were the nominalists trying to achieve?"

"The Scholastics were concerned with theological issues," Sophia confirmed. "But they were trying, much like Augustine, to reconcile Greek philosophy with Christian thought and since Aristotle had been rediscovered, they had to reconcile his thinking with theology and Neoplatonism. The nominalists disagreed with the realists about universals, but they shared the same general goal of understanding theological questions."

Sophia paused, trying to remember something she had read in the library.

"There was a nominalist named Berengar of Tours," she said. "He had a famous debate with Lanfranc, who was Anselm's mentor and a realist. Berengar was trying to understand what happened when a priest consecrated the bread and wine into the body and blood of Christ. Since he was a nominalist, he was trying to understand how the transformation could be brought about by words."

"And the Church tolerated that kind of questioning?" Hyle asked in surprise.

"Why wouldn't they?" Newman countered. "Logic and revelation both come from God, so they shouldn't be incompatible."

"Berengar wasn't questioning the sacrament of the Eucharist, Hyle," Sophia added. "He was trying to make the connection between the eternal and the physical, just like you were. But sometimes the nominalists were controversial. Anselm once accused Roscelin, the founder of nominalism, of heresy."

Hyle nodded and glanced over at Newman meaningfully.

"This is actually an even better example of nominalism versus realism applied to a theological question," Sophia realized out loud. "Roscelin claimed that you could just as easily say that the Trinity was three gods or three persons of God since 'gods' and 'persons' are just words."

"But that's tritheism," Newman said for Hyle's benefit. "The Council of Nicea determined that the Father, Son and Holy Spirit were of one substance—three persons of one God. To claim that they were three separate gods was considered to be a form of pantheism and therefore a heresy."

"Yes," Sophia continued. "Anselm said that anyone who can't understand how several individual men can be one man can hardly be expected to understand how three divine persons can be one God. For a realist like Anselm men are united in the universal that is 'man' just like the three individual divine persons of the Trinity were united in the universal that is God. These universals were real things to Anselm, not mere words that could be swapped arbitrarily, so he accused Roscelin of heresy."

"What did the Church say?" Hyle asked.

"Roscelin, of course, didn't think he was a heretic. Since 'gods' and 'persons' were just words to him, there was no significance of choosing one over the other. The church council that heard the case understood Roscelin's argument well enough to clear him of the heresy charge."

Newman shot back the same significant look he had received from Hyle at the start of the heresy story. Hyle gave a dismissive shrug.

"Roscelin didn't have to deal with Delacroix," he said.

CHAPTER THIRTY

IN THE DARK OF NIGHT

Early Friday evening, between dinner and the start of the unity meeting, there was a knock on the door of Newman's house. John let himself in and stood just inside the doorway, visibly uncomfortable about intruding on the communal meal.

"Come on in, John," Newman invited. "Don't be shy. We're just finishing."

The big man took a few steps forward.

"I have a message for you," he said. "You and Sophia."

"Ah, I see," said Newman, and got up, excusing himself from the table. Sophia did the same and trailed the two men to Newman's room.

Motioning for the other two to have a seat, Newman pulled out the chair from his writing desk and sat down, trying not to read too much into John's serious expression.

"What is it, John?"

"Sorry to interrupt your dinner," John mumbled. He cleared his throat. "Uh, Hyle said to tell you that he wouldn't be coming tonight."

"What? Why?" exclaimed Sophia. "He knows there isn't—" she caught herself, continuing in a calmer voice. "He knows we had some important things to discuss tonight."

John shrugged helplessly and fidgeted with the edge of his beard.

"Sorry," he said. "He said to tell you he was sorry, but he had a unique opportunity—I forget the exact words he used—but he said he had an opportunity to learn some important things that would help him with some big decision. He said you'd understand."

Sophia and Newman traded looks.

"Did he say anything more than that?" asked Newman.

"No. I don't think so. No."

"Did he already leave?" asked Sophia, gathering her feet under her chair to get up.

"Leave? Oh, you mean dinner?" John realized aloud. "He didn't come back to dinner with me. I don't know where he went, but I guess he went straight from work."

"Maybe he had a dinner invitation from another proctor," Newman suggested, mainly for Sophia's benefit. She gave him a dubious look. "Do you know if he was talking to any other proctors today?"

"No, I don't think so," answered John, scowling in thought. After a few seconds he had a visible revelation. "You know, he was asking me about the stockers yesterday, though." He shook his head. "I doubt he went with one of them though. He usually tries to avoid them."

"What are the stockers?" asked Newman.

"And why does he try to avoid them?" added Sophia.

"Oh, sorry. I forgot you probably don't know that much about the warehouse," John replied, now pulling at his beard with both hands as he thought. "Isaac—that's the old guy who runs the warehouse—has people divided up into two groups. There are the runners and the stockers. The runners, like me and Hyle, take carts out around the city and deliver food. The stockers stay at the warehouse and move boxes and help load the carts. At five bells all the carts are supposed to be back to the warehouse and the runners go home for dinner, but they close the door and the stockers stay inside. Hyle was asking me what they do after the runners leave and when they eat dinner."

John stopped, as if he had answered the question fully.

"And what did you tell him?" prompted Newman.

"I told him I didn't know."

"Do you think maybe he stayed with them?"

"I don't think so. I didn't see him in the warehouse when I left. I think he was already gone. Besides, like I said, he kind of avoids them."

"Do you know why?" asked Sophia.

"I think 'cause he got in trouble for asking too many questions when he first started working there."

"Can you tell us more about that?" Newman pressed.

"The first week he was there Hyle was asking the stockers about how much food there was and how long it would last and stuff like that," explained John. "The stockers are kind of like the managers. Well, not so much managers, because they don't give orders really, but they're the only ones who really talk to Isaac. I guess one of them complained to Isaac, so he went and talked to Hyle and told him the story of the Hanukkah lamp. Then Isaac told him that if he had time to ask questions he should do something more useful and made him mop the floor."

In spite of her concern, Sophia could not help smiling a little bit as she pictured the encounter.

"John, is there something else?" Newman asked. "You look like you have something more to say."

Glancing over at Sophia, John frowned so deeply that his face almost disappeared between his thick eyebrows and his beard.

"It's okay, Sophia's a proctor. Whatever you want to tell me you can tell her."

"You know I'm supposed to report to the magister if he does anything unusual," John said tentatively.

"Yes," Newman said. "But you told me, so I can tell him. Is there anything more?"

"Just that he was acting a little strange today," said John. "Nothing big. He just seemed to avoid the stockers a little more today and at lunchtime he was ahead on his route so he volunteered to sweep the floor."

"That doesn't sound so horrible," Sophia observed. John shook his head in agreement.

"Is there anything else?" asked Newman.

They asked John a few more questions and, determining that there was nothing more to be learned, let him go. He gratefully retreated from the room, thanking Newman for his offer to talk to the magister. Sophia and Newman stayed behind for a while speculating about where Hyle might have gone and whether they should worry or not. Ultimately they decided that there was nothing to be done but wait.

After the unity meeting Sophia made her trek across the common to Hyle's house. The residents of the house went to bed one by one, finally leaving her alone with the dying fire. The dark room and the crackle of the remaining flames conspired to lull her to sleep and eventually she put her head down on the table to rest. When she lifted her head again, the room was much darker, the embers in the fireplace glowing a sinister orange from deep within the blackened logs. Reluctantly she put on her cloak and headed back to her own bed.

CHAPTER THIRTY-ONE

SCHOLASTICS

Late on Saturday night, after the unity meeting, Newman and Sophia sat with Hyle at the round table in the common room. The guests had gone and the other residents of the house had gone to sleep. A fire crackled on the hearth erasing all memories of the chilly evening outside. Hyle had come to the meeting late and Sophia was sure that this was a calculated strategy to give him an excuse to sit in the back and avoid having to answer any questions about the previous night. John had come in the morning to tell them that Hyle was home in bed and planned to report in sick to work, going on to confide to Newman and Sophia that Hyle had come back very late and probably was not really sick at all.

When Sophia finally did ask the inevitable question and Hyle told her that he could not really say where he had been, he was both relieved and surprised at her uncharacteristic acceptance of this non-answer. She was full of nervous energy, spinning her empty mug absently on the table and jumping up frequently to check the tea kettle. Newman seemed not to hear her question, but in actuality he was ignoring it. He did not want to learn anything that he would feel obligated to report to the magister to get Hyle in further trouble, so he quickly changed the topic.

"Sophia saved the best for last—Aquinas."

He instantly regretted his choice of phrases. Sophia gave an uneasy laugh.

"Aristotelianism in general," she corrected. "Since Newman here likes Augustine and early Christian theology so much, our meetings have been skewed toward Neoplatonism, but if you take a broader historical view, Aristotle had just as big an impact on theological thought. Realism and nominalism was just a case study of a much bigger philosophical debate, essentially between the views of Plato and Aristotle."

Newman listened quietly as Sophia recapped their earlier discussion about the Islamic philosophers. She told Hyle about Al-Farabi and his early integration of Aristotle's ideas with Muslim belief, the reaction to Al-Farabi by Neoplatonist Al-Razi and then Avicenna's subsequent defense of Aristotle and further incorporation of Aristotelian ideas into Islamic theology. They discussed Al-Ghazali's *The Incoherence of the Philosophers*, an attempt to protect Islamic thought from the invasion of Aristotle's ideas led by Avicenna and other Islamic Aristotelians. Hyle was amused to hear that Averroes, writing in the twelfth century, had named his subsequent defense of Aristotelianism *The Incoherence of the Incoherence*.

"So Al-Farabi, Avicenna and Averroes were trying to do the same thing with Aristotle and Islam that Augustine did with Christianity?" Hyle asked.

"I think that's a fair assessment," Sophia agreed. "And they also influenced Moses Maimonides, a contemporary of Averroes, who did something similar in Judaism with his *Guide of the Perplexed*."

"It sounds like Aristotle had pretty much won out by the twelfth century," ventured Hyle.

"Not entirely. There was still a lot of Neoplatonism in Muslim philosophy. Averroes was probably the most faithful to Aristotle and the only Muslim philosopher more influential in the West than Avicenna. He thought that Avicenna had sold out to religion on some aspects of Aristotle's philosophy. By contrast, Averroes held fairly controversial views for a Muslim, like believing that the world was eternal instead of created and not believing in immortality after death."

Sophia paused for a moment, thinking.

"Actually he did believe in a sort of immortality, but it was very different from conventional Muslim belief or even other Muslim philosophers. Averroes thought when each person's potential intellect is actualized, it reaches a sort of universal truth or common soul, so he didn't believe that people have individual souls, he believed that through the intellect we all participate in the same universal soul in a sense."

"That sounds a lot like Plotinus," Hyle observed. "I thought you said Averroes was an Aristotle purist."

"You're right, but if Averroes reminds you of Plotinus, it's because Plotinus borrowed this particular idea from Aristotle rather than Plato. Aristotle had proposed that there were four different types of intellect, but this was one of the places in his metaphysics where he wasn't always clear and consistent about what these types of intellect were or how they interacted. It was an area of Aristotle's thought that many of the Muslim philosophers were interested in trying to clarify."

Sophia gave Hyle a summary of Aristotle's four causes, the different types of intellect, and some of the theories that the Muslim philosophers had proposed in order to build a more coherent philosophy from Aristotle's ideas about the intellect.

"Another idea of Aristotle's that's closely related to his theory of the four causes is the concept of potential and actualization. He believed that all change was a combination of the potential inherent in the thing being changed and the actualization of that potential by some agent. He saw potential as being more important than the actualization, although both were important. Aristotle applied this concept to motion, to the senses, to the intellect and even to the soul."

"So if I throw a rock," Hyle interrupted. "The rock has the potential to be thrown and I actualize it by tossing it. Are you saying that the rock is more important in this action than I am?"

"Yes, according to Aristotle. You just think of yourself as most important because of your point of view, but you and the rock are both inseparable participants in the same change. 'The road from Thebes to Athens is the same road as the road from Athens to Thebes,'" Sophia quoted, "Which way you see it depends upon whether you're looking at it from Athens or Thebes."

"'The path up the mountain is the same as the path down the mountain,'" Newman added.

"Exactly," Sophia said, pleased that he had remembered. "Aristotle applied this same idea to the intellect, but it's probably easier to see how it applies to the senses first. As with motion, both the observer and the thing being observed participate in the event. For example when you see an apple that's red, your eyes and the apple are both participating in the form of 'red', or as Aristotle might have put it, the apple has the potential to be red, and your eyes by observing it actualize that potential."

"So if a tree falls in the forest," Hyle began, "it has the potential to make a sound, but it doesn't unless someone actualizes that potential by hearing it."

"Yes, exactly! Sound can't exist without hearing. Flavor can't exist without taste. Now apply that same principle to epistemology."

Hyle shot Newman a look of mock distress.

"Does she come with a dictionary?" he asked in a stage whisper.

"Epistemology comes from the Greek word for knowledge, *episteme*," Sophia explained. "Epistemology is the branch of philosophy which is interested in understanding the nature of knowledge. What kinds of things are knowable? How do we come to know the things we know?"

"Do you remember what my original question was?" Hyle asked Newman with a playful look at Sophia. She smiled patiently and sighed.

"Bear with me for one more minute," she said. "Aristotle thought that the relationship between sensory data and thought was the same type as the relationship between an object and the sense that detects it. When thought 'senses' the data, they both participate in the same form. Plotinus took this idea and translated it into the intellect becoming unified with the One by the act of thinking about it and perceiving it, and Averroes also took this idea from Aristotle."

Newman, who had been listening quietly, finally spoke.

"Sophia, if you're still planning to talk about Aquinas, you better do it fast. It's late and I think Hyle's getting punchy."

"I do need to get to sleep soon," Hyle agreed.

"Okay. I just think that since Aquinas and the other thirteenth century Christian philosophers were first exposed to Aristotle through philosophers like Avicenna, Averroes and Maimonides, it's important to have a little background first." Turning to Hyle she continued, "I think you'll like Aquinas for his epistemology. His view of knowledge was that everything comes to us empirically first, through the senses. Without that empirical knowledge, according to his views, we wouldn't be able to even understand universal principles and concepts. That was a belief pulled directly from Aristotle. Aquinas said that when we're born we're a *tabula rasa*, a blank tablet, waiting to be written on by the act of empirical experience."

"That's a good start," agreed Hyle.

"Aquinas had taken on the task of his mentor, Albertus Magnus, of making Aristotle 'intelligible to the Latins,'" Sophia explained.

"You mean safe for Christianity," Hyle said.

Sophia shrugged off the comment and went on to explain some of Aquinas' ideas, tracing them back through various philosophers to Aristotle and telling Hyle that Aquinas had used Aristotle's philosophy and logic to lay out five proofs for the existence of God. She quickly summarized two that she considered less convincing. One was an argument that things in existence can be seen on a continuum of less perfect to more perfect, and something must be at the top of that scale. That most perfect being is God. As expected, this argument did not do much to convince Hyle.

"Another proof Aquinas develops is the teleological proof," said Sophia "The world seems to be perfectly suited for us to live in. How could it come to be so unless it was created for a specific purpose by a Creator?"

"That presupposes that the world is perfect, which I think is debatable," argued Hyle. "I'm sure it's also based on the idea that human beings exist as originally created, and therefore couldn't have adapted to fit their environment."

"Those are two of the weaker arguments," Sophia conceded. "His first proof was the proof from motion, and I think it's his best. His second and third follow a similar logic. Imagine you just stepped into a billiard parlor and saw all the billiard balls moving around on the table, bouncing off of bumpers and each other and falling into pockets. What would you say had happened?"

"I'd say someone was playing billiards."

"More specifically?"

"I'd say someone had just hit one of the balls."

"What if there was no one in the room? How would you know that someone hit one of the balls?" Sophia pressed.

"I suppose I wouldn't know for sure it was a person taking a shot. It could have been a cat jumping on the table or something, but something must have hit at least one of the balls to set them in motion."

"Have you ever seen one of those intricate patterns of dominoes that have all sorts of branches and curves and spirals? Even in something that complex you can trace the fall of each domino to one before it and the one before that and on up the chain."

"Cause and effect," Hyle said. Sophia smiled.

"Yes, cause and effect. And you can trace that chain of cause and effect all the way back to the first domino and even farther back to the person who pushes it down. The stars and planets are all in motion too, and even if you could assign the direct cause to other celestial bodies or crystalline spheres, or whatever was believed about astronomy in Aquinas' day, if you keep tracing the chain of cause and effect it will either go on forever or end in an ultimate first cause."

"And that ultimate cause of course is God," Hyle guessed, completing the argument.

"Yes, according to Aquinas. Aristotle called it the Unmoved Mover. For Aristotle it wasn't a spiritual or religious concept, but it also wasn't restricted to just physical cause and effect like motion either. In fact, at one point Aristotle gives a whole list of unmoved movers in different areas, but ultimately he thought that everything had to trace back to one original source. Aquinas borrowed that concept for his first proof of the existence of God. From the undeniable fact that there's motion on earth and in the heavens, and from the principle of cause and effect, we know there must have been a first cause to set them all in motion."

"But science has provided a different explanation for why the planets and stars are in motion," Hyle countered. "That energy was provided when the universe was created."

"True," said Sophia, "but that begs the question of where that force came from at the beginning of the universe." Hyle thought about this and Sophia continued. "A similar argument to the proof by motion can be applied to existence. If all things are material and have the potential to not exist, at some point they must have all not existed. Then there would be nothing to bring anything into being, which is impossible. Therefore, there must be something eternal as the first cause of being."

"Now that sounds like Avicenna and the argument you gave me about possible versus necessary being."

"It's very similar," Sophia admitted, "Many of the most powerful ideas Aquinas presented were not necessarily original. I think he's famous more because he was so thorough and logical in laying them out and he was the one who made these arguments so articulately for the Christian west. Moses Maimonides offered the same proofs for God's existence—the Unmoved Mover and the argument of possible versus necessary— and Aquinas was also influenced by Avicenna's idea that, in God, existence was the same as essence."

"What is essence exactly?" Hyle asked.

"The essence of something is what it is, as opposed to whether or not it actually exists."

"How can you say what something is if it doesn't exist?"

"Do you know what a centaur is?"

"Yes. It's a creature that's half man and half horse," Hyle replied, understanding the example even as he spoke. "So if I describe a unicorn or a dragon or some other mythical beast, I'm describing its essence, even though it doesn't exist."

"Exactly. Aristotle even went so far as to say that you can't say anything about the existence of something—you can only talk about its essence."

Hyle looked unconvinced.

"Think about it this way," Sophia explained. "We'd all probably agree that the chair you're sitting on exists, but how would you demonstrate to somebody that it exists?"

"I'd have them look at it or feel it, sense it somehow."

"That would tell them what color or shape it is or how hard or smooth it is. Those are all just properties of the chair. That's what it is, but none of those things are its existence. All you'll ever be able to say specifically about the chair is to give a collection of descriptions."

Hyle thought for a moment.

"That's a problem with Anselm's proof then."

Newman scowled slightly at this statement, but Sophia smiled.

"How so?" she asked.

"Anselm tried to prove the existence of God by using a description of his essence. Being able to imagine the most perfect being I can is no more a proof for its existence than being able to imagine a unicorn or a centaur and taking that as proof that they're real."

"Remember, you did accept that existence was more perfect than non-existence," Sophia chided, "and Avicenna and Aquinas believed that essence and existence were the same for God. Averroes didn't even believe that the distinction was real. But you'll be happy to know that Aquinas rejected Anselm's proof for the same basic reason."

Hyle expressed his happiness with a long, unstifled yawn.

CHAPTER THIRTY-TWO

ULTIMATUM

Afternoon on Sunday was dark and cold and patches of mist floated in the valley, the sun failing to break through the gray brown haze that still clung low in the sky. The weather had gotten worse as the day progressed, and the mist was beginning to turn to drizzle. Sophia scuffed along the road to Unity Hall between Hyle and Newman and put up the hood of her cloak. The energy of the previous night had drained away from her completely. Hyle had still not committed to staying in Asher, saying only that his answers to Delacroix would depend upon the magister's questions and Sophia had an ominous feeling about their impending conversation.

Ahead the wide curve of Unity Hall took its shadowy form, the two thin towers disappearing into the pale sky. People converged from all directions, pulling their cloaks closely around their necks against the weather. They mounted the broad stairs and Hyle got his first look at the interior of the building. Its scale was as imposing as a gothic cathedral. Although the ceiling was lower, the space inside was much wider, creating the same sense of vast openness. The building had been designed with acoustics in mind, and every whisper and every shuffling foot was audible as Newman led them up the aisle toward the front.

Despite its impressive size and acoustics the hall did not have the austere atmosphere of a cathedral. Cold stone arches had been replaced by huge wooden beams that ran up the walls like the ribs of an inverted ship to meet at the top of the vaulted ceiling. The knots and the grain of the wood shone through a polished golden finish, providing a welcome contrast to the weather outside. Between the ribs were tall narrow windows set with abstract patterns of stained glass in shades of pale blue, indigo, violet and red. They took their seats in the front row, near an odd structure that shared the center of the dais with the lectern. Newman had encouraged them to arrive early in order to get these seats.

"We call that the bullpen," Newman whispered to Hyle, nodding toward the box of railings. "That's where people go to contribute after the sermon."

He suspected that Delacroix might be planning to call Hyle up to contribute, and wanted Sophia to be nearby for support.

"I like to sit here so I can hear what they're saying," he explained truthfully, not wishing to worry Sophia any further and keeping his suspicions to himself.

Sophia had spent the morning in a last ditch effort to get a commitment from Hyle, arguing the virtues of staying in the city, summarizing the various demonstrations for the existence of God, and reviewing the different concepts of what could qualify as a higher power in order to help remove that barrier from his mind. She said nothing now, sitting in silence as if waiting for a death sentence.

It was not long before the rows of empty chairs were transformed into a sea of people, whispering and buzzing as ushers helped those still arriving to find open seats.

Eventually the ushers closed the doors, turning away a small crowd of people. Once the doors were closed, there was a momentary hush, followed by a renewed wave of whispering, which lasted for several minutes until a small door at one end of the dais opened.

Delacroix stepped into the room and people stood and clapped as the magister strode toward the front of the platform, grinning broadly and waving in acknowledgement of the applause. He stepped up into the pulpit and surveyed the crowd, smiling and nodding to the audience, for many long seconds, until finally he put his arms out and tried to quiet the crowd. His first words were barely audible above the commotion, but his commanding voice carried well, and one by one people began to sit down and the room grew quiet. The magister stood there a while longer, shaking his head in disbelief at the welcome he had received and still smiling broadly.

"Thank you," he said over the soft rustle and creaking of people shifting in their chairs. "Thank you. I am honored to be here among you all. The Prophet Asha, in his wisdom, has filled this city with extraordinary people. Let us pray together and give our thanks to God and to the Prophet Asha who performs his miracles on earth."

The magister led the congregation through a long prayer thanking God for finding them worthy and leading them to Asher, for giving them the Prophet Asha to guide them and asking for more guidance to help them to do the right things in the coming months. Although it was all new to Hyle, he noticed that many of the people around him recited the prayer along with the magister. When the opening prayer concluded, Delacroix began the sermon.

"He always starts with a story," Newman whispered to Hyle in explanation.

This sermon started with a movie Delacroix had seen some time during his adult years before the Union of Faith. It was a science fiction film in which humans had built robots that became smarter than their creators and eventually took over the world, enslaving the human race. He described another where the role of the robots was filled by an artificial intelligence that took over the networks, and another about a world where people had created machines to automate the running of their society only to die off and leave society unwittingly controlled by mindless machines. He invited the assembly to contribute their favorite stories along the same theme.

At first people raised their hands and he called on them, but soon people were shouting out titles of films and books.

"Why is this such a popular theme?" he asked as the voices petered out. "Why are so many stories made with this same idea? I will tell you why. To make a good movie, one that will really scare people, they have to be able to believe it. People can believe these stories because they have already lived them. Technology had already taken over our lives. Maybe not in the form of robots or artificial intelligence or great machines, but in other ways that you are all familiar with."

Delacroix went on to describe his image of the modern world as it had existed before the attacks. It was a world where people got their morality from television and the media. Where what one bought and who one voted for and even what one believed in was a function of how much someone else had spent on advertising. A world where a single person could hamstring billion dollar companies with a computer virus, where most people measured their value as human beings by how expensive their car was and how big their house was and how many electronic gadgets they could fill it with. It was a world, Delacroix said, where we could fly to the other side of the earth in a day or fly to the moon, but we could not prevent the destruction of our environment. A world where most of the fortunate people spent their time worrying about how to get rich or richer while the unfortunate worried about how to get food for their children. A world where celebrity gossip always made the news each day while torture, human trafficking and genocide went virtually unnoticed. A world so full of inventions and electronics and gadgets, and yet so empty of meaning that people have to find their happiness in bottles of alcohol or pills. Finally, he said, it was a world that had the intelligence to design weapons of incredible power—biological, chemical and nuclear—more devastating than the world had ever seen, but which had not developed the wisdom to refrain from building them and using them on one another.

"Over the last few weeks I have spoken with many of you," he said, sweeping his eyes across the hall. "Many of you mourn the loss of this world, but I see things differently. I believe God has given us a second chance. We do not need to mourn for those who have died or will die in the days ahead, for those who are justified will be waiting for us in the Kingdom of God. But we who remain, those of us who are among God's chosen, who received the word of his prophet Asha Zendik, have been spared. I do not know what lies in store for us, but I know that we are seeing the twilight of humanity as we know it. Perhaps we will remain here until the final Judgment Day, or perhaps we are meant to start the world afresh, like Noah after the Great Flood. The Prophet said something similar when I spoke to him last, just before the bombs began to fall. Will it be a new world or will we be helping to create the Kingdom of Heaven here on earth? If we are strong in our beliefs and faithful to our God, perhaps," he paused and surveyed the congregation. "Perhaps there will not be any difference."

The magister then asked people to come up and contribute and Hyle watched the process with interest. The first to contribute was a man who offered himself as an example of someone who had placed material success above all else, ultimately costing him his family through divorce. A woman stepped up onto the dais next and contributed her appreciation of living together closely with so many other good people and having the time to really work with them and get to know them. When she had finished a scattering of arms rose into the air. Delacroix scanned the room, but did not call on any of them. Instead he called on Hyle.

The first time Delacroix asked him up, gesturing toward the "bullpen," Hyle tried to politely decline. The second time the magister's voice and expression changed only slightly, but it was clear that he was not making a request.

"You better go," Newman whispered, but Hyle was already getting up.

Sophia squeezed his arm as he stood. Without looking back, Hyle circled around to the two steps up onto the dais and then stepped up again into the box. He faced the magister and put his hands on the railing, bracing himself physically in preparation for the questions he knew were coming.

The magister invited Hyle to share examples of how technology had caused problems in his life. There was a long silence while Hyle considered how to answer. He was concerned that Delacroix might be trying to draw him into a debate about technology. Perhaps the old man even knew of his history as a science writer.

"I can't really think of any at the moment," Hyle responded carefully.

"Come now, Hyle," the magister said. "You must be able to come up with some examples of why we're better off without technology."

Hyle took the bait. He replayed Delacroix's comment about not trying to change what should not and could not be changed and realized that he would probably not change anyone's mind, but he could not play along. A sea of smiling faces awaited his response.

"I'm not convinced that we are better off without technology."

Delacroix looked slightly surprised, but his eyes sharpened quickly.

"I would like to converse with you about this, Hyle. What did you think of the sermon you just heard?"

"I thought there were some valid points and I wouldn't argue with any of the examples, but I think they illustrate how people can make bad choices and let things ruin their lives, not why technology is inherently evil. The same argument could be made about money—'the root of all evil' as the saying goes. People can become obsessed with money and let it ruin their lives or drive them to do immoral things. On the other hand money can be used to feed the hungry, provide medicine to the ill and build churches or," Hyle added before he had a chance to think about what he was saying, "cities in the wilderness as refuges against nuclear attacks."

"Human weakness can surface in many different ways," the magister agreed, "and certainly technology has been used for some good purposes, but I detect a stronger anxiety behind your comments, Hyle."

Delacroix waited and watched Hyle patiently for a response. Hyle recognized this technique from his last discussion with the old man, except this time Hyle knew he could not try to outlast Delacroix without making himself look obstinate.

"Anxiety may be too strong a word, but there's something I don't understand. I can appreciate that people can get carried away by the pursuit of worldly things like money, power and material possessions, and that probably applies to technology too, but to me technology is just a collective name for tools. Even something as simple as a hammer is a piece of technology and you can use a hammer to build a new school or attack your neighbor, but that doesn't make the hammer good or evil. It seems that there's a specifically anti-technology agenda, and I don't understand why."

"Yes, we do have an agenda, as you call it," the magister confirmed. "It sounds like you consider it wrong to have an agenda, but an agenda is just a purpose, and anyone who does not have a purpose is wasting their life. Our agenda comes from the teachings of the Prophet Asha. All the material things you listed can distract us from God, but technology is particularly insidious because it seems to be beneficial while it slowly erodes our connections to each other and to God. It is exactly those connections we seek to reestablish here in Asher, and that is why we have consciously and willingly given up all of our modern technology."

This answer did not satisfy Hyle. He considered briefly doing what he knew would be wisest and conceding the point, but he could not bring himself to stay silent.

"Technology doesn't just seem to be beneficial—it *is* beneficial," Hyle asserted. He turned toward the congregation as he spoke to see if anyone was sympathetic to his views. "So far it has been nice living here, like an extended retreat, but what will happen if there's a fire, like the Great Fire of London or the Chicago Fire? As everyone is pumping away at the hand pumps and throwing buckets of water on twenty foot high flames, that's when you'll miss civil engineers, pressurized town water and fire hydrants. It's just past summer now. What will happen in the winter when you find out how poorly a fireplace warms a house and half of the population dies of some epidemic as happened to the Pilgrims at Plimoth Plantation? Then you'll miss your central heating and you'll appreciate the vaccines and antibiotics you take for granted. And when the crops fail as they did in the Irish potato famine? You'll have no transportation to leave or to bring food in. I do understand that technology can cause problems, but I think it's a mistake to think of only the bad aspects without considering the true benefits as well."

"Those aspects of technology that you describe Hyle are beneficial to save property and life," replied Delacroix. "But the purpose of life is not to preserve our possessions, or even to merely extend our lives. Quantity of life should not be mistaken for quality of life. People of faith are not afraid to die when it's their time. If we have a fire, plague or famine we will count on God to see us through or take us as He will. In contrast, look to your own examples to see the effects of technology. Where have you put your faith Hyle? In civil engineers and central heating and vaccines, or in God?"

Delacroix paused, giving an opportunity for a response, but Hyle chose to remain silent.

"This is the problem with technology. It pretends to be our friend, but it changes all of our values. We have sent a man to the moon, we have learned how to manipulate genes and make babies in a test tube, we have created machines and taught them to think, it's no wonder we feel like we don't need God anymore. We feel as though we are the gods in control of our universe. But obviously we missed something along the way. Look where we ended up. While our minds were racing forward, our souls lagged far behind. Where has all our technology gotten us? We can cure diseases and split atoms, but we cannot master the simple things like basing our lives on humility and love instead of competition and desire."

Again the magister paused to give Hyle a chance to speak, but Hyle knew there was nothing more to be said. He waited, watching Delacroix, wondering where the discussion would end.

"Our mission Hyle has been to help people to understand the Prophet's message, to give up their false gods—money, power and especially technology—to cast these things off and look at the world around them in a different light, to see their relationship with nature, the universe and God the way it was meant to be, unmasked and pure. Those who received the Prophet's message came here to Asher to escape the modern world for a week so that they could find the real world that lay beneath it. But things have changed now. That modern world has been ripped apart, people decimated by biological and nuclear weapons, symbols of that very technology we came here to escape. Now we have a new mission. We will live here until the time is right, until the world is ready for us. Then we will go back out there once more and help lift humanity out of the ashes. We will show the survivors how to live a life of quality. A life of love and service to God. A life of purpose and of value. We will convince them not to resurrect the old false Gods, or to think of themselves as new gods, but to find God in themselves."

The magister looked at Hyle sharply.

"Do you understand our agenda now?"

Hyle nodded.

"Good, then I must ask you a question. Knowing now what we stand for, do you believe your place is truly among us?"

This was the question Hyle had been waiting for and yet it took him by surprise. He had expected things to unfold differently. He stood there thinking, his jaw clenched. He glanced down at Sophia and nodded slowly. The people near the front began to clap, but Delacroix held out his hands and the sound quickly subsided.

"As you know, Hyle, we are a community of faith. If you are to live among us, I must ask you another important question. Do you believe in God, our Lord and Creator of all?"

Gripping the railing with sweaty hands, Hyle fought to breathe as his thoughts spun. He looked down at Sophia again and almost smiled as an image flashed into his mind of Sophia jumping up and yelling "your Honor I object!" This was certainly not the "belief in a higher power" that she had cited from the Union of Faith's charter and her face held a clear expression of surprise and betrayal. Yet Delacroix's question stood and a jury of thousands sat waiting quietly for his response. Hyle thought about possible versus necessary beings and the impossibility of creating something from nothing. He thought about the Unmoved Mover and the First Cause, about Roscelin and the nominalists and what the words God and gods and Creator meant. He thought about the secret room he had discovered below the warehouse. He looked down at Sophia one more time. She sat motionless, barely breathing, her eyes unblinking fixed on him.

"Yes," Hyle replied, still looking at Sophia.

He mumbled something afterwards, but it was lost in the swell of applause that filled the room. Delacroix smiled slightly and nodded toward the crowd as they clapped. It struck Hyle suddenly that the congregation was not clapping for him. They were applauding their magister and spiritual leader who had, in their eyes, saved another soul from the evils of the modern world. He watched the old man for a moment with a reluctant admiration before stepping down from the platform.

CHAPTER THIRTY-THREE

BETWEEN FAITH AND REASON

Torrential rain greeted the people leaving Unity Hall. A crowd gathered inside the open doors, watching the wind whip the rain down in blinding sheets, hoping that the storm would let up. A steady stream of the bravest and most impatient people filtered through the throng and disappeared from sight, swallowed by the downpour before they reached the bottom of the steps. Sophia hesitated at the door but Hyle pulled his hood up and stepped out the door without slowing. Trading glances, Newman and Sophia hurried after him. The steady hiss of rain and the poor visibility made conversation impossible, but the few glances Sophia got of Hyle's expression convinced her that this was for the better.

Inside Newman's house, Joel and Rachel, who sat at the table playing a card game with their children, watched the trio sympathetically as rivulets of water ran from their saturated clothes onto the floor. Rachel instructed the boys to fetch some blankets while Joel put a few more logs on the fire. After stripping off their outer clothes and wrapping themselves in the dry blankets, Newman pulled three chairs over to the hearth.

"Come on boys," said Rachel after looking at Hyle's serious expression. "Let's go finish this game in our room."

Sophia watched as Joel herded the youngsters into their room and closed the door behind his family.

"What's the matter?" she asked as soon as she heard the door latch.

"Delacroix," responded Hyle. "I really don't think he wants me here. That anti-technology sermon and asking me to come up afterwards—that was designed to show me in front of everyone that I don't belong here."

"Hyle," Newman said quietly. "You may be right that the magister picked that topic with you in mind, but I wouldn't look at it so cynically. He told me that if you were to stay here he wanted to make sure that there was no doubt that you were meant to be here. It makes perfect sense to me to get all the issues out in the open before asking you to make your final decision. That's exactly what the magister did, and you still decided to stay."

"We didn't get all the issues out," Hyle said, staring into the flames. "Not by a long shot."

"What do you mean?" Sophia asked anxiously.

"It seems to me that this anti-technology agenda is emblematic of a larger issue. There's a tendency here toward anti-intellectualism in general. I see it in Delacroix and most of the people in Asher and I think it's a natural part of organized religion. Anyone who asks you to take something on faith is also asking you to a certain extent not to think about it too much. It's always been that way with religion."

"How can you say that after we spent so much time talking about Aquinas last night?" protested Newman. "His comprehensive theology was probably the single greatest intellectual undertaking of the Middle Ages and one of the greatest of all time."

"I stand corrected. The Church tolerates intellectualism as long as it's directed at rationalizing Church doctrine."

"But the Church wasn't just focused on theology," argued Newman. "The university system as we know it today grew out of cathedral and monastery schools. You know thatt was the Church that founded the University of Paris, Oxford, and Cambridge, among others? In addition to theology, these universities offered studies in the arts. They had the *trivium* of grammar, rhetoric and logic and the *quadrivium* of arithmetic, geometry, astronomy and music. The Church was actually the sponsor of higher learning in the Middle Ages."

Hyle responded to this argument with a dismissive shrug.

"And," Newman continued, "around the same time Aquinas was researching Aristotle at the University of Paris, you have Roger Bacon at the University of Oxford doing work in mathematics, optics and astronomy, and emphasizing the importance of experimentation and observation. Even before that Robert Grosseteste was laying the foundation for Bacon."

"That wasn't the intention though," noted Sophia. "Study of the arts was supposed to prepare students to better understand and teach theology, but some students and faculty became interested in these topics for their own sake. Aristotle had become such a renowned authority that in some universities there were even conflicts between the school of arts and the school of theology. Ultimately radical Averroists like Siger of Brabant at the University of Paris, argued that theology and the arts could be pursued as separate endeavors without trying to reconcile them."

"Of course that's exactly what Aquinas did, right?" said Newman. "He reconciled Aristotle with theology."

"True, but that great theological project helped bring an end to the age of great theological projects that tried to integrate classical philosophy. Aquinas was the last great systematic theologian."

"What about Saint Bonaventure?" suggested Newman. "He was a contemporary of Aquinas."

"Maybe," Sophia replied, "but as an Augustinian, he was at a big disadvantage. Augustine is rich in imagery, but short on detail."

"But Bonaventure expanded on the theology of Augustine," Newman objected. "For example, he introduced the idea of exemplars—pure ideas that exist in God's mind as a template for things in the material world. God makes these exemplars available to us through his incarnation. As an exemplar, Jesus Christ gives us a chance to see into the mind of God."

"Like the right triangle," Sophia noted. "That does expand on Augustine a bit, but doesn't really explain how it works."

"That's where divine illumination comes in. Similar to the ideas of Plotinus or Al-Farabi, Bonaventure pictured divine illumination as an eternal light flowing down from God, making it possible for us to gain insight into the divine mind."

"There are a couple problems with that explanation though," said Sophia. "According to Aristotle, when our intellect understands something, our mind takes on that form, in a sense becoming the same as that which is understood. That would mean that as we receive divine illumination, our mind becomes identical with the forms of the divine mind and we become the same as God. That's a bit more than most theologians were willing to consider."

"That's why Bonaventure pictured divine illumination coming to us indirectly, like reflected light," Newman pointed out. "Although I agree it's not the most convincing solution."

"Another problem is that, in contrast to Augustine's view of the mind actively seeing knowledge, divine illumination is passive," said Sophia. "There's not much use for the human intellect in the process."

"But Bonaventure believed that in order to receive divine illumination a person must prepare through prayer, meditation and the exercise of virtues—not unlike Al-Farabi's criteria for a prophet."

"I suppose you could make the case that Bonaventure was the last great Augustinian to offer an alternative to Aquinas," allowed Sophia, "but in the end scholars were more attracted to Aristotle. It probably didn't hurt that Aquinas took a half step away from Augustine, arguing that although we still need divine help to understand God, the agent intellect is within us. In Aristotle remember, forms don't have independent existence. They co-exist within material things, like the form of the oak tree within the acorn. Aquinas applied this idea to humans, saying that the human soul was a form that conferred upon us the characteristics of living things, including our senses and intellect. In other words, he believed that the agent intellect was bestowed upon us by God from the beginning. This was a more naturalistic and autonomous view of the soul and the intellect than most theologians had previously suggested."

"Yes, I can see the appeal," Newman said. "I can see why Aquinas may have helped undermine the Augustinians, but how did he bring about the end of his own theology?"

"The Augustinians may have lost the intellectual battle in the thirteenth century, but they won the political war," Sophia replied. "They believed that many of the ideas of Aristotle contradicted scripture and Bonaventure made a point to quote Augustine in arguing that the rebel angels teach one to study science rather than sanctity. Bonaventure accused the Averroists of trying to teach a 'double-truth.' Four years before the deaths of Aquinas and Bonaventure, the Church issued the Condemnation of 1270, prohibiting the teaching of several ideas of Aristotle at the University of Paris. Seven years later another condemnation expanded the list of forbidden Aristotelian topics to over two hundred. The Condemnations were aimed mainly at the Averroists like Siger of Brabant, but included some ideas from Thomas Aquinas as well."

"I can see how that would put a stop to Aristotelianism," Newman accepted, "especially if a moderate like Aquinas made it on to the list. But then why didn't Augustinian Neoplatonism flourish again?"

"The success of Aquinas in integrating Aristotle with Christian theology put the last few nails in that coffin to such an extent that the next generation of Franciscans— Bonaventure's own order—completely abandoned the idea of divine illumination. Freed by Aristotle's logic from the blind adherence to Plato and by Church decree from Aristotle, the theologians of the next century were able to follow their own path. As a Franciscan, Duns Scotus carried on the fight against Aristotle, picking apart many of the arguments of Aquinas with meticulous logic. Another Franciscan, William of Ockham, took the ideas of Scotus even farther, stepping farther away from Neoplatonism. Ockham became an accomplished nominalist and his arguments were influential in putting the realism versus nominalism debate to rest."

"Is that Ockham of Ockham's Razor?" asked Newman.

"Yes. In fact he formulated that principle to combat realism. His argument was that we don't need to postulate the independent reality of forms in order to explain what we observed in the world. Given the choice between two equally valid explanations for something, the simpler explanation should be chosen and entities—such as forms— should not be posited unnecessarily. That principle is now known to us as Ockham's Razor."

"Interesting, I had heard of the principle but never knew the history behind it," said Newman. "I think you've also given me clarity on some of the events that happened after Aquinas and Bonaventure."

"Like what?" asked Sophia.

"Like the surge in mysticism and the Protestant Reformation."

"What exactly do you mean by mysticism?"

"Good question," Newman acknowledged "I meant the Christian tradition of making a direct connection with God. Mystics typically teach that by abandoning the material world and focusing on the soul one can unite in some way directly with God."

"That sounds like Magister Delacroix's sermons," observed Sophia.

"It does," agreed Newman. "Mysticism is a part of every religion though, and mystics go back to origins of Christianity with figures like Origen, Pseudo-Dionysius, and of course Augustine, in the first few centuries AD, up to Saint Bernard in the century before Aquinas and Bonaventure."

"That's Bernard of Clairvaux, right?" asked Sophia. "The one who talked about the 'mystical marriage' of the soul with God?"

"Yes. According to Bernard, we were created in God's image, but we lost aspects of that image after the Fall. Its core is still there in our souls though, obscured by all our materialism and worldly desires. Like Augustine, he believed that by seeking happiness in material things we make ourselves miserable, and our only chance for a happy existence is to abandon these things and rediscover that part of us that's in God's image."

"So what's the connection to the end of systematic theology if there's always been interest in mysticism?" asked Sophia.

"It may have created a vacuum that provided fertile ground for a revival of mysticism," explained Newman, "starting with Meister Eckhardt, who attended the University of Paris right in the wake of the Condemnations. He believed that the Father, Son and Holy Spirit were joined in what he called the Godhead, or the ground of God, and part of our souls shared this same common ground. In other words, a part of our soul was not created by God, but was actually one with God. Eckhardt taught and there should be no other purpose than finding this 'spark,' and because we're distracted by materialism, he encouraged followers to develop 'the highest virtue of disinterest.' It's an approach that I haven't seen anywhere else in Christianity, but shows up in Buddhism and eastern mysticism."

"I noticed you didn't refer to him as 'Saint Eckhardt,'" said Sophia.

"No, despite his caution about avoiding tritheism, he was being investigated for heresy when he died. But Eckhardt was a very popular preacher up and down the Rhine valley in Germany. He influenced a young Martin Luther, who in turn started the Protestant Reformation. Not too long after the Reformation the mystics Saint Teresa of Avila and Saint John of the Cross founded the Order of Discalced Carmelites and Saint Ignatius of Loyola founded the Jesuits."

A log slid off the stack of burning firewood with a thud, expelling a swarm of sparks. As if released from a trance, Hyle, who had been staring silently at the flames as the conversation rambled on, sat back in his chair and turned to Newman.

"You mentioned Luther and the Reformation," he said. "I know Luther tacked up a protest on some church door in Germany, but what exactly was he protesting?"

"Technically it was the selling of indulgences," Newman explained. "But the Church was embroiled in politics and there were a lot of other issues at the time. This was the era in which Machiavelli wrote *The Prince*. The Borgias had produced a string of popes and controlled the Papal States. Pope Julius II launched a campaign to oust the Borgias and also started rebuilding Saint Peter's Basilica, both of which required funding. Simony and selling indulgences were common practices."

"What's simony?" Sophia asked.

"And what's an indulgence for that matter?" added Hyle.

"Simony was the buying and selling of church offices or powers," explained Newman, "and indulgences were basically reduced sentences in the afterlife for sins which had been forgiven. They were given to people for their efforts to repent of sin by some type of charity, prayer or other good works, like donating money. Luther believed that spending money wasn't sufficient as a form of penance, and thought that the Church was overreaching its authority in presuming to choose on behalf of God who would be granted remission of punishment—let alone selling the privilege."

"No wonder people wanted to leave the Church," Hyle said.

"That wasn't Luther's intent though. There were a lot of people who wanted to see reform, but they didn't set out to split from the Church. In fact, many prominent figures of the day, like Erasmus and Thomas More, stayed loyal to the Catholic Church even though they supported reform, and although the legend is that Luther tacked his *95 Theses on the Power and Efficacy of Indulgences* on the door of Castle Church in Wittenberg, it's probably not true. It was a scholarly work that he presented diplomatically to the Church in an effort to change things from within."

"I gather that didn't work so well," Hyle ventured.

"Not really," conceded Newman. "The Pope wrote a rebuttal and the dispute escalated. Erasmus corresponded with Luther, debating points of theology and urging Luther to moderation, but Luther's views were irreconcilable with the Church. The printing press had just recently come into wide use, so the ninety-five theses were reprinted and distributed by reformers and helped turn widespread dissatisfaction with the Church into a movement. Eventually Luther received a warning from the Pope that he'd be excommunicated unless he recanted a long list of his claims. Famously Luther burned this warning publicly and was of course excommunicated."

"What was it that was so irreconcilable about Luther's views?" asked Sophia. "It wasn't just the corruption."

"No, it wasn't. His ideas were different from Church doctrine in many ways." Newman paused to organize his thoughts. "I suppose the major difference had to do with grace and salvation. Where Augustine had looked inward and up for a transcendent truth and Aquinas had looked for a rational basis for faith, the Church dogma of Luther's era may sound more familiar. That was the belief that, since the Fall of Adam and Eve, humans were born with sin, but if one had faith in God and lived a good and moral life one would be saved.

"Yes, that sounds very familiar," agreed Hyle, and Sophia detected a subtlety in his tone that said more than his words.

"In his youth Luther tried to live a perfect life of devotion to earn grace from God," Newman continued, "but of course, being human, he wasn't perfect and in his own mind kept falling short. There are different theories on exactly what changed, but maybe through a revelation from reading scripture, or maybe through the sacrament of penance, Luther realized that God offers the promise of forgiveness and all that's needed to accept it is to have faith in the word of God. *Sola fide*—by faith alone—became the main belief that separated Luther and John Calvin—the other famous Protestant reformer of that era—from the Church. They saw the Church as a human institution, which at best distracted people from scripture and at worst made the claim to speak for God. The Protestant reformers also took issue with humanists like Erasmus and More who believed that free will played an important role in salvation. Luther was very clear that it was only through faith and not through any human endeavor whatsoever, that salvation could be gained. This theology brought the focus back to the scriptures and back to the individual relationship with God, and the Protestant movement spread rapidly through Europe."

"Thank you," Hyle said, nodding slowly and staring into the fire as he spoke. Sophia watched him for a moment, studying his face. He seemed to be lost in thought and perhaps, she thought, also a bit melancholy. For a short time nobody spoke. The rain hissed gently against the roof, all but overcome by the warm whisperings of the flames among the firewood.

"What's the matter, Hyle?" asked Sophia softly when it became clear that something was troubling him.

He gave no indication of hearing the question, although she was certain that he had.

"Why the interest in Luther?" Newman asked, taking a different approach.

Hyle shrugged in response, as if to say that Luther did not really matter. He was trying to decide how to answer Sophia, plotting different conversations in his mind, trying out and discarding words and phrases, finding them all to be insufficient. His gaze shifted from the fireplace to the kitchen, past the cutting table, past the hand pump and basin to the window and beyond. Newman looked from Hyle to Sophia and then excused himself to go change into some dry clothes.

The storm had subsided but rain still peppered the glass, the drops collecting and racing in twisted paths down the pane. There was no more inspiration to be found outside than there had been in the fire and Hyle could not think of anything more eloquent to say than a simple statement of fact. He watched the door to Newman's room close and then turned to face Sophia.

"I've decided to leave Asher," he said. "Tonight."

CHAPTER THIRTY-FOUR

DECISIONS

Insistently the wind howled outside, blowing a spattering of raindrops against the kitchen window and whistling through the cracks as if the storm were searching for a way inside. Sophia stared at Hyle in shock, a torrent of half formed questions flashing through her mind. Her mouth opened and closed again, unable to find the right one to ask. Hyle tried to answer her unspoken question.

"I've been thinking about this for a long time, Sophia. I just couldn't quite bring myself to actually do it," he replied quietly. He watched the continuously shifting pattern of the rain on the glass as he spoke, unable to look at the disappointment and pain that Sophia's face projected. The guilt that filled him when he saw her reaction was slowly giving way to a directionless anger.

"Why?"

"Why couldn't I bring myself to leave?" Hyle responded, the anger breaking through into a scornful laugh. "If you don't know, I probably should have left earlier." His voice was soft, but there was an edge to it.

"No, why do you have to leave?" Her voice was louder, but sounded faltering and feeble in comparison.

"Because I really don't belong here. You helped me to rationalize a belief in God as some abstract first principle, but that's not what people here believe."

Sophia started to protest, but Hyle held up his hand.

"That's not the only reason. There's the anti-intellectualism. There's the fact that Delacroix doesn't want me here. And he's right. Sooner or later I'll try to change something here that I don't like and cause trouble for everyone."

"But this afternoon you told everyone that you wanted to stay," Sophia objected.

"I was afraid to say anything else."

"Afraid?"

Hyle leaned toward her and lowered his voice to a whisper.

"There are some things going on here that I don't understand, Sophia, but I'm not going to take any chances," he explained. "I'm going to leave quietly tonight without telling anyone."

He watched her face and the guilt returned, now accompanied by compassion rather than anger.

"I'd love it if you'd come with me, but I know you're happy here." His voice trailed off.

"What are you afraid of, Hyle?"

"I don't think the walls are here to keep people out, Sophia. I think they're to keep people in." In an urgent whisper he listed some of his reasons for concern, but Sophia shook her head in denial.

"This is crazy, Hyle. I'm sure there are good explanations for these things."

She got up and, wrapping the blanket around her, stepped toward Newman's door as she spoke.

"No, Sophia!" Hyle hissed. He stood up to catch her, but she was already knocking on the door.

When Newman entered the room it was immediately clear to him that the conversation had turned into some sort of serious dispute, so he continued buttoning his shirt and waited for someone else to speak.

"Tell him what you told me," Sophia said to Hyle, but he shook his head and Sophia saw anger flash in his eyes as she spoke. "I know you just wanted to talk to me, but I'm sure he can give you good answers to your questions. I can't. You can trust him."

"As your proctor, Hyle, I'll keep everything you say confidential," Newman assured.

"Even from Delacroix?" Hyle asked rhetorically.

"How about just until tomorrow?" Sophia suggested when Newman seemed to be having difficulty deciding how to respond to the question. Reluctantly Newman agreed, on the condition that keeping the secret would not cause harm to anyone or anything. Sophia looked at Hyle, hoping this compromise would be sufficient, but even after considerable prodding he was not willing to talk to Newman, so she decided to jump start the discussion.

"Hyle has decided to leave Asher," she announced.

Hyle glared at her, but the statement catalyzed the interaction she had hoped for. After Newman asked why and got the same explanation she had, he asked Hyle why this had to be kept secret.

"Because I'm not sure that Delacroix would just let me walk out of here," Hyle told him. "That's why I'm going to leave tonight, while you're keeping your end of this bargain. You can tell him whatever you want tomorrow."

"But you're free to leave whenever you want. Why sneak out at night?" Newman asked.

"I wouldn't expect you to understand. You've been brainwashed into thinking this is the perfect society just like everyone else here. Everyone's happy to do their job. Everyone gets along. I'm sure you can't imagine why anyone would even want to leave."

"You think we have to be brainwashed just because we get along?" Newman shook his head. "That's a pretty sad assessment of human nature."

"No. I think some disagreement and conflict is natural and healthy. This is a cult, Newman. It's a cult to Asha Zendik. Every night you all gather around and start with a prayer to him. Delacroix rules this city because he was appointed by the Prophet Asha. Nobody questions him, and everyone is happy as long as nobody asks any tough questions. You're all so busy 'conversing' and 'contributing' and giving each other 'clarity' and making each other feel good that nobody sees what's going on."

"What is going on?" Newman asked evenly, glancing over at Sophia and fighting back the urge to say something much stronger.

"Where should I start?" Hyle replied. "First of all, I think that Zendik knew about the attacks before they happened."

"Yes, he probably did," Newman agreed. "That's why people are calling him the Prophet Asha after all. He's been warning about the dangers of technology for years and talking specifically about our ability to destroy the world many times over."

"But I mean I think he knew specifically about when and where these attacks were going to happen. Delacroix made it sound like a wonderful coincidence that you were all here, but doesn't it strike you as odd that there was a global nuclear exchange on the same weekend that the Union of Faith happens to have retreats in remote locations all over the world?"

"No, that sounds to me like the attacks were revealed to the Prophet in time for him to schedule the retreats to protect his followers."

"Did he warn his followers that there was about to be a nuclear attack?"

"No, not specifically."

"Why not, if he had a revelation?"

"Maybe the Prophet Asha knew he had to schedule the retreats for that particular weekend, but the reason wasn't revealed to him," Newman suggested. "Or maybe it was just coincidence after all.

"Maybe it was just coincidence that he had radiation pills and bottles of nasal vaccine for the Mumbai Plague lined up for twelve thousand people," Hyle said. "Not to mention a variety of seeds for farm crops."

"Maybe he did know what was going to happen, but it was too late to warn everyone," Newman offered. "Or maybe he didn't think anyone but the faithful would believe him."

"I doubt that. Everything is in mint condition here," Hyle pointed out. "There's no rust, no worn parts, no weathered paint. It looks like most of the city was built this year and that must have taken several months at least. Zendik must have known at least that far in advance, but the Union of Faith has taken great pains to make this just look like an ordinary retreat."

"What are you talking about?"

"How are you going to feed eleven thousand people through the winter?" Hyle demanded. Newman, surprised by the question, shrugged helplessly and said nothing.

"The warehouse is big," Hyle continued, "but that's a lot of people. That building holds maybe two months worth of food, with rationing, but you know what? It's still almost full. How can that be?"

Looking from Newman to Sophia, Hyle smiled inwardly at his first small victory. Unable to propose an answer themselves, they both waited for his explanation, obviously pulled in by the mystery as he had been. They listened raptly as he told them how he had stowed away in the warehouse one night after the door closed and watched Isaac's crew of stockers using the padlocked wheel to roll aside some shelves along the back wall, revealing an elevator shaft. He had crept out and jammed a wad of paper into the lock to prevent it from closing fully and after several hours, once the stockers were finished replenishing the warehouse from below and had gone home for the night, Hyle had opened the lock and explored the secrets below ground. The elevator, he informed them, led down to a complex of large rooms deep underground, some as large as the warehouse itself.

"Most of them were packed with food," he told them. "Why would the Union of Faith build gigantic store rooms for food underground when there's plenty of space above ground for more warehouses?" Hyle felt another surge of satisfaction as Sophia and Newman shrugged and waited for his answer. "I can think of three reasons. First, they didn't want Asher to look like a place ready to survive a nuclear war. Admitting this was all planned months in advance would raise questions about how they knew and why more wasn't done to warn the world or prevent the attacks in the first place. Second, it would allow Delacroix and his trusted crew here to stage their own 'miracle of the lamp' by stretching the food supply to last through the whole winter. Nobody here would question that it was a miracle. You're all God's chosen people after all." The sarcasm was thick in Hyle's voice as he let all of his frustration spill out into this observation. "Third, I believe it was designed to be a fallout shelter if things went worse than expected."

"Just because they made some underground store rooms—" Newman began tentatively.

"Not just some, Newman. These are huge. You could fit the entire population of Asher down there. And it wasn't just food. I also saw antibiotics, barrels and barrels of fuel for lamps and cooking, and guess what else? There was one room with radiation suits and Geiger counters and another with racks of assault rifles and ammunition. Add to that the fact that everything here is human powered too—water pumps, hand carts, even the elevator—designed to operate after EMP. I think your Prophet knew exactly what he was getting you all into."

There was a long silence. Hyle had revealed his most damning evidence and watched Newman and Sophia as they thought through the implications of what he had told them. He recognized on Newman's face the slight scowl of someone in a deep search for ways to interpret information differently to avoid having to accept an unacceptable conclusion. Sophia was harder to read. She also appeared lost in thought, but looked more stunned than disbelieving.

"Now you know why I don't want to tell Delacroix that I'm planning to leave?" Hyle said quietly after some time. "I'm not sure that he'd let me go."

Newman opened his mouth to protest, and that was all the opening that Hyle needed.

"Are you going to tell me I can leave whenever I want? Well I can't. They keep the front gate locked at night."

"For security," Newman managed before Hyle cut him off.

"Security? Is that why you think a religious retreat in the middle of the Maine wilderness needs a huge wall around it?"

"According to Delacroix," Newman answered calmly, "the Prophet Asha is predicting the final battle at the end of days. If this was all planned in advance as you claim, then it would make sense to assure that the city was well stocked and protected."

"That may be part of it," Hyle conceded, "but I'm not talking about the doors being barred from the inside. They were locked. I lifted the bar and there was a lock hidden behind it, and I bet Delacroix has the key. Nobody can leave this place unless he lets them out. And who knows what would happen to somebody after he did let them out. It's another example of things appearing more innocent than they really are."

"Maybe the gates are locked for extra security," Newman said, allowing a hint of defensiveness to creep into his voice. "There's no reason to think that there's something underhanded about it or imply anything bad would happen to anyone who left."

Sophia nodded her head vigorously in agreement.

"Then maybe you can explain some other things to me," Hyle said, savoring the opportunity to argue all of the points he did not dare to bring up with Delacroix. "The guards who patrol the walls—more security to protect the city?"

Newman nodded, but he eyed Hyle suspiciously.

"Why do they live outside the walls then? You never even thought about that before, did you?" Hyle laughed, seeing Newman's expression. "Nobody else has either, and as far as I can tell, nobody interacts with any of the guards. They don't come to unity meetings or eat meals with anyone. They don't ever seem to set foot inside the city."

"The guards aren't members of the Union," Newman explained. "They were hired to provide security."

"But have you noticed that there are no stairs up to the top of the wall? I have walked it full circle. There's no way to get up there from inside. And the inside of the wall is surrounded by nice noisy gravel and well lit with more than a hundred oil lamps. Aside from making it harder to sneak over the wall at night, can you think of any reason to waste so much oil lighting the inside of the wall while everyone should be asleep?"

"Not offhand," Newman admitted, "but there may be a perfectly good reason. The guards are here to protect us, not to stop us from leaving."

"Are you sure? Have you ever talked to them? How do you know what is in their contract?"

"I don't, but I do know that hundreds of people left here as soon as they found out about the attacks."

"Yes, but how far did they get? Since no one's allowed back to Asher after they leave it wouldn't be at all suspicious if nobody ever heard from them again."

"This is ridiculous!" Newman said, shaking his head in disbelief.

"Hyle!" Sophia cut in, "What are you saying? Do you think the Union of Faith would have innocent people killed? Is that what you think?"

"I don't know. On one of my extra weekend shifts I asked around about the people from Madauros Village. Many of them are there, but the rest have disappeared. I'm not sure how deep this goes."

"What do you mean 'how deep this goes,' Hyle?" Sophia demanded.

"Sophia, do you believe me about what I saw under the warehouse?"

Sophia looked at him for several seconds and then nodded slightly.

"I can't imagine that you'd make something like that up," she said hesitantly.

"Then you have to believe that Zendik and the Union knew these attacks were coming long before they happened. Think about what that means. At best, he took advantage of the situation without warning anyone. At worst, he may have somehow had a direct hand in the attacks themselves, but in either case he was willing to let millions of innocent people die to achieve his goals."

"The Prophet Asha isn't responsible for what happened," Newman replied, raising his voice for the first time in exasperation. "This was a nuclear war between political powers. Nobody has anything to gain from something like that!"

"I disagree," Hyle said calmly, trying not to look too smug. "Your Prophet had everything to gain. You heard Delacroix's speech about creating the perfect society here while the world is destroyed and then rebuilding the world in its image. He believes you're destined to help create a new heaven on earth. What if that wasn't just a reaction to some unfortunate events? What if that was the plan all along?"

Sophia started to say something, but Hyle held up a hand and kept talking.

"Wait. Hear me out. Zendik has been preaching about how people have been led astray by materialism and technology and have abandoned their faith. If you were Zendik, and you wanted to fix things, what would you do? Here's one idea. You could isolate the parts that you thought were good and get rid of the rest. Just like weeding a garden. You round up all of the most faithful people you can find, bring them to secluded retreats all over the globe and arrange for the rest of the world to destroy itself in a nuclear war."

"You can't actually believe any of this," Newman insisted.

"Why, Newman? You think it's too crazy? There's a historical precedent. God already did this once before, remember? Remember the story of Noah and the Flood? You believe Zendik is a prophet of God and you believe God wiped out the entire earth once before for exactly the same reasons. Why is this so hard for you to believe? It's exactly what Delacroix says, isn't it? The people here are all God's chosen people, spared from the nuclear war as part of God's plan. Why shouldn't Zendik have had a part in that plan?"

Newman was silent. His dark eyes locked Hyle's with a cold intensity, but it was impossible to tell what he was thinking. Hyle returned the stare for several seconds and then looked away to Sophia.

"Personally I don't believe Zendik is a prophet of anything," he told her. "I think he's the crackpot leader of a dangerous cult. Whether he helped to bring about the nuclear war or not, he and his followers believe there's a final battle coming. With stakes that high, why would he give a second thought to getting rid of a few hundred unfaithful people leaving Asher or the inhabitants of Madauros Village if they threatened his plans? Or someone like me? I'm sure he believes that the members of the Union of Faith are really God's chosen people, but even if he's right I don't think I can stay here if those are the terms."

He took her hands and looked into her face. For the first time the finality of leaving truly registered and he felt his eyes misting over.

"I have to go, Sophia. I appreciate all the time you spent trying to help me to find a place here, but even without all of these suspicions I'm not sure I would have made it. I'm sorry."

She pulled him into an embrace and squeezed him until her arms trembled.

"No, don't apologize. I understand," she whispered. Then after a moment she said, "I promised when we came in here that we'd stick together."

"Sophia, you're happy here. I can't ask you to leave."

"You don't have to ask."

When Sophia announced her intention to leave with Hyle, Newman was too stunned to argue effectively. She reminded him almost apologetically of all the dangers that she and Hyle had faced together in the outside world—something, she explained to him, that he could not appreciate unless he had been out there—and she informed him of the promise she made just before they came into Asher. Newman tried to convince her to stay, but he could see that her mind was made up. In the end he found himself in the same farewell embrace that he had watched a few minutes earlier.

He extended a hand to Hyle and wished him luck. Hyle shook his hand and thanked Newman and then he and Sophia walked out.

As soon as they closed the front door, Newman pulled on his cloak and went to see Delacroix.

CHAPTER THIRTY-FIVE

OVER THE WALL

Outside a light rain was falling through the evening mist as Newman hurried along the path to the magister's cottage, in and out of patches of dense fog, his mind racing to outpace his feet. He had no idea what he was going to say when he got there. In the lantern light long shadows suddenly appeared and retreated back into the haze. When a dark figure, cloaked and hooded, glided quietly by in the opposite direction, it was not only the damp and cold that made Newman shiver.

Upon reaching the cottage Newman still did not know what he was going to say and hesitated just outside the door. He felt like the scrap of cloth that marks the center of a tug-of-war rope, pulled helplessly back and forth. He had made a commitment to the Union of Faith and Magister Delacroix, and in return he had been entrusted with the responsibilities of a proctor. He knew the magister's concerns about Hyle and Sophia, and now with her decision to go, despite all attempts to separate them and to assure that she was happy in Asher, those concerns seemed well founded. On the other hand he had given his word to Sophia not to say anything until the next day, and while he gave no credence to Hyle's conspiracy theory, he was disturbed by some of the things Hyle had discovered.

He turned around to leave, thinking for a moment that he would come back in the morning and report them both missing, keeping his word to Sophia, but he immediately felt like a coward for not facing his responsibility as proctor. He turned back again and knocked on the door. Nathan opened it, looking quite surprised to see him. He took Newman's cloak and ushered him directly into the magister's office.

Delacroix glanced up from a large book on the desk in front of him.

"Newman, please have a seat."

Newman sat down and waited while the old man ran his finger along several more lines of text before closing the book and pushing it to one side.

"Excellent timing, Newman. I was just going to send for you."

The statement caught Newman by surprise, but he felt an immediate wave of relief at the prospect that he might be spared from having to start a discussion that he was still unsure how to approach. His motivation for wanting to let the magister talk shifted quickly from relief to curiosity. Delacroix leaned across the desk. His characteristic smile faded and his blue eyes sharpened.

"I have just learned that Hyle did not come home two nights ago. He spent the entire night out somewhere. Do you know where he was?"

"No," Newman answered truthfully, although he suspected that was the night Hyle had spent in the warehouse and wondered if the magister knew.

"I want you to find out."

Newman breathed a silent sigh of relief. That meant that the magister was not testing him and really did not know where Hyle had been. He nodded his agreement.

Delacroix stared at him for several seconds before speaking again.

"I was a bit surprised at his choice this afternoon. I expected him to leave Asher, but perhaps it is for the better that he has decided to stay." Newman shifted in his chair but said nothing. "I am convinced that he is a danger to the organization. We need to find a way to keep him more isolated. I want you to find out where he was on Friday night. If he was up to something, that may be a good reason to keep him in confinement."

"He expressed some doubts to me about his decision," Newman said, venturing carefully into his reason for coming. "I think we could convince him to leave."

"No. That is no longer an option. He is a danger to our organization. Not just to Asher, mind you, but to the Union of Faith and all that it stands for, just as the Prophet warned. He may be more dangerous out there than here where we can keep an eye on him. Let us hope that the confinement solution works."

"What if it doesn't work?"

The old man looked off toward the wall thoughtfully and did not answer for a long time.

"Let's take things one step at a time," he said at last.

«« »»

Light still flickered in a few windows, but most of the city was asleep by the time Hyle and Sophia reached the wall and crouched in the shadows between two nearby houses. They traveled light. Under his cloak Hyle had concealed a small parcel of supplies that he had smuggled from the warehouse and in his hands he carried a cloth bundle. Beyond that they had only the clothes on their backs. Sophia clutched the base of her hood tight against the cold and watched her breath twist and spiral away, dissolving into the mist. The lanterns of the wall illuminated the fog with an eerie glow that made their light seem almost solid.

"Stay here," Hyle whispered. "I'm going to put out one of the lanterns."

In many evenings of walking along the wall on the way to or from unity meetings Hyle had seen a few instances of lanterns that had gone out and they did not seem to attract any particular attention. Even though the fog reduced visibility considerably, he preferred to climb the wall in darkness. When he reached the wall, midway between two lanterns, Sophia understood why. Although Hyle and the lanterns were obscured, she could see a distinct dark shape moving along the pale concrete wall toward one of the glowing spheres. Then it disappeared, swallowed by a sudden darkness.

When Hyle returned he suggested that they wait for a while to make sure that anyone who might care about such things had time to notice the extinguished lantern, satisfy themselves that nothing else was going on and move along. It was probably overly cautious, he realized, but they had all night to get across the wall and once committed they could not afford to be spotted.

It was not long into their watch when a shadowy figure startled Sophia, materializing only a few houses away. Stifling a gasp, she pulled her head back around the edge of the house and whispered into Hyle's ear what she had seen. Despite his recommendation to wait and watch he was clearly taken by surprise. They both moved back to the corner of the building and peered cautiously out. There was nothing. Puzzled, Sophia pointed in the direction she had seen the shape, shrugged and shook her head in bewilderment. A few seconds later the figure reappeared, stepping out from behind a different house, closer than it had been before. It paused and she could see the hooded head turning slowly toward her, searching the surrounding area. She pulled Hyle back out of sight motioning backwards. They moved along the wall, skirting around a bin for firewood and hid behind it, deep in the shadows, watching and waiting.

Time crept by. Hyle strained to see any signs of movement in the patch of dim light beyond the end of the building. Nothing. He was just entertaining the idea of creeping back up to the corner for another look when a voice behind him froze his heart in mid beat.

"Ah, there you are!" it hissed from only a few feet away.

Sophia gave a muffled gasp and pitched toward the bin as if the sheer force of the surprise had thrown her forward. His heart unfrozen and pounding furiously, Hyle wheeled and stood, ready to defend himself or run. Furtively he slipped one hand into the cloth bundle he carried in case it came to a fight. The figure was barely visible as a dark silhouette.

"I hoped I'd find you nearby when I saw the lantern go out," it said, still in a whisper.

Hyle's hand stopped just inside the first folds of cloth. There was something—

"Newman?" Sophia whispered from beside him.

"Yes. I'm glad I caught you in time."

"In time for what?" Hyle asked. "What are you doing here?"

The shadow was quiet for a moment.

"I'm coming with you."

"What? Why?" demanded Hyle.

"It's a long story," Newman said. He paused, but the silence told him that this was not a sufficient answer. "I don't believe everything you're claiming, Hyle, but I think you may be right to leave without telling anyone."

"That's nice, but it doesn't answer why you want to leave the city."

"After you left, I went to see the magister."

"What? You promised—"

"It wasn't like that," Newman protested. "I didn't break my promise. I didn't tell him anything about your plans."

Newman filled them in on his discussion with the magister and the old man's desire to keep Hyle in confinement.

"Even if I believed you, Newman, that still doesn't answer the question," Hyle insisted, with a hint of annoyance. "In here you made the rules, but once we're over the fence I don't owe you anything. If you want to come with me you'll have to do better than that."

"Hyle!" Sophia hissed in outrage.

He spun to face her.

"What? A few hours ago he was trying to convince us both to stay and now all of a sudden he wants to leave. Why the sudden change of heart? Even if he agrees I should leave, he should be telling us why he wants to leave too. Who is to say he's not going to sell us out as soon as we get outside?"

Sophia could only manage to make a guttural noise, sounding as if she choked on her response.

"If I wanted to turn you in I would have brought the magister," Newman replied evenly. "Or at least a lantern. That would have made it much easier to find you." He paused and sighed. "The reason I want to come is that it's the only thing I can do in good conscience. I promised Sophia that I wouldn't tell anyone that you were leaving until tomorrow, when it'll be too late to do anything about it. I won't break that promise. On the other hand, the magister is clearly worried about letting you go for some reason. Since I won't turn you in, I want to come along to mitigate any damage I may have done by letting you go. And if you're not going to let me come along, you should start thinking about how you're going to stop me from following."

"Hyle?" Sophia asked expectantly after several seconds.

"All right," he said, not sounding entirely convinced. "Let's go."

A few minutes later the three stood at the base of the wall at the edge of the gravel near the extinguished lantern. The nearest lanterns on either side were visible only as hazy points of light in the distance and the wall was only barely discernable above them as the complete absence of light. Hyle unwrapped his bundle by feel, looking down out of habit even though he could not see his hands, and removed his homemade treasure. In an unexpected rush of pride he wished it were lighter so that he could show off his handiwork—a grappling hook fashioned with two bent and crossed pieces of rebar from the school construction site. The arms were wrapped with strips of cloth from a spare blanket to dampen the sound when it struck the concrete of the wall and tied to a long rope. It was not as thick as he would have liked, but it seemed strong enough to hold his weight.

Hyle took a few steps away from Newman and Sophia, let out several feet of rope and swung the hook in a wide circle angled toward the top of the wall. As well as he could time it he released the rope when the grapple reached its apogee. It sailed away into the night and a second later he felt a tug in his other hand which held the end of the rope, followed quickly by a distant thump from the other side of the wall. His excitement growing, he pulled on the rope and was surprised to feel it catch almost immediately. He gave the line a quick shake and pulled again, retrieving about three feet of slack before the line caught once more and he cursed to himself, realizing what had happened. Too smart for my own good, he thought. The knots he had tied at regular intervals to help him climb the rope more quickly were making it more difficult to pull the rope back and tell when the grapple caught, but luck was with him in the end. After a great deal of jiggling the rope to get the knots over the edge of the wall one by one, the grapple caught solidly.

As they had planned, Hyle climbed up the rope first and Sophia held the bottom to keep it taut. Meanwhile Newman searched the darkness at the base of the wall for the extinguished lantern. Once he had retrieved it from its hook he held the rope for Sophia and then followed her up. The visibility was better at the top of the wall where a slight breeze had thinned the fog. High above, the moon appeared as a hazy disk of light fading gradually into a dark gray sky, casting just enough light to make out their surroundings. The top of the massive wall was protected by a narrow chest-high parapet on either side, creating a trench several feet wide for them to stand in, like the battlements of a medieval castle lacking only the crenellation.

When Newman reached the top Hyle immediately pulled up the rope, hung the grapple on the inner edge of the outside extension and pitched the rope over the other side. He had warned that this would be their time of greatest risk. The guards did not seem to have a regular pattern of patrols, but Hyle had seen them walking the circumference of the wall on several occasions. Within seconds of Newman's arrival Hyle was hoisting himself up onto the small parapet. He grunted softly, his arms struggling to hold his weight steady while his legs scrabbled against the concrete trying to get a foot or knee over the top. Precious seconds passed before he was able to pull himself over the top of the wall and drop down the other side.

Newman gave Sophia a leg up and she rolled expertly over the top of the wall and lowered herself down the rope. The few rays of moonlight that penetrated the cloud cover above faded away as she descended into the ground fog. She started when a hand touched her back. Hyle guided her to the ground and she stood in the shadow of the wall, able to see him next to her only as a dark outline. Above them the silence was split by the crash of shattering glass and a loud metallic clatter.

"What did you do?" Hyle hissed when he heard Newman scraping down along the wall a few seconds later.

"The lantern," Newman panted, dropping to the ground. "I lost it coming over the top."

"You warned them!" Hyle snapped.

Sophia knew that Hyle was right to be concerned. The sound would alert the guards and the broken lantern would be a clear sign that someone had been on top of the wall. It was a bad turn of events, but Hyle's tone was accusatory.

"It was an accident," Sophia whispered urgently, trying to diffuse the situation. She heard a snort in the darkness beside her and the soft whistle of a rope being whipped.

"Heads up," Hyle said in a low growl.

The grapple thudded into the ground nearby and Sophia heard Hyle shuffle toward it.

"Sophia, take my hand. Newman, take hers. We have to move fast. Don't lose each other."

Sophia felt for two hands in the darkness and as soon as she had them Hyle was pulling her blindly forward through the wet grass of the meadow. The ground was soggy and uneven and the best they could manage was a fast walk. Even at that pace they stumbled frequently. The first time it was Sophia, who caught her ankle in a small sinkhole in the field and pulled Newman down with her while Hyle kept hold of her hand, immediately helping her back up. Next it was Hyle. He pulled Sophia off balance, and unable to see where he had fallen, she tripped on his feet and fell on top of him. Newman stumbled over her. In the daylight, under different circumstances, it would have been comical, but Hyle cursed in the darkness as they disentangled themselves.

Eventually they learned how to work together, ready to brace each other within a split second, and the stumbles decreased. Sophia kept looking back into the darkness to check on Newman even though she could not see him. But she did see something else.

"Look back," she said, pulling back on Hyle's hand.

Two circles of light bobbed up and down in the distance behind them. They all watched for a moment, hypnotized by the dance of the lights, like will 'o wisps slowly approaching over the misty meadow.

"We must be leaving a trail through the grass," Hyle realized aloud. Three of them trampling down the grass would make their path obvious, and easy to follow quickly with light to see by. "Come on."

He dragged them forward, increasing the pace to a jog. Sophia stumbled right away, but he did not slow, straining to haul her along behind him until she was able to regain her footing.

The lights grew closer.

CHAPTER THIRTY-SIX

INTO THE FOREST

Night had fallen outside the city walls with the full force of nature and the darkness ahead of them was nearly impenetrable. Hyle felt it dragging them down like a ball and chain around his ankles. The scant moonlight that made it through the cloud cover allowed them only to see a few paces ahead, and only then with more concentration than the vague outlines were worth. The only useful light came from behind them, closing quickly.

"They're still gaining," Sophia panted.

"There are only two of them," Newman suggested from the back of the chain.

"Only two lights," Hyle corrected between breaths. "Could be more guards. And they have assault rifles. Not good odds."

The field seemed to stretch on forever. Hyle looked back over his shoulder more frequently, assessing how long they had before they were overtaken and considering their options as they ran. They could not go any faster without stumbling or losing each other and without light they could not hope to outrun the guards. Fighting seemed like a last resort, but it was starting to look like the only possibility. Maybe Sophia could continue in a straight line, trampling as much grass as possible, while he and Newman jumped off the trail to either side and surprised the guards as they passed. He checked back over his shoulder again. The lights were less than a minute from reaching them. It was time to act. As he opened his mouth to suggest the plan, something struck from the blackness ahead.

Stifling a yell, Hyle tore his hand away from Sophia and thrust his hands up, swinging them wildly from side to side in front of him to ward off whatever was grabbing at his face and arms. Sophia slammed into him from behind and gasped as she felt something brush against her face. Forewarned by his reaction, she was less surprised than Hyle and recognized more quickly what had happened. It was a long terrifying second of panic before rational thought caught up with primal response and Hyle realized that he was not being attacked. He had run headlong into the branch of a tree. Groping backwards for Sophia's hand, he led her onward.

"Duck," he whispered loudly as he stooped to pass under the branch.

As he plowed ahead Hyle was relieved to feel more branches whipping at his face and clutching at the arm he held out defensively ahead of him. They were entering the forest and the tall grass of the meadow, which held such clear evidence of their trail, gave way to a carpet of pine needles. Hyle cut to the left, guiding Sophia under branches and around tree trunks. The lights, which had been so close, began to blink out intermittently behind the dark trunks of trees, becoming more and more obscured until they disappeared altogether.

"Wait. I have to catch my breath," Newman said.

"Don't stop," Hyle advised, dropping his pace to a slow walk. "You won't be able to get going again."

The canopy filtered out the last rays of moonlight as they angled deeper into the forest. They moved into total blackness. With a sudden shiver Sophia recalled the time she had spent trapped in her basement, the only other time she had experienced a darkness so complete and inescapable. Before the attacks there had always been light from somewhere—houses, streetlights, cars, moonlight—even in her bedroom light filtered in around her drawn shades to join the glow from her alarm clock and the indicator lights of various electronic devices. She closed her eyes and opened them again. There was no difference and a wave of panic washed over her as if she had been buried alive by the darkness. Unnerving as it was, Sophia forced herself to appreciate the irony. In the open forest, in the middle of the Maine wilderness, she felt claustrophobic.

Closing her eyes, Sophia tried to make a game of it, focusing on her other senses. She inhaled the cool air deeply, savoring the evergreen scent and listened past the whipping branches and the labored breathing around her to hear the soft pad of their footfalls on the forest floor. And something else.

"What's that?" she asked, pulling back on Hyle's hand. "Listen."

A long silence followed. Hyle was just opening his mouth to say he did not hear anything when he did catch something in the distance. There was something familiar about the random pattern of low sharp sounds.

"Dogs!"

Sophia felt Hyle pull his hand free. There was some soft rustling, a metal scrape and suddenly they were blinded by a brilliant light. It was like looking into a flash bulb, but quickly faded to reveal a small flame at its center. Hyle held a small lighter to his chest.

"We're going to have to risk using this now and make a run for it."

Without waiting Hyle set off at a fast jog, the best pace he could manage, holding the lighter out to one side as he twisted and bobbed around trees and branches. The flame flickered wildly, giving them uneven glimpses of the forest ahead between instants of near blindness. The baying grew loud enough to hear again over the sounds of their flight.

"We can't outrun dogs," Newman said from the back.

Sophia was relieved to hear the effort it took Newman to make this observation. Her lungs were burning and her legs felt like rubber. She was even more grateful to hear Hyle's reply.

"I know," was all he was able to say, but his voice was confident, not desperate as she had expected.

A few minutes later she found out why when they reached the edge of a river. Hyle plunged straight in but Sophia hesitated on the bank.

"Does this trick even work in real life?" she asked skeptically, eyeing the water and wondering how cold it was. The river was low and wide and slow moving. Small rocks and huge boulders jutted up above the surface, just too far apart to provide a dry crossing.

"Sure," Newman said next to her. "It washes away your scent."

"Only one way to find out," said Hyle, apparently not hearing. He turned and started walking downstream, bringing the light with him. Sophia took a deep breath and stepped in. Icy water poured into her shoes. The water was only a foot or two deep, but after a few splashy steps she was soaked from the waist down.

After several minutes the river turned a gentle bend. Hyle stopped and let the lighter go out. When Sophia and Newman caught up he pointed to something. In the clearing between the forest on either bank, the perpetual overcast was once again visible, backlit by the moon. Framed against it was a mountain. A third of the way up the shadowy form a tiny point of light moved across it.

"Good thing we didn't take the road out of here. That's moving too fast to be people on foot," Hyle said, and paused to catch his breath. "If we follow this river, it should cross the highway sooner or later. I think there's enough light now that we can get back up on the bank and travel without the lighter."

With the dogs closing quickly they wasted no time splashing out of the water. Almost as soon as they stepped back onto land and into the cover of the forest a swarm of dark shapes broke from the woods a few hundred yards back along the river. The three fugitives watched from the shadows, anxious to see how well their tactic had worked, knowing that it was their last hope. At first the dogs ran back and forth along the bank barking, but soon their enthusiasm faded. The baying subsided and a couple of them sat down, the rest milling around with their heads to the ground. Their occasional howls of frustration were soon joined by a new sound. It was a high whining noise, very familiar, yet none of the three were able to place it before something exploded into the clearing.

A bright light suddenly illuminated the bank and the whine wound down to a low rumble. Dogs scattered and then began barking again, bounding excitedly around the dark shape behind it. A second light appeared, more slowly than the first, revealing in its path the pack of dogs and the object they surrounded. It looked like a cross between a miniature army jeep and a motorcycle on steroids. On it, between the four oversized knobby tires of the all terrain vehicle sat a man, turned partially around, evidently talking to the rider of the second ATV. He was pointing down the river.

Hyle cursed through his clenched teeth.

"Time to go."

Between the edge of the river and the tree line was a narrow strip of terrain that turned out to be ideal for traveling. It was nearly flat and reasonably well lit. They were able to set a fast pace, jogging for most stretches and occasionally slowing to pick their way through a stand of trees or stretch of boulders. To slow the dogs as much as possible they crossed the river back and forth several times, but traveled always downstream. The baying started up again not too long into their travels, but fell silent after only a few minutes, apparently stalled again at the river.

Several hours later, wet, cold and weary, the trio climbed a small embankment and stepped onto the shoulder of Route 11. They walked south, resting frequently. One car passed by them, the rumble of its engine giving them plenty of time to conceal themselves in the woods before it came into view. Other than that there was no sign of a pursuit. To the east the sky paled and grew orange. It was fully daylight before they found their first house. Two ruts and a narrow gap in the trees were the only indication of a driveway, and even on foot they nearly missed it—a small log cabin, set well off the road down a gentle hill and barely visible through the trees. There was no yard, only a small space where the trees had been cleared away. It was the perfect place to get a few hours of rest.

No one answered the first time they knocked, and after waiting a few seconds Hyle circled around the house peering in the windows. One large room took up more than half the interior. Toward the front were a couple arm chairs and an old television set topped with plastic cups and a beer bottle. A vinyl card table accompanied by a pair of mismatched chairs and stacked with more cups and bottles occupied the center of the room and a small kitchen area filled out the back corner. Two doors led to other rooms. Through one of them a bed was plainly visible. The other was small and dimly lit, presumably a bathroom. It appeared to be a summer cabin, so Hyle was taken aback by what he found behind it.

A large Quonset hut of corrugated aluminum sat about fifty yards away from the back of the cabin at the edge of a large clearing. A battered yellow plow angled out of the shadows. Behind the plow was an equally battered old pickup truck. The unfinished strips of tarnished metal that were riveted around the edges of the wheel wells where the rust had devoured the original body were the only signs of maintenance.

Newman and Sophia rounded the corner just as Hyle crossed over to the back door again.

"Nobody home?" Hyle asked, affecting surprise as he twisted the edge of his cloak around his hand.

"No," Newman responded innocently, and then he realized what Hyle was doing. "Hyle, what are you doing? This is someone's house. You can't just break in."

A wry smile spread on Hyle's face. His eyes did not leave Newman's face as he thrust his hand forward, shattering the glass of the back door.

"Don't worry," he laughed, "I'm sure his homeowner's insurance will cover the damage, and when the police come we'll tell them you were not involved. Right, Sophia?" Hyle glanced over at her as he reached through the broken glass and opened the door. She did not seem to appreciate the humor. "There's a truck in that shed," Hyle explained, deflated, and jerked a thumb over his shoulder. "Let's see if we can find the keys."

The interior of the cabin was musty, with a lingering odor of stale beer and cigar smoke. Newman entered reluctantly, stepping carefully over the shards of glass. The point of Hyle's joke had not been lost on him. This was no longer the world he left behind when he traveled to Asher. The old rules no longer applied. Still, breaking into someone's house felt wrong and the whole unspoken argument behind it made him uneasy. There was only one place for that type of thinking to lead in the end. He pushed the concern from his mind and began opening drawers in the kitchen.

A few minutes of searching established that the keys were not inside. The spartan furnishings provided few hiding places.

"I'm going to see if I can figure out how to hotwire it," Hyle announced after giving up on the search. Looking at Newman, as if reading his mind, he added, "Hotwiring, breaking and entering, grand theft auto—you're running with the bad boys now."

Newman was too tired for an argument. He made a feeble attempt at a smile and kept quiet.

"I thought we were going to rest here," Sophia protested.

"With dogs and ATVs behind us, we have to get further away."

"Hyle, we lost them long ago—"

"Maybe, but it won't take a genius to figure out that we followed the river to the highway, and put the dogs back on our trail again. And they can move a lot more quickly than we can."

Sophia opened her mouth to speak but did not get the chance.

"You think I'm being paranoid? That's what you thought back in Asher." Hyle snapped, immediately regretting how harsh his words had sounded. He was fighting exhaustion too and wanted nothing more than to lie down and take a nap. "I just won't rest easy until we're farther away," he explained apologetically.

"I don't need to rest easy, I just need to rest," Sophia said.

"Why don't you take a nap while I work on the truck?"

Sleep came quickly to Sophia. She fell into the bed, wet clothes and all, and was already drifting out of consciousness by the time Newman flopped down beside her. A loud noise woke her. She lay still, listening and staring absently up at the unfinished pine beams and the points of nails that protruded through the sheathing of the roof in small bursts of splinters. Gradually she became aware of a low rumble and then a few seconds later a roaring sound. As her thoughts became clear enough to get her bearings, she realized it was coming from the back. The truck, she thought with a wash of relief, and allowed herself to drift back to sleep.

The next time Sophia awoke, it was again a sound that had startled her. She had no sense of time. It might have been minutes or hours since hearing the truck start. Her mind, still saturated with sleep, decided that it must have been minutes and dismissed it as the same sound, but as she sank back toward unconsciousness, something felt vaguely wrong. The noise sounded far away. Had Hyle left, she wondered, with a detached curiosity as sleep tried to reclaim her thoughts. He'll be back. With that comforting thought she stopped fighting to stay awake. Then, as if the lights had been switched on in a dark room, she realized that this was a different sound. Sitting bolt upright in bed she strained to hear and almost immediately her fears were confirmed. The sound of dogs baying.

Newman's awakening was more traumatic. He had been in a deep sleep when Sophia woke him by yelling while simultaneously hauling him out of bed by one arm. She had dragged him to his feet and out of the bedroom before he heard the sound of the dogs and small engines approaching and comprehended what was going on. While Sophia threw open the back door, he dashed back into the bedroom to grab his waterlogged socks and shoes. It had seemed like a good idea to take them off when he went to sleep.

Inside the cab of the truck Hyle was sleeping fitfully. Earlier he had popped out the ignition cylinder and traced the wires back to the starter. With a little trial and error he had been able to get the right wires crossed and the starter turned over. The truck did not start up right away. It stalled on the first two attempts. The third time, by giving it just the right amount of gas, Hyle had been able to coax the engine to life and let it run until he was sure it was not going to stall. Satisfied that they had the transportation they needed, he rewarded himself by putting his head back to rest his eyes for a few minutes before collecting Sophia and Newman.

Hyle woke with an immediate sense of dread, knowing that he had fallen asleep. Sophia was pounding on the window. And he heard dogs. Not the distant baying they had heard the night before. This was the frantic barking of dogs that had found their quarry, coming from the other side of the cabin. Sleep was replaced by a surge of adrenalin. He twisted the wires together and fluttered his foot on the accelerator as Sophia slid onto the seat beside him. The starter cranked, the engine coughed several times and the truck shuddered. The engine stalled.

"Just like old times," Hyle joked, responding to Sophia's look of panic. "Hey, where's Newman?"

The starter continued to crank and Hyle tapped the gas pedal feeding the struggling motor more fuel.

"I don't know," Sophia said. "He was right behind me."

The engine roared to life. Hyle revved it twice and shifted into gear. Then things began to happen all at once. As the truck cleared the edge of the garage, Hyle and Sophia could see the back door of the cabin bouncing shut and Newman running gingerly toward them across the clearing, his shoes in his hands. A single dog came bounding around the far corner of the cabin, spotted Newman and accelerated toward him. Meanwhile in front, several dogs clustered at the front step of the cabin. They were barking excitedly, rearing up and scratching at the door. The first ATV came to a stop just off to one side of the ruts that passed for a driveway and the rider dismounted, slipped his assault rifle down from his shoulder and advanced slowly to the front of the cabin. The second rider was halfway down the driveway when the sound of an engine starting somewhere behind the cabin brought him to a stop.

Newman heard the dog snarling behind him. Not looking back, he accelerated toward the bed of the truck and dove in head first, flinging his shoes ahead of him and planting his hands on the sidewall to help him vault over it. As he swung one leg over, he felt powerful jaws clamp onto his other one. Teeth ground against the bone of his bare ankle. There was a brief tug of war as he tried to wrench his leg free and pull it into the truck while the dog threw its weight backwards and shook its head from side to side in an effort to pull him back out.

Seeing Newman's plight in the wide side view mirror, Hyle maneuvered the truck toward the back corner of the cabin as they approached it at increasing speed. He miscalculated, coming closer than he intended. The corner of the plow clipped the trim, tearing one of the boards free and an instant later the side mirror was torn off with a screech and an explosion of glass. The side of the truck scraped against the corner of the cabin before Hyle could pull away again and Newman's leg slammed into it hard. So did the dog. It collided head first with the back wall of the structure and released Newman's leg with a yelp.

In the driveway ahead Hyle could see two ATVs. The closest one was pulled off to one side toward the cabin. Its rider, in a dark jumpsuit and a closed full face helmet, stepped out in front of his vehicle holding an assault rifle. The other, with its rider still on it, was several dozen yards back. Hyle tugged on the wheel and swerved to the left toward the first figure. The man jumped easily out of the way as the truck sped by, but he was not the target. Glancing up off a tire, the plow blade caught his ATV solidly on the handle bars. The machine was dragged briefly and went spinning sideways out of the path of the truck. The second rider, seeing the plow bearing down on him, and stuck in a section of the driveway where the trees were too dense for his vehicle, abandoned his machine and dove for cover between some trees. The plow hit the second ATV head on, sending it somersaulting up the path. It flipped over, bounced off a tree and spun back into the path of the oncoming truck. The plow hit it again, pushing it on its side the rest of the way up the driveway to the pavement.

The view from the back was more worrisome. Newman felt a searing pain from the lower part of his left leg but did not have time to look at it. The corner of the house had caught it with great force, breaking the dog loose, flinging his leg into the bed of the truck and sending him sprawling. He was just pulling himself up to his hands and knees when the impact with the first ATV jolted the truck and knocked him flat again.

When he did manage to get to his knees, Newman saw that the dogs had abandoned the doorstep and were running through the woods beside the truck, looking for a chance to get close. The rider of the first ATV was running up the driveway after them, holding an assault rifle in one hand and pumping his arms furiously. The truck sped up again, but not quickly enough. Their pursuer had covered most of the distance that separated them and was still overtaking the truck even as it accelerated. He lunged forward to grab the tailgate with one hand and swung his weapon toward Newman with the other. Then came the big impact as the plow rammed into the second ATV.

The man had started to yell something, but Newman never heard what it was. The words were cut off in the first syllable as the truck lurched almost to a halt. Newman went reeling backward into the cab once more, but the pursuer, caught completely by surprise, slammed into the back of the truck at a full run. The tailgate caught him just under the ribs, freezing him in place, but his assault rifle continued to travel forward, clattering into the bed of the truck and sliding toward the cab. For a moment as the truck pulled away the man hung motionless as if suspended in air before collapsing to his knees and doubling over.

A shower of sparks flew up from the ATV as it skidded across the highway in front of the plow until the truck veered right and straightened out onto the road. Howling and barking, dogs poured out from the woods, quickly overtaking the truck. They leapt up along the sides of the vehicle, growling at Newman but unable to reach him. One dog jumped from the back and managed to hook its front legs over the tailgate. It scrabbled to get a purchase on the bumper with its back legs and propel itself into the bed. Newman grabbed one of his shoes and struck the animal with such a rapid succession of blows that it gave up and dropped back onto the highway. A few seconds later the last dog gave up the chase and stood in the middle of the highway howling after them in frustration.

PART III

Enlightenment
Ghosts in the Machine

CHAPTER THIRTY-SEVEN

REVOLUTIONS

Above the highway the sun burned fiercely behind its veil of clouds. The light brought out silver and blue hues among the dark pines that covered the rolling hills. Scattered through the forest were islands of deciduous trees, sometimes adding an isolated splash of color to the otherwise solid green sea of conifers that stretched to the horizon, other times enveloping entire hillsides in the red and yellow confetti shades of autumn foliage. The plow truck sped south along Route 11 and the small gray ribbon of asphalt was the only sign of human intervention as far as the eye could see.

Looking back through the window of the cab, Sophia watched Newman struggling to pull the leg of his pants up to look at his injury. He noticed her and gave her a thumbs-up and a weak smile, but she could tell he was hurt more then he let on. Below the knee his leg was a swollen mass of blood and purple flesh and his foot and ankle were streaked with red.

A few minutes later they crossed a concrete bridge over a narrow creek and on the opposite side found a place to pull the truck off the road into the woods. Behind the seat Sophia found a small first aid kit and some rags and after examining Newman's leg closely, she scrambled down the embankment to the stream and got some water to wash away the blood. Newman clenched his jaw as she scrubbed the wounds clean. She tried to apply antiseptic cream, but the blood was still flowing too freely, so she slathered it on some gauze pads instead and hastily taped them to the leg in an effort to staunch the bleeding.

Hyle surveyed the procedure with grim satisfaction.

"Now do you believe that I was right to be worried about Delacroix?"

Newman looked up at him, momentarily perplexed, and then looked down at his leg and the assault rifle lying next to him. "Maybe," he replied.

"Maybe? How much more proof do you need? We were just tracked for the better part of a day by armed men on motorcycles with dogs. You said yourself that he was worried about us. It's pretty clear they didn't want us to get away and they were very well prepared to stop us."

"I'll grant you that the magister was concerned about you both, especially you, Hyle, and maybe there were some things going on in Asher that were kept hidden from most people, but we don't know what the magister would have done if you had stayed. Part of the reason I let you go and came along with you instead of telling anyone is that I have my suspicions about the magister too. But you're jumping to conclusions saying that those men were trying to kill us or even keep us from leaving."

"What other conclusion could you possibly come to?" Hyle asked, incredulous.

"If they heard someone on the wall or in the field outside, maybe they thought we were raiders. Maybe they were just tracking us to find out who we were."

"That's really stretching it, don't you think?"

"I don't know," Newman replied evenly. "They didn't use their weapons. If they just wanted to kill us, why didn't they shoot at us?"

Hyle considered this. It was a reasonable question. Perhaps they had been worried about catching each other in the crossfire? He tried to remember where everyone was positioned, but it had all happened too quickly. The question raised the first shadows of doubt, but not enough to change his mind.

"Delacroix talks about preparing for a war and a final battle. If he knew we were leaving, wouldn't he assume that we had gone over to the enemy? Do you think he'd hesitate to kill us? By his logic, if we're the enemy, we deserve to be killed, and if we're with the good guys, we'll go to heaven, so either way it's okay."

"It's not that easy, Hyle. Believing in God isn't a license to kill," Newman said, shaking his head in disbelief at the idea. "I can't tell you for sure what the magister would have done. As I said, that's part of the reason I'm with you. But you never gave him a chance to explain himself. He offered several times to talk to you. He even gave you a chance yesterday to voice your concerns in front of the entire congregation. Why did you say that you felt you could be a part of the community if you had so many concerns? That was your opportunity to get answers straight from the magister about all of your suspicions."

"Newman, if my suspicions were correct that would have been an extremely stupid thing to do. Imagine what would have happened if I accused him of all the things I told you and Sophia about. Something like that," Hyle insisted, pointing back up the highway.

"So you lied?" Newman asked, sounding genuinely surprised.

"I gave him the answer that everyone wanted to hear. When you deal with fanatics, there's only one answer you can give—their answer."

"But how can you expect to change anything like that? You were given a chance to make a difference and talk openly about anything that bothered you, but instead you hid your concerns and lied in front of the whole congregation."

"Yes! I absolutely lied. I was afraid for my life," Hyle replied defensively.

"How can you expect to make a difference if you're not willing to stand up for your principles? You should ask Sophia about the trial of Socrates some time."

Sophia caught a quick glance from Newman that told her that he appreciated seeing Hyle on the defensive for a change. She could tell that he was goading Hyle and that his last comment had been calculated to draw her in on his side. It was not a serious accusation, but Sophia knew that Hyle was taking it seriously and she was convinced that the flush rising in his face was equal parts embarrassment and anger.

"But Aristotle left Athens rather than risk execution, and Galileo recanted before the Inquisition," she replied to Newman, hoping to defuse the situation.

"Right! Galileo did exactly the same thing in my position," Hyle agreed quickly. "Except that unlike Galileo, I decided to keep my damaging information to myself and leave quietly. Delacroix should be glad I did."

"I don't think that pursuing the truth is as damaging as you think, Hyle," objected Newman. "You have this preconception that religion is somehow opposed to finding intellectual truth, but it's not. Faith and intellect are two different roads to reach the same goal."

"Do you know what happened to Galileo?" Hyle asked.

"I know that he was teaching that the earth traveled around the sun and the Church asked him to recant. It was an unfortunate misunderstanding, but that happened four centuries ago."

"It was no misunderstanding," Hyle insisted. "The Church knew exactly what it was doing and so did Galileo. Galileo was trying to show people the truth and the Church was desperate to stop him."

"The Church may have been on the wrong side of the debate," Newman allowed, "but it wasn't fighting to suppress the truth. It was fighting against what it considered to be a heretical view."

"That's being far too kind to the Church," Hyle insisted. "It was probably around 1500 when Nicolas Copernicus first dared to think that the sun might be the center of the universe with the earth moving around it, and the official theory of the Church was that the earth was created by God as the immobile center of the universe. Copernicus discovered that his heliocentric model explained the movement of the planets better than the geocentric model that the Church taught, but the work that describes his theory, *On the Revolutions of the Heavenly Spheres*, wasn't published until 1543—four decades later. Do you know why?"

Newman shook his head.

"That was the year he died. He didn't allow it to be published until he was on his deathbed because he was afraid of what the Church would do to him."

Newman started to object, but Hyle ignored him and continued talking.

"And he was right to be worried. By the time of Galileo's trial almost a hundred years later, many scholars subscribed to the heliocentric model, but it wasn't widely accepted. The astronomer Tycho Brahe had collected a huge body of data on the motion of the planets and Kepler had used those data to improve the mathematics of the model and demonstrate that the planets moved in ellipses rather than circles. Meanwhile Galileo had gotten his hands on the telescope, which had just recently been invented, and improved it to the point that he could see that Venus had phases like our moon, which meant that it must pass behind the sun, and that Jupiter had moons of its own which showed that celestial bodies could orbit something other than the earth. He became convinced that, despite the teachings of the Church, Copernicus was right. He published his observations, started teaching that the earth moved around the sun and became something of a celebrity, but after a few years he was instructed by the Inquisition to stop teaching the Copernican theory. Giordano Bruno, another supporter of the heliocentric theory, had been burned at the stake after the Inquisition found him guilty of heresy a few years earlier, so guess what? Galileo stopped teaching the Copernican theory."

"Was that after the trial?" Sophia asked.

"No, that was just after a warning from the Inquisition," explained Hyle. "Then Galileo got a commission to write a comparison of the two theories, and after traveling to Rome, got what he took as permission from the Church to go ahead with the project, possibly by promising that it would come out in favor of the geocentric theory. His *Dialogue on the Two Great World Systems* was published in 1632, written as a dialogue between three characters, one who supported the geocentric model, one who supported the heliocentric model and one supposedly neutral, but not surprisingly the Copernican arguments were far more compelling than the geocentric ones. The Church immediately banned the book, stopped its sales and summoned Galileo to Rome and spent several months interrogating him. Why do you think the Church would spend so much time and money getting Galileo, who was almost seventy at the time, to recant his beliefs?"

"Because he was teaching what the Church thought was a heretical theory that was in conflict with the Bible," Newman ventured.

"No. Because they were scared," Hyle retorted. "It wasn't just the geocentric model that was at stake. The Church could see that their authority was being challenged even more broadly by the idea that you could find the truth by observing the world around you and thinking for yourself. That's why the Church wanted to make an example out of people like Galileo and Bruno and crush this little idea before it could spread. That's why this period is known as the Copernican Revolution. Not because the orbit of the planets was so significant, but because it changed the rules of how we discover what's true. It set the rules for empirical science and held them up in direct competition with the Church's authority. Not only that, but it raised questions about other teachings of the Church.

Suddenly earth and mankind were not at the center of the universe—we were relatively insignificant things hurtling through space on a little rock. How do you reconcile that with the belief that everything was created for our benefit? This was probably the single most important point in the history of science because it freed people to believe what their eyes told them and encouraged them to question what the Church told them."

"Look, Hyle, even if your cynical interpretation of history is correct and the Church tried to put a stop to Galileo and others because it saw its authority being challenged, that was almost four hundred years ago. People always bring up Galileo as evidence of how backwards the Church is, but remember that in those days doctors were treating people with leeches and shooting cannons off the city walls to ward off the plague. It's not fair to judge the actions of people back then against the knowledge and standards of today."

"Maybe so, but Galileo was forced to recant in 1633. He lived the rest of his life out under house arrest. Do you know when the Church pardoned him?"

"No," Newman confessed quietly, certain he would not be happy with the answer.

"In 1992, and they didn't do it lightly. It took four committees working thirteen years before the Church admitted it was wrong about Galileo. It was more than twenty years after we walked on the moon that the Church finally conceded publicly that they had been wrong. And do you really think the Church is staying out of matters of science? Look at creationism and all the associated attacks on evolution. These are dressed up as scientific discussions, but they don't have any scientific basis or motivation. Their only purpose is to stop the teaching of evolution because it conflicts with the Bible."

"No, I think their purpose is to give voice to ideas that they believe to be true. Evolution has a lot of holes in it, and challenging it should be every bit as acceptable as challenging the idea that the earth is the center of the universe."

"I'm not saying that scientific theories can't be challenged. They should be. What bothers me is the motive. Scientists challenge ideas when they think they've found a new idea that's closer to the truth. Galileo didn't challenge the authority of the Church because he was some kind of anarchist—he did it because he was defending what he believed to be true. Remember when we were discussing Aquinas, how the Scholastics believed that revelation and empiricism were just two different ways to get to the same truth? Galileo put that idea to the test by advocating the Copernican theory. The coexistence of revelation and empiricism turned out to be a nice idea, but wrong. They're not different ways to get to the same truth—they're different ways to get to different truths."

CHAPTER THIRTY-EIGHT

COUNTRY STORE

Newman sat quietly on the other side of Sophia, focusing on his knee and willing the pain to subside. Sophia had cleaned and bandaged the wounds the best she could. It was a significant injury, but not as bad as it had first appeared, and they had decided that his leg probably was not broken. Newman had insisted that he could walk, but as soon as he slid off the tailgate and put weight on his knee the manageable burning numbness transformed into pain so unexpectedly intense that his vision had gone black and starry. Next thing he knew, he was being helped into the cab of the truck and was only vaguely aware of Sophia circling back from closing the tailgate to slide in next to him. She glanced uneasily at the weapon beside her as they pulled back onto the highway and suggested that they stop at Danny's to trade it for some supplies. The thought of trading away their only protection did not appeal to Hyle, but he agreed that stopping at Danny's was a good idea.

Behind its dirty cloak the sun crawled toward the horizon. It dropped below the trees and the shadows were growing long before they reached the general store. They half expected to see the old man sitting outside in his rocking chair reading a book the way they had left him many weeks earlier, but the porch was empty when they pulled into the parking lot. Hyle took the rifle, still uncertain about trading the weapon, but certain that he felt better carrying it than leaving it behind in the truck. Newman watched through the windshield as they pushed aside the door which hung partially open in the doorway, Hyle in the lead and Sophia close behind. There were no lights inside. Except for a dim light coming from a doorway in the back, the only illumination was the daylight that filtered in with them through the open door.

Even before their eyes adjusted to the scant light Sophia was struck by an overwhelming wave of apprehension. She put her hand on Hyle's shoulder, stepping up close behind him.

"Hyle," she whispered.

He nodded.

The shadows began to resolve into empty shelves and empty racks. Empty peg hooks lined the walls. Everything had been cleaned out, even the useless souvenirs. The store was stripped bare. Their eyes scanned the room, but their attention was drawn quickly to the back, to the cooler where Danny had stored his guns. The chain was still looped through the two handles and held in place by the padlock and the doors were closed.

Hyle felt the grip on his shoulder tighten. The glass had been shattered. The weapons were gone.

Moving carefully and quietly they circled to the back of the room where fragments of broken glass lay strewn about on the floor beneath the empty cooler. Hyle cocked his head and listened. There was a high pitched sound coming from the back room—an electrical droning, like a fluorescent light with a bad ballast. He moved toward the sound, stepping cautiously around the outer edges of the field of broken glass and leaned into the doorway. For a moment he stood there in frozen horror. The sensation of motion behind him snapped him out of his stupor.

"Sophia, no!" he warned, wheeling and thrusting out his arm to stop her, but it was too late.

She clamped her hands to her mouth, muffling a gasp, and ran out of the store. Hyle watched her go, still stunned himself, and tried not to register the sound of retching. With a deep breath to steel himself, he looked back into the room. It was a small storage room occupying the back corner of the building. Two tiny square windows surrounded by shelves let in the gray remnants of daylight. A few items remained in this room, cans of paint, plastic letters for the changeable sign in front, mop heads, various cleaning supplies and a few other unidentifiable parcels.

In the middle of the room was a small table and seated at the table was a figure. Hyle had to study the corpse closely to be sure it was Danny. Only his upper body was visible above the table and Hyle forced himself to look at it with a medical detachedness. The old man's once thin frame was now horribly bloated, his flesh straining against the white sleeveless tee shirt. His skin, where it could be seen, was dark red, mottled with purple and covered with open lesions. A swarm of flies surrounded him like a cloud and covered his skin almost completely, giving the impression of a hideous bloated demon composed entirely of the crawling insects. Hyle staggered back from the sight and hurried out to join Sophia and Newman.

They piled back into the truck in unspoken consensus, wishing only to get far away from the general store. Unconsciously Hyle defaulted to the roads he knew, retracing their path westward across Maine as twilight gathered. There was little conversation. For a while they drove with no sound other than the hum of wheels on pavement, too disturbed to talk about what they had seen. It was Newman who broke the silence. He looked from Hyle's face with his jaw clenched and his gaze on the road unbroken to Sophia who looked physically ill and on the verge of tears. From their sparse descriptions, he had constructed a grotesque image that he could not shake and he decided that it would be better for them to face their demons together.

"What do you think killed him?" he asked, almost in a whisper. "Do you think someone shot him?"

Sophia nodded her head slightly, but Hyle disagreed.

"I think it may have been the Mumbai Plague," he answered, not taking his eyes from the road.

The lesions had not looked normal, Hyle pointed out, admitting that this was just his impression and that he was not drawing from any real medical knowledge. Wearing only a tee shirt in such cool weather also suggested that the old man might have had a fever when he died. Sophia brought up the missing weapons, and they debated whether the store had been emptied in an act associated with Danny's death or some time afterwards. Newman allowed himself to enjoy a small feeling of satisfaction as the tension melted away. In his head he said a prayer for the soul of the old man he had never met and resolved not to think about it anymore.

Miles passed without conversation until finally Sophia commented on the notable lack of people. There were no signs of life, not even the occasional lights in house windows or car in the distance that they had seen on their journey to find Asher. They talked about this for a while, giving Newman some of the details of that cross country trip, but they were unable to decide what to make of it, soon falling silent again. Newman slept and Sophia napped intermittently while Hyle continued to drive. In the early morning hours, with the hazy glow of the moon descending, they crossed the New York state line headed for Albany. Gas was running low, and as soon as he thought about stopping,

Hyle realized his stamina was running low as well. He found a place to pull off the ro_c into a wooded area, cut the engine and fell quickly asleep.

Sunlight filtered down through the leaves from high overhead by the time they were all awake again.

"Newman wants to know where we're going," Sophia said as Hyle emerged from the cab, rotating his head in an effort to stretch his sore neck. He joined them where she sat cross-legged on the forest floor next to Newman, who reclined against a large tree with one knee hiked up and his bad leg stretched out in front of him.

"That's a good question."

They had retraced their steps almost to the place their journey had started. Sophia, during the times she had been awake during the night, had been comforted by knowing the route and the idea that they were heading toward familiar territory, but now as they drew nearer, she wondered if familiarity was the only thing the area had to offer anymore.

"We ate the last of the food you gave us," Newman said, "and I don't imagine yours will last beyond breakfast, so the first thing we need to do is find some food."

"Yes, and gas. And water," added Hyle. "Finding clean water is even more important than food."

"But after that?" Sophia asked, picking up Newman's unasked question. "What next? Back in Asher we didn't have to worry about food and shelter and everyone had a job to do. Out here, once we take care of survival, assuming we can figure out how to do that, what else are we doing?"

Newman looked at Hyle expectantly.

"After survival," said Hyle slowly, after thinking for a moment, "what I want next is information. I'd like to find some place where we can look into what's been going on while we were locked away up there in isolation. We haven't seen any signs of people yet. I'd like to find some people. And after that, I want to find out what happened and what Zendik and Delacroix knew about it."

"And then what?" Newman asked suspiciously. "Why are you so intent on finding some link between the Union of Faith and the start of this world war?"

"I'm intent on finding the link because there are too many suspicious coincidences for there not to be one," Hyle replied. "And if I'm right and there is a link, we may be some of the only people in the world who know about it. As for what we do with the information, I guess that depends upon what we find out."

"We need a library," Sophia offered.

"There must be a good public library in Albany," Newman suggested.

Hyle shook his head. "Not anymore. We should avoid the cities anyway until we know what's going on. Unfortunately, that'll make it harder to find a good library."

"What about a college?" Newman suggested.

"Yes, that's a good idea," agreed Hyle, "if we can find one in a small town somewhere."

Sophia smiled. "I know just the place."

CHAPTER THIRTY-NINE

ROAD TO KNOWLEDGE

Twisting himself around to look behind the tree against which he rested and swinging his injured leg into a more comfortable position, Newman leaned forward, listening intently. Something was moving deep in the forest. He picked up the assault rifle from the ground beside him and pointed it in the general direction of the sound. Sophia and Hyle had gone out in search of food what felt like hours ago. After much discussion they had decided to leave the weapon with Newman in case he needed to defend himself or the truck. As soon as they had gone, Newman found that he was much more attuned to noises in the forest, and had been surprised on more than one occasion by how deceptively large a squirrel could sound crossing dry leaves. The current noise sounded like something large and it was drawing nearer at a steady pace.

As he brought the rifle stock to his shoulder and looked along the barrel in the direction of the sound he wondered what he would do if it were someone other than his traveling companions. Even if someone did try to steal the truck or threatened him with a weapon, he was unsure whether he would really fire. Maybe some warning shots to scare them off and signal for help. He was debating the virtues of shooting for kneecaps when Hyle and Sophia emerged from the underbrush.

"Jeez, put that thing down!" Hyle said, momentarily freezing in his tracks until he was sure Newman recognized him and set the weapon aside. Sophia approached, and stooping next to Newman, unfolded her shirt, dropping several large clusters of something green on the ground next to him.

"We brought you some grapes. They're a bit sour," she cautioned, "but they should hold you for a little while. And get some water in you."

"Make sure to wipe them off well though," Hyle added. "They may be coated with radioactive dust from the fallout. It's been long enough that we're probably okay, but we need to find some canned or wrapped food to be sure."

Most of the remaining daylight hours were spent looking for gas. All the cars they found, whether in parking lots or at private homes, had been siphoned dry. The gas caps were missing too, in some cases obviously torn from the string that tethered them to the car. Hyle suggested that this might be a convention adopted to mark the cars that had already been drained, and took it as a sign that finding gas might be even harder than they had expected. His fears were confirmed when they came across their first gas station.

"This isn't a good sign," he said as he looked down into the large pit at the edge of the pump area. It would have been over his head if he jumped in, and the gentle curve of a large tank could be seen protruding into it along one edge. He threw a rock against the side of the tank and the impact produced a hollow clang.

"Somebody went to a lot of work to drain this tank. No gas here."

They continued on, deciding to follow a course that would take them around the outskirts of Albany in the hopes of finding some untapped cars in the suburbs of the city. The gauge was reading empty as they reached a small development community. At the sight Sophia's eyes flooded almost before she felt the emotion hit her. Although the houses were a little newer and the damage a little worse, the cluster of homes atop the shallow hill reminded her of her old neighborhood. Newman merely stared in disbelief at his first sight of blast damage. Fragments of walls stood where they had been blown down or ripped away. Roofs lay atop piles of rubble if they were not missing altogether. Pieces of past lives lay scattered about on the ground everywhere—clothing, photographs, broken dishes, toys, papers—everything that had once been stored away when the houses were intact. With the assault rifle in one hand, Hyle jumped out and jogged through the fields of debris to check the nearest car they could see. The gas cap was missing.

It was the same with the handful of other cars in the development. After breaking this news to the others, Hyle started describing a plan to somehow bore through the bottom of the gas tanks to drain out anything the siphons had missed, but Newman suggested another idea. He pointed to a small garage that had collapsed in place and asked if there might be a car inside. They were able to determine that there was, and a few hours later with darkness approaching the truck had a half a tank of gas again, and a bed loaded with a variety of small treasures salvaged from the garage. Sophia did not question the usefulness of the hatchet and duct tape or even the garden hose and trash cans, but she was curious about Hyle's particular excitement at finding a bicycle pump and a chemical sprayer for the hose.

Almost immediately after they began driving again, they crested a hill and what remained of the city of Albany came into view in the distance. Newman surveyed the destruction in stunned silence. Sophia nodded empathetically, reliving the fear and horror she experienced when she first climbed out of her basement.

"It looks much worse when you get closer," Hyle said.

Sophia quietly agreed, and once more they recounted their trip into the center of the city, emphasizing details that they had not mentioned to Newman before. Hyle described the buckled streets and images of the shattered buildings. Sophia recalled the wall of notes and photographs, with the bunches of flowers and candles laid out on the ground below them. She thought too of the trails of smoke twisting up out of piles of rubble that had made her feel as though she were entering hell. Now the city was uniformly gray and cold, like the ruins of a long dead civilization. She was not sure which image bothered her more. They continued driving and talking, leaving the dead city far behind in the falling shadows. The topic of conversation changed and changed again and the blackness of another starless night had set in before Sophia realized that Newman had not spoken in a long while. She looked over at him. He was staring absently out the window.

"Newman, are you okay?" she asked gently.

He inclined his head a little and gave a small shrug.

"What's the matter?"

Newman shook his head slowly and shifted his gaze to the far side end of the windshield.

"I know. It's tough to see something like that even if you do know what to expect," Sophia said, "but things will get better as we get out into the country." She paused to watch his reaction. "It might help to talk about it. What are you thinking about?"

"What a mess we made," he answered after a long silence. "That's what I was thinking about. And wondering if maybe the magister was right about where science and technology have taken us."

"I can answer that one," Hyle said flatly.

"Science has moved too fast for us, Hyle. You think the Church was wrong to try to silence Galileo, but imagine if they had succeeded. Do you really think things could have turned out any worse than this?"

"It wouldn't have made any difference. It wasn't Galileo that challenged the Church, it was the idea that truth should be found by observation instead of revelation. And it was much broader than just the Copernican model. If it hadn't been Copernicus and Galileo it would have been someone else. The genie was already out of the bottle. In fact, about the same time Galileo was first getting into trouble with the Church, Francis Bacon was in England writing the *Novum Organum* which is generally considered to be the groundwork for modern science."

"Really?" Sophia exclaimed, and Hyle took his eyes off the road for a moment to look at her in surprise. "Do you know why he called it the *Novum Organum*?"

"It means something like 'new method' in Latin," he replied.

"But do you know what the old method was? It was Aristotle's *Organon*. His works on logic and knowledge that were taught in the universities from the Middle Ages up to Bacon's time were collectively known as the *Organon*. It was the authoritative work on almost everything not covered by theology."

"That makes sense," Hyle replied. "Bacon learned Aristotle at Cambridge and didn't have much use for him."

"But…" Newman began slowly, looking from Sophia to Hyle and back. "I thought that Aristotle was very scientific. Didn't you tell me he was a naturalist who thought it was only worthwhile to study things that could be observed?"

"Yes, that's true," Sophia replied. "He was scientific, especially compared to Plato, and I think he deserves to share a lot of the credit for modern science. The foundation he laid was taught for more than a thousand years."

"One of Bacon's first lines in the Novum Organon says that it would be foolish to believe that new progress can be made using only old methods," Hyle paraphrased. "That was exactly the problem Bacon identified. Aristotle was seen as such an authority that knowledge had not really advanced for two thousand years. He may have been ahead of his time, but by Bacon's age over-dependence on Aristotle was actually holding back knowledge. What the Church was doing actively to Galileo and astronomy, Aristotle was doing passively with everything else. That's why silencing Galileo, or Bacon for that matter, wouldn't have made any difference. The world had been stuck in a rut but it was ready to move on to a new way of seeing things."

"What did Bacon propose that was so different from Aristotle?" Sophia asked, with more than a hint of challenge in her voice.

"Probably the most significant was the principle of induction—that by making observations and looking for patterns, one could induce general laws of nature."

"Aristotle also taught induction."

"Maybe so, but by Bacon's time I think most people were more interested in analyzing what Aristotle thought than using his principles to think for themselves," Hyle replied, looking at Sophia pointedly. "Bacon also identified four patterns of thought that throw people off the track of real knowledge. One of these false 'Idols of the Mind' as he called them had to do with people having difficulty thinking in a new way if they were already indoctrinated into a particular school of thought, like Aristotelianism for example. Another had to do with the human tendency to see evidence that supports your views and ignore evidence that contradicts them. Bacon stressed the importance of making objective observations before inducing general laws."

"This is the beginning of British empiricism," Sophia remarked. When neither of the men responded, she explained, "The British Empire turned out a string of philosophers who believed that empirical observation was the main way we acquire knowledge."

"They sound like scientists to me," Hyle said, "and I don't doubt that he influenced them. Bacon had some high court position and he lobbied for the founding of a royal society for the promotion of science. The Royal Society of London wasn't founded until 1662, after Bacon had died, but he was regarded as a sort of spiritual leader."

"That's an interesting choice of terms," Newman observed.

"Ironic even, considering what the Society represented," agreed Hyle. "The Crown of England was officially promoting the exact type of thinking that had gotten Galileo in trouble with the Church only three decades earlier. With men like architect Sir Christopher Wren and physicist Robert Hooke as founding members, the Royal Society was held in high esteem and where clergy had been called upon to go investigate claims of miracles only years before, now it was scientists who were called upon to sort the truth from superstition. And their motto was *Nullius in Verba*—'on the words of no one'— which meant that they found truth for themselves, not in the authority of the Church or the Crown."

The last words were spoken as the truck decelerated and Hyle cut the wheel sharply, bringing them into the far side of a small parking area. As he swung the truck around, pumps appeared briefly in the headlights. He pulled forward slowly until he found what he was looking for, then got out and rummaged around in the back of the truck. Sophia saw him reappear in the headlights with the garden hose slung over his shoulder and jumped out to join him.

"This tank looks untouched," he said hopefully as she approached.

"How do you know it wasn't siphoned?"

"To siphon something you need the downstream end to be lower than the surface of the liquid to create the flow, and these tanks are underground. Getting gas out of here isn't as easy as siphoning gas from a car."

"You're not planning to dig a pit?" Sophia stated more than asked.

"No, I have a different idea in mind. I'm hoping we can pump it out."

Under the glare of the headlights Hyle removed the end of the spray head from the chemical sprayer, disassembled the bicycle pump and reassembled it, then used a large quantity of duct tape to attach the two.

"I turned the seal around in the pump," he explained in response to Sophia's look of curiosity. "Instead of pushing air it should pull it and create a vacuum."

The first attempt ended in failure. The pump did create a vacuum, but instead of pulling gas up the garden hose collapsed. The hoses on the gas pumps had been removed, apparently hacked off in an attempt to get gas from the pumps or held up in the lines. The small convenience store had been emptied completely, but Sophia found a coin operated air compressor behind the building. The hose was strong enough to withstand the vacuum, and their efforts were finally rewarded when gas began to trickle into the plastic bottle of the sprayer. One bottle at a time they filled the tank of the truck. When Hyle dragged one of the trash cans over and began filling that, Newman hobbled out of the truck.

"Are you going to take that with us?" he asked.

"I was planning to fill all of them," Hyle answered, gesturing toward the other trash cans in the back of the truck.

"Are you sure that's safe?"

"No, it's probably not, but this may be the last gas we can get."

Newman shrugged.

"Well, at least if something happens we'll go out in a blaze of glory."

They took turns pumping until all the containers were filled and tied them in place with the garden hose. The moon, a patch of fuzzy silver luminescence in an otherwise dark sky, was high overhead by the time they finished, but Sophia thought that they were close to their destination, so they decided to press on. She found her bearings when they intersected a small highway, and a little while later they turned onto the familiar country road into town.

Pastures rolled by, dotted with barns with silos and the occasional farmhouse. Eventually businesses began to appear—a pizza place, a department store, a couple fast food restaurants, a grocery store. Soon they found themselves in the center of town, an intersection of two roads lined with several dozen small storefronts set back behind wide sidewalks. Windows were shattered and many of the doors hung open, but the buildings showed no other signs of structural damage, and a few cars were still parked at the curb. Down a side street, a marquee announced the single film that had last played at the cinema. They turned right onto the broad main street, following the edge of a long common.

"Oak Drive will be the second road up here on the left," Sophia said, but her voice trailed off. Something materialized in the headlights where she had expected to see the intersection. It took a moment to realize what it was. What at first appeared to be a smooth white wall was actually a tractor trailer, overturned across the road at an unlikely angle.

"Right on the other side of that trailer," Sophia sighed. "That's okay. Back up. We can take some back roads."

"That seems like an odd place for an accident," Hyle observed as he followed Sophia's instructions to turn just in front of the truck onto the small street that looped back along the other side of the common. A tall church with whitewashed pillars rising from its steps overlooked this end of the green. They passed the church and turned away from town, following a short street among old colonial and Victorian houses before turning again. Just beyond the junction of three roads this way was blocked as well. A huge tree had fallen across the street, blocking it completely.

"Look at the stump," Sophia said. "It looks like it was chopped down, and it blocks all access to campus from this side of town. I think someone doesn't want us to go any further."

"Maybe we should take the hint," suggested Newman.

"It's a sign that there are people here," Hyle said. "That's exactly what we're looking for."

"Unless they shoot us as soon as they see us."

"We could leave you here if you like."

Sophia shot Hyle a look which clearly indicated that she did not appreciate the humor and then turned to address Newman.

"There's safety in numbers and we do need to find some place safe to stay. Sooner or later we're going to have to take a chance and deal with other people."

When Newman shrugged a grudging consent, Sophia guided them back through town, across the main street to another series of back roads. Here the streets were longer and the houses, interspersed with small businesses, were not as large or crowded together. There were no signs of life anywhere.

"Take a left here," Sophia instructed. "This will turn into the main road onto campus, assuming we can get across Broad Street.

They followed the road past a series of similar looking apartments to the intersection. Large houses lined their side of the main street facing undeveloped land on the opposite side. The way across was unobstructed. Hyle let up on the accelerator, creeping across the street and scanning the shadows for a possible ambush. The wide meadows on either side and a large pond to the left comforted him somewhat, but there were still plenty of trees to conceal sentries. The road began to climb. In the distance above, the silhouettes of buildings were just visible against the sky.

They passed a house, the first building close enough to be seen clearly from the road, and Sophia was suddenly transported back a decade to a time when she walked the campus as a student in the brilliant spring sunshine. The house, she recalled, was for special interest students. It was always changing names and themes. Last she could remember it was a residence for foreign language students who wanted an immersion experience. Ahead she could just make out a sign that read "Merrill House," and as the old stone building rolled by on the left she remembered nervously attending her freshman orientation there. It was comforting to be in a familiar place again. Sophia smiled to herself, lost in a sudden rush of memories—classes on the sunny quad, walking downtown on the weekend with her friends, lounging in the common room of her dormitory, studying in her favorite carrel on the top floor of the library—all the best scenes from four years of college life recalled in a jumbled flood of pleasant emotion.

Her reminiscence was cut short as the truck screeched to a sudden halt.

CHAPTER FORTY

ENCOUNTER

In the middle of the road, a figure had materialized out of the shadows. It was a young man dressed in dark clothes. His left hand was extended toward them, palm out, ordering them to stop. His right arm was at his side, with a pistol clearly visible in his hand. There was a sharp rap on the driver's window near the back of the cab and all three travelers jumped, looking for the source of the sound. A rifle barrel. It rapped on the window again and the dark shape holding it took a step forward and leveled the barrel across the front seat. Another shape moved on the other side of the truck.

Hyle put his hands in the air, showing them to the figure outside his window and Newman and Sophia quickly followed suit. The barrel of the rifle bobbed up and down. When Hyle recovered his wits enough to understand the gesture, he reached slowly for his door with one hand and cranked the window down.

"Who are you? What are you doing here?" demanded a voice from behind the rifle, clearly feminine but tough.

All three travelers began speaking at once, explaining that they had come from Maine, they had been attacked, they were just looking for a safe place to stay, used to go to school here, did not mean any harm, wanted to use the library, were hoping to find other people, and several other things in such rapid succession that the young woman actually laughed and told them to relax. Once she had established that they were traveling alone and wanted to stay, she seemed to relax herself, but not before commanding Hyle to pass the rifle out of the window stock first.

"If you're hoping to stay here, I'm going to have to talk to someone first," she said. "Turn off your lights and follow me."

She spoke a quick command to someone behind the truck and two dark shapes clambered into the back. The person who had first stopped them melted back into the shadows as the woman began walking up the center of the road, waving for them to follow. The road continued to rise and they followed it into a small parking lot behind a plain brick building. It was a box shaped structure cut into a hill that rose steeply away to cover at least one of the building's three stories in the front. They had come in to the rear of the building and Hyle was surprised that there was no loading dock and more surprised when Sophia informed them that it was the biology building which marked the edge of the academic quad. A figure emerged from a door in the back of the building and had a conversation with the woman. She came back to the window.

"He's going to go check with Dean Essex on what to do with you," she explained from a safe distance away. "Essex is pretty much in charge here."

"In charge?" Hyle repeated. "How many people are here?"

"I don't know. Probably close to a thousand now."

She went on to explain that the majority of the two thousand students had tried to find a way to get back to their homes, but quite a few had chosen to stay. Many of the townspeople, including most of the faculty that lived in town, had decided that it was safer to move up to the campus and there had been a slow accumulation of refugees from the surrounding towns.

After a while a man emerged from the back of the building and stepped up beside the woman with the rifle. He was a short, middle-aged man with a round face and a small moustache. His hair was literally hacked short, as if he had tried to give himself a haircut without the benefit of a mirror, and the moonlight reflected off the small round lenses of his glasses, obscuring his eyes. His attire, a rumpled broad striped oxford shirt and jeans, reminded Sophia afresh of both the casualness and the constant atmosphere of learning that had marked her time as a student. He exchanged a few quiet words with the young woman and then turned to the truck.

"I'm John Essex," he said. "Dean of the College. I'm now in charge of overseeing things here at Colgate. I understand that you're looking for a place to stay for a while." The travelers nodded as he continued, sounding intrigued. "And that you wish to use the library?"

"Yes we do," Hyle confirmed.

"That'll make Francis very happy," Essex said, smiling, and the woman gave an amused snort. "So until now you've been living in Maine. Are you traveling through on your way to somewhere?"

"We don't know yet," Hyle said.

"We might like to stay for a while if that's all right," Sophia added, leaning across him. Essex nodded thoughtfully.

"And where did your travels take you before you came here?"

With occasional input from Sophia, Hyle gave him a condensed account of their meeting and journey to find the retreat in Maine. They described the city of Asher and their stay there, but said nothing of the reasons for their departure.

"And you didn't run into any trouble on the way here?"

"We haven't seen anyone since we left Maine," Hyle answered quickly.

"That's a good sign. We've heard reports of armed looters, sometimes very dangerous and prone to desperate actions. Some of the faculty who live around here have holed up in their houses with their families, but most of us have banded together here for safety. We're pretty isolated now though and it's hard to get a gauge on what's going on out there."

Essex frowned thoughtfully. The young woman watched him, waiting for instructions.

"Put them up in West," he told her. "There are still rooms on the fifth floor, right?" She nodded and he turned back to the truck.

"You'll have to leave that with us," he said, pointing to the confiscated assault rifle. "No weapons on campus except for people on guard duty. And we'll have to put you to work unless you brought your own food. Do any of you have any medical experience?"

"No, sorry. And we don't have any food," said Hyle. "Could we trade something? Do you need gas?"

The dean nodded. "Yes. We send teams out scavenging every night, but they're spending more and more time looking for fuel and less finding food and supplies. How much do you have?"

"How much food would twenty gallons get us?"

"Twenty gallons?" Essex muttered, clearly taken aback. He scowled for a moment, mumbling some calculations to himself. "If I said that a gallon is about a night's work, I could give you a week of food—dinners—that's all we serve. And sometimes some bread to take for breakfast. That's being a bit generous, but I think it's fair."

"Good. You can take those four trash barrels in the back," Hyle said, pointing his thumb over his shoulder. "Those are thirty gallon barrels and they're at least two-thirds full. That ought to be good for a month's worth of food."

Essex exchanged a look with the guard.

"I thought it smelled like gas back there," she said, as she walked over and pulled the lid off of the nearest trash barrel. "Yeah, this one is definitely more than two-thirds full."

"Why are you trading away all of our gas?" Newman whispered while the conversation was going on outside.

"We can get more, I hope. Besides, unless we post a guard we'd probably lose it anyway."

The discussion was cut short as Essex appeared again in the window to accept the deal.

"You can park your truck down at Merrill," the dean said, pointing back down the road. "Rita can show you where." Wishing them good luck finding what they were looking for in the library, Dean Essex disappeared into the building again leaving the young guard in charge.

Rita jumped in the back and rode with them to the nearby parking lot and then they hiked back up to Olin Hall where she led them through the back door of the building and into a dimly lit corridor. It was unquestionably the hallway of an academic building. The light gray tiles of the floor still reflected the light of the single fluorescent light at the end of the corridor. The cinder block walls were painted in a pastel color indistinguishable in the dim light. They passed by closed wooden doors set in metal frames. Each door had a plastic name plaque and many had information or cartoons taped to the windows. Voices came from nearby, down a corridor to the right, but Rita pushed ahead through a door and led them up some stairs.

"Why did you choose Olin Hall to set up shop in?" Sophia asked as she helped Newman to get his footing on the stairs.

"We didn't," Rita responded with a laugh. "Those were just some other members of the night watch you heard. I'm taking you through the tunnels. They had those when you were here, didn't they?"

"Yes, I'm not that old," Sophia replied, feigning offense.

The tunnels had been built long before Sophia had attended the university. A pair of tee shaped intersecting tunnels connected the second floor of Olin Hall, which was buried beneath the hill in front, with the math building on one side and the chemistry building on the other. Sophia explained this to Hyle and Newman as they reached the second floor, traversed a small section of corridor and entered the tunnels.

"Yes, and don't forget that Lawrence, Lathrop and McGregor are all connected by above ground walkways. And we've made some more changes over the last few months. There are now tunnels that connect Wynn to West Hall, and West to East and Andrews. They're digging one from Andrews to Stillman now."

"Why are you building more tunnels?" asked Sophia.

"We want to be able to move around unseen. We have some very strict rules about light that you need to be aware of. All the rooms either have their windows boarded or have blackout shades. You're not allowed to have your lights on unless your windows are completely covered. There have been a lot of reports of paramilitary groups preying on pockets of civilization and we don't want to make ourselves a target for them or looters, so we block out light and try to use the tunnels as much as possible, especially during the day."

The tunnel was large, wider than the corridors of the building. The ceiling and walls were made of smoothed but unfinished concrete. The floor, also concrete, had been sealed and painted. It extended a few hundred feet, rising slightly and ending at a perpendicular passageway. A single fluorescent bulb at the intersection lit their way. A row of similar lights, the bulbs all dark, lined the passageway.

"You have electricity," Hyle realized aloud, pausing to examine the light as the rest of the group followed Rita into a new tunnel.

"Yes, but they loosened most of the bulbs to save on power."

"Where does it come from?"

"There's a cogen plant on the other side of campus and we have crews going out to bring back wood every night. That's one thing we have a lot of around here. We have water in the dorms too. It's untreated though. Just for showers and washing dishes and clothes. We have to get our drinking water from Wynn, this building up ahead," Rita explained, pointing up the tunnel. "There was a water purification system for the chemistry labs, so we make our drinking water here."

They emerged into another academic building, entered another corridor lit by a single fluorescent light and passed between laboratories to a stairwell at the other end. Under the stairs blocks of the concrete wall had been removed to create a hole just large enough for a person to step through.

"Coming through," Rita yelled into the opening. "I hope none of you are claustrophobic."

Being taller than average, Hyle had to stoop to follow her through the wall and he was very disappointed to find that there was no more headroom inside the tunnel. With the bare earthen walls braced by what seemed to be far too few planks, he was reminded more of a gopher hole than any place a human should be entering. Claustrophobia, he reminded himself, was an irrational fear of enclosed places and entering had been a completely rational act. Still, he could not help dwelling on how much less uneasy he would have felt if there had been a few more inches to straighten his neck out. Sophia waited for Newman to pick his way cautiously over the crude threshold and followed after him.

The light from behind faded quickly and they had to traverse a short section of the tunnel in complete darkness before a dim light appeared ahead. They stepped through a similar hole in the wall of a large basement. Round rust colored metal pillars at regular intervals held up the floor above them and a bank of coin operated washing machines and dryers lined the opposite wall beyond a pair of long folding tables.

"So you haven't seen any of these paramilitary groups around here?" Hyle asked, anxious to put the tunnel behind him.

"No, not here. But we did get a bunch of refugees from Cornell about a month ago. They had a big group of survivors there too, but I guess they got attacked by a pretty scary crew. The ones who made it here thought that they might have been the only ones who got out. That's why we're being extra cautious about light and everything. We can't hide forever, but I guess we're all hoping that things change for the better soon."

Rita led them up six flights of stairs, waiting patiently for Newman to take each step with his good foot while bracing himself on the railing. She asked if they had any news from the road and told them that she had heard theories of a foreign invasion, a military coup and bands of paramilitary groups, but that nobody seemed to have any first hand information.

When they reached their room, down a short hallway from the stairs, she pushed the door open to reveal a cramped square room with a lone window on the wall opposite the door. The window was covered with thick drapes. By the dim light filtering in from the hall, Rita took a blanket from the upper bunk and hung it over the top of the drapes, then came back and flipped the light switch.

"One bulb per room for now. Saves on electricity and spares more bulbs," Rita explained. She smiled slightly to herself as she registered the expressions on the faces of her three guests. They stood just inside the doorway staring up in awed appreciation at the light. Sophia marveled at this simple action—something that she had done unconsciously dozens of times a day only a few months ago now seemed like a testament to the ingenuity of the human spirit.

A lone fluorescent bulb sputtered to life in the ceiling.

CHAPTER FORTY-ONE

BUTTERFLY DREAMS

Through the darkness dim walls rose all around her. Water trickled down the cold stone as Sophia picked her way over the rubble along what was once a corridor. What was this place? An old factory perhaps? It was huge. The walls were in ruins and the roof had been torn away, yet there was no place low enough to see outside. The sky above was a uniform slate. In the twilight she strained to see the passage ahead. It turned a corner and ended abruptly. Another dead end. She turned back, more urgently now, and followed another passage into a small room. Three doorways stood as dark openings barely discernable in the gloom. She picked the center one at random and hurried through into another room. No exit.

Desperately she tried to climb up to get a look out of the maze, but her feet could not find a purchase on the slick stone. I'm dreaming, she realized suddenly. Relief washed over her yet the nightmare did not fade. She turned, and a dark figure suddenly stood next to her, large and featureless, its face hidden in the shadows of a hood. It should have been frightening, but somehow she knew that it was there to help her to find a way out. Did I create it? wondered the Sophia outside the dream. As she stepped toward the figure she heard a disembodied voice. "Everything is not what it appears," it said, and then the stranger turned and disappeared through the wall. Sophia touched the spot where it had vanished. The stone was cold. Solid. In her dream she closed her eyes, stepped forward. Nothing. When she opened them again, she was standing on the ledge of a high cliff, looking out across a plain toward distant mountains. A sea of earth the color of rust rolled beneath her and sunshine washed her face. She closed her eyes and breathed deeply, savoring the warmth on her skin. When she opened them she found herself lying in a warm comfortable bed.

At first she thought she was at home, but slowly she remembered where she was and pulled the covers tight around her, soaking in the warmth. Hyle was still asleep in the top bunk, but Newman was already awake, sitting on the edge of his bed.

He watched Sophia stir. For a moment he thought that she was going to go back to sleep, but then she opened her eyes and tried to blink him into focus. Amused, he observed her as she stopped trying to clear her vision, suddenly distracted by something.

"Music. Isn't it great?" he said quietly once she was able to keep her eyes open. "It's The Police, *Zenyatta Mondatta* I think."

He hobbled to the door, opened it a crack and craned his head to listen.

Sophia heard the murmur of distant conversation and a high gravelly voice singing. It was hard to make out the words, but she thought she heard something about an old car and a battery running down.

Newman let his smile broaden to a grin, pleased that he had been right, and closed the door again.

"How's your leg doing?" Sophia asked, watching him shuffle back to the bottom bunk.

"Fine, as long as I don't stand on it," Newman said with a wry smile. "It's stiff, but it doesn't hurt as much as it did yesterday. How about you? Did you sleep well?"

"Yes, I did. Very well in fact, but I had this strange dream," she replied, and proceeded to describe it to him in detail. "It seemed very realistic, but the weirdest thing is that I actually realized halfway through it that I was dreaming. I've never had that happen before. But even though I knew it was a dream on one level, it was still very realistic to the me that was in the dream."

Newman nodded knowingly.

"'Once I dreamt I was a butterfly. Now I do not know if I was a man dreaming I was a butterfly or am now a butterfly dreaming that I am a man.'"

"That's beautiful, Newman."

"It's Chuang Tzu."

"It sounds like a bunch of New Age crap to me," came a mocking voice from above.

"Good morning to you too, Hyle," Sophia replied, not quite sure whether to be amused or annoyed.

"Isn't it interesting," said Newman, ignoring the exchange, "that in your dream this figure tells you that nothing is as it appears, when on one level he could be talking about the walls, and on another he could be talking about the dream itself."

"See, what kind of tripe is that? 'Nothing is as it appears,'" Hyle said, leaning over the rail of the top bunk.

"Don't be so sure of yourself," Sophia warned, allowing annoyance to win momentarily. "How do you know that anything you're seeing right now is really is as it appears?"

"Because there's no other option. What we sense is what's real by definition. If we see something clear and it feels cold and wet it's water. If it's yellow and hot and burning up a log it's fire. Are you trying to tell me that maybe fire is actually cold and wet? What would that reality be based on?"

"But your senses can be fooled," Newman interjected. "I remember driving out to go hiking in the Rockies. When I first saw the mountains, I thought we'd reach them in another hour. I thought the same thing an hour later, and an hour after that."

"Put a straight stick in water and it'll appear to be bent," Sophia added, watching Hyle for his reaction. "And amputees sometimes feel pain in their missing limbs."

"Yeah, yeah. Phantom limb," Hyle replied, sounding unimpressed. "And don't forget about optical illusions and magic tricks. I get the point. The senses aren't perfect, but they're generally reliable and it's the best we've got."

Sophia smiled to herself. If Hyle thought he was going to have some fun causing trouble at her expense, she had her own ideas.

"But if you catch your senses being fooled some of the time, Hyle, how do you know they're not being fooled other times when you fail to catch them? How can you be sure whether what you're perceiving at any given time is real or not?"

There was a moment of silence before she continued.

"I'm sure you believe you're awake right now, but how can you be absolutely sure that you're not dreaming? What would you use as proof?"

Another silence as Hyle pondered the question. His impulse was to say that he could tell in the past when he was awake, and even after a realistic dream he would know when he woke, but he realized this was not a sufficient answer to be considered a proof. Sophia fought to keep herself from smiling as she watched him wrestle with the question.

"Let me raise the stakes even more," she said. "How can you be sure of anything? Anything at all?"

Hyle propped himself up on his elbow, now looking very intent.

"I'm pretty sure that one plus one equals two, even in my dreams."

"Interesting," Newman observed, "that the one thing you're sure of after all is a mental construct—something conceptual rather than something observable."

"And as internally consistent as mathematics may be, it's so highly abstracted from the observable physical world that it doesn't carry much weight in proving any sort of physical reality," added Sophia.

"I'm still working on that one," Hyle said. "But you asked if there was anything at all I was sure of and there is. One plus one equals two."

"Okay, mathematics does seem to be true," Sophia allowed, "but let me give you a hypothetical situation and challenge you again to prove to me that it's incorrect. Suppose that you were in the thrall of a super powerful being—an alien mind probe, a virtual reality program, a malevolent demon, whichever you prefer—whose only purpose was to deceive you at every turn. It could control everything you experience, and even make you believe that one plus one equals two when everyone knows it really equals three."

"I suppose I'd be completely screwed," Hyle said, not certain of what that proved.

"Not completely. Think," Sophia said, and could not help but crack a smile.

Hyle closed his eyes and shook his head dismissively, but Sophia had a feeling he was still considering the question. Newman was staring into space, obviously working on it as well. She caught his eye with a questioning look.

"Obviously it's not any sort of physical proof, so it has to be mental," he said, and detected a smile of encouragement from Sophia. "But if any thought can be a deception… But the act of thinking itself…"

Newman threw up his hands as he finished the thought and kicked himself for not recognizing it sooner.

"*Je pense, donc je suis*. Rene Descartes. I think, therefore I am."

"Or in Latin, *Cogito, ergo sum*. Exactly," confirmed Sophia. "The one thing that can be known for certain, because even being completely deceived presupposes a thinking being to be the object of the deception."

"I never understood why that was supposed to be such a philosophical landmark," said Hyle. "It's not as though most people doubt their own existence and need to have it proven to them."

"No," Sophia agreed. "That's not what Descartes was trying to do. He was trying to construct a new rational method of philosophy based on something that could be known with absolute certainty. The Reformation had challenged the authority of the Church which had previously been the one place you could go for certainty. Like Bacon, Descartes was dissatisfied with Aristotelian Scholasticism, but for all the reasons Newman just mentioned, he didn't feel that empirical observation was a reliable path to absolute knowledge."

"When was all this in relation to the trial of Galileo?" Hyle asked. "Because the Copernican Revolution obviously challenged the authority of the Church too."

"Yes, I imagine that was a factor too since *Discourse on Method* was published just a few years after the trial. That's where Descartes first introduced his method and then he expanded on it a few years later in *Meditations on First Philosophy*. But a bigger influence was probably the revival of skepticism. Maybe it was because the world was ready for a change, as you put it, Hyle, but in Descartes' day there was a resurgence of interest in classical skepticism. Around the time Descartes was born another French philosopher, Michel de Montaigne published his *Essays*, which raised the unanswerable question of what we can really know."

"Nothing is certain, not even that," Hyle quoted, recalling the discussion he and Sophia had before their flight to Maine.

"And remember Timon of Philius pointing out that any logical proof must start from a set of unproven base assumptions, which could only be proven with a new set of assumptions."

"So Descartes was hoping to defend knowledge against skepticism by finding one starting assumption that couldn't be challenged," Newman concluded.

"Exactly, and to make sure it was rock solid," Sophia continued, "Descartes subjected it to the most severe skepticism that he could imagine, even going so far as to hypothesize a demon capable of constructing an alternate reality in order to deceive him at every turn. In a sense Descartes did the skeptics one better and still came up with something undeniably true. His method was to assume nothing from history, past philosophy or even from his own personal experience. He wanted to build certain knowledge rationally, step by step, starting with his *Cogito* and using rigorous logic the same way that you'd construct a proof in geometry or algebra, testing each step with the harshest skepticism. Only if all the steps could survive the test of skepticism could the conclusion be considered to be reliable knowledge."

"That's reminiscent of Francis Bacon, except using logic instead of observation," Hyle pointed out. "Bacon identified his four idols that prejudice human thought and emphasized that observations must be made objectively. Starting with what should be indisputable observations, the goal of his method was to induce generalized theories that are more powerful and useful than just a collection of observations and then, having made these theories, test them to see if they could stand up to new observations. That ultimately evolved into the scientific method. So where did Descartes go with his method?"

"One thing he did was prove the existence of God," Newman answered, taking Sophia by surprise.

"That's a neat trick," Hyle quipped. "How did he manage to do that?"

"If I remember correctly," Newman said, smiling, "he started with an argument very similar to your water and fire example. He said that a thing is what it's defined to be. A triangle is a shape with three angles. It can't have four or it wouldn't be a triangle. A unicorn is a creature with one horn, whether it's real or not. By the same logic God must be perfect, whether you believe in Him or not. But we can't observe perfection in the natural world and there's no way to deduce it, so where does the concept of perfection come from?"

"You're going to say that humans are imperfect, and something imperfect can't create something perfect, right?" Hyle guessed. He leaned over the edge of the bed and saw the confirmation on Newman's face. "I think I've heard this one before. Isn't this just Avicenna's necessary versus possible proof warmed over?"

"It's a bit different, but the same general idea," Sophia agreed. "Descartes also used another argument that would probably remind you of Anselm's ontological proof."

"There's an obvious problem with the first proof," Hyle said. "Take your own example of the mountains, Newman. They kept looking bigger and bigger the closer you got to them. Presumably you finally reached them, but couldn't you have imagined going one more hour than you did and seeing them get even bigger? And yet another hour after that and seeing them get even bigger still?"

"Yes, I'm sure I could."

"So you can imagine something greater than what you actually perceived. You have a conception that didn't come directly from your experience."

"It's one thing to think of something larger. It's another to conceive of perfection," Newman pointed out. "Perfection isn't just an incremental improvement, Hyle. It's absolute. The analogy would be imagining mountains that were infinitely large, and I'm not sure I could do that."

"Are you even sure that we really can conceive of perfection then?" Sophia asked with a sly smile.

"Sure we can," Hyle replied quickly. "In fact, I think there's a better way to approach it, because I agree with Newman that we probably can't really comprehend infinity. But perfection's a lot easier than infinity. What's the definition of perfection?" he asked rhetorically. "It's to be without flaws. Zero is a concept that we humans are definitely capable of comprehending. To say that God is perfect is to say that he has zero flaws. Now you don't have to worry about comprehending infinity. Problem solved."

"That's very much like the Mu'tazilites," Sophia noted. "Those were the early Muslim philosophers—the 'men of unity and justice'—who reasoned that God defied positive description and could only be described in negation. On the other hand, Descartes argued that perfection is more than just the elimination of human flaws."

"After 'I think, therefore I am,' I'm surprised to hear so much squishy thinking in these supposedly rational proofs," Hyle said.

"I wouldn't be too hard on Descartes," replied Sophia. "Trying to prove the existence of God has led a lot of accomplished philosophers onto shaky ground."

"Gee, I wonder why that is," Hyle mused.

"All philosophical arguments can be challenged," noted Sophia, "and Descartes had his critics even in his day, but the rationalist method he developed was so influential that it's considered by many to be not just the foundation of rationalism, but the beginning of modern philosophy. The rest of his proof may not be as solid as the *Cogito*, but it's still very logical. His next step was to define a substance as that which exists independently of other things. The mind is a form of 'thinking substance' and there also appear to be physical substances. Beyond substances there are attributes—qualities or states which are dependent upon substances. For example, thinking is an attribute of a thinking substance and color and taste are possible attributes of physical substances. These things can't exist in the absence of a substance."

"I'm not sure that the mind needs to be separated from physical substances," Hyle said, "but aside from that it sounds reasonable so far."

"For now they do have to be separated because the *Cogito*—I think, therefore I am— directly proves the existence of a thinking substance, the mind, but not anything physical. Sensations could still be illusions, as in a dream. To prove physical substances, Descartes next reasons that something cannot come from nothing by itself. Then he gets to the part we were just discussing—that a cause must be at least as real and powerful as the effect that it creates and something more perfect cannot come from something less perfect. From this and the logic that Newman outlined a few minutes ago about things being what they are by definition, Descartes derives God as the perfect first cause. Because God is perfect, He wouldn't deceive us, and we can therefore believe mathematics and such things that can withstand the test of skepticism. And even though our senses may be imperfect and prone to error, we can even know that we're not deceived in believing that there's a real physical world out there that we can sense."

"So proving the existence of the mind and God was a necessary precondition to proving the existence of physical substances," Newman observed. A thought occurred to him. "If the thinking substances exist independently from physical things and Descartes equates thinking substances with human consciousness, is he essentially making a case for an immortal soul?"

"Yes," Sophia said. "Or at least setting it apart from the restrictions of physical things."

"I don't see the advantage in doing that," Hyle said. "Except that maybe he thought people would feel better about believing his theory."

"That may not be too far off, Hyle," Sophia replied. "Whether Descartes did it consciously or not, he neatly divided the world in half with the thinking substances falling clearly under the authority of the Church while the physical substances obviously fell into the domain of the new sciences as practiced by the likes of Bacon and Galileo."

"Sort of like what the Averroists were trying to do at the University of Paris a few centuries earlier," Newman noted.

"It's funny how the same ideas seem to keep popping up throughout history in different contexts," said Hyle, nodding in appreciation of Newman's observation. "I can imagine that Descartes might have created this split on purpose since he was a bit of a scientist and an accomplished mathematician."

"Really? He was a mathematician too?" said Newman.

"Absolutely. He invented the entire branch of analytical geometry. Remember in high school plotting things on graphs with X and Y coordinates? You can thank Descartes for that. In fact, they're called Cartesian coordinates after him."

"Descartes was very mechanistic in his view of the physical world," agreed Sophia. "He's supposed to have come to very similar conclusions to Galileo about the nature of physical substances."

"Really, what did they conclude?" Hyle asked.

"In *Meditations* he does a wonderful analysis of a piece of wax."

Newman started to laugh, but caught himself when he realized that Sophia was not joking.

"Descartes considers a piece of beeswax, which starts off with the smell of flowers and the taste of honey and has a particular shape to it. But after being out of the beehive long enough, the smell and taste may fade, it can be reshaped and even melted from a solid form to a liquid, so Descartes concludes that the only property a physical substance consistently has is that it's extended in three dimensions—occupying space in other words—and has the potential for movement. All other properties like color, taste and even shape are only attributes. They may change or be missing altogether."

"If the only property of physical things is that they occupy space, how does Descartes explain motion?" asked Hyle.

"God," Sophia replied simply. "He went back to the Aristotelian idea of the prime mover, setting things in motion, but only to start things off. According to Descartes, since God is perfect, once His will is put into effect, nothing further is needed. Like a watchmaker who builds and winds a watch, then lets it run on its own. He even believed that all animal behavior could be explained as essentially automated reactions to things the animals perceived in their environment."

"But he didn't consider people to be animals?" asked Hyle.

"Yes and no. He did actually make the same argument about people."

"I thought people were supposed to be thinking substances," objected Newman.

"Yes, they are. That's what Descartes thought made people special. They have physical bodies that react very much in the same ways that animals do. We take in the same sensory input—colors, sounds, tastes, we get hungry, cold, frightened, feel pain. But what makes us different from animals is that we have aspects of thinking substances as well, so we can resist our natural mechanical reactions. For example, we can resist pain or fear to defend a loved one or even something as abstract as a nation. And Descartes posed a very interesting question. Would it ever be possible to construct a machine that was indistinguishable from a human being?"

"Of course not," Newman said quickly, even as Hyle was beginning to nod his head.

"There are already robotic hands that can manipulate small objects and robots that can ride bicycles," Hyle countered. "And a computer has won on *Jeopardy* and even beaten a world chess champion."

"That's not being human though," objected Newman. He paused to think of a good counter-example and was briefly distracted by the music down the hall. The same voice was now singing a different song and because he recognized it, Newman was able to fill in the words. He chuckled at the irony. Even as the singer lamented about life, asking where the answer lies, the music in general, and the song specifically, gave Newman the answer he was seeking.

"Trivia is just a collection of facts and chess is very mathematical," he responded, "but a computer could never compose song lyrics, or write poetry. Not anything worth listening to anyway, with symbolism and imagery, because that's a non-standard use of language. A computer could never really understand concepts like beauty or love or devotion."

"Or develop a concept of God?" Sophia suggested and Newman vigorously nodded in agreement. "Descartes came to the same conclusions for very similar reasons."

"Maybe we're just not advanced enough in our programming yet," Hyle argued. "Or maybe it's because we haven't yet been able to characterize what it is that appeals to us about poetry and other arts, but that doesn't mean that it can't be done."

"That could be," Sophia allowed, "but Descartes would disagree. He'd argue that there are some ideas which can't come from our perception of the world and also can't be deduced by logic. The rules of logic themselves for example. How do we know something's logical—that it's impossible for something to exist and not exist at the same time? How is it that people seem to naturally have a concept of physical substances? Descartes would say that these ideas are innate, along with the capacity for abstract thought and the concept of God."

As she spoke Hyle swung his legs out of bed and lowered himself gently to the floor. He ambled sleepily over to the window and pulled the window coverings aside. The last cold light of day was fading and shadows of buildings covered the quad.

"This has all been very interesting," he said, looking out absently at the fading strip of rust colored sky, "but the certain knowledge I'm looking for is out there."

CHAPTER FORTY-TWO

THE LIBRARIANS

Hearing the pulsing of a bass line down the hall, Newman opened the door of their room and allowed the music to flood in. It was not yet dark enough to risk traveling outside, so with only a little effort he convinced Hyle and Sophia to go meet their neighbors before leaving for the library. They tracked the source of the music to a room three doors down and when Newman poked his head into the open doorway he was surprised to see the number of people that had packed into a room no larger than their own. Most were student aged men and women, although there was a woman at least as old as Newman sitting in the only chair in the room. On the desk behind her sat a silver haired man with thick glasses and a finger's width of gray hair on his chin. The remainder of the people sat on the beds and the floor or leaned against any available vertical surface. The conversation faded as one by one people looked up and noticed Newman standing in the doorway.

One of the students, who introduced himself as James, invited them to come in, but the best Newman could manage was to squeeze around to the inside of the doorway to allow Hyle and Sophia a clear view inside. James explained that he was the one who actually slept in the room and introduced many of his guests, leaving a few to make their own introductions. In turn, Newman introduced himself, Sophia and Hyle, telling the crowd that they had arrived early in the morning, going on to explain that they had been living in Maine and had come to use the library. After unsuccessfully trying to get Newman's attention, Hyle jumped in to steer the conversation to other topics, launching into a series of questions about the workings of life at the college.

Everyone had a job, they learned, and work started right after sunset. The older man managed food preparation in the dining hall, the woman had a security shift, and the students had a variety of roles. Some went into the forest to gather wood for the cogen plant, others traveled to surrounding towns to scavenge or trade for supplies. Many worked with groups trying to restore water or power, dig new tunnels or other civil engineering projects. James explained that he was the only one who would not be leaving for work soon, having been assigned a graveyard shift at the infirmary due to his background as a third year biology major.

Once the questions about Maine and why the trio had come to use the library had been left far behind in the conversation Hyle tried to extract Newman and Sophia from the room, but Newman made no motions of leaving, instead explaining his concern about trying to navigate the hill down to the library in the dark with his bad leg. Secretly concerned that Newman would reveal the details of their trip if left unsupervised, Hyle tried his best to construct convincing reasons that they should stick together, or at least find an excuse to pull Newman aside, but was ultimately forced to give up when Sophia stepped in to agree with Newman's rationale. In the end they talked for a while longer and Hyle and Sophia left just after dark as the crowd began to thin out.

The path down to the library turned out to be very treacherous. A light rain was falling, making the long grass slick, and almost no moonlight penetrated the clouds. After his feet slid out from underneath him, sending him skidding several feet downhill, Hyle grudgingly admitted to himself that Newman had made a wise decision. Fortunately Sophia could have found the way with her eyes closed and soon they were on the asphalt path that led to the library. The building was dark. Hyle stepped carefully into the blackness beneath the concrete portico feeling for the doors. He found the handles and pulled on them. The doors were locked.

"I thought there were supposed to be people living in here?" he hissed, referring to their recent conversation back in the dormitory.

"That's what they said," Sophia confirmed, uncertain why she felt the need to whisper outside the library.

The doors felt like glass and Sophia strained to see anything in the darkness inside. As her eyes adjusted she realized that there was something covering the doors on the inside. The glass windows on either side were the same.

"It looks like they've papered over the windows," she reported.

In the darkness Sophia jumped at the sudden sound of pounding on the glass. Hyle put his ear to the door to listen for a response. He thought he heard some whispered voices and shuffling, and a few seconds later he too jumped as a bolt snapped into place near his ear. The door cracked open.

"Who's there?" demanded a stern voice.

All was silent for a moment as Hyle looked back at Sophia and she looked into the shadows waiting for him to answer.

"Just a couple people who want to use the library," he answered tentatively.

"Really? Way cool," said the voice, and the door opened wider. A sliver of light filtered out from inside and framed a broad figure in the doorway. "Come on in."

They followed the figure inside. At his instruction Sophia closed the door behind and then they were led through some curtains that hung just behind the door. Stepping through it they were nearly blinded. A few fluorescent lights glowed between distant rows of books, but a bright light at chest level shone directly into their eyes from a few paces away. The figure strode quickly to the light and pointed it away from them.

"Sorry, security measures," he explained. "No worries boys, we have customers. They're here to use our library."

As the light spots faded from her vision, Sophia began to see the figure more clearly. She pegged him immediately as a perpetual graduate student. He appeared to be roughly her age—at least ten years too old to be an undergraduate. Although his wide face was freckled and his boyish appearance was enhanced by a short crew cut of red hair, wisps of gray streaked his long braided ponytail. The end of the tail was tied with a green bow and Sophia found herself thinking of a young Ben Franklin, although upon reflection she realized that this was probably more because of a semblance to the infamous kite rather than to Franklin himself.

The gooseneck lamp which had blinded her was now pointed mercifully downward to the top of a long counter that curved gently away. Behind the counter where normally the librarians would sit to check out books and sort through returns stood three more figures that looked like undergraduates. One still leveled a shotgun at her from behind a short filing cabinet. The other two were lowering their weapons, and a fourth figure watched them from between bookshelves on the other side of the lobby.

Hyle looked around.

"A little heavily armed for a bunch of librarians," he said with a nervous laugh.

"*Au contrair, mon frere,*" replied Ben Franklin, speaking to the entire room. "Now that we have managed to bomb ourselves back to the Dark Ages, this building contains a treasure more valuable than Fort Knox, and we, the Brotherhood of Leibowitz, are sworn to guard it. This building contains the cumulative wisdom of the human race. More than two millennia of knowledge—encyclopedias, scientific journals, news reports, history, books on just about anything you can imagine. We're here to secure that knowledge. It's already starting to get cold out. When the winter comes the cavemen will start looking for fuel to scavenge for their fires. If they burn these books they burn our past, our future, and our hopes of rebuilding. We're here to make sure that doesn't happen. If the Mona Lisa and Saint Basil's and the Empire State Building are all in ruins, at least we'll have photographs to remind us of what we created. Shakespeare, Monet, Gauguin, Milton—it's all in here in some form, and it's our job to make sure it stays."

Their escort swept his gaze around the room. Proud and inspired faces nodded in agreement.

"I'm Francis. Welcome to our library," he said, extending a meaty hand to Hyle. As they shook Francis' eyes darted back and forth between Hyle and Sophia. "Hey, did your friend find you?"

Hyle and Sophia exchanged puzzled looks. There was no way Newman could have beat them down to the library even if he had changed his mind about coming. Francis noted their confusion.

"A big dude. What was his name? Auld. That was it."

He watched their faces for recognition.

"A big black guy? Looks like a football player or maybe some kind of Special Forces soldier type? He was wearing a black tee shirt and some gray camo pants."

Hyle and Sophia shook their heads, mystified.

"That doesn't sound like anyone I know," Hyle replied. He looked at Sophia, who shook her head in agreement, and a knot began to form in his stomach.

"I don't think he was looking for us," she added, although for some reason she was not completely convinced that was true.

In his mind Hyle replayed the events since their arrival. Immediately his thoughts jumped to Newman telling the room full of strangers their purpose in coming.

"How long ago was he here?"

"Yesterday," Francis replied uncertainly, now looking as confused as Hyle and Sophia.

Hyle began to relax. "He must be looking for someone else."

"I don't think so. He described you two perfectly. A tall thin guy with short blond hair and an oriental looking woman with long hair." Francis stopped to think for a moment. "Were you guys traveling with an older guy with shoulder length wavy black hair and a small beard?"

"Yes, we are," Hyle said slowly and exchanged a concerned glance with Sophia. "But we weren't here yesterday. We got in late last night. He must have come sometime today."

"I don't think so dude. It was during the day, which is unusual, but unless I'm really starting to lose it, it wasn't that recently."

Hyle's stomach suddenly felt as if he had swallowed a bowling ball.

"What else did this guy say about us?"

"He said that you'd be coming from Maine—"

"Did he say 'would be coming' or 'came'?" Hyle interrupted. Francis caught the urgency in his voice.

"I—I—Now I'm not sure," he replied. "Sorry man. I don't remember his exact words."

"What else did he say about us? What else did he ask you?"

"That was pretty much it. The thing about Maine and describing the three of you and he said to let him know if we saw you."

"Did he say where he was staying or when he'd be back?"

Francis shook his head.

"This guy is no friend of ours," Hyle said. "Do us a favor. If he does come back, don't tell him you saw us."

"Okay, you got it. But this dude looked pretty determined. I'm sure we're not the only people he asked."

From behind Hyle Sophia put a hand on his shoulder and drew him backwards.

"Should we go warn Newman? Do you think he's in danger?" she whispered.

"Excuse us a second," Hyle said to Francis, and led Sophia a few steps farther away from the circulation desk. "No, he's in a building full of people. He should be as safe there as anywhere."

"What if this guy really did follow us from Maine?" worried Sophia.

"I don't know. It would have been pretty difficult without any of us noticing, but then stranger things have happened. Especially in the last couple of months."

"Maybe we should get Newman and leave here now before he does find us."

"No point in doing that," Hyle asserted. "If this is a bizarre case of mistaken identity, or this guy is from around here and saw us come in last night, there's no point in leaving. If he really did track us from Maine, I doubt he'd just give up the chase here if we left. If he did follow us I'd rather confront him here and determine the nature of his game than have him following around behind us out in some wasteland. But it's all the more reason to do what we came here to do as quickly as we can."

This analysis did not put Sophia at ease, but it was hard to argue against Hyle's logic. She shrugged a helpless assent and Hyle turned back to talk to Francis. The ponytailed guardian of the library was eager to help them find what they were looking for and became quite disgruntled when Hyle refused to tell him what that was. The computers that had stored the inventory of the library had all been fried by the EMP but Francis informed them that the brothers had built another one from scavenged parts and were in the process of creating a new directory, although it was not yet user friendly. They had also been forced to move some of the books around to make room for scientific journals that had been relocated from the science library, Francis explained, so it would be difficult to find some things without help. Despite this persuasion, Hyle insisted that he and Sophia would prefer to work alone, so the disappointed guardian showed them to the computer, leaving them with stern instructions to take great care with it and put everything back when they were finished. Not long into their research, Hyle had to go back and ask Francis for help finding copies of newspapers from recent years.

Pushing a cart loaded with boxes of compact discs, Hyle returned to the small alcove that held the computer and set to work with Sophia. He sorted through the disc boxes looking for major newspapers while she worked with the discs he set aside, searching first for references to Zendik, the Union of Faith or Madauros Village. After several hours of searching Sophia had not found any references to Madauros Village but there were hundreds of references to Zendik and his organization. As she came across these Sophia read the headlines aloud, pulling up the articles if Hyle expressed interest.

From reading these various stories, they were able to piece together a profile of Zendik that matched reasonably well with what they had learned in Asher. The earliest articles dated back to the year 2000 and referred mainly to events in California where he had staged a few anti-technology rallies and hosted interdenominational councils on a wide variety of topics. His attempts to put together a permanent interdenominational council of religious leaders met with only moderate success. Within a few years there was no longer any mention of an interdenominational council, and Zendik had evidently shifted his efforts to building his own organization from the ground up. He traveled widely in the United States and a few places in Europe, preaching the need for faith, the threat of technology, and the commonality of world religions. He was portrayed in many accounts as a very powerful and moving speaker. Within a few years of appearing on the scene he had founded the Union of Faith, launched a popular web site and weekly broadcast, and his organization had grown rapidly in membership from tens of thousands to several million. A recent article listed it among the top ten wealthiest non-profit organizations in the world. Zendik continued to travel around the globe, meeting increasingly often with prominent religious and political leaders in various countries. In the past two years he had traveled to several dozen locations in almost as many different countries. Even though there was no mention of Madauros Village there were several references to an estate and headquarters on a large parcel of private land in Arizona.

Their research for the evening ended when Francis poked his head around the corner.

"If you want to get some dinner, you'd better wrap it up. People are going to start queuing up soon."

A long line stretched out of the dining hall by the time they arrived. Newman had not been happy to hear about the stranger who was looking for them, or that Hyle and Sophia had gone ahead with their research instead of coming back to tell him. Almost everyone in the dorm room had left shortly after dark to go to work in some capacity or other, Newman told them, leaving him alone with the one student who had been assigned the graveyard shift at the infirmary.

"I don't think I would have been very safe at all, especially not knowing what to expect. It wouldn't have killed you to miss an hour or two of research to let me know about this," Newman grumbled as they took their place at the end of the line. "Did you at least find out something useful? Did you confirm your conspiracy theory?"

"Nothing that would convince you, I'm sure," Hyle replied. "But, yes, we did find out some interesting things. Zendik traveled a lot in the last few years and met with major government and religious leaders around the world. And the Union of Faith is extremely wealthy. It looks like he had both the finances and connections to involve himself seriously in international affairs."

"That doesn't mean anything. Lots of people are involved in international affairs without being involved in conspiracies."

"Maybe so, but care to guess the short list of where Zendik visited most often? London, Paris, Moscow, Tel Aviv, Beijing, New Delhi, Islamabad and of course lots of trips to Washington."

"So what does that mean?"

"I'll give you a hint," Hyle said through a grim smile. "Many of his meetings with political leaders in those cities included high-ranking military leaders."

"Military leaders are often present at big political meetings. What's so suspicious about visiting those particular places?"

"They're all the original world nuclear powers," Hyle explained. "The one thing they have in common is the atomic bomb."

CHAPTER FORTY-THREE

BODY AND SOUL

Everyone in line received a dinner doled out on traditional food service plates, a collection of plain white ceramic dishes occasionally sporting stripes of brown or green around the edge for variety. The trio of travelers watched quietly as the two servers handed plates out over a high glass counter in trade for gold colored tokens. At tables behind the counter, workers in assembly lines loaded more plates with carefully measured scoops of mixed vegetables at one station and then mashed potatoes at the next. At a third station each plate received a thin slice of meat and then finally a miniature loaf of bread. The queue stalled a few times when someone complained about getting a portion they thought was too small, but for the most part things moved smoothly and everyone seemed happy with the meal, particularly the meat. Handing the first server three of the tokens he had received back in the dorm, Newman informed Sophia and Hyle that the common practice was to save the loaf for breakfast the next morning.

As they crossed the dining hall to a quiet corner to continue their discussion, Sophia looked out over the low sloping brick walls that segregated the open area into small groups of tables. She was not sure whether to be relieved or disappointed to see no one resembling the stranger Francis described for them. The stranger was the first order of business once they sat down. In lowered voices they reviewed the possible explanations for why someone might be asking around about them but came to no conclusions. The discussion degenerated into bickering between Newman and Hyle, a replay of their exchange in the dorm when Newman had learned of the decision not to warn him about the stranger right away. In the end Newman admitted that he would probably have decided to stay in the dorm anyway and Sophia seized the opportunity to steer the conversation toward making plans for the following day.

Hyle laid out his intentions to look for any mention of Madauros Village or the Union of Faith in local Maine papers. When he mentioned also following up on the group's headquarters in Arizona, Newman informed them that he had heard from Delacroix that the organization had recently moved its headquarters to a place in southeastern Arizona, near the base of some mountains. Evidently this was another town like Asher, also in an unpopulated region, but Newman knew nothing more about it. When the discussion threatened to turn into another debate about the possible role of Zendik in the nuclear attacks, Sophia tried to change the topic again.

For a while Sophia entertained Hyle and Newman with stories of her college days. She fondly recalled one old philosophy professor who, upon noticing that one of his students had fallen asleep at his desk, set the clock ahead an hour and encouraged all the other students in the classroom to quietly pick up their things and sneak away to have class out on the quad.

"About fifteen minutes later the poor guy came tearing out the front door of Hascall

Hall, sure he was late for his next class. Of course we were all sitting there just outside the door and when he saw us—" Sophia did an impression of his reaction and laughed so hard that heads turned their way from nearby tables.

"That was one of my favorite classes," she said, after regaining her composure. "The professor had a great sense of humor. He was always telling jokes."

"I have a sort of amusing story you might appreciate," offered Hyle. "A long time ago there was this famous horse. If you asked it a simple math problem it would stomp out the answer. If you asked, 'What's two plus three?' the horse would stomp its hoof five times. It could do multiplication, division, even simple algebra. But one day his owner decided to really test his abstract thinking. He asked the horse, 'If I have a point at x equals one and y equals one and another point at x equals three and y equals three, what's the slope of the line that connects them?' The horse went crazy, broke its restraints and ran off into the wilderness never to be seen again. Do you know what the moral of the story is?"

Sophia and Newman looked at each other and shook their heads.

"Never put Descartes before de horse."

"Oh, that was awful," Sophia groaned and clutched her chest dramatically. "That one was actually painful—I like it. You get it, right, Newman? Analytical geometry? Okay, but do you guys know the old classic? Descartes is sitting in a bar and the bartender asks him if he wants another drink. He says, 'I think not' and promptly disappears."

"Sophia, how could you willfully misrepresent such a foundational piece of philosophy for the sake of mere humor? I am shocked," Hyle said, looking deadly serious. His face softened into a grin. "Although I suppose he had it coming. Anyone who decides to question their own existence rather than just believe what they see deserves a few good jokes at their expense."

"It all made sense to me," Newman said, a bit more seriously. "Besides, Hyle, you didn't seem to have any good arguments against it this afternoon."

"I was just being polite," Hyle countered. "Sophia already supplied one of the best arguments against Descartes. He split the physical world apart from the mental world."

"Why is that such a problem?" Newman challenged.

"Because you're stuck with some non-physical force outside the jurisdiction of science that's responsible for making things happen in the material world."

Newman shrugged, unimpressed with this objection.

"Actually, Newman, it is a significant problem," Sophia interjected. "In fact, the mind-body problem, or Cartesian split as it became known, is still a topic that's debated in various forms."

"It seems like it resolves a lot of problems by splitting out the physical world to be studied by science and leaving affairs of the soul and such to theology. Why is that a problem?"

"Raise your right hand for a second, Newman," Sophia said in reply, and Newman raised his hand. "Now if we were to try to explain what happened, you might say that I asked you to raise your hand, you heard me, decided to do what I asked and put your hand up, right?"

"Yes," Newman agreed.

"Here's the problem. My speaking is a physical event. Sound reaches your ears. Somehow it gets converted from a physical event into a mental sensation. How does that happen? How do physical sound waves cause a change in something non-physical? Then your consciousness—a thinking substance outside of and separate from the physical world—decides to put your hand up. How does your consciousness get your muscles to move? How does something non-physical interact with the physical world?"

"What did Descartes say?" asked Newman after thinking for several seconds.

"Actually, this is probably the weakest part of Descartes' entire theory," Sophia said.

"He believed that the non-physical and physical came together only in human beings. He didn't really provide a satisfying explanation, but he thought that the soul or consciousness and body interacted in the pineal gland."

Hyle nearly choked on his water trying to stifle a laugh. "See, that's the problem with invoking some mystical non-physical element into philosophy."

"Maybe the problem isn't with the mind-body split," Newman suggested. "Maybe it's with the expectation that everything has to be reducible to some physical cause that we can dissect."

"If you're willing to make that concession," Sophia said, "then there are some solutions to reunite the Cartesian split. One of them, called occasionalism, was proposed by Malebranche. He argued that God created both mind and body as separate but causes everything that occurs in both. The innate ideas we have we receive from God. If our hand goes up when we have the thought to raise our hand, it's because God has paired the two events, causing one event to happen 'on the occasion' of the other. To us it may appear that one event caused the other, but that's only because we're ignorant of the true cause behind both events."

"But that would completely defeat the idea of science," Hyle protested. "We couldn't have made the progress in understanding the world as well as we do if there were no laws of nature."

"Not necessarily," argued Sophia. "There are laws of nature, but only because God chooses to act in a routine and predictable way. The Ash'arites made a similar argument in medieval Islamic philosophy," Sophia noted. "According to Malebranche, God typically chooses to act in the most economical ways by default and these become the laws of nature. When one billiard ball collides with another, the other ball rolls away because that's the default for the will of God. We see that event and think one ball caused the other to move. Of course, God can choose to act in some other way, disobeying the laws of nature as it were, and that's the explanation for what we'd call a miracle."

"It sounds logically consistent, but it's not a very satisfying explanation," Hyle said.

"There were others who tried to formulate a more scientific model. In fact, there was a group at Cambridge University known as the Cambridge Platonists, which included Henry More and Ralph Cudworth. They believed that matter was inert, so in order for matter to have any sort of organization or motion, it would have to be acted upon by some sort of 'indiscernible spirits' or non-physical forces. These were ultimately an extension of God."

"That seems to be a fundamental problem with rationalism," Hyle commented. "It sounds like Descartes and Malebranche and the Cambridge Platonists all had to appeal to some concept of God to get the physical world to work out at all. If you're going to lay out a grand theory of the universe and you have to end it with 'and then God does the rest' it seems like a seriously deficient philosophy to me."

"Interesting," said Newman. "I was just thinking that any philosophy that reduces God to a set of mechanistic non-physical forces has so devalued the concept of God that you might as well not even use the name any more. And Descartes, even though he may have stayed close to the traditional concept of God in some ways, has Him going into retirement after creating the world. Only Malebranche seems to have retained any concept of a God who is at work in the world the way He's described in scripture."

"It's all just semantics to me," Hyle replied. "It doesn't matter what name or description you give your set of indefinable non-physical forces. If you have to resort to a supernatural explanation to make the world work, there's something wrong with your philosophy."

"It's a big challenge," Sophia said, "to explain how consciousness interacts with the physical world while preserving simultaneously the laws of science and nature and the concept of a God who is still active in the universe."

"Probably why nobody's been able to do it," Hyle said under his breath.

"Benedict Spinoza may have come closest," Sophia replied, "but his conception of God was so different from the accepted ideas of the day that he was not only banned from his own Jewish community, but also had the rare distinction of being excommunicated by the Catholic Church even though he was a Jew."

"Sounds promising so far," Hyle said. "What was his theory?"

"Spinoza argued that Descartes' thinking substance and extended substance could really only be one substance, by definition. Whatever existed, whatever form it took, was the stuff of the universe and thinking and physical extension were just two attributes of the same substance. We can perceive an apple as being red or being hard or being sweet, because those are all different attributes of the same thing. In the same way, consciousness and materiality are just two different ways of experiencing the same thing, which Spinoza said is God or nature."

"So which is it," Hyle asked, only partly joking.

"According to Spinoza they're the same thing," answered Sophia. "Starting with the Cartesian definition of a substance as that which requires nothing else to exist, Spinoza reasoned that the only thing that seems not to require anything else is the totality of everything. Anything else is described and understood in relation to other things. He also reasoned that if God is infinite, then He must be everything, because if there was anything God was not, He'd be excluded and limited. So for Spinoza, God is one and the same with the entirety of nature."

"I can see why his philosophy wasn't accepted by the religious community," Newman commented. "It's certainly very different from the biblical depiction of God."

"Maybe so, but he was also one of the first to argue that scripture was written by various authors as a popularized collection of instruction rather than a record of divine revelation. This was another way he got himself in trouble, but he was trying to establish that scripture was best understood by faith rather than reason. It was his way of trying to preserve some of the Cartesian split, separating the domain of reason and philosophy from the domain of faith and theology so that both could be equally valid ways of understanding the world."

"When was this?" Newman asked, as if he had just made some connection. "Simon's *Critical History of the Old Testament* was published in 1678 and I thought that it was the first textual criticism of the Bible to suggest that it might have been written by different authors. And Pascal made a very similar argument about reason and faith."

"Maybe Simon was the first to publish ideas which were being discussed at the time," Sophia speculated. "All these philosophies were published in the same few decades after Descartes' *Meditations*. Spinoza would have been before Malebranche and Simon and roughly contemporary with More, Cudworth and Pascal."

"You don't mean Blaise Pascal, the mathematician?" Hyle interrupted.

"Yes," Newman confirmed. "Pascal said that reason and faith were just two ways of seeing the same thing. He used the example of a 'trick picture' like the white candlestick between two black faces—something that may appear one way to you at first, but suddenly can be seen in another, equally valid way. Why do you sound so surprised, Hyle?"

"Because Pascal was one of the great figures in the development of science. In fact, pressure is measured in pascals because of the work he did on air pressure. One of the first computer programming languages was named after him too. Pascal's father was a tax collector, so Pascal built him a mechanical adding machine. It's considered by some to be the earliest computer. I didn't realize he was so religious."

"He may not have been originally, but he had a life changing experience one night crossing the Seine," Newman explained. "It was during a great storm, and Pascal had a revelation where he personally felt the presence of God—the God of Abraham, Isaac and Jacob, not of the philosophers and scholars, as he described it. After that experience he joined a Catholic reform sect that had revived interest in Augustine, moved into their monastery, recorded his thoughts and developed them into a defense of faith in an age of science. When he died he left behind all his notes and his friends collected them and published them as his *Pensees*."

"What a waste," Hyle said. "I wonder what other things he would have discovered or invented if he hadn't had this flash of revelation."

"'The heart has its reasons that reason cannot comprehend,'" Newman replied, quoting Pascal in his own defense. "Obviously he thought that helping people come to know God was more important than advancing science. Pascal subscribed to the Augustinian idea that you couldn't come to know God by logic—it had to be by revelation or inspiration—but you could make yourself more receptive by reading scripture or following the right kind of logic."

Hyle was still shaking his head in disbelief.

"Are you familiar with G.W. Leibniz?" Sophia asked. Hyle stopped shaking his head and nodded. "What do you know about him?"

"Another great mathematician," Hyle replied. "He invented calculus just before Newton did. He also developed mathematical logic and proposed a theory of kinetic energy." Hyle turned back to Sophia. "Why did you ask about Leibniz?"

"Because he was more than just a mathematician. He was also heavily influenced by Descartes and Spinoza and considered to be one of the great rationalist philosophers."

"It seems to be a common flaw with mathematicians of that era," Hyle noted dryly.

"Not surprising really," Sophia answered. "Mathematics seems to exist in pure form in the human mind and yet it correlates with nature. It makes sense that mathematicians should see our understanding of the world as coming to us through reason. But Leibniz also thought that there existed what he called 'truths of fact' in addition to 'truths of reasoning' or what we'd nowadays call synthetic versus analytic truths."

"You might," Newman said. "I haven't heard the terms before. What's the difference?"

"A synthetic statement is something that might be true out of a range of possibilities and you can't know if it really is or not until you check. An analytic statement must be logically true or false. For example, if I said that my neighbors are a man and his wife, that would be a synthetic statement. It might be true or it might not. But if I say that they're a bachelor and his wife, you can know without checking that my statement is false. That's an analytic statement."

"That makes sense," Newman said. "But why is that so significant?"

"It became significant to epistemology because it distinguished between two types of possible knowledge. It was significant to Leibniz because it helped form a foundation for the rest of his philosophy. Since some things logically exclude others, if follows that there are only some sets of possibilities that are compatible. Leibniz had a more traditional view of God than Spinoza, so to answer the question of how evil can exist in the world if God is good, Leibniz argued that God created the best of all possible worlds, emphasis on the word *possible*. That doesn't necessarily mean a perfect world, because that would be impossible, even for God. Granting creatures free will, for example, comes with the consequence that they may make imperfect choices and do evil. This idea was published in a work entitled *Theodicy*, a word he coined that has since become a term for the justification of God in the face of evil in the world."

"It sounds like a pretty naïve theory to me but it sounds familiar," Hyle commented sardonically. "Wasn't it one of two great classical works—*The Idiot* and *Theodicy*?"

Sophia groaned.

"No, the other major work Leibniz produced was *Monadology*," she said. "Although you might be happy to know that *Theodicy* was satirized pretty unmercifully in Voltaire's *Candide*."

"And is monadology supposed to be what, the study of monads?" Hyle quipped.

"Actually, yes." Sophia replied. "That was another term he coined. A monad is sort of a basic unit of activity. Most people of his day saw matter as inert and needing some external force to organize and move it, but Leibniz saw an inherent potential for activity in material things. Monads are the basic units of that potential or activity, a bit like non-physical atoms or miniature souls, except with a much broader range. The simplest monads make up inorganic matter and each human mind or soul is a monad. God created monads to be able to exist together in a pre-established harmony. Even God is a monad."

"See, this is the problem with rationalism," Hyle said. "Once you assume innate ideas, the next question is where did they come from, and the rationalist answer always seems to end up with God."

"Why is that a problem?" Newman challenged.

"Because it assumes that God exists."

"It's fitting that we were just talking about Pascal, Hyle. Have you ever heard of Pascal's Wager?"

"No, what was it?"

"Not was. It still is a wager that you can make. It goes something like this," Newman explained. "Either God exists or He doesn't exist. You can't know for sure which is the case, but what you believe will affect how you live your life. So how should you place your bet? If you say God doesn't exist and you're right, so what? Congratulations—you can live a meaningless life in a meaningless world and be right. But if you're wrong, denying God would be a big mistake. On the other hand, if you say that God exists and you're wrong, you lose nothing, but if you're right, you gain everything. How would you make your wager?"

CHAPTER FORTY-FOUR

DISTURBED SLEEP

Sophia awoke into darkness with her senses alert. The squeaking of the springs beneath her mattress reminded her where she was as she rolled over onto her elbow to listen. The three companions had come back from dinner and gone straight to bed even though the hallway was buzzing with activity. Sophia was not sure how long she had been asleep. It was quieter now but she could still hear the soft murmur of voices and a baseline thumping rhythmically somewhere down the hall. On the other side of the room one of the men was snoring. The room was black. Her eyes were automatically drawn to the only thing visible, a dim sliver of light that marked the bottom of the door. She was just registering two spots where the line faded back toward darkness when a sharp rapping on the door jolted her upright. Sophia recognized it instantly as the sound that had awakened her.

While she collected her senses and began fumbling with the blanket there was another series of knocks on the door. Now more awake, Sophia realized that the knocking was not as loud as she had thought. In a half whisper she mumbled something in the general direction of the knocking while she pulled her blanket around herself and swung her feet out of bed. In the darkness she felt for the doorknob and pulled open the door. Light flooded her eyes, obscuring the large figure that stood in the doorway. A strangled scream from down the hall stopped her heart. For an instant she was paralyzed until the sound of bongos and maracas rose up behind another short yell and she realized that it was only the start of a new song.

As her eyes adjusted to the light, the image in the doorway slowly resolved. Before her stood a large man, as tall as Hyle but much more muscular. His skin was dark, very nearly black, and his appearance was striking. He was wearing night camouflage fatigues in shades of gray and black and his belt held a pistol and a roll of black cloth that appeared to be a beret. Not only was he clean shaven, a state not as common as it had once been, but naturally handsome as well. Although his face showed some lines, it was difficult to place his age. His eyes looked as though they had seen a lot and had an intensity which, combined with his physical size, could have made him quite alarming. The trace of a smile helped to put Sophia somewhat at ease but she was still relieved to hear nearby voices down the hall.

"You must be Mr. Auld," she said extending her hand tentatively.

"Pleased to meet you," he said nodding. He looked like he was about to say more, but instead gave her a broad grin, as if they were sharing something wonderfully humorous. Coming from anyone else the Cheshire Cat smile of perfect white teeth would have seemed artificial or intimidating, but to Sophia it felt genuine.

"Auld," he confirmed, squeezing her hand lightly. "Nicolas Auld. And you must be Sophia."

Like his appearance, his deep voice hinted at a power much greater than his gentle tone conveyed. It seemed somehow familiar, with a soothing musical quality—a Caribbean accent perhaps—which helped to put her further at ease.

"I understand you were looking for us…yesterday," Sophia said, watching Auld's face closely as she added the last word.

"Yes, I have been looking for you," he replied. His smile faded, but he gave no other reaction to her statement. "I have come to tell you that you are in danger. You must not stay here too long."

The warning took Sophia off guard. Any fear of danger had come from the knowledge that there was a stranger asking around about them. That he had been looking for them to deliver a warning was enough of a twist, but she was also thrown by the slow soothing manner of his speech which seemed to conflict with the urgency of the message. For a moment, Sophia considered the idea that it might be some elaborate prank. And she realized that she still did not know when he had first come looking for them. Her mind spun with questions.

"Why? Who…?" she managed after several seconds of stunned silence.

Auld gave her a sympathetic smile.

"I'm sorry to surprise you like this. But you must finish your work here as quickly as you can."

There was another long silence. In the distance a piano and bass guitar had joined the bongos and a voice yelled out indiscernible lyrics. Sophia listened absently as she tried to process all the information.

"What danger?" she asked, choosing one of her many questions.

"The world is very dangerous now, Sophia," the large figure said. "Many people have been killed. Most people. Survivors are running around fighting each other without even knowing why." Auld shook his head sadly. "They never do. Human beings have been killing each other for countless decades for the gods they made," he said, glancing down the hall. "Time is not long before they will come here, and when they do, you must be gone."

"How do you know?"

"I cannot say. But trust an old soldier. You do not have much time."

Sophia tried to focus her sleep addled mind. From the song, backup vocals like a train whistle blowing over and over distracted her. She felt that she was missing something. Auld had said a lot and yet she felt as though her question were still unanswered. The confusion must have shown on her face.

"What's puzzling you?" he asked.

"Why us?"

A smile returned to the dark face and his eyes flashed before fixing her face with a penetrating gaze.

"Because you have come from Maine."

At first the reply seemed to make perfect sense, but as Sophia thought about it, she realized that she should have worded her question more carefully. It was not clear whether Auld meant that he had been looking for them because they came from Maine or whether someone else was after them for that reason. She assumed it had something to do with Asher, but before she could form another question in her mind, she found herself watching the dark form disappear down the corridor. From the other end of the hall, a guitar wailed and a falsetto voice yelled something over and over as the music faded away.

Sophia woke in the darkness with her heart pounding in her chest. Light snoring was coming from the other side of the room, but otherwise all was quiet. She rolled over onto her elbow to listen for a while and then, hearing nothing, turned over and went back to sleep.

CHAPTER FORTY-FIVE

BEATING THE TORTOISE

In the library, research was not going well. Despite her best efforts Sophia was only able to find a few new articles and none of them turned up any new information. She had said nothing of her visit the previous night, unsure by morning whether it might not have just been a dream. Nevertheless she felt a pressure to get results quickly. The only thing that kept her from getting frustrated was that Hyle already was and she felt an obligation to be supportive. When she could think of nothing more to try, Sophia yielded the chair to Hyle and stood behind him, watching as he tried different search parameters, pursued long shots and became more and more discouraged. She rested her hands on his shoulders, leaning in occasionally when some lead looked promising and patting his arm or rubbing his shoulders as if he were a prize fighter waiting for the ninth round bell when each lead came inevitably to a dead end.

Like a mother hen, Francis had been popping in regularly to check on their progress, asking if there was anything he could do to help. Even though he was able to retrieve most of the articles they were looking for, Hyle found his frequent interruptions annoying. Sophia on the other hand saw only a genuine interest in helping. She had been gently making the case with Hyle that they should tell Francis more about what they were trying to find, and once Hyle's frustration reached a critical level he finally agreed.

Enlisting the aid of the self-appointed head librarian was a turning point for the day. They told Francis that they were looking for information on the purchase of land in Maine and he set off cheerfully to search, returning quickly with a small pile of discs and bound volumes that indexed various financial publications. By dinnertime they had still not found any direct reference to the land near Madauros Village, but they had learned that the Union of Faith owned several holding companies.

When they were all seated around their table in the corner of the dining hall, Sophia finally got up the courage to tell Hyle and Newman about her encounter with Auld. They discussed it for a while, trying to think of a way to determine if it had really happened and decide what to do about it if it had.

"And you really can't say whether it was a dream or if it really happened?" Hyle asked for the third time.

"No. I told you. I really don't know. It seemed real at the time, but I don't remember going back to bed," Sophia answered, her usually calm voice mirroring some of Hyle's frustration.

Newman shot her a furtive wink.

"See, Hyle," he said, "this just goes to show that Descartes was right. You can't trust your senses."

"Oh, not that crap again," Hyle sighed and cradled his head in his hands, but when he looked up again Newman and Sophia were watching him expectantly. "You want to know why all this philosophical rationalism is a bunch of nonsense, Newman? Let me ask you a question. Do you think you could outrun a tortoise?"

The question had the desired effect, coming out of left field and clearly catching Newman by surprise. Now it was Hyle's turn to wait expectantly for an answer.

"Yes," Newman replied suspiciously. He looked at Sophia and was dismayed to see that she was nodding knowingly and smiling. "You know where he's going with this, don't you?"

"Sophia, no helping," Hyle cautioned. "Now, Newman, let's imagine you're going to race a tortoise from here to the next town. Since you're so much faster, it would only be gentlemanly to give the tortoise a good head start. Imagine that you let the tortoise get up to a crossroad off in the distance before you start out. With me so far?"

Newman nodded and gave a helpless shrug to Sophia.

"You quickly reach the intersection and close the gap between you and the tortoise. But while you were running to the intersection, the tortoise has plodded along a bit further to a tree up ahead. So now you set off from the intersection, but by the time you reach the tree, the tortoise has moved even farther ahead, next to a rock. By the time you get to the rock, the tortoise will have moved again. Every time you reach the place the tortoise was it'll have moved a little further in the time it took you to get there. You'll never catch it. So logically you can see that you could never win that race against the tortoise."

"That's Zeno's paradox," Sophia told Newman. "Originally it was Achilles racing the tortoise. There's another version with an arrow that always travels half the distance to its target but never hits it."

"Don't feel bad, Newman, Achilles lost too," added Hyle. "That's the problem with rationalism. Logic can get you into trouble every bit as much as the senses can. And what Zeno's paradox proves, assuming that you still believe that arrows can hit their targets and people can outrun tortoises, is that knowledge about how the world really works comes to us through observation rather than logic."

"That does seem like the logical conclusion," replied Newman pointedly. "But if logic isn't perfect and we have already established that the senses are flawed, where does that leave us?"

"I believe 'screwed' was the description Hyle used earlier," Sophia said throwing Hyle's words back at him as a challenge. Her eyes flashed mischievously.

"No, not necessarily," Hyle said reflexively. He had to pause for a moment to think about what it was that he really did believe. "Even though empirical observation isn't flawless and the senses can sometimes be fooled, we don't have to assume that they usually are. In fact, they usually are reliable, and even when they're not, we're constantly making new observations of things under different circumstances. We may see a bent stick in water, but when we pull it out, we figure out that it's straight. Everything we really know about the world we know from observation."

"Really? Everything?" Sophia asked, in a tone that sounded as if she had received an unexpected present. "The Scholastics said, '*Nihil est in intellectu quod non prius fuerit in sensu.*' Nothing is in the mind which was not first in the senses. Is that what you're saying? All knowledge comes to us first from empirical observation?"

The invocation of Latin eroded Hyle's confidence somewhat, but he nodded in agreement.

"We start off life as a ball of cells that develops into a human being," he stated. "There are ways to transmit physical information from parents to offspring, and maybe some psychological characteristics, but there's no way to physically transmit knowledge. It has to be acquired by our experience."

"So then you believe that the mind at birth is a blank slate, a *tabula rasa*, which is written on by experience."

"Yes, that's a very eloquent way of putting it."

"But how do you get to a concept like freedom or justice or love just by walking around and picking things up and looking at them?" Newman challenged.

"Or even more basic," Sophia interjected, "how do you even arrive at a simple concept like a plate or a chair? Our eyes just detect color and brightness. With no innate ideas, how would I ever come to the conclusion that this patch of tan underneath you is a chair? How would I be able to distinguish it from any other splotch of tan that might happen to pass in front of my eyeballs?"

"That's similar to asking how we can be sure of anything if we know that the senses can be deceived," Hyle replied after thinking for a moment. "The first time you saw a splotch of tan, as you put it, you'd have no basis to know it was a chair. But that's the key. Observation isn't a one time deal. At first sensation may be just an overwhelming confusion of colors, sounds, textures and all, but as we make more and more observations we begin to discern similarities and differences, to see patterns and to categorize things. We begin to put the visual patterns together with sensations of color, hardness, shape, temperature and build mental images of objects in the material world. If we always see people sitting on one type of object we'll associate it with that function. Eventually, by hearing the word 'chair' in association with the object we learn its name. Of course once language is developed that's a powerful tool for abstract thought and development of even more complex concepts like love and justice."

"But to be able to learn from sensation there must be innate concepts," Newman objected, "otherwise everything would merely be an overwhelming confusion of sensations. There would be no basis for discerning patterns or categorizing things. The mind can't start off as a completely blank slate or it would stay that way."

"There does need to be some pre-existing mechanism in the brain for finding patterns," Hyle admitted, "but it doesn't necessarily have to be a set of innate ideas." He tried to think of some purely mechanical way that the brain might recognize patterns but could not come up with a plausible explanation. Fortunately Sophia saved him.

"Let me ask a question that may shed some light on things," she said. "Remember Avicenna, the medieval Arabic philosopher? He proposed something called the 'flying man' scenario. Suppose a man came into existence all at once, fully developed, but in a void. There's no light, no sound, nothing to smell, taste or touch. He's even suspended so that he can't even touch any part of his own body. So with no sensation of any kind, what would such a person know?"

"At the very least he'd know that he existed," Newman responded immediately, recalling their discussion in Asher. "He should at least know '*Je pense donc je suis.*'"

"That's essentially the conclusion Avicenna came to, by the way," Sophia whispered to Hyle while Newman paused to think.

"And from there he should be able to follow the same path as Descartes."

"Not very far," Hyle said, interrupting Newman. "Where would he get the concept of a demon? And what would he be deceived about? Without any interaction with physical objects I'm not sure that he'd be capable of having concepts of anything at all."

"What about mathematics?" Newman protested. "The rules of math apply even in the complete absence of physical objects. As you said before, Hyle, one plus one always equals two. Same with the basics of logic, like the concept that it's impossible for something to exist and not exist at the same time."

"One plus one equals two what though?" challenged Hyle. "What things are you talking about? In order to have a concept of numbers you first need to have a concept of discrete objects to count. It's true that the more complex aspects of mathematics are derived abstractly, but they're built on basic principles that are learned from experience, just like language. Counting objects, adding them together into a group, dividing them into piles—after all, that's the way we teach children basic math skills. The same must be true of rules of logic. Without any external sensations I don't think this 'flying man' would even be able to count, let alone develop the concepts of thinking, of self or of existence to be able to say, 'I think therefore I am.'"

"This is exactly why Descartes was so important," Sophia pronounced. "By dividing the world into the physical and the non-physical, he framed several philosophical issues that tend to polarize people to this day. In a way, he revived the old debate between the Aristotelians and Platonists over the material versus the transcendental with yet another twist. Now it's the empiricists versus the rationalists."

"There must have been people who didn't accept Descartes," Hyle suggested.

"Sure there were," Sophia replied. "There were some who tried to ignore the Cartesian split by arguing that either the physical or the non-physical realm was primary while the other was just an artifact. There were others who tried to reunite the physical and non-physical worlds on equal footing by modifying Descartes and still others who rejected his philosophy altogether. In fact, as soon as *Meditations* was circulated, Pierre Gassendi wrote a serious critique of Descartes' metaphysics. Gassendi admitted that the senses were flawed, but argued that logic was also flawed. For example, he took the syllogism, a primary element of Aristotelian logic—Socrates is a man, all men are mortal, therefore Socrates is mortal—and argued that you can't make a statement like 'all men are mortal' unless you have examined all the cases, which is impossible since there are infinitely many. Furthermore, in the case of this example, 'Socrates is a man' isn't only a statement, but part of the evidence for 'all men are mortal' so this is a case of circular reasoning. By making the case against logic he was making a case against both Descartes and the Scholastics."

"So Gassendi was a skeptic, like Hyle?" Newman taunted. Hyle started to protest, but Sophia did not give him the chance, and he had to settle for staring at Newman like a wounded animal.

"A mitigated skeptic, yes. He used skepticism against Descartes and the Scholastics, but he said that even though we can't have certain knowledge, we do know how things appear to us, so he was a proponent of the new science of Copernicus and Galileo. Gassendi tried to revive Epicureanism, leaving out or modifying the parts that conflicted with Christian doctrine, but retaining the concept of atomism. And the atomistic principle that basic units of matter could come together in different ways to determine the properties of matter had an influence on John Locke, who drew on it to propose a theory of human learning from basic building blocks of perception very much like the one you just presented, Hyle."

"I'm actually familiar with Locke," Hyle said, pleased to be able to keep pace with Sophia for once.

"I am too," said Newman, "but I thought he was more of a social philosopher. I remember learning that his political ideas were part of the inspiration for the American and French Revolutions because he portrayed societies as contracts where government is in service of the people, and he reserved the right for people to revolt if government failed to serve them or abused its privileges."

"Yes, he's one of a handful of philosophers who made significant contributions to both epistemology and social philosophy," Sophia agreed. "And in both cases Locke built on foundations laid by Thomas Hobbes. Hobbes believed that there was nothing in the universe that was transcendent or non-physical, and he described society in his *Leviathan* as a collection of people who willingly hand over power to monarchs to ensure their safety and well being. Locke expanded on these ideas, and his social theory and empirical theory of knowledge are very compatible. Both theories place the emphasis on the building blocks, where people come together to form societies on the one hand and sense data come together to form knowledge on the other."

"I learned about Locke as one of the founding fathers of the scientific method," Hyle said. "If I remember correctly he helped establish the rules of objective observations for science."

"That's true," Sophia acknowledged. "In his *Essay Concerning Human Understanding* Locke divided the properties of physical objects into primary attributes and secondary attributes. He described primary attributes as those which were inherent properties of the object, like length or weight, and could be measured objectively. Secondary attributes, like color or taste, he believed were not inherent and could only be described subjectively because they could be experienced differently by different observers."

"That's an important distinction to make," Hyle noted. "What you can observe objectively versus what observations may be colored by your own perceptions."

"Yes, but his theory of knowledge went far beyond that. Locke argued, as you did, Hyle, that we start off as a *tabula rasa*, and as we have sensations they're stored and accessible to the mind as memories. All knowledge is built up from basic sensations in gradual steps by association of these memories. Locke believed that all we could know was that which we could sense. And another thing you and Locke agree on Hyle—he rejected the argument for innate ideas."

"And rightfully so," Hyle declared.

"Of course Leibniz wrote a rebuttal to Locke, cleverly entitled *New Essays on Human Understanding*. Locke clearly laid out the empiricist view that knowledge comes from the senses, but he also seemed to be bordering on a materialist philosophy that everything was ultimately reducible to some kind of physical phenomena, even the intellect."

"Which sounds entirely reasonable to me," Hyle said.

"But Leibniz presented this example. Imagine that you take the brain and magnify it to a size that we could walk around inside and see it at the microscopic level. Assuming it's all physical, just like a great machine, you might see all sorts of mechanical activities going on. Or maybe given our modern understanding we'd expect to see chemicals and electrical impulses shooting back and forth between cells. But do you know what you wouldn't expect to see?"

After a moment of silence Hyle realized that it was not a rhetorical question. He tried to picture the inner workings of the brain and what might be missing.

"An idea," answered Newman.

"Exactly," Sophia said. "An idea. Or a concept, or a visual image, or a memory. When we see a chair, we don't somehow draw a little picture of a chair somewhere in our brains or build tiny models. These things exist in a non-physical form in our intellect."

Hyle began to formulate an objection. While it was true that it was not possible to pinpoint individual ideas or memories inside the brain, it seemed like a leap to say that this meant that they must not be stored physically. He was about to make this case but Sophia was already on to the next point.

"The other thing Leibniz pointed out is that we're self-aware. If we assume knowledge is built through sensation as you and Locke have argued, Hyle, that could explain how we come to know chairs and apples and lumps of wax, and maybe even ideas like love and justice. But how do we know that we're seeing something? We don't just have the experience of seeing an apple—we're aware that we're seeing an apple. You can't see seeing. You can't see thinking, but we're aware that we're thinking when we do it. Of course Leibniz would say that we're dependent on some form of innate ideas for our self-awareness."

"It still seems to me that a good theory should be able to explain the world in purely physical terms," Hyle maintained, not ready to concede the point. Sophia decided to change tracks.

"I don't suppose you have heard of George Berkeley?" she asked. Hyle shook his head. "Berkeley was an empiricist who started with Locke's theory of knowledge but came to some interesting conclusions. Let me illustrate his theory by asking you a question, Hyle. Does justice exist? Or love?"

"It depends on what you mean by existence. Really they're just words. You could say that they exist as concepts in our minds, and we can point to examples out in the real world that fit our concepts, but they don't exist independently of us. I thought we settled that back when we were discussing the nominalists and realists."

"Fine, I'm just establishing common ground to start from," Sophia replied with the trace of a smile. "What about the chair you're sitting on? Does that exist?"

"Yes, of course," Hyle answered without hesitation.

"What about the concept of a chair that we have in our minds? Does that work the same way as a concept of love or justice?"

"Yes, they're all concepts that we can talk about abstractly. The concept part works the same way—it's just that the things they refer to are different. Love and justice are creations of our intellect that exist only in our conception and we project those ideas on things we see in the world. The concept of chairs exists in our minds too, but there are real chairs out in the material world, separate from our conception."

"Are you sure they're really different?" Sophia challenged. "How do you know that your chair has its own independent reality as opposed to something like love or justice?"

"Because I can sense it directly," Hyle replied cautiously. He knew that Sophia was driving toward some point, but could not figure out what it was. "I can see it, touch it, smell it, knock on it and hear what sound it makes. I suppose I could even chew on it to taste it. It's subject to all of my senses, and the senses are what we use to detect things in the physical world. You can't see, hear, smell, touch or taste love or justice. You can only talk about them as abstract ideas."

"Okay, Hyle, consider your chair for a minute, or an apple or lump of wax or anything you can apply your senses to. If you strip away all of its attributes, its length, its weight, its shape, its smell, its color and texture—everything that you can sense—what's left?"

"Nothing," replied Hyle. "What we can know about the physical world is what we can sense."

"Then if you agree that there's not some intangible aspect to physical objects beyond what we can sense, is it fair to say that physical objects are nothing more than just collections of attributes?"

"Yes, I suppose so," Hyle agreed hesitantly.

"Do you remember Aristotle's principle of potential and actualization where the apple and the eye both participate in the form that's called 'red'? The apple has the potential to be red and the eye actualizes that potential. Berkeley took this idea one step farther. He concluded that what we call an apple is nothing but a package of potentials or attributes. Without being actualized, the apple is nothing. For Berkeley, to be is to be perceived. Without perception there is no existence."

"That can't be true. If I am alone in my room and close my eyes, would my desk and chair and walls cease to exist?" Hyle asked rhetorically.

"There's a cliché that's often associated with Berkeley's philosophy. If a tree falls in the forest and no one is there to hear it, does it make a sound?"

"Yes, of course it does. And this chair will still exist, even if we all stand up and close our eyes."

"That's exactly why Descartes believed that our concept of matter must be an innate idea," Sophia explained. "It doesn't seem to be derived through observation or logic and yet it seems intuitively obvious. Berkeley solved this apparent conflict with common sense by explaining that everything is perceived by God, or more poetically, everything inheres in the mind of God."

"Sounds a bit like Plotinus," said Newman, who had been listening quietly.

"Sounds a bit like a cop out," Hyle amended.

"He's also known as Bishop Berkeley, Bishop of Cloyne." Sophia said. "Philosophy, science and religion were not so clearly divided in those days and Berkeley also did work in optics and perspective. Don't think you can just dismiss his ideas because they happen to involve God. Even if you leave that part out his philosophy has some important implications."

"Like what? If I close my eyes I can make Newman disappear?" Hyle quipped.

"No, think about it seriously for a minute, Hyle. You said that our concept of the chair was like our concepts of love or justice. What about the sensations that make up the concept of the chair?" Sophia pressed. "The patterns of color or hardness and texture or sensations of hot or cold—not the properties, but the sensations themselves—do these exist in our mind too, or do they have some kind of physical presence?"

"No, they exist as memories, like the concept of the chair, only much more basic," Hyle replied.

"So if you agree with Berkeley that what we call physical objects are just collections of attributes—which are known to us only as perceptions—and you agree that our perceptions exist only in our mind, what would ever bring you to postulate the existence of an external physical world? Why would you not conclude that chairs are in fact just concepts that we construct in our mind and project on the world just like love and justice?"

There was a long silence while Hyle tried to think of a good response. Before he could, Sophia decided to drive the point farther home.

"Here's another way to think about it. Berkeley claimed that an idea can be like nothing but another idea. Concepts like chairs and apples exist fully in our minds as ideas, right? We can discuss them abstractly without the object being present. If the object were present, what more would there be to say? Nothing. Anything you'd try to express would be an idea, a sensation, a mental image. That's all we have. We have no access to anything else."

Sophia allowed herself a satisfied smile as she watched Hyle struggle with this argument.

"This strikes me as one of those things like Zeno's paradox," Hyle commented at length. "It sounds logical, and may be hard to argue against, but common sense will tell you clearly that logic has gone wrong somewhere. If I close my eyes, my room is still there, and even if every human being were wiped off the face of the earth, this chair would still exist."

"The important question here isn't whether things exist. The question is where does reality lie? Is it somewhere 'out there', or is it in our minds?" Sophia asked. "I seem to recall that you took a position very quickly against the medieval realists, but I'm sure it was common sense to them that universals must have their own existence and reality independent from us. Now here you sit pleading common sense to defend the existence of some material world that lies beyond our senses, with no more basis to support your claim than the realists had. You believe that all we can know is what we can sense, and what we sense exists as mental images. If that's the case, what basis do you have for saying that there's something called the 'physical world' then?"

"If there's no external physical world that exists independent from us, then where do these sensations come from?" Hyle challenged.

"A good question, but you're changing the subject. The question is where does our concept of an independent physical world come from?" Sophia said. "It couldn't have been built gradually from the sensations themselves, because without already having a concept of an external world, we'd experience sensations only as mental activities— impressions of color, sound, texture. Is the concept of matter an innate idea? If you say yes, then you're conceding to Descartes and the next question you'd have to answer is where that innate idea came from. You know where Descartes said it came from."

"Yes," Hyle acknowledged with a sigh. "So that's not an option. I still don't think that the concept of matter or a physical world needs to be an innate idea."

The other way out then," continued Sophia, "which I'm sure would make Newman happy, would be to stick to the idea that there is in fact a material world—something that exists 'out there' somewhere beyond our perceptions even after we strip away all attributes. Something that causes all of our sensations and yet somehow lies beyond them. In other words, something transcendent that we can never fully understand or explain—the ultimate reality behind this shadow reality that we're able to perceive."

CHAPTER FORTY-SIX

GRAVITY

Sophia slept fitfully, plagued by dreams. She could not remember anything about them but vague impressions. The last dream ended with a voice calling her name, a voice she knew from somewhere. She took hold of this thread of familiarity and followed it, pulling herself slowly back to consciousness. Hyle was sitting at the foot of her bed watching her.

"Sophia, are you all right?" he asked in a hushed voice when she finally opened her eyes. She felt a gentle hand on her shoulder.

"I think you were having a bad dream."

She nodded groggily at Hyle. She felt exhausted. Her eyes scanned the dimly lit room but the rest of her body refused to even consider the thought of movement.

"Where's Newman?"

"He's down the hall with his buddies. It's almost dark already."

Sophia's eyes fell to the window. The barest traces of light filtered in around the edges of the makeshift drapes.

"Are you feeling okay?"

"Yes. Just a bad night of sleep. I'm really wiped. Give me a few minutes and I'll be fine," she replied and focused her will on stretching and eventually on standing up.

As soon as Hyle opened the door, she could hear the buzz of voices down the hall, louder than usual. When they reached the gathering room they paused in the doorway for a moment. It was clear that something was going on. Several excited conversations were happening simultaneously making it difficult to follow any of them. The faces of those who were listening appeared concerned.

"A couple of refugees came in from Syracuse this afternoon," Newman explained, sliding over to join them in the doorway. "Some paramilitary group just stormed into the city and wiped out several enclaves of survivors."

The warning from Auld immediately replayed in Sophia's mind.

"When was this? Does anyone know where they came from?" Hyle asked.

Newman shook his head, looking more sad than concerned.

"It happened last night. I don't think anyone knows where they came from."

They listened for a while as best they could to the different conversations. One group was debating whether or not the assault had been launched by the U.S. military. Most people in the small circle did not seem to believe that this could be the case, but one young man was passionately defending this possibility.

"Soldiers do what they're told," he said.

"They don't slaughter innocent people," replied one voice that emerged from the mass of protests.

"They would if they were given bad information. What if they were told that these were groups of terrorists or insurgents?"

There was another chorus of protests.

"It's happened before. Look at Vietnam. Or Iraq."

"But who would give them bad information. And why?"

No answer was immediately forthcoming. Sophia shifted her attention to another discussion.

"...heard that it was a military coup."

"So what about this general who's supposed to be in charge?"

"That's the problem. It's not clear who's supposed to be in charge. I thought there were two generals fighting over command."

"But the military is very structured. It should be clear who's in command."

"Not necessarily for the soldiers..."

"This isn't exactly the normal wartime situation."

"...They're far enough down the chain of command that maybe they don't know. Information in the military comes from the top down, so if someone decides to break away, they take their part of the communication chain with them."

"What about the Air Force and Navy?"

"What Air Force?"

"Shouldn't the government be redeploying them to land?"

"What government?"

"Most of our forces have been shipped off to Asia anyway. They're probably stuck fighting there..."

Three young women, still engaged in conversation, started making their way to the door.

"Where are they going next, that's what I want to know?" one of them was saying. One of her friends met Sophia's eyes momentarily.

"I'm sure that's what everyone wants to know," the student replied.

The sunlight was almost gone. The room was growing dark and one by one the conversations wound down and people made their way for the door in small groups. Eventually only James, Newman, Sophia and Hyle remained. James pulled down the shade, closed the drapes, instructed Sophia to turn on the light and then sat down at his desk.

"That's enough depressing news for now," said James, and began tinkering with some electronic equipment. "Okay, Newman, see if you can tell me who this is," James challenged as a percussion line consisting of a single rapidly repeated note emerged from two tall narrow speakers standing in the corners of the room. It sounded like a cymbal or maybe a steel triangle. Newman sat on the corner of a bed next to the desk and concentrated on one of the speakers as the lone instrument was accompanied by a low sliding note from an electric bass. The ethereal female voice that joined next had only sung three words before Newman had his answer.

You can dance...

"Laurie Anderson," he said in the long pause before the next lyrics.

"The man knows his music," James said appreciatively.

Meanwhile Hyle and Sophia hung back at the other end of the room talking quietly.

"I've been thinking about our discussion last night," Hyle said.

"Yes, and?"

"And I've decided that I don't like the whole perception-is-reality argument."

"You just figured that out now?" Sophia teased. "I could tell that last night."

"I know, but there has to be something wrong with it, otherwise modern science wouldn't work, when obviously it does," Hyle asserted. "It defeats the whole purpose of what Locke was trying to do."

"It doesn't really affect science," Sophia replied. "Berkeley himself said that if you accept his philosophy, nothing changes. Your observations are still valid—they just can't be reduced to purely mechanistic terms. Why, what is it you think Locke was trying to do?"

"I think he was trying to establish a Newtonian science of the mind."

"What do you mean by that?"

"I mean Newton's approach to the discovery of universal gravitation became the example of how to do science for the next several centuries," Hyle explained. "Newton found the basic force that governed the interaction of the planets, and I think that Locke was looking for something similar for cognitive science—a basic principle that held our knowledge together. The model of learning by association was his basic principle."

"'Nature and Nature's laws lay hid in night: God said, Let Newton be! And all was light,'" quoted Newman, who had just tuned into the conversation.

"That's very clever," Sophia said.

"Thanks, but I can't take credit for it. That's Alexander Pope. I read that in a Westminster Abbey guidebook when I was backpacking through Europe. It was supposed to be an epitaph for Newton's tomb. I have to confess though that I never really understood why people say that Newton was the greatest scientists of all time."

"He invented calculus and discovered gravity for starters."

"I know that, Hyle. Give me some credit. But you said that Leibniz also invented calculus, and that Copernicus, Kepler and Galileo had already established that the earth traveled around the sun."

Hyle nodded thoughtfully.

"I see what you're saying," he replied, the sarcasm disappearing from his voice, "but Newton did more than that." Hyle explained Newton's work in optics, including his use of a prism to demonstrate that white light was composed of different colors of light that could be recombined to make white light again. "But aside from gravity and maybe calculus Newton is probably best known for his three laws of motion. I'm sure you're familiar with those."

Science had not held much interest for Newman in school. He shook his head doubtfully, but once Hyle listed them Newman quickly realized that they were indeed familiar.

"The first law, the Law of Inertia, says that a body at rest remains at rest and a body in motion remains in motion in a straight line until acted upon by an outside force," Hyle recited. "Galileo actually laid a lot of the ground work for that one. The second, the Law of Dynamics, says that an external force imparts force proportional to its own force and inversely proportional to the mass of the body it's affecting. The third law, the Law of Reciprocal Action, says that for every action there is an equal and opposite reaction. These three laws were absolutely foundational. They helped make the advances of the Industrial Revolution possible and for most purposes they're still how we understand physics."

"It may be how you understand physics," Newman said. "Whatever physics I learned in high school I tended to forget as soon as my tests were over. Why were these laws so foundational?"

"Because they explain all the major factors that affect the motion of objects. The classical example is the billiard table explanation. A billiard ball will just sit there on the table until another ball collides with it and sets it into motion. That's Newton's first law. The faster the cue ball is traveling, the faster any ball it hits will travel. That's the first part of Newton's second law. Now imagine that you shot the cue ball at a bowling ball instead. You wouldn't expect it to move as much as a billiard ball would. That's the second part of Newton's second law. And when you shoot a ball into the bumper, it bounces back in the opposite direction with essentially the same force. That's Newton's third law."

"That all seems pretty obvious," Newman said, sounding unimpressed.

"Now it does, but it wasn't so obvious before Newton. That's part of the reason his discoveries were so important. Before him, the common belief was that motion was the natural state of matter."

"That comes from Aristotle," Sophia interjected. "And Descartes too. He proposed an elaborate series of vortices swirling around to explain the motion of the stars and planets."

"That was another revolutionary aspect of the theory of gravity," Hyle continued. "Once Newton determined that a body in motion would remain in motion in a straight line unless acted upon by an external force, he no longer needed to find a force responsible for pushing the planets around. Instead he had to explain why the planets move in orbits rather than straight lines. His breakthrough was to realize that the same force that held the planets in their orbits was responsible for causing things to fall to the earth. Gravity."

"How did he ever get from an apple falling from a tree to the idea that planets were held in orbit by the same force?" Newman wondered aloud.

"They're actually two examples of the same problem," Hyle answered. "Imagine you're standing on top of a tall mountain and you throw a baseball straight out as hard as you can. What would happen to it?"

"It would fall to earth?" Newman answered, uncertain of what type of answer Hyle was expecting.

"Yes, but what kind of path would it follow?"

Newman closed his eyes for a second to create a mental image.

"It would travel straight at first, but then it would curve down more and more toward the ground as it fell."

"Good. Now imagine that you shot it out of a cannon instead. Now what would its path look like?"

"It would be pretty much the same, except it would travel farther and the curve would be more gradual."

"Okay, now remember that the earth is round. What if you could shoot that baseball fast enough that the curve of its decent matched the curve of the earth? As the ball falls, the earth falls away at exactly the same rate. What would happen?"

A look of realization slowly spread across Newman's face.

"It would be in orbit," he replied.

"Exactly," Hyle confirmed, grinning. "The ball is shot out of the cannon traveling in a straight line. The force of gravity acts on it to try to pull it toward the earth, but if the ball is traveling at the right speed, the result is that the ball falls at the same rate as the earth curves away from it. It goes into an orbit. That's essentially what happens with the moon in the gravitational field of the earth. And with the earth in the gravitational field of the sun."

"So why isn't the moon affected by the sun's gravity?" Newman asked.

"It is, but gravity decreases as distance increases. The moon is much closer to the earth than it is to the sun, so the earth has the major gravitational effect on the moon."

"Then does the moon's gravity have an effect on the earth since it's so close?"

"Yes, it does, but distance isn't the only factor. The force of gravity of an object is also proportional to its mass. There are some pairs of stars that orbit each other evenly, but since the earth is much more massive than the moon, the moon does the traveling while the earth stays relatively still. The moon does have an effect on the earth though. It's the gravity of the moon that's responsible for our ocean tides."

Newman nodded appreciatively.

"I suppose I can understand why Newton gets so much credit," he said.

"That's just his impact on physics," Hyle said. "The theory of universal gravitation also influenced science in general. Newton followed Francis Bacon's program of science. He insisted that science be built on experimentation and objective observation, from these he used induction to form a general theory—in this case universal gravitation—and then corroborated his theory with new observations. Newton was able to use the theory of gravity to explain the orbit of the moon and comets, the ocean tides, and several other previously unexplained phenomena. The success of his approach helped shape the way modern science is done. But even more important than that, it was so clear and powerful an explanation of how the universe worked that the Church had no choice but to accept it or keep quiet. This was only fifty years after the trial of Galileo and it opened the door for real progress in all fields of science."

"But Newton didn't set out to undermine the Church," Newman protested. "He's supposed to have been a very religious man."

"Yes, that's true. Newton said that he wrote his *Principia*, where he lays out the laws of motion and the theory of gravity, not to challenge the existence of God, but to demonstrate and enforce the idea of a supreme being," Hyle agreed. "Although it seems to me that he did quite the opposite."

"Maybe his view was similar to Thomas Aquinas and the Scholastics," Sophia suggested. "That understanding the laws of nature was a way to catch a glimpse into the mind of God. Coming to know the maker by his works, as the saying goes."

"Maybe so," Hyle allowed, "but many people in Newton's day were convinced that mere humans were not meant to understand the hidden laws of nature because they were some sort of divine secret. Newton proved them wrong."

"That explains Pope's couplet then," Sophia said, fighting to suppress a grin. "You could almost say that God chose Newton as his prophet to reveal the laws of nature."

The discussion would have continued, but just as Sophia opened her mouth to say more, James called for quiet.

"I think I'm getting something," he said in a hushed voice.

Only then did Sophia realize that the music had stopped after the one song had finished. In its place was a soft hissing sound. James had one hand on a stack of electronic components, slowly adjusting a dial. With his other hand he moved a long wire back and forth over his head. Voices emerged from the white noise and James froze in place, in a pose reminiscent of the Statue of Liberty. It was a conversation, badly garbled and mainly one sided. The second voice was so faint that Sophia wondered if it was not just her imagination filling words in where she expected to hear them. Eventually, after many long seconds of tuning with limited success, static consumed the voices and the conversation was gone.

"So close," James groaned. "I really wish we could transmit. I hate having to rely on luck to catch anyone out there."

"Why can't you transmit?" Hyle asked, surveying the equipment.

"Dean Essex is afraid that it'll give our location away and bring trouble. Unfortunately he's probably right considering what happened to Doom."

"To what?"

"Doom. You know, the guy who does the Twilight Report?" James looked from Hyle to Sophia to Newman and saw nothing but blank faces. "You guys don't know about the Twilight Report? Oh man, Maine must be even more back woods than I thought. The Twilight Report is a pirate radio broadcast that comes on every Sunday. Supposedly the guy who does it was a soldier who went AWOL when he found out that his unit had been ordered to ambush other U.S. soldiers. He used to broadcast almost every night, but then one night the broadcasts just stopped. There was nothing for several weeks."

"What happened?" Sophia asked, almost in a whisper.

"We didn't know. But then one Sunday he was back on the air again. Turns out that someone wanted him silenced. They blew up all of his gear and he barely escaped with his life. Now he only broadcasts once a week for about an hour and he moves around from week to week so they can't find him."

"Who was it that attacked him?" asked Hyle.

"And why do they want to silence him?" added Sophia.

"Question one, nobody knows. Question two, whoever is the answer to question one wants to silence him because he's broadcasting information. Survival tips, news updates, that sort of thing. He must still have connections in the army because he seems to have some inside information about what is going on, but even he says he's guessing at most of it."

"Why is it called the Twilight Report?" Sophia asked.

"For one, because he always broadcasts at sunset. I guess he wanted to pick a time that everyone could tell even if they didn't have access to a clock. The other reason is a bit of gallows humor. He keeps talking about the twilight of humanity and how the human race is about to wipe itself out. The name is sort of an inside joke I guess. Thanks to Doom there's more radio traffic around sunset than any other time of day or night. I was hoping to catch something about the attack on Syracuse and get some idea of which direction they're heading."

"Maybe there will be something in the next Twilight Report," Sophia suggested. "We'll have to make sure to tune in on Sunday."

"That's almost a week away," James replied. "I hope we're still here by then."

The moon was shining brightly behind the perpetual cloud cover and Sophia could see her breath swirling away in short bursts as she picked her way carefully down the steep hill. The ground was slick, and she walked just behind Hyle with one hand on his shoulder until they reached the front steps of the library. Someone other than Francis opened the door, and seeing who it was, mumbled something in greeting and stepped aside to let them in. A paper and a stack of discs were waiting for them when they reached the computer. Hyle picked up the paper and scanned it. It was a list of references, and the third one, which was marked with an asterisk, corresponded to the disc on top of the pile.

The computer clicked and whirred to life flashing a succession of icons as it loaded various programs. Hyle inserted the first disc while Sophia took a closer look at the list. It contained references to sources, file names and page numbers and although she recognized a few newspapers and periodicals most of the publications were unfamiliar. The first disc, the one that was starred on the sheet of paper, was one of those. The indicated file turned out to be a list itself, a registry of companies and their subsidiaries. As Hyle scrolled through the massive file the names of many well known companies flashed by. There were giant corporations in every industry—food and beverage, entertainment, electronics, software, appliances, financial institutions and many of these marketed several household brands and services. Hyle was amazed to discover how many of these were in turn owned by larger mega corporations, but he was far more interested in what he found when he reached the page referenced on the paper.

Near the bottom of the page in italic script appeared a listing for the Union of Faith. Indented below it were entries for seven entities that the Union owned and operated. A few of them had names that clearly suggested that they were charities. Each name was followed by three letters in parentheses, and occasionally an asterisk, dagger or super-scripted number.

"Looks like the non-profits are listed in italics," Sophia observed. "And most of them are headquartered in the United States," she added, tapping the monitor below a "USA" in parentheses.

"Yes," Hyle agreed absently, "but what do you make of this?"

He pointed to an entry several lines above the Union of Faith and Sophia was surprised by the realization that the Union of Faith itself was not at the top of the list. It was included as one of four major organizations under the heading "New Concordance Enterprises." Each of the four had several listings below them comprising a mixture of non-profit and for-profit organizations and the letters after New Concordance indicated a foreign headquarters. One of the groups called "NCE Communications" evidently owned three radio stations, a publishing house and several other for-profit entities. It was less clear what the other two umbrella organizations did, but a few of the names listed below them caught Hyle's eye.

"It looks like this New Concordance is based somewhere foreign, presumably where the laws governing non-profits are more favorable. They seem to own some pretty diverse organizations. Check this one out," Hyle said. He closed the file and reached for the next disc in the stack. "Let's see what we can find out about them."

Some time later, as they were reading the first paragraph of an article about a free health clinic being opened by the Union of Faith in Chicago, Hyle heard someone shuffle into the alcove behind him.

"Hi, Francis," said Sophia, and the three exchanged greetings.

Hyle held up the handwritten list of references. "Thank you for this."

"*No problema.* Find anything useful?"

"I'm not sure yet. I don't really know what I'm looking for, and I'm just getting started, but there were definitely some interesting things in that first file—the one with the lists of companies and subsidiaries."

"Number one with a bullet," Francis agreed.

As they spoke, Hyle shut down the article they were reading and swapped the disc out for the first one.

"This is something I'd like to find out more about. You don't happen to know where this place is, do you?" he asked Francis, pointing to the title of the article he had just pulled up.

Francis squinted and leaned in toward the display.

"The byline says it's in India," he offered.

"Yes, I saw that, but do you know where this town is relative to any of the big cities?"

"Not at the moment," the librarian said. A smile slowly spread across his face, "But I will soon."

CHAPTER FORTY-SEVEN

GLASS HALF FULL

Even before Sophia was fully awake the next afternoon she knew that something was troubling her. Whatever it was felt important, but lay just out of reach of her memory. Briefly she was distracted by the notion that she could believe something to be important without having any idea what it was. After shaking the sleep from her thoughts, Sophia tried again to find the hidden memory but it skittered away into the shadows of her mind like cockroaches fleeing from a flashlight beam. Or maybe soot sprites, she told herself, unhappy with the image of cockroaches in her thoughts. She pictured the scene from one of her favorite childhood movies in which the small black puff balls with eyes scattered from an attic room when the door was opened. The last lone soot sprite ran chattering into the shadows and Sophia gave up altogether on trying to remember.

The two men were already awake, looking out the window and having a quiet conversation. Newman glanced back over his shoulder and noticed her sitting on the edge of the bed.

"Hi, Sophia. We didn't wake you did we?" he asked softly. "Good," he continued with a brief smile when she shook her head. "Hyle was telling me yet again about how the advent of science saved the world from the tyranny of organized religion and I was afraid he might have gotten a little too excited."

"We were discussing the early influence of science on society," Hyle replied defensively. "I was merely saying that Newton showed that we can discover the truth about how the universe works, and we can do it without appealing to the authority of the Church or invoking some 'indiscernible spirits' that ultimately conduce to God."

"And maybe more importantly people questioned the basis of the authority of the aristocracy," Sophia added. "The whole idea of Locke and the empiricists that we start life as a *tabula rasa* and are then shaped by our environment and experiences is hard to reconcile with a class who claim to be privileged by birth to lead others."

"Right, and this empowerment of the common man eventually led to the freedom and democracy that we take for granted," Hyle added, shooting Newman a satisfied grin.

Newman nodded in agreement though, and Hyle's expression quickly faded.

"Yes," Newman said, "and Voltaire was very much influenced by Locke and Newton during the time he spent in England. He became a harsh critic of the French government, and he and his contemporaries like Diderot and Rousseau, were considered to be founders of the French Revolution even if they didn't actually lead it. This was still at a time when Paris was the intellectual and social center of the world and every cultured person read French, so they were widely read all over Europe and western civilization."

"Wow, you two actually agree on something," Sophia said.

"Only to a point," replied Newman seriously. "I agree that science had a social and political impact, but I don't agree that it had the major impact on religion that Hyle claims it had. Newton himself was said to be pious, and just discovering the laws of nature doesn't mean that God doesn't exist or that scripture is somehow invalidated."

"But what Newton showed was that the universe could be explained mathematically in terms of predictable underlying laws," Hyle argued. "Imagine the universe as a great watch. Even without understanding what all of the springs and gears inside do, we can learn to predict where the minute hand and hour hand will be. Once we understand how the watch behaves, we can start to understand what each piece does."

"Do you really think the universe is that mechanistic?" Newman asked.

"Actually, yes. I think it's a pretty fair analogy. The way science progresses is by observing a system, whether it's something big like the universe or something small like a cell, then breaking it down and examining the components one factor at a time to understand how each one of them works. Sort of similar to taking a watch apart piece by piece to understand what each part does. The ultimate goal of course is to know how to put the whole thing back together. And the significance is that nature can be explained without needing to invoke God or anything supernatural. In fact it has to be or it isn't science."

"But if the universe is like a great watch, then doesn't there have to be a watchmaker?" Newman asked.

"That's one problem with a mechanistic understanding of the world," Hyle acknowledged. "Every time you find a cause you can always ask what caused the cause, *ad infinitum*. But that doesn't lead to the conclusion that God must exist. I can ask what created God just as well as you can ask what created the universe, and if you say that God always existed, I can say the same about the universe."

"There's another problem with a mechanistic understanding of the world," Sophia interjected. "Have you ever heard of determinism?"

The term sounded vaguely familiar to Hyle, but he shook his head.

"Let's imagine that Newman has a pair of dice and you have some sophisticated futuristic equipment," Sophia said. "As he rolls the dice you can exactly measure and calculate everything about them as they move—their orientation, speed and angle as they leave your hand, the distance to the table as well as its hardness and friction and all of those physical factors. Would you be able to predict how the dice would land every time?"

"If I knew all of the physical factors?" Hyle pondered aloud. "Yes. I could. It would just be a matter of making the right calculations."

"And does that principle apply on a larger scale?" Sophia pressed. "If you could somehow know all of the physical information about every molecule and particle in the universe right at this instant, and you had an infinitely powerful computer, would there be anything in the future that you couldn't predict?"

"If I understood all the laws of nature?" Hyle confirmed. "Then no, I don't think there would be."

"Even what I'm going to have for breakfast ten years from now?" Newman challenged.

"If I knew everything about everything in the universe as of this moment, yes. There would be nothing in the future that couldn't be calculated. The human brain may seem too complex for us to fully understand, but that's just because we don't have the right tools yet." Hyle paused to think of a suitable example. "It's like predicting the weather. At first people could only predict the weather a few hours ahead by looking at the sky or maybe a day ahead by noting pressure or temperature changes in the air. Nobody could have hoped to predict the weather a week away. But with satellites and computer models we can do that now."

"Hyle is a hardcore causal determinist in the tradition of La Mettrie and Laplace," Sophia told Newman. "Determinism is a natural outgrowth of the mechanistic view of nature developed by people like Descartes and Locke and Newton. In fact, it wasn't long after Newton's death that La Mettrie wrote *L'Homme-Machine*—"

"The Man-Machine?" Newman asked, translating.

"Yes," Sophia confirmed. "I'm sure you can guess from the title what his view of human nature was. And a very concise statement of determinism was framed not long after La Mettrie in a scenario known as Laplace's demon."

"What is it with philosophers and demons?" Hyle asked, shaking his head.

"To be fair, Laplace just proposed the scenario to illustrate a point," Sophia answered with a laugh. "He believed that the present state of the universe is the effect of its past and the cause of its future. It was only later that his example became known as Laplace's demon."

"So what was his example?" Hyle asked.

"See if this sounds familiar. Laplace proposed that if there were a sufficiently powerful intellect that could know all of the forces at work in the universe at the present moment, then for that intellect nothing would be uncertain and the future would be just as clear as the past."

"But where do these determinist droogs find any place for free will in a clockwork universe like that?" Newman asked. "Hyle may be okay with it, but the idea that everything can be reduced to some mathematical formula bothers me on several levels."

"It's not the role of science to make people feel comfortable with the world," Hyle replied. "That's what religion is for. Science is about finding the truth."

His mouth was already open before Newman caught himself. He knew that he was being baited and yet he had almost given Hyle the satisfaction of an angry response. Taking a deep breath that might have sounded a bit like a sigh, he abandoned his immediate response. In its place he remembered something even better.

"Hyle, I seem to remember you giving me a hard time back in Asher about the omniscience of God somehow depriving you of your free will, but you seem willing to accept determinism as a consequence of science."

"Of course, determinism presupposes cause and effect," Sophia interjected, watching both men closely.

Hyle, who had been considering Newman's argument, was clearly taken aback.

"Is there anyone who doesn't believe in cause and effect?"

"What about Malebranche and occasionalism?" Newman suggested, but Hyle shook his head.

"No, he believed in cause and effect. He just believed in a particularly useless version where God causes everything. But I think just about everyone subscribes to the scientific understanding of cause and effect."

"That's probably true," agreed Sophia. "But where does the idea of cause and effect come from?"

"From observation," Hyle immediately replied.

"Do you think so?" Sophia asked and the challenge in her tone surprised Hyle. "Can you give me an example of observing cause and effect?"

"Sure, just consider the billiard table analogy I used to explain Newton's three laws of motion," Hyle answered a bit apprehensively. "The cue ball rolls across the table until it collides with another ball, then the cue ball slows or stops and the other ball begins to move. The cue ball has caused the other ball to move."

"A classic example," Sophia agreed. "But where in that example do you actually see causality? You see one ball move, you see a collision and then you see another ball start to move, but can you actually observe a cause anywhere on the table?"

"No, of course you can't actually see causality itself," Hyle conceded. "Causality is a principle, not an object or action. But you can observe the effects of causality."

"How can you say that you're observing effects? Doesn't the word 'effect' already presuppose the idea of cause and effect? What you're really capable of seeing is just a sequence of events."

"But they're connected events—"

"Yes, I know. Connected by cause and effect, but that's circular reasoning. Where does the idea come from in the first place though? You've said that you believe, as John Locke argued, that all knowledge comes to us through experience. Assuming that's true, how do we come to believe in causality if we can't observe it?"

"By induction," Hyle replied, finally understanding the point Sophia was trying to make. "If you see that every time the cue ball hits another ball, over and over without fail, the second ball starts to move at the instant of the collision, you can induce that the collision caused the second ball to move."

"Induce?" Sophia echoed thoughtfully. "Induce means what exactly? To assume?"

"No, I'd define it as something more like generalize or postulate, or even discover."

"Even if we do see the same type of collision between billiard balls a hundred times, how do we get from there to causality? Why do we not just stop with the hundred separate observations?"

"Because the world has to work by certain rules. Causality is just common sense."

"Is this the same common sense that told people the world couldn't be round because half the people would have to be standing upside down and that the earth could not be moving or everything would blow off of it? I think common sense is just a term for the accepted wisdom of the day, unchallenged by critical thinking."

Out of the corner of her eye, Sophia caught Newman smiling.

"Now you're arguing semantics," Hyle charged, the volume of his voice rising slightly. He was growing annoyed with this line of argument that seemed to lack a salient point and even more annoyed at his own inability to illustrate so obvious a principle as cause and effect. He tried rephrasing his assertion to get around Sophia's semantics. "Causality is the logical conclusion of consistently seeing the same pattern repeated over and over."

"So since day always follows night, would you agree that it's logical to conclude that night causes day?" Sophia asked.

"No, of course not. You're purposely twisting my words and ignoring my point just to give me a hard time."

"Not that that's a bad thing," Newman interjected.

"No," Sophia replied sincerely. "Since causality is central to scientific understanding it's important to understand why we believe in causality and it's not clear to me that it's from induction or logic. So far common sense seems to be the closest explanation. I think this is a valid and important philosophical question, Hyle. Giving you a hard time is just a fortunate side effect," she added with a grin.

"Okay," Hyle said, softening a little at Sophia's smile. "I still say causality is the logical conclusion of observation, but why don't you tell us where you think it comes from? You obviously have something in mind."

"I do," she admitted. "Actually I've been developing one of the ideas of David Hume. Let me just ask you a couple more questions. Do you remember the difference between analytic and synthetic truths from our discussion about Leibniz?"

"I think so," Hyle replied. "Analytic statements can be verified by logic without reference to the physical world, like saying that a cat can't be both alive and dead at the same time. A synthetic statement is one that can only be verified by observation, like saying a particular cat is dead."

Out in the hallway another conversation was going on. Voices passed by the door on their way to work for the evening.

"Yes, very good. So in the absence of observation only analytic statements can be certain truths. That's important, but they also have another interesting property. It's impossible to imagine an instance where a true analytic statement might not hold true.

The human mind can't even conceive of a time when it's both raining and not raining or a bachelor who is married."

"That makes sense so far," Hyle agreed.

"Then consider your example of observing the billiard balls over and over. Observing events that seem to be constantly conjoined in time and space leads to the assumption that the earlier event caused the latter one. But just because the balls have always moved when struck by other balls, there's no guarantee that they'll do so the next time you observe them. As Hume would say, the future is under no obligation to mimic the past. And in fact you can imagine a situation where one ball stays completely still after being struck by another one."

"I can imagine it as a fantasy, but I can't imagine it in real life," Hyle replied.

"But even if you never expect that it would really happen, just being able to imagine a counterfactual situation is enough to demonstrate that it's not an analytic proposition. With cause and effect, it's always possible to imagine a scenario where the effect doesn't occur the same way it has in the past."

"So you're saying that causality can't be derived by observation or by logic," Hyle said cautiously.

"Exactly. That was Hume's argument."

While Hyle considered this, Sophia picked up a shoe and held it out. "Consider another example. What will happen if I let go of this?"

"It'll fall."

"How do you know?"

"The law of gravity," Hyle asserted stubbornly.

"Would you have made a different prediction if you had lived before Newton?"

"No," Hyle sighed. "Even though I might be able to picture it hovering in place or even turning into a mushroom, I'd say that I know that the shoe will fall because shoes always fall when you drop them."

"The future is under no obligation to repeat the past," Newman reminded him.

"But in this case it always does," Hyle replied, pointing to the shoe.

"You mean it always has in the past," Sophia corrected. She waited for a moment for the implication of her statement to sink in before continuing. "And what if we were in a space station and I let go of this shoe?"

"I'm beginning to understand why Socrates was forced to drink poison hemlock," Hyle said in a stage whisper to Newman. "Okay, I concede that occasionally our observations may lead to incorrect conclusions about cause and effect and even that causality can't be derived from observation by strict logic. So where does that leave us?"

"David Hume was a skeptic, Hyle," explained Sophia. "A skeptic in an age only decades after Newton when it seemed that science would sooner or later discover all the workings of the clockwork universe. Hume is regarded by many to be the most influential philosopher to write in the English language because he so effectively attacked the basic assumptions about knowledge that lay at the very foundation of science. After demonstrating that causality can't be derived from observation or from logic, he explained that it was a mental habit, nothing more than a mode of thinking that's useful in making sense of the world. He also identified two other principles—resemblance and spacio-temporal contiguity—as things that can't be logically or empirically derived but that the mind assumes in order to make sense of the world."

"That doesn't seem so horrible a conclusion," Hyle said pensively, still trying to think through the significance of this philosophy.

"The point is that we can't be certain of anything," Sophia explained. "Any claims about discovering the laws of the universe have to be discounted because our epistemology is dependent upon our psychology. Any knowledge we may have of the external world is mediated by our perceptions and founded on uncertain habits of thought. And even if you assume causality to be true, Hume argued that every answer would only lead to more questions. If you say that it's gravity that causes the planets to orbit the sun, then you must discover what causes gravity."

"That's true," Hyle agreed. "There are always more questions to ask in science. Every time you identify a cause, you can ask what caused the cause and lead yourself into an infinite regress. There's always one more unanswered question, which is what seems to lead so many of your philosophers to God in the end. But that's what science thrives on—answering those unanswered questions. It may be an infinite task, but it's like a light growing brighter in a dark room. Every time we answer a question we push back the darkness a little farther."

Sophia smiled.

"Almost the exact words of David Hume," she noted. "He said that science only allows us to push back the boundary of ignorance a little farther."

"That seems like an overly skeptical way to look at it. I agree that there will always be more questions to ask, but it's a matter of how you look at it. Is the glass half full or is it half empty? You could say the darkness is infinite and the glass is half empty. But if you look at the knowledge that we do have, and the fact that it's increasing all the time, you'd say that the glass is half full."

"I think Hume would have said that the glass is half empty, but you might as well drink it anyway. Being a skeptic his glass was certainly half empty. As a starting point he believed that everything comes to us through the senses, but he carried this idea farther than Locke had. In *A Treatise on Human Nature* and *An Enquiry Concerning Human Understanding* Hume argued that because all we can know are perceptions and the memories and ideas built from them, everything we know has been passed through the filter of our senses and processed into some format that we can understand. If there's a real world out there we don't have any direct experience of it at all. Hume even argued that we couldn't support the idea of a 'self' since we can't observe a 'self' any more than we can observe causality. All we are is a collection of sensations. Like one of Berkeley's material objects, if you strip away all of our sensations, ideas and memories, there's nothing left."

"That glass isn't half empty. It's completely empty," Newman remarked.

"It would be if Hume had ended up like the Pyrrhonists, whose skepticism led them to question everything," allowed Sophia, "but Hume came to a much more livable conclusion. After thoroughly demolishing the idea that we can know anything with any certainty, he concluded that the best thing we can do is act on what we perceive. Whether or not they exist in some real material world, strawberries still taste sweet to us when we eat them. Shoes still fall when we let go of them. As long as we don't mistake these perceptions for some kind of ultimate knowledge about the universe, we may as well go along as we always have. It would be foolish to refuse to eat strawberries just because we can't prove with certainty that they're real. That's what Hume meant by 'reason is the slave of the passions' by the way, which is probably his most famous and most misunderstood quote."

"I can see why Hume is so influential," said Hyle, who had been listening quietly. "His logical arguments must really appeal to philosophers, while his conclusions have no practical impact on scientists. I just hope you're not going to spoil it by telling us that after all this work he appealed to some concept of God to give his philosophy a happy ending."

"No, definitely not. Hume's happy ending was deciding that he was comfortable with uncertainty. He was actually as tough on religion as he was on science and in fact was suspected of being an atheist. Without completely closing the door on the possibility of miracles, he pointed out that they generally occur in less civilized societies and eras and noted that miracles claimed by a variety of competing religions serve to discredit each other. He also spent the better part of a thesis refuting the teleological argument for the existence of God. One of the arguments he used is the same one you just stated Hyle— if one can claim that God always existed, the same could be said about the universe."

"I think Hume has just become my favorite philosopher," said Hyle.

"There are those who argue that it's not so clear that he was an atheist though," warned Sophia. "His *Dialogues Concerning Natural Religion* challenges the teleological proofs for God but also makes some compelling arguments in defense of religion, and he has one brilliantly crafted quote which could be taken by a devout Christian to acknowledge the role of miracles in their faith or by an atheist as a criticism."

"That's disappointing," Hyle replied. "What was the quote?"

"He said that the Christian religion was started by a miracle and now cannot be believed by any reasonable person without one."

CHAPTER FORTY-EIGHT

A SENSE OF PURPOSE

Music was playing once again as they left Newman behind in the dorm to do their research in the library. When Sophia made it clear that she would not accept his usual excuses for not coming, Newman had confessed that he was working on a project. Even though he would say only that it involved James and some of his friends, he swore Hyle and Sophia to secrecy with a promise that they would learn more soon. Although Hyle did not seem very interested, Sophia was intrigued by this secret and ran through various possibilities in her mind. By the time they reached the library, Sophia had forgotten about the uneasy feeling she had experienced upon waking up.

Francis greeted them with even more enthusiasm than usual.

"Hi, Sophia, how are you doing? Hey, Hyle."

Sophia noticed him glancing over her shoulder. She turned to follow his gaze just in time to catch several members of the Brotherhood looking away and focusing intently on something else. Francis escorted them back to the alcove, giving them an update on the progress the Brotherhood was making in updating the science library materials as they walked. He caught Sophia lightly by the shoulder as Hyle took his place at the computer.

"Just a minute," he whispered, "Wait right here, I have something for you."

As he hurried away Sophia realized that his energy seemed to be covering nervousness and despite trusting Francis, she began to grow nervous herself. When the librarian returned, he was holding something behind his back and Sophia noticed that his rosy complexion seemed a shade darker, particularly around the ears. She could feel the blood pulsing rapidly at the base of her throat and hoped that he did not notice.

"Remember a couple days ago when you were down here and we were talking about some of the things we missed?"

Sophia nodded and Francis pulled his hand from behind his back to display a distinctive can of diet soda.

"Well, here you go," he said with a small laugh.

For a moment Sophia could do nothing but stare at the can. Her hands reached out mechanically and accepted the gift as her brain worked itself through a mixture of surprise and relief.

"Thank you, Francis," she said as soon as she could find her thoughts again. "That's really sweet. How did you even…. And it's cold too!"

Francis grinned broadly, not lifting his eyes from the can.

"I have my connections," he said with a shrug.

"Well it's really wonderful. Thank you, Francis."

Sophia looked at the large man's ruddy face then back down at the can. There was an awkward silence.

"He's really fanatical about this, isn't he," whispered Francis at last, poking a thumb toward Hyle, who was bent over the computer just out of earshot.

"Yes," Sophia said nodding thoughtfully. "I think maybe it gives him a sense of purpose. To be doing something."

"I know what you mean. That's part of the reason I came back here," Francis said sympathetically. Then in answer to Sophia's look of surprise he explained, "After the surprise attack, I went back to the city to look for my folks. I didn't find them—that whole part of the city was pretty well flattened."

"I'm sorry, Francis."

Francis nodded his head in appreciation and shrugged. "I was pretty lucky though. I was hitching and got a good ride almost all the way there so I made it in a day. And once I knew, there wasn't really anywhere for me to go but back here, so I just turned around and started walking."

"You walked back here from New York City?" Sophia asked, looking at him with a newfound respect. "That must be at least two hundred miles!"

"Yeah, it took me almost a week," Francis laughed. "I got back just in time for the second round of attacks, and when I realized that this really was the end of civilization as we knew it—" He paused for a second, thinking, and shrugged. "I guess I just wanted to do something to hold onto part of it, so I came here to the library and began recruiting people."

The two looked at each other, Francis done speaking. Sophia nodded empathetically, trying to think of something to say.

"What about you?" Francis asked, saving her. "Did you—did you lose anybody?"

"No, not really. My mother died in China giving birth to me and my father died a few years later after we moved to the States. He was in ill health and so we moved in with his brother in Boston. It was really my uncle who raised me, more or less."

"That must have been tough."

"It was okay," Sophia replied. "I was too young to remember my parents but I could tell I was a burden for my uncle. He owned a small shop in Chinatown. He was single by choice because he had no time for romance or a family so I mostly tried to stay out of the way." Looking around the library she added, "My best friends were books in those days, so I think I understand how you feel."

"What are you going to do now?" asked Francis, glancing over at Hyle and then down at the soda can. "I mean long-term. Are you—are you planning to stay around here?"

The warning from Auld seemed to ring in her ears. "I'm not sure. I'd like to, I think, but…" She tried to explain the mysterious visit from Auld out of context and instead ended up giving Francis a detailed account of their travels since the time Hyle had rescued her. She described the massacre they had discovered at the hospital outside Albany, the make-shift community at the department store and their narrow escape to Maine and many of the details of their long stay at Asher. Francis was particularly interested in the account of the fortune teller, their flight from Asher and the account of Auld's warning.

"It sounds like you're fated to keep traveling," he concluded, as if he were handing down a sentence.

"Do you believe in fate?" Sophia asked him.

"I don't know. But I believe there are some things that we just have to accept."

Sophia nodded. "I know, but I feel so adrift sometimes. I envy you. You're doing something. I feel like I'm just wandering from one place to the next with no purpose."

Francis put a sympathetic hand on her shoulder. "Remember, 'All that is gold does not glitter, not all those who wander are lost.'"

Looking up from the computer, Hyle glanced back to see Sophia smiling up at the big librarian. His face clouded over. "Hey, Sophia. Are you going to help me tonight or what? I could use a second opinion over here."

"I have to go see how they're doing with the science journals," Francis said, backing awkwardly out of the alcove.

"Okay," Sophia responded. "Thanks for this," she added, holding up her diet soda.

The soda was almost back to room temperature when she cracked the tab and sat down at the workbench, but to Sophia it tasted like ambrosia.

"What have you got?" she asked Hyle.

"First thing is this," he answered, bringing up a news article on the screen. It was coverage of a court case a few years back in which several members of a paramilitary separatist group were charged with killing a rancher and his family after a dispute over property lines. Hyle pointed her to one of the closing paragraphs. It said that investigators were trying to determine how far up in the organization people had been involved in the planning. It also said that they were looking into the possibility that the organization may have received financial backing from the Union of Faith. There had been a prepared statement from Zendik denying the charges. "The Union of Faith does not support this type of violence. It is for God alone to pass judgment and punish transgressors," he was quoted as saying.

"I wonder what type of violence they do support," Hyle mused. "Nuclear war maybe?"

"This is interesting, Hyle, but why do you need a second opinion?"

"Not for this," he answered. "It's an overall pattern. I noticed something a little odd about all these articles. There doesn't seem to be any mention of Zendik before the year 2000."

"That was a big year for him," responded Sophia. "That was when he put together the interfaith councils and started holding demonstrations. Maybe he just wasn't newsworthy before that."

"That may be," Hyle allowed, "but it's not just that I haven't found any articles on him before 2000. It's that I don't remember seeing any mention of him at all before that year. Usually you get some kind of biographical information, where the person grew up, where they went to school, what they did before the particular topic of the article, but I haven't seen any of that about Zendik. Nothing at all. It's as if he didn't exist prior to 2000."

Sophia thought back through her own reading and slowly absorbed the truth of the observation.

"Wow, you're right," she said. "What do you suppose it means?"

"I have no idea. But if it really is true there must be a reason. Want to help me take a more careful look?"

Hyle and Sophia spent the rest of the evening looking through articles. They found nothing.

CHAPTER FORTY-NINE

FRAMEWORK

Presented with the observation that information about the Prophet did not seem to exist prior to the year 2000, Newman offered a list of possible explanations they had already considered, but when pressed was not able to draw on his tenure with the Union of Faith to provide any insight into Zendik's background and made it clear that he thought the whole endeavor was a waste of time. Even Hyle seemed to be tiring of this debate and had merely shrugged off the comment. Sophia looked from one to the other. Hyle was busy teasing apart the small cubes of venison in his stew, as if he hoped to fool himself with the illusion of more food, and Newman still seemed to be looking for something to say.

"We headed down to the library before I got a chance to ask you what you thought of Hume," Sophia said. Although she addressed the remark to Newman, she was gratified to see Hyle abandon his culinary project for a moment to glance over.

"I didn't like it at all."

"But that's not the point, is it?" replied Hyle. "If Hume wanted people to like his philosophy it would have been about eternal happiness in paradise or some such nonsense."

"Doesn't the argument that we can't really know anything bother you, Hyle?" Newman asked incredulously, ignoring the jibe.

"I suppose it would if I took it too seriously, but Hume himself came to the conclusion that we might as well live according to our perceptions of the world. Even if we can't have certain knowledge in some abstract philosophical sense, I'm still convinced that I exist and that this is really a chair that I'm sitting on. My knowledge may not be certain, but if I'm wrong, at least I'm in good company because I think that's essentially what everyone believes."

"That's a page taken from Thomas Reid," Sophia interjected. "He appealed to common sense as a defense against Hume's skepticism."

"You said that common sense is what told people that the world had to be flat," Newman reminded her.

"Reid had a more formal understanding of the term. Essentially the idea was that whatever experiences we share universally are what is to be considered true, and that to deny the truth of such experiences leads to contradictions. Reid and the Scottish School of Common Sense were probably more influential than Hume in his day, but their arguments really don't have the philosophical depth of Hume's. Of course Reid also said that principles of common sense are believed universally, with the exception of some philosophers and the insane."

"There must be some path to certain knowledge," insisted Newman. "I still like the Scholastics' idea of coming to know God through his works."

"Reid would be pleased to know that we have all three parties represented in this discussion," Hyle remarked to Sophia.

"As good as Hume's arguments are," she replied, ignoring Hyle's comment, "they do leave room for us to have certain knowledge—within limits at least."

"Really? I don't see how," Hyle said.

"Recall Hume's claim that we jump to causality from the observation that two events are constantly conjoined. That principle of constant conjunction itself relies on something else that can't be perceived. What do you need to assume to say that two events are constantly conjoined?"

After pondering the question for a moment Hyle shook his head and looked over at Newman. When neither of the men ventured an answer, Sophia rephrased her question.

"To say that one billiard ball moves first, and then a second one moves, what concept do you need to already have? What concept are you drawing on when you say 'first this then that' or 'before' and 'after'?"

The silence did not last long this time around.

"Time," Newman answered. "You'd need to have a concept of time, and you couldn't observe that on the billiard table either. Time is another idea that you can't get from empirical observation."

"And space for that matter," Hyle added, nodding appreciatively. "To see a ball move you need to see it go from one place to another. In fact, to talk about motion you need to have concepts of both time and space, since the ball has to move through space as a function of time. But time and space are both things that you can't directly sense."

"Yes, space and time are the two so-called 'pure intuitions' used by Immanuel Kant to illustrate that there must be some *a priori* modes of understanding in place before we can make any sense of the world whatsoever. He used the term 'pure' to indicate that they can't be derived from experience, so in other words must be innate. In addition to space and time, Kant outlined twelve similar 'categories of understanding' in his *Critique of Pure Reason*."

"Twelve? Like what else?" asked Newman.

"He grouped them into four sets—quality, quantity, modality and relation. These are all fundamental and universal ways that we perceive things that can't be derived from experience. For example, the three categories of modality are actuality, possibility and necessity. A man may possibly be married or not, you can confirm whether or not he actually is married, but if he's a bachelor he's necessarily unmarried. And the three categories of quantity are unity, plurality and totality."

"I don't see why you couldn't learn those by experience," Hyle remarked.

"You already had a proof for at least two of the categories. Cause and effect is one of the three concepts included under relation," Sophia explained, "and if you agree with Hume's argument that the future is under no obligation to repeat the past, there's no way to derive necessity from experience. And without totality, where would you get a concept like infinity? No amount of counting will get you to infinity, so that concept can't come from physical experience. In fact, Kant believed that arithmetic was an *a priori* concept derived from time and geometry was an *a priori* concept derived from the pure intuition of space."

"I understand how you can derive geometry from a concept of space since geometry is all about describing general rules for figures in three-dimensional space," Hyle said, "but how did he get arithmetic from time?"

"Because arithmetic starts with the number sequence—one, two, three, and so on. Counting is like a progression of numbers over time. It's not as obvious," Sophia admitted. "Kant is widely regarded as the most influential philosopher since Plato and Aristotle, but some of his ideas are pretty complex and his writing style makes them all the more difficult to understand."

"I thought you said that Hume was the most influential modern philosopher," Hyle said, a touch defensively.

"No, I said Hume was probably the most important philosopher to write in the English language. Kant was a German contemporary of Hume. But Kant did give credit to Hume as the philosopher who 'aroused him from his dogmatic slumbers.' It was in an attempt to answer Hume's skepticism that Kant developed this philosophy."

"I must be missing something then," Hyle said, "because it doesn't seem like much of an answer. All he did was expand the things that we can't learn empirically from just cause and effect to a whole list of these pure intuitions and categories. What does it matter how many different things we have to assume to make sense of the world? Whether it's one or fourteen, Hume's basic argument still applies."

"The idea of pure intuitions and categories of understanding is only a part of Kant's whole philosophy," Sophia explained. "But it's a critical part, so it's important to understand that there's a big difference between it and Hume's explanation of things like causality. Hume presented causality as a habit of the mind. In other words, something we come to expect after observing it many times. What Kant argued is that these pure intuitions must be in place before we can even have any meaningful perceptions. Try to imagine a world where things don't occupy space or exist in time. You can't do it. Without already having concepts of time and space, experience would be nothing more than a bunch of unassociated sounds and lights and textures. It wouldn't even qualify as knowledge."

"Okay, but…" Hyle frowned pensively, trying to understand the importance of the distinction, "they're still unfounded assumptions, even if they precede the senses."

Sophia shook her head.

"Let me try to explain it this way," she said. "Kant called this his Copernican revolution, which is actually not a bad analogy. Copernicus moved the center of the solar system from the earth to the sun. Kant moved the center of knowledge from the physical world to the intellect. His argument is that space, time and categories of understanding aren't properties of the natural world that we can discover through experience. They're not properties of the natural world at all. Instead they're structures that we impose on the natural world in order to make sense of it."

"Then if he agreed with Hume that things like cause and effect aren't part of the natural world, how does the idea of pure intuitions lead to certain knowledge?"

"Don't think of these as some quirk of being human that may vary from one person to another. For Kant these are prerequisites for any kind of knowledge whatsoever, whether you're talking about a human being, an animal, an extra-terrestrial, or I suppose even an artificial intelligence. In other words, they form a common ground between any beings that have knowledge. If you accept Kant's philosophy as true, it becomes possible to make synthetic statements about the physical world with the same level of certainty we have with analytic statements."

"I suppose I can see that," Hyle conceded. "But even if you can go from an analytic statement like 'a bachelor must be unmarried,' to a synthetic statement like 'a bachelor must exist in time and space,' that doesn't tell you anything new about the world. Besides, you have to assume Kant's philosophy is true to make that kind of statement in the first place."

"I never really thought about it that way," Sophia confessed. "Still, the point is that it's possible to have certain knowledge of the physical world, and we all share the same framework for gaining that knowledge. It's true that you have to assume Kant was correct to believe this, but if you reject his philosophy you'd have to explain how we come to have a conception of time, space, causality, necessity and all of those."

"So then how is Kant any different from Descartes or Leibniz?" objected Hyle. "This sounds just like the same rationalist argument warmed over—you have to assume pre-existing ideas in order to explain how we come to know things."

"To some degree that's true," Sophia agreed, "although the hard-core rationalists believed that logic like analytic statements were the only path to certain knowledge. But then Hume dismissed analytic statements as 'truths about words'. If you want to find out if a man really is married or not, no amount of logic is going to help you out, you have to go out into the world and find out through experience. Kant agreed with this argument that knowledge can't come to us through logic. It can only come to us through experience, mediated by our senses. His pure intuitions and categories of understanding are merely frameworks that can't be filled in except through experience."

"They're like an empty loom that lets us weave a tapestry of knowledge from the threads of our experience," Newman suggested.

"That's a very poetic way of saying it, yes."

"That seems like a nice compromise between rationalism and empiricism," Newman said, "but it still has a major problem. If our knowledge is limited to what we experience through our senses, then we can never have knowledge of anything but the physical world. It fails to address all the most important aspects of life."

Hyle gave an emphatic shrug.

"That compromise is one of the things Kant is famous for," Sophia replied. "He blended rationalism and empiricism to create the most tenable rebuttal to Hume's skepticism of any philosopher to date, but to do that he had to place limitations on both philosophies. In addition to throwing out the idea that we could gain knowledge through pure logic, he also showed that empiricism has limits. Our sensory perceptions can only show us the world as it appears, not as it truly is."

"What? Why can't we just have a physical world and leave it at that?" Hyle demanded. "What's wrong with believing that what we can sense is all that there is and that things are really how they appear to be?"

"That could be the case if you believe that the senses give us an accurate picture of the world as it really is."

"You're not going to bring back all the Cartesian arguments about how our senses can be fooled are you?"

"No, this time I want to take you much further down the rabbit hole," Sophia said with a grin. "For the sake of discussion let's start with the world of things as they actually are. Kant called this the noumenal world in order to distinguish it from the world of sensory phenomena. So, Hyle, your challenge, if you want to get rid of the distinction between the phenomenal and noumenal, is to demonstrate that what we experience through our senses is an accurate representation of the noumenal world."

"It's not a question of demonstration," Hyle objected. "There's no reason to believe that there's anything beyond our senses."

"But there's no reason to believe that there isn't either," countered Newman.

"Even if there was something that existed beyond what we can sense, there's no point in discussing it."

"Why not?" Newman objected.

"It's immaterial," Hyle replied, and Sophia rolled her eyes.

"Let me give you an example," she said, pointing to the utensil in Hyle's hand. He held it up in front of him, looking at it suspiciously. "Now think back to Locke. You see something in your hand, right? You can feel that it has hardness, texture, temperature and all those physical properties. Either there must be something outside of you, some object 'out there' stimulating those sensations, or you're making it all up yourself and there is no spoon. Or anything else for that matter."

"No, obviously there is an object that I'm sensing," Hyle replied, putting the spoon back down. "But why does it have to be any different than it appears to be?"

"Imagine that we're sitting in a field," Sophia told him. "I take a picture of a tree behind you in the distance. When I show you the picture the tree appears hazy and has a red tint to it. Maybe it was foggy over by the tree and the leaves are turning, or maybe the camera was out of focus and the picture was taken through a red filter. How would you tell the difference—without examining the camera?"

"I'd turn around and look," Hyle replied, wondering what was wrong with such an obvious answer.

"What if you could only look through my camera?"

"Obviously that wouldn't help. It's the accuracy of the camera that's in question in the first place." As Hyle spoke Sophia's analogy became clear. "So you're saying that since we can only look at the world through our senses, we'll never know how accurately they portray the objects that cause our sensations." Sophia nodded as Hyle thought through the implications. "But since logic can't tell you the nature of the real world either, we'll never know whether or not there's any difference between the phenomenal and noumenal worlds."

"Exactly the conclusion that Kant came to himself," Sophia confirmed, surprising Hyle. "Empiricism can explain the phenomenal world since we can understand it in terms of time, space and the categories of understanding. That's why science is so successful in the physical world. By definition science can't tell you about anything outside the phenomenal world, but Kant did believe that logic could give you some clues about the nature of the noumenal world. That's where there's room for morality, God, free will, the immortal soul and other things that don't seem to conform to the laws of the phenomenal world. That's also why science never made any progress in metaphysics."

"So Kant neatly boxed off all the superstitions into the noumenal world where science couldn't bother them?" asked Hyle pointedly.

"In a way, yes he did. But to be fair he also argued that the existence of God cannot be proven. He did believe in God though and said that he had to 'remove knowledge in order to make room for belief.' Kant wrote a sequel to the *Critique of Pure Reason* called the *Critique of Practical Reason* in which he developed a method for determining clues to the nature of such things in the noumenal world by applying logic to the patterns we can observe in the phenomenal world."

Hyle shot a look at Newman.

"Do you have any idea what she just said?"

"Take free will for example," said Sophia, smiling. "Kant argued that we can't imagine not having free will. Our whole concept of morality and responsibility is centered around a belief in free will. It's not really a proof of free will, but if free will can't be proven or disproven, at least this is a reason to tend toward believing in it."

"Ultimately though, doesn't separating off a noumenal world from the phenomenal world lead to the same kind of problems as Descartes splitting things between mental and physical substances?" Hyle asked.

"People have made that argument, yes. But the Cartesian split was truly an either/or division while the division between the noumenal and phenomenal exists just in our perceptions. We may not be able to perceive the noumenal or how it interacts with the phenomenal, but that doesn't mean there can't be any interactions."

"But any evidence for a noumenal world is circumstantial at best," Hyle pointed out. "I'm still not convinced it's necessary to assume anything beyond the material world."

"Then how do you explain where we get the ideas of time and space?" Newman pressed.

"I'm not sure," Hyle admitted, pausing to think about it. "Here's the problem—I can't remember whether or not I was born with a concept of time and space. Who can? So what's to say that we couldn't have learned these somehow through experience when we were very young?"

"How? You can't sense time or space," Newman reminded him.

"True, but you can't sense the noumenal world either. Why couldn't there be some yet to be identified mechanism of learning that explains how we develop those concepts? At least that would be consistent with the rest of our experience of how we learn things."

"A very similar case was developed by John Stuart Mill, not too long after Kant," Sophia said, nodding appreciatively.

"I can understand the natural inclination to defend materialism, especially for a scientist," Newman allowed. "But really you're just choosing one set of assumptions over another."

"That choice can be guided by experience though," Hyle countered. "Go back to Ockham's Razor—the simplest explanation is probably the best, and any explanation which postulates unnecessary entities, like pure intuitions or noumenal worlds, without evidence should be avoided. It just seems to me that the split between physical and mental, or phenomenal and noumenal, is an artificial one—an artifact of philosophy and logic, like Zeno's paradox. Conceptually it seems like less trouble to just stick with the physical world and explain the appearance of the mental or noumenal as artifacts."

"Conceptually there's something even easier," Newman suggested. "You could assume that everything is noumenal and the appearance of a physical world is the artifact."

"But that would mean that everything I think is physical really exists just in my mind," Hyle objected, "You'd be a figment of my imagination, Newman, just like Sophia was saying about my spoon."

"Actually that is a valid philosophical position, Hyle," Sophia noted. "It's called solipsism. Solipsism is the belief that only oneself exists."

"Solipsism isn't the only possible conclusion though, Hyle," Newman insisted. "You think that a non-physical world could only exist in your mind, but you're basing that conclusion on the traditional idea of a physical human body with a brain that's thinking things up. That wouldn't be true in a non-physical world."

"That's just too crazy to even think about."

"Actually Fichte, a younger contemporary of Kant, developed a similar theory," Sophia said. "He drew on Hume's argument that the self can't be experienced any more than causality can, and argued that we create the world in our intellects according to the laws of nature."

"I bet that philosophy leads to its own set of logical problems," Hyle replied, "but even if it's completely airtight, logically it's so far from our actual experience of life that it's only useful as a topic of dinner conversation."

"And there in a nutshell you have the central debate of epistemology," Sophia said. "The only thing people seem to agree upon is that we have sensations. On the one hand you can argue that they're relatively accurate representations of a real material world, or on the other hand you can argue that they're purely mental constructs and the material world is just an illusion. Or you can try to find some compromise the way Descartes and Kant did. The problem is that none of these explanations ends up being completely satisfying on both an intellectual and an emotional level. On top of that you have to explain how science has been so successful in understanding the physical world and yet failed so abysmally to prove or disprove the existence of God or free will or make any progress in metaphysics. Of all the philosophers who have taken a shot at this problem, Kant came the closest."

CHAPTER FIFTY

HELENA

It was dark and the room was abnormally quiet when Sophia awoke the next day. A dim sense of unease grew to concern and pushed the fog of sleep from her mind as she recalled waking earlier when a dismal gray light had filtered in around the edges of the blackout drapes. The two men had been awake then and she had asked them to let her go back to sleep to try to make up for a restless night of half-remembered dreams.

Now it was too quiet. Although she was still tired, Sophia got herself out of bed and padded down the hall. She was pleased to find Newman and James talking quietly. The room had been emptied of the typical pre-work crowd and it sounded like they were the only three people on the floor. Newman informed her that she had just missed Hyle who had set off for the library after listening to James scan unsuccessfully for radio transmissions.

"We were about to listen to some music. Any requests?" James asked, clicking through directories on a handheld player while Newman looked over his shoulder.

Sophia shook her head drowsily.

"How about Alan Parsons?" suggested Newman, pointing to the screen.

"Sure, which album?"

"Whatever you want. Surprise me," Newman replied.

James was pensive for a moment and then selected a track and cradled the player into the amplifier rack.

"I'm going back to our room to sleep a little more," Sophia told Newman. "Don't let me sleep through dinner though."

The music caught her attention as it faded in and she lingered in the doorway to listen. The first sound reminded her of a telegraph typing out the same pattern over and over in a rhythm almost like Morse code. Sophia wondered if it was coincidence that James had chosen this song just after working the radio. The telegraph was soon joined by a powerful chorus of horns and rolling drums that sounded like the dramatic scene of a horror movie. With an involuntary shiver Sophia turned away down the hall. Their room was dark but Sophia did not bother to turn on the light. She committed the location of the bed to memory and closed the door.

As soon as the door latched behind her there was a knock on the other side.

Sophia jumped back, startled by the sound. There had been nobody outside a moment ago. The music down the hall reached a crescendo, a frenzy of horns, guitar and kettle drums, and Sophia could feel her hand shaking on the door knob. More knocking. Sophia drew a deep breath for courage, turned on the light and let her eyes adjust. Then she opened the door. The dark face and bright grin of Nicolas Auld filled the doorway.

"Oh, it's you," Sophia said with a sigh of relief. "Where on earth did you come from?"

"I am sorry if I startled you," he replied, looking more amused than apologetic. "May I come in?"

Something in the back of Sophia's mind told her that it was not wise to invite a relative stranger into her room. She still knew nothing about him. Yet there was never any real question. For some inexplicable reason, she could not imagine that he would ever do her harm. Even knowing him for only a few minutes Sophia trusted Auld almost as much as Newman and Hyle. She opened the door wider and stepped aside.

Auld hesitated awkwardly in the doorway, shifting his weight and looking as though he did not understand the gesture. Sophia felt the increasing burden of an uncomfortable silence.

"Please, come in," she said after a moment, motioning him into the room. The smile returned Auld's face.

"Thank you," he said, brushing past Sophia and walking to the desk below the window in the back of the room. He leaned lightly against the wood veneer writing surface and watched Sophia for a moment without speaking.

"How is the research going? Is your friend finding what he needs?" he asked at last.

"It's hard to say," she answered slowly. The question took her by surprise. "I'm not sure he even knows what he's looking for." Being evasive made Sophia felt a bit guilty and she was surprised at how much Hyle's secrecy had rubbed off on her. She considered asking Auld why he wanted to know, but somehow that seemed inappropriate, so she said nothing. Auld looked at her thoughtfully and the silence grew to fill the room. She was suddenly reminded of the feeling she had once at the end of a semester, waiting and watching while one of her professors read through the first few pages of the term paper she had just turned in.

"How are you feeling?" asked Auld at length. His melodic voice immediately put her back at ease. "You look tired."

"Yes, I am. I didn't sleep very well last night."

"Bad dreams?"

Again Sophia was taken aback by the question.

"Yes. Well, maybe. I had a lot of dreams, I think, but I don't really remember them. They may have been nightmares though because I didn't get much rest."

"Perhaps they were trying to tell you something," Auld suggested, and Sophia got the distinct impression that he would be grading her on her response. She could not tell if he was serious or not. She shook her head uncertainly and opened her mouth, but could not think of what to say.

"Come with me," Auld said, standing quickly. "There is someone I think you should meet."

Sophia considered asking who he wanted her to meet and where he wanted to take her, but suspected that she would not get a useful answer. Auld had pushed off the desk, passed her and disappeared out the door before she had decided whether or not to say anything, let alone go with him. Cursing silently to herself Sophia grabbed her shoes and hurried out the door.

She caught up with Auld as he was entering the stairwell. Sophia followed him down several flights of stairs, lit only at the landings by the narrow windows in the door to each floor. Even a few steps behind Auld her head was barely higher than his, yet he moved with the grace of a dancer and she noticed that she could not hear his footfalls at all above the sound of her own shuffling bare feet. Auld was wearing the same gray camouflage as the evening before, and as they approached the halfway landing of each floor where the light struggled to reach, Sophia focused on the back of his dark head, afraid that he might fade away into the shadows and leave her in her bed again wondering if it had all been a dream.

When Auld reached the first floor and stepped into the hallway, bringing her eyes once again level with his shoulder blade, Sophia was still convinced that she was awake. He stopped and indicated an open door, gesturing for her to go inside.

"This is Helena," he told her. "Tell her about your dreams. Perhaps she can even help you figure out what they mean."

Sophia stepped into the doorway and paused to look around the room. It was arranged differently from the others she had seen. The only furniture was a black lacquered coffee table in the center of the room. Posters covered all the walls. Most had the names of bands, but Sophia recognized one movie poster that showed Dorothy and her three companions in front of the Emerald City and another with strange green characters cascading down behind a man in a leather trench coat. One striking poster directly across from the door featured a single red rose on a black background, with the letters "DM" in the corner.

Beneath this black poster, an undergrad sat on the edge of a mattress that seemed to serve both as a bed and as seating. She was taller and thinner than Sophia and her pale complexion was made all the more striking by her choice of fashion. Her straight black hair was pulled away from her face into tight pigtails, which stuck out from the sides of her head like bicycle handlebar grips. Heavy mascara encircled her eyes. Her clothing was a continuum of black from blocky shoes that seemed to have been inspired by combat boots to fishnet stockings, a leather mini skirt and tee shirt. Only the tee shirt had any color other than black, in the form of the three white letters "NIN". Sophia stared at the shirt for a moment before realizing that the third letter was reversed.

"Hi. I'm Sophia Xiao. My—my friend," Sophia began, settling somewhat awkwardly on the term and gesturing behind her, "thought that maybe you could help me figure out a dream I had."

"Hi, Sophia. I'm Helena. Nice to meet you," the young woman said in a high rapid fire voice much brighter than her appearance. Sophia gave a little smile and nodded in greeting, still looking around the room. "Oh, where are my manners?" Helena said, falling backwards across the bed and stretching to reach something against the back wall. "Here, have a seat." She flung a large brown object across the table. It landed across Sophia's feet with a plop in an amorphous heap. "So you're having problems with dreams? I'm not sure what I can do for you, but it can't hurt to tell me about them anyway. Go on, sit down. It won't bite you. It's just a beanbag chair."

Sophia looked doubtfully at the shiny brown globule but lowered herself into it anyway. The beads inside shifted out from under her until she was sitting almost on the floor. After finally getting herself settled she realized that the only thing more awkward than sitting in the beanbag chair was the expectant silence in the room.

"I don't really remember having any dreams last night, but I did have one a few nights ago," Sophia offered. She went on to recount the last dream she could clearly recall, describing how she had wandered through the old roofless factory, the desperate feeling of being lost with no way out, the mysterious figure that had appeared and the realization that she was dreaming.

"You realized that you were dreaming and you actually watched yourself in the dream?" Helena asked excitedly when Sophia explained the experience. "Lucid dreaming. That's what that is."

"So do you know what the dream means?" Sophia asked. She turned to catch Auld's reaction and was surprised to see that he was not there.

"No idea. I don't really interpret dreams, although it might be kind of fun. Maybe it was the lucid dreaming your friend wanted you to tell me about. I do know something about that and it's not easy to do, I can tell you that. I've been working on it for years and I've only been able to do it a couple times myself. Have you done it before?"

"A few times, yes. But I don't think—I mean, I didn't say anything about that to him," Sophia objected. She looked over her shoulder again. The doorway was empty.

"Well, still, here you are," Helena said. "I don't believe in luck or coincidences, so you must be here for some reason. It's like being characters in a book, I think. To them everything seems to be just a bunch of unconnected chance encounters, but really everything is important. Every name and every event has some meaning. Everything happens for a purpose. Life is the same way. So maybe the reason you're here is to learn about lucid dreaming. Have you ever left your body?"

Sophia would have laughed if she had been sure she heard the question correctly. By the time she replayed it in her mind she could see that Helena seemed to be waiting for a sincere answer.

"Not to the best of my knowledge," Sophia replied diplomatically.

"Well you should keep working on your lucid dreaming. That's the first step to astral travel. Next time you realize you're dreaming try to pick somewhere you want to go and go there in your dream." Helena paused for a moment, looking thoughtful. "Hey, you could come visit me!"

"Astral travel? I'm not sure I'd want to do such a thing even if I could."

Helena twisted her face into an expression that was a blend of horror and sympathy.

"Of course you would," she insisted. "It's the most wonderful experience! Well, at least it's supposed to be. That's what I've read anyway. When you can leave the confines of your body you become part of something greater than any of us. Like a higher level of consciousness. That's where the word *ecstasy* comes from you know. In Greek *stasis* means to stand and so ecstasy means to stand outside of yourself. *Ex stasis*—standing outside yourself. Ecstacy. It's an opportunity most people would die for. Promise me that if you have another lucid dream you'll try to go somewhere."

Half stunned by the verbal onslaught, Sophia nodded her assent.

"Good. Now do you have any other abilities that I should know about? Like any kind of extra sensory perception or anything like that?"

"No. I'm just a normal person."

"Maybe. But maybe you have talents that you're not even aware of. Like lucid dreaming," argued Helena. "Have you ever had the phone ring and known who it was before you answered it? Or planned to call a friend and had them call you just as you were headed for the phone?"

"Maybe once or twice by chance, but not really, no."

"Have you ever worried suddenly about friends or close relatives and later learned that something bad happened to them right at that time?" Sophia shook her head. "What about dreams? Have you ever had anything come true that you dreamed about beforehand?" Sophia shook her head again and Helena began to show signs of discouragement. "Have you ever felt like you knew exactly what someone was thinking, or how they were feeling?"

"Yes, sometimes. But I think everyone has had times they felt like that," Sophia replied automatically. When she thought more about it however, she realized that this was something she had considered a strength at work. "I guess maybe I'm better at that than most people, but I don't think it's because of ESP or anything. I think I must just be more attuned to the subtle facial expressions or tones of voice that people use."

"Or maybe you have a latent ability in telepathy and you just don't realize it," Helena suggested. "You should try to develop it." She lay down across the mattress again and searched for something out of sight just beyond the edge. When she sat up again she was holding a deck of cards. She removed the rubber band that held them together and handed the deck to Sophia.

"Do you know what those are?" she asked.

Sophia looked at the cards. They were oversized, with a light blue pebbled pattern on the back and the deck was about half as thick as a normal deck of cards. She turned it over. The facing card had three thick black wavy lines that looked like a symbol for water, but turned ninety degrees. Sophia thumbed it aside and moved it to the back of the deck. The next card had a circle, and the one after that had a star. She thumbed through the rest of them. There were more of those shapes as well as some squares and plus signs.

"Yes," Sophia answered. "These are the cards they use to test for psychic abilities."

"Right! Zener cards. I practice with them all the time. Go ahead and shuffle them and we'll test you."

Sophia shuffled the cards.

"Okay, but don't get your hopes up."

"We might as well not even test you with an attitude like that," Helena chided. "If you don't believe in yourself you'll kill any ability you might have. That's called the sheep-goat effect, you know. People who don't believe in ESP—goats—score lower on average on these tests than sheep—people who do believe. Even the attitude of the experimenter can throw things off. The problem is that most paranormal effects are so small that it's easy to dismiss them. But that's where you have to start. Think of it like weightlifting. If you walked into a gym and tried to pick up a two hundred pound weight you probably couldn't budge it, but if you started off small and worked your way up, one day you probably could." She took the cards back from Sophia and put them face down on the coffee table between them. "So remember, you're just trying to beat the odds here, not match everything."

"And what are the odds?"

"There are five types of cards, so if I reshuffle after each guess you'll have a one in five chance. A test is usually twenty five guesses, so the mean chance expectation is five hits."

"What do you usually get?"

"It depends on the day. Some days I can focus better than others. Last week I got twelve. That's my record. I seem to be doing better in the last few months, ever since… you know," her voice trailed off. "Maybe there were too many radio waves interfering or something." Helena shrugged and tapped the top of the deck. "Go ahead. Concentrate on the first card. Take your time. When an image forms in your mind, tell me what it is."

Feeling a bit silly, and thankful that nobody else was there to see her, Sophia stared at the back of the card and tried to picture the symbol on the other side. She tried to push aside her self-consciousness to keep her mind open and give the trial a fair shot.

"Circle," she said at last.

Helena turned over the card. It was a star.

"That's okay. Keep concentrating," she said as she shuffled the deck and placed it back on the polished black surface of the table. The next guess was a miss as well, but Sophia matched a square on the third guess. A short time later, when she got her fifth match with eight guesses left to go, Sophia found herself more excited than she would have expected at the prospect of beating the odds. In the end she got seven hits.

"That's excellent," Helena told her excitedly. "See what you can do when you believe in yourself?"

Sophia smiled, but shook her head. She liked the idea that she had tapped some hidden power to match the two extra cards, and Helena's enthusiasm was infectious, but it was difficult to believe.

"Probably just beginners luck."

"Don't say that," Helena protested. "There's no such thing as luck. Only things we don't understand yet. You have potential—we just have to develop it. Let's try telepathy next and after that I can show you how to try to influence physical things. I have been using dice recently. I used to practice cloudbusting, but that's not really an option anymore."

"Cloudbusting? What is that?"

"Haven't you ever tried it?" Helena's voice transitioned rapidly from shock to reverie. "It's great to do on a summer day when the sky is blue and the sun is shining and there are a few wispy white clouds floating by. You find some place to lie on your back and pick out a small cloud to focus on and try to get it to dissipate."

"And what do you do with the dice?"

"I try to get them to roll ones. It's not as much fun as cloudbusting, but it's good practice. Let's test you on telepathy now," Helena said, shuffling the deck and laying it back on the table. "Just like last time, except now I'm going to draw a card and look at it and you focus on what I'm thinking, okay?"

Sophia watched her pull the top card off the deck and stare at it, her eyes widening slightly as if she were trying to burn a hole through it with her gaze. Sophia's guess was a miss. When her next two guesses missed as well, Helena decided to switch methods.

"Instead of looking at the card and sending you a picture, I'm going to put the card down and visualize it. Let's see if that helps. You might be attuned to a different kind of thought patterns or something."

After looking at the next card, Helena placed it face down next to the rest of the deck. She placed two fingers on each temple and squeezed her eyes closed as though straining to force her thoughts out toward Sophia. It was such a stereotypical image that Sophia had to choke back a spontaneous laugh and cover it by pretending to clear her throat. Helena continued to concentrate unperturbed by the noise and Sophia closed her own eyes to focus on the card, mainly by blocking out the image of Helena. When she got a hit, Helena concluded that this method worked better for Sophia and repeated it for the rest of the guesses.

It was several hours later when Sophia was startled by a familiar voice.

"There you are!"

Hyle stood behind her in the doorway and shot her a furious look as soon as she turned around.

"We've been looking all over the building for you! I was starting to worry that something serious had happened. I never expected you to just wander off without telling anyone to go play dice games."

"This isn't a game," Helena retorted, looking affronted. "We're practicing telekinesis." Newman appeared in the doorway behind Hyle as she spoke.

"And talking," Sophia added quickly. She could feel her face flush. "About all sorts of things. This is Helena. Helena, this is Hyle and that's Newman, the guys I came here with."

"Nice to meet you," Helena said. "Sophia is just being modest by the way. She has a lot of undeveloped empathic and telepathic ability. I'd watch what I was thinking around her if I were you," she added with a grin.

"It's a good thing it's an undeveloped ability," Hyle replied, "because she wouldn't want to know what I'm thinking right now." He made it sound like a joke, but Sophia knew him well enough to take the comment at face value.

"I did match nine out of twenty five Zener cards," Sophia said, picking up the deck to show to Hyle. "That's well above the expected average."

"Just once?" Hyle asked. It was as much a prediction as a question.

"That was my first try with Helena looking at the cards." Sophia could not quite bring herself to explain that Helena was projecting her thoughts. "But I got seven out of twenty five before that without either of us looking at them. The average should be five."

"So you beat the average twice? That's all it takes to convince you that you have some kind of latent psychic ability?" Hyle gave Sophia a look of utter disappointment. "That's just luck. You'd need to get that kind of score consistently for it to be meaningful." Sophia was about to object, but Hyle held up a finger. "Tell you what. If you can do it again three more times and get above five each time I'll give you my dinner and I won't say another word about it."

Everyone was looking at Sophia. She scanned the room, thinking. Helena seemed uncertain about the idea.

"What if she loses?" Newman asked Hyle.

"No consequences. She can keep her dinner, but I get to say 'I told you so.'"

"Okay, it's a deal," Sophia said determinedly. She handed the deck to Hyle. "Go ahead and shuffle it and give it to Helena."

They repeated the telepathy test with Helena looking at the top card and then closing her eyes to project her thoughts to Sophia. Hyle caught Sophia's eyes and shot a meaningful look at Helena, with her fingers against her temples, once her eyes were closed. After seven straight misses, Helena launched into an explanation of the experimenter effect—a phenomenon in which negative energy from non-believers determined to debunk psychic abilities had been demonstrated to dampen the abilities of their test subjects. Hyle said nothing, but it was clear from his expression what he thought of the argument.

Sophia only got four hits.

CHAPTER FIFTY-ONE

BREADCRUMBS

Rolling dunes stretched out before Sophia, forming a vast wasteland of pale sand, mottled with shadows. It was cold in the desert at night. Although there was nothing in sight to suggest a reason for alarm, somehow she knew that there was little chance she would make it across alive. It was not until she looked up that she discovered the source of her unnatural fear. Around the broad silver moon the dark shapes of three vultures floated noiselessly, and Sophia knew in that instant that they were waiting only for her. Suddenly the view shifted and Sophia found that she was watching herself from a distance as her form picked its way around the rocks that dotted the bleak landscape. She remembered that this was a special thing—that the real Sophia was supposed to try to go somewhere, but she could not remember where. For a moment she found herself back in her bedroom listening to Auld's warning that they should not stay too long and then everything faded.

It was still light out when Sophia got out of bed feeling reasonably well rested, although the vague impression of another disturbing dream tugged at the back of her mind. She was pleased to see that both men were still asleep. Hyle had been extremely unhappy to learn that it was another visit from Auld that had brought her to Helena the previous night. After that discovery Sophia had endured a patronizing lecture about talking to strangers which she tolerated partly because she did not wish to cause a scene in front of Helena, but also because she knew that Hyle was right.

Things had gone downhill from there. She had assumed that Helena knew Auld, or at least had seen him at her doorway. When neither of these assumptions proved to be true, she noticed a subtle shift in the conversation. It was not until they were almost to the dining hall, when Newman had asked her about sleepwalking, that she had realized what he and Hyle were thinking. They were beginning to question whether or not Auld was real. She could almost picture the looks they must have been giving each other behind her back. Fortunately, when the two men did wake up, nobody mentioned the adventure of the previous night.

It was not until she was walking down to the library with Hyle that Sophia had a sudden memory of her dream. The fragment she could recall was only a brief image, but with it came a surge of fear almost as fresh as the original nightmare. The image of vultures floating across a moonlit sky evoked an involuntary shudder. Sophia clutched Hyle's arm and looked up. Behind the cover of the dust clouds Sophia thought she could make out a full moon.

When Hyle asked what was wrong, Sophia shrugged it off, fairly sure how he would respond to hearing about another dream. Any further mention of Auld was out of the question.

"How many more nights of research do you think you have?" she asked, trying to sound casual.

"I don't know. I'm starting to run out of leads. I didn't really find out much of anything last night, but we still have another three weeks of free food, so I figure I'll keep plugging away until I need to get a job. Why?"

"Just curious," Sophia answered, wishing she could get Auld's warning out of her mind.

Once inside the library Hyle got right to work. He was pleased to see a slip of paper with several references waiting for him. Most were dead ends or led to information that was relevant but not new. The last reference however, one that appeared to have been hastily scribbled onto the bottom of the page, led to something altogether different. It was a short article in a California newspaper.

"Sophia, have you seen Francis?"

"Tonight? Not yet."

"Come take a look at this," said Hyle, pointing to the article and reading. "The deceased, a man known as Anderson Poimen, was described as a reclusive psychologist who was best known for a 1992 book on cult deprogramming. He was lost at sea and presumed dead after his small sailboat was caught in a winter storm off the coast of southern California."

The article did not mention the man's age or birth date, but the photograph showed him to be well on in years. There was nothing in the article to suggest why it should be of interest.

"I don't get it," Sophia said. "Why are you showing me this?"

"I was hoping you could tell me. I thought at first maybe this was someone who got in the way of the Union, but look at the date."

"January 3rd, 2000?"

"Yes, that's a couple years before the Union of Faith was founded."

"Let's see if we can find Francis," Sophia suggested. "Maybe he gave you the wrong reference by mistake."

They found Francis on the lower level of the library overseeing the reorganization of several dozen rows of shelves to make room for another set of journals that had been relocated from the science library. When Francis returned with them to the computer alcove, rather than clear things up as they had hoped he deepened the mystery.

"I didn't write that," he told them, looking at the last entry on the list of references.

"Are you sure?" Hyle asked without thinking.

"Yeah dude. Pretty sure I'd know if I wrote it. That's not even close to my handwriting anyway."

"Who else would it have been?" asked Sophia. "Do any of your guys know what we're working on?"

"I don't think so." Francis shrugged. "I sure haven't told anyone."

"Did anybody else work on these computers since last night?" Hyle inquired.

"I haven't seen anybody outside the Brotherhood of Leibowitz in here since you left last night man. We use the computers a lot during the day, but I told everyone not to touch your stuff."

"Probably one of your guys just needed to jot down a quick note," Hyle suggested.

"I don't know man. I told them not to touch your pile," Francis insisted.

While Hyle continued to interrogate their librarian host, Sophia let her eyes wander across the pile of books, papers and jewel cases until her interest was caught by one particular disc. Of all the media spread out across the desktop, this was one that she did not remember either of them viewing. A quick check confirmed that it was not on the list of references.

"Do either of you speak German?" Sophia asked a few minutes later.

Rather than answer, Francis and Hyle crowded around the computer. Near the top of the screen was the lower half of a black and white photograph which showed the torsos of several people. The rest of the screen contained German text arranged in three columns. The name Zendik was scattered throughout the article and was highlighted in yellow. In the center of the screen, also highlighted, was a single instance of the name Poimen.

For a moment no one spoke as they each tried to make sense of what they were seeing.

"Do you have a German to English dictionary?" Hyle asked Francis at length. "I took a couple years of German in high school."

By the time Francis reappeared with a dictionary, Hyle had translated enough of the words at the start of the article to get a general idea of the topic. Zendik was addressing a large crowd at a university in Berlin. With the help of the dictionary Hyle was able to confirm that the theme of the oration was the familiar topic of technology and faith before he skipped down to the paragraph of interest. This he pieced together slowly, looking up many of the words and testing out different translations with Sophia and Francis until they made sense in context. Gradually a coherent story emerged.

Someone had caused a commotion early in the sermon, apparently addressing Zendik from the back of the hall. The young man, a graduate student in the psychology department, claimed that the speaker was really named Poimen. He reportedly yelled "I know your secret" several times as he was being escorted from the building by campus security. The article concluded that the student was a troubled youth and may have been opposed to the sermon's anti-science message.

Scrolling up to the top of the article, Hyle studied the face of Zendik, shown in the photograph shaking hands with some German official. He captured the image and saved it before pulling the disc out and replacing the article from the California newspaper. The photograph from the California article showed a man who looked many years older than Zendik. He was pale, with thinning salt and pepper hair in sharp contrast to the picture from the German article of a man with a thick mane of snowy hair, a perfect smile and a tanned face that radiated vitality. Despite the initial impression that these two images had no characteristics in common there was a certain resemblance.

"They must be the same person," concluded Hyle, studying Sophia's face. He met her skepticism with a series of arguments about the similarities of different facial features, especially the eyes, which he argued were the most difficult to alter. After debating the idea for several minutes, finally the other two had run out of objections and Hyle was particularly pleased to finally see Sophia nodding slowly as though grudgingly accepting that it might be true.

"Think about the timing. It all fits," Hyle declared excitedly. "We have never seen any mention of Zendik before the year 2000, even back in Asher. Poimen disappears, Zendik appears a few months later. He must have staged his own death."

"And had plastic surgery?" Sophia asked incredulously.

"And spent some quality time tanning on a beach, looks like," added Francis.

"Maybe. I don't know. But you can see that they're the same guy, right?" When nobody objected to this assertion, Hyle went on. "And it's not just the timing that fits. It can't be coincidence that this Poimen wrote a book on cult deprogramming and here's Zendik building what essentially turns into a worldwide cult. Do you think you have his book here, Francis? We should see if he published any articles too."

The remainder of the evening was spent searching for publications.

"Here's the author index," Francis told them, leaving them at a shelf of thick books arranged by year and then by section of the alphabet. The books contained references to scientific articles published in that year, listed alphabetically by author. Hyle and Sophia, who were quite familiar with such research, had worked through more than a decade of volumes by the time Francis returned to inform them that the library did not have Poimen's book. The first article they found attributed to an A.E. Poimen was on the effects of growth medium on the cell wall of *Saccharomyces cerevisiae*. The next one however was on the role of group dynamics in assessment of truth statements, and it became the first to be recorded on a list of articles to retrieve. After apologizing and explaining that the journals from the science library were currently in disarray making it difficult to find anything quickly, Francis promised to have a stack of articles waiting for them the following evening. Even without the articles they were able to glean some information about Poimen's research interests. As they accumulated the titles of the articles and the journals in which they were published, a pattern emerged. The earliest publications shared the general theme of social interaction within a group and its impact on individual behavior. The next few also appeared to be studies of groups, but the exact topic was more esoteric.

"I have no idea what this one is about," Hyle admitted, "but if he had to publish in something called the *Journal of New Consciousness* it must be pretty interesting."

Sophia knew Hyle well enough to understand that 'interesting' in this context was not a compliment.

The last two articles had been published in the *Annals of Parapsychology*, and both titles included the same interesting term.

"What is 'collective solipsism'? Isn't that an oxymoron?" Hyle asked Sophia.

"Yes, solipsism is the belief that you're the only thing that really exists, so I don't see how it could be collective."

Francis did not remember ever seeing *Annals of Parapsychology* and after a search of the piles of science journals on the lower level failed to turn up anything, Hyle and Sophia decided to end their work for the night. They packed away their notes, carefully reshelved the small stack of volumes from the author index, and thanked Francis for his help. Hyle was almost to the door when Francis called them back.

"Hey, wait, before you go I have something else for you," he said, waving them back urgently. "I almost forgot with this whole photograph secret identity staged death thing." Francis led them over to a large atlas that lay open to a map of India. "Remember you wanted to find out about the town that biotech company was in? Well check this out."

CHAPTER FIFTY-TWO

CONSPIRACY THEORIES

In the dining hall, Sophia listened to the two men talking, but her attention was not entirely on the debate. Hyle was filling Newman in on their recent discoveries in the library and expanding on what Newman had dubbed "the grand conspiracy theory." Occasionally Hyle called on her to verify some piece of information they had seen in the library, which she did, or back him up on some part of his theory, which she did not. She was too busy trying to figure out—what? That was the problem. It was not even clear what it was that troubled her. And troubled was too strong a word. At first she thought it might be another dream that she was trying to remember. It was the same kind of vague awareness, but a dream did not feel like the right explanation. Eventually she realized that it was the conversation itself—not just the one at her table, but all around them.

There was an undercurrent of nervous energy not usually present in the normal buzz of dining hall talk. Was it concern about the attacks in Syracuse? Again, that did not seem right. There had been no more news in the last few days, and although people were still edgy, this was different. One table in particular drew her attention. At it, five students were engaged in an animated discussion, dominated by a stocky blond boy with a moustacheless Abraham Lincoln beard and a Hispanic girl with hair that cascaded down almost to her waist. It was too far away to catch anything they were saying, and from the way they leaned in, Sophia assumed they were talking quietly anyway.

"Think about it," Hyle was saying, "It's the perfect biological weapon if the goal is to kill as many people as possible. High rate of transmission, high mortality, slow onset." Newman shrugged, and Hyle's voice climbed a few decibels in response. "That doesn't happen naturally, that's what I'm saying. Toxins aren't contagious, bacterial agents can be treated with antibiotics, and viruses have a very fast onset. It's easier to quarantine people. This has got to be an engineered virus. Something with a delayed onset."

"Why is that so important?"

"Two reasons. First, it's easier to quarantine people if there's a fast onset of symptoms. You catch them early before they have a chance to infect too many other people. That was exactly what caused the problem in India, right? By the time everyone realized that it was an epidemic, the horses were already out of the barn. They tried to close the borders, but it was too late. In fact, the U.S. suspended international travel and sealed its borders too, but a week later it started popping up here. Those measures might have been implemented in time if the symptoms didn't take so long to manifest."

Again Newman shrugged and this time Sophia realized that his mind was not really on the debate. Hyle increased the fervor of his arguments, desperate to find the clearest chain of logic to convince Newman that he was right. But Sophia saw the real problem. It was not that Newman was unconvinced. What Hyle took to be an obstinate stance or a debating tactic was actually much less calculated. Newman was not unconvinced— he just did not care.

"The second reason is epidemiological," Hyle continued. "If you want to spread an epidemic you need contact between people. You've heard of Ebola, right? It's a very nasty virus. Wipes out whole villages in Africa in no time flat. But it kills people so quickly that they don't have time to spread the disease. You have to have a certain population density to spread disease. A certain rate of human to human contact. The faster the agent kills people the higher the rate of contact needs to be and the more likely people are to be spared if the population is below this threshold. The ideal biological agent will be spread far and wide before anyone knows it's coming. It would have a very low population threshold."

"So that's why you think the Mumbai Plague was a biological weapon?" Newman asked.

"Not *was*, is. It's probably still smoldering out there, waiting for a wind to pick up and whip it up into a brushfire. All it would take is one carrier to show up here," Hyle glanced uneasily at Sophia and read the expression on her face. "Sorry. I'm not trying to be sensational, but it's true. Besides, like I said, I think we were already vaccinated."

This was one of the parts of the grand conspiracy theory that Sophia found most interesting. Hyle had tried to convince her that Tandava Labs had not only created the virus now known as the Mumbai Plague, but also a vaccine for it. The steps required to make a vaccine—identifying the virus, isolating it, learning how to grow it up in large quantities, purify it, render it non-infectious, and formulate it for delivery—took considerable time and effort, he had argued, particularly for a nasal formulation like the one they had been given in Asher. The fact that Tandava Labs was one of the early purchases of the New Concordance Enterprises supported the idea that the company would have had several years to participate in the conspiracy, and engineering a biological weapon would have given them the knowledge to design the vaccine against it.

"Just look at the facts, Newman," Hyle pressed, recapping his argument. "There's no question that Zendik purchased Tandava Labs—a biotechnology company that specializes in vaccine manufacture. What does a church want with a biotech company? Zendik makes frequent trips to India. Probably checking on the progress of his little project. Then, when it's ready, he lets it out into the world."

"How?" Newman asked. "And why?"

"It could have been any number of ways. Maybe he smuggled some vials out himself. Maybe some zealots volunteered to be infected. Maybe they convinced someone to test the vaccine and gave them a placebo instead. Whoever was the first carrier wouldn't have to go far though. Mumbai, with more than twenty million people, was only a short car ride away."

This was the information that Francis had pointed out in the atlas. It had triggered a new flurry of research into Tandava Labs and the first reports of the Mumbai Plague.

"As to why, it all fits together. It's the step that puts everything else in motion. Tensions are already high in that part of the world. As soon as the Plague starts to pop up you get a bunch of trigger happy nuclear powers pointing fingers and accusing each other of deploying biological weapons. The disease kills a large enough portion of the population in Asia to create crises within a few short weeks, and on top of the war, throws the military in all those countries into disorder. It's the perfect time for Zendik to call on all those generals he kept meeting with. All it takes now is one missile launch to start an all out nuclear war."

Newman listened impassively and Sophia tried to read his mood. She had heard Hyle's theory all the way back from the library. It made a certain amount of sense to her, but it was a bit too much to absorb. Perhaps that was how Newman felt, although she thought he had seemed distracted even before the discussion got underway. When she caught a subtle exchange of glances between Newman and the long haired girl sitting with Abe Lincoln, Sophia began to formulate some conspiracy theories of her own.

"Meanwhile, Zendik builds a series of secluded communities, far away from population centers," Hyle continued, "and stocks them with vaccine, medicine, weapons and enough supplies to feed an army through the winter. Then he gathers all his faithful together just before the Plague starts to burn out of control and the missiles start to fly."

There was a brief silence as Hyle watched Newman and waited for a response.

"Well, what do you think?" he demanded. Newman responded with another shrug. "What's that supposed to mean? You don't think it makes sense?"

"It makes as much sense as any explanation, I suppose," Newman allowed.

Hyle waited for him to say more. He expected to hear some objection, but none came.

"Don't you care? What I'm trying to tell you is that I think Zendik wasn't only involved in the nuclear attacks. I think he was behind the Mumbai Plague too. If you think I might be right about all of this, doesn't it matter to you?"

For the first time that evening Sophia saw Newman truly engage himself in the conversation. He looked at Hyle for several seconds before answering.

"No," he said, very deliberately.

There was another long, awkward silence with Hyle shaking his head in stunned disbelief and Newman staring resolutely at him. Eventually Newman pushed away from the table and stood up.

"Sorry, Hyle, I'm really tired. I'm going to head back to the room to get some sleep. I promise that we can talk more about this tomorrow."

When Sophia woke the next day she had a sense that something was out of place, but this time she was sure that it was not a dream. The first thing she noticed was that she had slept later in the day than usual. The sun had very nearly set and light was already turning from orange to gray. Both men were still asleep, which was also odd, since typically one of the three of them would have been awake by this hour. Finally it dawned on her—there was no music. Quietly she slipped out of the room and down the hall. James was not in his room and the light was off. There were a few voices from elsewhere on the floor, but the dormitory seemed to be strangely deserted.

Still sleepy and with the nagging concern that she might be dreaming, Sophia hurried back to her room and was relieved to find Newman awake and Hyle stirring. After assuring Newman that she was okay and had not been sleepwalking, he finally listened to her description of the unusually quiet halls. It was nothing to worry about, Newman told her, reminding her that he had been working on a secret project with James and some others.

As they each ate the apple muffins they had saved from dinner, Sophia and Hyle tried to get some hint about the nature of the project, but Newman would only tell them that people were taking a day off from work and that they would see why soon enough. Sophia watched the two men as the conversation progressed, Hyle appearing intrigued, but in a hurry nonetheless to get through the surprise so that he could get back to work in the library, Newman apparently stalling for time. Darkness fully covered the campus by the time they were ready to leave.

Outside the dormitory a few flakes of snow danced their way earthward in the narrow shafts of light that escaped around the edges of the blackout curtains. In silence Newman led them along the path across the quad, abandoning the path when it turned right, and continuing straight, up a grassy incline. Passing into the shadow between two dormitories they focused every thread of perception on the nearest suggestion of a human shape until vision became entirely useless and they were forced to navigate by sound and feel. A gentle breeze came in gusts, peppering their cheeks with tiny darts of concentrated cold that dissolved into wetness on contact. Beyond the buildings a broad expanse of grass spread out behind the quad and sloped uphill to the edge of a forest. Just before entering the forest, Newman stopped and turned around to face the other two.

"Your question deserves a better answer than I could give last night, Hyle," he said. His voice was low and measured, and even though Hyle was impatient to hear what came next, a part of him cursed Newman for breaking the silence. "I have something I want to share with you," Newman continued, addressing both of them. "It's something I hope the two of you will enjoy, or at least appreciate. A surprise. But first I want to explain why I don't care whether or not there was a conspiracy." He paused, unsure of exactly how to continue.

There was a flood of thought and emotion inside Newman, a rising swell that had lifted him up and tossed him about like a boat in a hurricane. How could he explain this as a positive force? Something vital? Language seemed wholly inadequate to the task. Especially to the task of explaining this to a scientist. He drew a long breath, conscious of the path the icy air followed deep into his lungs.

"Your theory may be right, Hyle. I don't know. But what's done is done. The question for me isn't how we got here. I'm more interested in where we're going. Maybe this all happened for a reason. Not a reason you'll find in news articles in the library, but a higher reason. Maybe this was meant to be a course correction for the human race." Hyle scowled and shook his head slowly, but did not interrupt.

"When we were in Asher, I read a book that always makes me think of you, Hyle. It was called *On Religion: Speeches to its Cultured Despisers*." Newman paused to let Hyle absorb the title. "It was written by a hospital chaplain named Friedrich Schleiermacher in 1799, right at the height of the Enlightenment, at that time everyone was infatuated with science. Philosophers had taken over moral instruction, proofs for the existence of God had failed to bring the certainty that they sought, and religion no longer seemed relevant. It was held among the intelligentsia to be nothing more than an outdated set of superstitions that humanity had outgrown. Schleiermacher wrote his speeches directly to these people with the goal of reforming religious thinking and reintroducing it to the mainstream. He made the case that religion can't be understood by logic. It has to be experienced through intuition or feeling."

This idea captured just exactly what Hyle disliked most about religion. In his mind he framed several replies, all of them caustic, but somehow the chill breeze on his face seemed to whisk these thoughts away like so many snowflakes before they could be spoken aloud.

"Each person is a microcosm, a finite reflection of something greater and infinite," continued Newman. "We're at once separate from the universe and a part of it. As individuals we're finite and separate from the universe. We experience it and study it as if it were something foreign. But we are at the same time a part of the vast, infinite universe and a reflection of it. That's where Schleiermacher says that religion comes from. It's this intuition, this sense that we're part of something greater and the desire to find a connection back to it."

A plume of mist drew a long sigh behind it. This was not going as well as Newman had hoped. What had seemed so clear when reading the words of the *Speeches*, what he could feel again as a powerful truth in his heart, now defied expression except in the most abstract and cryptic statements. Sophia would understand what he was trying to say, but Hyle had the ability to make anything sound ridiculous. Hyle had been listening quietly so far, but how long would his patience last? There was never any real possibility that even the most perfectly chosen words would somehow lead Hyle to an epiphany and turn him suddenly religious. Newman chuckled silently at the thought. Still, he had dared to hope that it would be possible to make a connection, with the right illustration or a good example, which would lead Hyle to discover this feeling in himself, if only in some small way. At least coming out here to have the discussion was a good idea, Newman thought. The silence of the night was definitely making Hyle more receptive.

"I know you don't agree with the Prophet about technology," Newman continued suddenly, hoping he had found his illustration. "Or maybe you agree with his premise, but you don't see it to be any loss if faith should be diminished by technology. But I think that even the Prophet may have missed a part of the picture. Technology doesn't separate us from faith—it separates us from nature. All the most basic conveniences of modern culture were designed to protect us from nature. Houses kept us cool in the summer, warm in the winter and safe and dry in the fiercest storms. Cars brought us hundreds of miles without ever having to walk a step through a meadow or down a forest trail. Grocery stores brought food to people who never touched a hoe or sowed a seed or picked fruit from a tree. Technology separates us from nature. That's what science is all about, isn't it? Dissecting nature, boiling it down to basic principles, describing it in equations so that we can control it—that's the purpose of science. Science is the sword that we wield to protect ourselves from nature and keep it at bay. You may not care about the loss of faith, but stop and listen for a minute, Hyle. If you're quiet long enough I bet that even you will find something out here that you were missing."

Hyle cast his eyes across the field and into the darkness beyond, blinking often to clear the snowflakes that lit on his eyelashes. There was a vastness in the impenetrable night, a sense of infinity. The wind stirred the forest behind him, setting bare branches clattering and scraping and tree trunks squealing and groaning in protest. The cold had tightened the skin against his face. His cheeks felt like leather and his breath appeared in pinwheels of mist that drifted away just in time to be replaced by a new frosty burst. The small patch of luminous sky concealing the moon was slowly torn away by a low, dark storm cloud, and for a moment he had the sensation of being all alone in the world. A chill deeper than the wind shook him and he turned back to search for the outline of Newman against the forest.

"Can't you feel it? The power of nature?" Newman asked, mistaking Hyle's silence for disagreement. Hyle, in turn, missed the trace of desperation in Newman's voice.

"Yes," said Hyle. His response was barely audible. A series of memories washed over him even as he spoke. Stumbling, lost and alone in the blackness of the forest, not remembering who he was or where he had come from—if there had ever been a time that he had felt the presence of God it was that night that began this whole dark adventure. He had experienced something powerful beyond logic and reason that night, but not something he wanted to seek union with. If it was God, it was the God of the Old Testament—powerful, mysterious and unpredictable. Something born of fear and awe.

"Yes," he repeated, "I do feel something, but maybe not what you feel."

Content with this small victory, Newman decided not to pursue the details.

"Let's keep walking," he said, and set out along the tree line at a slow pace.

For a long time the only sound was the wind in the trees, punctuated occasionally by the distant cries of a small animal. It was Sophia who broke the silence. Something caught her attention in the woods. At first it was just a feeling that she had seen something out of the corner of her eye. The next time she thought she knew what it was—a point of light. Yet when she tried to find it again it was gone. The third time she was sure.

"There's a light up there in the forest," she said, reaching ahead to put a hand on Newman's shoulder as she stopped.

"I know," he replied. "That's where we're going."

CHAPTER FIFTY-THREE

NATURAL PROGRESSION

Cutting into the forest, they followed a narrow trail away from campus. Not so small once, the parallel ruts made by the traffic of heavy tires were still discernable beneath the scattering of weeds, even in the flickering torchlight. Except by hikers, the road had not been used for many years and the forest was slowly reclaiming its loss. Branches twisted tentatively into the space above, and patches of undergrowth crowded along the edges. Here and there the brush was bold enough to grow right out into the road, obscuring one of the ruts entirely.

A torchbearer inclined his head slowly in a silent greeting and motioned them further in, toward the next point of light. He wore a theater drama mask. Flames danced on the white ceramic surface, bringing an eerie animation to the leering grin painted on it. The next torchbearer was worse yet, the mouth of his mask twisted into an expression of agony and despair. Sophia shivered as they walked past. Comedy and tragedy alternated as they made their way along the trail, from one island of flickering light to the next, deeper and deeper into the woods. Eventually they came to a place where the road cut sharply left and disappeared into darkness.

As they hesitated at the edge of the road a shape broke from the shadows beside Sophia.

She fumbled backwards and let a truncated shriek escape before she realized what had startled her. A mime, complete with grease paint face and black and white striped shirt, stared back at her with wide eyes, hands clamped to his cheeks and mouth opened wide in a silent scream.

"Oh, God, you scared me," Sophia hissed, wondering in the back of her mind why she felt compelled to keep her voice to no more than a loud whisper.

The mime pouted and hung his head in shame. Then, as if suddenly struck by a wonderful idea, he sprung to life again with a wide grin, leaping off the road toward the light and beckoning for them to follow. He led them through a stand of trees, the light growing brighter with every step until they emerged into a clearing. They found themselves standing at the edge of a quarry. Light radiated from the quarry floor. In the distance, at the edge of the shadow, the walls dropped nearly twenty feet straight down, but at their feet it pitched away at an angle that was steep yet manageable for walking. Logs had been set into the earth along the grade, forming concentric semi-circles around the small bonfire at the bottom. Several people already sat upon the crude benches whispering to each other in pairs and small groups. A safe distance behind the fire a series of sheets tied to a rough wooden frame blocked the rest of the quarry floor from view. The mime swept his arm out over the range of seating, bowed, and trotted back into the woods.

"It's just like an old Greek amphitheater," Sophia whispered as they took their seats near the center, one row back from the bottom.

Newman grinned. "That's the idea."

"Do you know what the show is going to be?"

"Yes."

The grin widened and Sophia was struck by a sudden thought. She had not seen Newman this happy since they left Asher and she felt herself becoming infected.

"Fine, keep your secrets," she told him. For a while she contented herself with watching the flames dance in the bonfire and the pulsing orange glow of the coals beneath them. She traced the firefly trails of the sparks as they rose to meet the darkness and tried to tell whether the tiny dabs of white that fluttered down around the edge of the firelight were ash or snow. Every now and then she would look back over her shoulder to watch a group of new arrivals pick their way down the slope, but it was never long before her eyes were drawn back to the flames.

"You really can feel something, can't you?" Sophia said at length, still speaking in a reverent whisper. Out of the corner of her eye she could see Newman gently nodding in agreement. "You know, there's a philosophy that's very much like what you were saying about being a part of nature and yet separate from it."

"Spinoza?" guessed Newman.

"No. Well, yes, but no. Spinoza made the case that God and all that exists must be one and the same. The philosopher I'm thinking of is Schelling. His philosophy is really concerned with Nature. Nature with a capital N. Schelling believed that all aspects of reality—matter, life, spirit—were all aspects of Nature and that Nature itself isn't static. Nature is constantly expressing itself through the act of creation, constantly developing, and human beings are the pinnacle of Nature's development. When we create, Nature is expressing itself through us."

"I like that," Newman said.

"I can appreciate getting back to nature," Hyle conceded, pausing to look around at the darkness that enshrouded the fire, "although I can't really picture nature as an evolving organism. It sounds like Schelling misappropriated Darwin's theory of evolution somewhere along the way."

"It does," Sophia agreed, "except that Schelling published his *Philosophy of Nature* long before Darwin."

"Maybe Darwin was inspired by Schelling," suggested Newman.

"Actually it's more likely that Darwin was influenced by Hegel," replied Sophia. "Hegel borrowed heavily from Schelling, and while Shelling was popular in certain circles, Hegel was the preeminent philosopher of his day. In fact, there's a saying that all philosophy since Hegel has just been a series of reactions to his work."

"He must have made some pretty impressive renovations of Schelling's philosophy then," Hyle commented.

"Yes, he did actually. He applied Schelling's idea of Nature to history, but as part of a more complex and far-reaching philosophy."

"How does that work?" Newman asked, balancing his question somewhere between defensiveness and curiosity.

"Remember the Divine Intellect of Plotinus?" Sophia asked. "If you were to cross that with Schelling's concept of Nature you'd end up with something like the Geist of Hegel's philosophy."

"Geist is German for spirit," Hyle noted, "as in poltergeist."

"Yes, except in this case it's Geist with a capital G," explained Sophia, "and it translates to something more like World Spirit. Sometimes it's translated to Idea, again with a capital, but whatever term you choose, it's this thing that constitutes reality for Hegel. Actually, 'thing' is a bad choice of words—the ground of reality for Hegel is something in between a universal spirit and a pure intellect. But unlike the Neoplatonists, Hegel saw everything as changing. Geist isn't static, and it's not just changing haphazardly. It's evolving—developing toward an end—that's another idea he shared with Schelling."

"Why was that idea so popular?" Hyle questioned.

"It was part of the backlash against science, I think, to offer an alternative theory to the clockwork universe of the Enlightenment. Hegel was very critical of scientific method." Sophia's speech accelerated in pace with her enthusiasm for the topic. "It seemed to him that the scientific process is a self-fulfilling prophecy. Scientists start with a materialistic world view and define the rules for acquiring knowledge to be rigorously materialistic. Accordingly the tools of science are designed to find material causes, so then when scientists set out to learn about the world, is it really any big surprise that the explanations they find are materialistic?"

"I suppose that if you believed the world is essentially spirit or divine intellect or whatnot, you'd be a little biased against people who believe that the world is physical."

"A fair point, Hyle," Sophia allowed. "Hegel's world view may have pre-disposed him to his ways of thinking too—that could probably be said of everyone—but he also had another complaint against science that I think strikes a chord with many people. His complaint was that science just describes things instead of explaining why things happen."

"What's that supposed to mean? The whole goal of science is to explain why things happen."

Hyle studied the miniature flames reflected in Sophia's eyes as she stared thoughtfully into the fire.

"Give me an example of something that science explains," she said at last.

"Since we were just talking about Newton recently, how about gravity? It explains why apples fall to earth and why the planets circle the sun."

"Okay, good," Sophia said. "So what does the law of gravity say? Objects are attracted to each other with a force proportional to their mass and inversely proportional to their distance?"

"Yes," Hyle agreed. "The square of their distance, technically."

"Would you say that it's an accurate description of how large objects behave?"

"Yes. Good enough to land rockets on the moon."

"Aristotle believed that to truly understand something you must understand all of its causes—the material cause, the efficient cause, the formal cause, and," Sophia drew a breath, pausing for emphasis, "and this is where science falls short—the final cause. The final cause is the teleological cause. The purpose. The law of gravity is just a description of the way things are. It may have taken a great deal of perception and insight to notice the pattern, and it has great predictive power, but it just describes what is so. Not why it's so. It's akin to saying that birds fly and fish live in water. That's not an explanation. It's just a statement of the way things are. Why aren't objects attracted to each other independent of their weight? Or why don't they repel each other instead of being attracted?"

"That's just the way nature is," Hyle replied.

"Maybe so, but it's sort of like telling a kid 'because I say so' when she asks why she can't have ice cream for breakfast, lunch and dinner. It's not a satisfying answer. It's not an explanation. It would be more meaningful to tell the child about health and nutrition."

"The same is true of any explanation though," Hyle countered. "If you ask a priest why something happens, he'd probably tell you it's God's will. Then if you ask why it's God's will that innocent children should die horrible deaths, you'd get something trite like 'the Lord moves in mysterious ways.' Really what that means is 'because God said so.' Sooner or later any chain of cause and effect will come to the cause we can't explain and we have to throw up our hands and say that this is just the way things are."

As he was speaking, Sophia was shaking her head. "Not necessarily. According to scientists, even if we do adjust our theories from time to time as we learn more, the laws of nature themselves are absolute and eternal. Just like God or Platonic Forms—eternal and unchanging. The key to Hegel's philosophy is that the ground of his reality isn't static."

"I don't see how that would make a difference."

"Let me see if I can explain it. It's a pretty complex philosophy though so bear with me."

People continued to fill the amphitheater and their quiet conversations blended with the wind in the trees to create a constant background of white noise. Hyle nodded at Sophia's request, and Newman perched on the edge of the log, leaning forward to see her face as she spoke.

"Geist or the World Spirit is the totality of everything that exists. Instead of a static clockwork universe, all of reality takes the form of this Divine Intellect or spirit. Nature is part of Geist, which is why it follows rational laws, and we're part of Geist as well. Hegel said, 'The real is the rational and the rational is the real,' which means that as rational beings whatever we perceive and whatever we conceive is a part of reality. It's similar to Parmenides' claim, 'That which can be conceived is that which exists.' Our art, culture, science, religion, economics, political systems—everything that we do—is an expression of Geist. Hegel was the first to introduce a historical perspective to philosophy. He argued that Geist, as measured by the yardstick of human culture, changes over time, and the changes aren't just random. The changes represent an evolution."

"Evolution toward what?" asked Newman.

Hyle scoffed. "What stage of evolution have we achieved by nuking ourselves back to the Stone Age?"

Although this was clearly a rhetorical question, Sophia smiled and addressed it nonetheless. "It's hard to say. Hegel would answer that you can't really understand the significance of your own time. In his words, 'The owl of Minerva spreads its wings only at the setting of dusk.' Obviously the owl of Minerva represents wisdom, so what Hegel is saying is that any given era can only be understood in hindsight, with the full knowledge that has been gained over the course of the age."

On hearing this Newman was momentarily possessed by a distant expression and silently mouthed the words of the quote to himself.

"In fact," continued Sophia, "people can't truly understand other eras of history, or even really influence their own period of history. According to Hegel, everyone is a product of their time. Everyone gets swept away in the *zeitgeist*—"

"The spirit of the time," Hyle translated, nodding.

"Yes. For example, there will never be another Mozart or Beethoven. People can write classical music now, of course, but they'll always seem a bit like imposters, trying to imitate a style that's no longer part of our *zeitgeist*. Conversely, Copernicus and Newton couldn't have foreseen the impact that their discoveries would have on culture and society. The impact of those discoveries can only really be appreciated in hindsight and moreover our perception of things is always colored by the ideas of our age. Nobody can stand outside of history and judge it objectively."

"Makes sense so far," said Hyle, "but if the real is the rational and the rational is the real, how can we have such diversity of beliefs about what is real? Christians, Muslims, Buddhists and atheists can't all be right."

"You have struck on a critical part of Hegel's theory, Hyle. We're part of Geist and an extension of Geist, but we don't feel the connection. Often we don't even feel the connection to each other. But we're aware of something missing. We have a sense of disconnectedness, or alienation—"

"That sounds a bit like Karl Marx," Newman noted.

"It is," Sophia agreed. "Remember that quote about all modern philosophy being a reaction to Hegel?"

"Can we stick to Hegel?" Hyle asked, making no attempt to hide his impatience.

Sophia smiled and with an apologetic glance to Newman, continued. "Most people don't feel the connection to Geist. Geist expresses itself mainly through isolated cases which we recognize as genius. These are people who have the ability to tap into the universal nature of Geist and express it in an individual instance. A great poem or a great painting, for example, should make us think of something greater than just the individual subject it presents."

"Philosophers are always trying to find universals," Hyle commented under his breath.

"True. Hegel listed philosophy as another example of the expression of genius, although for him the best example came from Christianity."

The connection was immediately clear to Newman. "Jesus as a man is an individual, and as the Son of God is an expression of something universal."

"Exactly, but the expression of Geist isn't always so benevolent," Sophia continued. "Figures like Caesar and Napoleon are also expressions of Geist, although maybe not in the same way. Geist uses their ambition to bring about change, usually causing their undoing in the process. All the while the common person is just a helpless victim of history."

"That's a pretty depressing thought," said Newman.

"Unfortunately it's hard to have a philosophy of history that doesn't account for war," Sophia replied. She could see another comment beginning to form on Hyle's lips, and anticipating his request to stay on topic she quickly added, "But even though individual people may suffer the horrors of war, it's toward some end. At least that's what Hegel would say. Our disconnection from Geist and from each other leads to alienation and conflicting ideologies. But this conflict is part of the evolution of Geist and it doesn't just happen randomly. It's resolved through something Hegel called the dialectical process or the dialectic—a cycle of thesis, antithesis and synthesis."

"Do these conflicts always have to be resolved on the battlefield?" Newman asked, a hint of despair in his voice.

"According to Hegel they often are, but not always. For example, do you remember the debate between the realists and the nominalists about universals? How can we all use the word red to describe an apple and mean the same thing? The thesis of the realists was that the universals themselves—like redness—had a reality of their own. Universals had their own independent existence as a sort of pure Platonic form. The antithesis was provided by the nominalists, who argued that universals were just words, with no special status. Now you have the thesis and antithesis—a conflict of ideas. Abelard provided the synthesis. According to Hegel, a synthesis melds the two competing ideas, retaining aspects of both sides, but changing both ideas in the process. Remember Abelard's solution? He said that words were just words, as the nominalists argued, but that universals did exist, as the realists said—except they existed as concepts in the mind. His synthesis answers the objections of both sides in one package that's radically different from the original thesis and antithesis.

"Plato is another example. Before him you had philosophers like Thales, Parmenides and Democritus whose thesis was that everything that exists is reducible to some basic element which is immutable and that change is an illusion. Heraclitus staked out the antithesis. 'You cannot step into the same river twice.' Everything is constantly changing and permanency is an illusion. Plato synthesized these two world views into his idea that the material world is a finite and changeable shadow of a transcendent and immortal world. But as soon as a synthesis is established and accepted, it becomes the thesis of the next guy who comes along, like Aristotle in this case. And the dialectic cycle repeats—thesis, antithesis, synthesis. Another good example is Kant and his synthesis of rationalism and materialism—"

"Are we getting close to the part where you give us the explanation of life, the universe and everything that's more satisfying than science?" Hyle interrupted.

"You have all the pieces now," Sophia responded with a taut smile. "If you can answer Newman's question about what Geist is evolving toward, you'll understand the basics of Hegel's philosophy."

The challenge caught Hyle off guard, and for a while he just stared at Sophia.

"Seems like it should be evolving toward the ultimate philosophy," Hyle suggested after a while.

"That makes sense," Newman concurred. "But what is it?"

"If Geist is evolving, then the ultimate philosophy should be the endpoint of evolution," Hyle said, glancing at Sophia for some indication of whether he was on the right track. Her expression was encouraging, so he continued. "And the driving force behind this evolution is this dialectic process, so the ultimate philosophy would be a thesis that doesn't have an antithesis. The last word in philosophy, ideology, and politics as it were."

Nodding in approval at this conclusion, Sophia asked "What would be necessary to have a thesis with no antithesis?"

This time it was Newman who rose to the challenge. "If alienation and conflict are caused by our separation from Geist, we'd need to become unified with Geist somehow."

"How can we be separate from Geist?" Hyle demanded. "I thought we were part of Geist."

"We are. As I understand it, we're an extension of Geist, but we're not conscious of it and it's not conscious of us. Maybe we're the extension of Geist that represents awareness and exploration and our goal is to discover Geist. In a way it would be Geist gaining self-awareness."

"That sounds nice, but I have no idea what it really means," Hyle said.

"Think of it this way," Newman replied. "Remember Avicenna's flying man, suspended in the dark with no light, sound, and unable to even touch any part of his body to any other part? You questioned whether this flying man would even be aware of himself or anything else, including the idea of existence. Remember?"

Hyle indicated that he did.

"Now imagine that whatever magical restraints held this flying man's limbs apart were suddenly released. He might feel around in the darkness of his void until eventually his fingers touch some other part of his body. Wouldn't he use his fingers to touch and learn everything he could?"

"Makes sense," Hyle agreed. "I certainly would."

"By analogy, if Geist is the flying man, we're the fingers. So the ultimate state must be Geist gaining self-awareness through us." Newman concluded.

"That's it," Sophia confirmed. "Hegel called this the Absolute Idea, or just the Absolute."

"This philosophy actually makes some sense," Hyle allowed, "aside from the fact that there's no more reason to believe in Geist than there is to believe in God. But at least once you get past that assumption it seems logically consistent. It also fills the religious need to believe that our final reward is some end state of perfection. I'm not surprised Hegel was influential."

By the time he finished speaking Hyle was no longer addressing the other two, pulled away by his own thread of thought. He stared into the bonfire and half-listened as they discussed Hegel's influence on Marx, who Newman seemed to have read or at least studied. Sophia explained that Marx was considered one of the Left Hegelians. Those were followers of Hegel who tended toward atheism and revolutionary views, inspired by the idea that as an expression of Geist, we have more progress to make. Hegel himself was of the mind that the Prussian state he lived in was not far removed from the Absolute Idea—a view embraced by the Right Hegelians who tended toward Hegel's Protestant values and nationalism.

"Of course many of these people wouldn't have called themselves Hegelians at all," Sophia qualified, but Hyle did not hear her. He was busy tracing back through their conversation and picking out pieces of a jigsaw puzzle.

The evolution of Geist, the owl of Minerva spreading its wings only at the setting of dusk, individual expressions of genius—these were all pieces that he turned around in his mind. Now he added the fact that Hegel had believed his Prussia to be near to the Absolute Idea, and this brought him to his first realization. To claim to understand the whole of history, Hegel would have had to believe that history had come to an end. Or at least his era had. The larger realization followed quickly—if Hegel's philosophy is about Geist coming to know itself, isn't that exactly what his philosophy achieves? Hyle knew immediately that this was what he had been struggling to see—Hegel created a philosophy that not only predicted that history was progressing toward some final chapter, but he also wrote the story in such a way that his philosophy *was* the final chapter. Hyle was simultaneously amazed by the audacity and impressed with the brilliance of it all. He turned back to Sophia to share his insight.

At first Hyle thought his timing was good because he had caught Sophia and Newman during a break in their conversation. Then he noticed that nobody was talking. All the conversations had stopped.

The only sound was the crackle of the fire and the creaking of the branches in the darkness beyond.

CHAPTER FIFTY-FOUR

MIDNIGHT FESTIVAL

In the black void beyond the fire a shape coalesced, gliding silently toward them. From the other side of the fire another came, at first nothing more than the merest suggestion of motion, then the vague outline of a human form, advancing slowly until at last, in the warm light of the flames it resolved itself into a young woman in a dark flowing dress. She paused in the wide space in front of the bonfire, apparently unaware of the audience that encircled her only a few dozen paces away. Presently she was joined by a man in a sport coat who hailed her with a soundless greeting. As he closed with her, more figures emerged from the shadows that concealed the far end of the quarry.

In ones and twos they came, until the makeshift stage was filled with a sizeable crowd, all going about various activities in total silence. Some interacted with each other, nodding and gesturing enthusiastically in mute conversation. One man read an invisible newspaper, turning the pages carefully and snapping the crease into shape before starting to read again. A short distance away another man appeared to be mowing his lawn. Farther on a group of people stood shoulder to shoulder, lurching and swaying. Most had one hand up at head height, clutching something for support, but one typed away intently on an unseen keyboard. Others washed dishes, walked dogs, shopped and acted out a variety of office scenes. A pair of women jogged slowly around the entire ensemble, chatting and occasionally pointing into the darkness. As they circled back between the crowd and the bonfire, all activity stopped suddenly and everyone looked up into the sky.

The bonfire exploded in a supernova of white light. Sophia, who had suspected that the two women were more important than the rest, had just caught a glimpse of one of them throwing something into the fire before she was blinded by the sudden burst of brilliant light. The scattered whispering of the audience stopped abruptly as everyone tried to process what they were seeing as the afterimage of the flash faded. The actors, reduced to dark silhouettes, stood motionless for a few seconds that seemed frozen in time and then, some with arms outstretched as if pleading to heaven, they crumpled, melted, withered, to the ground.

A few gasps issued from the audience, and far in back someone began sobbing. The whispering returned with a furious intensity, like a gale through a wheat field and then subsided again when one of the figures raised itself slowly from the ground. It hugged its knees to its chest in a fetal ball for a moment before pulling itself unsteadily to its feet. It was not until it was standing that the audience could see the white bones painted on the black bodysuit and the skeletal mask. One by one more skeletons rose from the ground and they began to shuffle slowly and aimlessly around. When two in the fore-ground encountered each other, they studied one another for a moment and then removed their masks. Others followed suit, embracing or mouthing solemn conversation and gradually gathering into a single large group. One of them bent down and retrieved a suit coat from the ground, brushed it off and put it on. Others moved to do the same, and as the last of them donned their human attire, a young woman stepped away from the crowd toward the audience. It was the long haired Hispanic woman from the dining hall.

"And so we rise, like Phoenix from the ashes," she said, spreading her arms like a televangelist. The other actors melted back into the shadows as she spoke. "Pale and trembling, like fragile wraiths, all but lost in the smoking ruins of our burned out world. We have lost much, but we have survived. Many have died where we have lived, and it is fit that we should grieve for them, but not tonight. Tonight we will not mourn the dead," she said, her voice swelling dramatically, savoring each word as it was spoken. "Tonight we join in celebration. A celebration…of what it means…to be…*alive!*"

As if suspended on her outstretched arms the final words of the oration hung in the air for several long seconds only to be blown aside by a fury of percussion that made the audience jump in unison. A wide curtain was raised in front of the bonfire, blocking all direct light and in the relative darkness a hundred heads turned together to find the source of the sound. At the top of the quarry a young man was largely concealed by shadows from the two large cylinders in front of him. His hands flew across the surface of the bongo drums, flickering in and out of existence in the shifting glow of reflected firelight like a mongoose and cobra caught in a strobe light. From behind the curtain a half dozen shadowy figures raced out of the darkness, circling in from both sides, a torch blazing in each hand. They wore the same black body suits as the actors, but without the bones, and had dark coverings over their faces, drawing attention away from the performers to the torches. To the frenetic rhythm of the bongos the torches spun, raced past each other, arced, stopped dramatically, snapped back into motion in a carefully choreographed display somewhere between a dance and a martial arts kata. Tracing a mesmerizing path through the night, the flames darted to and fro as though they were the participants in the dance and the humans in the flickering light behind them were incidental. The bongos stopped in sync as the six performers dropped to a one-legged kneel, torches outspread.

Someone far to the left of the audience clapped tentatively and a scattering of others joined in as the performers bowed and retreated backstage and the curtain was lowered to reveal the bonfire once more. Newman, who was most inclined to show his appreciation of the routine, could not quite bring himself to break the relative silence with applause. It would almost, he thought, detract from the impact. He was convinced that was why the first performance was met with silence—in this case it was the highest expression of appreciation—and it appeared that most of the audience shared this conviction with him. He did lean over and whisper to Sophia and Hyle an amusing anecdote about the first rehearsal being done in robes until one of the performers almost set himself on fire.

The next few acts had less flair and showmanship than the first two. There were several readings of poetry and prose and a few folk songs. During these performances Newman leaned over frequently to relay some tidbit of information, explaining "That's Emerson," or "I think she wrote that herself," or, enthusiastically, as three new performers stepped forward into the firelight, "I like this one a lot."

One of the three performers carried a cello and a small stool. He brushed long wavy hair back from his face over his shoulders as he took a seat on the stool and fidgeted with the placement of his instrument. The second performer stopped beside the cellist and raised a violin to his chin. Sophia looked at Newman inquiringly and he nodded, confirming that it was James who held the violin. "He wrote the score for this," Newman whispered. The third performer, a pale young woman with flowing blonde hair, almost ethereal in a diaphanous white dress, took a few steps beyond James and the cellist. Glancing briefly at the sheet of paper in her hands she announced to the audience, "Kubla Khan, by Samuel Taylor Coleridge."

The violin played a serene, uplifting melody, buoyed by long rich notes from the cello as the speaker slowly recited the first lines of the poem.

In Xanadu did Kubla Khan
A stately pleasure dome decree:
Where Alph, the sacred river, ran
Through caverns measureless to man
Down to a sunless sea.

The instruments maintained the same theme as the second stanza of the poem expanded on the idyllic description of Xanadu, but then shifted in tone as the third section began. The notes of the cello contracted, building gradually toward a staccato and those of the violin climbed in pitch throughout the lengthy passage as the young woman painted the image of a savage chasm in a cedar grove. The music reached its crescendo as the poem depicted the eruption from this chasm that flung rocks 'like rebounding hail' and then subsided into a minor key which added a dark gravity to the last couplet of the section.

And 'mid this tumult Kubla heard from far
Ancestral voices prophesying war!

For the fourth section of verse the strings retreated further to a melancholy variation on the opening score. Accompanying the fifth and final long section of the poem the violin and cello returned to the original theme and expanded upon it, the violin soaring higher and the cello weaving in and out of a complex baritone. Meanwhile the reader, now speaking in the first person voice of the poet, painted the picture of a damsel from a vision whose symphony and song would revive within the poet the ancient sunny dome and caves of ice.

And all who heard should see them there,
And all should cry, Beware! Beware!
His flashing eyes, his floating hair!
Weave a circle round him thrice,
And close your eyes with holy dread,
For he on honey-dew hath fed
And drunk the milk of Paradise.

A last lonely note from the cello lingered, powerful yet wistful. When it finally died away the brief silence was overwhelmed in applause. Newman turned to his companions, clapping vigorously and raised inquiring eyebrows although Hyle was nodding appreciatively and it was clear from Sophia's awed expression what she thought.

"What did you think?" he asked nonetheless.

"Even I recognized that one. We had to read it in high school, but I have to say the music added a lot," Hyle replied, trying not to look overly impressed.

"It was amazing," Sophia answered, addressing Hyle as if she were correcting him.

Newman quickly agreed. "I almost feel guilty clapping," he said, "like we should have just kept quiet and reflected on it for a while."

"Maybe we should try snapping," Hyle offered, smirking and doing a passable beatnik impersonation. Sophia shot him an icy look, prompting him to add, "Next time I'll wear my beret and bring some clove cigarettes."

The clapping tapered off as the next performers appeared from behind the bonfire just in time to save Hyle from Sophia's response. There were more folk songs, more poetry readings and nothing at all to make Hyle wonder if his comments had been unfair. When a mime took the stage—the same one who had guided them to the top of the outdoor theater—Newman stood into a crouch and shuffled in to whispering range.

"I'm up next. I'll be back in a little bit." To Hyle he added, "I helped pick the opening number. I think you'll like it."

With that cryptic comment he stood up with his back to the stage area and ascended the aisle that led back behind the spectators into the woods. As Newman disappeared into the night that shrouded the top of the hill, the mime suddenly discovered the audience and reprised the silent scream he had given Sophia after startling her. Eventually, after climbing invisible stairs and escaping from invisible boxes and the like, the mime was pulled off stage by a giant invisible hook to the sound of tepid applause.

Newman appeared from the other side of the fire, carrying a guitar and flanked by two young women. One of them Sophia recognized immediately as the long-haired beauty who had introduced the evening. She felt her chest tighten as she was gripped by an unexpected surge of antipathy. Even as the animal part of her snarled at this young woman merely for being beautiful—no, not just for being beautiful—for being beautiful and *knowing* it, the rational part of Sophia tried to uncover the source of these unusual emotions. She generally looked for, and found, the good in people, but Sophia was convinced that this girl deserved her disdain, and it puzzled her that this should be so. She traced the feeling back to her grade school days when looks and arrogance were all one needed to be popular, and just hoped that Newman also saw this girl for what she was. It was with this final notion that the emotive and logical sides of Sophia quickly agreed not to pursue the line of thinking any further. By the time Newman was strumming the opening chords of a song, Sophia had relaxed considerably and she was able to smile, understanding Newman's parting comment when the opening line of the song made reference to the trial of Galileo.

Sophia was forced to admit to herself that the dark-haired singer had a very good voice and carried the poppy folk song well. The other young woman provided back-up vocals and harmony for the chorus, and even Newman joined in near the end of the song. The crowd clapped with reasonable enthusiasm when it was over and Hyle leaned forward holding both hands out and snapping with gusto. Newman spotted him easily in the front row and grinned back. Beside Newman, the lead singer bowed slightly a few times and waved graciously at the audience.

"Thank you for joining us tonight," she said at last. "We hope you enjoyed it. We plan to do this again next month, when we will be producing Shakespeare's *A Midsummer Night's Dream*. In the meantime, remember each day to appreciate this gift of life we've been given. Seize the day! Make your lives extraordinary!"

To wind down the evening, she called all of the performers forward to join in a few final songs. People picked their way down through the seated spectators. As figures crowded onto the makeshift stage, eclipsing the bonfire, the audience gave them a long ovation.

With Newman leading on guitar, the assembly launched into a rendition of *American Pie*. By the end of the first chorus, everyone in the quarry was singing. Hyle enjoyed the sing-along, but found it too sappy to allow himself to be moved the way some people obviously were. He observed more than a few glistening eyes as the song drew on, despite the addition of so many off-key voices and the mumbling which nearly obscured the middle verses.

The night ended with *This Land is Your Land*, again with everyone joining in. To the left of the audience people put their arms around each other such that whole rows were locked into a single line of bodies, swaying back and forth in time to the music. This idea spread through the crowd and soon Sophia found herself with her arm around Hyle, lost in the experience, unencumbered by any judgment of the event. All thoughts of the long-haired girl had been washed away, and the feeling that now rose in her chest was one of a deep, soul-nourishing warmth.

Sophia realized that for the first time in a very long time she was really, truly happy.

CHAPTER FIFTY-FIVE

ROMANTIC NOTIONS

Snow no longer fell in light flakes that floated gently on the wind. Sticky clumps plummeted out of the sky and clung to the individual blades of ankle deep grass where they landed. In the diffuse moonlight such resolution was lost and the wide sloping field bordering the forest took on the appearance of a desert with shallow rolling dunes of white sand. When Sophia emerged from the woods with Newman and Hyle, a dark trail cut directly across the field toward the dorms, made by the trampling feet of the many people who had left the quarry before them. She hesitated for a moment, then turned and started walking slowly along the tree line. If either of the men had asked why, she would have had a hard time explaining it, but she had a feeling that the night should not be over yet—as if there were something yet to come or something left to do perhaps. Nobody asked.

Maybe I just don't want it to end, Sophia considered, invigorated by the sting of the cold wind. She paused occasionally to catch snowflakes on her tongue as they sauntered aimlessly along the edge of the field and discussed the evening in hushed voices. Sophia traced back through the evening, trying to determine what was causing her sense of incompleteness. She remembered one thing but dismissed it immediately. When nothing more convincing came along she stopped and turned to Hyle.

"You were just about to say something to me before the performances started," she prompted.

Hyle scowled for a moment, trying to recall what they had been talking about. "Oh yes, that. We were talking about Hegel."

"Yes," Sophia confirmed, but it did not feel like what she was looking for.

"I had just realized that if Hegel believed that you could only understand a historical age when it was over, and he was claiming to understand all of history, does that mean he believed that history had come to an end?"

A quiet snort of laughter emanated from Newman's direction.

"No, I'm serious," Hyle protested. "Look at it another way. He believed that the ultimate goal of Geist—the *telos* that Sophia was talking about—was for Geist to come to know itself. And we're extensions of Geist, right? So as soon as Hegel formulates his philosophy, humanity has therefore discovered Geist. In other words, Geist has come to know itself through humanity and the end goal is achieved. Hegel's philosophy is a self-fulfilling prophecy."

"There's a certain arrogance to Hegel if you interpret his philosophy in that way," agreed Sophia. "Of course some scholars made entire careers of arguing about how to interpret him. You know, the other thing that's sort of ironic about Hegel is that even though he pioneered the concept of historical perspective, his philosophy was clearly a product of his own *zeitgeist*."

"Really? His philosophy sounded pretty unique to me," Hyle observed.

"Except for the similarities to Schelling," Newman reminded him.

"Hegel wasn't just influenced by Schelling either," added Sophia. "Fichte had already developed the concept of thesis, antithesis and synthesis, and Hegel was also influenced by Fichte and Kant's moral philosophy as well as the general backlash against science. And of course he thought the Prussia of his own time, right at the end of the eighteenth century, was pretty close to the ideal state. That argues for someone who was well entrenched in their own time, and it does support the interpretation that Hegel may have believed he was living near the end of history."

"That's also the time of Sturm und Drang and the Romantic Movement," noted Newman. "Those would have been part of Hegel's *zeitgeist* as well."

"Sturm und Drang?" Hyle repeated. "Sounds like a school for wizards." It was the type of joke he made mainly for his own amusement. If someone else got it, so much the better. When nobody laughed he added more seriously, "That translates as 'storm and urge' more or less. Was it a revolutionary movement?"

That did get a laugh from Newman. "No, far from it. It's usually translated as Storm and Stress by the way, and it was a late eighteenth century German artistic movement which focused on intense emotions. Goethe is probably the most famous artist associated with it. Are you familiar with the Romantic Movement? It grew out of Sturm und Drang."

"I can't really say that I am," Hyle confessed, "but at least I've heard of that one."

"It was a reaction to the Enlightenment," explained Sophia. "Part of the backlash against science I mentioned. The Romantics were people who found the logic and science of the Enlightenment to be too..."

"Sterile," Newman chipped in when Sophia paused to find the right word.

"Yes. Too sterile I suppose. I think Newman described it well earlier. The Enlightenment was all about man versus nature. The Romantics wanted man to be part of nature again. Schelling was one of the patron saints of the Romantic Movement, as you might imagine. The Romantics put an emphasis on spirituality and setting aside cold logic for emotion and experience."

"A basic premise of both movements was that in order to really appreciate life," Newman added, "in order to fully experience being human, you had to experience the strife of being a part of nature—the conflict, the fear, the sense of awe. You must know William Blake's poem *The Tyger*?"

Hyle was fairly sure he had heard it in high school. He was struggling to remember when Sophia recited the first lines.

> *Tyger! Tyger! burning bright*
> *In the forests of the night,*
> *What immortal hand or eye*
> *Could frame thy fearful symmetry*

"I love that poem," she said.

"It's a wonderful poem," Newman agreed, "and a wonderful example of Romantic poetry. Blake uses the tiger—a mysterious and powerful hunter—to strike a chord of fear and awe in the reader, not just for the tiger, but for nature and God as well."

"You sound like my high school English teacher," replied Hyle. Newman accepted the comparison with a smile.

"A lot of great artists came out of that period," he continued. "We heard some of them tonight. Composers like Beethoven and Schubert, poets and writers like Coleridge, who wrote *Kubla Khan*, Wordsworth, Byron, Shelley and Keats are all considered part of the Romantic Movement. You can even see the theme carried into the music of Wagner and the transcendentalism of Emerson and Thoreau in the early half of the nineteenth century."

"This is all very interesting," Hyle said, "but what does it have to do with Hegel?"

"You asked if it was a revolutionary movement," Newman replied. "In a way the whole aesthetic movement was a revolution. It was a reaction against science and rationalism. Remember Goethe's *Faust*? Faust makes the deal for his soul with Mephistopheles because as a scholar he has already learned everything that science can teach and he's still unfulfilled. There are other parallels too. The idea of a World Spirit or Geist is a Romantic notion, and the principle of thesis, antithesis and synthesis boils down to the Romantic view that life is a struggle. Romanticism is all about freeing the human spirit from restrictions, whether they're external restrictions from governments or internal restrictions from rationalism."

"That sounds like both a foundation and a point of departure for Hegel," Sophia observed. "One of the ideas Hegel drew from Kant and Fichte was his idea of freedom. Not like the American idea of liberty though. This is more akin to moral autonomy— the freedom to choose your own actions. Hegel traced the progress of humanity through history in terms of freedom, from Egypt where the Pharaoh alone was free, to Greece where the citizens were free but most people were not citizens, to his own Prussia where all were free. And Hegel thought that freedom could only be truly understood when it was taken away or constrained, which ties back to that idea of struggle being important for the human experience."

"Why did Hegel pick Prussia at the end of the eighteenth century as an ideal state?" Hyle asked. "That would have been just after the Revolutionary War when America became the first modern democracy."

"That's the point of departure I was talking about. Hegel was very nationalistic. He believed that willing allegiance to a strong nation state was a step beyond just having freedom. And being a Christian state, Hegel saw that in Prussia all were free because all were equal under God."

"If freedom rather than equality is supposed to be the measure of our social evolution, then it seems to me that there's one step beyond Hegel's Prussia still to be made," Hyle ventured. "What about freedom from the restrictions of Christianity? That's just another set of laws that most people had no part in determining. I'd think that stepping outside the restrictions of Judeo-Christian tradition and making our own moral code would be the highest level of freedom possible."

"I can think of at least one philosophy that goes far beyond even that," Sophia said.

"What would that be?" Hyle asked.

"It's a somewhat pessimistic modification of Kant," Sophia explained. "Remember the phenomenal and noumenal realms? Kant believed that we could never know the nature of things in the noumenal world because all our information from the noumenal world gets filtered through our senses and our *a priori* pure intuitions. Since we organize things into our framework of time and space, they're properties of our phenomenal world, but not properties of the noumenal world—the 'real' world we can never know."

"Are you going to tell us how to free ourselves from the phenomenal world now?" Hyle asked sarcastically.

"Actually, yes, more or less. This was a competing philosophy to that of Hegel. Arthur Schopenhauer wrote *The World as Will and Representation* early in the nineteenth century— in 1818 I believe, and the next year when he was appointed to teach at the University of Berlin he scheduled all his classes opposite those of Hegel."

"So it was literally a competing philosophy," Hyle noted.

"Yes, but it didn't compete very well. Nobody came to Schopenhauer's classes since Hegel was already established as the greatest active philosopher in Europe at the time. But Schopenhauer got his recognition in the end, a few decades later."

"You mentioned space and time being properties of the phenomenal world," Hyle noted. "What is the significance of that?"

"Schopenhauer reasoned that in order for there to exist two separate things, they must be separate in either time or in space. If they occupy exactly the same space at exactly the same time, then they really are one."

"So if time and space don't exist in the noumenal world, the noumenal world must be one," Newman concluded. "An undivided whole."

"Exactly," Sophia confirmed. "Kant had believed that objects we sense in the phenomenal world correlated to objects—'things as such'—in the noumenal world, but Schopenhauer came to a different conclusion. Schopenhauer envisioned it as a sort of blind impulse—an energy or force—but not a force like you find in physics. In fact, he specifically avoided the term force and chose 'will' instead."

"As in '*The World as Will and Representation*,'" Hyle realized aloud.

"Yes. Now causality is another intuition that's a property of Kant's phenomenal world. Schopenhauer reached a similar conclusion about causality. Since it exists in the phenomenal world, we can't say that things in the noumenal world cause sensations in the phenomenal world. Therefore, Schopenhauer concluded that they must be the same thing experienced two different ways. It's a bit like Parmenides. Or Spinoza. Remember that Spinoza concluded that Descartes' thinking substance and extended substance must be two different aspects of the same unity? According to Schopenhauer, we as human beings are just manifestations of will. Everything that exists is a manifestation of will— we just perceive it all as the material world."

"I understood everything you just said, but I still have no idea what you're talking about," Hyle said.

"Here's an example. You know yourself in two different ways. In the first way you're a physical body with the same general properties as a chair or an apple or a rock."

"Hey, what are you implying?" Hyle objected.

Sophia chuckled. "I wasn't implying anything about your intelligence. I mean weight, length, color. In that way you exist as a physical object. But what makes us different from those things is will. The other thing that makes you you is what you can control through your will. What makes your hand move, for example, is your decision to make it move. Your body is the boundary of what your will directly controls. You can experience yourself both as will and as representation."

"So our bodies are the phenomenal representation of our will?" asked Newman.

"Exactly right," Sophia replied. "Now, before Hyle asks what all this has to do with freedom, let me explain that Schopenhauer had a dim view of life, although he had a sense of humor about it. He was a bit of an old curmudgeon. He once described life as a comedy that has all the elements of a tragedy. We suffer through our trials in life, but in the end we're no worse off than anyone else, so we're not even afforded the dignity of a tragic hero. The problem is that we're made up of will, so we desire things. We want a bigger house, better job, or maybe it's respect, or avoiding pain. Whatever it is that we want, we're constantly wanting, constantly planning, trying to manipulate things and people to get it. And because our plans frequently fail, life is generally unhappy—at least according to Schopenhauer."

Newman interrupted and rattled off four sentences as if they were a familiar list of principles. "Life is suffering. The source of suffering is desire. Release from suffering comes from eliminating desire. Desire can only be eliminated by a path of right-thinking." Then he added, "So the ultimate freedom, according to Schopenhauer is to free ourselves from desire."

If Newman could have seen Sophia's face more clearly in the dim moonlight he would have seen an expression near to amazement. "Yes. That's right. Exactly," she said in a half-whisper. "Have you read Schopenhauer?"

"No. Those are the Four Noble Truths of Buddhism. Did Schopenhauer study Buddhism?"

"He did, but it's thought that he had developed most of his philosophy already. That's what he claimed anyway. Translations of Buddhist and Hindu texts started becoming available not long after Schopenhauer's philosophy was published and probably helped it become more popular. But even if he did hear about some Buddhist principles, Schopenhauer's philosophy is very well grounded in Plato and Kant."

"It's interesting that two entirely different cultures followed completely different paths and still arrived at the same conclusions," Newman noted.

"Yes it is," Sophia agreed. "Schopenhauer seems to be the link between eastern and western philosophy. What's more, he also provides a link back to the Romantic Movement we were just discussing."

Sophia paused, and took the silence as a tacit expression of interest.

"Schopenhauer believed that only the saints of various traditions are able to deny desire, but the rest of us can get a temporary reprieve through aesthetics. Art, poetry, music are things that we appreciate for their beauty alone. We don't want to possess them or manipulate them—just appreciate them for what they are. And in so doing we leave our desires behind, at least for a little while, and get a taste of the peace that would be possible if we could rid ourselves of desire permanently."

"I bet Schopenhauer was very popular with artists," Newman said.

"He was. Especially musicians. He recognized that literature and painting are representational, reflecting things in the phenomenal world. But music doesn't correlate to anything in the phenomenal world, so Schopenhauer thought this was the highest form of art. He is supposed to have inspired many artists. In fact, Wagner—" Sophia broke off. A sudden chill rippled down her back.

"What's that?" she asked in a hushed voice. They all listened.

"I don't hear anything," Hyle whispered after a few seconds. But almost as soon as he finished speaking he did hear something. It was a sensation more than a sound at first. A low rhythmic throbbing reverberated in his chest. Gradually the pulsing grew more intense and rose in pitch until it was just barely enough to detect audibly.

The three companions turned in the direction of the sound and searched the darkness. Then Sophia saw them. One by one they slipped into a patch of clouds backlit by the moon. One, two, three dark shapes flying in formation, approaching rapidly.

"Helicopters!" Hyle hissed. "They're helicopters! Come on, let's move!"

CHAPTER FIFTY-SIX

BLACK HELICOPTERS

Moving unconsciously back into the edge of the forest as they spoke, Sophia, Hyle and Newman held a short but furious debate as the three aircraft advanced and began their descent. Hyle wanted to make a beeline for the truck and leave as quickly as possible. Newman made the mistake of challenging the assumption that the helicopters were necessarily a threat. He was not able to discern much of what Hyle and Sophia said in response because they were yelling over each other, but their vehemence made it clear that they were quite comfortable with the assumption. Sophia wanted to warn someone, but Hyle pointed out that they were short on time.

"We already went through this in Albany, remember?" he shouted, grabbing her by the arm. He started pulling to get her to move, realizing at the same time that he was not sure what direction to go.

"Francis!" she yelled back. "We have to warn Francis!" Before Hyle could object, she added, "It's on the way. This way," and she began moving, now leading Hyle as he held onto her arm.

It was a stroke of good fortune that Sophia had chosen to turn the direction she had when they left the forest. Turning the other way would have cut them off from the library and the road that circled below campus toward their truck. Cutting straight across the field would have left them in the open, silhouetted against the snowy ground. They hurried back toward the dining hall, clinging to the edge of the forest as the helicopters closed obliquely and then passed by them not more than two hundred yards away. As they raced, slipping and sliding down the access road toward the library, the choppers began their vertical descent into the middle of the quad.

The glass of the library door oscillated dangerously under Sophia's pummeling fists before it finally opened to reveal Francis, standing between the curtains of the improvised entry way, holding a pistol.

"Three helicopters—just landed in the quad!" she said, gasping to catch her breath.

He waved them into the library. "You can hide on the lower floor. There's a service room—"

"No, we're leaving," Hyle cut in. "We just came to warn you. There's still time if you want—"

"We're not going anywhere," Francis declared in an authoritative voice. "Right boys?"

"From behind the barrier there came a mixture of yelled and murmured assent.

"Good luck to you Sophia—to all of you. I hope you find what you're looking for at the end of your journey."

"Thank you for everything," Sophia choked out, leaning in to hug him goodbye. "Be careful."

Francis held her for a moment. "Don't worry about me. We all have to die some time, so we might as well make it count for something." Then, raising his voice he yelled back to the curtains, "Today is a good day to die!"

This was met with louder cheers and chanting from inside.

Francis clapped Hyle firmly on the shoulder, embraced Sophia once more quickly and closed the door. The chanting faded, but the trio of travelers could still hear it as they started to make their way further down the hill to the road. Sophia had to cling tightly to Newman's arm. Her eyes were too watery to see the path.

The trio followed the road past the library, and as the way began to gently curve and rise, lights flashed among the tree branches ahead of them, growing brighter as headlights approached along a crossroad. With no place to hide and little time, all they could do was take a few steps off of the road before the headlights came into view. They stood frozen in place, three dark shapes against a background of white snow, each holding their breath, until the lights continued uphill, passing the end of their road. Fortunately the lights continued past Merrill House, where they had left their truck, and farther up the hill toward the main campus.

Upon reaching the intersection, they turned in the same direction and jogged uphill along the tire tracks, hoping to cover the short distance to their truck before another vehicle appeared. Gunshots sounded from somewhere on the other side of campus, near the dining hall, just before they reached the truck. Seconds later, a gun battle erupted much closer, near the spot where they had first talked to Dean Essex. A minute later they were sliding across the cold vinyl of the familiar bench seat. There was another exchange of gunfire. Several short bursts of automatic weapons fire were followed by an unsettling silence. Just as Hyle reached for the ignition, the front windshield was bathed in light.

"Oh crap! Get down, don't move!" he hissed, sliding down in the seat.

The windshield was covered with a thin layer of snow, blocking the source of the light from view. Newman murmured a prayer that the snow would also conceal them from whatever was approaching. They all watched, not daring to breathe, as the light grew brighter. Shadows wavered across the snow as the light source bounced gently up and down. Hyle kept hold of the wires, ready to spark the ignition if anyone approached. The light continued to draw closer, shifting, seeming for a moment to be fading only to shift again and appear brighter still, and then finally veered past them, following the road uphill. A large truck, briefly visible through the side window, blurred by them and screeched to a halt behind the other set of headlights.

"Go! Go!" Sophia urged, and Hyle touched the wires together, stepping on the gas even before the wipers had a chance to clear away the snow. He remembered to leave the lights off, but in his excitement he stepped too heavily on the accelerator. The engine roared to life. As the pickup lurched across the lawn that separated the parking lot from the road, Newman kept a watch out the back window.

The first tire slipped over the edge of the curb, tilting the cab, and the corner of the plow struck asphalt, leaving a showering trail of orange sparks in its wake. Squinting through the frost smeared window, and trying to distinguish the unplowed road from the surrounding white terrain, Hyle risked a quick glance into the rearview mirror. There was no sign of pursuit, but his relief was short-lived.

"Hyle, look out!" Sophia warned.

Ahead, another set of headlights bore down on them. The wipers cranked frenetically across the windshield, scraping a maddeningly small area of frost away with each pass and it was too difficult to make out the road. Hyle flipped on the headlights, hoping to see some escape route or at least surprise the oncoming vehicle.

"There," Sophia said, gesturing. "Left!"

The road forked right and left. Hyle saw it. He cut the wheel and pumped the brakes, but the truck continued to slide forward. Tires gripped the pavement and the pickup lurched sideways, barely in time to keep from going off the road and just seconds before the oncoming headlights could reach them from the other fork. Three hearts froze as that vehicle—a long, black sport utility vehicle—slowed to take the turn behind them. The advantage of momentum helped them widen the gap as the SUV nearly doubled back around the tight corner, and Hyle pushed their speed as fast as he dared to go. It was a straight shot now to the road out of town, but Sophia's mind was racing, trying to recall the layout of the campus roads in case their route was cut off. Just as they passed the library, her fears were realized as another source of light appeared in the road ahead.

"There should be another road to the left," she said, trying to quickly estimate speeds and distances. She was not sure that they would beat this new vehicle to the turnoff. Newman let out a distraught sigh of disbelief when the light appeared ahead of them, but when he spoke his voice held a different kind of disbelief.

"It looks like a motorcycle!"

That revelation removed any indecision from Hyle. There was an SUV behind them and a motorcycle in front of them with a plow blade to meet it. He kept his foot on the accelerator.

"There! Turn!" Sophia directed, pointing ahead to the left.

Until the second they got to the intersection it was too close to call. Hyle pumped the brakes and cut the wheel just before the side road, sending the truck into a controlled skid. The motorcycle had already shifted to the far side of the road to avoid them, passing behind them just as the tires gripped and they started to accelerate again into the turn.

"Crazy bugger," Newman muttered as he watched the motorcycle fly by them in the narrow lane between the edge of the road and the corner of their rear bumper. The large rider leaned against the backrest of the bike as if he were out for a leisure ride on a summer day. The only one of the three who had ever ridden a motorcycle, Newman alone could appreciate how truly unbelievable this was. He had once toured across the country with a group of his friends and considered himself a fairly skilled biker, but he was still cautious about riding in the rain and knew it was insane to even consider taking a bike out in the snow. It was incredible to him that this guy was not long dead. What happened next did nothing to change his opinion.

Through the rear window he watched as the motorcycle slowed and spun out in front of the sport utility vehicle. Somehow the guy managed to keep his bike upright as the back end slid out in a wide fishtail, bringing him to a stop sideways across both lanes. Amazingly the SUV slowed and came to a stop in front of him. A single shot was fired as the back end of the motorcycle swung out again, sending a rooster tail of snow up behind it, elegantly illuminated by the headlights of the SUV. The motorcycle sped off the way it had come and the sport utility accelerated after it. Newman twisted backwards to make sure the pursuit carried them past the turnoff.

"We lost them," he said, breathing for what seemed like the first time in several minutes.

Sophia guided them south onto Broad Street, which divided the campus from the town, and soon Hamilton disappeared from sight in the rearview mirror.

They drove for a long time in silence, the headlights off again. No one asked or cared where they were headed. Flakes of snow continued to fall in large lazy clumps, but with the engine warm the dashboard heater melted them as soon as they hit the windshield. The town quickly gave way to sparse neighborhoods and then to farms dotted along rolling hills. They had just crested a large hill when Newman broke the silence.

"Wait a minute! Go back, I thought I saw something."

Hyle kept driving as he processed Newman's statement. "What did you see?"

"Just turn around!" snapped Newman.

Reluctantly, Hyle stopped the truck and performed a three point turn. As they approached the top of the hill, Newman instructed him to slow down, and searched the trees on the side of the road. They came to a spot where the hill sloped away sharply, creating a gap in the tree line.

"There!" Newman pointed, but Sophia had already seen it.

"Oh my God," she whispered.

Far off in the distance, a thick column of smoke swirled like ink against a luminous gray sky. Below the smoke, an orange glow covered the top of the hill where the college had been.

PART IV

Shadows of Doubt
The Persistent Illusion

CHAPTER FIFTY-SEVEN

LOOKING BACK

The overwhelming sensation of whiteness met Sophia's eyes when she woke, cold, stiff and disoriented. Nearby, to one side, a loud sound jarred her to full consciousness. She was already sitting when she woke and raised her head from Newman's shoulder to locate the sound. To the left sat Hyle, his head toppled back between the headrest and the driver's side door, snoring furiously with his mouth agape. The cab of the truck was shrouded in snow and bathed in vanilla light.

Trying to retrace the path that led her to the present, Sophia's mind jumped through memories. The escape. The helicopters. The warning not to stay too long. The flames on the hill. She pushed back the sudden urge to cry. There had been enough tears the night before. She told herself that it was now a time for strength, that there was nothing to be gained by grief, but secretly she was simply afraid of sliding into despair. Stubbornly she refused to think of Francis, or Helena or James, or the scores of familiar faces that swarmed around her mind. Reflexively she fanned her hand in front of her face as if dispersing a cloud of gnats, willing her eyes to reverse their flow and become dry again.

Somehow they had escaped. There had been no further pursuit. At first they had driven fast, too fast, the pickup fishtailing wildly several times when the rear wheels lost traction. But when it became clear that they were not being followed, Hyle had turned the headlights off. With the sparse light illuminating a monochromatic world, progress thereafter had been painfully slow. She was not sure how long she had been asleep, but Sophia calculated that they could not have gone more than five or ten miles before daybreak.

Beside her Newman stirred. He woke cold, stiff and hungry. Looking over at Sophia, his eyes quickly lost their haze and he put a comforting arm around her shoulder.

"Are you okay?" he whispered.

Sophia had a vague memory of falling asleep in a similar position. She nodded her head, once tentatively, then again more certainly, more to convince herself than Newman. Together they assessed their situation, speculating about the time of day, the amount of snowfall, how and where to find food, and any other reasonable topic that specifically avoided discussion of the attack. The sticky snow had clung to all the windows, obscuring the view even through the vertical window behind the cab. As they talked, Newman rolled down his window, letting the sheet of snow slough off against the door. The world outside was miraculously white. Even the sky seemed to be a lighter shade of gray. Open ground sloped gently upward away from the truck and the stubble of a fallow field poked up through the plain of white giving some indication of its depth. Not more than an inch Newman concluded, explaining to Sophia that they had pulled onto the edge of the field behind an old roadside farm stand when the sky had begun to lighten.

Eventually their whispered conversation woke Hyle and a third set of opinions was added to the mix. It was agreed unanimously that food was their first priority. This was driven less by Hyle's careful review of the basic requirements for survival than it was by Newman's stomach. A lengthy debate about whether or not to drive during daylight hours ended with the compromise decision to set off at twilight, which appeared to be only a few hours away.

"And then what?" Sophia asked. "Assuming we find some food, then what?"

"We should go back and check for survivors," Newman said, looking delicately at her.

There was never really any debate. They talked over the danger, the best way to approach undetected and what they might find, but they each realized it was the right thing to do. In the end they agreed to look for food briefly until it became fully dark, then head back to Colgate. When this line of discussion had run its course and gaps of silence overpowered the conversation, Sophia returned to her original concern.

"If we don't find anyone there," she said, "or even if we do," she added slowly, trying to pull her thoughts together. Not all those who wander are lost. She considered the words. They seemed so profound—when applied to someone else. She felt herself sliding. "What are we doing? I mean not tomorrow, or next week. What are we doing with our lives? What's our goal? What's our purpose?"

Hyle's face tightened. He had no wish to be hard on Sophia, but he could see where the discussion was heading.

"You know my goal. I want to get to the bottom of whatever is going on. After that? It depends on what we find."

Without taking his eyes from the dashboard Newman replied. "Whether we find anyone back there or not, I'd like to rebuild, either there or some other place like it. There have to be little communities like that all over the country. I'd like to find one, settle down and start rebuilding."

"I can't settle down until I know what's going on," Hyle declared.

As if he had not heard, Newman went on developing his line of thought. "I don't mean to say that everything that happened wasn't tragic," he continued carefully, "but it does bring us an opportunity. We have a chance to start civilization over again the way it should be. The way it should have been. Before this war everyone was worried about car payments and promotions and putting braces on their kids' teeth. Now, for the first time in my life I see people being more concerned about each other, and I believe that as horrible as everything was, maybe this really was our Great Flood. Maybe everything that happened, happened for a reason."

"It didn't happen, it's *happening*," Hyle interrupted. "And maybe you believe that God has spared you, but I don't think I have a reservation on the Ark. To stretch your analogy a little further, if this is our Great Flood, then the death squads and maybe the Mumbai Plague are our rising flood waters and I intend to keep swimming for land until I find some or get sucked under. Anywhere we try to settle now will become a target until this truly is all over. Our best chance for survival is to find a place that'll sustain the three of us and just hole up there until this is all over."

Newman shook his head, but Hyle continued, "No, I'm not suggesting we do that. I'm not sure we could even find such a place. A lot of people are probably holed up in their houses already, and who knows how long we'd be able to compete with them to scavenge for food or even how long we'd need to? That's why I want to keep moving and looking for answers."

"What other answers do you need?" asked Newman. "I thought you already had everything figured out. What could you hope to gain by spending another week or two in a library?"

The question seemed to take Hyle by surprise and for a moment he did not respond. Newman watched patiently, giving him time to consider it carefully.

"I do think I know what's going on, generally at least," Hyle replied. "I think I know who, and at least part of how, but what I don't know is why. Or when it'll all end."

"You're not going to figure that out by reading old newspapers," Newman pointed out. "Even if you did, what would you do with that information?"

"It would depend on what I learned. You can never tell what you're going to do with information until you have it," Hyle replied. "And as to where to get it, you're right. It won't come from a library. There's only one place to get the information we need now."

His eyes darted back and forth between Newman and Sophia.

"Arizona."

CHAPTER FIFTY-EIGHT

SHACKLES

Refracting through the dust layer, the sun transformed the horizon to a blood red strip that faded into shades of burgundy and purple to the north and south. The world was suffused with an orange glow that was at the same time beautiful and disturbingly alien. Under a leaden sky shadows crept unevenly across the fallow field, cast by the thin line of trees that marked its edge. In such a light it was difficult to make out subtleties of expression, nonetheless Hyle tried to gauge the reaction to his suggestion.

Sophia was uncharacteristically impassive. This disappointed Hyle. He had hoped that she would indicate some support for his idea, or failing that he had at least expected her to show some interest, but she was still too sleepy to focus on such a serious issue. Newman did not say anything immediately, but his stomach emitted a hungry growl that seemed to percolate through him and end up expressed on his face.

"I think you need to let it go, Hyle," he said at length. "Try to think about something positive for a change. Ever since I first got to know you back in Asher it seems like you've had a chip on your shoulder and I've been trying to figure out why. I don't know if I did something to offend you, or maybe the Prophet or Delacroix rubbed you the wrong way. I know you don't like their views on technology, but there's more to it than that. Maybe you have something against religion in general. In any case, it's clear to me that you're driven by more than just some academic quest for answers. It seems more like a personal vendetta to me."

"Wow, I've been psychoanalyzed," Hyle joked, attempting to brush the accusations aside, but to no effect. Like a venomous serpent, coiled and swaying in the path before him, they held their ground. His initial impulse was defensive. Reflexively he cataloged the main points of the case against him and began outlining counterarguments and supporting evidence to address each one.

"That's a lot to respond to," Hyle said. He stared out the window and ran his fingers absently through the blond stubble on his chin. "To begin with, it has nothing to do with you. Even though I disagree with you on just about everything, there's no reason for me to hold a grudge."

Newman seemed satisfied with this answer, willing to take it at face value, but Sophia heard more than just the words. Hyle was sincere, and yet, when he said that he did not hold a grudge, something lurked in the shadows behind those words hidden even to him.

"I suppose maybe you're right. Delacroix definitely rubbed me the wrong way, and Zendik too from everything I read about him." Hyle fell silent. It was not much of a confession, but even this small admission about Delacroix and Zendik caused him to question his defensive position. He hesitated, subconsciously stuck between two paths. The scientist inside him awakened and he resolved to turn the lens of his microscope back upon himself.

"It's not just that they don't like technology. Everyone is entitled to their own opinion.

What bothers me about Delacroix and Zendik is that they mislead people. They ignore the benefits and sensationalize the bad aspects of technology to turn people against science."

"People always present one-sided views in support of their cause," Newman pointed out.

"No, that's not my point," Hyle replied. His voice had gained an edge, but it was passion rather than anger. He was beginning to see the conversation as a tool. Something in the original accusation had struck a deep nerve and now Hyle saw an opportunity to explore some of his most fundamental beliefs—beliefs that he had always held and yet never consciously expressed before. A complex and sweeping idea began to coalesce amidst his scattered thoughts.

"They're opposed to technology because they think it encourages people to put their faith in human ability and draws them away from God. That's exactly why I don't like religion. It teaches people to be dependent and subservient."

"Religion does tend to emphasize humility," Newman agreed, "but a lot of great people have been very religious, including many scientists."

"Maybe they were great in spite of religion," Hyle replied, waving his hand to dismiss the argument. "Christian values certainly don't encourage people to excel. Self-confidence is perilously close to pride, which is a sin. Instead you're supposed to be humble and obedient and wait for God to solve all your problems for you."

"I think that's a little extreme," said Newman.

"People often present one-sided arguments," Hyle replied with just a hint of a smile.

"Why do you think Christianity teaches those kinds of values?" asked Sophia, suddenly engaged in the discussion.

"Slavery," Hyle said simply. He had already been considering exactly this question. "Historically Christianity starts with the slaves in Egypt and it's easy to see why it's the perfect religion for slaves. First of all, it offers comfort for a downtrodden people. The whole message of the Judeo-Christian faith is, 'Don't worry that your life is crap, there's something better waiting for you after you die.' Originally the idea of heaven was meant to console people who had nothing in this world but suffering. Nowadays it encourages people to accept their lot in life, even though we have the freedom to change things for ourselves."

"God helps those who help themselves," Newman offered as a reminder. "Christianity doesn't teach you to neglect your life—just to keep it in perspective."

"Maybe it depends on who's doing the teaching," Hyle allowed, "but look at what the Bible teaches as virtues—humility, sacrifice, unquestioning obedience. Those are the characteristics of slaves. Christianity takes all the attributes that are forced on slaves and turns them into virtues. That way people can feel good about their oppression. Even if they can't have enough food to eat or a warm shelter, at least they can feel virtuous about their suffering."

"And if you look at how God is typically described," Sophia interjected, "He has all the characteristics that we'd wish for him to have. He's omniscient, omnipotent, benevolent and loving and active in the world. That's what led Feuerbach to conclude that God was really just a projection of mankind's inner nature."

"Man created God in his own image," Hyle interjected.

"Yes, and Marx said that religion was the 'opium of the people,'" Newman added. "It's true that religions generally do offer people comfort and something to look forward to beyond this world. It's also true that Christianity teaches people not to be too proud, but the greater message is to treat others with love and respect. It's not that you should roll over and accept anything that happens to you."

"That may not be the intended message, but it's the result," Hyle argued. "This is what really bothers me about all organized religion. It's a source of comfort for people who can't find any meaning or value in life otherwise. People who have already failed to make it in life on their own terms, or who never dared to try, are perfectly happy to accept humility and obedience as virtues. They're happy to label pride and independence as sins because those are traits they don't have. Religion is the systematic embrace of mediocrity. And Christianity is a downright celebration of mediocrity. It's all about not asking for too much, not sticking out from the crowd, not making waves, accepting what life hands you—even if it's crap—and being thankful for it. I think it's an insult to humanity."

"That's a common mistake, Hyle," Newman replied. His face acquired the expression of a parent explaining to a child the necessity of bedtime. "People often mistake love for weakness. They think businessmen who are willing to lie and cheat and step all over other people for their own gain are strong and people who are honest and humble and put others ahead of themselves are weak. But I think it takes more inner strength to sacrifice what you want for the good of someone else."

"Of course you do—because you have bought this whole Christian ethic hook, line and sinker. But you don't have to be ruthless to be independent. You just have to be willing to think for yourself. My problem with this whole set of slave ethics is that it brainwashes people to be subservient followers. Look at the imagery 'the Lord is our shepherd.' Congregations are flocks. Jesus is even called the Lamb of God. Is that what we're supposed to aspire to? Being sheep? The problem with sheep is that a large flock can be completely controlled by one well-trained sheepdog."

Hyle was nowhere near finished, but he stopped suddenly. Sophia was smiling at him, but not in a way that indicated agreement. She looked like she was party to some inside joke.

"What?" he asked.

"You sound just like Nietzsche, Hyle," she said. "Or at least a mild version of him."

"A mild version?" Newman exclaimed.

"Yes. Believe it or not Nietzsche was even more cynical. But he made essentially the same case about Christian morality in *Beyond Good and Evil*. In fact he even called it slave morality, or sometimes herd morality."

"Herd morality," Hyle repeated, testing out the words. "I like it."

"Feuerbach also thought that faith in God blinded people to their own abilities," Sophia continued, "but Nietzsche took it to the next level. He saw the stifling effect that Christian morality has on human achievement but he thought it was motivated—at least subconsciously—by jealousy. According to Nietzsche, people in the lower classes use slave morality to fetter the wealthy and powerful. Forcing everyone to live by laws and values based on equality, humility and sacrifice is how the weak level the playing field. Since the weak can't excel themselves, out of jealousy, they make sure that no one else can either."

As Sophia spoke Hyle nodded vigorously, adding, "I once heard a theory that the reason the ancient Greeks accomplished so much in all aspects of civilization was that they didn't have any organized religion. They worshipped the various different gods, but there was no uniform set of religious strictures or expectations for them to follow, so they were free to pursue their own ambitions."

"There may be some truth to that," Sophia agreed, "but Nietzsche also attributed the success of the ancient Greeks to the right combination of intellect and passion, represented by Apollo and Dionysus. Dionysus represented passion, love, mysticism and spirituality. The followers of Dionysus allowed themselves to be possessed by the god for mystical experience. Of course Apollo was the god of light, representing the arts and knowledge in sciences and intellectual pursuits, characterized by a measure of self-control. According to Nietzsche, the height of Greek culture was when the influence of Apollo was on the rise and mixed with the Dionysian forces. You can imagine how a culture driven by both passion and intellect could achieve so much in so many areas. But ultimately the influence of Apollo became dominant. Passion was constrained with credos like 'nothing to excess'—ideas which have the same dampening effect as slave morality—and Greek culture suffered as a consequence."

"So Christianity isn't the only thing Nietzsche had a problem with?" Newman asked.

"Oh no. He had a problem with anything that got in the way of people realizing their potential. That's central to his philosophy," Sophia explained. "You must at least have heard of his concept of the 'will to power' or the *übermensch*—the superman?"

"Superman?" Hyle repeated. He shrugged apologetically and shook his head. "Not unless you mean the comic book character."

"They sound familiar," Newman replied.

"The will in will to power comes from Schopenhauer," Sophia explained. "Supposedly it was reading Schopenhauer that turned Nietzsche into a philosopher. Before that he had been following in the footsteps of his father, who was a Lutheran pastor."

"You're kidding," Newman interjected.

"No, not at all. But Nietzsche identified with Schopenhauer, especially his description of nature as being full of conflict and devoid of any sort of teleological evolution, as opposed to philosophers like Schelling and Hegel. Nietzsche liked the idea of the will as a driving force, but disagreed with Schopenhauer's view that will derived from some kind of mystical absolute reality. Instead Nietzsche believed that what you see is what you get. There's no supernatural or metaphysical world beyond the one we live in and experience."

"So Nietzsche took everything pessimistic in Schopenhauer and threw away the only optimistic parts?" Newman commented.

"Essentially, yes," Sophia acknowledged. "Nietzsche is often misunderstood as being one of the most skeptical and pessimistic philosophers ever. Some of the most powerful elements of his philosophy are pretty dark, but Nietzsche himself believed that we needed to confront this darkness in order to come out the other side."

"Come out the other side to what?" asked Newman.

"Self-realization."

"I don't get it."

"That's because you don't have the whole story yet," Sophia explained. "Nietzsche saw a world full of people who had been swindled out of their lives by a barrage of false ideals. Religion, metaphysics, the "golden mean" of moderation and all sorts of other similar ideas convince us to go quietly through this life trying to please our invisible masters while we look for our happiness in some transcendent world. The slave morality of religion is the major culprit, and the worst part is—not only does the slave morality teach us to lead polite, quiet, drab, meaningless lives—but we don't even really believe the original premise anymore. People don't really believe in God."

"That's just not true though," Newman responded. "The vast majority of people believe in God."

"In the same sort of bland, non-committal way they believe that the purpose of life is to have a nice house in the suburbs, serve on the PTA and write a few checks to their favorite charities. Just because they go to church one hour a week and check 'yes' on a survey that asks if they believe in God doesn't mean that religion gives their life meaning. Most people just go through the motions because they don't know any other way to live."

Newman shook his head, and was going to object, but Hyle spoke first.

"If people really believed that their reward for all eternity is based on their deeds in this life, why did we have so many lawyers and corporate managers and so few Mother Teresas? And what happens nowadays when somebody shows up claiming to be the second coming of Jesus? We lock them up in an insane asylum. Nobody takes it seriously."

"That's exactly what Nietzsche means when he says, 'God is dead,'" Sophia interjected.

"Nietzsche is quickly shaping up to be my favorite philosopher," Hyle commented.

"I suspect you'd like Auguste Comte too on this count," Sophia told him. "Comte is the one who said that culture—and actually individuals as well—go through three stages in trying to explain the world. The first is an animistic or religious stage. The second is a metaphysical stage. The third is science."

"I'd agree with that," Hyle said.

"I was sure you would," Sophia replied, "and Nietzsche may have been influenced by Comte initially. Nietzsche respected science for removing the blinders of religion. He also liked that it was empirical and based on individual observation, but ultimately he came to believe that science was looking for an absolute truth that wasn't so different from metaphysics or religion."

"If he didn't believe in science, philosophy or religion, what did he believe in—nothing?" Newman asked.

"Nothing absolute," Sophia corrected. "He introduced the concept that has become known as perspectivism. He said, 'There are no facts, only interpretations.' Basically he believed that there are many ways to view any situation, and no one view can be labeled true over others. For example, you can judge a piece of music by how it makes you feel, or you can describe it mathematically as a sequence of tones of varying duration. Both are valid."

"Doesn't that mean that he'd have to consider Christianity a valid perspective?" Newman argued.

Sophia considered this. "I suppose it's one perspective, but what Nietzsche would definitely not consider valid is the exclusive claim on truth that Christianity makes. There's no room for that in Nietzsche's world. There's no God's eye view of some absolute truth, whether from scripture or science. No transcendent heaven or Platonic ideal realm. There are no rules. It's just us and our interpretations. What you see is what you get."

"That's a depressing idea," Newman commented.

"It can be," Sophia agreed. "And it's fertile ground for oppression. Anyone who claims to know some absolute truth will find themselves with many willing followers. The world as Nietzsche sees it is depressing enough that most people are happy to keep deluding themselves with the comfort of religion or metaphysics rather than face up to it. Who wants to confront the idea that they've been living according to a set of oppressive values and going through the motions of an empty life in order to claim some eternal reward that doesn't exist?"

"That sounds pretty pessimistic to me," Newman said.

"Nietzsche might have been the ultimate pessimist if he had not introduced his concepts of the superman and the will to power in his classic work *Thus Spoke Zarathustra*. Stepping out of the comfort of unquestioned beliefs and absolute truths is frightening—too frightening for the vast majority of people—but those who are able to do it become liberated. It's the will to power that compels these rare people to follow a separate path. Will to power drives us to pursue our passions without constraint. It's the driving force that's shackled by the slave morality. It's the passion to compete and excel. Nietzsche's superman is someone who dares to throw off all the conventions and restrictions of the world and follow his will to power."

"So instead of trying to live together harmoniously Nietzsche would rather have a world full of ruthless business tycoons and world conquerors?" Newman objected.

"Will to power and superman are unfortunate translations that way," Sophia said. "Will to power has less to do with power than with self esteem or self fulfillment. Maybe personal empowerment would be a better term. 'Dare to become who you are,' Nietzsche said. That could mean a great artist or world explorer—anyone who is devoted to pursuing their greatness, following whatever gifts they may have. It'll be different for everyone. Goethe was the closest candidate for a superman that Nietzsche ever mentioned. And Socrates, as much as Nietzsche disliked his philosophy, would have to be considered a superman because in his passionate pursuit of philosophy, Socrates was willing to disregard the conventions of society and follow his principles, even to the point of death by his own hand. But a superman could just as easily be a business tycoon or conqueror. Nietzsche wouldn't have cared about any loss of harmony they might cause. In fact, he believed that competition and strife aren't only a natural part of life, they're what drive those who excel and what move civilization forward. Individuals may lose out in the conflict, but society as a whole gains."

"That sounds a bit like Hegel," Hyle noted, "with his idea of thesis and antithesis conflicting to produce something greater in the end."

"A bit," agreed Sophia. "Except Hegel works on the sweeping scale of nations and eras. Nietzsche's will to power is a much more personal motive force than some universal Geist. I suppose Nietzsche is a bit like Hegel individualized in that regard."

"I still don't see it," Newman said. "It seems to me that without some higher purpose than filling our own selfish desires, life would be too empty to be worthwhile."

"I think Nietzsche would argue that the higher purposes of religion and philosophy have people looking for meaning in all the wrong places. That's why most people don't have very fulfilling lives," Sophia explained.

"Life is what you make it," Hyle said. "That's his point."

"Yes. Life has no meaning but that which we give it," Sophia agreed. "There's an aspect of stoicism in Nietzsche. He might believe that life is inherently empty, but instead of hiding from the fact, he wants us to look into that void and stare it down. He also had a good dose of Dionysus in him. He appreciated aesthetics and believed in living life with passion. We need to make our own meanings, find our own passions, and then live our lives with gusto by following them to the full extent of our being. In fact, his ultimate test is the principle of eternal recurrence. Suppose a demon visited you in the night and offered you the chance to live your life over again, what would you say?"

"I'd say, 'Oh look, it's another demon—there must be a philosopher nearby,'" Hyle quipped.

"Probably inspired by Descartes' demon," Sophia acknowledged, "but really, what would you say?"

Hyle and Newman were both silent as they considered the question.

"What if you had to repeat your life over and over for eternity," Sophia continued, "and it was to be exactly the same every time? Nietzsche believed that if you followed your will to power and lived your life to its fullest potential, you'd jump at that offer. If you can't imagine living your life such that you'd take that offer, you have to ask yourself who is the bigger pessimist, you or Nietzsche. So, what would you say to the demon?"

Neither man answered.

CHAPTER FIFTY-NINE

AMIDST THE RUINS

A plume of smoke still spewed from the ruins of their old dormitory. The trio had encountered the acrid odor even before reaching the edge of campus. Now as they stood below the broken walls, rising like giant shards of shattered glass above them, the smoke was so thick that it tasted like chewing on ash with every intake of breath. Newman mumbled a quiet prayer for any souls that might have been lost. Sophia and Hyle just stood in numb silence.

Skirting around the academic buildings, they made their way to the middle of the quad, alert for any sound or movement. Although Sophia did not admit it to herself, as they approached the wreckage of the dormitory they had slept in just one night earlier, she was also alert for sounds of movement from inside the rubble. The memory of being trapped beneath the debris of her own collapsed home squirmed below the surface of her mind, threatening to become a conscious thought.

A thick mass of storm clouds covered the moon, blocking all but the few bravest rays of moonlight. The absolute black silhouette of the collapsed dormitory building could be seen only against the near-black of the sky. Snow lay in light gray patterns in the open spaces around them, but beyond the dark edges of the quad the earth was hidden by impenetrable shadows. Even if they had been in possession of a flashlight they would not have dared to use it. Off in the distance, a loose brick or stone clattered, followed by the noise of a small avalanche.

They each froze, fearing that someone lay in the darkness waiting for them. It required little imagination to picture a sniper scouring the darkness for a moving target or a guard ready to raise the alarm to summon a squadron of soldiers against them. For some span of time that seemed infinitely too long to measure in seconds, they waited, and when enough time had passed to convince them that they had heard nothing more than loose rubble surrendering to the force of gravity, they waited longer just to be sure.

It was Sophia who first moved tentatively toward the dark circle of earth surrounding the building. Both men fell in beside her. The three inched forward, straining their eyes to keep track of each other and reaching out occasionally to confirm the shapes they thought they saw. As they pressed forward slowly the air grew warmer and the smoke became a physical force, stinging their eyes and blurring what vision they still possessed. When Hyle caught his toe on a fragment of concrete it was only the slow pace that prevented him from pitching forward.

"Watch your step," he whispered.

For the next several minutes they moved cautiously forward, probing ahead with their feet and stepping over patches of debris until it became difficult to find clear spaces in which to stand. When they were forced to find footing on uneven chunks of concrete in order to progress Hyle was tempted to ask what exactly they thought they were doing, but thought better of it and resolved to let things run their course. It was not long after his decision that Sophia found something.

She was a few steps ahead of Hyle, picking her way through the rubble when her shoe got snagged. She bent down to free her shoelaces from the jagged end of a rebar strut when her fingers brushed something that did not feel like concrete. Before her mind could process the information further, she had reflexively reached out to feel around. It took her a moment to realize that her hand was grasping an arm. The sensations hit her like a bomb blast. Unlike the concrete and metal, it yielded slightly to her grip. It was cold, and something sticky had permeated the fabric that covered it. In the process of flinging it away from her, she could feel its movement restricted by a joint still attached to something that lay buried in the debris below her. She stifled a scream and staggered backwards.

Newman and Hyle heard what sounded like a whimper. Hyle, who was closer, was moving to help Sophia when they collided. She threw herself into his arms and buried her head in his shoulder.

"I want to go now," she murmured. "I want to go."

"Sophia! Are you okay?" Newman asked. "What was it? Are you hurt?"

With his arms folded around her, Hyle could feel Sophia struggling first to inhale, then to regulate her breathing. He was immediately torn by two conflicting emotions. The first was something akin to joy, although more complex. In that distant life before the bombs fell, there had been very few girlfriends. He blamed this on his busy life and told himself that romance was not important to him, but knew that in reality it was just because he was not good with women—or people in general. Those rare individuals who demanded nothing in return provided his only friendships, and the few relationships he had enjoyed seemed to have fallen out of the sky. He had done nothing to initiate them. Now, holding Sophia, he felt the stirring of a passion that he realized he had kept suppressed ever since the cabin on the way to Maine so many weeks ago. Added to this was a strange element of pride. The mere act of comforting her made him feel like a Knight of the Round Table.

The other emotion was guilt. Sophia had come to him hysterical with shock and horror and he felt the ultimate cad for not thinking exclusively of her. He chided himself for being selfish, but could do nothing to shut off the flow of positive emotions, which only served to compound his guilt.

"She's fine! Just give her a minute," he snapped, maneuvering Sophia carefully away from the collapsed building, and away from Newman.

"Hey, I was concerned, just like you," Newman said as he scrambled through the debris to catch up with them. Back on solid ground Hyle reluctantly let go of Sophia.

"I know," he replied. "Sorry. We're all a bit tense."

Sophia explained what had happened in terms general enough to allow her to keep blocking the memory as she spoke. "I want to go now," she repeated.

Only a few dozen steps back in the direction of the truck Sophia stopped them.

"Wait. There's one more place I have to see."

Traversing the quad in the opposite direction, they followed a path between one of the academic buildings and the chapel, both of which remained intact. The moon disengaged from the darkest patch of clouds as they walked. This small blessing made the snowy path less treacherous once it began to descend. Sophia found herself struggling to suppress both dread and hope as with each step the blackness of the library emerged farther from the night. From the dark silhouette the building appeared to be whole. Launching herself into a series of controlled skids and stabilizing herself with one hand on the handrail, Sophia accelerated down the path, skiing to the end of the railing.

At the end of the short walk that led to the library the view was clearer. In place of the entryway, which had held the paper-covered glass doors, an explosion had ripped a jagged hole. From the blackness beyond, a thin stream of smoke issued, spilling upward from beneath the eaves like an inverted waterfall cascading into the sky.

No one spoke on the way back to the truck. They maintained the silence until they were several miles away from campus.

"Are we going to stop soon?" Newman asked in a voice barely above a whisper.

"I wasn't planning to," Hyle replied. "I was going to keep on going until we ran out of darkness or gas, whichever comes first. Why?"

"Aren't you planning to go back?"

"No."

"But now that we know there are no soldiers we have to go back. We have to go back in the light and look for survivors," Newman said. He hesitated and then added, "Or at least give those who didn't survive a proper burial."

"We know there were at least three survivors," Hyle answered. "And I'm not planning to do anything more to jeopardize them. We don't know that the soldiers are gone. All we know is that we didn't get ourselves killed tonight—a fact for which I am extremely grateful and plan to do nothing to change."

"We can't just drive away," Newman protested, addressing his appeal as much to Sophia as to Hyle.

"Don't you see? This is the only thing that stands between civilization and complete anarchy. It's people like us making the choice about whether to do our best to help others or just look out for ourselves."

"Sorry, I'm not going to be swayed by a Three Musketeers versus the forces of anarchy speech. If I have a realistic chance to help somebody out, sure I'll do it. But if you're talking about going back in the daylight where we'd be sitting ducks for anybody with a gun, I think you're crazy. Any survivors who were in any shape to move would have cleared out of there already and any who couldn't are beyond our help anyway. We have no hospitals to take them to. And as for burying the dead, what are we going to do? Dig them out of the rubble so we can bury them in the earth?"

"What if it were you back there, Hyle? Wouldn't you want to know that someone would be willing to go back there for you? Wouldn't you want to know that someone would be willing to give you a proper burial?"

"Now? Of course I'd like to think you'd do that for me. Ask me again when I'm dead though and you'll get a different answer."

Out of the corner of his eye Hyle could see Sophia's head swivel to him with a speed that indicated shock at his response. Newman said nothing.

"Tell you what," Hyle said quickly. "Why don't we just find some place close by to pull off the road and get some sleep and we can figure this all out tomorrow?"

They continued only until they came to a small plot of undeveloped woodland, where Hyle drove the truck into a gap between two trees. In order to be ready for a quick escape and to see anything that might approach from the road, he backed the truck in. His last memory before closing his eyes to try to sleep was the vision of pristine tire tracks in the snowy road, ending abruptly and veering off into the woods.

An engine woke Sophia. It was the low throbbing sound of an idling motor and it was very close. The sound roused her from a deep and pleasant sleep. It was the one bright spot in a night filled with vague nightmares and uncomfortable half sleep. She had been dreaming that she was in some other time and place. A warm breeze ruffled her hair playfully. Small plumes of golden dust rolled away from her feet as she walked, sparkling in the sunlight. She travelled along a path of dry packed earth. Patches of scrub brush, spikes of aloe and stunted Joshua trees broke the monotony of the golden landscape. She knew that Newman and Hyle were somewhere nearby even though she did not hear or see them. Nor did she look. The knowledge that they were with her was enough. Confirmation was not important. She was heading somewhere, but the destination was also unimportant. She was enjoying the walk. Birds were singing and a wide blue sky stretched out before her. The sun baked her skin and permeated through her, warming her body and her spirit.

When at first something had intruded from the world outside this scene, that part of her mind which was observing the dream had not wanted it to end. She was curious about her destination, but the walk alone brought her a sense of joy and peace that she had not known for a long time. But something was wrong.

The dream dissolved, replaced in her awareness by an ugly noise. Slowly she identified it for what it was and then, realizing its proximity, ascended several levels of consciousness to sit bolt upright in the cab of the truck.

On the road, no more than a dozen yards away, a rider straddled a stationary motorcycle. The large figure wore a long leather riding jacket, leather pants, gloves, and heavy boots, all of black. His helmet was black as well, with a reddish gold tinted visor that glittered in the pale daylight. Stopped directly in front of them, framed by the two trees that marked the gap they had use to back into the woods, the motorcycle idled, the low rumble of its engine pulsing through the cab of the truck. The rider was looking directly at her.

A chill ran through Sophia. She realized in the back of her mind that this was not only from the situation, but from the temperature as well. The small amount of heat there had been in the truck when they had gone to sleep had long dissipated and her feet were numb with cold. For a long moment her thoughts were frozen too. She stared at the rider and he looked at her. No thoughts came to her mind until he touched his visor with two fingers in a small salute, gunned the engine, and accelerated out of sight.

CHAPTER SIXTY

A HARD LOOK AT TENDER THOUGHTS

Not a single thought stirred in Sophia's mind the entire time the motorcycle was stopped in front of her. As if the movement of the departing biker had broken some spell that held her mesmerized, she suddenly remembered Hyle and Newman. By the time the men were awake the motorcycle was long gone.

"This isn't another appearance of your phantom from Colgate is it?" Hyle asked.

"I know what I saw," insisted Sophia. "I mean, it's true that I was asleep, but—" she stopped, looking for evidence even as she began to second guess herself. The latent heat of the asphalt had melted the snow from the road, so there were no tracks to corroborate her story. The best she could do was to try to convince the men with a detailed description of the rider and motorcycle.

"I thought I heard something when I first woke up," Newman chipped in, a bit too tentatively to be convincing.

"Relax. I was just teasing," Hyle said. He gave them both a broad grin, but despite this assurance, failed to convince Sophia that it was entirely a joke. "We'll have to risk moving, if only a mile or two, just to be on the safe side."

Sophia nodded, grateful that Hyle was at least uncertain enough to want to relocate the truck.

"And where will we go after that?" she asked.

"I'd still like to go back," Newman stated. "I feel like we owe it to those people."

"We paid off our debt in advance with barrels of gas and our assault rifle," Hyle said adding, "both of which I am particularly missing at the moment."

"That's not what I meant. I meant the debt that we owe them as friends. I realize you spent most of your time in the library, but I got to know quite a few people there. It would really mean a lot to me to go back."

Hyle still felt this was a bad idea, but Newman's sincerity stopped him from stating this fact in the first terms that popped into his mind. He was almost persuaded to give serious thought to Newman's argument, and was cursing himself for even considering something so colossally stupid, when Sophia saved him.

"I can't go back there," she said. "Please."

Newman did not say anything, but exhaled deeply and melted back into his seat.

"I'm sorry, Newman," she said. "I understand where you're coming from, but I just can't do it."

"Do you?" he asked. It was not a challenge. He seemed appreciative.

"You're a good soul," she responded. "That's one of the things I like about you."

"And I have no soul," Hyle said.

"That must be why you like Nietzsche," suggested Newman.

"You're very logical though and we need that just as much." Sophia chuckled, grateful for a change of topic. "Funny you should mention Nietzsche, Newman. I was just thinking that you two reminded me of William James. His philosophy was a sort of Americanized version of Nietzsche. In his book *Pragmatism: A New Name for Some Old Ways of Thinking* he divided philosophy into two camps, and the two of you are almost perfect examples of them."

"What were they, religious versus scientific?" Hyle guessed.

"Essentially, yes. Maybe spiritual would be more accurate than religious. He called them the tough-minded and the tender-minded. The tender," Sophia said, looking at Newman, "come from the rationalist tradition. They're romantics who are driven by principles and ideals. They believe in some unifying cosmic order and tend to be religious, or at least spiritual, optimistic, and believers in free will. They also tend to be dogmatic."

Hyle snickered.

"The tough-minded," Sophia continued, turning toward Hyle, "come from the empiricist tradition. They're materialists in their view of the world. They're likely to be irreligious, pluralistic, fatalistic, pessimistic and skeptical."

Newman smiled at Hyle and raised his eyebrows.

"I'm not sure about pessimistic and skeptical," Hyle commented. "It's all relative I guess. I'm sure I appear that way to one of the soft-headed."

"Tender-minded," Sophia corrected.

"What do you mean by pluralistic?" Hyle asked.

"In this case it means someone who believes that there are many different views of truth, like Nietzsche for example," Sophia answered. "Someone who says things like, 'It's all relative.'"

"That's the one part of Nietzsche I didn't buy," Hyle answered. "I believe that there are unifying truths. I just happen to think they'll be revealed by science rather than by metaphysics or scripture."

"Not everybody will fit perfectly into those categories," Sophia acknowledged, "but if you look back through history you'll see that it's pretty easy to put most philosophers in one camp or the other."

"Which one was he?" asked Newman.

"A little of both actually. James classified himself as a pragmatist."

"Is that a separate school of philosophy?"

"Yes. It was started by the work of Charles Sanders Peirce on knowledge and meaning. William James expanded Peirce's epistemology into a full-fledged philosophy and popularized it. But it was probably John Dewey who most famously put pragmatism into action."

"Is that the same Dewey who was the education reformer at the start of the twentieth century?" asked Newman.

"Yes," Sophia confirmed. "Like James—and Nietzsche for that matter—Dewey blended psychology and philosophy, but Dewey was more interested in the social implications of both. He criticized the ivory tower tendency to debate great ideas without ever taking action—something he called the 'spectatorial view of knowledge'— like watching a sporting event instead of going out and playing the game yourself. Peirce, James and Dewey were contemporaries, and each contributed to pragmatism in a different way."

"Doesn't pragmatic just mean practical?" asked Hyle. "How's that a philosophy?"

"It has to do with how we understand truth," Sophia replied. "Peirce was a mathematician and pioneer in the field of modern logic. He was very interested in how we learn, and he came to realize that the way we actually learn couldn't be described by the classical explanations of deduction and induction."

"Sorry, what's the difference again?" Newman interrupted.

"Deduction is the process of deriving new knowledge from a self-evident set of truths. It's the hallmark of rationalist philosophy. Descartes' *cogito ergo sum* is a classic example of deduction. Induction is deriving facts and general principles from individual observations. It's the hallmark of empiricism and science. For example, Newton sees that everything falls to the earth, realizes that the moon and planets can be seen as more or less falling perpetually in a circle, and induces the law of gravity."

Newman nodded, satisfied with the explanation.

"Learning is the attempt to find explanations for new situations and experiences that are outside our knowledge base," Sophia continued. "There's an element of induction because we're trying to explain something we have experienced, so naturally we'll compare it with our past experiences and observations. On the other hand, Peirce realized that this wasn't just a random process. Not all hypotheses are equal. We tend to prescreen our hypotheses against the general principles we believe to be true and this is a form of deduction."

"That sounds like the scientific method," Hyle observed.

"It does," agreed Sophia. "Peirce believed that something like the scientific method is the approach we use for all our learning. But this business of deduction and induction is only good enough to get you to a decent set of hypotheses. You then have to decide which ones are true and which ones are false, and this is the area that led Peirce to lay the foundation of pragmatism. Looking at it from this angle he came to see knowledge as an ongoing process where truth is a functional test. An idea that functions well to describe our experience is true, and what can be called reality is the end point of a sufficient amount of information gathering and reasoning."

"That makes sense. I can see how that idea of truth would be called pragmatism," Hyle said. "You said Peirce also pioneered modern logic. What exactly is it that makes his logic modern?"

"Modern logic is a way of applying mathematical thinking to facts," answered Sophia. "It's a system for building or analyzing complex ideas and statements using simple components like A and B, A or B, if A then B, and such. Peirce analyzed what meanings we assign to terms we use. One of his significant conclusions was that two terms are different only if they lead to some different consequence or conclusion. If they lead to the same result then they are for all practical purposes the same thing."

"You say po-tay-to, I say po-tah-to," Newman said.

"Yes, exactly."

"Seems like common sense to me," Hyle said.

"A lot of great ideas seem like common sense to us after the fact," Sophia pointed out. "But this was a pretty important observation. It's one of the ideas James expanded to address issues of metaphysics, like the questions of free will and the existence of God."

"Those choices both have major implications," Newman observed, struggling to see how pragmatism might be applied.

"Yes they do," agreed Sophia. "But what James did was invert Peirce's principle. Take the case of free will as an example. You can argue that we have free will, or you can say that we live in a deterministic world and that our sense of free will is just an illusion. James made the point the either option is a valid model. We can't choose one over the other on the basis of how well it explains our experience. If you look at the implications of each option to our future however, you'll see some big differences. If you believe in determinism you believe in a world that has been set on a path that can't be changed, which is kind of depressing. If you believe in free will, you believe that your action in the world can make a difference. You believe in the possibility that the future can be made to be better than the past, and you're given a sense of meaning to your life that you can be an active participant in the world."

"I take it James believed in free will," Hyle commented.

"In this case he wasn't so much arguing for free will as he was trying to demonstrate that the basis for choosing what to believe about free will isn't a function of reality. It's a function of utility. Calling an idea true is like paying it a compliment that says it's a useful way to view the world." Sophia thought for a moment before going on. "Yes though, he did believe in free will. He was very much an individualist. He sometimes likened pragmatism to the Protestant reformation because it put the power of philosophy in the hands of the individual. You can see that in his study of psychology as well. It focuses a lot on how our consciousness is personal, active and selective."

"Wait," Hyle interrupted. "Is this the same William James that wrote *Principles of Psychology*? The one with the bear?"

"Bear?" asked Newman.

"Yes," confirmed Sophia.

"He set up the first experimental psychology lab in the country at Harvard before psychology was really a separate field," Hyle said.

"And his younger brother was Henry James, the novelist," added Sophia, directing this fact to Newman.

"Must have been some interesting dinner conversations in that house," Hyle said.

"Bear?" Newman repeated.

"He wrote an article that questioned the prevailing belief about emotions, using an encounter with a bear as an example," Hyle explained. "Most people thought that you saw a bear, then you experienced fear, then you decided to run. James flipped this around and argued that you see the bear, then you have a physical response—fight or flight in this case—then you experience this state as fear." Hyle looked over at Sophia. "Although now that I know James was a philosopher, I'm surprised he didn't use a demon."

"He came to philosophy through psychology," Sophia said, acknowledging Hyle's comment with a thin smile. "That's one of the many similarities between James and Nietzsche. They were both attracted to psychology and philosophy even though they had no formal training in either."

"They don't seem that similar to me," Newman noted.

"They had the same mix of spiritualism and empiricism." explained Sophia. "They were born within a few years of each other, so both were influence by Emerson and the Romantic Movement on the one hand, and by science and especially Darwin on the other hand. Even though they had the same influences and came to the same general conclusions about the nature of truth, they developed very different perspectives from this common ground. Where Nietzsche saw pluralism as a reason to reject all beliefs and invest everything in the individual, James saw it as a reason to tolerate many views and pick from the best among them—a little from column A, a little from column B— whatever works best for you."

"I think I like James better," Newman said.

"That's because you're one of the soft-headed," said Hyle.

"Tender-minded," Sophia corrected.

"I think James was one of the soft-headed too," Hyle said, as if he had not heard Sophia.

"Yes, he did consider himself one of the tender-minded," she confirmed, emphasizing the last two words.

"Ha! I knew it! I bet I can tell you how his review of faith goes too." Hyle waited for a reaction from Sophia. She watched him expectantly. "I bet he said that science and religion are both capable of fully explaining the world, but since the existence of God can't be proven or disproven, you might as well believe in God since it'll make you happier."

"That's actually pretty close," Sophia admitted.

"Just close?" Hyle asked, clearly disappointed.

"Why do you think he chose a life of faith, Hyle?" she prompted.

"For the same reasons everyone else does. It's easier to believe that someone up there is watching out for us, waiting to reward us for all our suffering and make everything work out in the end."

"You're not wrong, but you haven't given James enough credit as a scientist. His philosophy isn't as simple as 'believe whatever makes your life easiest.' When I said 'whatever works for you' it has to work logically and mentally, not just as a convenience. It has to fit with your best understanding of the world. James would certainly not recommend turning a blind eye to facts just to make life easier. He was well aware of the evils and imperfections in the world. His is a God of finite power, leaving us to use our free will to make a positive impact on the world. But he does see science without faith as leading to materialism, determinism, and fatalism whereas faith allows us to believe in something that will survive us. Like free will, it can give life meaning and be empowering. In the absence of any empirical argument pragmatism led him to choose faith."

Newman smiled at this assessment. "I definitely like James better than Nietzsche."

"I like the idea of pragmatism," Hyle said, "but I think James took a little too much from column B."

CHAPTER SIXTY-ONE

BARE NECESSITIES

Sinking low in the sky, the sun descended through the haze toward a line of trees in the distance. Newman's growling stomach had been joined by two others. It had been two days since their last meal, and the hunger pangs that had come and gone at first no longer went away, remaining as a persistent reminder of the need to find food or perish. Pointing out that the human body could survive several weeks without food but only a few days without water, Hyle suggested that they eat handfuls of snow. Newman and Sophia dutifully complied, but knowledge about the superior importance of water did not help them feel any better about their hunger. By mutual agreement they abandoned their normal precaution of waiting until darkness to travel and set off in the first shadows of twilight.

Less than a mile away they spotted their first prospect, an old farmhouse set back only a few dozen yards from the road. Hyle wanted to leave one person in the truck, but they could not agree on who would stay behind, so all three approached the house together. Boards creaked underfoot as they climbed the sagging stairs and crossed the porch. A fresh coat of red paint on the heavy door only served to highlight the clapboards which had faded from white to light gray. They knocked several times and waited for a response, listening for any sounds within. Hearing nothing, they went around to the back where two wooden steps led up to an unpainted screen door. Behind it the inner door hung ajar.

"Looks like it was kicked in," Sophia noted, pointing at the splintered wood on the jamb.

The pantry had been cleaned out. A search of desk drawers and other likely hiding places for snacks revealed nothing edible. Under the cushion of an armchair Hyle found a jackknife and Newman returned from a search of the bedrooms with a couple blankets he had found in a drawer below one of the beds. Hyle eyed the blankets with disappointment.

"At least we'll be warm when we starve to death," he said.

A mile down the road the scene was replayed at another farmhouse where there was nothing worth taking. They did not get to enter the third. The two men were walking toward the front porch. Sophia had finished sliding across the bench seat and was just emerging from the passenger side when a shotgun blast split the evening air. Across a fallow field a murder of crows took wing, chattering nervously as they escaped in a swarming cloud. Out of the corner of his eye Hyle saw Sophia falling backwards into the truck. He threw his hands into the air and began backpedaling.

"We don't mean any harm!" he yelled to the unseen gunman. His eyes scoured the dark shapes of the windows but the light had faded too much for him to distinguish open from closed or to make out the shape of the shooter or the gun.

"We're just looking for food," Newman added.

Another shot exploded from the direction of the house. A spray of snow and dirt erupted from the ground a few paces in front of Newman. Hyle swung quickly around the driver side door crouching low.

"Are you okay?" he hissed to Sophia. For a horrifying second she lay motionless on the seat, one arm draped over her head. There was no blood. No sign of damage to the truck. Then she twisted around to look at him and nodded vigorously, as if to convince herself. She pulled her feet in just in time for Newman to scramble in the door. Hyle slid up onto his seat, started the truck and backed at full speed down the long driveway. Not until they were back on the road and driving forward again did they breathe a collective sigh of relief.

"I'm not so hungry anymore," Sophia said.

This comment seemed unusually funny all of a sudden and Sophia found herself unable to stop laughing. Her laughter infected Newman and Hyle and soon they were all exchanging fits of uncontrollable laughter. Every time it seemed to be dying down, one of the three broke into giggles and triggered another wave of laughing. It ended only when Newman started falling behind on his breathing and Sophia realized that her stomach hurt worse from laughing than it had from being hungry.

Night settled in and they continued to drive, heading generally west and looking for some place other than a house that might have food. They found a country convenience store but the windows were smashed. The interior had been stripped of everything except the last remnants of some food that had long ago rotted in the cooler. Hyle tried to use his makeshift bicycle pump siphon to get fuel from the minivan and the small convertible that had been abandoned in the parking lot, but their gas tanks were as empty as the store. It was Sophia who had the first good luck of the night. In the console between the two front seats of a minivan she found two granola bars and a baggie full of Cheerios.

An impromptu feast was held in celebration, using the hood of the truck as a dining table. These small epicurean treasures were divided into three equal portions. The Cheerios tasted dry and chalky but nobody complained. The granola bars were wonderful.

After the humble dinner they set out again, not daring to check out any more houses, but stopping at derelict automobiles and the occasional small business. The only useful item they found was a small flashlight.

"Just finding food is going to become a full time activity, isn't it?" Sophia worried aloud as they pulled away from the offices of an auto salvage yard empty handed.

"People can only live on the leftovers of civilization for so long," Hyle noted. "Eventually things are going to run out."

"That's why we need to find a good place to settle down," Newman said. "If we want to survive when there's nothing left to scavenge, we need to learn how to hunt and fish and grow crops. We should learn to do that now while we can still find a little food left to tide us over."

"Well, I'm going to Arizona," Hyle said. "I'll be happy to drop you off any time you want."

Sophia frowned and glared at Hyle through squinted eyes.

"I don't want to split up," Newman replied evenly. "We're better off if we stay together. I just think it should be a group decision."

Once again Sophia found herself in the position of arbiter between the two men. She was too tired and hungry to make a choice, but any hope she had of waiting out the situation evaporated when Newman asked, "What do you think, Sophia?"

She shrugged and shook her head vaguely. "I'm not sure."

The idea of settling in somewhere made a lot of sense to her but something about it did not feel quite right.

"I'll give you one reason I'm going to keep going," Hyle said. "Even if I do have to learn how to hunt or grow crops I'm going to do it some place warmer. This is what they call nuclear winter. It's what, early November? Already there's an inch of snow on the ground. We had killing frosts more than a month ago. Imagine what it's going to be like in December or January. Even if we don't find any answers in Arizona at least we won't have to worry about freezing to death."

Sophia recalled her dream of walking in the desert. She nodded slowly, almost able to imagine the warm sun on her face again.

"What are we going to do for food in the meantime?" Newman challenged.

"It's probably about two thousand miles," Hyle calculated. "If we can average twenty miles an hour for ten hours a night, give or take, we could make it inside of two weeks. There's a chance we'll run out of food or gas before we get there, but that's a chance I think we have to take. If worse comes to worst we can stop however far we get and learn how to hunt and fish there."

It was clear to Newman that Hyle was just rationalizing and that the real reason he wanted to go to Arizona was his fanatic quest to find some wrongdoing on the part of the Prophet. Still, the argument about surviving winter in the north was convincing. A quick glance at Sophia told him that she was having similar thoughts. Newman said nothing more and they kept driving.

Several hours later they came to a gas station. It was clear even as they pulled into the pump area that someone had been there before them. Several thick metal disks of various sizes lay on the pavement leaving matching sized holes uncovered. Hyle got out anyway but did not bother to turn off the engine. He stood by one of the holes and looked down into the blackness. There was still an odor of gasoline although it was not strong. Just to be sure he dropped a rock into the hole. His fears were confirmed when he heard clattering, rather than splashing, come from the bottom of the tank.

The sky behind them had brightened to a rusty orange band when they found an isolated place to stop and rest. Sophia slept poorly, troubled by the aches and rumblings of her empty stomach. Even though the sky was covered by the ever present layer of brown smog the light was somehow brighter and more annoying. It seemed every time she started to doze off one of the men would keep her awake by tossing and turning, and as soon as he stopped the other one would start. When darkness came it was almost a relief to admit defeat and end the struggle to fall asleep.

This night was much like the night before except with more intention. It started with a plan to follow rural highways to Ohio, passing to the south of Buffalo and cutting across the northwest corner of Pennsylvania on the way. They became very efficient at searching, going thoroughly through a car in a minute or two and a small business in five or ten. Although they worked together well and fell into a natural routine, Hyle did everything he could to encourage and improve upon this efficiency. In response to a casual inquiry from Newman, he had been forced to admit that they had covered less than a hundred miles the previous night and he was determined to make it across the Ohio border before sunrise. They were more selective about stopping for vehicles and businesses, passing by if a door stood open or windows were smashed. Most of the stops yielded something that was deemed worthy of salvaging and gradually the toolbox behind the cab filled with potentially useful items. Finally they found a candy bar and a bottle of water, which were divided into three meager breakfasts.

Rounding a bend on a deserted stretch of highway a few hours later, a deer broke from the woods along the edge of the road. In a concession to speed and safety Hyle had resumed the use of headlights. He saw the deer at a distance, but his reaction time had been dulled by a lack of sleep and the hypnotic rhythm of wheels on pavement. They closed with the animal too quickly to stop. It froze in the headlights. Hyle stomped on the brake and cut the wheel hard to the right, then pulled it back to the left. The truck lurched off the pavement and fishtailed along the sandy shoulder before coming to a stop parallel to the road.

"Whoa," Hyle said. "Sorry about that. That scared the hell out of me."

Sophia nodded in agreement. Newman, who was also breathing heavily, had his attention focused on the forest on his side of the truck.

"Good thing you kept it on the shoulder," he said. "There's a pretty good drop off here."

It was hard to judge the exact distance and angle, but the forest floor dropped away into shadows all along the right hand side of the road.

"Looks like somebody else wasn't so lucky," said Sophia. She pointed up the road.

At the edge of the area illuminated by the headlights two dark skid marks failed to follow the road where the curve tightened, instead leading off the pavement to a gap in the otherwise uniform underbrush. When they pulled up for a closer look it was clear that a car had gone off the road there. Small fibrous bushes rose several feet high along the shoulder in both directions, but in this spot most of the bushes had been shorn away and the remnants crushed. Weeds had taken the opportunity to fill in the gap, but they were not enough to conceal the original damage to the undergrowth. Retrieving a flashlight from the glove compartment, Hyle got out to look down the slope.

"There's still a car down there," he reported.

Armed with the flashlight and two lighters they made their way down to the car. A few feet in, just beyond the brush, they had to scramble down a waist high embankment, but then the ground sloped away more gently and they could walk normally. The car was a small sedan. Its front end was wrapped solidly around a thick pine tree. As Hyle approached the side of the car he could see the remains of the driver slumped against the steering wheel.

"Go back and get the crow bar. See if you can pop the trunk while I check out the inside," he said, giving Newman a significant look. He was not sure if Newman could make out his face in the darkness or if he or Sophia had guessed what had been left unsaid, but nobody questioned his instructions.

Neither of the doors would open, but Hyle was able to lean through the passenger window to search the glove compartment, center console and back seat, carefully avoiding the desiccated corpse. He discovered that the keychain held a small blue LED flashlight that illuminated when the button was held. Aside from this, there was not much of value in front, but the back and floor was piled with overstuffed duffle bags, packs and a large cylinder which turned out to be a sleeping bag. Hyle was in the process of heaving a long, heavy duffle bag out through the window when the trunk popped open. His curiosity about what was inside the bag ended abruptly when Newman yelled.

"Yes! Yes! Thank you God!"

When the latch gave way and the trunk popped open Newman had expected to see a spare tire and jack. He hoped to see something useful like a gas can, a flashlight or a first aid kit, but what he actually saw under the flickering glow from his lighter caused him to first stare in silent disbelief, and then to shout exuberantly, grabbing Sophia into a bear hug expression of joy. When Hyle came around the corner hauling a bulky bag in one hand it was just as well that Newman could not see his face in the dark.

Letting go of Sophia, Newman pressed his palms together in front of him in a gesture of prayers answered, pumped his fist and looked skyward. Sophia, who had finally processed what she was seeing, hopped up and down clutching her hands together tightly like a child waiting to open presents on Christmas morning. The trunk was filled with food. There were no grocery bags or boxes. Cans of ravioli and Spaghettios, vegetables and beans, tuna fish and corned beef and pumpkin pie filling and soup were jumbled haphazardly among boxes of dry breakfast cereal, pasta and crackers and bags of coffee, trail mix and cookies.

The heavy bag turned out to be a tent, and the other bags in the back seat contained more camping equipment and clothing. When these were removed they revealed more bags and other items that had been stacked on the floor, including a camp stove and a full five gallon gas can. A quick inspection of the packs and duffle bags revealed all manner of gear and warm clothing required for an extended stay in the wilderness.

As they busied themselves transferring these items to the truck, they concluded that the owner of the car must have survived the first nuclear attacks and then hurriedly cleaned out his cupboards of all non-perishables, or perhaps he had visited a grocery store before the shelves had been cleaned out. The food was the most precious commodity, so they stacked it in the small space behind the seat of the truck, selecting a few things to set aside to eat on the road. When the pile threatened to obscure the back window, they covered it with a blanket to guard against the chance that someone might spot their hoard and be incited to violence out of greed or necessity. What could not be hidden behind the seat was put in the toolbox. The remaining bags of camping supplies were thrown into the bed of the truck. Despite the bounty the car had already yielded, they made one more trip back down the hill to check the tank for gas. It was empty, presumably lost through some rupture underneath the car.

Good fortune increased their selectivity once they got under way again. They did not bother to stop at any more businesses and made better time, crossing the border into Pennsylvania by morning. After an uneventful day of sleep in the service bay of a muffler repair shop, they resumed their travels. Signs for Erie increased in frequency and then disappeared, replaced by signs for Cleveland. In the early hours of the morning, still under the full blackness of night, they crossed the border into Ohio, approaching the outskirts of Cleveland before turning south. It was not until they had circled around Columbus that the sky lightened in the east and they began looking for a place to stop. It was just after dawn that the snow began to fall.

CHAPTER SIXTY-TWO

MASTERS OF SUSPICION

Instant panic gripped Sophia as soon as she opened her eyes. She could see nothing. Her first thought was that she had somehow lost her vision. It was terrifying. Rejecting this explanation, if for no other reason than to temporarily preserve her sanity, she decided that she was in a darkness so complete that it was equivalent to blindness. Her fear abated only slightly. Even as a child Sophia had never been afraid of the dark, but this was a blackness more absolute than anything she had ever experienced. In a flash of insight she realized that there had always been some source of light somewhere, however weak—a nightlight, the light filtering in from under the door, the illumination of streetlights slipping in around the edges of blinds, even the luminous glow of a watch face or the few meager photons of moonlight that penetrated the fabric of her tent when camping. She remembered a having similar revelation as they fled into the Maine woods from Asher and her panic diminished slightly.

Deprived of vision, her mind turned to other faculties of memory, touch and sound. In rapid succession she remembered finding food, crossing into Ohio, parking in the empty lot behind an old warehouse, the snow still falling. She felt the pressure of the seat below and behind her. She heard breathing on either side of her. She felt the tightness in her chest dissipate.

It was the combination of snow covering the windows and the fact that night had already fallen, she realized, that had created such darkness. This discovery in turn triggered the realization that she had slept better than she had in many nights. She credited this in part to a full belly. Although they had exercised restraint the previous night after finding the cache of food in the wrecked car, they had allowed themselves the luxury of eating well. The night air chilled the skin of her face, but she felt the comforting bulk of the sleeping bag about her legs and waist and the heavy insulation of a blanket around her shoulders, supplemented by the warmth of bodies on either side.

Reaching across Newman, Sophia fumbled for the handle and opened the door. To her great relief, the dome light came on, putting her fears permanently to rest. When Newman woke up, blinking against the light, she ushered him out the door, sliding out behind him to assess their current situation. The cloud cover made the night extremely dark and snow adhered to all but a thin strip at the top of the passenger window, creating the darkness that Sophia had experienced upon awakening. In the glow from the cab of the truck, Newman inspected his footprints in the ankle deep snow and then looked up at the sky. Snow was still falling at a steady pace. Large clumps appeared out of the darkness and plummeted to the ground with a lack of grace unbecoming of snowflakes.

"Hyle isn't going to be happy about this," he said, and Sophia thought she saw just a hint of a smile.

This prediction turned out to be accurate. When Hyle emerged from the truck a short while later, he muttered several choice words before joining his traveling companions at the tailgate.

"Looks like we're not getting anywhere tonight," he said in lieu of a greeting.

His mood lifted when Sophia handed him a small container, which he suddenly connected to the scent he had been noticing but had not registered.

"Careful, it's hot," she warned. He thanked her and inhaled deeply, savoring the aroma before taking his first sip of coffee from what was apparently a vegetable can wrapped in a sock for insulation.

"You can thank Newman," Sophia said. "It was his idea."

"We probably should have saved the Sterno for something more important than coffee," Hyle replied. He mitigated this comment with another long sip.

After a long silence Sophia wondered aloud how long the storm would last. They debated this for a while, undisturbed by the fact that none of them had any real knowledge. How much snow might accumulate? How long would it take to thaw? The opinions varied, but none were very optimistic. Would it be followed by another storm? Sophia ventured that it was too early in the year to expect another storm soon.

"We're in a nuclear winter," Hyle pointed out. "Who knows what to expect?"

"Besides, it just snowed a few days ago," Newman added.

"How much do you think it'll have to melt before we can travel again?" Sophia asked. She tried to keep her voice level, but she was afraid of hearing the answer her own mind was supplying. Hyle shrugged.

"There won't be any snow plows clearing it for us."

"But we have a plow."

"Doesn't really help us." Hyle replied. "If we have traction enough to use the plow we can just drive. The plow would only help the next guy."

"So how much snow will have to melt?" she asked again.

"Pretty much all of it."

They watched the snow fall. As the coffee dwindled the wind seemed to grow colder.

"It's freezing out here," Sophia announced at last. "I'm going back in the cab where it's warm."

Hyle and Newman followed her to the truck and for a while they sat in another awkward silence, deriving their only comfort from the shelter the truck provided against the wind. As if it sensed this, the wind picked up and whistled angrily around the edges of the doors.

"I feel bad for the people stuck outside of Asher who weren't smart enough to head south," Sophia said, staring out the window.

"As Isaac Asimov said, 'Intelligence is an accident of evolution and not necessarily and advantage,'" Hyle replied. "I wonder what Darwin and Wallace would say given how far we came only to nearly kill ourselves off as a species."

"I know Darwin, of course, but who's Wallace?" asked Sophia.

"Alfred Wallace was a naturalist who came to some similar ideas about evolution," Hyle explained. "He and Darwin corresponded about their theories. They both presented papers in London, but it was Darwin who became famous for writing the compelling account of evolution in *Origin of Species* in 1859."

"Nietzsche would have been just starting his academic career around that time," Sophia noted.

"God is dead," Hyle said, "and Darwin helped to kill him."

"I never understood why evolution needs to pose any sort of threat to religion," interjected Newman.

"It wasn't evolution that bothered the Church," Hyle replied. "When *Origin of Species* came out there wasn't much protest. It was twelve years later when *Descent of Man* was published that Darwin really made some waves."

"What was the big difference?" asked Newman.

"For one thing *Origin of Species* was just about animals," Hyle explained. "*Descent of Man* brought humans into the picture. Remember, in those days people generally considered human beings to be a special creation, separate from the animal kingdom. Darwin dragged human beings back down to earth, into the animal kingdom, and subjected us to all the forces and natural instincts and drives that govern animals. You can imagine how well that went over outside of scientific circles. And of course Freud had a field day with it."

"Freud?" asked Newman.

"And Marx," Sophia added.

Hyle and Newman both looked at her in surprise.

"Yes, Marx, Nietzsche and Freud were all influenced by Darwin for similar reasons," she said. "In fact, they're sometimes referred to together as the 'masters of suspicion' because they each attacked the widely held beliefs in their respective areas of interest. First there was Marx on economics claiming the bourgeois have defrauded the laborers of their rightful control of the means of production, and that all of our rules and cultural institutions are reflections of the values of those who control the economy, designed to keep them in power. Next Nietzsche applies the same principle to morality, claiming that everything we value and think of as good and moral is designed to keep the weak and ineffectual in power, as if it were a huge hoax perpetrated on the strong by the weak. Finally Freud comes along in psychology and applies this thinking to our knowledge of ourselves, claiming that our actions are governed, at least in part, by subconscious instincts and drives that we're not even aware of."

"In each case the things we think we're in control of are actually controlled by some hidden force," Hyle realized aloud.

"But how did Darwin inspire that?" asked Newman.

"Marx, Nietzsche and Freud were all atheists," Sophia explained. "One of the things that's appealing about Darwin for an atheist is that the theory of evolution gives you teleology without the need for a designer. In a way, Hegel set the stage for Darwin with the idea of a dialectic struggle between conflicting ideas resulting in a synthesis that's superior to either one. That's really a form of evolution, but with Hegel there's a spiritual aspect that's very compatible with religion. Darwin takes this one step further. By proposing the forces of natural and sexual selection, he takes any element of the supernatural or spiritual out of the equation."

"It's like Copernicus all over again," Hyle added. "First science comes along and challenges the idea that earth is the center of the universe. Then Darwin comes along and does the same thing with human beings. He demonstrates that we're not the center of the universe and that we're subject to the laws of nature just like all the other animals."

"Yes, there was certainly that aspect," Sophia agreed, "but for the masters of suspicion there's a more unifying theme. Darwin's theory of natural and sexual selection proposes invisible forces that work behind the scenes. Species, or individuals, don't progress because they've chosen the right path. They progress because nature—without any need for them to even be aware of it—has driven them down the right path. The common theme between Darwin, Marx, Nietzsche and Freud is that we're controlled by forces that we don't even know are there. The real sources of power are hidden and subversive. Nothing is the way it appears."

"I don't know," said Newman. He shook his head slowly, not because he failed to understand the concept, but because he was unconvinced. In his younger days Newman had been very interested in the idea of communism, which had exposed him to Marx. It appealed to him that a society could work together for their mutual benefit without competition. That seemed to him to be the next step up the ladder of social evolution, albeit one that humans were arguably not ready for yet. He had read many passages describing the ideas Sophia presented in her analysis of Marxist thought, yet he had never seen Marx as a 'master of suspicion' and he struggled with this new perspective.

"It's a bit ironic," he realized aloud, "that Marx and Nietzsche both rejected religion. Marx saw religion as a tool of the empowered ruling class, used to placate those who were being subjugated. He wanted to overthrow this system in favor of one where people worked together for the good of the whole. Nietzsche, on the other hand, saw religion as a tool of the weak, who used it to create just the type of egalitarian society Marx advocated while Nietzsche himself advocated the self-centered wealthy bourgeois lifestyle that Marx sought to overthrow."

"That's an interesting observation," Sophia remarked, "although I think you're being a bit unfair to Nietzsche."

Newman shrugged.

"Anyway, I get the idea of hidden forces in society, but what's the connection between Darwin and Freud?"

"Freud was all about repression," Hyle explained, "and Darwin, especially with sexual selection, found something worthy of being repressed."

"I don't really know that much about Freud," Newman confessed. "All I really know are the pop culture references like 'tell me about your mother,' and analyzing dreams."

"He started off as a neurologist," Hyle said. "He opened up a practice in Vienna to treat hysterias—things like paralysis of a limb or blindness. Many of these things were caused by neurological damage, but it was known at the time that some percentage of these cases weren't traceable to neurological damage."

"How could they tell that?" asked Newman.

"Neurology was well enough established that they could tell some of these hysterias didn't fit the pattern. For example, if something comes and goes it may not be nerve damage. Or a classic example is what's called glove anesthesia where the patient experiences paralysis of just the hand from the wrist down. The nervous system doesn't work that way. If nerve damage caused a hand to be paralyzed the arm would be affected too. It was clear that there was some psychological component to these hysterias, but it wasn't clear what the cause was."

"And Freud figured it out?"

"Yes, with some help. Freud had a colleague named Breuer who he talked to regularly about their cases. Breuer had a patient he referred to by the pseudonym of Anna O. She credited him with coming up with a 'talking cure' because when she talked to him she felt relief from her symptoms even without any other treatment. Freud and Breuer made a study of these hysterias and formulated a theory of repression which they published together in 1895. Freud expanded the theory in a series of books and publications after that."

"That's the origin of psychotherapy," Sophia added.

"The explanation Freud found for repression," Hyle continued, "is that there's a part of us that's driven by our animal instincts and desires. This is the part that's controlled by the pleasure principle. It wants instant gratification. It wants to maximize pleasure and minimize pain. Freud called this the id. But we couldn't be a civilized society if we were driven solely by the id. It would be chaos, so society imposes restrictions on our desires."

"They come to us in the form of laws and morality," Sophia clarified. "And here's the influence of Darwin again. Pleasure is the reward that nature gives us for doing the things we have to do as a species to survive. The id is tied up with our animal nature."

"Right," said Hyle. "So to live in civilized society, the desires of the id must be balanced by the superego. The superego is the part of you that's responsible for making sure you obey morality and law. It's essentially your conscience. In between the id and the superego is the ego. The ego is the conscious part of the mind which is constantly trying to arbitrate between these two opposing forces. The catch is that you're not really consciously aware of all the influences of the id and the superego. They work behind the scenes too. The id is selfish. It's constantly in search of pleasure and instant gratification without any consideration of the social cost. The superego is constantly trying to keep it in check. It's a battle of 'I want, I want, I want' versus 'no, no, no', but the key thing is that this battle happens in the subconscious. We're not aware that it's going on."

"But we make choices like that consciously," Newman objected. "A couple years ago the guy down the street was selling a beautiful motorcycle that I almost bought, but I thought it over and decided against it because it would make it tough for me to keep up with my rent."

"Of course we make conscious choices," Sophia said. "Freud didn't claim that everything happens in the subconscious. It's just that not everything happens in the conscious mind either. For example, there's the whole mid-life crisis pattern of men buying sports cars and motorcycles to recapture their youth. Could that have had any part in your desire to buy?"

"Or maybe you were trying to impress a particular young lady at work," Hyle added, stealing a glance at Sophia. He gave the suggestion a moment to be considered before moving on. "The point is that much of what influences our decisions happens behind the scenes in the subconscious."

Newman shook his head in denial, but said, "All right, fine. But what does this have to do with repression?"

"The ego tries to keep the peace," Hyle explained. "It tries to find compromise and walk the middle path between the id and the superego. But sometimes it runs into a desire that's too powerful to forget and yet too unthinkable to act upon. In cases like these the ego operates subconsciously too. It works behind the scenes to repress the idea—to keep it out of the conscious mind. This keeps the peace at the conscious level since you're not aware of the desire or the conflict it creates, but it causes all sorts of turmoil at the subconscious level.

"It's repressed, but it's not gone," Sophia added. Hyle nodded.

"And that's what causes the problem," he continued. "It bubbles up somewhere else. In the case of hysterias it bubbles up as a physical symptom."

"Including blindness and paralysis?" Newman asked incredulously. "There must have been something pretty serious going on for that to be just psychological. Is that why Freud was so fixated on sex? Of all the things that needed to be repressed in his day and age, I bet sex was at the top of the list."

"Exactly," Sophia said. "That's where the oedipal complex comes from. The only thing worse to deal with than sexual desire is a taboo like desire for your own mother. Freud developed this complex theory of sensual pleasures that people fixate on in stages from infancy to sexual maturity."

Hyle waved his hand dismissively. "Much of what Freud theorized is open for debate. There was a lot of speculation in his work. But most people would agree that conflict between our animal instincts and the demands of society matches pretty well with experience. And he developed the very important idea of an active subconscious portion of the mind where this psychic war is going on."

"That's where the idea of dream analysis comes from," Sophia noted. "Freud thought that there were clues to what was going on in our subconscious represented symbolically in our dreams."

"I think the whole business of dream analysis is a bit like fortune telling," said Hyle. "A person who is smart and creative enough can always come up with something that fits the situation. Still, you have to give credit to Freud for breaking a lot of new ground. Whether or not I agree with all his theories, Freud did have major insights, and is probably one of the most influential thinkers of the twentieth century."

"And why he's counted as one of the masters of suspicion," Sophia noted. "Arguably he's the most damaging one, because with Marx and Nietzsche at least we have the possibility of seeing through their hidden influences. With Freud we can never be sure what is going on in the subconscious."

"That's pretty depressing," Newman said.

"It's worse than that," Hyle added. "If you believe Freud we can never really be happy either. The id and the superego are in constant conflict. We'll never behave selfishly enough to completely satisfy the desires of the id and we can never behave with the moral perfection required by the superego. Our only option is to try to please both and to fail on both accounts."

"And you wonder why I hate science," Newman said. He opened his mouth to say something more, but ended up just shaking his head. Hyle and Sophia too seemed to have run out of words. For the moment they sat in silence, watching the snowflakes accumulating on the windshield, blotting out the last remnants of light.

CHAPTER SIXTY-THREE

MILITARY INTELLIGENCE

Throughout the night snow continued to fall. Frigid air slowly penetrated the blankets and warm clothing. To stave off the cold and make use of their normal waking hours of darkness, the three travelers set about increasing their stock of fresh water by collecting and melting snow. Since the accumulation prevented any plans to travel by truck, as they worked they debated the idea of exploring the area on foot. Hyle was nervous about leaving the truck unguarded with so much food and survival gear in it, but nobody was comfortable with the idea of splitting up. For a long time there was no resolution.

In the end boredom won out. The three of them together explored the warehouse they had parked behind and then, finding little of interest, moved on to other buildings nearby. There were a few houses scattered among industrial buildings but there was nothing to salvage in any of them. Signs of looting were everywhere. Windows were smashed in every structure, doors stood open, and in one of the houses the looters seemed to have made a point of overturning every piece of furniture possible. Eventually Hyle was able to extract a little gasoline from a snow blower and lawnmower in one garage, but other than this and a few scattered tools they found nothing useful.

Despite having little to show for their efforts, the search did achieve its primary purpose. It kept them moving and warm, and gave them something to talk about other than the possibility of being marooned for the entire winter. Finally, as dawn approached, they started the truck to warm the cab and ate dinner. Newman brewed another batch of coffee, and this time Hyle's only reaction was to warm his numb fingers by the camp stove. Since there was a plentiful supply of water in its delicate frozen form, they had instant oatmeal and condensed soup and then settled into the cab to sleep, clinging to the sensation of warmth inside and out.

This became the pattern of life for the next handful of days. The storm faded, and after two frigid days failed to melt any snow, another storm passed through, adding a few white powdery inches on top of the dingy, well-trampled parking lot. The scavenging hunt was extended in a new direction each night, every day without any sign of recent human activity emboldening them to travel a little farther. They recovered just enough gasoline to justify their habit of running the engine to warm the cab every day before they slept, a few books, including a tattered copy of *The Wizard of Oz*, which Sophia had always wanted to read, and a large charcoal grill, which Hyle wrestled back from several miles away while Newman toted a bag of charcoal briquettes and a squeeze bottle of starter fluid. That morning, before going to sleep, they feasted on grilled Spam and asparagus.

Sharp rapping startled Hyle back to consciousness. He had fallen asleep with his head against the side window, his position causing the sound to be amplified through his skull like a gunshot. He woke in a panic, squinting through sleep addled eyes into the daylight at the silhouette of a person, arm clad in a camouflage jacket, and pistol pointing into the truck. Muttering a string of curses he fumbled blindly behind him for Newman and Sophia.

"Wake up! Hey! Get up!"

The gun bobbed up and down at the window. It took Hyle a moment to recognize the significance of this motion. Hand trembling, he turned the crank to lower the window. A thin sheet of snow fell inward onto his leg. The figure beside him was a young man and the jacket he wore bore a military insignia. He wore a cylindrical army style cap pulled low such that his eyes were concealed in shadow. The cap was also camouflage. Snow was still falling and the light seemed dim, even considering the storm clouds and the perpetual haze.

"Good morning sir," said the young man. "How are you doing?"

Mind racing, Hyle tried to figure out the situation and how much danger they were in. The question took him by surprise. What in words sounded like a casual greeting conflicted with the serious tone of voice. And the gun.

"Fine, I guess," Hyle replied. His eyes shifted from the man's face back to the barrel of the gun. "Is something wrong?"

"Is everyone in here okay?" the man asked, ignoring Hyle's question. He gestured forward with his gun as he bent down for a better look inside the truck, staying one step back behind the cab and away from the door. This tactic reminded Hyle of the procedure police officers used in a traffic stop. His panic subsided slightly with the hope that the soldier was just doing things by the book. With the current state of chaos he could certainly not be faulted for playing it safe. Nonetheless Hyle kept his eyes on the gun and the soldier rather than turn to look back into the truck. He heard Newman make some guttural noise that passed as a positive response and Sophia answer yes.

"Do you have any weapons?"

"No," Hyle answered. He then hastily added, "No sir. We don't have any weapons."

The soldier moved his pistol away from the window and made a gesture behind him. When he turned back he kept his gun lowered.

"Hi, I'm Sergeant Decker. "Sorry if I startled you," he said displaying his gun briefly in front of the window and then dropping it out of sight again. "We saw signs of activity in the area. Are those your footprints all over the neighborhood?"

Hyle nodded and relaxed a bit.

"We're just checking to make sure the area is clear and everyone is okay."

"Plus we smelled coffee," added a new voice from behind the truck. The statement sounded as if it were directed to Decker as a reminder.

"Yes," Decker acknowledged with a sigh. "And Private Perez smelled coffee. He misses his cup of joe in the morning. We were hoping maybe we could barter for some."

Hyle looked at the others. Newman was nodding and Sophia raised her eyebrows and pursed her lips in the facial equivalent of a shrug. When the three travelers got out of the truck it became clear that the soldiers had indeed been playing it by the book. A Humvee was parked in the street, blocking the access road to the parking lot. Two soldiers stood on the other side of it, one leaning an assault rifle against his shoulder. In addition to Perez there were two other soldiers deployed in the parking lot, one on either side of the truck at a greater distance. Decker motioned for the two nearby soldiers to come in.

"This is Private Franklin," he said, pointing to a heavyset young man. "And this is Private Manly." Decker indicated a short, serious looking woman. "Yes, the only woman in our squad is named Manly. Don't go there," he warned, and the soldiers, including Manly, chuckled.

While Sophia and Hyle did the bargaining, Newman busied himself at the back of the truck brewing more coffee. The mere act of opening the bag seemed to drive the value higher as the soldiers caught the fresh aroma. They opened with an offer to trade cigarettes for the coffee. Sophia jumped in to take charge of the negotiations.

"Sorry, none of us are smokers."

"They're good currency for bartering," Decker told her. "Cash is no good anymore. These are the next best thing." He held out the pack in his hand and tapped it for emphasis. "Good as gold. Maybe better."

Sophia was aware that he was watching her closely for a reaction. She kept her face expressionless, giving him no satisfaction.

"Not here," she said. "Sorry. What else have you got?"

"How about tequila?"

"No thanks," she replied without hesitation.

This drew a scowl of concern from several of the soldiers. Clearly cigarettes and alcohol were two reliable forms of currency in the new world economy in which they operated. She read equal parts dismay and disbelief on their faces.

"We're looking for things that'll increase our chances of survival, not decrease them," she said.

"What we really need is a gun," Hyle suggested.

"No way," Decker said before anyone else could respond. "Weapons and ammunition are off the table. Gas too. It's got to be something else."

"What else have you got?" Sophia asked.

Decker rattled off a list of items, supplemented by suggestions from his squad. Sophia listened, expressing reserved interest in a few.

"Are you sure about the gas?" Sophia suggested once the ideas stopped coming.

"Absolutely. Gas is off the table."

This drew a rumble of protest from some of the soldiers.

"But Sarge...." Franklin began.

Decker wheeled on the private, unsympathetic to the look of desperation he received. His tone alone ended the argument. The words were unnecessary.

"Not for coffee," he said. "For something more important, maybe. If your life was on the line," Decker said, and then paused thoughtfully for a moment," maybe I could spare a gallon or two."

The squad snickered at this, and the chastened soldier, despite turning red, seemed to be able to appreciate the sergeant's humor.

In the end Sophia was only interested in three items—antibiotics, a mess kit, and food rations—and she drove a hard bargain to get them, trading an unopened bag of coffee for a mess kit and a ten day course of antibiotics. As soon as the deal was struck and the items traded, Sophia opened negotiations for fresh brewed cups of coffee. Right on cue, Newman who had been listening from the back of the truck, walked up and handed Sophia a soup can full of coffee. She sipped it as they bargained, rejecting Decker's first few offers—first roadside flares, then a hunting knife.

"How about a Mylar emergency blanket?"

"We have plenty of warm blankets and clothes."

"We could trade you one MRE per cup," Decker offered after a brief huddle with his troops. When Sophia did not respond to this offer he added, "And we'll throw in a deck of cards."

Hyle leaned over toward Sophia. "MRE stands for 'meals ready to eat.' They're rations."

"You have yourself a deal," Sophia announced and she and Decker shook hands ceremoniously. The soldiers opened the back of the Humvee and began rummaging through supplies, arguing among themselves about which MREs tasted the worst. Hyle quietly collected the rations and cards and put them in the truck while Newman distributed coffee.

"So what are you guys doing in this area?" Hyle asked. "Looking for survivors?"

"No, I wish that was the case. We were cut off from a convoy," Decker explained. His expression grew somber. The soldiers drew in around the three travelers in a rough circle to listen to their leader tell the tale. "We were at Fort Benning down in Georgia when the first strikes were launched. We were scrambled right away of course, but it took a couple days for the Army to decide what to do with us. We ended up guarding a petroleum refinery in Louisiana. They called in the Corps—the Army Corps of Engineers that is—so that we could supply the troops with fuel."

"I thought we had big stores of fuel underground somewhere down on the Gulf Coast," Sophia said.

"No ma'am. What you're thinking of is the strategic petroleum reserve, and that's just crude oil. It still needs to be processed. We have big reserves underground like you said—two in Texas and two in Louisiana—but we need refineries to make them into gas and oil we can use. There are only a handful of refineries left in the country, mostly around the Gulf of Mexico. That's why we had gas problems every time there was a big hurricane in the Gulf. So our job was to guard this refinery until they got it back online. Out of the four they were working on, ours was the first to go back into production."

The pride in his voice was unmistakable. The other soldiers grinned, and a couple uttered affirmations under their breath.

"That was a couple weeks ago," the sergeant continued. "We've been guarding fuel convoys since then. We were escorting a big convoy to Chicago when we were attacked."

"Attacked?" asked Newman. "By who?"

"Not sure," replied Decker.

"The rebels, no doubt," said Perez.

"We were coming around a bend in the main road through a small town when the convoy stopped. We were at the back, so we didn't realize what was going on at first. Then we heard that the front had been hit by RPGs."

"Rocket propelled grenades," Manly explained to Sophia, in response to her blank expression.

"We came under some small arms fire, but it was hard to see where it was coming from. We singled out one of the buildings and returned fire, but then the tanker at the end of the convoy, not very far from us, took a direct hit. There was a fireball that I'm still going to see in my nightmares if I live to be ninety. Long story short, we came under more intensive fire, plus the fire from the tanker started to spread our way. There was no way forward through the wreckage. And if that wasn't enough there was a chopper that was taking potshots at us. So we backed up to try to find our way around through side streets, but the chopper followed us and any time we'd slow down they'd toss a grenade. By the time we were able to shake the chopper we were completely separated from our unit. We've been trying to hook back up with whatever is left of the convoy, but no luck so far. At least nobody in the squad was injured, thank God. So that's our story, what about yourselves?"

"We were with a group of survivors at a college in upstate New York," Sophia answered. "But then a few nights ago we were attacked too." She went on to describe the enclave at Colgate and give a superficial account of the attack. Newman and Hyle filled in some of the details that she was unwilling to speak aloud.

"I'd heard that the rebels attacked civilians, but I'd never talked firsthand to anyone who'd actually been through something like that. Hard to believe."

"Who are these rebels?" asked Newman. "We have been so cut off we don't have any idea what's going on, or even what started any of this."

"Join the club," said Perez.

Decker inclined his head to acknowledge this comment. "Good intel is hard to come by these days. That's for sure. The story goes something like this. You know about the war and everything that was going on overseas, right?"

"Yes," said Newman. Sophia and Hyle both nodded.

"The president had just committed to sending U.S. troops over there to sort things out. Seems like when he made his trip over there to meet with the coalition leaders, one of the breakaway nations decided it'd be a good time to cause some trouble. You know the nukes aren't locked down there they way they are over here. Some of these countries are so unstable that any farmer with an oxcart and a shotgun can grab a missile for himself."

"This wasn't no farmer and an oxcart," interrupted Franklin.

"Probably true," Decker admitted. "It looks like the first nukes that were launched started overseas and were designed to pull in as many countries as possible. And they think that the first ones to hit the U.S. actually came from a nuclear sub. A lot of those countries had it much worse than we did with the Mumbai Plague, and the chain of command even in some of the more civilized countries was pretty weak, so we got ourselves caught up in a full scale, worldwide nuclear war. But as far as I've heard, no country claims to have started it. It looks like it must have been some sort of coordinated terrorist plot. Whoever started this clearly had some kind of inside help in a lot of the national militaries."

"Even ours," said Perez.

"Even ours," confirmed Decker. "There's one conspiracy theory that one of our generals broke off with a bunch of Army divisions and maybe some other of our armed forces. I can't believe that's true, but the rebels are sure well armed and it does add up that there was some help from inside our borders at the start."

"I even heard that some of our cities was hit with our own nukes, and that's why they didn't get shot down," added Franklin.

"And there was another air burst over the Midwest just a few days ago too," Decker added, "so somebody is still tossing nukes even after all this."

The soldiers finished their coffee and Decker said his goodbyes and shepherded them back down the driveway. The Humvee rumbled to life and rolled out of sight down the street beyond the warehouse. Sophia listened to the drone of the engine until it was lost among the soft sounds of branches and dead leaves rustling in the gentle breeze. For a while she watched the snow dance in eddies across the parking lot, glad for the company of the two men who travelled with her yet feeling more alone than ever.

CHAPTER SIXTY-FOUR

RELATIVELY SPEAKING

In the darkness, Newman sighed. "It seems like this is where all the problems of modern society got started," he said. "Rejecting religion, shortcomings notwithstanding, leads you to this wasteland of uncertainty."

More than a week had passed since the bartering session with Decker and his squad. They had long since stopped speculating about whether they would be trapped all winter or debating whether trying to go to Arizona was a calculated gamble well worth taking, as Hyle maintained, or whether staying near Colgate to look for survivors and re-form a community, as Newman argued, would have been a better option. This conversation had been replayed over and over again in various forms until, like rival chess masters, they could see every argument so many moves ahead that it was pointless to continue because it was obvious that it could only end in a stalemate.

Over the last few days, milder weather had moved in, and although nobody dared to speak it aloud, it brought renewed hope that the roads would soon be navigable again. The supply of food from the wrecked car, through judicious portioning, was less than half depleted, and with all the local buildings explored as far as they dared to range, the books all read, and as many naps as one could wish in a lifetime, the biggest challenge was maintaining their sanity. The trio had been entertaining themselves with conversation, returning eventually to their discussion of Darwin, Freud, Marx and Nietzsche.

"There are always certainties we can fall back on though," Sophia pointed out, "like *cogito ergo sum* and Kant's pure intuitions."

"But weren't Kant's original pure intuitions space and time?" asked Hyle. "I think Einstein demonstrated that space and time aren't absolute either."

"Is that relativity?" Sophia guessed. "All I know about relativity is $E=mc^2$. What does that have to do with time and space?"

"It's funny, that famous equation is actually just a small, albeit important, sidebar in Einstein's paper on special relativity. I could probably explain relativity in a minute or two," Hyle offered, "but you need to know some of the history of physics to fully understand it."

"We're not going anywhere," Newman pointed out. "Let's hear the full version."

"Okay," Sophia agreed, "but before we get into that could we run the engine a bit? I'm freezing."

After some scraping in the dark, the engine rumbled to life and the cab of the truck was washed in the pale blue glow of the dashboard lights.

"All right," Hyle began, "for the most complete version I'll have to start before Einstein. Most people think that Einstein invented the idea of relativity."

"Didn't he?" Sophia interrupted.

"The idea of relativity was around long before Einstein," Hyle told her. "What he did was find a very creative and elegant way to apply relativity to a new situation in order to solve some major quandaries in physics. You already understand the principle of relativity, but it's important that you hold on to it, because before we're done you'll have to abandon your current beliefs about time and space."

"That sounds like a pretty tall order," Newman said. "Don't assume I know anything about relativity."

"But you do," Hyle insisted. "Arizona is hot relative to this place, but cold relative to the sun. You're large relative to an ant, but small relative to the earth. Anything that's measured can only be measured in comparison to something else. Henri Poincaré, one of the scientists who was struggling with the same questions Einstein ultimately answered, proposed a scenario to illustrate this. Imagine that while you were sleeping, everything in the universe grew to ten times its original size. I mean everything—not just cars and people, but molecules and atoms as well. Would we be able to tell the difference?"

Sophia and Newman thought about this for a moment.

"Sophia, you can imagine that a demon enlarged the universe if you'd like to make it a more philosophical scenario," Hyle said, pausing to laugh at his own joke. "The answer is that there's no basis for telling since everything is still the same size relative to everything else in the universe."

"Okay, that makes sense," Sophia said, "but what does this have to do with physics?"

"Einstein published his first paper on relativity in 1905, but the story really starts much earlier than that," Hyle told her. "Galileo and Newton had developed the laws of motion that covered physical objects—balls rolling down inclined planes, arrows fired from bows, objects falling to the earth, the orbits of the planets and that sort of thing. You deal with relativity in this branch of physics all the time. Sophia, imagine that you had a baseball right now. You give it a little toss two feet into the air and catch it. What kind of path does it take?"

"It just goes straight up and straight down," Sophia answered hesitantly. She had the sense that this was a trick question, but decided to give the obvious answer anyway.

"Would you agree, Newman?" Hyle asked.

"Yes, straight up and down," Newman confirmed.

"Good," said Hyle. "Now, Sophia, imagine that you and I are driving down the highway at sixty miles an hour. What happens when you toss the ball? Is there any difference?"

"No," Sophia answered. "It still goes straight up and down."

"Let's ask Newman what he thinks." Before Newman could answer, Hyle added, "Newman is standing at the side of the road. We pass by him just as you throw the ball up in the air. What kind of path does the ball travel, Newman?"

Newman considered this. "It would be an arc. If it leaves her hand when you pass me you'll travel down the road a bit before it lands in her hand again."

"Exactly right. And at sixty miles an hour we're traveling just under a hundred feet per second relative to you. So for Sophia the ball travels straight up two feet and down two feet. For you it takes a different path, describing an arc that's more than a hundred feet long. Which one of you is right?"

"Newman must be right," answered Sophia, "because we're really moving. The ball just appears to us not to be moving since it's in the car with us."

"So Newman's standing still?"

Sophia nodded slowly. Something in the tone of Hyle's voice told her that the trick question was about to be revealed.

"I beg to differ," Hyle said. "I think Newman is actually hurtling through space at almost seventy thousand miles an hour—relative to the sun at least. What would happen if we reran the scenario with Newman standing on the surface of the sun while we flew by at thousands of miles an hour on the surface of the earth?"

"It would be the same answer," ventured Sophia, "except the arc he sees would be much longer."

"Exactly," Hyle acknowledged. "And the sun and our galaxy are moving relative to other galaxies. The point is that, just like size, motion is relative. You and Newman are both right. You're just looking at the same event from two different frames of reference. We're always assuming a frame of reference. Always. In the truck, which is your frame of reference, the ball just goes straight up and straight down. The only reason you think that we're 'really' moving, Sophia, is that you use earth as your default frame of reference without thinking about it. You've lived your whole life on earth, and it always appears to be stationary, at least relative to everything else around you. That's an illusion though. Earth is in motion relative to other astronomical bodies, and in physics there's nothing special about earth as a frame of reference."

Hyle watched the other two. There were no objections, but he could see that they were not totally convinced either.

"To make it even more clear, let's take away the earth," he suggested. "Let's say that Sophia and I are about to play catch on the upper deck of an intergalactic cruise ship. Just like before she tosses the ball up and catches it. Newman is sitting on a space station ahead of us. Just like before, we close the gap with Newman and then go past him just as Sophia throws the ball up. First question—will either of you see anything different about the path of the ball compared to the scenario on earth?"

"No," Sophia answered. Newman shook his head as well in agreement.

"Right, Newman will still see an arced path relative to him and Sophia will see the ball just go up and down relative to her. Second question—if we're in the blackness of space, with nothing else around, who's to say whether we're flying and Newman is standing still, or whether we're standing still and he's flying toward us?"

"You can't tell," Sophia answered.

"It's all relative," added Newman.

"Right again," said Hyle. "One more illustration before we move on. Let's say we're closing in on each other at a hundred miles an hour. And let's say that Sophia has a fastball that's sixty miles an hour. If she throws me her fastball, how fast will it be going when I catch it?"

"Relative to you or to Newman?" asked Sophia.

"Ah, you're catching on," replied Hyle. "Relative to me."

"Sixty miles an hour."

"What if you threw your fastball to Newman?"

"One hundred and sixty," Newman answered.

"Yes," agreed Sophia. "It should be the speed of my pitch plus the speed of the ship. Oh, I mean the speed of the ship relative to Newman."

"Now you understand physics as it was right up until a few decades before Einstein," Hyle said.

"I have a feeling the plot is about to become more complicated," said Sophia.

"Yes indeed," Hyle agreed. "The complications start in the 1860s with the work of James Clerk Maxwell. With the laws of physics well established for material objects, Maxwell was working on a second branch of physics that had to do with electricity and magnetism."

"The ancient Chinese were interested in magnetism and electricity," Newman noted.

"So were the ancient Greeks," added Sophia.

"True," Hyle said. "The phenomena were well known, but the efforts to explain them intensified in the eighteen hundreds. What do you know about magnets?"

"They have a north and south pole," Sophia answered.

"And opposites attract," said Newman.

"But how?" asked Hyle. "It originally appeared that they somehow reached out through space and pulled on each other through some sort of 'action at a distance.' That's what Newton called the action of gravity. We'll come back to that. But you probably know more about the forces generated by magnets."

"They generate magnetic fields, don't they?" Sophia remembered. "We did a lab in school with iron filings sprinkled onto a piece of paper over a magnet. You could see the magnetic field radiating out of one pole of the magnet and looping back to the other."

"Right. It had been established that magnets generate magnetic fields and that objects are subject to the attraction of the magnet if they're inside the magnetic field. It had also been established that a moving magnetic field could generate electricity. That's the principle of electric generators, by the way. Magnets spinning inside a coil of copper wires produce electricity, like the turbines spinning in a windmill or hydroelectric dam. James Clerk Maxwell thought that nature should be symmetrical. If magnetism could produce electricity, he thought electricity ought to be able to produce magnetism. He worked out a series of equations—now called Maxwell's equations—which describe the two-way relationship between magnetism and electricity."

"That's amazing." Sophia said. "He just expected nature to be symmetrical, then went out and proved that it was?"

"There were some theoretical reasons too, but yes, a major reason for looking for the conversion of electricity to magnetism was his suspicion that nature was symmetrical. And the conclusion that came from these equations led to a revolution in physics. Maxwell imagined a magnetic field moving and generating an electric field which also moved, generating a magnetic field again. He theorized that these moving fields would be self-perpetuating—magnetic creating electric, electric creating magnetic and so on— and move through space in the form of electromagnetic waves. He calculated the speed of these waves and guess what he came up with?"

Sophia shook her head and Newman shrugged.

"The known value for the speed of light," Hyle said. "Previously there had been no connection between optics and the field of electricity and magnetism. Newton thought light was a particle, but Maxwell's equations explained light as being an electromagnetic wave. So in one elegant set of equations, Maxwell not only unified electricity and magnetism mathematically, but he also discovered an unanticipated connection with light."

"That sounds like a major achievement," Sophia commented.

"It was, but it took a while for Maxwell's theory to gain traction. In 1887 Hertz demonstrated electromagnetic waves in the lab by generating and receiving radio waves, and this helped convince the skeptics. This is when the problems in physics began to surface."

"There was a problem with Maxwell's equations?" asked Newman.

"The problem wasn't in the equations. It was with their implications. First, light waves—in fact all electromagnetic waves—travel at a known speed we call c, which is about 186,000 miles per second. But 186,000 miles per second relative to what? Second, waves need a medium. Waves in the ocean are in water, sound waves are vibrations of air, earthquakes are essentially 'earth waves' but electromagnetic waves didn't vibrate in any of these media. Both these problems led scientists to propose a theoretical substance called the ether that existed all through the universe."

"I heard about relativity in high school even if we didn't study it," said Sophia. "I've never heard of the ether. Do we know it by some other name?"

"I can't tell you yet," Hyle replied. "That would ruin the suspense. What I can tell you is that since light travels through space, the ether would have to exist everywhere. This naturally led to the question of whether the earth moved through the ether—creating a sort of 'ether wind' that would blow in the opposite direction of earth's motion—or whether it carried some localized ether along with it, the way earth carries the atmosphere along with it. Which alternative was actually true could be determined by observing starlight."

"How does that work?" asked Sophia.

"Imagine you're swimming across a river," Hyle said. "You swim away perpendicular to the shore, but the current is moving pretty fast. When you get to the opposite bank you'll be somewhere down river. Even though you were trying to swim straight ahead, your actual path across the river will be at an angle. It's the same thing with light. If starlight, for example, were trying to get to earth through an ether wind, it would come to us at an angle. If it came through an 'ether atmosphere' it would come straight. You can determine which is the case by observing stars at different times of year. Remember that the earth is speeding around the sun in an ellipse, so it reverses direction every six months, relative to stars outside our solar system. If there were an ether atmosphere, starlight would come from the same angle all the time, but if the earth moves through the ether causing an ether wind, the starlight would come from a different angle now than it would six months from now because the ether wind would be blowing in the opposite direction every six months. Like the river reversing flow and pushing you upstream instead of down. Astronomers observed that they did, in fact, have to aim their telescopes at different angles to see a star at different times of the year. This is called the aberration of starlight."

"So there is an ether wind?" Sophia asked incredulously.

"That's the conclusion scientists came to around the end of the eighteen hundreds," Hyle answered. "For many years scientists tried to detect and measure the effect of the ether wind. Then in 1887 Michelson and Morley published what is probably the most famous negative experimental result in the history of science. They performed an elegant experiment where a beam of light was shot at a half-silvered mirror set at a forty five degree angle to the light. Being half-silvered, the mirror allowed half the light to go straight through while the other half was reflected by the mirror to travel perpendicular to the source beam. The beams were reflected back and forth a few more times to increase their travel time, then recombined and sent to a detector. This whole apparatus was set on a block of marble, which was floated in a pool of mercury to dampen vibrations and allow it to be turned."

"It sounds very complicated," Newman observed.

"They spent many years perfecting it before their famous experiment."

"Are you going to explain how it worked?" Sophia prompted.

"Yes, of course," Hyle said. "The idea was that one of the paths would be aligned with the flow of the ether wind while the other was perpendicular to it. Since the light paths were perpendicular to each other and the device could be rotated, they didn't even need to know which direction the ether wind was blowing. They could just rotate it and measure the results in several orientations. When one of the light paths ended up aligned in the direction of the ether wind it would take longer to make its trip than the light that was perpendicular to it."

"Wouldn't the effects of going against the ether wind be cancelled out by the effects of going with it in the opposite direction?" asked Newman

You might think so, but actually the light would spend more time 'swimming against the current' then it would getting a boost back, so it doesn't actually cancel out."

"Even so, light moves incredibly fast," Sophia objected. "How could they measure such a small difference?"

"They couldn't clock it like you would with racing cars," Hyle confirmed, "but they came up with another method. When two beams of light are combined they create what is called an interference pattern. Imagine dropping two pebbles into a pond side by side. Where the ripples overlap, a pattern is created called an interference pattern. Constructive interference is where the crests of the two waves meet. The resulting crest will be twice as high. Destructive interference is where a crest and a trough meet and cancel each other out. Light waves behave the same way, and the height of the wave corresponds to how bright the light is. By looking for changes in the interference pattern of the two beams of light in their detector, Michelson and Morley could tell if one beam of light was traveling at a different speed than the other. What they found was that, no matter which way they pointed the apparatus, they didn't see a difference."

"So one set of experiments proved that there is an ether wind and another one proved that there isn't one," concluded Newman.

"This was exactly the crisis in physics around the turn of the century," Hyle confirmed. "In an attempt to explain the Michelson-Morley experiment, a couple scientists working independently came up with the same explanation. FitzGerald and Lorentz suggested that maybe the resistance of the ether wind compressed physical things. The path would have to be compressed by just the right amount to allow the light traveling against the ether wind to travel more slowly, yet because it was traveling a shorter distance, arrive at the same time as the perpendicular light beam. Lorentz worked out the mathematics for what is now called the Lorentz contraction, or sometimes the Lorentz-FitzGerald contraction. Remember Henri Poincaré's scenario of the whole universe getting larger? This is a case of the whole world getting shorter in the direction of the ether wind. If all the measuring sticks get shorter by the same amount, how would we ever know? It may not surprise you to know that Poincaré corresponded with Lorentz about this problem in physics. Between them they had developed many of the fundamental ideas that Einstein incorporated into special relativity, but they were still trying to explain things in terms of the ether. It was Einstein who took the radical step of declaring that the ether didn't exist."

"I knew it!" said Sophia. "I knew I'd have heard something about it in school. But if the ether doesn't exist then what does light travel at speed c relative to?"

"Everything," Hyle answered cryptically. "Which creates yet another problem. Think about our game of catch on the intergalactic cruise ship. Instead of a ball, imagine that Sophia is holding a flashlight at the back of the deck. When she switches it on, I'll see the light coming at me at 186,000 miles per second. But guess what, even though we're closing with Newman at a hundred miles an hour, he will *not* see the light coming at him a hundred miles an hour faster. It'll come at him at exactly the same speed. We'll both measure it as traveling at speed c."

"How can that be?" asked Sophia.

"What Einstein really stated was that the laws of physics for electromagnetic waves were valid in any frame of reference, just as the laws of motion for physical objects are," Hyle explained. "In that regard it's a very conservative and sensible idea. The catch is that in order to make sense of it you have to abandon your ideas of time and space being absolute. In Einstein's relativity it's the speed of light which is absolute. Time and space end up being relative."

"I should clarify though that what Einstein published in 1905 was what we call his theory of special relativity. It only applies to frames of reference in uniform motion—moving straight without speeding up or slowing down—relative to each other. It wasn't until 1916 that he formulated a theory of general relativity that could handle any relative motion. By the way, 1905 was a big year for Einstein. In addition to special relativity he published three other papers, two of them were of major significance."

"All well and good," said Sophia, "but for the moment I still don't understand how you and Newman could both see light moving at the same speed from the back of our spaceship."

"Fair enough," Hyle conceded. "Before I try to answer that, let me establish the parts that work the way you'd expect. Light still has one thing in common with the baseball analogy. If Sophia were to shine a flashlight at a mirror two feet above her, in our frame of reference on the spaceship the light would travel straight up and bounce two feet straight back. But in your frame of reference, Newman, if we're flying past you, the flashlight will have moved from the time the light wave leaves the bulb to the time it bounces back. From your perspective, the light will travel at an angle up to the mirror, and come back down at an opposing angle. The light will have traveled a greater distance in your frame of reference—just like the baseball."

"But how can it go a greater distance while moving at a constant speed?" demanded Sophia.

"Remember when I said you'd have to hold on to the idea of relativity because it was going to challenge everything you believe about time and space?"

"Yes," Sophia replied. Newman nodded.

"Well, this is that part. The apparent conflict is that, for Newman in his frame of reference, light travels further than it does for us in the same amount of time, and yet Einstein says it travels the same speed for all observers. If both statements are true, there are only two ways to resolve it. Want to take a guess?"

The offer was met with silence.

"I'll give you a hint. We measure speed, like the speed of light, in terms of units of distance per unit of time, like 186,000 miles per hour or one foot per nanosecond. Distance and time."

"Because distance and time are relative?" Sophia asked. "I'm guessing that's the answer because of your hint but I'm not sure I understand the concept."

"Yes, distance—or space more accurately—and time are what are relative in Einstein's theory of relativity. Go back to the spaceship and flashlight example. For Newman, we're the ones moving, and from his frame of reference, our time will appear to move more slowly and we'll appear to be compressed in the direction of our motion. Actually I shouldn't say 'appear.' We really will be compressed and time really will move slower for us, as viewed from Newman's frame of reference."

"It must be a pretty minor change," speculated Newman. "We don't notice it in our daily lives."

"It is minor," Hyle confirmed. "The speeds we measure in our daily lives are very slow compared to the speed of light, and you have to be moving at a significant fraction of the speed of light for time dilation and the Lorentz contraction to be noticeable."

"Lorentz contraction?" interrupted Sophia. "So Lorentz and FitzGerald were right after all?"

"In a way," Hyle confirmed. "Remember that their mathematics worked quite well to explain the properties of light. It was just that they worked things out on the assumption that there was an ether wind. Einstein used the same equation to explain the behavior of light in terms of relativity based on different frames of reference—an explanation which didn't require an ether wind—resolving that conflict. Our frame of reference on earth is moving relative to the stars, which explains the aberration of starlight. On the other hand, the light in the Michelson-Morley apparatus was all in the same frame of reference, regardless of the direction it was moving."

"But the effects become more noticeable the faster you travel?" asked Newman.

"Yes, if you express velocity, v, as a fraction of the speed of light, the Lorentz contraction is the square root of one minus v squared."

"Sorry, Hyle, I'm a math atheist," Newman said. Sophia laughed in commiseration.

"It's not that bad if you take it piece by piece," Hyle assured him. "I'll keep it simple. Let's say that our spaceship is moving eighty percent of the speed of light relative to the space station. Our velocity is 0.8 times the speed of light, and squared that would be 0.64. So now we have the square root of the quantity 1 minus 0.64. That's the square root of 0.36 which is 0.6. There's your correction factor."

"So if you're going eighty percent of the speed of light relative to me, your meter stick would appear to be only sixty centimeters long?" ventured Newman.

"Sixty centimeters, yes," Hyle confirmed. "But it wouldn't *appear* to be sixty centimeters long to you. It would *be* sixty centimeters. It's not an illusion."

"What would that feel like for you in the spaceship?" asked Newman.

"No different," Hyle replied. "I'll try to explain it in a minute, but first I need to take a break to answer the call of nature."

As it turned out, nature had a surprise in store.

CHAPTER SIXTY-FIVE

THE CALL OF NATURE

Outside the truck a light snow was falling. Barely enough to dust the ground, the wind pulled it from the trees and the warehouse roof, whipping it this way and that, creating the illusion of a blizzard. A million tiny points of reflected light, like blue pixie dust in the glow of the LED flashlight, twisted and danced, occasionally swirling into tight little whirlwinds that looked almost as if some magical creature was about to form out of thin air. Blinking constantly, Hyle slogged across the parking lot to the corner of the warehouse. Through the shifting curtain of snow he could just make out the cab of the truck, faintly illuminated by the dashboard lights. A few more steps took him out of sight beyond the edge of the building.

On the side of the warehouse, an access road ran between the parking area in the rear and the street. It was bordered by an abandoned lot, along the edge of which a jumbled wall had formed over the years. Rounding the corner, Hyle swept his flashlight across a dumpster, a stack of rotting pallets and a pile of broken lumber. Somewhere behind those, hidden in the absolute darkness rested an assortment of fifty five gallon drums, some so rusted that their forms seemed to defy gravity, and an old car with its roof staved in. The missing tires might have been four of the several dozen in an unorganized pile nearby. Any space that people had not filled with their cast off relics, nature had been happy to fill in with scrubby bushes and the occasional stunted tree.

A few dozen paces down the alley, still relatively near the back, was the only feature on this side of the warehouse—a side door that exited at waist height, opening onto a concrete landing. The landing and the ramp, which led directly away toward the street, were surrounded by a tubular steel safety railing. Stopping there, in the corner formed by the platform and the warehouse wall, Hyle paused to puzzle over the peculiarities of human nature that had led him there as he relieved himself. With only two people for miles around, and they on the other side of a warehouse wall and in almost total darkness, it was not modesty that compelled him to the corner, he realized, but some animal instinct that drove him to seek a sheltered place to perform this vulnerable act. In parallel with this active line of thought, a sudden amorphous foreboding bubbled up from his subconscious. Apprehension inspired him to finish quickly, even as he wrote it off to too much psychoanalysis and a primitive fear of the dark.

Retrieving the flashlight from between his clenched teeth, Hyle completed his mission and turned to head back to the truck, but a movement stopped him in place before he had even taken his first step. From the shadows at the periphery of the blue light only a few paces away, a large dog watched him warily, apparently also stopped in its tracks, its lead paw resting gingerly on the ground in mid step. Barely discernable in the monochrome light, its dark coat was supplemented by a slightly lighter color along the compact muzzle and lower legs, in the characteristic black and brown pattern of a Rottweiler.

For a while the two creatures stared at each other, motionless. The dog displayed no signs of agitation or aggression yet, Hyle noted—no growling or barking—but it also showed no sign of backing away, even though it was not the one cornered. Never having owned a dog, subtleties of canine behavior were lost on Hyle, but its posture did not put him at ease. Ears pulled back, it was stretched low, as if trying to slip under a fence, its eyes locked on his eyes. Time passed and nothing transpired to break the stalemate.

"Hey boy," Hyle said dubiously in a voice as calm and soothing as he could muster. Moving slowly, he stepped forward, extending the back of his hand for the dog to smell in a gesture of good will. The Rottweiler's lips curled and it emitted a low growl of warning. Hyle stepped back and withdrew his hand. The dog's behavior was puzzling. Was it defending its turf? If it intended to attack there had been plenty of time for it to size him up and get on with it. If it was scared of him, nothing prevented it from fleeing.

The mystery was resolved when a second animal shape moved into the island of light. Skirting along the wall of the warehouse, a mongrel not quite as large as the Rottweiler padded up beside it, stopping one step back. Even in the poor light Hyle could see that the animal had fallen on hard times. A large piece was torn from one ear, patches were missing from its matted coat, and a dark wound covered the length of one foreleg. From the direction of the abandoned lot a German Shepherd closed in, taking up a position at the Rottweiler's other flank. This is what the dog had been waiting for, Hyle realized. It was keeping him trapped in the corner. These animals were not protecting their turf—they were hunting.

It was only a matter of time—and not much time—before they overcame their uncertainty and began to close in. With diplomacy no longer an option, Hyle resorted to intimidation. Shaking the flashlight and waving his free hand, he took a stomping step forward and yelled, "Heeyah!" The German Shepherd backpedaled, but the Rottweiler took only a half step back, settling its weight on its haunches and bracing itself for combat, ready to spring. The smaller dog was unfazed. But that was not the worst of it. As the blue light bounced around the alleyway, Hyle caught sight of several more dark shapes closing in behind the three dogs. This new bit of information explained why they were not intimidated and changed the situation dramatically, erasing any thought of fighting.

The attempt at scaring them might have bought a few more seconds while the pack sized him up, gathering their collective confidence to attack. Scenarios flashed rapidly through Hyle's mind as he considered his options. He was fairly sure how it would play out if he did nothing. The pack would inch forward, gaining courage bit by bit, until finally one of them—probably the Rottweiler, who appeared to be the alpha—leapt in for an attack. As soon as that first daring assault was launched the rest would jump in, quickly and mercilessly. The thought of yelling for help crossed his mind, but with no weapons in the truck, he could not picture what Newman or Sophia could do. Besides, he worried that the dogs might be able to sense the distress in his call and set upon him all the more quickly. And, being completely honest with himself, although it wasn't enough to risk his life unnecessarily, there was even an element of pride that argued against calling for assistance. He imagined trying to explain to Newman, and especially Sophia, why he had ventured so far from the truck, and resolved to keep quiet for the moment. Fighting was clearly not an option. He also ruled out making a break for the truck. Dogs were natural hunters and they would seize the advantage of attacking from behind.

It was then that he realized the good fortune of whatever instinct had brought him to the corner formed by the protruding concrete landing. His best bet was to get to the door above and behind him. Once safely inside the warehouse there was another door he remembered in the back of the building, near the spot they had parked. The flaw in this plan was that the end of the ramp was a good distance away, and getting there would expose him to being flanked by the pack. Instead he decided to try to make it over the railing, taking an extra second to pull together a hasty plan. Turning slightly sideways but not taking his eyes, or the light, off the Rottweiler, he reached up for the railing. The Rottweiler snapped its head upward to follow the movement of his hand, but otherwise none of the dogs moved. Yet.

Out of the corner of his eye, Hyle tried to gauge the height of the concrete landing, knowing he would only have one shot to get a toe hold and that falling would ultimately be fatal. Drawing a deep breath, eyes still locked on the alpha dog, he jumped, pulling himself up by the upper railing while his foot sought purchase on the edge of the platform. His toe banged off the bottom railing, failing to find a surface. The flashlight beam skewed wildly and Hyle struggled to hold himself aloft with the strength of his arm. Sliding under the rail, his foot found the landing and he twisted to face the pack, swinging the light back in line. In the few seconds of darkness the pack had closed in, the Rottweiler now directly below him. Tempted to kick at the dog's head, Hyle realized that this could trigger an attack by the other dogs which would try to drag him off his perch by the arms and legs. Instead he kicked his leg upwards, swinging it over the top railing, momentarily turning his back on the pack. The Rottweiler leapt.

As his lead leg cleared the bar, Hyle laid his chest on the surface and pitched his weight across it, hoping to retain his grasp on the rail to break his fall, but willing to fall on his tucked head rather than risk an extra second for a better landing. It was the right call. His trailing leg described an arc out and over the Rottweiler, which jumped to intercept it, catching the edge of his pant leg, but unable to hold on. Hyle felt a tug on his pants, like a nibble on a fishing line, before crashing to the snow-laced concrete on the other side of the safety rail. The light went out. Hyle fumbled for the keychain in the darkness, found it, aligned it in his hand and held down the button. The bared teeth of the mongrel were suddenly illuminated just inches away, the dog's muzzle wedged sideways between the lower rail and the landing, snapping at his face. Hyle spasmed backwards, struggling to breathe. Recovering his wits, he pulled his hand and legs away from the railing and lay there inhaling slowly for a moment before pulling himself to his feet.

On the far side of the railing the dogs took turns leaping up to bark or growl at him while he tried the door. Locked. With one eye on the pack, Hyle examined the door. It was steel, with a steel frame with a guard plate over the latch. Short of finding a key miraculously hidden nearby, there was no chance he would be escaping that way. He ran the flashlight beam over the warehouse wall, finding it as smooth and windowless as he remembered. If anything the flat roof now seemed higher off the ground than it had been when he last saw the building in the daylight. The Rottweiler managed to hook its legs across the middle railing and held itself up, rear legs scrabbling madly against the side of the concrete platform, as it wedged its head between the rails and snapped at Hyle from a foot away. It was then that Hyle decided to yell for help.

In the truck, Newman and Sophia were still trying to make sense of relativity. More accurately, Sophia was trying to make sense of relativity, restating and summarizing what she thought she had understood while Newman reclined with his eyes closed, voicing an occasional question or agreement.

"What was that?" he asked, interrupting Sophia in mid-sentence.

"Aberration of starlight?" she asked. "It was—"

"No. I thought I heard something."

"Like what?"

"Like maybe—" Newman paused, thinking back and becoming more sure as he tried to analyze what he had heard. When he spoke again his voice was serious. "Like someone shouting."

"Hyle's been gone a while," Sophia realized aloud as Newman sat up, grabbing the flashlight from the dash with one hand while opening the door with the other.

"Stay here. I'm going to go see if he's okay."

"Wait Newman—" Sophia started, but cut herself off as she realized that she was talking to the closed passenger door.

Striking a balance between caution and speed, Newman jogged toward the alley, careful to keep the flashlight beam as close to his feet as possible. As he ran, leaving behind the white noise of the truck's heating fan, he could hear the sound of barking from the side of the building. Stopping at the corner, he poked his head around and saw immediately that the alley was awash in a cobalt glow, which meant that Hyle was still there and at least capable of holding down the flashlight button. The second thing he noticed was the group of large, dark shapes surrounding the light. One leapt up at it, snarling and barking, accompanied a second later by another, casting giant shadows at him as they blotted out the light.

In the queer blue light details were difficult to make out, but the leaping shapes seemed to Newman to be large enough that Hyle would be knocked down, if not by one, certainly by two. Without waiting, Newman charged ahead, waiving his own flashlight and yelling.

"Newman! No!"

There was something not quite right about the voice. By the time Newman realized that it was out of place—slightly higher and farther back than he expected—and too steady for someone being attacked by wild animals, he had closed most of the distance at a speed too fast to stop.

"Up here! Jump up!" Hyle yelled, banging on the railing as the pack of startled dogs turned to confront Newman.

With a running leap Newman planted his foot on the lower bar of the railing and climbed it like a ladder, grabbing the top rail with his free hand, and stepping on the middle rail with his other foot. As he swung his lower foot upwards to vault the railing, Newman felt powerful jaws clamp down on his foot, stopping his momentum. For a second he teetered, with his torso leaning over the railing, counterbalanced by the German Shepherd pulling him earthward by the foot. In a second Hyle was there, pulling Newman toward him while the other dogs jumped up in a frenzy, trying to help the German Shepherd bring him to ground. Finally the deadlock was broken as Newman fell forward onto Hyle and the German Shepherd fell back to the pavement, holding Newman's empty shoe in its mouth.

"Thanks," Newman panted as he rolled off of Hyle and found his footing.

"You okay?" asked Hyle.

"Yeah, I—it just got my shoe. I'm okay." Newman stopped to take a few deep breaths before continuing. "Sorry. This wasn't much of a rescue I guess. Are you okay?"

"Fine, but I think we're stuck here. The door is locked."

Newman focused his flashlight on the door, then repeated the same survey that Hyle had, searching the warehouse wall and evaluating the distance to the roof.

"Fortunately dogs are too stupid to think of circling around to the ramp," said Hyle. "They just keep trying to find a way through the railing."

"Ants aren't too smart either," Newman pointed out, "but they always seem to find your picnic sooner or later."

As the dogs snarled and barked on the other side of the safety railing, the men scoured the alley and searched their intellects for some means of escape. Occasionally a dog would move around the corner to the long side of the ramp and Hyle and Newman would taunt the pack from the corner to draw it back. The best plan they could come up with involved one of them acting as a decoy while the other made it safely back to the truck. Neither one was in a hurry to put it into action.

Through the swirling snow Sophia watched Newman disappear around the corner of the warehouse. When he did not reappear to signal for help or indicate that everything was okay, she realized that the heating fan was blowing loudly enough to block out most sounds from outside. As soon as she shut it off she could hear baying and her already rapidly beating heart began hammering. She rolled down the window and listened for a moment, and then, hearing no voices, decided that she needed to act quickly. Sliding behind the wheel, she shifted the truck into gear and accelerated cautiously, cutting the wheel gently toward the side of the warehouse. The tires spun in the shallow snow, but slowly the truck gained momentum and turned, until she was crossing the back lot at a fair speed.

"What's she doing?" asked Newman, watching the lights bouncing over the parking lot.

"Looks like she's bringing the truck."

"Yes! Go Sophia! That's a much better rescue."

The truck appeared at the end of the alley and for a moment the wash of the headlights overwhelmed the flashlights, distracting the pack. Although the front wheels were cut hard into a turn, the pickup continued in a straight line, sliding into the stack of pallets with a muffled crash. The headlights disappeared behind the dumpster. Hyle sighed in disbelief.

"At least we have a better chance if we need to make a break for it," he said.

"Think we'd be safe if we could get into the bed?" Newman suggested.

"Only if we get desperate. Maybe if they find the ramp we could jump the rail and make a run for it."

The dogs milled about, splitting their attention between their quarry behind the railing and the new curiosity at the end of the alley. When the door of the truck opened, the Rottweiler tore itself away from the platform and advanced to the head of the pack.

"No, Sophia!" Hyle yelled.

"Get back in the truck!" Newman shouted, waving the flashlight to warn her away.

Sophia seemed oblivious as the two men continued to yell. She walked purposefully toward them, the small flame of a lighter providing a sphere of fluttering orange light around her and showing the determination in her face. When she was about ten feet away and still closing, the Rottweiler shifted its weight back to spring. Newman found himself unable to yell. All the air seemed to have been sucked from his lungs and he braced for what would come next. He started to scramble over the railing.

A geyser of fire erupted from Sophia's hand, shooting through the darkness and catching the Rottweiler square in the face. With a horrified yelp it sprang sideways and sprinted to the back of the pack, turning back just in time to see the stream of flame appear a second time, bathing a second dog in fire. It too sprinted away in fear and pain and suddenly the entire pack was backpedaling. With a few more blazing jets at the nearest dogs to convince them, the pack finally broke into a full run, fleeing down the alley and into the street.

Newman jumped down and grabbed Sophia into a bear hug. "That was brilliant!"

"Get into the truck," Hyle said, jumping down from the rail to retrieve Newman's shoe. "They may be back soon." As they clamored into the cab he agreed, "That was amazing! Using lighter fluid to make a flame thrower—that was pretty inspired. I don't think I'd have come up with that."

Sophia grinned. "I'm just glad it worked. Are you both all right?"

"Yes. We're fine," answered Newman. "But I have to say, I'm really starting to dislike dogs."

CHAPTER SIXTY-SIX

HOUSES ON SHIFTING SAND

Newman put his shoe back on. He had been drying his wet sock under the heating vent as they retold the story of the run-in with the dogs from every angle until the excitement had died down.

"So, Hyle, next time you hear nature call, don't answer," Newman suggested as he tied his shoe.

"I don't think that's really an option," Hyle replied, laughing. "But I certainly won't go so far and maybe I'll take Sophia's flamethrower."

"We should also make sure to keep the heater fan off and the window cracked whenever anyone leaves the truck," Newman suggested. "With all that noise and us talking, we almost didn't hear you yell."

"That reminds me," Sophia said. "We never got our explanation of what it would feel like to be in a spaceship traveling close to the speed of light."

"Right, you never told us why you wouldn't get compressed the same way the meter stick does," added Newman.

"You're still thinking in old school Newtonian terms," Hyle explained. "Remember that in relativity either one of us can equally claim to be the stationary frame of reference, so if Sophia and I were on the spaceship we wouldn't feel all compressed or like we were moving in slow motion. For us, you'd be the one moving and you'd be the one compressed and experiencing time dilation. Your meter stick would measure sixty centimeters when we measured it. The frame of reference we experience personally is always the stationary one. The Lorentz contraction and time dilation always happens to the other guy. In other words, between our different frames of reference, we can agree that light travels at one foot per nanosecond, but we can't agree on how long a foot is or how long a nanosecond lasts. We're trading in the absoluteness of space and time for the absoluteness of the speed of light."

"I understand the general concept," Newman said, "but I still don't quite see how it works."

"I warned you that it would be hard to abandon your old ways of thinking," Hyle replied. "It takes some time to really think through it all."

"What if you and Sophia had stopwatches?" Newman proposed. "I go flying by you with my own stopwatch. Just as I pass you we all start our watches, and just as I pass Sophia we all stop our watches. Do you mean to tell me that your stopwatches would agree on how long it takes me to get from you to her, but my stopwatch would say something different?"

"Yes."

"How can that be?" asked Newman, in a tone somewhere between disbelief and distress. "Ten seconds is ten seconds. How can there be time dilation if we agree on how much time elapsed?"

"Just like one meter is one meter," Hyle reminded him.

"But this time you're looking at my stopwatch. You're reading something from my frame of reference," objected Newman.

"Yes, you're right. Good catch," said Hyle. "But that's a different problem altogether. That's another idea you'll need to let go of. Things that happen simultaneously in one frame of reference don't happen simultaneously in another."

"Needless to say," said Sophia. "I don't get it."

"Trying to change your whole world view isn't easy," Hyle sympathized. "Imagine now that Newman is still on his space station, but that Sophia and I are each in separate spaceships of exactly the same design. We pass by each other going the same speed, but in opposite directions, right next to the space station, and let's just say that Sophia is travelling backwards."

"Why do I have to be the one going backwards?" Sophia objected.

"Don't answer that," advised Newman. Hyle laughed and obliged, pretending not to hear the comment.

"In Newman's frame of reference," he continued, "we appear to be moving the same speed in our opposite directions, so the Lorentz contraction is the same for both of us. He'd see the nose of my spaceship pass the nose of yours, Sophia, just as the tail of your ship passed the tail of mine. But in my frame of reference, I'm standing still, Newman is moving past me, and Sophia is moving past twice as fast. In my frame of reference, Sophia's ship is shorter than mine, due to the Lorentz contraction. Since it's shorter, it would be impossible for those two events—the alignment of our noses and the alignment of our tails—to occur at the same time. For Sophia, my ship would be the shorter one. What's simultaneous for Newman isn't simultaneous for me or for Sophia."

"So how does that apply to the stopwatch example," Newman asked. He was hovering on the edge of understanding, but the concepts were still a bit overwhelming.

"In the example with the stopwatches, it becomes a question of when each of us thinks that the event of Newman passing me and the event of Newman passing Sophia actually occurs. The answer is that they occur at different time intervals in our two different frames of reference. Since our spaceship is shorter for Newman than it is for us, he'll measure off less time to travel that interval than we would. If we could sneak a look at his stopwatch, we'd see that he marked off less time than we did."

"But what if Newman went on a long voyage through space at speeds near the speed of light?" asked Sophia. "In our frame of reference, if time moves slower for him, would he be younger than us when he came back and re-entered our frame of reference?"

"That's a great question, Sophia," said Hyle. "That's basically the famous twin paradox, and the answer is yes. If you had a twin, Sophia, and we put her on a round-trip spaceship to a galaxy far away traveling at a high fraction of the speed of light, she'd experience significant time dilation. From our perspective time would move more slowly for her than it does for us. So when she came back she'd actually be younger than you were."

"From our perspective?" Sophia noted. "But since all frames of reference are equally valid, then time should move more slowly for me from my twin's perspective and when she returns she should appear younger to me and I should appear younger to her. That's why it's impossible, right?"

"No, it's actually possible," Hyle insisted, baffling Sophia. "Remember that special relativity requires each frame of reference to be in uniform motion in order for them to be equally valid. In this case, the space traveling twin is changing directions to return to earth, so it's no longer uniform motion. Now the frames of reference aren't equally valid, and because earth is in uniform motion, the space traveling twin really will be younger than the one who stays on earth."

"But earth isn't in uniform motion either," objected Sophia. "It's revolving around the sun."

"True, but it's so slow compared to the speed of light that it might as well be in uniform motion."

"If you traveled faster than the speed of light could you go back in time?" Newman asked.

"No. Time moves at different rates in each frame of reference, but it always moves forward. It's impossible for anything to go faster than the speed of light."

"How do you know it's impossible?" Newman replied.

"By definition," explained Hyle. "It's built into the theory of relativity."

"Seems kind of arbitrary to me," said Newman.

Hyle opened and closed his mouth a few times in unfocused exasperation, not sure quite where to start addressing this objection.

"It seems that special relativity covers a lot of ground," observed Sophia, trying to shift the topic. "What does general relativity add?"

"I'm no expert," Hyle confessed, "General relativity is much more complicated. After special relativity it took Einstein eleven more years to work out the theory of general relativity in order to account for all types of motion. One of the major outcomes was a new theory to account for gravity."

"What was wrong with gravity?" Newman asked.

"What Newton proposed was a good mathematical solution, but it didn't really explain what gravity was," Hyle clarified. "To make a long story short, Einstein realized that the effects we attribute to the mysterious force we call gravity could actually be understood in a different way. Once again this requires some radical thinking. He used non-Euclidean geometry to explain gravity in terms of curved space-time."

"How can time be curved?" asked Newman. "Let alone space?"

"And what is non-Euclidean geometry?" added Sophia.

"Let me start with Sophia's question," Hyle answered with an understanding laugh. "Remember all those geometry proofs you did in high school? That's the standard geometry developed by Euclid in ancient Greece, and most of it can be derived from just a few basic principles. One of those principles is that only one line can pass through two points."

"I remember that," agreed Sophia.

"Well it happens to be wrong," Hyle said. "If you think of space-time as curved, then more than one line can pass through two points. That's the foundation of non-Euclidean geometry. From there you can derive a whole alternative system of geometry."

"I still don't see how space can be curved," said Newman.

"Think of the path a plane takes from one city to another. Did you ever notice that they look like arcs on a flat map? Those are actually straight lines from the curved surface of the earth. Let's say you wanted to fly from one place on the equator to the exact opposite side of the earth on the equator. If the earth were a perfect sphere, it would be just as fast to go across the North Pole as it would be to follow the equator—they're both halfway around the world. Now you can have more than one straight line that passes through two points."

"I suppose that makes sense," Newman said.

"Good, because that's a good analogy for curved space-time."

"Why do you keep calling it space-time?" asked Sophia.

"Because in relativity, time is a fourth dimension," explained Hyle. "Since time and space both change depending upon the frame of reference, it's mathematically useful to link them together into one set of coordinates. Instead of plotting the location of something in three dimensions, you also need to plot it against time."

"So what does that have to do with gravity?" Sophia asked.

"Einstein developed a theory in which matter distorts space-time. The more matter, the greater the distortion. We see that distortion as gravity. The common analogy is the ball on a sheet. Imagine a taut sheet with a heavy ball placed in the middle of it. The sheet represents space-time and the ball represents a planet or a star like the sun. The mass of the ball will create a depression in the sheet that decreases the farther away from the ball you go—just like gravity. If you were to roll a small ball past the large one, the small one might get caught in the depression and circle around it. If it were going at just the right speed, it would even go into orbit."

"There was a huge funnel at the science museum when I was a kid," Sophia said. "It rolled these big steel balls around the top of the funnel and they seemed to go around and around forever."

"Like those funnels that you donate coins into," added Newman.

"Yes, exactly," Hyle confirmed. "That's like the effect of a massive object on space-time. It creates the effect we call gravity."

"If we move at such slow speeds compared to the speed of light, how do we know that any of this is real?" Newman asked. "It seems to work logically, but completely conflicts with common sense."

"That's because your common sense comes from your experience," Hyle replied. "You've never experienced anything remotely near the speed of light. When Einstein first proposed relativity there were no tools to test his theories, but in the decades that followed, more advanced technology allowed many experiments to be performed and they all confirmed the predictions of relativity. It's one of the most tested theories in physics. Time dilation has actually been demonstrated with planes flying at high speed around the earth carrying very sensitive clocks. The traveling clocks return from the trip a bit behind the earth bound clocks. And the theory of general relativity predicted the existence of black holes."

"What exactly is a black hole?" interrupted Sophia.

"It's a region caused by an incredibly massive body which creates gravity so strong that even light can't escape."

"And those weren't observed until after Einstein came up with relativity?"

"Right," Hyle confirmed. "Relativity also predicted the results of another experiment done back in the nineteen forties with muons, which are particles that travel at speeds very close to the speed of light. Muons are known to decay at a certain rate. Scientists went to the top of a mountain and counted the number of muons reaching earth from outer space. Then they counted the number of muons that reached sea level. Based on the rate of decay, about fifty percent of the muons should have decayed over that distance, leaving only half surviving, but the actual measurement was more like ninety percent. That's because in our frame of reference time moved more slowly for the muons, so fewer of them had decayed."

"If Einstein couldn't do any of these experiments, how did he come up with relativity in the first place?" Sophia asked.

"He was trying to explain the conflicting results of all those experiments we discussed, but he didn't do experiments himself. He was famous for using so-called 'thought experiments' where he imagined different scenarios and tried to figure out how to explain them. For example, he asked himself what it would look like if he could run alongside a light wave at the speed of light."

"I'm amazed that he was able to just think this all up," Sophia remarked.

"It's mind-boggling," said Newman. "When Hyle explains it everything seems to make sense, but if I actually try to think about it on my own it makes my head spin."

"Einstein was truly exceptional," Hyle agreed. "What's even more impressive is that he also helped unravel a whole other set of problems unrelated to relativity and became one of the foundational figures in quantum physics."

"Why, what else did he figure out?" asked Sophia.

"It's a bit complicated."

"You might as well tell us anyway," Sophia insisted. "I'm still too full of adrenaline to be able to sleep for a while."

"I'm not even sure where I'd start."

"Treat it like a story and tell it from the beginning like you did with relativity," Newman suggested. "I always enjoy learning more when it's presented as a story."

"Good idea," Hyle agreed, and then fell silent for a minute. He ran his hand back and forth across the blond stubble on his chin as he thought. "Let me start with a prologue. Newton's physics enjoyed great success for two centuries, explaining a wide variety of physical phenomena, and Maxwell's equations were a huge advance in understanding electromagnetism. But problems began to appear in one corner of traditional doctrine as people uncovered things that couldn't be explained by the well established rules of physics. By the first years of the twentieth century it was clear that there were some major problems with classical physics."

"Like what?" asked Sophia.

"First there was the problem of explaining why atoms were stable. Second there was the photoelectric effect. Third there was the problem of spectral lines. And last but not least there was the ultraviolet catastrophe.

"Spectral lines and the ultraviolet catastrophe?" Sophia repeated. "Sounds more like a horror story than science history."

"It does," Hyle acknowledged, laughing. "But it's pretty safe. Let me start with atoms. The Rutherford model depicted atoms as being something like miniature solar systems with the protons and neutrons clustered together in the center like the sun, providing most of the mass, while the electrons orbited like planets at a great distance from the center."

"That's the way I remember atoms from high school," noted Newman.

"That model explained many aspects of atoms that earlier concepts of the atom couldn't explain, but it still had one significant problem," Hyle replied. "There was no explanation for why the electrons didn't get pulled into the nucleus, collapsing the atom in the process. Similarly, the photoelectric effect is explained by Maxwell's theories, but what scientists observed didn't match the predictions of theory. Imagine two metal plates separated by a distance inside a vacuum tube. If you shine light on one of the plates, the metal absorbs energy from the light and discharges electrons which flow to the other plate. If you wire the plates to a battery and detector to make a circuit you can measure the current in the photoelectric cell. Classical theory said that since light energy is spread out across light waves, it should take a while for an electron to absorb enough energy to be ejected from the atoms of the metal. It also predicted that the color of the light shouldn't be important. What was actually observed though was that electrons were ejected immediately, and that color did make a difference. The higher the frequency of light, the more energy in the current, and below a certain frequency of light no electrons were ejected at all. The ultraviolet catastrophe was—"

"Wait," Sophia interrupted, "Aren't you going to finish explaining the photoelectric effect first? Why does the color of light make a difference?"

"Who's telling this story? I'll come back to all that, but first I want to get to the ultraviolet catastrophe."

Newman elbowed Sophia and shushed her with the type of glare a child might get for talking in church.

"You know how metal glows when you heat it? Like when a blacksmith heats iron?" Hyle asked. "First it glows a dull red, then orange, then yellow, then white. At the atomic level, picture the iron atoms absorbing energy in the form of heat and the energy causing the electrons to vibrate at increasing frequencies. This increasing vibration in turn causes electromagnetic radiation—in other words, electromagnetic waves, or in this case light—of different frequencies. The same general principle holds true for all elements. Here's the catch though. You might think that the color changes gradually and evenly the more energy you add to the system, but that's not what's observed. Actually light is only emitted at certain wavelengths."

"Wait," Sophia objected. "How did you get from frequencies to wavelengths?"

"Sorry. Frequency is inversely proportional to wavelength—the bigger the wavelength, the lower the frequency. Red light is on the long end of the visible spectrum with a wavelength of about 650 nanometers and blue light is near the short end at about 450 nanometers. Ultraviolet light is even shorter, at about 280 nanometers. Since they're all electromagnetic waves traveling at speed c, which one would send waves past you more frequently?"

"Ultraviolet. I get it. Shorter wavelength means higher frequency of waves passing by."

"Right," Hyle confirmed. "So back to spectral lines. The point is that as the atoms in the blacksmith's iron bar absorb energy, they emit light of increasing frequency and decreasing wavelength. The critical thing to know is that there are gaps in the spectrum. The atoms don't emit every wavelength of light along the way. They skip over some wavelengths. Each element has a different pattern of these so-called spectral lines, separated by gaps in the spectrum where no light is emitted. This is counter to Maxwell's equipartition theorem, which said that energy in a system should be evenly distributed across all the possible ways it could be. Spectral lines were an anomaly, but it was a similar problem that really made it clear that there were fundamental problems with classical physics and ultimately inspired the breakthrough that evolved into quantum physics. That problem was the ultraviolet catastrophe."

"It must have been a pretty big problem to be called a catastrophe," Newman noted.

"True enough," Hyle agreed. "Trying to figure out how things fit into a theory is a normal part of the evolution of science. The spectral lines probably seemed like the type of detail that theories typically figure out over time, but in the second half of the nineteenth century, an idea was introduced that made things worse instead of better. This idea was a theoretical object called a black body. A black body is a perfect absorber and emitter of electromagnetic radiation, and the problem was that as a black body was heated, the amount of energy given off, according to the equipartition theory and classical physics, should begin to approach infinity, with most of it in the ultraviolet spectrum and beyond. This was clearly impossible, but all attempts to resolve this problem with classical physics failed. It became known as the ultraviolet catastrophe."

"So Maxwell was wrong?" Sophia asked.

"No, no. Maxwell wasn't wrong," Hyle said, "but there was something missing about our understanding of electromagnetic energy. It turns out the theory only needed a very minor tweak, a tiny adjustment. What was surprising is that this tiny adjustment ended up changing all of physics and spilling over into philosophy and pop culture as well."

"That doesn't sound very minor," Sophia observed.

"Let me continue and you can be the judge. A physicist by the name of Max Planck was able to change the equations for light to resolve the ultraviolet catastrophe. He did this by adding a correction—a 'fudge factor.' That number, which is known as the Planck constant for obvious reasons, changes a bit depending upon the units of measure you're using, but it's so small relative to most things we measure that you have to go past the decimal point and roughly thirty zeros before you come to a digit that's not zero. Planck himself was supposedly not very happy with the solution. He solved the problem mathematically, but there was no scientific explanation for it. But if you go in the other direction and ask what the math says about the world, it says that energy isn't continuous. Energy is packaged into little bundles that can't be subdivided. It's quantized. The bundles are so tiny that they don't have any impact on most of physics, but when you get down to the atomic level and start talking about that size of particles and energy, quantum mechanics starts to make a big difference."

"Sort of like the way relativity doesn't make a difference until you hit speeds closer to the speed of light?" suggested Sophia.

"Yes, exactly."

"But how did that solve the ultraviolet catastrophe?" Newman asked. "And where does Einstein come in?"

"Planck determined that electromagnetic energy was equal to his constant times frequency—the frequency of atomic vibrations or light waves. Looking at energy in this new way, the Planck constant, as small as it is, makes the highest frequencies require too much energy to be likely to occur. This shifted the emissions from a black body out of the high frequency ultraviolet range and solved the ultraviolet catastrophe. What's more though, the Planck constant also provided the key to solving the other three problems I mentioned. Neils Bohr used the Planck constant to modify the Rutherford model of the atom, adding the restriction that electrons could no longer orbit wherever they liked but instead could only orbit at certain distances from the nucleus. The distances were a function of the Planck constant. Bohr theorized that in these stable orbits, electrons didn't vibrate or give off electromagnetic energy. They only did this when they shifted from a higher energy orbit to a lower one. These shifts explained the observance of spectral lines, and in fact the patterns of spectral lines correlated with the electrons and orbits in the atoms of different elements in Bohr's model. The stable orbits explanation also meant that electrons couldn't spiral ever closer to the nucleus and implode the atom since they were obligated to stay in their orbits. The Bohr model of the atom solved two more problems with classical physics, but again there was no explanation for why certain electron orbits were stable—it just worked out mathematically."

"So that leaves the photoelectric effect," noted Sophia. "I'm guessing that was also explained somehow by Planck's constant?"

"Yes," Hyle confirmed. "Care to guess who solved it?"

"This must be where Einstein comes in," guessed Newman.

"Yes, it was Albert Einstein," Hyle confirmed. "Planck unraveled the ultraviolet catastrophe in the year 1900. Remember that Einstein had four papers in 1905? One of them was on the photoelectric effect. In that paper, Einstein proposed that light traveled in little quantized particles, which we now call photons. Photons explain why electrons in a photoelectric cell can be discharged immediately. All they need is for a photon to collide with them. It also explains why the color of light makes a difference. Color correlates to wavelength and frequency. Remember that energy equals frequency times the Planck constant. Red light, with its high wave length and low frequency has relatively low energy. Photons of red light may not have enough energy to ever discharge atoms in a photoelectric cell. Blue light, with a short wavelength and high frequency, carries a lot of energy relative to red light. Photons of blue light are much more likely to expel electrons in a photoelectric cell and create a current with more energy. After Einstein proposed this, Compton demonstrated that light loses energy when it discharges electrons. The decrease in frequency when this happens, known as a Compton shift, is because the photons of light lose energy when they collide with electrons just like a cue ball loses energy when it collides with another billiard ball."

"Wait," Sophia interrupted. "All through your explanation of relativity you were talking about light waves. Now you're saying that light is actually a particle?"

"Yes and no. Einstein does, in fact, talk about light waves in relativity and light quanta in explaining the photoelectric effect. This is one of the confusing aspects of quantum physics. Light has properties of both a particle and a wave. At the crest of a light wave, where the wave is strongest, you're most likely to find a photon. And higher frequency waves have more energy."

"That makes sense, kind of," said Newman. "But I still don't understand how light can be a particle and a wave at the same time."

"Neither do I," Hyle confessed. "But it is."

CHAPTER SIXTY-SEVEN

THE BEST THINGS IN LIFE

Under cover of the murky shadows of impending nightfall, the trio finally set out on the road again. To the west, the rough location of the sun was marked by a blood red patch of horizon, ringed by shades of orange and purple. The remainder of the sky was a familiar oppressive brown haze, deepening into a merciful black in the east. Snow lingered on the undeveloped parcels of land, the trees and the rooftops, but a steady rain had cleared the pavement, leaving only ridges of slush here and there on the road. The wheels of the truck cut through these with a gratifying thump and heavy splatter against the wheel wells, sounding very much like progress.

Anxious to make up for lost days, they took to the interstate highway, traveling with the headlights on. Although food was beginning to run low—with only a quarter of their original stock remaining, enough for about a week—they were more concerned about covering ground before the next blizzard came, and so passed by several opportunities for scavenging in favor of a full night of driving. The plow had been removed to improve gas mileage. With the lights on and the roads increasingly clear of snow, they made good time, skirting around Indianapolis sometime around midnight. There were no signs of people anywhere.

Interstate 70 proved to be largely clear of traffic, taking them to the outskirts of St. Louis before their luck ran out. Green road signs had guided them through a maze of interstates north of the city, but it was also one of those signs that almost led them directly into the Mississippi River. It was a small one, indicated the route number and some mileage information.

"Good, 270," Newman confirmed, squinting into the darkness to read it as they approached. "We can turn south once we're past the city."

"Look out! Stop!" Sophia yelled, interrupting Hyle's reply to Newman.

What caught her attention lay just beyond the sign—a dark fissure in the pavement running in a straight line across their path. Small chunks of pavement stood upended along the edges of the crack, and beyond it the road disappeared. Hyle switched on the high beams and got out to investigate, his passengers close behind. They stood atop a trestle, beyond which the roadway canted downward, out of the illumination of the headlights. The sound of water was just discernable above the thrum of the truck's engine.

"I think that's the Mississippi down there," said Newman. "Looks like we're going to have to find another way across."

Nearly an hour later and about ten miles to the south, with the sky growing pale on the horizon, they approached the river again on another interstate that led to St. Louis and on to Tulsa. Farther south the sky started rumbling, adding urgency to the quest to find a crossing, but their luck at this bridge was no better.

A simple beam design, the bridge was composed of two separate spans, one for each direction of traffic, running side by side. Each span was broken into thirds by huge concrete piers that rose out of the river to support the roadway. The middle third was missing from both spans. Across the Mississippi, the iconic Gateway Arch of St. Louis, built to welcome travelers to the West, now only added to their frustration.

"This one's out too?" Sophia said, her disbelief evolving into concern even as she spoke.

Hyle sighed. "I was really hoping to get across the Mississippi before morning," he said. "And before the storm hits."

"It looks like that other bridge is out too," noticed Sophia, pointing down river where two trussed sections of bridge tilted down into the water.

"What do you think caused them to collapse?" Newman asked. He was working through his own suspicions, but he decided not to speak them aloud yet.

Beyond the Arch, a few tall buildings stood intact amid the jagged remains of the St. Louis skyline, just visible as a collection of dark forms against the pre-dawn sky.

"If the city was hit with a nuke, it must have been farther west," Hyle concluded. "Some of the buildings seem to have survived, so I doubt that's what knocked down the bridges. Somebody must have blown these up."

As if to emphasize the point, a low rumble rolled in from down river. "Are you sure that's thunder?" asked Sophia. "It doesn't sound quite right."

"No, it doesn't," Hyle agreed. "I think that's artillery. There's no storm coming in. We're driving closer to some place that's getting shelled."

As they sat in the truck surveying the damage, there was a howl from up the river, like a hurricane suddenly descending upon them. In the first instant it was unclear what could cause such a cataclysmic sound to rise from nowhere, but a second later two fighter jets streaked by, flying low and following the course of the river. Within seconds they were gone, the roar of their engines fading into the darkness. The boom and rumble continued to the south.

After a brief discussion the travelers decided to backtrack, turning north and accepting the risk of driving during the day to get farther away from the potential war zone. Passing the highway that had initially brought them to the area and the first blown bridge, they continued north along the beltway, covering ground quickly in the growing daylight.

Leaving behind the system of interstates that crossed and ringed the St. Louis area, they took to state roads, following the river north and west through suburbs, past the grassy slopes of towering levees, moored barges and yet another demolished bridge, before finally finding a crossing over what turned out to be the Illinois River, a tributary to the lower Mississippi. The framework of green girders that supported the narrow deck appeared undamaged and there was no sign of any guard. Crossing the bridge brought them to an immediate choice of north or south. They continued north along the west side of the river, through lightly settled areas and farmland, looking for a place to rest. Eventually they found a ranch style house on a wooded hill above the road and performed only a cursory search before surrendering to sleep.

A strange sound woke Sophia with a start. Dim light infiltrated the room around the drawn shades and curtains. Next to her, Hyle slept fitfully in the double bed, but Newman, who had lost the coin toss, seemed to be missing from the extra mattress they had dragged into the room.

"What's the matter?" mumbled Hyle in a sleep laden voice.

"What's that sound?" she whispered back, straining to decipher the hissing sound that seemed to come from somewhere within the house.

She got out of bed, stepping carefully on the mattress in case she had been wrong about Newman.

"Newman's missing," she reported, still keeping her voice low. Hyle muttered something inarticulate, and from the tone, most likely indecent, as he climbed out on the opposite side of the bed.

Cautiously they opened the bedroom door and stepped out into the main living area. The mysterious sound grew louder, clearly coming from behind the closed door adjacent to the bedroom.

"Newman?" Sophia called over the noise. "Are you taking a shower?"

A few seconds later the sound stopped abruptly. "Hello?" Newman answered from inside. "Just a minute." In far less than a minute Newman opened the door, towel around his waist, water dripping slowly from the long strands of black hair plastered to his face and shoulders. Hazy warm air billowed out of the bathroom. "That was amazing. Who wants to go next?" he asked. "There's a kerosene generator behind the house," he explained, pointing toward the low humming sound, which was now audible with the shower off. "The house has well water with an electric pump and an electric heating element on the hot water. I figured I'd try to get it going while you slept in."

"What if somebody hears the generator?" Hyle objected.

"Who's going to hear? Anybody driving by won't be able to hear it over their engine. Someone would have to be walking along the street, or maybe bicycling. When was the last time you saw that happen?"

"Fair enough," Hyle conceded. "In that case, Sophia can go next."

A while later, showered and refreshed, they all sat in the open kitchen at one end of the living area, eating provisions from the truck by the light of an incandescent bulb. They had chosen the house in part because, although it was largely obscured from the casual passerby in the street, they had noticed that the front door hung opened, suggesting that nobody currently lived inside. The drawers and cabinets had been cleared of all food and most useful supplies, but the furniture and bedclothes were untouched. With running water and electricity, it was the closest they had been to the comforts of home since the nearly forgotten days before the war.

"Let's hit the road," Hyle said as they finished their meal. "I think we're probably thirty miles or so north of St. Louis, and with the battle, or whatever is going on to the south of the city, I was thinking maybe we should find a route west to Kansas City before we head south again."

Sophia nodded, silently indicating that this seemed like a reasonable plan, but Newman just stared at the table for moment without replying.

"You know, Hyle," he began at last. "I was thinking, this is really not a bad place to stay." Hyle started to object, but Newman put up his hand. "Wait, let me finish. We may not be far enough south that we avoid snow altogether, but it should be milder here. We've got electricity and running water—well water, which should be potable and won't run out. We've got the river right across the street where we can fish and maybe salvage items that float downstream. We're surrounded by woods where we can get firewood and this is a small enough place that the fireplace could actually heat it reasonably well. The land here is fertile, so we could grow crops in the spring."

Sophia said nothing but watched Hyle with interest for his response.

"Having a hot shower was wonderful, I'll admit," he said, "but what happens when the kerosene runs out? We're having enough trouble finding gas. Imagine how hard it would be to find kerosene."

"Maybe we could build a windmill or a water turbine," Newman suggested, quickly enough that it was obvious he had thought this out in advance. "The wiring is already routed to the emergency generator, so it shouldn't be that hard to swap in a different energy source. You already told us how to do it. A generator is just an electric motor running in reverse. All we need to do is salvage an electric motor and find some blades to turn it."

Hyle shook his head but did not respond. Before he could think of a reply, Newman made a preemptory suggestion.

"How about we stay until the kerosene runs out and see? There's that town just south of the bridge where we might find a motor—we need to look for gas anyway."

"At least we'd have a comfortable place to stay while we're treasure hunting," Sophia agreed.

«« »»

It was five days later when the kerosene finally ran out. The town a few miles to the south was small, and to Newman's great disappointment, they had been unable to locate a suitable electric motor for his windmill. In fact, they had not had much luck in any category of scavenging. Most of the houses had been thoroughly looted already. There was no food anywhere, and all vehicles—including the boats docked up and down the river—had been drained of fuel. Between lawnmowers, outboard boat motors, and a single small tractor buried in a collapsed barn, they had managed to find a little more gas than they had used.

In the end, these facts did nothing to change anyone's mind. Newman was still in favor of settling down, expressing his faith that they could find suitable components for a windmill if they expanded their search, and reiterating the advantages of fresh well water, proximity to the river, fertile soil and the abundance of firewood.

"Besides," he pointed out, "if we run out of gas or get snowed in and want to give up on this place, we could just take a boat and drift down river."

"If we wanted to settle down, those would all be good reasons to stay here," Hyle agreed. "But I don't want to settle down. Not yet. I'm still convinced that your Prophet knows something about what happened and I won't be satisfied until we have a chance to confront him and find out what he knows."

"But what if you're wrong?" Newman countered. "We only have a few days of food left. You'd be gambling on finding more food on the road, not to mention gas. What if you're wrong and all that risk is for nothing?"

"There's risk no matter what we do. Maybe there are no fish in the river, or not enough to get us through the winter."

"But what if you get there and find out he had nothing to do with it? You said that this was a good place to settle down, and you'd have left that behind."

"If I'm proven wrong, I'll admit it and move on. People are adaptable. I'm sure we could find a good place to settle down there."

Sophia watched the conversation like a tennis match, saying nothing, her head moving back and forth between the two men as they spoke. Newman and Hyle, each realizing that he was unlikely to convince the other, had agreed to abide by whatever Sophia decided in the probable event that they ended up deadlocked. This could not have been more fair, since she had been going back and forth on the decision all week. She considered each argument carefully, hoping for something to tip the balance.

"Remember when we were talking about Nietzsche?" Hyle asked. "Remember the challenge that Sophia told us about—if a demon gave us a chance to relive our lives exactly as they happened, would we do it? Well, I've decided that I would, even with the war and everything. I don't want to just go along for the ride, hoping to get safely to the end. I don't have any real regrets in my life, but if I didn't chase down this mystery I'd never be satisfied with myself."

"Really? You don't have any regrets?" exclaimed Newman. "Must be nice."

"Regret is a useless emotion. I'm not saying that there aren't things I'd do differently, but I believe that if you make the best choices you can with the information you have at the time, you have nothing to be sorry for. Even if you screw up, there's no sense looking backwards and wishing you could change what can't be changed. But what you can do is you can recognize those points in your life when they come up. This is one of them. If I sit back now fishing for catfish and gathering firewood when people are out there killing each other and somebody may be conspiring to wipe out all human civilization, how could I ever be happy with my choice?"

"There's another way to look at this," Newman suggested. "Whether you believe it's just random chance or part of a higher plan, as horrible as this is, it has given humanity a fresh start. Maybe this isn't something that we're supposed to interfere with. You might write it off as coincidence, but I believe we've been spared and that it's more than good luck that brought us to this place."

"Just to play devil's advocate, if there really were some kind of divine providence, maybe we were spared specifically so that we could go confront Zendik. That would make more sense than being spared so that we could live in a cozy cottage in southern Illinois, never to be heard from again."

"But you don't believe that anyway," said Newman. "You think this is some huge global conspiracy. If it really is, what do you think will happen if you confront the Prophet? If you're right, do you think you'll just have a nice chat and talk him out of his plans and he'll just call the whole thing off?"

"I don't know," Hyle admitted. "But I have to try something. The Union of Faith has twelve cities like Asher scattered around the globe where the people inside have no idea what's going on in the world outside. The world outside has no idea what's going on in the Union of Faith. We're some of the only people alive who have seen both. I can't just forget about that and do nothing."

"The Prophet believes we're headed for the final battle between good and evil," Newman replied. "If you're going there to confront him, are you sure what side you're on?"

"I'm not convinced that the world needs to be remade according to his vision. If someone is decimating the human race, then I'm against them and on the side of humanity. I'll leave it to the theologians to figure out which side that is. Besides, that's why you need to come along—to keep me honest."

Newman sighed. He felt drawn to the house in a way that was as powerful as it was irrational, and the idea of leaving filled him with foreboding, but he had to admit the logic of Hyle's arguments.

"What do you think, Sophia?" he asked. She took a moment to gather her thoughts, although her mind had already been made up.

"I think that if there's any chance we can put an end to whatever started this war, we ought to give it a shot. With all of its flaws, I was rather fond of the world the way it was."

CHAPTER SIXTY-EIGHT

FEARFUL SYMMETRY

Night was falling as Newman said his goodbyes to the house, still uncomfortable with the decision they had made. Sophia gathered blankets and a few changes of clothing while Hyle waited impatiently at the back door. The sound of an approaching engine caused them each to stop, trading glances but not daring to speak, until the vehicle had raced by and the drone of the engine had faded into the distance.

"Figures," Hyle said as he followed the other two out the door and closed it behind them. "We stay here for almost a week without seeing a single sign of another living person and then, just as we're about to leave, some car goes tearing right past our front door, headed the same direction we're going."

"That wasn't a car though," claimed Newman. "That was a motorcycle." Sophia and Hyle traded glances. He seemed to read her thoughts.

"If it's just coincidence, they'll be long gone at the speed they were going. If someone's following us, there's not much we can do about it. Best to leave now and just keep a lookout."

"Are you sure it was a motorcycle?" asked Sophia. Newman nodded.

"It was a big engine, but it was definitely a motorcycle."

"It went by so fast all I could make out was the—I forget the term—*neeeeooooowwwmm*," said Sophia, doing her best impression of the passing vehicle.

"Doppler shift," Hyle prompted.

"That's right. I forgot the term, but I do remember that it's caused by the sound waves being compressed in front of the speeding vehicle to cause a high pitch, and stretched out behind it to cause the lower pitch, right?"

"Yes, basically. It works the same way for light too," Hyle noted, swinging himself into the driver's seat. "Have you ever heard of redshift and blueshift?"

Sophia shook her head and slid in beside Hyle as he worked the wires and got the truck started.

"Light from distant stars and galaxies gets shifted toward higher or lower frequency depending upon whether they're moving closer to us or farther away," he continued, once they were on the road. "Most galaxies show a shift toward lower frequencies. That's called 'redshift' since the light shifts toward the red end of the spectrum. The prevalence of redshift is why scientists believe the universe is expanding, because it indicates that most galaxies are moving away from us."

"Are there any instances of blueshift?" asked Sophia.

"Yes. The light waves from the edge of a spiral galaxy that's spinning toward us will have a blue shift relative to the light waves from the edge that's spinning away, for example."

"I thought light was a particle," chided Newman.

"It's a particle and a wave," Hyle answered, not entirely sure whether Newman was joking.

"You mean scientists haven't been able to figure out which one it is yet, right?" asked Sophia.

"No," Hyle replied. "They've figured it out. Light's a wave and a particle. It's both."

Hyle paused to survey the confused expressions of his two companions.

"That makes no sense," objected Sophia. "They're opposites. Light should either travel in a continuous wave or it should travel in discrete particles."

"The path up the mountain is the same as the path down the mountain," Hyle answered, trying only half-heartedly to suppress a grin.

"The road to Thebes is the road to Athens," Newman added helpfully.

Sophia glared at them both.

"Are you planning to explain this?" she demanded.

"Quantum physics is even weirder than relativity, but it all makes sense when you understand it," Hyle told her. There was a short silence while he collected his thoughts. "On second thought, I'm not sure I can promise that, but at least I could try to give you the complete picture."

"It's always good to have realistic expectations," Sophia said with a laugh.

"Historically there was always some question about whether light was a wave or a particle," Hyle explained. "Newton originally thought that light was a particle but Huygens thought it was a wave. Then around 1800 Thomas Young did an experiment that convinced most people that light was a wave. It's called a 'double slit experiment' and it's been repeated under many different conditions since he first performed it. If you take a dark surface and make two small parallel slits in it very near each other, then shine a light through the slits, onto a surface on the other side you can do this experiment. For example you could take a piece of glass, paint it black, score it with two razor blades, then shine light through this onto a wall. Now if light is a particle, you'd expect to see two separate parallel lines of light on the wall behind the slits."

"I'm not sure I'd expect to see anything in particular," Newman protested.

"Picture it as a miniature version of a carnival game," suggested Hyle. "The game has a big sheet of plywood with two slits in it—each one just about wide enough for a baseball to pass through. If you throw baseballs at the slits, some will hit the plywood and bounce off. Others will go through either one slit or the other and continue in a straight line to hit the wall. The places where they hit would be two lines, one behind each slit. Now if light is a wave, you'd get a diffraction pattern. Imagine throwing buckets of water at the two slits. Some water will splash back, but what goes through will fan out from each slit and the splash from each slit will overlap with the splash from the other slit. When you shine a light through the razor slits in your black painted glass, you should be able to tell whether light is a particle or a wave depending on whether you see two distinct lines or an interference pattern."

"You mean the same kind of interference pattern as in the Michelson-Morley experiment, where waves that align would be brighter and waves that are out of sync would be darker?" Sophia asked.

"Yes, exactly," Hyle confirmed, pleased that she had remembered those details.

"So that's what Young must have seen," she concluded.

"Right again. So for the next century most people were pretty well convinced that light was a wave. Then Einstein comes along and solves the photoelectric effect by saying that light is a particle."

"But doesn't the two-slit experiment prove that it's a wave?" Sophia asked.

"Yes, but it doesn't prove that it's not a particle," replied Hyle. "When you observe the pattern through two slits you see a wave interference pattern, but here's where it gets interesting. When you cover up one of the slits, you get the single line that you'd get from particles. If light is a wave, how can you explain that? Now you might be wondering what would happen if you used a very weak light source—something that would only emit a photon every few minutes or even hours. What pattern would show up in the two slit experiment if the photons have to be travelling one at a time through the slits?"

"I was just about to suggest that," Sophia said in a purposely unconvincing tone.

"If you use photographic film instead of the wall, you'll get a spot showing up at each place a photon interacts with the chemicals in the film. If you direct that weak light source through a single slit, a line will appear on the film, dot by dot. If you direct the light toward a double slit however, an interference pattern will develop slowly, dot by dot."

"But if a photon goes straight through a single slit, how—what—" Sophia started, but then gave up and shook her head. Newman nodded sympathetically.

"This is why quantum physics isn't merely an adjustment to classical Newtonian physics," Hyle explained. "It's a whole new way of looking at things. In a sense, the photon goes through both slits, but not in the way that a baseball goes through the hole in the plywood. Do you remember how I said that there was a higher chance of finding a photon at the peak of a wave? What that means is that sometimes you'll find one, but sometimes you won't. That's a big departure from classical physics. You don't find probabilities in classical physics."

"I think I get it!" Sophia exclaimed. "The wave diffraction pattern is like a probability distribution. The photons have more of a chance of hitting the film where you'd expect to find bright bands in the pattern and less chance where you'd expect to find dark bands."

"Exactly," Hyle confirmed.

"But wait a minute," said Sophia. "I understand how the photons could build up an interference pattern one dot at a time, but what are they interfering with if they go through the slits one at a time? There's only one photon."

"The answer is open for debate," Hyle replied, "but the most generally accepted explanation is called the Copenhagen interpretation. It's a set of rules Neils Bohr and Werner Heisenberg proposed as a result of their collaborations in Copenhagen about two decades after Einstein's paper on the photoelectric effect. The first part is Bohr's so-called complementarity principle, which says that it's necessary to use characteristics of waves and characteristics of particles to describe the nature of light, but that a given experiment will only observe one characteristic or the other. I can explain this a little more in a minute, but if it makes you feel better, one way to think of it is that light exists as a wave until it's forced to decide. If you set up an experiment to detect wave behavior you'll find a wave. If you set up an experiment to detect particle behavior you'll find a particle."

"Why can't scientists just set up some kind of detector on each slit to see which one the photon passes through?" Sophia asked.

"Have you ever heard of the Heisenberg uncertainty principle?" Hyle asked in reply.

"I've heard of it, but I don't really know what it is."

"How would you detect a photon? It's the smallest quantum of electromagnetic energy. If it interacts with anything that could detect it—whether it's a photographic film or a human eye—it'll be absorbed in the process. If you try to detect it through collision—like with electrons in a photoelectric cell—you'll change its path or energy. That's true for electrons and subatomic particles too by the way. These are such small quantities of matter that any attempt to detect their nature actually changes part of their nature. The Heisenberg uncertainty principle states that you can't know all the properties of a quantum system at any one time because the mere act of observing the system will change it. This is radically different from the clockwork universe of classical physics where every force and every particle was thought to be traceable back through history."

"Observation is supposed to be the basis of science," Newman noted. "With every-thing in quantum physics being probabilistic and uncertain, doesn't that raise questions about the very nature of science?"

"Not really," Hyle replied quickly. "It did force a change in how science views the world at the most fundamental level, but quantum physics doesn't really change any of the mechanics of Newtonian physics at the macroscopic level. Remember, most of the things we deal with every day are composed of gazillions of atoms. If you flip a coin it's very uncertain whether it'll land on heads or tails. If you flip a billion coins I can tell you with a high degree of certainty that half will land on heads and half will land on tails. It might not be exact down to the last penny, but it'll be half to as many decimal places as you're likely to ever care about. Quantum physics can actually be described very accurately by equations and mathematical models. They're just based on probability. When you have a large enough system of atoms and electrons, the uncertainty decreases to the point that you arrive back at classical physics."

"I still don't get what's happening with the photon and the two slits though," said Sophia. "How can you explain that with an equation?"

"Quantum physics uses a wave equation, which describes the chances of all the various possibilities for the photon. In the two slit experiment the wave equation would predict a high probability of finding the photon impacting the film where the interference pattern is bright and a low probability where it's dark. At the instant of detection the wave equation is said to 'collapse' to a single possibility. Before that though, you can't even really talk about a photon at all—it's just a collection of unrealized possibilities described by the wave equation."

"If a tree falls in the forest and nobody's there to hear it, does it make a sound?" Newman suggested.

"Yes, something like that. In the quantum physics version the tree exists as both fallen and unfallen and in various states of falling until it's observed. When you observe it, odds are highest that the wave equation will collapse around it being a standing tree or a fallen tree, but there's a small chance that the wave equation will collapse around the tree in a state of falling. Then it will make a sound."

"This is a lot like Aristotle's idea of perception," Sophia noted. "The potential in objects is actualized by the event of observation."

"Except with Aristotle, the properties of objects were an inherent part of the object," Newman added. "With quantum physics it seems that everything is random."

"Not random," Hyle corrected. "Probabilistic. By the way, Einstein hated the Copenhagen interpretation of quantum physics. It was just this type of thinking that led him to make his famous quote about not believing that God would play dice with the universe."

"This just applies to tiny things like photons and electrons though, right?" Sophia asked. "The tree was just an analogy?"

Hyle did not answer right away. "This is where things get interesting," he said.

"Things already got interesting a while ago, remember?" Newman pointed out.

"You keep using that word," Sophia added. "I do not think it means what you think it means."

Hyle gave Sophia an admiring smile. "Even more interesting. How's that?" he amended. "A young doctoral student named Louis de Broglie decided that if waves can be described as matter, then matter should be able to be described as waves. He was able to derive equations for so-called matter waves, which are the same type of probability equations that we discussed for photons and electrons, so in principle everything is governed by the same type of probabilistic equations."

"So I could pass through two doorways at the same time just as long as nobody was looking?" Sophia challenged.

"I don't know about that, but theoretically you could walk through a wall," Hyle answered. "Atoms are mostly empty space. If the size of an atom, as determined by the orbit of its electrons, were as big as a football stadium, the nucleus would be about the size of the ball and the electrons would be something like mosquitoes flying around the bleachers. Theoretically if all the electrons in all the atoms of your body shifted in just the right way at just the right time, you could walk through a solid wall."

Sophia laughed and started to object, but Hyle stopped her.

"That actually happens at the quantum level. It's called electron tunneling. People who design circuit boards for computers have to be careful because if they make the circuits too close together electrons that are supposed to be in one part of the circuit can actually appear in a circuit next door. They don't actually tunnel through the material between the circuits, of course. It's the wave equation that determines where you'll find the electron. The probability centers on it being in the circuit, but there's some small chance it'll be found outside the circuit. If there's another circuit close enough, it can be actualized in that circuit where it's not supposed to be and cause problems."

"If that's true, why can't I walk through walls?" pressed Sophia.

"It goes back to the billion coins analogy. The odds that all the electrons in all the atoms in your body would do exactly what you needed makes it statistically so improbable that it might as well be impossible—like the odds of a billion coins all landing on heads. Even bacteria are far too huge to move through solid walls. On the other hand, there's a way to tie the high level of uncertainty of the quantum level back to the macroscopic world. It's a scenario proposed by the physicist Erwin Schrödinger."

"Schrödinger's cat?" Sophia guessed.

"Are you familiar with it?" asked Hyle.

"Somewhat, but I don't really understand it," she confessed.

Newman shook his head slowly. He recognized the reference, but had never heard it explained.

"Imagine that you put a cat in a box along with a radioactive element, a Geiger counter and a special container," Hyle said. "Geiger counters detect particles that are emitted from radioisotopes as they decay and usually transfer that detected energy to an audible click for each particle. Instead of clicking though, this Geiger counter has been wired to send a signal that releases a hammer, which in turn smashes a vial and releases cyanide gas. If you close the lid on the box, the cat will be trapped inside with this device and will live only until the first radioactive particle decays and is detected by the Geiger counter. Then the container will be smashed open and the cyanide gas will kill the cat."

"I hope nobody has actually done this experiment," Newman said.

"No, it's a thought experiment. There would be no point in doing it, as you'll see in a moment," Hyle assured him. "Let's say that the radioisotope in this scenario emits particles about every two hours on average. If you check the box in one hour, there's a roughly even chance that the cat will be alive or dead. Whether or not a particle decays is determined by a wave equation though, so until someone opens the box and observes the system, the state of the entire system is in what's called a 'superposition state' where it's governed by the wave equation and all possibilities are still undetermined, so the cat in the box is both alive and dead. Once the box is opened and the contents observed, the wave equation collapses, the particle is determined to have decayed or not decayed and the cat is determined to be alive or dead. To the outside observer, it's just a fifty-fifty chance of finding the cat alive or dead. The interesting question is what's happening in that box for the hour that nobody outside observes it."

"That seems like Zeno's paradox to me," Newman objected. "Something that makes logical sense, but is clearly not true. There must be a better explanation than the cat being both alive and dead."

"No. As crazy as that sounds, that's the Copenhagen interpretation of quantum physics and it's still the most widely accepted interpretation by far. There were a few famous dissenters from this interpretation though—Einstein and Schrödinger to name a few. Schrödinger is the scientist who developed the wave equation in the first place and won the Nobel Prize in 1933 for his work. He proposed this scenario to question the Copenhagen interpretation by demonstrating that it led to ridiculous consequences."

"And he did an admirable job," Sophia said. "So why do scientists still believe the Copenhagen interpretation?"

"Let me answer that with another scenario that's a little more technical. It involves a concept called quantum entanglement. Quantum physics led to particle physics and the discovery that protons, neutrons and electrons, which had been thought to be the most basic particles, are actually made up of smaller subatomic particles. You've probably heard of the quark, which is one of many types of subatomic particles that group together to form the atomic particles."

"I've heard the term, but I didn't know exactly what they were," Sophia replied. "So they make up protons, neutrons and electrons?"

"Yes," Hyle confirmed. "Quarks are held together by a property called spin, the same way that protons and electrons are held together in the atom by what we call charge. Given enough energy, you can blow these particles apart and send the quarks flying off in different directions. That's the type of thing they do in supercolliders in order to learn about subatomic particles. When the particles separate, they retain their opposing spins, so their properties are 'entangled.'"

"Before you go on," interrupted Sophia, "I'm not sure I quite get what you mean by that."

"Imagine that I have two gears that mesh and spin together," Hyle explained. "One spins clockwise and the other spins counterclockwise. If I pull them apart and tell you that the one in my right hand is spinning clockwise, what could you tell me about the one in my left hand?"

"It must be spinning counterclockwise," replied Sophia. "Okay, I get it now."

"The key is that, because of the Heisenberg uncertainty principle, the spin of each particle isn't determined until it's observed," Hyle continued. "In 1935, the EPR paper by Einstein, Podalsky and Rosen used quantum entanglement to demonstrate that the Copenhagen interpretation of quantum physics violates one of the principles of relativity. If you break apart a pair of these subatomic particles and allow them to travel in opposite directions, and then measure the spin of one of them, thereby collapsing the wave equation for that particle around a particular spin, according to the Copenhagen interpretation you'd have to believe that you also instantly and simultaneously collapse the wave equation of the other particle to the opposite spin, even if it's hundreds or even millions of miles away. This would require information to travel faster than the speed of light—something that's forbidden in relativity in order to prevent problems with the order of events and causality in different frames of reference. Einstein called this instant resolution of quantum entanglement 'spooky action at a distance.' The alternative, which Einstein favored, is that the spins were determined all along and the uncertainty of the wave equation is an incorrect thesis of quantum physics."

"That's favored by me too," remarked Sophia, "in case you were wondering."

"Unfortunately, your opinion is several decades too late to matter. Quantum entanglement was just a thought experiment, like Schrödinger's cat, until 1964 when Bell's theorem was introduced. Bell developed a mathematical method that demonstrated that between those two alternative explanations there was a statistical difference which could be measured. In 1982, Alain Aspect figured out how to actually perform such an experiment. The results suggest that Einstein was wrong. It seems that the spin of paired subatomic particles really is undetermined until that property is measured for one of them, thereby instantly determining it for both."

"So to summarize," said Sophia, "according to modern science, time and space are no longer constant, many straight lines can pass through two points, light can be a wave or a particle—depending upon what you're looking for, you can never know all the properties of subatomic particles, cats are alive or dead until they're observed, and information travels instantly across the universe. Did I miss anything?"

"I think that covers the basics," Hyle said, laughing.

Newman shook his head.

"I'm beginning to really appreciate Newton," he said.

CHAPTER SIXTY-NINE

THE DREAM OF ARIADNE

Concealed in shadow, high walls rose up on either side. How far up they ended she was unable to tell, but a faint gray light filtered down from somewhere above. Cold concrete, they were streaked with the stains of dripping water. Moving forward cautiously but steadily, she walked and walked some more. Time behaved strangely here. She felt that she had been walking for hours, maybe days, yet could not remember the passage of time. She was not tired. Pressing forward, she waited for understanding to come.

The sky grew lighter over time. It had been the sky all along she realized, dark and overcast and backlit by the moon, but now the sun was rising. The sky seemed closer now too. The walls were shorter. What had been concrete in the night was now something less solid in the light. Something... not walls at all, she recognized. She was in a corn field with huge rows of stalks on either side, almost twice her height, dark and irregular with gaps of light gray light between them. Walking on, she came to a gap where another corn row merged in from an oblique angle before curving out of sight. Something rustled in that direction. Quickly she passed it by, only to come upon a similar gap, and then one on the other side, before arriving at a place where a wall of stalks blocked her way, marking the end of the path. Not a cornfield—a corn maze.

Recalling the story of Theseus in the labyrinth of the Minotaur, Sophia was just wishing that she had a thread to show her the way out when she realized that the walls on either side bent away at right angles, creating a path in each direction along this new wall. In the three-way intersection was an object. Drawing closer, Sophia could see that what had at first appeared to be a sundial was actually a compass of a sort. Even in the dull gray light from the sky, a shadow was visible behind the gnomon. When she rotated the horizontal surface of the dial until the shadow pointed at the word 'morning,' the compass told her that she had approached from the east and could now choose between north and south. Without hesitation she chose south and resumed walking.

Some uncertain time later, after passing several paths to either side, she arrived at another tee intersection. Again there was an object, but she could not make it out until she got very close. It was roughly the same size as the sundial but very different—metal, bright red with yellow and green and black. She could make out a large wheel sticking up. It was a tractor—a child's riding toy that had been knocked over on its side. A bright yellow seat hovered between two large wheels on one end of the red body and pedals stuck out near the base of the other end. There at the end of the path it marked another choice, right or left. Sophia puzzled at this. The tractor, before being tipped over, would have been headed left. She chose that direction.

Continuing onward she passed more paths to either side and again came to the end of the row with a choice of turning right or left. Once again there was an object in the intersection. This one was a doll house. It was large. It would have stood taller than Sophia except that it had been broken apart—reduced almost to rubble. It looked as though it had been sheared diagonally from the roofline on the left to the bottom on the opposite side, leaving the first floor largely intact. A fragment of the second floor remained in the back corner with a splintered wall jutting up around it. A perfectly intact living room set and model television circled a coffee table on a braided rug, but amid the rubble of the upper floor, beds, dressers and miniature clothing were strewn about the ground among fragments of wall and floor. The roof lay overturned a few feet farther away. Sophia took in all this detail in a few seconds, but the sight disturbed her for reasons she could not quite identify. Choosing a new direction quickly, she turned right, putting the ruined doll house behind her.

Time continued to behave erratically, bringing her, after some interval of minutes or hours, to a new object to mark the end of her path, far bigger than all the others. It spanned the width of the path and was as tall as the walls of corn. More rustling sounds issued from the other side of the corn row and Sophia got the distinct feeling that she was being watched. As she hurried closer to the object, she determined that it was a small booth, like a guard shack. Or a toll booth. It blocked her way entirely, save for a small gap to the right. In this opening between the wall of the shack and the wall of corn stalks, two translucent panels hovered, filling the space from ankle to waist high, very much like a subway. There was a man in the booth. Sophia studied him as she approached, and he watched her, smiling amiably.

"Curiouser and curiouser," she said to herself, surveying the booth and toll gate. There was no place for a token or a pass card. The man, noting her puzzlement, leaned forward and adjusted the flexible neck of the microphone on his counter.

"Where are you going, Sophia?" he asked in a tinny voice from the other side of the green glass.

The question took her by surprise. For one thing, she could not remember telling him her name. But time was moving so strangely that she could not be sure she had not already spoken with him. Somewhere in the back of her mind she had known all along, but now she was fully conscious, that this was a dream. In this part of the dream it had not been established whether this was the beginning or middle of their conversation. But the question bothered her for another reason. It seemed to be a broader question than just a curiosity about her travel plans. It made her wonder where she was heading in her life. What was her purpose? Why was she in this place? Some parts of it were vaguely familiar. She felt as though she were missing something important.

"That way," she said absently, pointing across the gate while puzzling through her thoughts. "To the south."

"Of course you're going to the south dear," the man said gently, "but what is your final destination?"

Somehow in the way of dreams Sophia knew immediately that this question was the reason she was here. With this question the mental balance shifted. Although Sophia still wondered at the philosophical implications of the question, she now understood that the man's interest was literal, and suddenly she did not trust him. Without changing its appearance, his friendly smile transformed into something smug and sinister, and she knew with that same dream-certainty that she had come the wrong way. She felt trapped by her own stupidity. How could she turn back? She would look like a fool to have come all this way only to turn around and retrace her steps. Clearly people were supposed to pass through the gate. What would the man think if she turned back? Was it even allowed?

She almost decided to answer the question and pass through the gate despite her misgivings, but somehow she could not bring herself to speak the words. A debate broke out between two lines of thinking.

"Why should I care what this man thinks? Who cares if I look foolish? Turn around. Go back," said the one.

"Don't rock the boat," said the other voice. "Go through the gate the way everyone else does. Face up to your fears and stop being foolish."

"That man isn't what he seems," argued the first voice. "Don't play into his hands. Who knows what he'll do if you answer his question?"

"Who knows what he'll do if you don't?"

Sophia turned and looked back the way she came. She felt as though she had traveled a tremendous distance and yet she could see the broken doll house down the path. Perhaps it was not so foolish to turn back. She took a step in that direction, resolving to tell the man that her destination had changed, but she never did, because at that moment a massive dark shape appeared near the doll house, filling the path.

An improbably large black bear entered the intersection and turned in her direction. It paused, raising its snout to sniff the air, then moved along the path toward her at a deliberate pace.

Sophia looked back at the gate and wondered if the man would open it for her now. She did not think so. She wondered if she could jump the gate and at the same time was still afraid of what lay beyond it. She looked back up the path.

The bear charged.

In a moment of inspired desperation Sophia turned to her right and plunged through the corn row wall. Beyond it was a tightly planted field of corn. Stocks and leaves obscured her view, limiting her to only a few feet of visibility. She plowed forward, running as hard as she could, warding the plants away from her face. The bear emitted an angry roar and gave pursuit. Sophia could hear it behind her—a continuous low growl punctuated by the pounding of its gigantic feet on the ground. It sounded like it was right behind her, but she dared not risk breaking her stride to look back. She fled through the corn field with the bear at her heels, never gaining, never falling behind, until the field ended suddenly, giving way to a city street.

People thronged the sidewalk, jostling each other as they hurried along on their business. Beyond the curb, taxi cabs blared their horns in a futile attempt to ward off traffic congestion, and across the street another sidewalk filled with people was bordered by small shops and brownstones. Sophia pushed her way into the crowd on the sidewalk and hurried along with it for a while before daring to turn back. The last thing she saw was a puzzled bear on the sidewalk, searching the crowd for her in vain while people stepped casually around it.

Waking, Sophia found herself in the cold cab of a truck with Hyle sleeping to her left and Newman to her right. He was awake and quietly eating a granola bar. Memories of the conscious world came flooding back to her. She remembered driving for hours in a drizzling rain, trying to find a crossing over a second river which had turned out to be the actual Mississippi, talking for most of the night as usual before finally closing her eyes. She looked outside. The sky ahead was lit with a dim brown light which grew lighter and orange at the horizon to the left. To the right the sky was still dark. Somewhere outside there was a low thrumming sound that reminded her of the bear growling as it chased her, except that this noise was fading away into the distance. It sounded like a motorcycle.

CHAPTER SEVENTY

THE ENDS OF LOGIC

Every part of her body was numb when Sophia woke. It was late afternoon and the cold of the outside world had managed to find its way through the blanket that covered her and seep into every extremity. The only thing that did not seem to be frozen was her stomach, which ached. Hyle and Newman were both outside, leaning against the fender of the truck and talking. Sophia rummaged through the stores behind the seat, selected an individual sized box of raisin bran, and slid out of the cab to join them.

"We were just enjoying the nice weather," Hyle said. There was an odd mix of sarcasm and sincerity in his voice.

"I'm still cold," Sophia responded.

Although notably less frigid than it had been in the northeast, it was by no means warm.

"At least the rain has stopped," offered Newman.

Sophia looked up at the sky. The black storm clouds were indeed gone, but the omni-present brown-gray haze still covered the sky from one flat horizon to the other.

"Wasn't the sky blue once upon a time?" she asked.

"Somebody got up on the wrong side of the truck," Newman observed. "What's put you in such a bad mood?"

Shaking some dry cereal out into her palm and tossing it into her mouth, she chewed as she considered the question.

"I didn't realize it was so obvious," she said.

Just below the surface of her conscious thoughts, beyond the cold and hunger, there was anger and frustration. She recalled waking briefly in the morning and then remembered her dream. The dream had disturbed her—that was part of the problem. The motorcycle was another part. Newman claimed to have heard nothing, even though she could still hear the sound fading away after his reply. The men clearly thought she was crazy back at Colgate when she had seen Auld and they had not. How could she tell them she was hearing phantom motorcycles and having vivid lucid dreams? Certainly this was the source of her frustration, but it ran even deeper. It was not just the fear that Hyle and Newman would think her crazy if she shared these things with them—it was the fear that they might be right. They both watched her, waiting for an answer.

"I don't know," she lied. "I just feel lost." True enough. She felt her eyes welling up and fought to hold back tears. "I just had a bad dream and it was so realistic—" her voice caught and she stopped to control her breathing. "It was so realistic, and the real world seems so wrong, and I—I don't know where I'm going. I don't even know what's real sometimes. I've been hearing things—"

"It's okay," Newman said, and he reached to put a calming hand on her shoulder. "You're just rattled from having a bad dream. That's all."

"No!" Sophia jumped back from Newman's hand as if his touch were poisonous and then shook her head apologetically. "No, it's more than that. It's everything."

"Look, Sophia, we understand," Newman insisted. "We're all lost. I'm sure we all have some survivor's guilt to contend with. The lives we knew are gone and we're trying to figure out how to start things over. It's okay to be shaken up and confused from time to time, but things will settle down and you'll feel better."

"What's real is real," Hyle added. "You'll figure it out over time. If you were able to survive Berkeley, Hume, Schopenhauer and Kant, this is just a speed bump."

In spite of herself, Sophia laughed.

"What's real is real," she repeated thoughtfully. "You may laugh, Hyle, but your relativity and quantum physics are no help. I actually care about things like that. That's why I took so much philosophy in college. I felt that science had the material world pretty well figured out and I was interested in philosophy to learn about metaphysics. Now I learn that in modern science everything is relative and uncertain. It doesn't help."

"The same thing I said about Descartes applies here though," Hyle said. "Nobody really doubts whether or not they exist. It's the same for physics. You can go back to Newtonian physics and that'll get you through life just fine. The average person doesn't worry about things at the quantum level or at the speed of light."

"The average person doesn't care about metaphysics either. But I do."

"There are all sorts of New Age interpretations of quantum physics to be had," Hyle told her, "but if you want to get back to reality, go back to your philosophers like James. Truth is what's useful day to day."

"I don't know," Newman objected. "Pragmatism leaves me cold." He looked at Sophia who nodded slowly in agreement.

"Quantum physics has been around long enough that someone must have developed a philosophy to account for it that's based on materialism and logic," suggested Hyle.

"I suppose analytical philosophy might qualify," Sophia said. "I'm not sure that it was developed in response to quantum physics, but it's certainly based on materialism and logic and I suspect that the minds behind quantum physics and the school of analytical philosophy were all influenced by some common ideas. Now that I think of it, the entire endeavor makes more sense in light of your history of quantum physics."

"Really? How's that?" asked Hyle, secretly pleased to see the old Sophia back so quickly.

"The equations of quantum physics yielded some very strange conclusions," she answered. "In places where the mathematics seems to conflict with common sense, it would be natural to question why scientists tend to believe mathematics."

"And analytical philosophy answered that?" asked Hyle.

"That was its goal, yes," confirmed Sophia. "Analytical philosophy has its roots in work done by the German mathematician Gottlob Frege on logic in the late eighteen hundreds. Frege developed symbolic logic, which essentially changed logic from an exercise in human thinking and common sense into something that could be represented precisely and mathematically, independent from human thinking. What Frege hoped to do was demonstrate that mathematics could be derived from logic. This pre-dates quantum physics and I wonder if it didn't enable it in a way."

"Why do you say that?" asked Newman. "Seems like symbolic logic makes things more concrete while quantum physics does the opposite."

"Mathematics is very structured and logical," Sophia agreed, "but everything in math starts with some premise that has to be assumed, so in a way it's just out there on its own, not connected to reality. There had been a philosophical debate about whether math was just a reflection of human thought—how we structure and understand the world, along the lines of Kant's belief—or whether it was somehow independent of human thought. If math could be demonstrated to be based on logic it would be anchored in truths that transcend the structure of the human mind."

"Isn't it enough to know that math always works?" asked Hyle.

"Pragmatically, yes," agreed Sophia. "But I think most people assume that math is somehow logically true, independent of humanity, sort of like what the realists believed about universals. Science has always used mathematics to describe nature. Look at your examples, from Copernicus and Newton, who found new explanations for how nature worked by developing equations to match their observations. Same for Lorentz, Planck and Bohr. But in some cases, like Maxwell and de Broglie, who were looking for mathematical symmetry, and Einstein who changed his entire perspective to make sense of the Lorentz equation, it almost seems that the math comes first and then nature is made to fit the equation. I wonder if scientists would have put so much stock in math as a description of nature if they didn't believe it to have an independent reality, impartial and disconnected from human psychology."

"Did Frege succeed in establishing mathematics on the basis of logic?" Hyle asked.

"No, but he broke lots of new ground in the effort and opened the door for Bertrand Russell and Alfred North Whitehead. Russell is arguably the most influential philosopher of the twentieth century. He laid out the claim at the start of the century that arithmetic and probably all of mathematics could be based on logic. Then with Whitehead he published the *Principia Mathematica* from 1910 to 1913 in three huge books where they developed the proofs."

"So they succeeded?" Hyle guessed.

"Not exactly," Sophia said. "It looked as if they might have until 1931 when Gödel published his incompleteness theorem. His theorem demonstrated that any logical system would either be too weak or incomplete to explain mathematics, or it would necessarily contain contradictions. The demonstration of this is very similar to the Liars Paradox wherein I make the statement, 'I am lying.' That statement can never be true. Gödel constructed the same type of statement in formal logic, effectively using the tools of formal logic to demonstrate that the effort to build an entire mathematics based on logic wasn't possible. The effort to build mathematics on a foundation of logic actually ended up calling into question the logic and consistency of mathematics itself."

"In that case, why do you say that Bertrand Russell is so influential?" asked Hyle.

"First of all, someone doesn't need to be one hundred percent right to be influential," Sophia pointed out. "The theories of Newton may have been supplanted by those of Einstein, but I'm sure you wouldn't debate Newton's influence. And although the quest to anchor mathematics on logic ultimately fell short, it changed the focus of philosophy for the better part of the twentieth century. Even if that were all Russell did he would have had a huge influence. But he also applied the same analytical approach to language. One of the revelations of this work was that many of the problems we initially think of as philosophical problems are actually just problems with misuse of language."

"With so many philosophers writing in different languages, it's hard to imagine that none of them noticed something like that before," noted Newman.

"Not really," Sophia told him. "It was the development of symbolic logic that helped clear up some of the issues that are common to all language. For example, if I tell you that bulls have two horns, is that a meaningful statement?"

"I suppose so," answered Newman. "I'm not sure quite what you mean."

"Would you say that it conveys information?" Sophia clarified.

"Yes."

"And if I say that unicorns have one horn would you say that statement is meaningful too?"

"Yes," Newman replied, a little more slowly.

"And that's the way our language makes it appear," she agreed. "The problem of course is that unicorns aren't real. If I were to construct this sentence in symbolic logic, it would translate to something like, 'There exists such a thing as a unicorn and that thing has one horn.' When I phrase it that way it becomes clear that this statement is false and nonsensical. We get into trouble because, when we use words that describe things, most of those things correlate to objects we can experience in the real world, and our language builds in that assumption. Then when we talk about something like unicorns, that built-in assumption confuses us into believing that they exist simply because the word exists."

Hyle waved his hand excitedly to interrupt. "Wait, who was it that argued that God must exist because we can imagine him?"

Newman sighed. "That was Anselm's ontological proof," he said, knowing exactly where this was headed.

"If you apply this logic to Anselm's proof," Hyle continued, "you'd say, 'There exists such a thing as a god and it's perfect.' Then it would be clear that you're granting the property of existence to something you're able to imagine, just like you grant a horn to something you can imagine, even if neither actually happens to exist."

"There's an entire movement of philosophy that would agree with you, Hyle," said Sophia. "Have you ever heard of logical positivism or the Vienna Circle?"

Both men shook their heads.

"The Vienna Circle was a group of philosophers that gathered in Vienna in the 1920s and included Rudolf Carnap, Moritz Schlick, Otto Neurath, Hans Hahn and several others, including Kurt Gödel. They were heavily influenced by the *Tractatus Logico-Philosophicus* by Ludwig Wittgenstein, who in turn was influenced by, and studied with, Bertrand Russell. The *Tractatus*, which became a hugely popular and influential book while Wittgenstein was still quite young, essentially argued that all the problems with philosophy were actually language problems, and that if we could just understand language thoroughly, all these problems would resolve themselves and disappear. The Vienna Circle took up this banner, and their brand of philosophy became known as logical positivism."

"You mean to say that all the great debates of classical philosophy are just questions of semantics?" asked Newman, clearly skeptical.

"Their argument was that for something to be philosophically meaningful it has to be a logically positive statement," Sophia explained, "positive in this case meaning true. If the truth or falsehood of a statement couldn't be verified by correlation to what we observe in the real world, the logical positivists believed that there was no sense discussing it. It was literally nonsensical. They attempted to resolve statements clearly into three categories—logical truths which are absolute, empirical truths which are probabilistic, and opinion which is relative. To the logical positivist, things like Plato's forms or Kant's noumenal world are the philosophical equivalent of unicorns and dragons. They sound real because of the way we use language, but they have no bearing on the real world."

"But that presupposes that verifiability through physical experience should be the sole criterion for determining what's real," Newman objected. "That's not a philosophical development. It's merely a tool for empiricists to be more precise about their philosophy, just like science is."

"The logical positivists were very enamored of science," Sophia acknowledged, "but they were focused on philosophy. A.J. Ayer argued quite strongly that the goal of logical positivism should be to entirely eliminate metaphysics from philosophy. Carnap said something similar. Even Willard Van Orman Quine, who did more to undermine the logical positivists than anyone else in his day, agreed that the goal of modern philosophy ought to be the elimination of metaphysics in favor of the study of language and symbolic systems."

"How did Quine undermine logical positivism?" asked Newman.

"Generally, he argued against the sharp distinctions that are necessary for logical positivism to succeed. For example, Carnap had embarked on a project to describe objects symbolically, to try to free science from debates about epistemology, similar to the project to base mathematics on logic. In his system an apple could be objectively described as being round, red, sweet, hard, and so on. The problem, as Quine pointed out, came when you tried to describe location, which ultimately can't be objective—it has to be relative to something else. Another example is Quine's observation that there are problems with the distinction between analytic and synthetic statements."

"Really?" Hyle asked. "That seems like a fundamental part of logic."

"Yes," Sophia agreed, "but Quine noted that analytic statements, which are supposed to be independent of experience, can really be understood only through language-based concepts that are learned through experience. You might argue that it's impossible for a bachelor to be married, but that's based on a contextual understanding of the term 'bachelor.' We only know that bachelors are unmarried because that's the way we use the word in language. There's nothing inherently logical about it, or even permanent. The definition of words can evolve over time."

"Isn't that the whole point of using symbolic logic though?" Hyle suggested. "Every-day language may be vague or subject to change, but it should be possible to pick specific definitions and nail them down in a logical language."

"That's not as easy as it sounds," Sophia replied. "How would you define the word 'game,' Hyle?"

"A game is—" he paused to think through a good definition. "A game is an activity where two or more parties compete according to a predetermined set of rules."

"So would warfare be considered a game," asked Sophia, "if both armies adhered to the Geneva Conventions?"

"I should have said, 'Where two or more parties compete for fun,'" Hyle amended.

"Is professional football played for fun?" countered Sophia. "For that matter, is solitaire not a game just because it doesn't involve more than one person? If children play catch, is it not a game because they're not competing?"

"You can probably find examples that challenge any definition of many words," Hyle admitted, "but that doesn't mean that they don't have a commonly understood meaning."

"The game example is one that Wittgenstein used," Sophia said. "Back when his *Tractatus* was first inspiring the logical positivists, he ascribed to the picture theory of words. In that theory a word is just a label or picture that stands for something in the real world, but he abandoned this idea later in his career. His *Philosophical Investigations* was published posthumously and often contradicts the *Tractatus*. He came to regard words as being less rigidly defined—more like tools that could be used differently in different situations. Wittgenstein explained this with the analogy of a family resemblance. That is, someone in a family may have several physical traits—eyes, hair, nose, build, freckles and whatnot—that make them look like their mother and their father and their sisters and brothers, but it may be a different set of traits in each case. They can all resemble each other even if there's no single trait that every one of them has in common. A concept like 'game' works the same way."

"That must have been a significant roadblock for the logical positivists," noted Newman.

"Yes," Sophia confirmed, "and it only gets worse from there. Forget about complex concepts like justice—or even bachelor or game—there are problems even with the most basic words. Wittgenstein believed that we only understand words through their use."

"Why is that so different from saying that we learn words through experience?" asked Hyle.

"Consider Avicenna's flying man," said Sophia. "If you opened a portal and let him observe a city, would he see buildings and cars and people? Would he hear taxi horns and people talking? Or would he just experience an incomprehensible blur of colors and sounds? Even if he watched long enough to realize that yellow blotches move by in similar patterns, and eventually came to observe what we call a taxi, what would cause him to ever assign a label or word to it? To what end if there was nobody to talk to? Wittgenstein concluded that words gain meaning only through use. The point is that language is an inherently public activity and not something that someone can derive simply from their own empirical experiences. Furthermore, words and language require a shared context. Wittgenstein said, 'If a lion could talk, we could not understand him,' because of course we don't share the life experience of a lion to be able to make any sense of his view of the world."

"It sounds like Wittgenstein did to language what Einstein did to physics," Newman observed. "He made everything relative."

"I never thought about it that way," replied Sophia, "but it's not a bad analogy. Quine shared a similar view of language, and both philosophers tied language closely to knowledge. Another of Wittgenstein's famous sayings is, 'The limits of my language mean the limits of my world,' and Quine pointed out that a language can only be fully understood by translating it into the context of a richer language. The way we learn foreign languages is by translating all the terms and phrases into our own native language."

"But then how can we fully understand our native language?" asked Newman.

"Exactly the point," agreed Sophia. "We can't, which is why language is understood only in the context of mutual experience, and that always leaves a little room for doubt and disagreement. Quine extended this concept to all knowledge in general. Building on the pragmatism of James and Dewey, he explained epistemology as a 'web of belief' in which every concept we have is tied to other concepts. When we're introduced to a new concept that conflicts with our existing knowledge, we must choose whether to reject it, or to displace something from our web and rebuild that section of the web around the new belief. That's partly why Ockham's Razor appeals to us."

"Because a simpler idea will do less damage to our web of belief," Hyle realized aloud, completing the thought. "A simpler explanation requires less rebuilding than a complex one."

"Exactly," acknowledged Sophia. "Further, ideas that exist on the fringes of your web may be only connected loosely to a few ideas and easily displaced, but the ones that are fundamental to the way you see the world will be close to the center and difficult to change. For example, I don't know much about dinosaurs, so if Hyle corrected one of my beliefs about dinosaurs, I'd probably just switch to the new belief without thinking much of it. On the other hand, I'd have a tough time abandoning the idea of cause and effect, even in the face of a really compelling argument, because so much of my experience is built around it."

"Like the idea that time and space aren't constant?" suggested Newman. "Every time I try to really think about that, I can feel my web of belief ripping right down the middle."

CHAPTER SEVENTY-ONE

FLYING WITHOUT INSTRUMENTS

Realizing she had fallen asleep, Sophia jerked herself suddenly upright, lifting her head from Hyle's shoulder. Newman was dead to the world with his head against the window, but Hyle was awake, leaning over the wheel and staring into a night lit only by the amber glow of the running lights. A dashed line to the left of the truck and a solid line to the right were the only features that could be clearly discerned.

"Sorry, Hyle, I didn't mean to fall asleep on you. How long was I out?"

"I don't know. Maybe an hour," he replied. "You drooled on my shoulder by the way. It's okay though," he added with a laugh. "We should probably find a place to stop and sleep soon but I want to see if we can get a bit farther before dawn."

Despite Hyle's good humor Sophia felt guilty about falling asleep. Newman had announced his intentions to take a nap and it fell to her to keep Hyle awake and entertained as he drove.

"I just want to get through this next town," Hyle said, pointing at a sign. "Then we can stop." Sophia was unable to make out the text in time, but the white letters looked like the name of a town followed by some roundish single digit of mileage.

They played the restaurant game for a while—a game in which one person played the food critic who named two ingredients that did not go well together. The other person played the chef who had to work them into a three course meal in which each ingredient was used in at least two dishes. The goal was to think up appetizing dishes and describe them in such detail that the food critic was forced to give your restaurant a good review. Newman refused to participate. Since they were restricted to a limited supply of cold boxes and cans of food in real life, he not only found it to be perverse, but also complained enough to ruin the fun, forcing Hyle and Sophia to play it only when he was asleep.

"Peaches and sauerkraut," Sophia suggested. "I hate sauerkraut," she added with a grin.

After thinking for a few minutes Hyle offered a sauerkraut soup with potatoes and kielbasa to start. For the main course, he concocted a quiche with sour cream to mute the bitterness of the sauerkraut and bacon and peaches to add some savory and sweet flavor. Hyle was of the opinion that every dish could be improved by the addition of bacon. To cap it off, Hyle described a dessert bowl of peaches in cottage cheese and cream with honey.

Sophia only gave him three stars, but her stomach started churning.

They played several more rounds, and Sophia was trying to figure out what to do with anchovies and grapefruit when Hyle brought the truck to a sudden stop in the middle of the highway. Sophia had just enough time to notice an unusually dark patch in the asphalt right in front of them before the headlights switched on, flooding the roadway. Newman lurched forward bouncing his head off the dashboard before regaining consciousness.

"Ow, bugger, what was that?" he asked, rubbing his forehead.

"Bridge is out," Hyle told him.

"Bridge?" Newman asked incredulously, thinking back on the terrain he had seen before falling asleep. For the entire night it had been the same. Mile after mile of flat farmland and gently rolling hills extended as a black mass in all directions to meet at the horizon with a sky that was only a few shades lighter. Occasionally a farmhouse or silo could be made out against the near black of the sky.

"Overpass," Hyle corrected. "The interstate crosses over a state highway down there and the deck of the overpass has collapsed.

"We need to find a place to stop soon anyway, Newman," Sophia said. "We're getting low on gas and it's getting close to morning. She pointed out the back window of the truck where the sky was noticeably lighter.

Hyle backed the truck up and cut across the grassy median and oncoming lanes and went the wrong way down the entrance ramp for the eastbound lanes. Maneuvering around a small car that faced them near the bottom and past a few other derelict cars, he crossed another median to join the southbound lanes of the state highway. Even though they had seen only a couple other vehicles using the roads since leaving their house by the Illinois River, Hyle felt compelled to drive on the right hand side of the road when he could.

"Looks like we're entering civilization again," he said, pointing ahead to the dark trademark shape of a fast food sign. "We need to cut south anyway. Let's get through town so we know what's behind us and then find a good place to sleep. We can try to find some gas before we set out again tomorrow night."

They passed by a few small buildings and what they determined to be a strip mall, judging from the open space for a parking lot and a large sign with a dozen or so smaller signs beneath it. As was often the case along state highways, the median strip disappeared and the highway became the main street into town. For several miles they drove through a mainly residential area, with houses set back from the road in the center of wide yards. Occasional businesses were scattered among the houses and side streets appeared in abundance. A gas station at the corner of one intersection had been thoroughly excavated.

Although they had to change lanes several times, they were able to get well into the town before getting stuck. A municipal building with large neoclassical columns was the first suggestion that they had reached the center of town. By the time they reached the first stop light, the side streets had become wider and more frequent and the houses had been replaced with commercial buildings, sometimes only slightly larger than houses. At the second traffic light, a few cars sat abandoned where they had been waiting for the light to change. The oncoming lanes were clear, but a tractor trailer had been crossing the intersection and cut them off without enough room to squeeze through, so they were forced to turn back and take the nearest side street to circle around.

It turned out to be an unfortunate choice. Although most roads in this part of the country were fairly straight, this particular street turned multiple times in each direction. Before coming to their first intersection several miles later, they had lost their bearings, turning onto the new street knowing only that they were headed either generally toward town or at least generally south.

The next crossroad was no better. A tall and narrow three story brick building that stood on one of the four corners of the intersection had partially collapsed. Most of the structure was still intact, but the front had fallen away in an avalanche of brick across the road ahead of them. A smaller portion of the side facing them had also crumbled away, allowing a cutaway view into a first floor apartment, and scattering debris into the street to their left.

Newman suggested taking the street to the left since it was their best chance of finding their way back to town. Sophia wanted to turn around and find a safe place to sleep. Hyle was determined not to turn back, despite the fact that the first gray light of morning had fully arrived. He considered taking the left turn, but was afraid of risking the tires. Ultimately he convinced his two passengers that they were best off taking the right turn even though it probably led out of town, arguing that they could come back in the evening if necessary.

No more than five minutes later they were forced to turn again. On the right hand side of the street a high wrought iron fence ran the perimeter of a large property. Set back from the street across an expanse of brown grass flecked with frost was a large squat industrial building of brick and glass. It was difficult to tell whether it was a factory or a prison or a school. On the left was a side street and beyond it a house surrounded by a white stockade fence. Only the second floor was visible over the whitewashed boards, and Newman was sure that he saw someone watching them from behind one of the windows. He pointed this out to the others but by the time they looked nobody was in sight.

The road ahead, which lay in between the two fences, was blocked by a tractor and an overturned flatbed wagon of hay. Bales of hay in an early stage of decomposition were scattered into the intersection. The front of the tractor touched the stockade fence less than a foot from the corner. It appeared that the driver of the tractor had misjudged the turn, or perhaps had tried to turn around in the middle of the road and had cut the turn too tightly in an attempt to miss the fence. By a matter of inches the tractor was now pinned between the fence and the overturned trailer.

There was little choice but to take the left hand turn and see where it led. Sophia had an uneasy feeling about continuing and argued unsuccessfully that they should find a place nearby to stop for the day. The men both wanted to get a bit farther out of town and convinced her to give it just a little more time. When they spotted a sign pointing the way to a state highway at the next intersection, Sophia knew she had lost any hope of stopping. The state road, when they reached it, looked no different from most of the other roads in town aside from the single yellow line running down the center. Judging from the shading of the sky, the route ran roughly east to west. Hyle turned the truck west toward the dark horizon. Although the light was still dim, it was sufficient to see stalled cars and other obstacles in the road and they made good time. In the space of a few miles the occasional businesses gave way entirely to houses and the houses spread farther and farther apart, giving way to farms.

It was here on the edge of farmland that they came upon a delivery truck stopped in their lane. A little closer the opposing lane was blocked by an SUV, but there appeared to be just enough room to squeeze through. As they approached the vehicles, slowing to maneuver between them, two people stepped into the gap from behind the SUV. They were dressed in camouflage fatigues. The first soldier held up his left hand in a motion to stop while holding an assault rifle up in his right. The other, also holding a rifle, banged his free hand on the side of the truck. A second later the back door of the truck rolled up revealing a third soldier sitting behind a very large gun on a tripod and a fourth soldier squatting behind a folded chain of ammunition.

Newman muttered something indecipherable under his breath.

"Don't tell them where we're going, Hyle," Sophia said.

"Oh man," Hyle muttered. "This does not look good."

"Don't tell them where we're going," Sophia repeated, more urgently. "We have to get out of here. We can't let them know where we're going."

One of the soldiers was walking toward Hyle's window. He paused to look at something on the front of their pickup truck.

"Hyle!"

"Okay," he hissed. "Okay."

"We have to get out of here," Sophia pleaded, looking back and forth between the tall rows of withered corn on either side of the highway.

"Not with that thing trained on us," Hyle said through gritted teeth as he started to roll down the window.

It was only a small comfort that the soldier did not point his weapon into the cab as he approached. He was a young man, who looked barely into his twenties. His thin build and large ears would likely have attracted ridicule in his grade school days, but his combat fatigues and his weathered face combined to give him a predatory look.

"Good morning," he said. There was a tinge of southern drawl in his voice. It was friendly but he did not look at them. Instead his eyes searched around the interior of the truck as he spoke. "How y'all doing?"

Hyle nodded to acknowledge the greeting. "Fine," he answered. The other two said nothing. "Getting low on gas and food," he added, trying to fill the silence and sound casual. Their meager supply of food was still hidden behind the seat by duffle bags, blankets and a sleeping bag.

"What's in the gym bag?"

Hyle turned involuntarily. He was relieved to see that no food or valuable supplies were visible.

"Just some camping gear. And that one is a tent," he added, pointing at a longer bag. The soldier nodded, apparently not very interested in the answer.

"And where are you folks headed?" From his right Hyle heard a soft intake of breath.

"Texas," he half lied. The route would take them through Texas. The soldier locked eyes with him for the first time.

"What's in Texas?"

"Warm weather." Hyle answered. It sounded a little more like a question than he had intended. The young man studied his face. "We're just trying to get somewhere warm before the winter really sets in," Hyle added.

"Come quite a long way from Maine," the soldier ventured.

Hyle felt his heart stop and Sophia's hand tighten on his knee. Thoughts and questions flashed through his mind. He recalled the escape from Asher and from the cabin where they had first found the truck, the warning of the soldiers back in Ohio and a separate warning from Sophia back at Colgate. Could these soldiers have been on the lookout for them? Was it possible that their description had been communicated so widely and so efficiently when most means of communication were in shambles and even the military seemed to be disorganized and fragmented? Why else would there be a road block on a small state road in the middle of Kansas? He remembered the soldier pausing in front of the truck and cursed himself as he realized that they had left the license plate on, no longer obscured by the plow.

"Maine?" he asked, trying to sound surprised. "Why do you say that? Oh, the license plate." He forced a laugh and studied the soldier's face, but it was inscrutable. "The truck's come a long way I guess," Hyle continued, "but Sophia and I were in New York, near Albany, when the bombs went off." He immediately kicked himself for using her name but the soldier did not seem to react to it.

"All right, just wait right here," he said. He took a couple steps backwards from the window, then turned and walked back to the other soldier, keeping an eye over his shoulder. They talked for a while but their voices were too low to overhear what they were saying. The one who questioned them gestured in their direction several times. Sophia was sure that he was pointing at the license plate. The other soldier unclipped a walkie-talkie from his belt.

"Hyle, we have to get out of here," she pleaded. "You have to do something."

"What? What am I supposed to do?" he snapped. "Pop up the bullet proof shields? Activate our cloaking device? If I so much as turn the wheel or throw the truck into reverse that guy behind the machine gun could cut this truck to pieces before we moved ten feet."

"If they wanted to kill us they would have done it already," Newman reasoned, looking at Sophia. "They'll probably question us a little more and then let us go when they realize that we're not any sort of threat."

"No, Newman, I don't think they will," Sophia responded, struggling to retain her composure.

"I'm with Sophia on this one," Hyle agreed. "If I could figure out a way to bail out of here I would. I just can't."

"You don't really think these guys have anything to do with Asher do you?" Newman shook his head in disbelief. "That's a thousand miles away and nobody there even has a cell phone—even if cell phones still worked—which they don't."

"This guy has a walkie-talkie," Hyle pointed out. "He must be talking to someone."

There was a three way conversation between the two soldiers and the walkie-talkie, and then the first soldier began walking toward the truck again. This time he held his rifle in both hands. It was not pointed at them directly, but Sophia noticed that his finger was inside the trigger guard. About halfway to the truck he stopped. Hyle gripped the bottom of the wheel where his hands were still out of sight, ready to duck down, cut the wheel and stomp on the accelerator if the soldier opened fire.

It was Sophia who heard the sound first. It was a low pulsing sound, growing louder while increasing in pitch and tempo. It was a sound she had come to know well. As she turned to look out the back window she heard a separate sharp noise, like a gunshot, and saw a motorcycle speeding toward them from town. The front wheel was small and extended far ahead of the handgrips, raising the front end of the bike and pitching the rider back in his seat. Like the machine, the rider was large and solid. He was dressed all in black and there was something odd about his face. He was accelerating as he approached the roadblock.

As the biker drew closer, the details of his appearance became clear. Black boots were all but covered by black leather pants with a fringe along the outside of the legs. A matching coat of leather with a similar fringe on the arms covered his upper body. His face was not visible. It was behind a gas mask. The single filter jutted out like a snout in the front, giving him the appearance of a bug-eyed alien creature.

Another shot was fired and this time the source was clear. Behind the motorcycle and also traveling at high speed was a Humvee, painted in the flat olive green of an Army vehicle. A soldier hung out the passenger side trying to aim a rifle, but as they closed with the roadblock he gave up, pulling his body and the weapon back inside as the Hummer began to slow. The biker continued straight down the middle of the road, as though he intended to thread the narrow gap between the stopped vehicles at full speed, with no regard for the two soldiers who stood in it. One was already starting to scramble out of his way, seeking cover behind the SUV. A few seconds before the motorcycle reached them, Hyle decided to make the biker's life a little easier.

"Get down now!" he said, turning the wheel hard to the right and slamming the accelerator.

The machine gunner turned his head from the motorcycle to the truck and back. That second of indecision was enough to allow both to pass safely out of his arc. Out of the corner of his eye Hyle saw the soldier try to swing the heavy weapon around toward them but it was too late. Newman had his eye on the rider as he sped through the gap between the delivery truck and the SUV. On the back of his black jacket was an angel. It rose from a sea of flames, white with feathered wings spread to either side and a trident raised over its head, like Zeus ready to throw a lightning bolt.

The truck plowed into the corn, mowing down the stalks by the side of the road. Hyle began to cut the wheel back to circle around the delivery truck but Sophia grabbed it and pulled in the other direction.

"No! Go through the field!" We have to lose them in the corn," she said.

They drove fast and blind, bouncing across the field with a continuum of corn stalks disappearing beneath the hood. Newman kept a watch out the back, but the road was soon lost from view down a crooked trail of flattened vegetation. They drove and drove, the staccato of corn stalks disappearing beneath the hood the only measure of time. The truck lurched and briefly there was a patch of emptiness.

"It's a road!" Sophia exclaimed.

Hyle threw the wheel to the right and pumped the brake. The tail of the truck swung out and the yellowing stalks of corn beat against the side of the truck and streamed sideways across the windshield. Once the vehicle stabilized they plowed blindly through the field for several more seconds before crossing the road again at an oblique angle. It was a single lane road of packed earth heading roughly in the opposite direction they had been going when they encountered the roadblock. Now with the benefit of daylight and a clear view ahead Hyle stomped on the gas. The engine roared and a plume of dust rose up beyond the tailgate. Newman kept a watch out the back. Through the cloud of dust he saw movement in the field behind them.

"They're coming," he said. His voice was surprisingly calm.

The fuel light came on.

The road ran straight ahead as far as they could see. They flew past several dirt roads that crossed theirs at perfect right angles before Newman saw the Hummer break from the field far behind them, almost out of sight. It reappeared on the road from the opposite field.

"They've spotted us," Newman said.

The truck lurched again, this time crossing a narrow paved road, and another like it soon after. The fields grew smaller, and where there had only been a few scattered farmhouses in the distance, now a rough line of houses stretched from right to left ahead of them. Beyond the houses something blocked the road. As they bore down rapidly on this area it became clear that they were approaching a residential street and the object ahead was a derelict car.

"They're gaining on us, Hyle," said Newman. There was a bit more urgency in his voice.

A hard road crossed their path at a right angle, and the truck bounced up onto the pavement. Hyle stood on the brakes, spinning the wheel left and skidding into the intersection, before speeding off down the street as quickly as he dared. They took the next turn and several more turns, eventually coming to a small highway just about the time they allowed themselves to believe that they had lost the soldiers. Here the buildings were small and spread out, the majority commercial, with a few houses interspersed.

"We should try to hide in the town," suggested Newman, pointing down the road to the right.

"No," Hyle said and turned the opposite direction. "I want to get as far away from here as I can before the gas runs out. They may be based in that town."

Sophia felt a knot in her stomach and felt the hairs on the back of her neck stand on end.

"Wait! Quiet! What's that?" she interrupted.

The men listened but heard nothing above the engine of the truck.

"There," Newman said, pointing backwards. "A helicopter."

It was flying low and heading away from them, back in the direction of town. It quickly disappeared from view.

"A helicopter. And no gas," Hyle lamented.

Small businesses flashed by on either side. Ahead a huge sign marked the Normandy Mall and several dozen smaller signs below it carried the names of large chain stores and restaurants.

"In there," Sophia directed. "We can hide in the crowd."

The parking lot was nearly full. Hyle nodded and pulled in. They found a spot away from the highway and pulled the truck in between two other large vehicles. As soon as they cut the engine they heard the sound of another motor approaching. A Humvee came into view on the main road. This one was painted in desert camouflage colors and had a machine gun mounted on the roof behind a metal plate. Through the windows of the adjacent van, they watched the Humvee as it picked its way past stalled cars at a moderate speed. When it passed the entrance to the mall the travelers gave a collective sigh of relief. They looked at each other but said nothing until finally Hyle instructed Newman to grab some tools and remove a license plate from the front of a local car while he removed the rear Maine plate from the truck. Sophia slid out the passenger side, crouched down, and vomited.

"Oh great," Hyle said. "Now it'll be obvious someone was here recently." Newman glared at him.

"Really, Hyle? Are you seriously going to yell at a woman for throwing up?" He put his arm around Sophia to comfort her.

"At the moment I'm less worried about hurting someone's feelings than I am about staying alive," Hyle retorted. Newman stayed with Sophia while Hyle busied himself changing license plates and muttering under his breath. He noticed with dismay that all the cars he could see had their gas tank doors popped or pried open.

"Come on," he said. "We need to get inside and find a place to hide until dark."

They grabbed the flashlight and a few supplies and headed for the mall. The main glass doors were smashed, allowing easy entrance. Inside was dark and musty with a faint stench of urine.

A new sound outside sent them scrambling for cover. From the safety of the shadows and the protection of the information desk they watched as a helicopter appeared. It followed the roadway from the direction of town and swung out over the parking lot, flying directly over their truck before continuing on along the highway.

CHAPTER SEVENTY-TWO

ALIENATION

The emptiness of the mall was overwhelming as they walked slowly along the wide central hall, their path paralleled above by the railings of a second and third floor. Beyond those, a dirty skylight allowed some light to filter in, but the flashlight was still necessary to make out the names of many of the stores let alone see inside them. Like most places they had seen since leaving Maine, the stores had been stripped clean of everything that had not been vandalized. Empty shelves and bare racks stretched back to the end of the flashlight beam in one large department store. The only exceptions were a few specialty stores that were closed, with their entrances barred. Hyle shone the light into a small shop called Langrom's Leather Goods. There was evidence that someone had taken a saw to the grill in a failed attempt to break in. A rack just beyond the security gate held a dozen black leather riding jackets, a large red circle containing a stylized letter A emblazoned on the back of each. Newman laughed.

"Mass produced anarchy apparel. Somebody's missing the point," he commented.

"Maybe so," said Hyle, "but they must be pretty happy now."

After checking out the few surrounding stores they retreated to WonderWorks. Most of the toys there had been removed, and those that remained had been vandalized beyond use. Stepping over a smashed train set they headed for the back where they found a stock room with an unlocked door. A lockable back door opened into an access corridor, giving them a possible escape route if anyone approached from the front. Convinced that this was as good a place to hide as they were likely to find, the trio settled into the stock room to rest. After making contingency plans for various scenarios in which they were discovered, they decided to sleep in shifts, Newman volunteering to take the first shift, since he had slept in the truck. He switched off the flashlight and they sat in the darkness for a while, but Hyle and Sophia were unable to sleep.

"What do you think we'll find when we get to Arizona?" Sophia asked after a short silence.

"I expect it'll be a lot like Asher," ventured Hyle. "Big concrete walls, lots of houses and the latest in medieval technology."

"If we even get in. We were only invited to Asher," Newman reminded them. "And the Prophet may not care to let us in to accuse him of some conspiracy theory."

"If those guys at the roadblock had any communication with Zendik, he'll definitely let us in," Hyle replied. "If not, we'll just have to play it by ear when we get there."

"I hope we get in," said Sophia. "I'd really like to settle this one way or the other. I'm tired of all the useless speculating."

"See, Sophia, you're just like me," said Hyle. "You're driven to find answers."

"Everyone wants answers, Hyle," replied Newman. "We just look for them in different places."

"Yes, but Sophia and I are willing to accept that uncertainty is part of life and then go out and look for our own answers. I think that's why science and philosophy are so similar."

"Actually, Hyle, I think it was the quest for certainty that attracted me to philosophy in the first place," Sophia said. "That's why I've always had a soft spot for metaphysics and had a hard time digesting relativity and quantum physics."

"If you don't like the uncertainty of relativity and quantum physics, I can't imagine telling us about analytical philosophy and logical positivism helped much when you ended them with Gödel's theorem and Wittgenstein," Hyle replied. "Or was that just revenge?"

Sophia responded with a weak laugh.

"No, that was unintentional."

"Even before we got to Gödel I was thinking that there had to be something better," said Newman.

"Analytical philosophy and logical positivism weren't the only game in town even when they were popular," Sophia replied. "Henri Bergson and Edmund Husserl, for example, went off in a different direction."

"Bergson sounds familiar," said Newman. "Where have I heard his name before?"

"Do you know the phrase *élan vital*? That's from Bergson."

"Yes, that's it. Good call."

"Bergson coined the term because he didn't believe that natural selection was sufficient to explain evolution and felt there must be some sort of driving life force behind it."

Hyle snorted.

"Bergson also distinguished between our artificial conception of time marked in minutes and hours from the way we experience it as a free flow of sensation," Sophia continued. "In a way he anticipated one of the observations of Wittgenstein because Bergson believed that philosophy gets into trouble by mistaking time and mobility as things that can be cut up and studied, rather than seeing them as progressions. That's the source of our problems reconciling causality with free will.

"Sounds like some squishy thinking to me," Hyle observed.

"Bergson's philosophy had many elements people found attractive, but it was also controversial because it wasn't always based on rigorous philosophy or science," Sophia conceded. "Husserl was more scientific in his approach, which he called phenomenology."

"What's that, the study of phenomena?" asked Hyle. "I've never even heard of it."

"Essentially, yes. Husserl was a mathematician who originally set out on a mission to put mathematics on a solid foundation based on induction and empiricism in the tradition of John Stuart Mill. A strong critique by Frege convinced him that this was a dead end, so he did an about-face and set off in a new philosophical direction—not just new for him, but new for philosophy."

"Between all the different variations on empiricism and rationalism and Wittgenstein claiming that understanding language would unravel all the mysteries of philosophy, I'm surprised there was any direction left," Hyle quipped.

"Believe it or not, you're on to something, Hyle," replied Sophia. "Husserl rejected both epistemology and rationalism to strike out in a novel direction. Actually, rejected is too strong a term, but he was willing to set them aside in order to start fresh, much the same as Descartes started by doubting all his prior knowledge. Like Descartes, Husserl was looking for some basic unit upon which to build scientific certainty. He determined that it's our conscious experience which is basic and undeniable, and he wanted to study it without getting bogged down in whether that experience corresponded with some external real world or pre-existing frameworks in our mind or other philosophical baggage like that. He set aside all these questions, in a method he called 'bracketing,' in order to stay focused, and this line of philosophical inquiry became known as phenomenology."

"I get the idea of bracketing, but I still don't really understand what is left for phenomenology to study," Newman said.

"If I see an image of an apple, empiricism will want to find out if it's a photograph of an apple or a real apple and measure the wavelength of the red light it reflects," Sophia explained. "Rationalism will want to determine whether the concept of an apple pre-existed in my mind somehow and the way that concept relates to oranges and pears. The slogan of phenomenology is, 'Back to the things themselves.' Phenomenology wants to know what is going through my conscious mind at that very moment. For example, even though I'm only looking at the apple, I experience it as a three-dimensional object and I anticipate its texture and taste. I'm focused on the apple and less focused on other things. One of the discoveries of phenomenology, along the lines of William James, is that consciousness is intentional—that is, that it's always directed at something. Husserl hoped that by examining our experiences in such a way, and without pre-supposing any philosophical framework, we'd discover more about how we experience things and find some basic rules and commonalities in these experiences."

"Sounds like this work would have been of more use to psychology than to philosophy," Hyle observed.

"Merleau-Ponty was a phenomenologist in the tradition of Husserl who did take things more in a direction of psychology and science. One of his insights was that philosophy tends to overlook the fact that, because we exist as physical beings, our positions and the interaction of our bodies with the world influence our perspectives and experiences. But Husserl definitely had more of an impact on philosophy. Along with Nietzsche and Kierkegaard he laid the foundations for existentialism, and one of his students—Martin Heidegger—became one of the most influential philosophers of the twentieth century."

"Didn't you say that about Bertrand Russell?" Hyle asked rhetorically.

"And Wittgenstein," added Newman.

Sophia sighed. "Yes, I probably did."

"And I thought Kierkegaard was alive long before the twentieth century," Newman said.

"Not that long before, but yes, he published most of his works in the middle of the nineteenth century, about a century before existentialism became popular."

"How is it that you're both so familiar with Kierkegaard?" Hyle asked. "I've heard the name, but I don't really know anything about him."

"I know him as the father of existentialism," answered Sophia.

"And I know him because he's one of the figures who helped reinvent Christian theology," Newman explained.

"How is it possible to reinvent Christian theology?" asked Hyle. "I would have thought that once you got the Bible and hashed things out at the Council of Nicea everything was pretty much decided."

"You must not have been paying much attention in Asher then," Newman replied. "The Bible gives us some history and guidance, but it leaves a lot of questions unanswered. Medieval scholars like Aquinas and Augustine tried to work out some of the answers, but like science and philosophy, it's a never-ending pursuit."

Although nobody could see it in the darkness, Hyle rolled his eyes at the comparison. "What did he do that was so revolutionary?"

"Kierkegaard felt that the Danish church had become an impersonal institution," Newman explained. "It emphasized ritual but missed the point of religion—the relationship with God. The Church had made it too easy to be a Christian in his opinion. All you had to do was show up on Sunday and participate in a service and you could walk away feeling like you were a good Christian."

"Sounds pretty similar to Martin Luther's objections," noted Hyle.

"Don't forget that Hegel was popular in Kierkegaard's time," Sophia added, "so the philosophy was impersonal too. Hegel was concerned with the evolution of societies through time and allegiance to the state, and not much interested in individuals."

"Yes," Newman said, agreeing with both comments. "And Kierkegaard found this all to be completely out of touch with the individual experiences of the ordinary person. He saw life as uncertain and paradoxical—maybe even by design, as a test of faith—and yet we have to make choices and act. His writings tend to emphasize personal experience and emotion. In his best known work, *Fear and Trembling*, he develops the theme of the dread that one feels in facing up to existence. For Kierkegaard, to exist is to be created separate from God—to be fallible and sinful. Out of the despair of existence he finds faith, which is the key to his relationship with God. It's something that he sees as uncertain and stressful but necessary. And I think, Hyle, you'd appreciate that he didn't believe that logic or proofs were of any use in helping you to get closer to God."

"Yes, I can get behind that," Hyle agreed.

"He felt that we could never really understand something as infinite and transcendental as God when we're finite and mortal. Kierkegaard coined the term 'leap of faith' to illustrate that you could never remove that chasm of uncertainty—you just had to leap across it."

"Kierkegaard was disenfranchised with religion in the same way as Nietzsche," Sophia pointed out. "But where Nietzsche rejected religion Kierkegaard found a way to reclaim it."

"That's a theme that's repeated in one form or another by the great theologians of the twentieth century too," said Newman. "I imagine Kierkegaard influenced Karl Barth for example."

"I'm not familiar with Barth," Sophia confessed.

"Barth was a Christian theologian who was influential in the early part of the twentieth century. He believed that religious studies of his day were missing the point. Barth believed that God was alien and unknowable for the same reasons that Kierkegaard did. We're mortal and material and God is immortal and infinite. Attempts to understand the Bible in its historical context for example, or to interpret different cultural aspects of religion, are a waste of time at best, if not outright blasphemous, because they're really attempts to subsume God into some finite human endeavor. The only way God can truly be understood by mortals is by revelation. Barth often described the world of humanity as a circle and God as an infinite line that's entirely separate and inaccessible from the circle. The only exception is a tangent where they touch at one point."

"And that point represents Jesus?" Sophia guessed.

"Absolutely right," said Newman, pleased by her perceptiveness. "God and the finite world of humans intersect in Jesus, who is a form of revelation. For Barth, the proper way to read the Bible is to try to get into the heads of the Apostles and other authors and understand things through the eyes of their revelation."

"We read a couple modern theologians in my college intro to philosophy and religion course," Sophia said. "I'm trying to remember their names."

"Probably Martin Buber, Reinhold Niebuhr or Paul Tillich," guessed Newman.

"Actually all of those names sound familiar," said Sophia.

"Martin Buber was a Jewish theologian who wrote in the early twentieth century. A main theme of his teaching was about the different ways you can participate in a relationship. You have an impersonal relationship with objects that you use, like your car or a broom, where you think of them only as means to an end. It's possible to have the same type of relationship with other people, and Buber thought that was a big source of our problems. Instead, he wanted us all to engage each other fully in what he called an 'I-Thou' relationship where all facades and safety mechanisms are gone. And of course God is the archetypal Thou."

"Yes, *I and Thou* was definitely one of the books I read," Sophia remembered.

"I think that's the only book Buber wrote," said Newman, "but Tillich and Niebuhr, who were both Protestant theologians, wrote quite a few throughout the middle of the last century. Niebuhr framed most of his teaching around trying to explain and solve the problems of modern society. According to Niebuhr, God granted us free will to act autonomously. Although we're limited, finite and fallible beings, we were created in God's image and so we have the desire to do good and to transcend this human condition. Niebuhr celebrated this struggle but also warned of a pitfall—if we express our free will and drive to transcend our limitations on our own, our pride will blind us to our imperfections and our work will become twisted and corrupted. Even noble endeavors like democracy can be undermined in practice by the pride and flaws inherent in us."

"Like absolute power corrupts absolutely?" Sophia quoted.

"Something like that, yes," Newman confirmed. "The alternative is to acknowledge our flaws and dependence on God, use the example that He provided us in Christ, and try to live to those ideals. Even though we can't ultimately succeed, as a goal it'll keep us on the right track."

"That sounds a bit like a Platonic form," noted Sophia. "It reminds me of Augustine."

"Augustine was very perceptive about human nature," Newman replied. "Both Niebuhr and Tillich took a page from Augustine in that regard. I think it was even more conscious and direct with Tillich. His views were similar to Niebuhr's, but Tillich was more philosophical in his approach, and addressed the impact of different philosophies. I wish I had talked to you Sophia before reading Tillich. I probably would have understood him better."

Sophia laughed. "I'm sure you didn't have any problems understanding what you read."

"Actually, one point I took away is a bit like Plato's cave. Tillich was dismayed by the apparent victory of nominalism over realism in modern thought. He believed the concept of universal ideas still had the power to keep us from spending too much time studying shadows. In this light, he examined Christ and the other major symbols of Christianity, arguing that symbols aren't just abstract representations of something else, they're actually active participants in the thing they represent."

"I'm not sure I understand what you mean," interrupted Sophia.

"The American flag, for example, isn't just an abstract symbol of our nation," Newman explained. "It's something that we use in the daily life of the nation. Kids in school pledge allegiance to the flag. The symbol helps to define the thing it's a symbol of. In that same way, the symbols of Christianity can be a vital part of the Christian tradition without being caught up in historical debates and literalism. You can see that in Tillich's concept of God. He saw a problem with the modern concept of God as a supreme being, which he called 'theological theism.'"

"What other concept of God is there for a religion?" Hyle asked.

"In the modern era it's difficult to accept the image of an all-powerful tyrannical creator that ultimately controls our fate," Newman answered. "According to Tillich, this is the God that Nietzsche pronounced dead. In its place Tillich argued that God is being itself. It's the view of God that's left when the biblical image of God is forced to retreat, but the biblical image of God is still a powerful symbol that can point us to something universal and transcendent. Tillich argued that God is the 'ground of being' and we all participate in being, therefore we all have a direct link to God."

"That sounds like a blend of Meister Eckhardt, Spinoza and Heidegger," Sophia noted. "So Tillich's idea is to use the symbols of Christianity to overcome our natural alienation from being?"

"Yes. Tillich found the current human condition one in which our existence as finite beings makes us stand apart from God even though we're connected. It's this alienation of modern society he sought to address, and part of the solution is to focus on this common ground of being. In fact, one of his more popular books is called *The Courage to Be* where he used Kierkegaard's concept of dread as that which must be overcome by the courage of self-affirmation."

"And thus we come full circle back to Kierkegaard," noted Hyle. "And I think I understand now how he helped to reinvent Christian thought," he added, anxious to wrap up the topic, "but, Sophia, didn't you say that he also influenced philosophy?"

"Yes, although after listening to Newman I'm not sure whether he influenced philosophy or just anticipated modern society in the same perceptive way that Nietzsche did. In any case, his connection to philosophy is with many of the same themes Newman just explained through theology. The theme of alienation is picked up by Heidegger, Camus, Sartre and the other existentialists."

"Isn't Heidegger one of the most influential philosophers of the twentieth century?" asked Hyle.

"I know it's too dark for you to see me, Hyle," answered Sophia, "but I want you to imagine me glaring at you."

CHAPTER SEVENTY-THREE

THE SOUND OF INEVITABILITY

Although it was too dark to see, Hyle could clearly picture Sophia glaring at him. They all laughed quietly.

"But yes," she continued, "Heidegger was very influential. He started off with phenomenology as a student of Husserl, but soon struck out in his own direction. Heidegger is really the father of modern existentialism, although he'd object to the title. He thought the existentialists erred in focusing on the self."

"I thought Kierkegaard was the father of existentialism," Hyle said. "Existentialism has almost as many fathers as the twentieth century has most influential philosophers."

"Glare," answered Sophia. "Fine, Kierkegaard is the grandfather of existentialism and Heidegger is the father."

"What does that make Husserl?" asked Hyle.

"His teacher," Sophia fired back. "Anyway, like Husserl, Heidegger believed that philosophy had been on the wrong track, pretty much since Plato and Aristotle. Rather than focusing on the nature of reality or knowledge, Heidegger backed things up to even more basic questions. Why is there being instead of nothing? What does it mean to be? Heidegger doesn't really try to answer these in any metaphysical way, but like Husserl, he wants to understand them by studying the human experience. Heidegger considers Being, always with a capital B, as the ground of existence, similar to Tillich's concept of God. Being is populated by beings, always with a small b, such as objects, creatures and people. Nothing, with a capital N is the absence of Being."

"And how long did it take Heidegger to come up with this groundbreaking philosophy?" asked Hyle.

"Glare," said Newman.

"Actually Heidegger described his ideas as the end of philosophy and the start of thinking. If you think this is basic and obvious stuff, I'm not sure Heidegger would disagree. But he'd point out that it was neglected for a couple millennia of human development. Heidegger coined the term *Dasein* to describe individual human beings in order to avoid all those philosophical preconceptions like consciousness, soul, self, mind, experience and the like, which tend to disconnect us in some clinical way from our personal involvement in being."

"What does that mean, 'the one'?" ventured Hyle.

"I've always heard it translated as 'being there,'" answered Sophia. "Heidegger talks a lot about 'being in the world' not like being in a place, but as being engaged in something, like being in science or being in politics. He developed a whole theory about the stages we go through in our relationship with the world which does involve something called the One, or the They. We're not *Dasein* when we're born into the world. We're born into a particular culture, and that culture—through interactions with our parents, our teachers and friends and the indirect interaction with all the people we don't know—

unavoidably shapes who we are. *Dasein* is an active participant in this society which Heidegger calls the One or the They. The One is what determines what is acceptable and what *Dasein* can and cannot do. *Dasein* is at the same time controlled by the One and also a participant in it."

"That's like Tillich's concept of symbols," observed Newman.

"Sounds like Heidegger was talking about the Man," said Hyle in a failed imitation of a sixties hippie that landed somewhere between Bob Dylan and Kermit the Frog. Sophia chuckled.

"Something like that," she agreed, "except for Heidegger the One isn't a repressive institution to be free of, although people often make that mistake. The first stage of involvement with the world is what Heidegger calls undifferentiated. In this stage *Dasein* lives happily oblivious that there's any such thing as the One. Then *Dasein* realizes that they'll die and they have to face Nothingness. They face that dread that Kierkegaard describes and in their anxiety they think, 'This can't be all there is, there must be something more.' That angst drives them to the next stage which is inauthenticity. Here *Dasein* tries to change who they are and live in some other way. The typical midlife crisis isn't a bad example of this. A guy gets to middle age and starts thinking about his mortality so he gets divorced and finds a younger wife, buys a sports car or a motorcycle, takes up kickboxing or whatever in order to try to change who he is. It doesn't work, of course. When it doesn't work they experience a sense of what Heidegger calls 'fallenness' where they feel lost and come back face to face with the angst they tried to avoid. Now *Dasein* can go in one of two directions. If they try to avoid that dread again they find some other inauthentic path. Maybe our midlife crisis guy joins the Peace Corps or sits down to write the great American novel, but in the end he'll be back at that experience of fallenness. This time though he accepts his mortality. Here *Dasein* stops trying to overcome it by being something it's not and embraces who they are. Now *Dasein* can go back to accepting that original life they were born into and embrace it as their own choice. Heidegger calls this being authentic."

"That sounds like Nietzsche and his demon," Newman said. "The one who offers you the chance to live your life over again exactly as it happened last time."

"Yes," agreed Sophia. "The point though isn't about living life over. It's about making the choice in this lifetime in order to overcome the anxiety and absurdity of the world. In the end, according to Heidegger, it's in this authentic relationship with the One— rather than through science, philosophy or theology—that we find meaning in our everyday lives. One of the things that can get in the way of that proper relationship is technology."

"I hope you're not going to get all anti-science on me like our friends back in Asher," Hyle said.

"Cell phones, computers, email and such, were not around when Heidegger wrote about technology, Hyle. I'm sure these things only bolster his case, but he used the term in a broader sense. Technology for Heidegger is a way we approach objects, as means to an end. And we can approach people the same way. He used the term *bestand* which means stock, like the type of stock you'd have found in this stock room. When we fall into the old trap of thinking of ourselves as thinking things or as chosen beings, we tend to treat everything in the world as stock for our use. Eventually that attitude rubs off on our interactions with other people."

"Like Buber's distinction between I-it and I-Thou," noted Newman.

"Yes, except for Heidegger, even seeing objects in the world as stock was wrong because it removes us from the relationship."

"Do you mean I'm supposed to have an I-Thou relationship with my push broom?" asked Hyle.

"Sort of," Sophia answered seriously. "If you're sweeping the floor there's a good chance that you're thinking of something else. Daydreaming about something you'll do later maybe. Heidegger would argue that you're missing out on the experience of sweeping, although he wouldn't use the term 'experience.' You and the broom and the floor are all part of a unified system, and to be authentic you should participate in it fully instead of trying to escape from it by daydreaming. Throw yourself into the task, appreciate the quality of the broom in your hands and take pride in your work and live in the moment. Be there."

"So I'd be justified in seeing a push broom as an even trade for Newman?" Hyle asked.

"Not exactly," replied Sophia. "You might need to improve your relationship to both, but Heidegger does distinguish between people and objects because people have the ability to use language. In keeping with the twentieth century focus on language, Heidegger applied the same type of analysis to language as he did to being and determined that words have lost the original intensity of their meaning over time. Think about the word love for example. The first time the word was used it meant the type of earth-moving first love with fireworks and a chorus of angels. Now people might say they love pepperoni pizza. Heidegger said, 'Language is the house of Being,' by which he meant that language is how we preserve and express and share the memory of Being. Language grants *Dasein* the power to ask questions about Being and ultimately makes us the custodians of Being."

"That's a pretty attractive philosophy all in all," Newman commented.

"I suppose I can see why he's among the many most influential philosophers of the twentieth century," Hyle allowed.

"Thanks for that, Hyle," Sophia said. "I hesitate to mention that one of his greatest influences was on Jean-Paul Sartre, who became extremely popular and more directly influential than Heidegger."

"We read Sartre in my high school French class," Newman said. "Camus as well."

"Are they similar?" Hyle asked. "I've heard of them both, but never read anything by either."

"Camus wrote several novels, but we read *The Plague* and *The Stranger*, which are probably his best known," replied Newman. "He won the Nobel Prize for Literature for *The Stranger*. The main theme of his work was that life is absurd because we're driven to find meaning in our lives but the world itself is meaningless."

"Yes," agreed Sophia. "He even opens one of his essays by stating that the only real philosophical question is suicide. The title of that essay is *The Myth of Sisyphus*—Sisyphus of course being the Greek king who was punished by Zeus by being forced to eternally roll a bolder uphill only to have it fall back down before it reached the top. That should give you a clue about Camus' answer. He took the stoic view that one shouldn't give in to the absurdity of life by suicide, but should instead rebel against it. He's generally considered an existentialist, but he didn't agree with the label."

"Is there anybody who actually calls themself an existentialist?" asked Hyle.

"You know, it's funny that so many existentialists rejected the title," Sophia said, taken aback by the question. "I think Sartre may have accepted it for himself though, which is fitting since he's the first person most people would think of if asked to name an existentialist. Simone de Beauvoir also developed a lot of the same themes, although she tends to be overshadowed by Sartre."

"But she wrote *The Second Sex*, right?" Newman interjected. "She and Sartre were in a life-long relationship. I'm sure they both influenced each other."

"True, they were both authors and philosophers," agreed Sophia.

"What did Sartre write that I might have heard of?" asked Hyle.

"His first major work was the novel *Nausea*, which happens to be a study in phenomenology," Sophia replied. "It's about a man who realizes that the world is totally indifferent to him and he can't escape his own freedom. Sartre wrote the plays *Flies* and *No Exit*, as well as some philosophical works, the most famous of which is *Being and Nothingness.*"

"Being and Nothingness sounds like Heidegger," noted Newman.

"There's a clear influence," Sophia confirmed, "but some significant differences too. Sartre developed a concept called 'facticity' which is a bit like Heidegger's One. Facticity is the collection of historical facts that influence who you are. But unlike Heidegger, Sartre believed that you can exercise your freedom despite your facticity. The problem is that people are afraid to face up to their freedom and often choose to hide behind moral or social conventions, which Sartre called 'acting in bad faith.' He famously said that we're 'condemned to be free' because the world supplies us with no inherent meaning and we have to make our own. It's very similar to Heidegger's authenticity except for Sartre it's embracing something individual and personal."

"Seems like a very fine line between nihilism and existentialism," Hyle observed.

"The nihilist doesn't believe anything has meaning," explained Sophia. "The existentialist believes he can create his own meaning."

"So an existentialist is just a self-deluded nihilist," Hyle concluded.

"If you—oh, watch out," Sophia gasped suddenly, scrambling past Newman. Their conversation ended with the sounds of Sophia throwing up in the darkness.

CHAPTER SEVENTY-FOUR

IMPROBABLE ESCAPE

In a world where watches had long ago stopped, where the television and radio stations were silent, where people no longer rushed to work in the morning, where even the sun was difficult to see behind the layer of dust that choked the sky, time was no longer measured in minutes and hours. It was measured only in periods of light and darkness. In the absolute darkness of their hiding place in the stockroom it was nearly impossible for Newman to tell how much time had passed between hearing the heavy breathing of his sleeping companions and hearing sounds from somewhere outside the mall.

The sound of an engine had come and gone twice since he started his watch. In the busy world the mall was built to serve, that sound would have been drowned out by the voices of shoppers, by background music and the metal whine of the escalators and elevators. Outside it would have blended with the noise of scores of other vehicles, all melting into an unnoticed background like the trill of insects in a country summer. Now those sounds were gone. The sound of a single engine was muffled but distinct. Twice it had crested nearby and then faded into the distance. Newman was unsure whether it was the same vehicle or even whether it was traveling in the same direction. But the third time was different. The third time the sound did not fade. It just ended.

Newman listened for a while, debating whether to wake his companions. Again he heard the sound of an engine in the distance, growing louder. Again the sound crested and disappeared without fading. He struggled to make sense of it. Only when he heard several more engines approaching did he understand what he was hearing. The vehicles were closing on the mall at high speed and then dropping to low speed nearby, the near-idle of their motors too low to hear through the walls. They were gathering outside.

"Wake up," he hissed, leaning forward and reaching his hands out in opposite directions. His left hand connected with something solid, and slid from Hyle's back up to his shoulder to start shaking it while his right hand probed farther until it found Sophia's ankle.

Hyle woke partially, asked some groggy unintelligible question, and then remembering their situation and realizing the significance of being roused, snapped fully awake. Meanwhile Newman shuffled closer to Sophia and scooped her up into a sitting position while he explained what was going on. By the time he finished there was nothing to be heard outside.

They waited. Sophia tried closing her eyes and opening them again, but there was no difference. Aside from the sound of their breathing and the slow drip of water somewhere in the distance, all was quiet. They waited. Time passed.

Eventually the silence was broken by a low pulsing sound, initially distant but growing closer and louder and finally settling into position somewhere very nearby, echoing off of the side of the building. It was the unmistakable reverberation of a helicopter. Against this new backdrop of noise they listened and waited.

"I hear voices," Sophia whispered at length. They grew louder as the trio listened. Several different voices yelled to each other, still far away, but getting closer. It was impossible to make out what they were saying, but it was always brief, often monosyllables. Within a few minutes everything became clear. There were several groups of people methodically working their way through the mall.

"Check in there," a voice directed. Then from a little farther away, "Clear up here."

"Clear," from a slightly different direction.

"Schumer, Wills, up the escalator. Roth, Hoffman, in here."

They were in the store now, no more than fifty feet away. Sophia tried to quiet her breathing and wondered if it was really as loud as it seemed to her.

The doorknob rattled.

"Locked," reported a voice from the other side.

"Saito are you in position?" asked the leader. The reply crackled through a walkie-talkie, nearby and distinct.

"Negative sir. But I see the entrance to the service corridor just ahead."

As quietly as he could Hyle opened the back door and tugged on Sophia's hand. She pulled on Newman's. They moved quickly, executing one of the scenarios they had planned and reviewed before sleeping. Hyle paused in the corridor until he heard the soft click of the door closing behind them and then continued down the hallway in a direction that led away from the main gallery.

They reached the door at the end of the corridor and Hyle placed his hand on the pushbar.

"They're probably watching the exits," he whispered. "Be ready to hide, run or surrender depending on what we see. Ready?" Sophia squeezed his hand in response.

"Yes," Newman whispered back.

Light appeared at the far end of the corridor. The source was around the corner where the service way led back to the main gallery. The light was growing brighter as it bounced up and down the wall. Hyle pushed open the door and stepped through, pulling Sophia with him, and then things happened quickly.

As soon as they emerged from the building the sound of the nearby helicopter filled the air and they were blinded by the daylight. Even though the sunlight was dampened by the perpetual brown haze it was sufficient to blur their vision. A voice shouted excitedly from somewhere to their right. The thrum of a land vehicle engine approached from the left.

Hyle, who was the first one into the light, was the first one to be able to see clearly. They were standing on a narrow sidewalk. Behind them, the plain metal door of the emergency exit had closed. There was no handle on this side—no way back. In front of them was the parking lot. The nearest cars, which were the only nearby cover, were at least thirty feet away, across the two lanes of road that circled the mall and the grass divider which separated the roadway from the parking area. To the right was a covered entryway into the mall in front of which an olive drab Humvee sat facing the sidewalk. Its doors were opened to provide cover for the soldiers who watched the entrance. On the side nearest them a crouching soldier stood up, pointing toward them and yelling, the assault rifle in his other hand arcing down to level at them. Tires squealed from the left as the vehicle that had been speeding toward them down a nearby row of parked cars emerged into the road and took the corner at high speed. The pickup truck angled across the lanes to bear down on their position. Hyle stepped backwards and pushed Sophia toward the wall with his outstretched arm. His mind raced, trying to process the feeling that he was missing some important piece of information.

Amid a screech of rubber the truck skidded to a stop next to them, its tires just touching the curb. Thin trails of smoke drifted away from the rear wheels. For a second the cab was empty as the driver ducked down out of sight and then the door was flung open. It was only upon seeing the familiar bags behind the seat that Hyle realized that this was their truck.

"Get in," the driver ordered. His voice was deep and thickly accented. No one moved. The driver was a large man, solidly built and muscular, with skin so dark it nearly matched his black leather jacket. A large chrome pistol rested in his lap.

"Auld! It's Auld!" Sophia exclaimed.

From the right the soldier shouted as he ran toward them, "Stop right there! Don't move!" He kept his rifle aimed in their direction as he ran. The open door of the pickup provided partial cover but little comfort.

"Get in. Now!" Auld repeated.

"It's Auld, from Colgate," Sophia explained, shoving Hyle toward the truck. Hyle jumped forward as if awakened from a trance. Sophia scrambled in after him and Newman behind her.

"Are you following us?" Hyle demanded. "Did you—"

"Get down and listen carefully," interrupted Auld. As he spoke the truck leapt forward. His voice still held that musical quality that had so captivated Sophia, but now it also carried an authority that bore no questions. They tucked their heads down as best they could, with Sophia mainly on Hyle's lap and Newman still struggling to squeeze in farther and get the door to latch. There was a short burst of automatic weapon fire ahead of them.

"I am going to bring you around the corner," Auld continued. "There is a dumpster there—"

A second burst was accompanied by the sound of glass shattering. Sophia's face was stung in several places and Newman, with the top of his head pressed to the dashboard, felt a spray of little shards burn into the back of his neck. Risking a quick glance up, he saw that the safety glass of the windshield was spider webbed and there were two bullet holes on the passenger side where their heads might have been had they been sitting upright. Tires squealed. The truck veered around a corner and raced along between rows of parked cars.

"There is a dumpster there with a fence around it. You will only have a few seconds to get out and hide inside. I will lead them away. Hide there and watch until you are sure they are all gone."

They made another hard turn at the end of the parking lane and circled the outside of the lot. The soldier who fired on them gave up and ran back for the Humvee.

"Then follow the sun west through the fields for a few hours. When you come to a dried up creek bed, follow that southwest a few more. You will see a farmhouse with a metal silo and a green barn. A green barn. Under the haywagon there is a storm shelter stocked with food."

From the other parking lot, the squeal of tires signaled that the Humvee was in pursuit.

"Wait there until I come for you, however many days it takes. Cover your tracks. Do not come out until I come for you."

The truck came to an abrupt stop. This time there was no protest from the tires.

"Get out, now!"

Newman opened the door, half-tumbling out of the truck, and then took two staggering steps to a tall chain link fence. As Sophia and Hyle piled out after him he lifted the latch and squeezed through the gate. The truck was already in motion as Hyle swung the door closed, and within seconds of latching the gate behind them the Humvee rounded the corner. At the opposite end of the mall complex a helicopter rose above the roof of the building, arcing in their direction. Angular and armored, it was clearly a military craft, but smaller and possibly older than the well-known Apache and Blackhawk models. Below it a black SUV raced around the perimeter of the parking lot.

The trio watched things unfold from inside the fence. They were next to one of the many eateries surrounding the mall. The restaurant was set back into an undeveloped field leaving the front of the building flush with the outer edge of the parking lot. The dumpster was set off to one side, and to block the unsightly view, it had been enclosed in a six foot high fence covered on the inside with a fine green plastic mesh. This had the effect of allowing the three travelers a clear view of what transpired outside while keeping them relatively invisible. Only if the helicopter were to fly directly above them would they be spotted.

Apparently they had made it to cover in time. All attention seemed to be on the pickup truck, which continued along the road that ringed the outside of the parking lot. Auld drove quickly along the straight stretch of road while the pursuing Humvee, which had rounded the corner, paralleled his path on the inner road, closing the gap. Well beyond the pickup, at the far end of the parking lot, the SUV sped along a perpendicular path on an intercept course. The helicopter swung into position ahead of it and then tipped forward, accelerating toward Auld.

The racing engines of the truck and the SUV, the roar from the engine of the Humvee and even the continuous thunder of the chopper's rotors were suddenly drowned by a new sound. With a blaze of light, machine guns on either side of the helicopter opened up on the road. Just as they did, the truck made a right angle turn between two rows of parked cars. A continuous stream of bullets shredded pavement in two rough lines where the truck had been. The back end of the truck fishtailed and slammed into a little hatchback. The sounds of shattering glass and scraping metal were barely audible above the sound of the guns. As the helicopter shot past the dumpster, flying low, it was already starting to bank, and a second later it was lost from view behind the restaurant. Recovered from the turn, the pickup accelerated toward the inner road, closing on the Humvee, which braked hard as it overshot the end of the parking lane. The SUV was late to the party and just rounding the corner at the distant end of the lot.

Auld reached the end of the lane and made another hard right, just behind the Humvee which began to accelerate toward him in reverse. As Auld sped away, the Humvee backed into the parking lane and reversed direction again, pulling back onto the inner road in pursuit. The pickup disappeared from view behind the restaurant, followed shortly by the Humvee. There was another burst of machine gun fire. The helicopter streaked back into view, still flying low and once again decelerating for a turn. The SUV blew by in the opposite direction just in front of the dumpster. Engines roared and tires squealed. The three travelers could do nothing but listen. Sophia had to remind herself to breathe.

An engine approached from the far side of the restaurant and the pickup blew by with the Humvee in hot pursuit. The SUV appeared on the inner road a few seconds later. Auld executed several more turns, timing them perfectly to allow one of his pursuers to overshoot if they were close or giving him enough time to reach the end of the parking lane and reverse direction up the next before they closed. The helicopter hovered at the far end of the lot, waiting for him to make a mistake.

"Unbelievable, he's playing Pac Man with them," Hyle said.

It was clear that the two land vehicles were trying to trap Auld inside one of the parking lanes. It was less clear what Auld was trying to accomplish. Several times he got enough of a lead that he could have made it to an exit only to turn and cut back in a different direction. Finally a new vehicle appeared. A tan Humvee rounded the corner underneath the helicopter.

Auld was on the inside road, headed in the general direction of the chopper and directly toward the new Humvee. The SUV was close behind him and the olive drab Humvee paced him on the outside road, now hanging back enough that it had time to stop when he made his next move.

"Oh no," Sophia whispered, seeing all his escape routes cut off.

The pickup turned one more time, but rather than cutting into a lane of parked cars, it fishtailed to a stop sideways across the inner road. The tan Humvee approached from the far side and the SUV was on a collision course on the near side. Two shots exploded from the cab of the truck and then it lurched forward into the parking lane. The SUV, which had been braking in a vain attempt to stop before colliding with the truck, continued forward, jumping the narrow sidewalk by the mall and glancing off the wall of the building amid a shower of sparks and back into the road before ramming into the oncoming Humvee. In the meantime, the olive Humvee had moved into position to block the outer end of the parking lane. The pickup sped toward it and then, halfway along the row of cars, it bootlegged into a three quarter turn, skidding to a stop across the lane. With the passenger side and the back end of the truck toward the Humvee, Auld jumped out and stayed low, running between cars and disappearing from view. Behind him the front of the helicopter dipped and it began moving. Sophia buried her head in Hyle's shoulder.

The machine guns opened up on the path Auld had followed. The roof of a sedan evaporated in a shower of glass and metal and the van next to it rocked and shook as if caught in an earthquake. The path of destruction continued to the next cars, pulverizing them with an invisible barrage of lead. A few rows away, Auld popped his head up from behind a station wagon. He aimed his oversized pistol in a two handed stance, squeezed off a string of shots, and dove away just ahead of the machine guns. The helicopter lurched and tipped farther forward, angling toward the ground. Already flying low, it lost altitude, skimming the tops of vans and trucks as it streaked over Auld's last position. Several lanes away it plowed into a row of parked cars and the lot was rocked by an explosion. An expanding ball of fire obscured the site of impact.

"No way," Hyle said under his breath. "That's impossible."

A few seconds later the pickup was speeding back down the parking lane. It turned away from the SUV and the tan Humvee which were just disengaging from the crash. The truck raced along the side of the mall and disappeared behind the flames and black smoke which covered the center of the parking lot. The two Humvees chased the truck. Not long after they were out of sight the SUV pulled away in the opposite direction around the mall. The sound of engines faded. Eventually the only sound was the crackling of flames and the slow creak of burning metal.

CHAPTER SEVENTY-FIVE

WELCOME TO THE MACHINE

Noon had come and gone by the time Sophia, Hyle and Newman decided that the coast was clear. To be safe, they stayed between the dumpster and the restaurant when they circled the fence to the edge of the field and kept low through the chest high grass and weeds as they left the mall behind. Crossing a narrow dirt road took them into a corn field and from then on they were in farmland. There was no sign of pursuit.

Although the sun itself could not be seen, its position could be determined as a bright patch in the dust layer, almost overhead. They walked toward this patch, occasionally deviating to skirt around the open ground of fallow fields. Hyle led the way with Sophia in the middle and Newman bringing up the rear. They spoke very little at first. The rustling as they pushed their way through stalks of wheat and corn prevented whispering, and they were unwilling to speak any louder.

When the mall was far enough behind them, they tried to make sense of what had happened there. Now firm believers in Auld's existence, Hyle and Newman peppered Sophia with questions, but it soon became clear that she knew almost nothing about him. She could only retell the story of her encounters with him at Colgate. They traded theories about Auld's military training, about why he might have followed them, and about the intention of the soldiers who had flushed them out of the mall, but none of it made much sense. Eventually they returned to silence.

Late in the afternoon they came across the creek bed. It was not entirely dry. At its peak the flow might have formed a formidable stream, just a bit too wide to jump across. Now a small rivulet of clear water wound its way along the bottom of the wide path between the banks. Drained from walking, Sophia stopped to wash her face in the cool water before they moved on. It was near dark when they spotted the barn. The light had faded to the point that it was difficult to confirm that it was green until they were inside the farmyard.

The front of the barn faced a sprawling white farmhouse. Off to one side a hay wagon rested, overflowing with a load of hay bales. A few bales had toppled off of it onto the ground, and obscured behind them was a narrow bulkhead. There was just enough room under the wagon to swing the double doors open. Newman passed the flashlight to Hyle. It was now their only possession. Hyle switched it on and descended.

"Come on down," he called from the bottom. It's a pretty good ladder. Just take it easy."

Once Sophia and Newman were safely down and the bulkhead was closed Hyle gave them a guided tour with the flashlight beam.

"The back shelves are stocked with food," he said, running the light across them. It was beginning to dim noticeably. "There's a camp toilet there in the corner and three sleeping bags rolled up over there with some padding." He pointed to a couple switches on the wall by the ladder. "Ventilation works, but the light doesn't. And of course the flashlight is dying. Once we get some food I'll switch it off and leave it here on this shelf so you can find it if you need it."

"Not a bad place to stay for a while," observed Newman.

Sophia headed straight for the sleeping bags and began unrolling one. Hyle pried up the pull tab on a can of ravioli, opened it and handed it to Sophia.

"Here, try to eat something before you go to sleep," he said.

"Just hearing you open that can is making my mouth water," Newman said.

"That's a positive development," replied Hyle. "Maybe you're trainable after all."

Sophia saw the puzzlement in Newman's expression. "I believe it's a reference to Pavlov's dogs," she explained.

"Sorry, Hyle, I don't think that works on humans," Newman responded. He and Hyle each picked a can of food from the shelves.

"Of course it does," Hyle scoffed. He switched off the flashlight before it could fade away on its own. "How do you think they trained you to wear clothes and eat with a fork and knife? Society is just a web of positive and negative reinforcements for different behaviors."

"I'm sure nobody actually believes that," replied Newman.

"Actually, Newman, quite a few people do believe that," Sophia informed him. "Behaviorism was one of the first major schools of psychology. It's gone in and out of favor, but it always has a following."

"Behaviorism is what helped make psychology into a real science," Hyle asserted. "In the late nineteenth and early twentieth century there were a few people like Ebbinghaus doing focused research on perceptions and memory, but most of psychology consisted of people extrapolating elaborate theories from general observations, like Freud and Jung. Psychology was more like philosophy than science. In fact, you may remember that Sophia knew William James—one of the foundational figures in psychology—primarily as a philosopher. Even the more lab-oriented psychologists like Wundt, Titchener and the like approached psychology through introspection. They studied sensation, memory and emotion in order to figure out what was going on inside the mind. The goal of behaviorism was to make sure that psychology was based more strictly on observation and less on speculation."

"And Pavlov started this whole movement?" asked Newman. "I get the bell reference, but what exactly did he do in these experiments?"

"No, Pavlov didn't start behaviorism," Hyle replied. "And his discovery was something of an accident. He was studying digestion in dogs and measuring how much they'd salivate under different feeding conditions. During these experiments he noticed that sometimes the dogs began to salivate before the food was even in their mouth. In pursuing this he discovered that they could associate a variety of other stimuli, including the sound of a bell, as signals that they were about to be fed. Pavlov even showed that the dogs could associate one stimulus with another stimulus and still get the response of salivation, although each step away from the primary stimulus made the response weaker and the association more tenuous."

"So the dogs learned that the bell meant that their dinner was coming?" Newman summarized.

"They associated the bell with food and that caused them to salivate," corrected Hyle. "Nobody said anything about learning."

"What's the difference?"

"Salivation is an unconscious response. To demonstrate learning, the subject needs to have a choice of actions," Hyle explained. "That was investigated by Thorndike, who was doing experiments with cats around the same time that Pavlov was experimenting with dogs. Thorndike put cats in a puzzle box where they had to pull a loop to open the door. When they did, it freed them from the box and they got a treat. Then Thorndike would put them back in and repeat the study. At first the cats would yowl and scratch and bite at the bars until accidentally they pulled on the loop and got free. Thorndike showed that generally, the more times he put a cat in the box, the quicker it got out."

"First Schrödinger and now Thorndike—scientists seem to have a thing for cats in boxes," Sophia noted. "I don't want to hear another word about philosophers and demons." Newman chuckled.

"But the conclusion is that the cat learns how to get out of the box, right?" he asked.

"No," Hyle answered. "The other thing Thorndike observed is that even though the general trend is for the cat to get out of the box more quickly, sometimes it would take much longer than the previous time. Thorndike concluded that the association between the stimulus of being trapped in the box and the response of pulling on the loop was strengthened through repetition, but that there was no understanding on the part of the cat. If the cat had learned how the box worked, it would have pulled the loop right away every time. Thorndike formulated these observations into the law of effect, which states that given all the different responses an animal can have to a certain situation, ones that are closely followed by some type of satisfaction will be more likely to be repeated in similar situations."

"So that's the basis of behaviorism," Newman surmised.

"Not quite, but almost," Hyle told him. "That and maybe some of James' pragmatism set the stage for John Watson, who's regarded as the founder of behaviorism. He published a paper in 1913, which is now known as the 'behaviorist manifesto,' in which he laid out the basic theme of behaviorism. His stated purpose was to remove from psychology all the vague and unquantifiable terms like satisfaction, desire, hunger, consciousness—all those introspective and private concepts of the mind—and focus instead only on what could be observed and measured."

"A bit like the logical positivist movement in philosophy," noted Sophia.

"Yes, very similar," Hyle agreed. "Behaviorism built on Pavlov and Thorndike, but cut out any discussion of satisfaction and terms like that. Watson believed so strongly in the power of behaviorism that he famously claimed that if you gave him twelve infants, regardless of their social or ethnic background, and a controlled world to raise them in, he could pick one at random and turn it into a lawyer or doctor or beggar man or thief."

"Where does B.F. Skinner fit in?" asked Sophia. "His is the name I usually associate with behaviorism."

"Skinner followed Watson and became the central figure in the field. He did a lot of pioneering work, wrote a foundational textbook as well as a couple popular books and evolved Watson's original explanations for behavior. For example, Watson believed that learning could be boiled down to a muscular reflex that was caused in response to a stimulus."

"That's ridiculous," Newman objected.

"Did you know that when you stick a fly's foot in a sugar solution, it'll stick out its mouthparts and start trying to drink?" Hyle responded. "You can do this as many times as you like and it'll always work. The fly is just a little biological machine. Descartes had it right—that is, until he went and ruined a good theory by trying to stick a soul in our pineal gland."

"But that amounts to biological determinism," Newman protested. "It might work for flies, but humans are clearly much more complicated than that. We have free will. We create works of art and appreciate beauty and have desires. We fall in love. Psychology can't succeed if it ignores these things. Not everything can be reduced to numbers or put under a microscope."

"Those were the big challenges for behaviorism," Hyle admitted. "The behaviorists were able to explain a lot of animal—and arguably human—behavior, but the muscle response explanation was too limited to even explain the behavior of Thorndike's cats. A cat in Thorndike's box didn't always use the same paw for example. Skinner modified Watson's theory to say that a type of behavior, rather than a specific muscular response, was being strengthened when it resulted in a reward. Skinner did a lot of work to understand operant conditioning, which is the process of strengthening a type of behavior, called an operant, through a program of trials and rewards. And it's important to note that the reward could be a treat or it could be the cessation of something negative. Skinner believed that operant conditioning could be used on people to improve society."

"Hyle, did you ever read *A Clockwork Orange*?" asked Newman.

"No, but I watched the movie. Does that count?"

"Isn't it pretty clear that using brainwashing to try to improve society is wrong?"

"No," Hyle immediately replied. "And by calling it brainwashing you've already rendered your verdict that it's a tool for some sort of sinister purposes. Using operant conditioning to engineer society isn't some wild scheme—we do it all the time. How do you think parents get their kids to behave? Spank them or send them to their rooms when they're bad and give them candy or praise when they're good. The parents with spoiled brats are the ones who don't understand operant conditioning. And lest you think it works only on kids, consider managers in the workplace. Praise, recognition, promotions, warning letters, demotions—it's all the same thing. Skinner wasn't opening a debate about whether operant conditioning should be used in society. It already is. He was just trying to help us get better at it."

Sophia could tell that Hyle believed what he was saying, but even in the darkness, without the benefit of seeing his face, she could sense something more. He was deliberately choosing his wording to provoke a reaction from Newman. She could almost hear the satisfaction in the silence between his words.

"There is some debate though," she interjected. "Skinner's behaviorism depends upon a particular theory of learning in humans, but it doesn't entirely correlate with what's observed. Alfred North Whitehead once challenged Skinner at a dinner party to explain verbal behavior—in other words, language—through behaviorism. Skinner spent the next couple decades developing a theory which he published in the book *Verbal Behavior*. When Noam Chomsky was asked to review it he wrote such a well-crafted rebuttal that it ended up becoming at least as well known as the book itself. Even though much of the review was just argumentative, Chomsky did make some solid points."

"Like what?" Hyle asked.

"Like the fact that children learn to talk at the same age in all cultures despite differences in how much reinforcement they get. Children whose parents fuss and fawn over every word don't learn to talk more quickly than those in cultures where children are largely ignored, despite what should be a significant difference in operant conditioning. Grammar is also hard to explain solely by behaviorism since parents focus on meaning and generally don't reward grammar. Finally, children who are isolated from other humans when they're young may never be able to learn to communicate. This suggests some type of neural development that happens during early childhood rather than just enforcement of certain verbal behaviors by parents and peers."

"I'm not sure anyone has a fully defensible explanation for language," Hyle objected.

"It's not just language though," replied Sophia. "Piaget also showed that children go through developmental stages based on their age. If they're too young there are concepts they're just incapable of grasping, no matter how many examples you give them. Just like Chomsky's point about language, this shows that neurological developments in the brain are a prerequisite to certain types of learning."

"Fair enough," Hyle conceded. "That may demonstrate flaws in Skinner's explanation for learning language, but even the most radical behaviorist wouldn't expect to be able to teach a newborn to walk. The fact that children may go through stages of mental development that determine their capabilities doesn't mean that behaviorism should be tossed out the window."

"Maybe not, but at least it calls into question your conclusion that humans are nothing but biological machines," Newman pointed out. "If learning is necessarily dependent on some type of mental development then, to have a full explanation of human behavior, you need to deal with some of those introspective things which are beyond the scope of behaviorism. And one of them just might be free will."

"Don't think you can escape determinism that easily, Newman," Hyle said. "There has always been a debate about whether it's nature versus nurture that shapes our behavior. I think almost everyone acknowledges that both have some influence. The debate is about how much of a role each plays. Behaviorists come down hard on the side of nurture. Since that seems to lead to determinism, you want to swing toward nature as the main influence. Have you ever heard of sociobiology?"

"No, and I have a feeling I'm happier that way."

"When I was in college I read a book called *The Selfish Gene* written in the seventies by Richard Dawkins," Hyle said. "It was an interesting twist on the idea of natural selection. Of course genes aren't literally selfish, but his point is that natural selection can be viewed as happening to pools of genes rather than individual organisms. The organisms are just hosts for the genes. For example, you might think that natural selection would weed out altruism since organisms inclined toward altruism are more likely to get killed off. But from a genetic standpoint, an altruistic mother who risks her life to defend her offspring is more likely to spread her genes to the next generation than a mother who abandons her offspring to flee and save herself."

"The problem with biological determinism—whether it's behaviorist or genetic—is that it removes moral responsibility," Newman objected.

"The modern courts were full of cases where the defendant's crimes were blamed on society or genetics," Sophia agreed.

"Don't confuse biology with morality," replied Hyle. "Science just tells you how things are. It doesn't make any claims about how things ought to be. That's for the philosophers and theologians to argue about. On the other hand, E.O. Wilson believed that there might be a biological use for free will—or at least the belief in free will. Wilson popularized the field of sociobiology, which argues that many of our social and cultural conventions are driven by genetics," Hyle explained. "Our genes have a built in mutation rate—a certain error rate when they're copied. Sometimes this leads to problems like genetic diseases, but it also creates the possibility for beneficial new genetic combinations that could lead to evolution. A certain amount of randomness in our behavior—which might be mistaken for free will—could introduce the same type of change agent into society."

"How can a gene influence society?" asked Sophia. "They just determine personal traits."

"You're thinking of genes as things that determine physical traits—like the color of your eyes—but they can also influence behavior," Hyle explained. "There are more and more studies linking genetics to things like violent behavior or the tendency toward religiousness. They may even be responsible for a sort of genetic memory."

"But genes are just segments of DNA," Sophia objected. "If your life starts as a single cell with one set of genes from your mother and another from your father, how can there be any memory included in strands of DNA?"

"I don't know," admitted Hyle, "but I remember reading about a study someone did with prairie dogs. They isolated newborns and raised them in an artificial environment. They had never seen the outside world, but they had an extreme fear of cross-shaped shadows."

"Which means what?" asked Newman. "Were they vampire prairie dogs?"

"No," Hyle said with an exaggerated sigh. "It's the shape of shadow a hawk would cast. They were born with an instinctual fear of their natural predator. If it wasn't learned from their environment it must have come from their genetics. And think about humans. Can you name a couple things people have an irrational fear of?"

"Spiders," Newman answered.

"And snakes," added Sophia.

"Just about any creature will run from a big predator like a mountain lion or a bear, but snakes and spiders aren't large enough to be scary. Yet there is an evolutionary reason we should be afraid of them."

"Because they're often poisonous," Sophia concluded.

"Right. And genetics may be behind incest taboos, religious beliefs, dietary rules and a wide range of other cultural institutions which improve the chances for a social group to survive. You'll notice that these social traits are conserved fairly well across many different cultures and geographic regions."

"That might explain Jung's idea of the collective subconscious," Sophia realized aloud. "Did either of you ever read any Jung?" She paused for a moment and took the silence to mean that neither of the men had. "He developed the idea of extroverts and introverts," she continued. "In his view our personalities are shaped by conscious and unconscious forces. Some of the unconscious forces are in turn shaped by our individual personalities and experiences, but another set of forces is innate in all human beings. Jung called this the collective unconscious, and it includes things like fear of the dark, which seem to be common to most people and cultures. You could imagine that fear of the dark would have an evolutionary advantage if it kept our ancestors from exploring the dark lairs of predators or wandering too far from the campfire at night."

"It does sound sort of similar," Hyle agreed. "Where did Jung go with this idea?"

"He was concerned largely about the development of individuals," Sophia explained. "He saw the collective unconscious as a basic part of human nature that helped determine who we'd become. Like Freud, he believed that the unconscious could be unlocked by the interpretation of dreams." Sophia said. Memories of the old warehouse and the shattered doll house flashed into her mind and she pushed them aside. "This was all critical to Jung's idea of individuation. According to Jungian psychology we each have a drive to reach our own personal destiny, but we can't accomplish this until we get all the aspects of our mind—both conscious and unconscious—into balance. The analysis of dreams helps us to bring out the subconscious aspects of our psyche so that we can achieve that balance in order to reach our maximum potential and become who we are meant to be."

"That kind of psychobabble is exactly why behaviorism became popular," Hyle observed.

"Jung also suggested that the collective subconscious is the source of archetypes which recur through different cultures," continued Sophia, choosing to ignore the remark. "For example, the wise old man, the tyrannical ruler, the trickster—these are all archetypes that you can find in the folklore of many different cultures and which provide a common baseline for individuals to identify or contrast themselves with as they develop. They may also be useful in helping to interpret dreams. And speaking of dreams, I really need to sleep," she added. "I can barely hold my eyes open."

"I'm not sure why you'd bother to hold them open anyway," Hyle quipped. "It's pitch black in here. But I could use some sleep myself."

"We all could," Newman agreed.

The two men unrolled their sleeping bags in the darkness and made arrangements to leave the flashlight on a low shelf where they all could reach it.

"Since we'll probably want the light for either the food or the toilet I'll leave it right up here by your head, okay, Sophia?" Hyle said, but there was no reply. She was already asleep.

CHAPTER SEVENTY-SIX

BETWEEN THREE DOORS

Time distorted, stretching and folding back on itself. By the time she realized where she was, Sophia could not remember where she had started or how long she had been walking. Familiar walls of pale concrete flanked her, stretching forward and backward into the shadows. The cold gray walls were streaked with the fossilized remains of the water which had trickled down them over the ages. A few were still slick with moisture and her feet splashed through shallow puddles as she walked. Looking up, the walls extended into darkness. Sophia thought she could remember the luminescent gray of an open sky. Or was that a different dream?

She continued on, her footfalls on the damp cement floor the only sound. At one point she wondered how it was that she was able to see if there was no moonlight lighting the way from above. Looking down she was only partially surprised to find that her mind had filled in this gap by placing a flashlight in her hand. The beam was fading so she banged it with the palm of her free hand. Encouraged to try harder, the battered flashlight emitted a brighter beam, revealing a door ahead, which Sophia opened. She found herself in the center of a room, square and featureless, with a door in each concrete wall. Turning around, Sophia was unsurprised to see that the door had closed behind her. She reached for the handle, knowing what she would find. It was locked.

Even if she could remember where it led, turning back was no longer an option so she checked the other three doors. Behind each one lay a corridor exactly like the one that had led her to the room. With nothing to distinguish between them she picked one of the doors at random and continued on. It led her to another room, exactly the same as the one she had left. Again the door behind her locked and three new doors opened onto identical passages. Again she picked one at random. This continued for some time, a sequence of doors, corridors and rooms, disappearing into shadows around the edges of the perpetually fading flashlight beam.

Sophia grew increasingly tired, yet she pushed herself forward, door after door, struggling just a little bit more with every step. In the back of her mind—the part outside of the dream—Sophia wondered why her dream self should be tired at all. She also wondered if things would change soon because the dream was beginning to bore her. The thought that she might be going in circles crossed her mind. Inside the dream that possibility registered with a wave of despair and she almost decided to give up and lay down on the floor, cold and wet though it was. She resolved to try just one more door.

The room she entered was the same as every other room except that this one had something in it. There was some tall thin object of a slightly paler gray off to one side of the right hand door. Sophia approached it, banging on her flashlight with her open palm. The light brightened to reveal a sundial. It seemed familiar but Sophia could not think of where she might have seen it before. Examining it, she realized that what had at first appeared to be the shadow of the gnomon did not move as she moved the flashlight. Instead it was an arrow, like the single hand of a clock. An arc was carved into the surface, just inside the outer edge and covering two thirds of the circumference. The word 'noon' was inscribed at the center of the arc. At the left appeared the word 'sunset' and 'sunrise' was carved at the opposite end of the arc. The arrow pointed to a position beyond the arc before sunrise. It also pointed toward the door. The curiosity this device inspired was enough to encourage Sophia to keep going a little longer, taking the door and the passageway behind it to another room.

This room had an object near the far door—a child's riding tractor. This she did remember from another dream. Through the tractor door and down the corridor she came to a third room, and in it was the shattered doll house she expected to find. Taking the left hand door it marked, she found herself in yet another room of the same design. In the center were two armchairs, facing the opposite wall and turned toward each other at a slight angle. Sophia's curiosity at what lay beyond the three new doors was overwhelmed by her fatigue. She shuffled toward one of the chairs and collapsed into the cushions. It was an old fashioned wing chair with thickly padded arms scrolling outward. Her head slid across the high back until it came to rest comfortably against one of the wings, her body listing to one side. She allowed the exhaustion to consume her, content to slip out of consciousness and out of the dream.

"Don't give up now. You're nearly there," said a voice, shocking her back to the room.

Sophia looked around and was startled to find somebody sitting in the other chair. It had been empty when she sat down a few seconds earlier, she was sure of it. The figure was dressed all in black with its face hidden in the shadows of a hood.

"Almost where?" Sophia asked.

"You'll know when you get there," the shadowy form replied.

"But I don't even know where I am."

"Nobody does, really."

"Who are you and why are you here?" demanded Sophia.

"Where is here?"

Sophia thought about this. She was unsure how to answer. "Here in my dream," she replied at last.

"Ah, lucid dreaming. Well done, Sophia." The voice that replied was distinctly more feminine than it had been before. The figure reached up and pulled back its hood to reveal a pale face framed by black hair. Pigtails stuck straight out from either side.

"Helena?"

Helena briefly flashed a thin smile and inclined her head in acknowledgement but her eyes were filled with sorrow.

"What's the matter?"

"This will be the last time I can visit you, Sophia."

"What do you mean? Did you visit me before?" She remembered Helena—the real Helena—from Colgate and knew that she must be dead, so at first the statement confused her.

"Are you saying you have visited me in other dreams?"

Helena nodded solemnly.

"I'm sorry," Sophia told her. "I don't remember."

"You'll remember this one," replied Helena. "That's all that matters."

"Is that why I won't see you again?"

Helena nodded once more.

"So what do I do now?"

"What were you trying to do before you came to this room?" Helena asked.

"I was trying to find my way out," replied Sophia, realizing as she spoke that she was answering a rhetorical question. "And you're here to cheer me on?" she guessed. "I don't suppose you can give me any clues?"

Helena just looked at her and said nothing.

"That's what I thought," Sophia said, and forced herself up out of the chair. "This is one of those things I have to figure out for myself, right? Let's see what's behind door number one then," she said crossing the room to try the door on the left. She was completely unprepared for what she saw. Based on her previous experience she half expected to see another dark corridor ending in yet another door. From her discussion with Helena, and the fact that Helena had appeared to break the monotony of the dream in the first place, she suspected that this door might be different, but what she beheld was so unexpected that it took several seconds for her mind to make sense of what she was seeing.

A broad highway originated from the door and ran away in a straight line to the distance. It was fresh black tar with bright yellow lines in the center. Fields of some nondescript yellow-green crop filled out the view on either side, but what caught Sophia's immediate attention were the guardrails. What appeared to be guardrails in the distance resolved in the foreground into a row of silver posts. Each cylindrical post was topped with a glowing dome of blue glass. On the horizon, at the end of the road, was a huge futuristic metropolis reminiscent of the Emerald City. Coke bottle skyscrapers of twisted cobalt glass rose into the sky above an expanse of green and blue bubbles of varying sizes. As she studied it Sophia was able to make out hundreds of small dots, like a cloud of gnats, flying around the expanse of buildings. Just as she realized what they were, something flew overhead and continued down the road—a sleek metallic object sharing the same rounded design of the city, three red tail lights glowing behind it. She watched it diminish as it followed the road toward the horizon.

It was all marvelous, but the most inexplicable thing in the scene, and the first that she noticed, was the man in the foreground wearing the white lab coat. He was not more than ten yards away and yet he seemed to be unaware of her. He was examining one of the posts and held in his outstretched hand what appeared to be a sonic screwdriver—a small silver cylinder pulsing at the tip with blue light. The man in the lab coat was Hyle.

Sophia knew at once that she was looking into a different dimension or a different world somehow, but it only dawned on her slowly how it was that she knew this. First, Hyle was unaware of her despite how close he was. Second, the road and even the flying car which had traveled it seemed to extend right from the wall of the room. Finally, although the sun shone on Hyle and the magnificent city in the distance, none of the light spilled into the unlit room Sophia occupied. She was somehow equally sure that if she stepped through the doorway there would be no coming back. She considered stepping through to greet Hyle and leaving Helena and the dark room behind, but then remembered the other two doors. Reluctantly she turned away.

"That was unexpected," Sophia said, attempting to keep her tone light. Somewhere in the back of her mind Sophia noted this casual façade, amused that even her dream self was concerned about keeping up appearances. Helena only shrugged slightly and watched her.

"Let's try door number three," Sophia said as she crossed to the other side of the room.

This door opened onto another improbable outdoor scene. The grass which stretched out from the other side of the threshold was brilliant green, scattered with an abundance of wildflowers, their dazzling colors glowing in the bright sunshine. The sky above was sapphire. In a wide glade, ringed at a distance by trees with lush green foliage, below the arc of blue, people milled about in pairs and groups both small and large, some strolling, some standing and some sitting in circles. In the foreground a small group sat in a circle around the edges of a white ground cloth, a lavish feast spread out between them. Everyone wore white robes with golden trim, and even the picnic blanket was made of white fabric edged with gold tassels. In this circle of picnickers sat Newman, engaged in lively conversation, holding an apple in one hand. Sophia watched the scene for a while. Every face she examined was joyous and she felt a strong urge to step across the threshold and join the revelry. It was only the remaining door that prevented her from doing so. With a great mental effort she tore herself away from the scene and crossed to the third door.

"Truth be told," she said to Helena, "I'm a little afraid to open this last door." Helena gave her a thin smile but said nothing.

Sophia opened the door. Beyond the doorway lay a vast private library. It reminded Sophia of an old English library and was exactly the sort of place she would have had in her house if she had been wealthy enough to live in a mansion. Sets of high backed chairs of dark brown leather were arranged around small reading tables. Wooden shelves ran floor to ceiling in all directions, filled with books. A wooden ladder on a rolling rack leaned against the left hand wall, granting access to the upper rows of shelves. The room was lit with a warm and calming yellow light.

In the foreground was an immense wooden desk of polished mahogany. Its bowed sides met at thick legs which curved back out to meet the floor on wide padded feet. On the writing surface, stacks of thick leather bound tomes were arranged around the blotter, where a figure hunched over a parchment, laboring intently on some project with a quill pen. The billowing sleeves of their white shirt tapered at the wrist and then flared into frills at the cuff. The face of this person, which had been obscured by long black hair as they wrote, was suddenly revealed when she sat up to stare pensively into space. Sophia found that she was looking at herself as she might have been a few centuries earlier. She smiled at this other version of herself for a moment before turning away.

Returning to the chair next to Helena, she sat down, confused. The three doors remained open and from her vantage point in the chair Sophia could see each of the three scenes. Through one the road led to a futuristic city, boxed in by the door frame. Hyle had moved to a new post and continued to examine it with his strange device. Through another Newman was still talking happily, now carving a large watermelon. Ahead of her, the other Sophia scribbled furiously, hard at work on her magnum opus.

"If I choose one of these I can't come back, is that how it works?" Sophia asked.

"Is that what you think?" replied Helena.

"Yes, somehow I think that's the way it works."

"Then you're probably right."

"But they all look good for different reasons," Sophia protested. "Am I supposed to pick the scene I'm in? Is this supposed to be symbolic, telling me not to live someone else's life? I don't understand, Helena. Which one am I supposed to pick?"

"I can't tell you," Helena answered. She watched Sophia's reaction with sympathy. "You have to figure it out. This is your dream."

"Yes, but my dream put you in here for a purpose," Sophia reasoned. "And I don't think it was just to keep me from falling asleep in the chair. You're going to help me solve this."

When Sophia made this last statement it was not speculation. It was an imperative. She was trying to take control of her dream. That part of Sophia which was outside the dream watched anxiously to see what would happen next.

Helena stood up. She turned to Sophia and smiled, although there was still a trace of sorrow in her eyes.

"Goodbye, Sophia," she said, turning to go.

"Wait!" Sophia called out, but before she could say more the most remarkable thing happened. Somehow, without changing her form, in a way that could only make sense in a dream, Helena left through all three doors at once.

CHAPTER SEVENTY-SEVEN

THE DYING OF THE LIGHT

Yelling after Helena, Sophia woke with a start. Someone was shaking her. She opened her eyes but they saw nothing. Panic crushed in on her until she realized that someone was speaking to her softly.

"Are you okay, Sophia? Are you awake? You were calling out in your sleep." It was Newman.

"It sounded like you were yelling for someone, but we couldn't make out what you were saying," Hyle added.

Sophia explained that she had been calling out for Helena, and ended up recounting the entire dream.

"I've been having very vivid dreams ever since—" she broke off, looking for the words. "Ever since the holocaust. Some I remember clearly and some I just remember as fragments or vague impressions, but I think I remember being stuck in those dark corridors before. What do you think it means?"

"Maybe someone's trying to tell you something," Newman suggested.

"You mean the ghost of Helena is communicating to Sophia through her dreams?" Hyle asked incredulously.

"I don't know about that," answered Newman. "But divine revelations often come in the form of dreams. And who's to say that Helena's spirit couldn't communicate with her in her dreams?"

"That's ridiculous," Hyle said. "I'm not a big fan of Freud and Jung, but if you have to go somewhere with this, blame it on the subconscious, not some sort of supernatural phenomenon. Since civilization was blown apart a few months ago, no wonder she feels like she's walking around lost in a dark building with no way to get out. The scene of you sounds like a cross between you leading the flock at Asher and the summer party where you said the two of you met. I appear as a scientist in a futuristic city since we have been talking science and technology recently. That could also explain Helena's exit. It sounds like the two slit experiment with light. Sophia's mind probably pulled all these different ideas together from her subconscious. You don't need to read anything supernatural into it."

"Maybe, but how can you rule it out, Hyle?" Newman demanded. "Unless science can prove things like parapsychology and the supernatural don't exist, aren't you forced to consider them as valid possibilities?"

"That's not the way science works," Hyle responded. "Those subjects aren't even fit for science to consider."

Sophia heard the edge in his voice again and she knew where it came from. She felt that she could almost look into his mind. He was performing for her, tearing down Newman's beliefs so that he could be right and win the competition. It did not occur to her to be flattered. This was just Hyle on his own little stage and it was starting to annoy her.

"How does science work then?" she asked. "I'm curious to know what you think the rules are."

"A common misconception is that science sets out to prove things," Hyle said.

"You mean it doesn't?" Newman exclaimed. "I thought that was the basis of science."

"No. According to one of the early models of science, scientists make a series of observations and then use them to induce general laws of nature from the pattern of individual examples. Having a sufficient number of examples that supported the theory was considered to be proof that it was true. I personally appreciated the whole mission of the analytic philosophers, but that's one place where they got it wrong. They claimed that for something to be true, it had to be verifiable through observation. By this criterion they would have said that Newton was right and gravity was true."

"But then along comes Einstein," Sophia interjected.

"Right, Newton was one of the greatest scientists of all time and gravity one of the most successful theories in science, verified by observation for centuries, but ultimately it was demonstrated not to be true. That's why Karl Popper famously revised the scientific method. Instead of a criterion that something had to be verifiable, Popper said that for something to be scientific it had to be falsifiable. He also argued that science starts with conjecture drawn from observation, rather than direct induction from observation. It's a subtle difference, but the idea is that no amount of observation is sufficient to formulate a natural law. Instead we start with a hypothesis. That gets circulated around the scientific community where some experiments may lend credence to it, but also where scientists who are skeptical can perform experiments to try to falsify it. That's why the criterion of falsifiability is critical. One experiment can invalidate the whole theory."

"Like the Michelson-Morley experiment," prompted Sophia.

"Yes," Hyle agreed. "The key though is that no theory is ever proven to be true. It just becomes more and more likely the more people fail to disprove it. The other important point is that scientific discipline isn't a result of personal integrity or open-mindedness on the part of the theorist. Although those are beneficial, it's due to the convention of exposing ideas to critique by others. And that's why the supernatural isn't a fit field for science. Just as Hume said, these things always seem to happen in isolated areas where they can't be reproducibly observed. There's no opportunity to falsify them."

"Be careful with that," Sophia warned. "You know where Hume led us."

"So basically you're saying that science doesn't know anything for certain," Newman said.

"Yes," Hyle allowed, "although what we have are the best available explanations for everything. Uncertainty is the price we pay in order to leave the possibility of improvement over time. Each time a new theory supplants an old one science gets closer to the truth about how nature works."

"Do you really think so?" Sophia asked. "Have you ever read Thomas Kuhn's *The Structure of Scientific Revolutions*?"

"No, but I suspect you're about to make up for that."

"Kuhn was a science historian," Sophia continued on cue. "His work, especially on the Copernican revolution, led him to the conclusion that science doesn't progress in the gradual way that most people think. Instead it goes along not making any progress until there's a major change in thinking. He popularized the term 'paradigm shift' to describe this change."

"There are certainly theories that have a big impact on science," Hyle acknowledged, "like the heliocentric solar system of Copernicus or gravity or relativity, but I wouldn't go so far as to say that science doesn't progress apart from them. Most of what we've learned about nature has been the result of countless smaller experiments and discoveries."

"That's the classical view, yes," said Sophia, "but Kuhn saw the history of science playing out differently. He argued that science is based on paradigms. A paradigm isn't just a theory. It's a world view. When you hear the phrase 'think outside the box' the paradigm is the box—and most people don't even realize they're in one. Science can't question everything all the time. In fact, when scientists do research most things are taken for granted and only explanations within the narrow field of study are questioned. Something like the earth being the center of the universe seemed so obvious in the days before Copernicus that nobody would even think to question it. All science was done within that framework and all results were interpreted on the basis of the sun orbiting the earth, whether consciously or not."

"I suppose I'd agree with that," said Hyle. "Sounds a bit like Bacon's false Idols of the Mind, but I don't see the problem yet."

"According to Kuhn, science goes through stages. The period where there's a working paradigm he called normal science or 'puzzle solving.' This period can be very productive, but contrary to Popper, Kuhn said that when an experiment ran counter to the popular paradigm it was typically the experiment that was called into question rather than the paradigm. A single experiment might be enough to disprove a small hypothesis, but paradigms are much more durable, and often for irrational reasons. Scientists will go to great lengths to defend their paradigm."

"Because our paradigms are near the center of our web of belief," Newman concluded.

"Exactly. Think of Ptolemy and the intricate calculation of epicycles to explain away the retrograde motion of the planets in a geocentric solar system. Or think of scientists making up the ether to try to explain the behavior of light before relativity. Only when enough of these anomalies build up do people start to question the paradigm. This stage is called crisis, and out of the crisis emerges a competing paradigm which can explain the anomalies."

"Again, I don't disagree," Hyle said. "That seems like a pretty good account of how science progresses."

"Except that science doesn't necessarily progress," Sophia replied. "The new paradigm explains the old anomalies. It'll do a good job explaining some things, and scientists who hop on the bandwagon will make great progress explaining things in these areas. But the new paradigm will also have its own set of problems. When scientists choose to follow a new paradigm it's not based as much on evidence as it is on persuasion. And one of the distinguishing features of a paradigm is that it's an exclusive world view. It's completely incompatible with other paradigms. The scientists in one paradigm can't even understand or speak the language of another. Kuhn likened it to a religious conversion—a leap of faith—where once you change you can't go back. It's like the picture with the two faces and the candlestick. You can either see the faces or the candlestick, but not both at the same time."

"Now I have to disagree," Hyle said. "Most of that sounds accurate, maybe even the part about paradigms being incompatible, but I still think that science progresses. A new paradigm needs to be able to do more than just explain the anomalies of the old paradigm. It has to be able to explain more than the old paradigm did. That's progress."

"The most cynical interpreters of Kuhn would disagree," Sophia responded. "In their view science just hops from one paradigm to another, trading one set of accomplishments and flaws for another. The less cynical, possibly including Kuhn himself, would argue that each new paradigm does explain more than the previous one and therefore provides a more useful model. As long as you don't need to claim that you're any closer to the truth you may be content to call this progress."

"Of course a better model gets us closer to the truth," Hyle protested.

"Look at quantum physics," replied Sophia. "It explained the anomalies of classical physics, but it certainly resulted in a very strange view of the world and the cost of believing in it seems to be an agreement to not ask too many questions. Who's to say that some better theory won't come along and make all the quantum weirdness go away and leave us all shaking our heads about why we would have believed something so strange in the first place? In the end science may be just another world view, no better and no worse than any other."

"Do you really believe that? Or do you just have a philosophy for every occasion?" Hyle replied. "You can quote all the philosophers and argue every side of a question, but do you actually believe anything for yourself? Are you saying that you believe your dreams are supernatural just because science may work by paradigms? Do you think some new paradigm is going to come along in which ghosts and ESP are neatly explained and we can know the position and momentum of an electron at the same time?"

The question took Sophia by surprise. She knew Hyle well enough to understand that he was overreacting because she had called his beliefs into question, so she knew better than to take his bluster personally, but the words stung nonetheless.

"I don't know, maybe," she replied at length. "A lot of scientists thought Jung's collective subconscious was a bunch of nonsense, but you've helped explain it through sociobiology. Who knows what we'll believe in the future?"

"When was Jung doing his work?" asked Newman, eager to change the topic.

"He was a contemporary of Freud and supporter at first," Sophia answered. "I think he published one book early in the twentieth century and a few more in the middle. But he split from Freud early on. Why do you ask?"

"When we were talking last time and you mentioned the trickster archetype it reminded me of Claude Levi-Strauss. He came to some similar ideas in social anthropology by studying myths. He saw the same elements in myths across many different and unrelated cultures and thought they must have some common origin in human thought. The trickster figure is one of those. It's supposed to mediate between two polar ideas and help reconcile them. For example, the coyote and raven are supposed to mediate between life and death."

Hyle snorted. "How is that supposed to work?"

"Herbivores represent life and predators represent death. The coyote and raven are scavengers, so they're in between and have elements of both. The point is that Levi-Strauss had this same idea of looking for common patterns of human thought, and he was influenced by Saussure who did something similar with linguistics around the end of the nineteenth century. I just thought it was interesting that all these different disciplines used the same sort of approach."

"Congratulations, Newman," Sophia laughed. "You have applied the principles of structuralism to discover structuralism itself."

"I'm not entirely sure what you just said," Newman confessed.

"You looked at researchers in several diverse fields and found an underlying pattern which united them. That's essentially what structuralism seeks to do within a field. Those early psychologists Hyle mentioned for example, the ones who used introspection to try to understand the structure of the mind, were structuralists. Jung, Saussure, Levi-Strauss were also structuralists because they were all looking for similar patterns across different sets of data, whether they were individual psychologies, languages or cultures. Structuralism stands in contrast to reductionism, which is the main mode of scientific research." Sophia had a sense that Hyle was waiting to interject and hurried to finish her point. "Take biology for example. A common scientific approach is to say that in order to understand animals you need to understand their anatomy, which means understanding organs. But organs are composed of cells and in order to understand cells you need to understand molecules. Molecules are composed of atoms and in order to understand those we need to understand the relationship between protons, neutrons and electrons. But those in turn are made of subatomic particles, so ultimately we need to understand quantum physics."

"That's not all there is to science though," Hyle objected.

"No, of course not," agreed Sophia. "Knowledge benefits from both pursuits. It's like a digital picture. Reductionism gives you better and better resolution. Without it the picture would be too blurry to understand. On the other hand, you'll never see the whole picture if you only stare at the pixels. Your explanation of sociobiology fits the description of structuralism. Structuralism has also had an impact on modern philosophy, influencing people like Jacques Lacan, who applied it to Freudian psychology, Michel Foucault who applied it to the power structure of social institutions, and ultimately Jacques Derrida."

"What do you mean 'ultimately' Jacques Derrida?" Newman asked.

"Derrida started and was the major figure in a school of thought called deconstructionism. He began from the premise that most people are looking for some source of meaning, some ultimate Truth with a capital T from which all meaning flows. For Plato it's the transcendent world of the Forms. For Aristotle, Locke, and modern science it's the material world and the laws of nature. For Christians like Augustine it's God. According to Derrida, all attempts to find meaning are characterized by this goal of finding some central source. The different schools of belief just move it around and rename it. Even structuralism, which attempts to cast a wider net than the classical methods, ends up being trapped in the language of those methods."

"What's that supposed to mean?" asked Hyle.

"For example, the search for a higher form of reality or ultimate Truth tends to be characterized by pairs of words you can call binaries, in which one word is favored over the other. Body is viewed as inferior to soul, action inferior to thought, becoming inferior to being. These relationships parallel the belief that we live in an inferior world from which we search for a superior Truth. Derrida critically analyzes the language used in various works of philosophy to demonstrate that the texts are self-contradictory. He doesn't believe there's any ultimate Truth to be found and shows through his analysis of language that philosophy is incapable of finding one, and that even if it could find some ultimate Truth it wouldn't be able to express it to anyone."

"Why is that?" asked Newman.

"Derrida believed that words are too vague to convey precise meaning. In fact, one of the things he tries to demonstrate is that, since words are just signifiers for things and ideas, they're imprecise and end up only referring to other things and ideas. Ultimately we just chase ideas around in a circle but never get to any final goal."

"If he believed that language was useless, why did he bother to write anything at all?" asked Hyle.

"A fair point," acknowledged Sophia. "There are some who dismiss Derrida as a parlor magician doing sleight of hand with language, but others regard him as brilliant. He was aware of the possibility that his own techniques might be used against him and was a master of manipulating language. Much of his work includes double meanings, clever puns and other techniques that make it very difficult to pin him down. If you argued that people couldn't agree on a single interpretation of his work, I think he might be happy with that conclusion."

"French philosophy sure took a turn for the depressing in the twentieth century," noted Newman.

"Deconstructionism is supposed to be liberating, like existentialism," Sophia clarified. "I agree with you though. In the modern age, science and philosophy undermined organized religion to the point that Nietzsche declared that God is dead. Now in the postmodern age philosophy seems to have devoured itself and undermined science in the process. Wittgenstein and logical positivism destroyed metaphysics, reducing it to problems of language, and then Derrida undermined structuralism and language. Analytical philosophy reduced empirical philosophy to mathematics and then Gödel demonstrated that mathematics can't be a complete set of knowledge. Kuhn called science into question—"

"What are you suggesting?" asked Hyle. "Should we go back to living in caves and hunting mammoths with our spears?"

"Have you looked around the world recently, Hyle?" Newman interjected. "We seem to be heading in that direction."

Light filled the room, temporarily blinding the two men as the flashlight beam bobbed around in the corner before coming to rest on the toilet. Sophia shuffled over to it, retched and switched the light back off.

"Sorry," she said. "I'm still not feeling that well."

"Wait, turn that back on," Newman exclaimed. "What's wrong with your face?"

"What the hell is that?" Hyle said, enunciating each word.

"What? What is it?" she asked, the fear in her voice rising.

"You have—spots," answered Newman.

"On your hands too," Hyle added. The clinical tone of his voice frightened Sophia even more than Newman's uncertainty. Sophia examined her hand under the flashlight. The back was covered by a dozen red spots. They were the size of chicken pox but not raised or itchy. A few of them glistened with blood that was seeping through her skin. She switched the light back off.

She whispered, "Oh God, what is that?" There was a long silence. Sophia steadied her voice. "What is it?" she demanded.

"I don't know," Hyle said. "Probably just—"

"Stop it!" Sophia interrupted, shouting. "Stop it! Don't you dare say that it's nothing! I can tell what you're thinking. You think I'm going to die. Just tell me what it is!"

Hyle's lips pressed together so hard they disappeared altogether from his face. His throat constricted and for several long seconds no words—not even breath—would come out.

"Tell me," Sophia demanded again, her voice softening. "Just tell me the truth, Hyle."

"The Mumbai Plague," he answered. He spat out his reply quickly as if even the name of the disease were contagious and held his breath again. A sharp intake of air in the darkness was Sophia's only response.

"No, Hyle," objected Newman. "That can't be true. We all got a vaccine for it in Asher. Besides, how could she have it but not us? We never even saw anybody with it."

"We have no idea how well the vaccine works," Hyle said.

Sophia began crying quietly. Newman moved to put his arms around her.

"No! Get away!" she shouted. "I don't want you to get it too. Get back! Both of you. Get away from me."

Hyle, who was already standing, did take a few steps back toward the ladder, but Newman refused.

"No," he said simply and wrapped his arms around her. "We're not going anywhere. At least I'm not. We're not going to leave you alone."

For a moment Hyle said nothing. He became acutely aware of the sound of his breath in the darkness. He felt the pulsing of his heart. Then with a long silent breath he stepped forward quietly.

"If we were going to catch it from you we probably already have it," he said, and crouched down to find Sophia's knee and rest his hand on it reassuringly. "We won't leave you."

"We should go try to find some help," suggested Newman.

"Even if we could find somebody there's no real cure," Hyle replied. "It had a high mortality rate even when the hospitals were open."

"What's going to happen?" Sophia whispered. "How long do you think I have?"

"I don't want—"

"Tell me, Hyle," she demanded. "I want to hear it. Tell me the truth. Everything."

Hyle sighed.

"It's a hemorrhagic fever, like Marburg and Ebola, except with a much longer incubation. It can take about a week for signs to start to show, but then it's only a few days. The virus basically eats you from the inside out. I'm sorry, Sophia."

She found his hand in the darkness and Hyle tried not to flinch at the touch. Squeezing it, she said, "Don't be. You saved my life, remember?"

Hyle wanted to say something more, but nothing worked. He just squeezed her hand in return until she lay down to go to sleep. Eventually Newman and Hyle slept too.

Time passed without any ability to measure or even estimate its length. The flashlight faded with each use until it was gone. Sophia slept most of the time and Hyle and Newman were quiet for fear of waking her. In the silence and blackness they returned to sleep quickly and life fell into a routine. They fumbled around in the darkness, eating, sleeping and waiting to die.

PART V

Twilight
All or Nothing

CHAPTER SEVENTY-EIGHT

DEUS EX MACHINA

Sunlight poured into the shelter and a large figure appeared suddenly, leaping down to bypass the ladder and landing solidly. The shock through the floor of the structure woke Hyle. Newman, who had awakened when the hatch was opened, squinted into the light in a vain attempt to identify the silhouette.

"Good, you made it," said a familiar deep voice.

"Auld!" Hyle exclaimed, allowing his relief to be displayed unchecked. "You scared the bejeezus out of me."

Sophia reacted only by moaning as if she just wanted someone to turn out the lights and let her get a few more hours of sleep. This triggered Newman's memory.

"Auld, get out. We've been infected with the Mumbai Plague." He gestured with both hands to wave Auld away. It then occurred to him to examine his own hands, which were still clear of the red spots that covered Sophia's skin. Hyle was also unblemished. The only part of Sophia that was visible was the side of her face and it was still marked with the lesions.

"Not to worry," Auld replied and approached Sophia. She roused slowly.

"Auld?" she asked groggily, lifting her head from the sleeping bag.

Newman gasped and clamped his hand to his mouth. At the top of the sleeping bag where her head had been, the light colored fabric was covered with some dark material.

"These are purpura," Auld proclaimed after taking Sophia's hand and examining it. "It is not the Mumbai Plague. This is radiation sickness."

"What? Are you sure?" Hyle asked.

"Yes." Auld reached over to the head of the sleeping bag, ran his hand across the black mass, and then pulled something up. Between his fingers he held some of the dark material. "Hair loss is one of the signs."

"Radiation?" Newman exclaimed. "That's good news—right?" He felt a sudden twinge of guilt at the wave of relief that he experienced. Auld seemed to read this.

"For you? Yes. For Sophia, maybe. It could still be fatal, but it is better than the Plague."

"I didn't mean—"

"We need to get her to some help," Auld continued, interrupting Newman. "I will go find a car."

"What happened to our truck?" asked Hyle.

"It blocked an RPG for me," Auld replied with no trace of humor.

"Do you know where we can go for help?" Newman asked.

"The best bet is to keep going to Arizona."

"What's this all about?" Hyle demanded. "Why are you helping us? And how do you know where we're going?"

"Hyle!" Sophia mustered her strength to sit up fully and glare at him.

"Sorry," he said, looking from her to Auld. "We're grateful of course, but I can't believe that it's coincidence that you just showed up here in the middle of Kansas in the nick of time to save us. I think we deserve an explanation."

Sophia started to object, but Auld silenced her with a wave of his hand.

"It is okay. I do not blame you for wondering, but it is a long story."

"We don't have time, Hyle," concluded Newman.

"If we're heading for Arizona a few extra minutes isn't going to matter a whole lot," Hyle argued. "And I'd like to know who I'm traveling with."

"That is fair," Auld agreed. "Ask me what you like and I will answer."

"We don't have to—" began Newman, but Hyle interrupted him.

"How long have you been following us?"

"I followed you all the way from Colgate."

As Auld spoke Sophia listened closely to his words. His answer seemed honest, but she was convinced that he was holding something back, and suspected that he had been following them for much longer. She tried to remember when she had first been aware of the sound of a motorcycle engine in the distance.

"And why us?" Hyle asked.

"I am interested in you because the one who calls himself Asha Zendik is interested in you."

"The Prophet?" Newman asked.

"Yes."

"Why is the Prophet interested in us?" Hyle demanded. "Is it just because we left Asher?"

"He has foreseen a prophecy, or so he believes," Auld explained. "It is of three travelers who have the power to undo his plans."

This was another half truth, Sophia realized. She had the impression that each answer Auld gave was an intentional and carefully crafted evasion. He also seemed to be aware that she knew this and was unconcerned by it. In fact, if anything he seemed to be amused, although she could not tell if it was in some conspiratorial way directed at her or whether he considered this word play some form of sport. Maybe both.

"We know about the prophecy, but how do you know about it?" asked Newman.

"I was watching Zendik long before the war."

"Then I gather you want to stop his plans?" Hyle guessed.

"Yes."

Hyle smiled appreciatively, but Newman's face darkened.

"I already told you Hyle—I'll have no part in killing the Prophet or anyone else."

"I have no intention of killing Zendik," Auld responded. Half-truth.

"Do you know what his plan is?" asked Hyle.

"I have some information I can share, but his plans are very complex and difficult for a man to decipher." Carefully constructed evasion. Sophia could tell that Auld was particularly pleased with his wording of this one.

"Let me ask you this then," Hyle continued. "Do you believe his plans involved orchestrating the nuclear attacks?"

"Yes," Auld replied.

"What about the Mumbai Plague?"

"That as well."

"Do you have any actual evidence, or is this just speculation?" challenged Newman.

"I know some things, but it is not what you would call conclusive evidence. However, I have other reasons for my certainty."

"And why can't you share these reasons?" asked Newman, clearly skeptical.

"It would not be good policy for me to reveal my sources. You will just have to trust me."

"I can't believe that," Newman stated. "Why would he do such a thing?"

"That is what you need to figure out."

"You mean 'we,'" Hyle corrected.

Auld shrugged. Even the shrug was evasive Sophia thought, with a grudging appreciation.

"You are planning to go with us?" confirmed Hyle.

"Yes, I am."

"Why are you so interested in the Prophet?" asked Newman.

"I prefer to call him Zendik," Auld replied. "He has been at work on a large conspiracy, in some form or other, for a very long time and I am the only one who fully understands the extent of his deception. I have been watching him, waiting for an opportunity to expose him and end his plans."

"That seems a bit arrogant, thinking you're the only one who knows what is going on," observed Hyle.

"You will have to forgive me. Sometimes knowledge begets arrogance, is that not so?" Auld locked his eyes onto Hyle who shifted uncomfortably.

"Why didn't you just go to the authorities?" asked Newman.

"If the guy has enough contacts to start a nuclear war what do you think the police would be able to do? Or the FBI even?" Hyle answered. "What I want to know is how was he able to convince so many people to pitch the world into a nuclear war."

"I know you learned a great deal about Asha Zendik and the Union of Faith in your research," Auld replied, "but I think you know very little of who he was before this."

"We found the titles of some of his research papers under the name of A.E. Poimen," Hyle said. "Some pretty wild stuff about hypnosis and telepathy and things like that."

"Yes, but before his interest in things paranormal he had another career and another name."

"Another name?" Hyle repeated incredulously. "What was it?"

"He was a biochemist at a university out in California, specializing in psychology," Auld replied. "He went by the name of Eno Anderson. For several decades he did average work, but then suddenly his luck changed dramatically. Within a few years he invented two pharmaceuticals, one of which became the best selling anti-anxiety drug on the market. He could have retired comfortably on the royalties from the lesser of the drugs, but chose to continue his work. Over time, he became more and more interested in the physical and environmental conditions that affect learning, and soon became an expert on the effects of psychotropic drugs on learned behavior and mental conditioning."

Auld paused to let the meaning of his last statement sink in. Hyle's was the first expression to reveal the light of understanding. Sophia was close behind. Before Hyle could speak, Auld nodded, confirming their unspoken conclusion.

"In the late seventies, he was approached by the government to do some highly classified work in the general areas of deprogramming and programming— brainwashing. He worked for them for over a decade. No doubt he acquired many useful skills and contacts. By the early nineties, he and the government parted ways. His ideas had become too radical to be of use to them, and he found them to be too restrictive. They gave him a new identity as Anderson Poimen. He published a book to give himself some credibility and set himself up as a professor in a small Midwestern university. Somehow his fringe research never seemed to run out of government grant money. That brings us to the part you know. His sailboat disappeared, his body was never recovered and a little while later Asha Zendik appeared in the world."

"Why would somebody stage their own death just to start up a religious movement?" Newman challenged.

"Maybe he felt that he couldn't effectively preach an anti-technology agenda if people knew he had been a scientist," suggested Sophia.

"Maybe," said Newman, "but staging your own death is a bit extreme."

"So is a full-scale nuclear holocaust," pointed out Hyle. "Besides, we're talking about somebody who thinks he can contact alternate dimensions through hypnosis. Staging your own death seems downright rational compared to that."

"I still don't buy it," concluded Newman.

"It all fits though," Hyle argued. "We already confirmed that he met with all the military, political and religious leaders necessary to orchestrate a global nuclear war."

Auld nodded.

"If he developed some kind of advanced brainwashing technique," Hyle continued, "maybe that's how he got all the key people to cooperate with his plan."

"But why?" objected Newman. "Why orchestrate a nuclear war? He was already rich. If he wanted fame or power he could have just brainwashed the right people. I still don't see any reason to believe he's behind the nuclear attacks. There's no motive."

"You're right," Hyle conceded. "We still don't know what he's after, but everything else fits. If we can figure out what he's trying to do I'm sure we'll find his motive for starting the nuclear exchange."

"This is why we need to go to Arizona," Auld said.

"And because you think there's somebody there who can help Sophia?" Newman asked, allowing his suspicion to bleed through into the tone of his voice.

"Yes, of course. Zebulon will have someone who can help her," Auld replied.

"Zebulon?" Newman repeated. "That name sounds familiar. I suppose I must have heard it in Maine." A thought occurred to him. "Will we be able to get in? We're not welcome back in Asher you know."

"Zebulon is exclusive and walled like Asher," Auld explained. "It is built in the foothills of a mountain, but outside the walls is a large settlement of pilgrims and refugees who were denied entrance."

This answer bothered Sophia. Auld implied that there was someone in this settlement outside Zebulon who could help her, but there was something left unsaid. There was some caveat or loophole buried somewhere in his words. He met her eyes and gave her a reassuring smile, as if asking for her trust. For some reason she did not understand, she was willing to grant it.

"Have you been to Zebulon? Do you know how to get there?" Hyle asked.

"I have not been inside, but I know how to get there, yes."

"That's a lucky break," Hyle noted, addressing his comment to Sophia and Newman. He turned back to Auld. "Sophia and I spent quite a while trying to find Asher even though we were only a few miles away. All we knew about this place was that Zendik had set up camp somewhere in southern Arizona. Knowing they way should make the trip much quicker."

"If we can find gas," Newman reminded Hyle. "Every car we've seen around here has been siphoned."

"Leave that to me," said Auld. "I will be back in a while. A few hours. Tomorrow latest. Just make sure she eats something."

Without waiting for a reply Auld took a few large strides toward the ladder and ascended. A few minutes later a motorcycle engine started nearby and then faded into the distance.

"That was interesting," Hyle said, breaking the silence. "I'm glad I was wrong about the Mumbai Plague, Sophia. I'm sorry. I really thought—"

"It's okay, Hyle," she said.

"We'll find you some help in Zebulon and you'll be feeling better in no time," Hyle said confidently.

"Auld has you completely snowed, doesn't he?" observed Newman.

"What do you mean? You don't think he was telling the truth?"

"I don't know. I just get a bad vibe from him. If he didn't claim to know the way there I would have suggested going without him."

"A bad vibe," Hyle echoed, laughing. "What do you think, Sophia?"

"I think he was telling the truth, but he was definitely holding something back. Just about every answer was a carefully worded half-truth, understatement or double meaning."

"That's what I mean," agreed Newman, "He has some kind of hidden agenda, and I feel like he's trying to manipulate us. I can't deny that he helped us out, but that doesn't mean I have to trust him. We don't know the guy from Adam."

CHAPTER SEVENTY-NINE

THE GIFT OF FIRE

Yawning and stretching, Sophia struggled to shake off the fatigue she had felt since waking. She had eaten a decent meal accompanied by plenty of water in the hopes that this would help her to feel better, but it had not. A gray light still lit the shelter from the top of the ladder shaft at one end, although it was much dimmer than when Auld had arrived. This was in part due to the fact that Auld had rolled the hay wagon back over the opening when he left. Hyle had interpreted this to mean that Auld felt it was safe to leave the doors open as long as the wagon was in place, and since the flashlight was long ago dead, nobody argued with this conclusion.

They had been talking on and off, jumping back and forth between a limited set of topics—Sophia's health, Auld and the Prophet. Unless they addressed her directly Sophia mostly rested and listened to the men talk.

"I don't know why you find it so hard to believe," Hyle said, returning to the argument he had been having on and off with Newman ever since Auld left. "Religion is probably responsible for more wars than any other cause in history."

"And science has developed weapons to help us kill more people more quickly when we do go to war," Newman retorted. "Do we have to have the science versus religion debate again? It goes nowhere."

"I'm always happy to have that debate, but that wasn't my point this time. This isn't science versus religion. What I'm getting at is reality versus your idealized perception of religion. If you can't believe that Zendik could be behind a nuclear war, it's because your view of religion is skewed. Some of the worst bigots, some of the most hateful, judgmental, vindictive people I have met have considered themselves religious."

"I don't doubt that there are people like that, Hyle, but that's not the message of any religion, and certainly not the Union of Faith. Look at the name—union—it's supposed to bring people together. That's the driving force behind every religion. Just because some people don't get the message doesn't mean that religion is bad. The problem isn't with religion or even my conception of religion—it's with individual people." Hyle shook his head.

"Okay, so religion unifies people. To what end? I think Nietzsche got it right and most churchgoers were just going through the motions every Sunday out of some vague sense of obligation. Maybe your parish priest or pastor or whatever was able to get people to donate cans for the hungry or collect clothes for the poor, but his efforts to do good in the name of God have to be weighed against the guy who is willing to strap on a bunch of explosives and blow himself up in a crowd of civilians in the name of God. That's the big problem with religion—once you think you have God on your side, everyone else becomes inferior. Or worse, they become enemies of God—pagans, infidels, heathens. Killing them becomes justified. Is it really so hard to believe that the Prophet thinks that he has God on his side? Delacroix was convinced we were chosen by God to come to

Asher. That means that everyone who didn't come wasn't chosen. They're the pagans, infidels and heathens. No mercy for the enemies of God. Historically that's been an excuse for repression, gay bashing, racism, sexism, genocide, terrorism and outright war. Look at the Crusades and jihad in the Middle East. Or take Northern Ireland. There you've got Protestants and Catholics—both Christian sects who are supposed to follow the teachings of Jesus Christ—blowing each other up in the name of God."

"Now you're mixing politics with religion," Newman pointed out. "None of those conflicts were just about religion. No doubt rulers and rebels and politicians co-opt religion to call people to arms, but that doesn't make religion bad. Remember your argument in Asher about technology? You can use a hammer to build a school or to kill your neighbor. It isn't the hammer that's good or evil. Even though it can be corrupted, the basic message of every religion is one of tolerance and unity. Religion teaches people how to live together, and every society has some form of religion. That can't be coincidence. It must come from some higher source."

"It does unify groups of people and teach them to live together," Hyle allowed, "but at the expense of outsiders who don't fit within the group. Isn't it interesting that the same religion wasn't given to everyone? People tend to be whatever religion is dominant in their family, community and part of the world. If you're American or European you're likely to be Christian. If you're Israeli you're likely to be Jewish. If you're from elsewhere in the Middle East you're likely to be Muslim. People don't believe religions because they're some revealed truth. They believe them because it's part of their culture."

"I suspect you'd find that atheists are more prevalent in less observant families, in liberal areas of this country and in industrialized countries where technology has undermined faith compared to other places," Newman argued. "They're also prevalent in universities where groups of intellectuals find it fashionable to congratulate themselves for escaping the superstition of less intelligent people. Who would admit to being devout in such an environment? Maybe atheism is just a cultural phenomenon rather than some rational belief."

"There's an alternative explanation for religion that doesn't involve anything supernatural," Hyle said. Newman laughed at this, but Hyle continued. "Did you know that neurologists have identified the temporal lobe as an area that controls religious feeling? There are cases of people who experience brain damage who become extremely religious."

"There may be some part of the brain that influences love too, but that wouldn't mean that love doesn't exist," Newman objected.

"There's no question that religion exists," Hyle clarified. "The question is what it's based on. You asked why all cultures have some type of religion. I say it's because humans are predisposed to it, just the way we're predisposed to a fear of snakes and spiders. People needed to make up stories to explain why it gets dark at night, why the sun and stars are in the sky, why there's disease and death. The gods were made up to explain all these things that seemed too magical to comprehend in any other way. The first gods in our Western recorded history—the Egyptian, Greek and Roman gods—were modeled on people with supernatural powers. They frequently walked the earth and had human failings. Once we created the gods we immediately set about trying to figure out how to get them to do what we wanted. We offered sacrifices and rituals and certain behaviors so that they'd protect us from sickness, drought, starvation. The only problem is that gods are fickle and sometimes everything we did was ignored. People still got sick and died, crops still failed. It didn't quite add up. We needed a better model—a better paradigm to use the scientific analogy—and along comes the God of the Jews."

"Wait," Newman interrupted. "Are you trying to say that the whole Judeo-Christian tradition came out of some effort to improve upon Greek and Roman mythology?"

"Greek and Roman religion," Hyle corrected. "Mythology is what you call a religion you've decided not to take seriously. To me it's all mythology."

"Fine," conceded Newman, "but even though some doctrines can be debated and change within a faith, religions have to be based on fundamental beliefs that can't change. You don't really believe that religion changes the same way science does, do you?"

"Why not? Science and religion are both collections of ideas. Why can't ideas evolve the same way organisms do? In fact, Richard Dawkins coined the term 'meme' to describe ideas in terms of genetics. A meme is analogous to a gene—it's like a thought virus. Some thoughts are hatched and die shortly afterwards, but some catch on in a host and spread like wildfire. Many of these memes are in competition with each other. Capitalism and communism, empiricism and rationalism, Judaism and Christianity—these are all such successful memes that they're the equivalent of scientific paradigms. You can't believe wholeheartedly in both at the same time."

"And you think Judaism was just a better paradigm than pantheism?" Newman asked skeptically.

"Sure. First of all you get the convenience of one-stop shopping. No more praying to one god for a bountiful harvest and a different one to find true love or cure a sick relative and a yet another to bring you victory in battle. Second, this new god is omniscient, all powerful and perfect, unlike the Greek pantheon. Third, followers of this new god are promised a reward in the afterlife."

"I don't think people shop around and pick the religion with the most benefits," Newman countered.

"Not like you'd shop for a car, no," Hyle agreed. "But look at it from a marketing perspective over the long term. Religions come and go. It's a fact that people do leave one faith to join another. Why? If you sacrifice your ox and your crops still fail, you might begin to question the gods. The great thing about a reward in the afterlife is that nobody can come back from the dead to tell you it's all a crock. Moving the reward to the afterlife makes it impossible to disprove. It makes the meme harder to kill. And this idea was first marketed to conquered people and downtrodden slaves. Who could be more receptive to the idea that they'll find paradise in the next life? Of course it also had immediate benefits in the real world as well. It brought people hope and unified them, gave them dietary laws to help health, social rules to promote order."

"Hyle, it almost sounds like you're saying that religion can be beneficial," said Newman.

"For primitive downtrodden slaves with no concept of self-government, absolutely."

"And you think somebody just invented a new religion because they thought it would serve them better than pantheism?"

"No, that's not the point," Hyle replied. "It could have been intentional, by someone who wanted to rally their people for example, but it could just as well have been a random evolution of ideas. Wherever the ideas came from though, they went through the same type of natural selection that species do. Only the fittest ideas survive."

"I still don't think such a radical change can occur in a religion," Newman said.

"Here's one example I learned from you," Hyle offered. "Judaism was very successful, but exclusive. For this monotheism to really spread it takes Jesus to preach a more universal message. And you told us that it was Paul who determined that one didn't have to be Jewish to be justified by God. It was enough to have faith in Jesus. Just like the genetic mutation that allowed sea creatures to first breathe on land, or enables an avian virus to infect humans, this one mutation in religious thought was enough to allow this brand of monotheism to spread across the world. If you want another example, consider Martin Luther posting his theses on the church door and starting the Protestant faith."

"I take the point that religion can change around the periphery of its core beliefs," Newman conceded, "but neither of your examples is quite on par with jumping from the Greco-Roman pantheon to Judeo-Christian monotheism, and I'm not convinced that Paul or Martin Luther really intended a radical change."

"What about the Council of Nicea?" Hyle asked. "Before that there was a debate among Christians as to whether God, Jesus and the Holy Spirit were three separate deities or somehow the same—basically a choice between pantheism and monotheism. Of course, rather than pick either of the logical alternatives, they decided to try to create a monotheism where three things are actually one thing."

"After you told us that light can be a wave and a particle at the same time, you're going to call the concept of the Trinity illogical?" Newman countered.

"Fair enough," Hyle conceded. "I suppose I have to give you that one. But the point is that a large group of Church leaders gathered to make an official decision about the relation of Jesus to God. Every time the Catholic Church canonizes a new saint it's a smaller version of the same thing. These are ideas that are discussed and debated and consciously chosen."

"Even if these ideas do change as you say, God chooses to act in this world through people," said Newman. "I'd argue that it's God's will that things unfold this way."

"Of course you would," Hyle replied. "That's one of the things I find so frustrating about arguing with people about religion. It's been through a couple millennia of evolution so now there's an answer for every question. It's like Santa Claus."

"Santa Claus?" Newman asked with an incredulous laugh.

"Yes, the tradition of Santa Claus is like Christianity on training wheels," said Hyle. "They both feature a benevolent magical old guy that nobody ever sees who can always tell if you're being naughty or nice and rewards you accordingly. Any time a child asks some logical question that would help lead them to the conclusion that Santa Claus doesn't exist, a crafty adult comes up with some explanation to keep the child's belief intact. Why don't we see Santa Claus? Because he lives far away in the North Pole. Not unlike living far away in the heavens. Why don't we see him when he comes on Christmas Eve to give us presents? Because he waits until you're sleeping. Not unlike waiting until you're dead to give you your reward of paradise. Magical flying reindeer, elves to help him make toys—over time the story gets enriched and improved. It's the same with religion. It keeps changing and improving the answers until it finds the ones that people can't disprove."

"Or maybe it had the answers all along and you just weren't around to hear them," suggested Newman.

"Maybe, but I doubt it," Hyle answered. "Do you believe that the earth was created in six days?"

"You mean literally in six days, like starting on Monday and resting on Sunday?"

"Yes."

"Not necessarily," Newman said. "It may be that what was translated as day originally referred to a longer period of time. If you look at the sequence of events in the Bible it parallels the sequence of events that science describes pretty well. God starts with, 'Let there be light' which could be the Big Bang. On day two He creates a firmament which is similar to the gases condensing to form planets. On day three He gathers the waters in one place to form the land and sea, similar to the cooling earth of science. On day four He divides the light in the firmament to days and seasons and creates the sun, moon and stars, which establishes earth in the solar system. On day five He fills the seas with creatures, which is where science believes the first life began, and on day six He creates the animals of the land and finally humans, which reflects the order of evolution science plots. If you took each of these days to be eons, the Bible wouldn't be that far off of current science."

"I guess you were paying attention in science class after all," Hyle allowed. "But what you just demonstrated is the type of rationalization that allows the Bible to be creatively reinterpreted so that nobody can prove it to be just plain wrong. That's the evolution of religious thought in action. Religion has been retreating from logic since the dawn of time. If I tell you that I have a hard time with the idea of God as an old guy with a white beard sitting up on a cloud, you'll tell me he's a supernatural force that's everywhere and nowhere. Philosophers try to prove the existence of God with logic and every one of them fails. So does religion die? No, instead the faithful start to argue that if religion can't be based on logic, then you need to reject logic and take a leap of faith. Now if you ask for facts and proof it looks like treason. God exists outside the laws of nature so that science can never question religion. Brilliant! Historians and archeologists discover that various accounts in the Bible are inaccurate? That's okay—it's because that part wasn't meant to be taken literally—it's figurative, just like the six days of creation. How can you tell which parts are figurative? Whichever ones you can prove are wrong. The rest is literal. If something bad happens we can explain it away by saying that we can't presume to know the mind of God. But in all other areas religions claim to know the mind of God on a regular basis."

"I'm not sure what you're getting at, Hyle," Newman replied. Sophia noted the edge in his voice. In the past he had always seemed to enjoy this type of discussion. Even in these sparring matches with Hyle, Newman seemed to take everything in stride, but Sophia could tell he was reaching a limit. "First you complain that religion is inflexible and followers have to accept the dogma unquestioningly," he continued. "Now you say it changes and you're complaining about that. I don't necessarily agree with your view, but even if you're right you've made religion sound very similar to science, where you consider it a virtue that ideas change when they're discussed and debated. I also think you're making the mistake of treating religion—or at least a whole religious faith like Christianity—as the equivalent of a theory like gravity. Religion is more than that. It's a collection of beliefs. It's a world view. You may be able to disprove a scientific theory with the right collection of facts, but you wouldn't disprove all of science or the entire branch of physics. You can no more expect to disprove all of religion or an entire religious faith."

"The difference is that in science there are very strict criteria for picking one idea over another, with the goal of getting closer to the truth," Hyle argued. "In the rest of pop culture—including religion and politics—choosing between ideas is a popularity contest where the most appealing memes and the best marketing win. In that type of free-for-all, anything goes to protect and promote the ideas you cherish."

"What's the difference between that and scientists defending a paradigm?" Newman interrupted.

"The search for truth," replied Hyle. "Look at the Council of Nicea again. You have Church leaders voting to determine the divine nature of Jesus and which breakaway sects are heretical and which are canon. That's one difference between science and religion. You can't determine the truth by a vote, but it's not a bad way to run a political movement. You may say that the creation of the earth in six days was figurative, but no Christian I know would suggest that the miracles or resurrection of Jesus were figurative. That's another big difference between science and religion—religion is unwilling to question its core beliefs. A third difference is that religion changes specifically to undermine other faiths—or at least Christianity does."

"What's that supposed to mean?"

"Most scholars agree that Jesus wasn't born in December and the birth of Jesus wasn't celebrated for centuries after the founding of Christianity. It was Pope Julius I in the fourth century AD who founded Christmas on December 25th. That's a matter of historical record. Christianity was fighting for attention at the time against a number of pagan religions that had end of year celebrations around the winter solstice, not the least of which was in Rome where Saturnalia ended on December 25th. Christianity was able to penetrate the Roman religious market much more successfully once it was able to offer a competitive holiday."

"And Easter is supposed to have come from the Teutonic goddess Eostre or Ostara, the Assyrian goddess Ishtar or the ancient Greek goddess Astarte, depending on who you ask," Newman added. "They were all ancient fertility goddesses and there were spring celebrations in their names. But several Christian faiths don't celebrate Christmas or Easter, so again, what's your point?"

"My point is that religions are basically thought viruses that are competing with each other, and Christianity has been particularly virulent because it has either consciously undermined or unconsciously absorbed the features of its competitors. It built in self-perpetuation by making it a mission for followers to spread their beliefs and save non-believers. It sent missionaries out to convert people from other beliefs and it refined the concept of heresy to decrease the chance followers would be lured away by other ideas. And it's not just other religions—Christianity has actively opposed science as well. Look at Galileo."

"Oh please," Newman interjected. "Let's not go back to Galileo."

"Fine," conceded Hyle. "Then what about the Scopes monkey trial?"

"More recent, but also ancient history."

"Intelligent design?" suggested Hyle. "Another example of how the ideas and tactics change, but the intent doesn't. Instead of suing to prevent the teaching of evolution, proponents of intelligent design dress up the creation myth and try to pass it off as a scientific theory. Religion has always opposed science."

"Clearly you see it that way, Hyle, but I knew several scientists who were also religious. The two don't always have to be in conflict."

"I think they do though," Hyle insisted. "It's built right into the foundation of Christian belief. Look at the story of the Garden of Eden. Adam and Eve are living in blissful ignorance and are forbidden from eating from the Tree of Knowledge. But then the serpent, who is supposed to be Satan in disguise, talks Eve into taking an apple from the tree. Once Adam tastes it they're cast out of paradise and made to suffer a mortal life in what we'd call the real world."

"In some translations it's the Tree of Knowledge of Good and Evil," Newman pointed out.

"Adam and Eve didn't learn morality though," Hyle argued. "That's probably a merism, meaning everything from good to evil. It's like saying you did something from A to Z. Regardless, Adam and Eve are punished for acquiring knowledge and the agent who helped them to do it—Satan—is considered to be evil. And you know what really bothers me about this story?"

"I suspect you're going to tell me," Newman said.

"Why did God stick a Tree of Knowledge in the Garden in the first place? That's like tossing a carving knife into the playcrib with your baby or handing your toddler a metal fork and turning him loose in a room full of open electrical sockets. Then when the inevitable happens, although God could have just forgiven Adam and Eve instead of casting them out of the Garden, it's Satan who gets all the blame."

A sound in the front of the shelter distracted Hyle from continuing. Newman leaned around him to look. Auld stood there, leaning against the base of the ladder.

"How long have you been there?" Newman demanded sharply.

"Just a few minutes," Auld replied. "Do not let me interrupt. It sounds like a very interesting discussion." His rich, deep voice was soothing, despite Newman's resistance. "Please, go on."

"Okay," Hyle agreed. "I was just going to compare the story of the Garden of Eden to the story of Prometheus. In the Greek tradition, Prometheus was a titan who felt sorry for humans, who were being kept in primitive conditions by Zeus as a punishment for giving him poor sacrifices. To correct this situation, Prometheus stole fire from Zeus and gave it to mankind, allowing arts and civilization to blossom. In the Garden of Eden, Satan gives knowledge to mankind as an act of evil and corruption. In ancient Greece, Prometheus is a hero who gives knowledge to mankind to liberate and civilize us. The culture in which Prometheus is a hero gave us the Golden Age of Greece—Aristotle and Plato, Pythagoras, Hippocrates, Sophocles, Archimedes. The culture in which Satan is evil for doing the same thing gave us a period of history known as the Dark Ages."

"Are you trying to say that Satan should be considered a hero for giving Eve the apple?" asked Newman.

"That wasn't my point. I was just demonstrating that Christian mythology clearly considers knowledge to be evil where ancient Greek culture considered it to be good, and you reap what you sow," Hyle clarified. He stopped for a moment, overcome with a delayed sense of déjà vu at Auld's remark about the conversation sounding interesting, remembering his own very similar comment on a very similar discussion. "Now that you mention it though, Newman, my college roommate dated a girl who had a very interesting version of the story of God and Satan. I think it was derived from some old Christian cult, but I don't remember the name. She believed that the earth was created by an imperfect and tyrannical god, which is the reason for all the wrath and punishment of the Old Testament. According to one version of this story, that god was supplanted by a benevolent god who is responsible for the change of tone in the New Testament, but she believed that it was all still the same god and the benevolent act was just a ruse to keep people in line. In fact, she thought that all of reality was nothing more than an illusion to keep us under control and keep this god in power."

"That sounds like a variant of Gnosticism," Newman said. "The Gnostics believed that the earth was created by a demiurge who was a fallible reflection of a greater being," Newman explained. "A bit like Plato where there's an ideal transcendent world and an imperfect reflection which is the material world, but in the case of Gnosticism it's complete with an imperfect god who creates it."

"That could be it," agreed Hyle. "Did the Gnostics also believe something about our souls being like light trapped in the earth?"

"Some did, yes. In one version of Gnosticism the material world is used as a tool by the powers of darkness to trap fragments of light. Our bodies are part of the earth and material world, but our souls are of that transcendent realm of light. The material world is like a prison—sometimes depicted as more like an illusion or intoxication that distracts us from seeing our true situation—and keeps us from rejoining the realm of light."

"Yes, that's it!" Hyle exclaimed. "So I guess she was some modern version of Gnostic—my roommate's girlfriend, that is. She took the typical Christian idea that God and Satan are battling for influence over humans and turned it upside down. Except she preferred the name Lucifer since it means 'bringer of light.' That was one of the points she cited to make the case that Satan was actually the good guy who was trying to free us from the oppression of a tyrannical god—much like Prometheus did."

"Do you realize that in Hesiod's original version of the story Prometheus wasn't the hero?" asked Newman. "He was responsible for bringing the wrath of Zeus upon humanity, and the story was an illustration of what would befall you if you crossed the gods. It was Aeschylus who recast Prometheus as a hero in *Prometheus Bound*. The story of Satan has been creatively reinterpreted in the same way. Milton casts him as something of a tragic hero at the beginning of *Paradise Lost*, and William Blake tried to redeem Satan in *The Marriage of Heaven and Hell*. These are interesting as stories and character studies, but they're in conflict with not only the Bible, but all other religions that have a version of Satan. They all portray him as a corrupter of humanity and a master of deception."

Auld joined the conversation for the first time.

"History is written by the winner," he said, and Sophia, who had been listening quietly, realized with some surprise that he was as engaged by the conversation as she was.

"Exactly," Hyle agreed. "I was taught in school that America won the Revolutionary War largely through the cunning and bravery of the colonists. But in a British museum I went to, the American Revolution was one small display of many, and it listed the aid of the French and Spanish as the main reasons for losing the American colonies. The story you hear depends upon who's in power. American culture is portrayed as an evil corrupting influence in many foreign countries, especially in dictatorships. Individual empowerment and freedom are ideas that a dictatorship can't tolerate. Neither can Christianity."

"Are you just trying to be provocative, or do you actually believe that God is some type of malevolent dictator?" Newman asked. The edge that Sophia had heard in his voice was now clear enough for Hyle to notice, although that did nothing to temper his response.

"I don't believe in God, Newman. Maybe it's just a convergent evolution of two sets of memes that are designed to control the behavior of people, but Christianity shares with dictatorships all the elements that are required to keep people in line. If you want to set up a dictatorship, the first thing you need to do is establish a powerful leader and demand loyalty—the God of the Old Testament fits that bill nicely. Since no dictator comes to power by claiming to be evil, it helps to portray this leader a strong defender of the people against some opposing force—like the Pharaoh. To help people to endure hardship without defecting, make sure they're focused on a higher goal like the good of the state—or in the case of Christianity, the afterlife. If anyone fails to show their loyalty you have to get rid of them, preferably making an example of them at the same time— just as Satan is cast out of Heaven and Adam and Eve are cast out of the Garden of Eden. The next step is to seal the borders, control the media and education, and create a fear of outsiders and suspicion of their ideas—the Bible tells us that it's the only source of information to be trusted and warns us not to listen to those crafty philosophers. Then, make sure to reinforce that fear of outsiders by blaming all the bad things that happen in the dictatorship on the infiltration of outside influences—thus human suffering is the fault of Satan, not God. Next, to make sure that no revolutionary ideas develop inside the regime, make sure you have secret spies everywhere and that nobody knows who might be an informant—but if you happen to be omniscient and omnipresent then you can skip the spies. Finally, all this fear mongering may be effective, but it also breeds resentment which can spill over into revolution, so you may want to rehabilitate your image into one of a benevolent ruler who has the good of the people at heart—much like the God of the New Testament."

Hyle paused to wait for a response from Newman. When none came, he rolled on.

"You know that old joke that if something feels good it must be a sin? It's not a joke. The seven deadly sins are all things that people might naturally desire, but self-fulfillment runs counter to the idea of sacrificing yourself for the good of the regime. Pride is an especially dangerous sin because it prevents people from being subservient. It makes you think you have the right for something better."

Hyle paused again.

"Come on, Newman, don't you have anything to say? Or should I assume you're in complete agreement?"

"Does it matter what I say, Hyle? Clearly you're very pleased with your argument. I should probably let you think you're the first one to come up with something like this, but you aren't. Religion has been the target of many philosophers. Marx called it the 'opiate of the people' and Engels developed the theory of the false consciousness of the worker where the masses help uphold the rules of society that are created to suppress them. And Sophia told us what Nietzsche had to say on the subject. The argument is centuries old, but as you pointed out, Hyle, religion is still here. It's still a powerful force in the world and I believe it has a positive impact on the world."

"It is easy to talk," Auld said. "Choosing how to act—that is where the difficulty lies. If Prometheus offered fire to you, would you accept it?"

"I would," answered Hyle immediately. "In fact, I might take the apple from the Garden of Eden, even knowing the consequences. What about you?"

"It is what you think that is important," Auld replied. The response was delivered to sound like the humble deferral of an outsider intruding on their conversation, but again Sophia caught that undercurrent of double meaning. She realized that he was looking at her.

"Yes," she answered. "I think I would."

"And you, Newman?" Auld asked.

"Do you mean the Prometheus of Hesiod or the Prometheus of Aeschylus?" replied Newman. It was a rhetorical question.

"Interesting," Auld observed. "You are the only one to ask that."

The question was left unanswered.

CHAPTER EIGHTY

A QUESTION OF TRUST

Newman and Sophia were asleep by the time Hyle returned to the shelter. This disappointed Hyle, since he had hoped to show off the amazing vehicle he had brought back for them. The fact that Auld had been able to find such a piece of technology in the middle of nowhere, in the ruins of the civilized world, had impressed Hyle further than he had believed possible. Despite his enthusiasm he decided to let his two companions sleep. Auld chose not to join them in the shelter, instead sleeping up in the barn, saying that he was more comfortable being on his own.

It was Auld who woke them all the next morning, gathering the remaining food from the depleted larder. A barely perceptible light sifted in from the open hatch.

"We need to travel light," said Auld. "One sleeping bag for Sophia only." For the men he took three lightweight Mylar survival blankets from the supplies in the shelter.

Getting Sophia up the ladder was a team effort. She had been able to keep her food down and told them that she was feeling better. Although she was shaky when she first stood up and had to catch herself on Newman's shoulder, she insisted on climbing the ladder by herself. Nonetheless, Hyle and Newman preceded her, Newman lying on the ground so that he could extend his arm down and Hyle ready to offer his hand to pull her over the top as she emerged. Auld stayed below, ascending a few rungs behind her in case of a slip. All the precautions turned out to be unnecessary, but she did lean gratefully on Hyle for support once she reached the surface.

The barn door stood open and Hyle escorted Sophia inside. Newman and Auld came in behind them. Just inside the door on one side of the hay-strewn floor was a motorcycle. It was a chopper style with a tall reclining backrest behind which Sophia's sleeping bag was attached by crisscrossed bungee cords. Large saddlebags flanked the rear wheel. The paint job was black except for the extended gas tank, which was adorned with a scaly red dragon, flames leaking from its nostrils and streaming back across its leathery wings. The main attraction however was the other vehicle.

It was a car of sorts, constructed on a frame of tubular aluminum. Small and low, it reached just above Hyle's waist at the highest point. The top surfaces of the vehicle were all covered with small rectangles of black bordered with silver. Hyle explained that the low, flat design maximized the surface area for the photovoltaic cells, which comprised what would have been the hood, roof and trunk on a standard car. These appeared to be the only solid surfaces. A thin fabric, like the type used for camping tents and ski jackets, enclosed the frame and protected passengers from the elements. Plastic windows provided visibility out the sides, and in the narrow gaps between the solar panels to the front and rear. The sides zipped down the middle like tent flaps and all around the edges, so that they could be removed entirely. Designed to be light weight rather than street legal, lights, windshield wipers, bumpers, mirrors and other such features were absent. Hyle pulled back one of the unzipped doors.

Inside the car, two bucket seats rested directly on the floor, which was made of the same nylon material, stretched tightly over the tubular frame. A miniature steering wheel flanked by a single dark LED display and a toggle switch marked the dashboard, and a flimsy metal arm rose from the floor between the seats for shifting gears. Behind the driver and front passenger, who would have to extend their legs horizontally almost to the front of the car, was a narrow bench seat, its edge starting only a few inches behind the front seats. Hyle explained that the car, which stored its energy in a series of twenty eight compact batteries under the chassis, was expected to have a top speed of fifty miles per hour and a range of over three hundred miles, not including the continuous charge from the solar cells. They had the capacity to charge the batteries fully over the course of a sunny day.

"How do you know so much about it?" inquired Newman.

"It's a prototype," Hyle explained. "Auld found it with a placard on the roof in the display room of a little engineering company. What do you think?"

Newman nodded his approval.

"It looks like a go-kart wearing a rain coat," remarked Sophia. Hyle laughed.

"It's a beautiful day and we have a full tank of electrons," he said. "Let's roll."

Soon they were on the highway with the farm and storm shelter far behind. The sky was the same overcast they remembered, but compared to the cramped darkness of the shelter the openness was liberating. It was also a refreshing change to travel by daylight. Auld had assured them that it would be safe and promised to act as a scout. He raced ahead on his motorcycle, sometimes disappearing from view despite the flat terrain and straight roadway. By mid-morning they had angled southwest around Wichita and picked up a state highway heading west. Although they never got close enough to see the city, they were able to guess its fate from the familiar black soot that clung to the abandoned vehicles in places that the rain had missed. This far away from the city the roads were fairly clear of such obstacles and they covered ground quickly. An LED display, which scrolled between a speedometer, a reading of battery charge, and a few other numbers nobody could identify, had them traveling at a top speed of fifty eight miles per hour. Not long after turning west their luck changed. It started with a few drops of rain on the plastic windshield.

The sky had been growing steadily darker as they travelled west and the light rain that began to fall was quickly replaced by a serious rainstorm. The lack of windshield wipers made visibility difficult and Hyle had to slow to a frustrating pace. As they entered the next small town along the highway Auld flagged them down from a gas station, where he sheltered from the rain under the canopy that covered the gas pumps. Hyle pulled up next to him and zipped opened the door.

"Keep on going as far as you can and I will catch up," Auld instructed, raising his voice a bit to make sure that he could be heard over the hiss of rain in the background. "Just keep following the highway until you need to stop."

"How's he going to find us?" Newman wondered aloud as they pulled away.

"He followed us all the way from New York," Hyle pointed out. "He should have no problems finding us somewhere farther up this road."

"How do we know he's really going to try to find us?" Newman asked as soon as the fear popped into his head. Hyle gave him an uncomprehending look. "I mean, how do we know we can trust him?" Newman clarified. "He's got all our supplies. What if he doesn't come find us? We've got nothing."

"First of all, he hasn't got our supplies—he has supplies from the shelter that he sent us to in the first place," Hyle pointed out. "Second, we don't have nothing—we have a car that runs without gasoline which he found for us while he's still riding a motorcycle and has to scrounge for gas. And third, he followed us all the way from New York and saved us at the mall. Why would he go through all that effort just to ditch us somewhere in Kansas?"

"I don't know," Newman admitted. The argument made sense, but it did not completely comfort him. "I still don't trust him. He seems like he's up to something."

"Maybe so," replied Hyle, "but he's helped us every step of the way. I don't see that we have much choice but to trust him."

They drove on for another hour or so in the steady rain before the storm worsened and the hard rain became an all-out deluge. Water hammered the windshield so hard that the passengers worried about the integrity of the plastic and the seams that held it in place. Eventually they found a small truck stop off the road and took shelter by the gas pumps, just as Auld had. Newman offered to get out and check out the shop while Hyle recovered from the mental exhaustion of driving. Hyle gratefully accepted.

The building was a plain concrete shell that had inexplicably been painted the color of concrete. Its design could have been described as utilitarian, but Newman's first thought was ugly. There were two doors in the front. One led into a small diner, the other to a convenience store, although customers could walk freely between the two sides.

Everything of value had been taken and anything that was not useful or was too large to carry away had been smashed. Newman's feet crunched across fragments of glass from the large front window, mixed with porcelain shards from plates and coffee cups, and bits of plastic from signs. The destruction was so severe that his mind reeled as he tried to comprehend the motivation of the vandals. The diner had a service bar with a kitchen area stretched out along one side and stools for the patrons along the other. Rotating red vinyl padded seat cushions topped the chrome stools that had at one time been bolted to the floor, but all eight of them had been uprooted. Chunks of concrete still clung to the bolts protruding from the bottom of a few that lay scattered on the floor. One of the stools had apparently been used as a sledgehammer to demolish the bar. It was still wedged between two pieces of splintered pressboard. Formica sheets hung down from the shattered bar like peels of a banana.

Newman took all of this in within the first seconds of stepping through the door and it hit him with such force that he found himself moved to tears. For a moment that diner seemed to symbolize the entire world and he was swept away by the hopelessness of it all. Reflexively his thoughts turned to Sophia, who was asleep in the back seat of the car. He didn't think of her face, as he would have preferred, but instead pictured the patches of her scalp that showed through her increasingly thin hair.

By the time Newman emerged from the building Hyle was on the verge of leaving Sophia in the car to make sure nothing had gone wrong. He was surprised when Newman took a detour on his way back to the car to walk to the edge of the service area and stick his face out into the torrential rain. After several seconds he pulled his face back in and shook the water off like a dog, sending a shower of water droplets flying in all directions from his long black hair and beard, then rubbed his hands over his face before getting back into the car.

"Everything okay?" Hyle asked. Newman nodded slowly.

"Yes," he answered. "I'm just—tired." Then, without looking into the back seat, he leaned his head back and closed his eyes.

The trio napped on and off, lulled to sleep by the continuous white noise of the rain. Eventually the storm relented. For a while they were surrounded by a normal rain, then a light patter, and then a mist, the sky growing a little lighter with every stage. As the sky was beginning to grow darker again with nightfall, the sound of a motorcycle approached. Sophia, who had been sleeping most of the afternoon, was the first to hear it.

"Auld's here," she said, rousing Newman from a troubled sleep. A moment later the motorcycle rumbled up beside them. Auld dropped the kickstand, leaned the machine onto it carefully and dismounted. With a nod in the general direction of the car he turned and walked into the truck stop. He was gone for quite some time and Hyle found himself in the familiar position of debating when to go in and see if things were all right. No sooner had he mentioned this to Sophia and Newman than Auld emerged from the doorway. He pointed to the car, held up three fingers and motioned for them to come join him.

They entered the door on the diner side from which Auld had summoned them, and Sophia, with Hyle supporting her, walked over to join Auld behind the shattered service counter. Newman stopped in the doorway. The floor had been swept. Not a single shard of glass or plastic could be seen. On the kitchen side of the counter four of the stools were arranged in a semicircle around the large stainless steel grill. The other four had been pushed into a back booth between the seat and table, two to a seat, where they resembled four alien patrons gathered for breakfast. Aside from the broken bar, the only obvious sign of disorder was a pile of debris on the grill. Auld stood beside this, and after a closer look Newman realized that it was actually a pile of wood and paper. In one hand Auld held a lighter, a rolled up tube of newspaper in the other. He lit the tube as Sophia approached.

"Would you like to do the honors?" he asked, gesturing toward the paper and kindling protruding from beneath a rough teepee of wood scraps. Sophia accepted the tube from Auld just as the flame began to blossom and she applied it to the base of the pile of firewood. As the flames began to spread across the top of the grill, Auld retrieved the rolled up tube of paper and held it up into the large ventilation duct above the fire until the smoke began to follow that upward path. He tossed the remaining paper onto the fire.

"A hot meal, some light and a warm place to sleep," he said, grinning broadly.

True to his word, Auld miraculously produced a mess kit from his saddlebags and proceeded to cook a hot meal of powdered scrambled eggs and corned beef hash. As they ate, he set to work on something else and when questioned would only tell them that it was something for Sophia. He heated water in the broad aluminum cup that came with the mess kit and crumbled a few things into it. He also dropped larger chunks of something into it, one of which looked like a small pad from a cactus plant. Then he put it to one side of the grill and let it rest while he ate his meal.

The three travelers continued to ply him with questions. Auld held up a finger while he finished chewing his food and swallowed.

"It is rude to speak with one's mouth full," he said. "And I am hungry." And he took another mouthful of food.

Each one of the trio reacted in a slightly different way to Auld's refusal to answer their questions. Hyle became more and more curious. Sophia could almost sense his mind collecting data, running through theories, discarding some and enhancing others. Newman became increasingly annoyed. He wanted the answer, but he was less curious about what Auld was making and more concerned with the principle demonstrated by the fact that Auld refused to answer them. For her part, Sophia was amused. She was curious of course, but mainly she was entertained by observing the interactions of the other three. Auld particularly intrigued her because she could not quite figure him out. Sophia tried to remember if he had ever given a straight answer to any question and wondered for a moment if he was a pathological liar, incapable of telling the truth, but she discarded this idea. It didn't fit. Auld was completely conscious of what he was doing. He seemed to be amused by this game of evasion and even more so by Newman's increasing annoyance. And as before he also seemed to be aware that she knew what he was up to and even that she knew that he was aware.

Auld made a small production of finishing his last bite of food and opened his mouth as if to speak. Instead, he stood up and produced a hip flask from his pocket and carefully poured the contents of the cup into it. The last few ounces of golden brown fluid he poured into the cap.

"It is an herbal remedy. It should help you feel better," he said, offering the cap to Sophia. Again she got that sense of a secret withheld. "I want you to take one capful each morning and each evening until it is gone."

Sophia studied the liquid in the cap. It was pale brown with a tinge of green and the cap was growing hot between her fingers.

"Drink now," Auld commanded, and without thinking further, she did. It tasted like grass with a terrible aftertaste. Her face clearly displayed her epicurean assessment. Auld laughed heartily.

"Yes, it is bitter, but it will make you better."

"What's in it?" Hyle asked out of genuine curiosity.

"It is a secret."

"How did you find all the herbs you needed?" asked Newman, and his suspicion was as clear to Sophia as Auld's amusement.

"The same way I found the storm shelter and the electric car."

"Where did you learn to make it?" Hyle tried, sensing that it was pointless to follow up on Newman's question.

"Tribal knowledge," replied Auld. It was not clear to Hyle whether he was meant to take this answer figuratively or whether Auld was implying that he had some connection to ancient shamanistic lore from his African heritage. Auld grinned making it quite clear that he was pleased with the ambiguity. He paused and studied Hyle's face.

"You do not believe in herbal remedies, do you?"

"Most of them don't go through any formal testing," Hyle began diplomatically, "so it's hard to know which ones work and which ones don't. But of course aspirin was discovered because of a folk remedy."

"Tell me, do you believe in Sophia's gift?"

"Gift?" asked Hyle. His bewilderment was matched by that of Sophia and Newman. "What are you talking about?"

"Sophia sees things that other people cannot see. Is that not true, Sophia?"

"I—I—" Sophia stammered. At first she intended to say that she had no idea what he was talking about, but as she looked at Auld, who waited patiently for her response, her mind flashed from the cards with the stars and squares, to Helena sitting cross-legged on her bed, and then to the dream and the three doorways that had seemed to be trying to tell her something. Her denial softened. "I'm not sure what you mean," she said.

"Do you not feel sometimes that you can almost tell what people are thinking?"

"Yes," Sophia nodded. "But I've always been good with people."

"Perhaps you are more than just good," Auld suggested. "I understand that you did quite well with Helena's Zener cards."

"Not reproducibly," Hyle interjected. Auld ignored him.

"And do you not sometimes have very realistic dreams that seem to be telling you something?"

"What? How do you know? Did I tell you about those back at Colgate?"

"You are quite special, Sophia," Auld answered softly. "Just accept that and be comfortable with it."

Although none of the trio was really satisfied with this response, the bewitching mix of musical accent and authority put an effective end to the conversation. Auld smiled and studied their faces one by one, almost daring them to ask him something more. Sophia caught herself placing odds on whether Newman's distrust or Hyle's natural rebelliousness would take up the dare, but neither did.

"Have any of you ever fired a gun?" The sudden change in topic took them all by surprise, but they eventually managed to communicate that none of them had.

"You need to learn some self defense," Auld said. "Come, I will teach you."

"No thanks," Newman replied immediately. "I have no interest in shooting anyone." Hyle and Sophia both nodded in agreement.

"Even if your life depended upon it?"

"Even if my life depended on it," Newman confirmed. Auld looked to Sophia and Hyle and then back to Newman.

"Even if Sophia's life depended upon it?" Newman's answer came much more slowly.

"Not if anyone's life depended on it," Newman insisted. Again Auld looked to Hyle and Sophia.

"Hyle, come. You, at least, are practical."

Hyle looked at Sophia and Newman and hesitated. After several long seconds he stood up and fought off the urge to apologize to his companions.

The two men went outside and the next half hour was punctuated with occasional gunfire. Auld was demonstrating how to reload when Newman emerged from the building.

"Sophia is going to sleep now," he announced. "Maybe you could play with your guns another time."

"Very well," Auld agreed. He studied Newman's face. "You do not seem to like me," he observed. "Why is that?"

"I feel like you're not telling us the whole truth most of the time," Newman replied at length.

"Sometimes that is for the better."

"No, it's not," responded Newman.

"Do you want the truth about the herbal remedy then?"

"Yes, that would be nice for a start."

"It does nothing at all. It is just bits of harmless plants boiled in water."

"What?" Newman exclaimed. "Then why did you give it to her?"

"Because if she believes that it does something it will make her feel better."

"The placebo effect," Hyle realized aloud. Auld nodded.

"The what?" Newman asked, looking pointedly at Hyle rather than Auld.

"The placebo effect," repeated Hyle. "It's a phenomenon that's observed in clinical trials of experimental drugs. In most scientific experiments you try to keep all the variables constant except the one thing you're trying to test, and you usually run something called a control, which is a test where that variable is held constant or is set to zero. When testing new pharmaceuticals, the control is a fake drug that doesn't have the active ingredient in it. That's called a placebo. Some people are given the test drug and others are given the placebo, but nobody knows which they're getting. The funny thing is that in some trials, a statistically significant portion of the people taking the placebo feels better. It's some psychosomatic mechanism where the expectation of the patient that they're getting treated with a beneficial drug actually triggers some natural biochemical process which makes them feel better."

"So basically you lied to her," Newman accused, glaring at Auld.

"No, I told her it would make her feel better. It will. You may tell her the truth if you think it is the best policy."

"You betrayed her trust," amended Newman.

"I did not betray her trust," Auld replied calmly. "I rewarded it."

CHAPTER EIGHTY-ONE

WILL AND REPRESENTATION

The thunderstorms of the previous day were long gone and the morning was as close to sunny as anyone could remember seeing for months. Although the perpetual dust layer still shrouded the sky, the usual gray was tinged with a friendlier shade of brown and the warmth from the sun managed to seep through. They crossed the border into Oklahoma, fulfilling one of their objectives for the day. Auld and Hyle had plotted a course that would take them diagonally across the panhandle of that state and the northwestern tip of Texas on the way to New Mexico. According to the meter that monitored the battery power of the car, the charge was almost two thirds full. Hyle was not sure how much to trust this since it had been below one third when they had stopped the previous evening and he was fairly sure solar panels did not charge by moonlight, even if there had been any moonlight to speak of, but he decided that there was nothing to be done but to keep an eye on it and keep on driving. Sophia and Hyle chatted between long periods of silence. Newman said very little.

"Why are you so quiet this morning?" Sophia asked. Newman shrugged.

"He's still mad at me for trashing on religion," guessed Hyle.

There might have been a grain of truth to this, but Sophia knew it was not the real issue. Although she was physically weaker and had needed both men to help get her to the car, she felt more alert than she had the previous day. Nonetheless, they had been trying all morning to avoid the topic of her health. Everyone knew that Hyle was baiting Newman and on this particular occasion it was a welcome diversion.

"Mad? No. More like sorry for you," Newman said. "I think when you choose to be an atheist you lose an entire dimension of life that you can never experience. Like watching the first part of *The Wizard of Oz* in black and white—people didn't know what they were missing until they saw Oz in color."

"I didn't choose to become an atheist," Hyle replied with an incredulous laugh. "I came to the conclusion that religion didn't make any sense after learning all the facts. You can't choose what to believe."

"Sure you can. People do it all the time."

"You mean if I asked you to believe that the earth was flat, you could just decide to believe it?"

"Maybe," Newman replied. Hyle turned to look at his face just to make sure he was serious.

"That's ridiculous. Now you're talking about just deluding yourself. Maybe that explains some things about religion. Sane people allow the facts to dictate their picture of reality—not the other way around."

"I'm not so sure it's that black and white," Sophia commented. "Most of the things you take as facts Hyle are probably from unsubstantiated sources. I'm willing to bet you haven't performed your own experiments to confirm relativity or quantum physics. You never met George Washington and weren't around for the last ice age. How do you know any of those things are real? You have to take a lot on faith yourself, Hyle. I think you just happen to believe your sources more than you believe Newman's sources."

"A fair point," Hyle conceded, "but that's because my sources are better. And besides, that still doesn't constitute choosing to be an atheist."

"One point at a time," said Sophia. "What do you mean your sources are better?"

"I mean that history and science are open to the public for criticism and revision. They may not be perfect, but all the information is there for anyone to examine and decide for themselves. The source of truth for Christianity is the Bible. People believe it because it claims to be the sole source of revelation of God's word, but that's circular reasoning. If I told you I was now the sole source of wisdom in the universe, after you were done laughing you'd ask why you should believe me. If I told you 'because I said so and I am the sole source of wisdom in the universe' I doubt that would sway you very much. Somehow that works for the Bible though."

"It's more than that," Newman said. "What we learn in the Bible fits with what we experience in our lives."

"Because you all work so hard to maintain the shared delusion," replied Hyle.

"Hold on'" Sophia interrupted before Newman could object. "Hyle, you've decided that religion is unnecessary because you believe that science offers a complete explanation for the world, right?"

"It's not complete yet," Hyle amended, "but I believe that it's the only tool necessary to ultimately explain the world, yes."

"How did that scientific world view come to be?"

"Do you mean for me or in general?"

"Either."

"Observation," replied Hyle. "I suppose it's the same in either case."

"Dogs and cats observe things," Sophia pointed out.

"Empiricism," Hyle corrected. "And logic."

"And what makes you think that empiricism and logic give you the most accurate view of the world?"

"Because they yield explanations that fit most closely with what we actually experience."

"So you're defending empiricism and logic as the best means of understanding the world based on the fact that they yield the best empirical and logical fit with experience?" asked Sophia. "How is this any less circular than the Bible claiming that it's the sole source of God's wisdom?"

Hyle was silent as he struggled to find an answer to this question. Before he could think of anything Sophia continued.

"I think that at some point early in your life you had to take the same type of leap of faith into empiricism that Newman did into religion. Remember Arcesilaus? 'Nothing is certain, not even that.' We've seen with Hume and Descartes that if you follow empiricism to its logical conclusion it leads to total skepticism. What prevents that? Maybe it's just because we all work so hard to maintain our shared delusion."

Newman made a half-hearted attempt to suppress a laugh and ended up making a sound somewhere between snorting and choking.

"I'm not convinced that science really can explain everything eventually," Newman said once he had recovered.

"It can only explain the things it can observe," replied Hyle. "So if you mean things like finding the soul hiding in the pineal gland, I agree. But for anything that can be observed, I believe that science can ultimately find a good materialistic explanation."

"Speaking of Descartes and the mind-body problem, what about determinism?" asked Newman. "Do you really not believe in free will?"

"I don't know," Hyle answered. "It's a beautiful idea but it's completely unnecessary. Not only that, it contradicts almost everything we believe about the world. I don't know of anyone who doesn't believe in the law of cause and effect, including people who are very religious. Even if you believe in a prime mover who pre-existed the world, once that prime mover sets things in motion there's no room for free will. For us to have free will we'd all have to be prime movers, existing outside the laws of nature. You may not like determinism, but it's a perfectly valid explanation for things."

"But all cultures have some concept of morality," argued Newman. "And morality is dependent upon the ability to choose a course of action. Belief in free will is fundamental to human thought. How could it not be true?"

"Hume made a similar argument," Sophia observed. "Of course he also said that for free will to be truly free it would have to be unaffected by anything—including punishment for immoral action—so it ends up being almost equivalent to randomness."

"I'm talking about the type of free will we experience every day," said Newman. "Scientific explanations are supposed to be based on our observations and experiences. If I want to raise my arm I observe that I think about raising it then it goes up. That's part of my experience. Regardless of whether you believe in determinism, you're forced to behave every day as if free will exists. You have the experience of constantly choosing your course of action. You can't just ignore it and have an explanation of the world that claims to be complete."

"Are you suggesting that we have no choice but to believe in free will?" Hyle asked. He flashed the trace of a smile before becoming serious again. "Just because you feel like you have a choice doesn't mean that it's true. It could be that the human mind is wired to give us the sense of free will even though we're actually predetermined to act in the way we do," he suggested. "The idea of free will is that when you choose one course of action you have the feeling that you could have chosen a different course of action instead. The problem is that you can never put that to the test. Nobody can go back in time and put themselves in exactly the same situation to see if they could have chosen a different action. That fact prevents us from proving free will, but it also prevents us from building conclusive evidence against it."

"Have you ever heard of Buridan's Ass?" Sophia asked.

"No," Hyle admitted. Newman shook his head.

"It's a philosophical problem that dates back to Aristotle, but Buridan's version is best known. Imagine a donkey placed halfway between a pail of water and a bale of hay. Because it has no basis for choosing one over the other it dies of both starvation and thirst."

"It'll go for one or the other based on whether it's more hungry or thirsty," said Hyle.

"It's a thought experiment, Hyle," Sophia pointed out, even though she knew he was being purposely obstinate. "You can substitute two equally attractive piles of hay and he'll just die of starvation if you prefer."

"Either way it doesn't sound right," Newman observed.

"No, but that doesn't mean it's wrong," said Hyle. "Relativity and quantum physics are counterintuitive too, but they bear up pretty well when put to the test. It would be nearly impossible to do an experiment to test Buridan's Ass, but if you could it might turn out to be true."

"What about quantum physics?" asked Newman. "Since determinism is based on cause and effect, doesn't quantum physics defeat determinism?"

"You mean because of quantum indeterminacy?" Hyle asked.

"At the very least quantum indeterminacy defeats the main premise of determinism," noted Sophia. "The scenario of an omniscient being knowing the position and momentum of every particle in the universe as a starting point is now known to be impossible."

"That may throw a wrench into the hardcore definition of determinism," Hyle conceded, "but it doesn't establish free will. There's a bit of randomness at the quantum scale, but at the scale of human beings the statistics are so tiny that we're essentially operating under that old definition of cause and effect."

"What scale is human thought?" Newman asked. Hyle considered this.

"It may well be that the physical mechanisms of thought are affected by quantum physics and indeterminacy," he conceded. "That might give you enough randomness to keep Buridan's Ass from starving, but it doesn't give you free will. If some random percentage of the times that you tried to raise your right arm your left arm went up instead, I wouldn't call that free will. Randomness isn't freedom. It's just randomness. And remember that there might be an evolutionary advantage to that randomness because it creates new behaviors, just like mutated genes can create new physical traits."

"I still don't think it's valid to ignore the fact that we have the perception of free will," Newman insisted. "Why should we dismiss our experience of free will as an illusion but then turn around and accept the five senses upon which empiricism is built?"

"Because you can build an entirely coherent explanation of the world based on the feedback from the five senses and without the need for free will."

"But what if it's the wrong explanation?" Newman persisted. "Newton built an entirely coherent explanation of physics without the need for relativity."

"It's really part of a bigger question," Sophia interjected. "How does the mind work? Science still doesn't have a good answer to that question, and until it does the issue of free will can't be determined—no pun intended."

"I think we actually do have a pretty good understanding of how the mind works," Hyle objected. "Neurologists have mapped lots of activities and functions to specific locations of the brain and we were able to build computers that could recognize faces and outthink chess grandmasters."

"An interesting choice of words," Sophia noted. "Do you really believe that a computer thinks? Does it understand what it's doing?"

"As much as we do."

"Do you believe it's possible to build a computer that's equivalent to the human brain in all mental aspects?" Sophia asked Hyle.

"Yes, absolutely," he replied. "Our minds are just biological symbol manipulation machines. Mathematics is symbol manipulation which follows very strict rules. That's why it was one of the first successes in computing. Logic can be expressed mathematically. Words in language are symbols that represent ideas according to certain rules, but the rules are much more complex. Visual images that we remember are just another kind of symbol. Are you familiar with the Turing Test?"

"It sounds familiar," Sophia answered. Newman shook his head.

"Alan Turing was a British mathematical genius who helped crack German codes during World War II," Hyle explained. "He devised what is called a Turing Machine, which is a device capable of performing complex algorithms by performing a couple simple operations on ones and zeros. Turing determined that it would be possible for such a machine to be capable of computing anything that was computable. He didn't actually build a machine, but he came up with the principle that is the basis for digital computers. The Turing Test is a test in which you have a human participant converse in some type of blinded fashion with another person or with a computer. If the computer is sophisticated enough to be indistinguishable from the human it can be said to be intelligent."

"Has any computer ever done that?" asked Newman.

"Not completely," admitted Hyle. "There used to be a competition every year to try. Several computers have fooled naïve participants in text based conversations, but there hasn't been one that could fool a panel of experts. There's no reason a computer can't win though. It's just a matter of having enough programming complexity."

"Hyle, do you understand Chinese?" Sophia asked.

"No, why?" he answered, intrigued by the apparent non-sequitur.

"Let's say that I stuck you in a closed room with a big notebook filled with strings of Chinese characters. Every so often a card comes in through a mail slot in the room. These cards have strings of Chinese characters printed on them. You're instructed to take each card, and match the string of characters to one listed in the big notebook. Each string in the notebook has a number next to it and you're instructed to then go to the big catalog of pre-printed cards and look up the card with the right number. You're to take that card, which is printed with different Chinese characters, and push it back out the mail slot. Unbeknownst to you, the characters on the cards that come in the mail slot are questions and the characters on the card prescribed by your big notebook are the corresponding answers. By using this system you're able to have a clear and intelligible conversation with a native speaker of Chinese who is sitting somewhere outside the room. Does this mean that you understand Chinese?"

"No," Hyle admitted.

"That's John Searle's Chinese Room argument against strong artificial intelligence by the way," Sophia said.

"Clearly I don't understand Chinese in that scenario any more than I do in real life. But I'm just part of the whole system."

"Do you mean to tell me that the room understands Chinese?" asked Sophia.

"In a manner of speaking."

"That's an unusually imprecise statement coming from you, Hyle," Sophia noted. "What we're trying to establish is whether or not a computer can be equivalent to the human brain in all mental aspects. One aspect is understanding language—not just reproducing it—but actually understanding what we're saying."

"No, and I take the point," acknowledged Hyle. "In this scenario the Chinese Room is just manipulating symbols. It's mimicking what goes on in the brain the same way a computer can but without the understanding."

"And no amount of complexity will create that understanding," Sophia added.

"Maybe," said Hyle. "But what exactly does it mean to understand a language? You need to know the rules of the language, which is something that a sufficiently good computer program could handle. So what's missing in the Chinese Room?"

"To really understand a question in Chinese—or any language—you need to understand not just the structure of the language, but each of the words," Sophia explained. "Words are very complex symbols that represent things or ideas which may themselves be composed of other things or ideas. The human mind is able to sift all of these levels of complexity and invoke the word in the context of all that it represents."

"So what if a computer had access to a huge database of human experience?" asked Hyle. "What if every word was cross referenced with pictures and sounds and definitions in a huge interconnected web such that every time it evaluated a word for a sentence, it referenced several levels down this web before using the appropriate rules to choose the best word. Would the computer then understand its sentence?"

"No, because it would still just be manipulating symbols without understanding them," Sophia replied, but she was dissatisfied with her answer even as she gave it.

"But you defined understanding as the ability to associate symbols with specific pieces of information in a database of information to put them in context. Maybe what you call understanding is illusory just like free will," Hyle suggested. "Maybe the experience of understanding you have is just a symbol itself for the vastness of the database you have in your mind."

"I'll have to think about that," Sophia replied. It still did not feel right to her, but she could not put her finger on exactly where the argument might be wrong, so she decided to try a different approach. "If you built the smartest computer you could imagine and gave it all the data in the world and asked it, 'What are you?' what do you think it would say? Would it understand that its thoughts were actually a series of ones and zeros and electrical circuits?"

"Are you aware that your thoughts are a series of electrical impulses and firing synapses?" Hyle countered. "If our brains are just physical then it stands to reason that someday, when we have figured out how they work, we'll be able to build a machine with the same properties. We're aware of hunger and tiredness and believe them to be physical phenomena. Why should thought be any different?"

"It depends upon how you define thinking I suppose," Sophia mused. "But there are still some pieces missing. A computer may be able to manipulate symbols in order to think like a human being, but the meaning of those symbols had to be determined somewhere. Computers get their symbols directly from people. It's human beings who create meaning. Computers just manipulate the meanings that we feed them."

"But then what is meaning?" asked Hyle. "It should be similar to understanding. If a computer could create a new word by picking a previously unused combination of syllables and attaching it to a new collection of symbols that it notes are conjoined at a high frequency, wouldn't that be just like a person coining a new word?"

"Possibly," Sophia allowed. "But I still think there would be something missing from computers. There are aspects of our consciousness that transcend thinking."

"That's because you're stuck on the idea of a mind-body problem," said Hyle. "I don't think there is such a problem. It's a false construction like Zeno's paradox with Achilles and the tortoise. Maybe those aspects of our consciousness which you believe to transcend thinking are merely side effects of working brains, like heat given off by a working engine or ripples on the water of a pond. The idea that they're something transcendent is illusory—like echoes in a circular room—they seem to come from somewhere else when it's really just us speaking."

"That doesn't cover it," replied Sophia. "There are properties of consciousness that are definitely intentional. As William James pointed out we have the ability to focus our attentions. Not just by turning our heads, but by deciding where to pay attention. We can strain to hear a faraway sound or tune out noises that are nearby to focus on reading a book. Without that regulatory function we'd be overwhelmed by an onslaught of sensation."

"A computer can determine where to spend its processing resources."

"Maybe so, but we actively choose to do it."

"So now we're back to debating free will?" Hyle asked.

"No, there's another point there. We're aware that we're making the choice. It's that self awareness I have a hard time picturing in a computer. You might program a computer to refer to the bundle of hardware that makes it up as 'I' but that's not the same thing as being self-aware." Sophia paused and reflected on this. "On the other hand, I'm not sure exactly what we mean when we use the word 'I' either. Wittgenstein said that this word was one of the most misleading representational techniques in our language. What I'm getting at though is that I believe there are aspects of human consciousness that can't be imitated by a computer."

"I understand your point," Hyle acknowledged. "You might even be right, but I still believe that the brain is just a biological machine and someday we could build a machine that's comparable in all aspects of its complexity. I suppose we'll just have to disagree on this point because it's clear that nobody is going to be building any computers for quite a while now. There are just some things that we'll never be able to understand in our lifetime."

"Maybe we're not meant to understand them at all," Newman suggested.

"There's nothing in the physical world—which is all I happen to believe in—that can't eventually be understood by science," Hyle replied.

"That's not necessarily true," said Sophia. "Remember the Gödel Incompleteness Theorem?"

"But that just applies to mathematics," Hyle replied.

"What do you think computation is? You've just finished arguing that the human brain is essentially nothing more than a complex computer." Sophia pointed out. "That would mean that we have a pre-programmed inability to fully understand ourselves. If you grant that we think in some way other than purely mathematical computation that helps a little, but we still end up in the same place."

"How does that help at all?" Newman asked.

"Have either of you read *Gödel, Escher, Bach* by Douglas Hofstadter?" asked Sophia. Although Hyle recognized the title as one of the many books on his list to read, neither of the men had read it. "It's a very interesting book about mathematics, symbolic logic, computers and artificial intelligence."

"That sounds exciting," Newman said, in a tone that suggested exactly the opposite.

"Actually it's written in a style which makes it very enjoyable," Sophia explained. "The author tackles these topics through dialogues between several characters, which is a technique I find makes tough intellectual topics much easier to digest. It also features characters popping up and down different levels of reality and is full of subtle self-referential humor."

"I love stories with self-referential humor," Hyle said, "but what do you mean by different levels of reality?"

"It's similar to what we were just talking about with computers," Sophia replied, "when you asked if I was aware that my thoughts were electrical impulse and synapses firing. That represents one level of meaning, but the patterns at that level are compiled into a new level of meaning which might come across as sensations, syllables of sound or bits of visual patterns. Those then get compiled into an even higher level of meaning and the bits of sound become words. Then words become sentences and sentences describe concepts."

"That sounds like the principle of emergence," noted Hyle. "It's an idea that's used in several different fields of science to describe higher-order patterns that arise from simple components and are more than just the sum of the parts."

"Exactly," agreed Sophia. "I remember reading a great example based on an ant colony and an anteater."

"This should be interesting," Newman commented under his breath.

"Imagine a colony of ants where each ant goes about its business, occasionally bumping into other ants and trading signals about where to find food, or running about in a panic when an anteater happens by. From the ant's eye view, so to speak, each ant is only aware of what's going on around it and whatever little communication it gets from the other ants it comes across. The anteater sees things at the level of the colony though. Hofstadter imagines this anteater interacting with the whole colony, or ant hill—which he calls Ant Hillary—as if it were a single entity. The anteater can read the emotions of Ant Hillary by the pattern of ants. For example, it can tell that Ant Hillary is upset if he gets too close since Ant Hillary begins to change shape very rapidly. The point of this is that we can interpret the same physical phenomena at different levels of meaning. That ties back to Gödel because, although a given symbolic language that's powerful enough to explain mathematics may have a built-in contradiction, it's possible to build a higher level language to understand the original language, including resolution of the built-in contradiction."

"Somehow I suspect it's not that simple," Newman said.

"The higher level language is also symbolic," noted Hyle. "It would contain the same type of built-in contradiction."

"Exactly," Sophia said. "So we may be able to understand the limitation of mathematical logic from the viewpoint of some higher level of understanding, but that level will also be necessarily limited. My point in all this is that maybe we won't actually be able to explain everything with science given enough time. It may be that part of our minds will always be unavailable to us to understand. In fact, many of the intractable philosophical problems seem to stem from a few concepts that we have a hard time fully understanding."

"You mean like consciousness?" Newman suggested.

"Yes, but also things like infinity and time. For example, both science and religion are challenged to explain why we're here. Why is there something rather than nothing? How did the universe come to be? You can answer these questions with God or with the Big Bang, but invariably someone will ask what came before those."

"Time started with the Big Bang," Hyle explained.

"And according to Augustine, God created time," Newman added.

"Okay, but then where did God come from?" Sophia persisted. "Did he pre-exist before time? What does that even mean? And where did all the material for a universe come from before the Big Bang? Do you see? These may be questions we can never answer. Maybe free will comes from us operating at a higher level of meaning than we can understand. We can only understand one level down from where our brains operate. Maybe we really aren't meant to understand everything about ourselves, and I'm not sure that's a bad thing."

CHAPTER EIGHTY-TWO

FINDING THE WAY

Hyle tried to gauge the exact position of the sun through the haze as they passed a sign that placed them thirty miles outside of Albuquerque. They were driving west on the interstate into the setting sun and with no headlights on the car he was trying to decide whether there would be enough visibility to catch up with Auld. When they had stopped for an afternoon meal a few hours back, Auld passed up the food, instead making plans to ride ahead and find a good campsite south of the city. Lunch had taken longer than expected and now Hyle was racing against the fading sun.

A median of bare earth scattered with nearly dead wild grasses divided the interstate into two lanes in each direction. The occasional billboard or fast food sign mounted on an extra tall pole accompanied low buildings strung out along either side of the pavement. Beyond this strip of civilization brush and low trees punctuated the flat dry land. As they approached Albuquerque, the buildings decreased in frequency, the highway gained a concrete divider and an extra lane, and the flat land began to rise up. Long low hills loomed ahead, dotted with dark bushes in numbers insufficient to cover the red earth. Soon the buildings were gone altogether and the hills closed in around the highway.

"Did we take a wrong turn somewhere?" asked Newman, looking around at the towering hills.

"I don't think so," Hyle replied, sounding a little less certain than he intended. "Albuquerque should be just another five or ten miles."

"Doesn't look that way."

As they continued Hyle began to question the route himself. To make matters worse the road wound between hills, and anytime they were not heading directly west it was closer to night than to day. In a matter of minutes however, they broke out into flat terrain again and passed under an elevated highway. The buildings reappeared, exits became frequent and there were indications that they were approaching the city. The highway gained a fourth lane, but the traffic increased accordingly, forcing them to weave back and forth more often to avoid stopped vehicles.

To the north, the collapsed ruins of a few large hotel buildings passed by and there were signs that a fire had burned through the area. To the south, the structures were intact and no more than two or three stories high, but most of what could be seen was still open space. From reviewing the map with Auld, Hyle knew that they would cross Route 25 to Las Cruces in the middle of Albuquerque so, having seen no evidence of a skyline or city center, he was taken by surprise when the sign appeared ahead of them in the fading light. He had to break hard and weave around a sedan in order not to miss the turn. From the depths of sleep Sophia groaned in the back seat. She propped herself up and stared groggily out the window as they followed the exit ramp around and down to the southbound route.

"What's that sound?" she asked. The electric motor was extremely quiet, and the only sound from the car was the low whine of the tires on pavement.

"What sound?" Hyle asked. After listening for a moment, Sophia answered her own question.

"Helicopter," she whispered, pointing up the road.

"Stop us next to that semi," advised Newman.

Hyle pulled around a tractor trailer into the rightmost lane and stopped. To their right, beyond a narrow breakdown lane, a retaining wall held back the bottom few feet of a hill and provided cover. The sound of the rotors seemed to be coming from somewhere along the road ahead and was growing louder.

"It's going awfully slow," Newman remarked. "Seems like they're looking for something."

Sophia found herself holding her breath as the pulsing of the helicopter grew louder. Its approach seemed to take forever.

"It sounds like they're right on top of us," she yelled. A few seconds later the car was flooded with a brilliant white light and buffeted from above. The sides flapped under the windstorm of the helicopter blades.

"Hold still," Newman shouted over the sound of the pounding rotors. "They can see our legs through the window."

Everyone froze. The light stayed on them for several seconds. Then it swept away toward the trailer beside them and disappeared behind it. Before they had a chance to be relieved, it was back, shining through the windshield. They sat motionless, squinting and blinking in the bright light that flooded the car. It shifted to the rear window and the car was illuminated from the back. Suddenly the light vanished and all was dark. The sound of the helicopter engine retreated slowly behind them.

"I feel like I just survived a close encounter with an alien spaceship," Hyle said. He was able to speak in a loud voice rather than yelling as he craned around Sophia's head to watch out the rear window for a glimpse of the helicopter. Before any of them were able to spot it against the darkening sky Newman noticed something. Odd patterns of light played along the inside of the car. They were diffuse and shifting, playing across what remained of Sophia's long black hair. He observed the same sort of patterns around the edges of the window inside the car. In the few seconds it took his mind to make sense of what he was seeing, the light grew brighter and the shifting resolved along a single axis, as if the source were bouncing up and down. Newman spun in his seat to look forward. Two points of light bore down on them from the road ahead.

"Hyle! Turn around!"

Hyle turned, saw the headlights and cursed under his breath.

The lights were too intense to be ordinary headlights. Staring into them, it was hard to get an accurate sense of distance, but they also appeared to be too far off the ground. Sport lights atop a pickup truck was the first explanation that crossed Hyle's mind, but he had no time to think about it. The vehicle was closing rapidly and unless it slowed—which it showed no signs of doing—in a matter of seconds it would be right on top of them. Literally, Hyle realized. Their car was little more than three feet off the ground. From the height of the lights he pictured a monster truck with huge tires raising the chassis enough to clear their hood.

"Back up!" Sophia shouted, even as Hyle tried to find the gear.

"Come on, hurry!" urged Newman.

A rhythmic mechanical squealing grew louder with the approaching headlights.

"Put it in reverse—reverse!" Newman yelled.

"It won't go," Hyle said, trying to quell the panic that threatened to render him useless.

The ground began to vibrate. The squealing was joined by a deep rumble and the lights closed quickly to within fifty yards.

"Get the switch!" Sophia shouted. "The switch! You didn't start it!"

Hyle found the toggle and flipped it up. The LED began to glow but it was impossible to tell if the engine was on. Even had it been a gasoline engine the sound would have been drowned by the machine noise approaching them and the vibration would have been masked by the shaking of the pavement. It was clearly much more than a pickup truck and only a few car lengths away. As it closed, the focus of the lights began to clear the top of the car, allowing them to see. In the shadows of the light, movement caught Newman's eye. A continuous motion started at a height well above their heads and moved rapidly downward. It was a huge metal tread.

"It's a tank!" Newman shouted. "Go! Go!"

The gearshift clicked into position and Hyle slammed down on the accelerator. The treads of the tank closed within a few yards as the car jumped into motion, and the barrel of the tank's long cannon drew even with the front of the car, looming many feet above them. The car sprinted backwards, paralleling the retaining wall.

"Sophia, get down!" Hyle yelled, trying to see around her through the back window. Newman watched as the treads held at a steady distance for several heart-stopping seconds, and then started to slowly pull away. The whine of the car's transmission made itself heard above the din as the vehicle reached top speed in reverse. Hyle scoured the shifting twilight and shadows for an opening in the traffic to their left large enough to make it through at high speed. He wasn't sure if the tank was still gaining on them and didn't dare spare the second to look. It was all he could do to hold their course steady in the narrow slot between the retaining wall and cars in the adjacent lane. Executing a smooth turn in reverse at such a high speed would be extremely difficult, but it was only a matter of time before they encountered another car blocking their path. Hyle knew that any error in skill or judgment that prevented them from escaping the lane soon would be his last.

As they passed the back of a small station wagon Hyle made his move, cutting the wheel hard. The back end swung into the gap and glanced off the front bumper of a van, whipping the front end around. The back half of the car was clear of the lane, but Hyle and Newman were half in and half out. The rear wheels screeched against the pavement but the car was pinned against the van. Hyle flung the wheel around in the opposite direction. The car lurched backwards past the van into a gap in the third lane before their back end slammed into the side of a sedan. The tank rumbled by, flinging chunks of asphalt into the air behind it.

Another tank followed closely behind the first, and then another and another. The trio watched, not daring to move and barely daring to breathe, as fourteen of the huge metal machines rumbled by, each spewing a rooster tail of pavement in its wake. It was quiet in the car well after the rumbling and squealing of the tanks had faded into the distance.

"Sorry," Hyle said at length, "I couldn't shick—shick the—sift the stick." He drew a deep breath. "Shift the stick," he corrected. Newman burst into laughter. He only laughed louder as Hyle tried to explain that the gearshift was electronic and would only work when the car was powered on. Soon Sophia was laughing at Newman and was only able to stop when her laughter gave way to a fit of coughing. Hyle recognized this as a hysterical response and gave up on explaining anything. He focused instead on trying to control his annoyance and the involuntary shaking of his muscles in order to get them moving out of the city again. The whole encounter had lasted no more than five minutes but it seemed noticeably darker.

There was no further sign of the helicopter. When everyone had calmed down again they discussed this fact and agreed that it was likely scouting ahead of the armored column, looking for the best path through the city. Newman recalled seeing a sign warning that the right lane ahead was under construction, which might have provided an obstacle free path for the tanks.

"That's probably why the helicopter was so interested in us," Hyle realized aloud. "They were trying to determine how difficult it would be for the tanks to roll over us."

"They must have decided it wasn't too difficult," noted Sophia.

"And I'm inclined to agree," added Hyle.

"We were playing dead," Newman noted. "They would have had no reason to suspect that there were people in this car. Since we only started moving when they were right on top of us, I'm not sure if they ever even saw us."

"Didn't see or didn't care," Hyle said. "Either way they're long gone in the opposite direction. We just need to find Auld before it gets too dark to see."

It was only a few miles later that they spotted a small fire by the side of the road. Already the highway was back down to two lanes in either direction, one of them chewed up by the passage of the tanks, and although they were still passing exit signs for city streets, the breakdown lane had given way to a dirt shoulder bordered by a sporadic guardrail. In a flat, open area, Auld's distinctive motorcycle was parked on the shoulder, pointing toward the fire a few dozen yards away from the road. Hyle maneuvered the car across the choppy pavement and past the motorcycle to the edge of the campsite. The two men helped Sophia out of the car and over to the campfire. Auld sat on the far side of the fire. He had already pitched the tent for Sophia.

"I thought you were supposed to scout ahead to make sure it was safe," Newman said as they approached, accosting Auld from the other side of the flames.

"Yes," Auld agreed. "I did."

"We were nearly killed by a bunch of tanks just a few miles up the road."

Auld listened while Newman, with some assistance from the other two, told the story of their near-death encounter with the tanks. As he narrated Newman became less angry and increasingly distracted by Auld's cooking project. The fire burned in a pit several feet deep and on either side of the pit was a stack of rocks. The headless carcass of some medium sized animal was positioned over the fire on a long spit. Its skin glistened in the firelight and every now and then fat dripped off into the flames with a crackle and hiss. Newman's rant turned into a story and ultimately ended with a non sequitur.

"What are you cooking?"

"A pig. It is almost ready."

"Where did you find a pig?" asked Newman.

"Or a spit for that matter?" added Hyle.

Sophia coughed.

"There is a fence back there," Auld answered, pointing a thumb over his shoulder into the darkness. "That is where I shot the pig. There was a loose fence post nearby."

The spit was indeed a long piece of metal, square in cross section and open on one side with small tabs of metal punched out of the opposite side to serve as hooks to hold barbed wire.

Sophia's cough turned into a fit of hacking that ended when she spat something dark onto the ground.

"What was that?" asked Hyle. "It looks like blood."

Newman bent down to examine Sophia where she sat by the fire. A line of dark liquid ran down from one corner of her mouth.

"Are you okay?"

"I'll live," she answered reflexively, instantly regretting her choice of words. It was bad enough that she was not convinced it was true, but the pained expression on Newman's face almost made her forget her own plight. There was a difficult silence as they each looked at the other, not knowing what to say.

"Newman, come help me with the other end of the spit," Auld called out. "She will be fine."

Auld set about carving the pig, first producing a speed limit sign from the shadows to use as a serving platter. He also had a small cook pot full of biscuits hidden in the stones by the fire to keep them warm. It was a delicious meal and Sophia seemed to gain some strength from it. They continued to retell the story of their near miss with the tanks as they ate, adding new details and perspectives. Hyle confessed how nervous he was about keeping the car straight as they backed away at high speed. When he mentioned that he wanted to look back to see how close the tank came but didn't dare take his eyes off the road behind them even for a second, Newman described the barrel of the cannon disappearing out of sight over the roof of the car before they started to pull away.

"Someone was watching out for us," he said, pointing up toward the sky.

"Then *someone* should have had us park in a different lane unless he was trying to scare the crap out of us," Hyle said. "I like to think *someone* did some pretty good driving to get us out of that jam alive. If you go and give God all the credit for everything that turns out well, you leave nothing but table scraps for us humans."

"It looks like they went right up this road," Sophia said quickly in the hopes of averting another debate. Auld nodded.

"I'm surprised the helicopter didn't spot you," added Hyle.

"It did," replied Auld. "They put the spotlight on me. I waved. They flew away." He studied the faces of his audience in the firelight, especially Newman's. "Tomorrow we will stay close together," he assured them, going on to explain that tomorrow they would cut west across the mountains and, if they got an early start, could make Zebulon before nightfall.

Sophia excused herself to go sleep in the tent while the men helped themselves to a second serving of dinner. They talked little, and only then in low voices so that they would not disturb her. A while later, when heavy breathing could be heard inside the tent, Newman turned pointedly to Auld.

"Is there really help for her in Zebulon?"

"Yes."

"Will they be able to cure her?"

Auld stared at Newman, clearly debating how to answer this.

"Much depends upon Sophia," he replied. "But I believe that things will turn out well."

"What do you mean you believe?" Newman hissed. "You led us halfway across the country instead of looking for help. You'd better more than believe."

Hyle opened his mouth to say something but Auld silenced him with a sidelong glance.

"I cannot guarantee the outcome of human affairs any more than you can," he said. "But I can tell you that this is the place that she must go."

"How can you be so sure?" Newman challenged. "How do we know you're not just leading us on a wild goose chase while she gets closer to dying every day?"

Seeing the tension in Newman's face as he spoke, Hyle fought to maintain his own composure.

"I told Sophia that she had a gift."

Hyle regarded Auld through slitted eyes. "Wait, you want us to believe that you have some kind of magical gift too?" Auld shrugged and inclined his head in a gentle nod.

"Prove it," said Hyle. He found suddenly that he was at war with himself. He had been the biggest advocate of Auld back at the shelter, trusting him from the very beginning. There were some logical reasons, but Hyle realized that it was largely a character judgment, or perhaps, more cynically, a leap of faith. He was not sure why it should be the case, but he felt betrayed.

"It does not work that way," said Auld.

"Why not? If you have some super human powers, do a demonstration for us," Hyle demanded.

"I cannot."

"Why?"

"Hyle, if God himself spoke to you out of a burning bush, you would spend the rest of your life looking for where the speakers were hidden." Before Hyle could object Auld stood up. "It is time to sleep. We must get up early tomorrow." He walked over to the tent. Orange reflections of the campfire danced on the edge of darkness as he settled in under his survival blanket and the open sky. Hyle stood up a moment later.

"I'm going to go sleep in the car," he said. "Should be warmer in there."

Newman rose quickly and caught up with him.

"Hyle, are we doing the right thing?"

"What do you mean?"

"I mean, how do we know he's telling the truth about Zebulon? What if he doesn't know where it is?"

"I don't see what option we have," Hyle said. "Either we drive around aimlessly on our own or we trust him. Even if he doesn't know, what's the difference?"

"We could find a good place here."

"What's the point of that?"

"To make Sophia comfortable," explained Newman. "I don't think she has many days left."

"We're going to find her some help," Hyle insisted.

"She's scared to die," Newman said. "We're her friends. We need to help her come to terms with it."

"No," replied Hyle immediately. "I'm not going to make it easier for her to die. There are all sorts of psychological studies to show that the will to live sometimes makes the difference between living and dying."

"Have you looked at her recently, Hyle? She's lost a lot of weight and most of her hair. She can't keep food down. She can't even walk without assistance and now she's coughing up blood."

"Yes," Hyle answered, straining to keep his voice level. "That's why we need to get her some help quickly."

"Maybe it's her time Hyle."

"It's not her time," Hyle hissed. "And don't you dare hand me any crap about her going to a better place."

Newman nodded. "Fine. Okay." He locked eyes with Hyle. "But what if she dies in the back seat tomorrow?" He put his hand on Hyle's shoulder. "She deserves better than that."

With a sudden revulsion, as if he were brushing away a spider, Hyle's hands shot out and caught Newman solidly on the chest, sending him sprawling backwards into the dirt.

"She deserves better than to have you give up on her," he said, turning his back on Newman and stalking off into the darkness.

The fire had nearly burned itself out before Hyle returned to the campsite. Newman was sitting on a rock, watching the orange glow pulsing in the embers. Standing next to him, Hyle stared into the fire too until Newman finally looked up at him.

"I'm sorry," Hyle said. "Sorry for what I did—but that doesn't change my mind." With no reply or reaction from Newman, Hyle turned around and headed for the car to sleep. Newman went back to staring at the dying flames.

CHAPTER EIGHTY-THREE

FROM EAST TO WEST

Even at such an early hour of the morning, when the predawn light was beginning to crawl across the eastern sky, flies had already found the remains. Newman had been awakened by the purely biological need to empty his bladder and had walked out of the campsite away from the road. About the time he had planned to stop something caught his eye in the distance, so he kept walking. It was the fence Auld had mentioned, but there was something more. In the scant light it had been impossible to tell what it was until he was within a few feet. At the bottom of one of the fence posts was a pile of entrails and mounted on the top of the post was a pig's head. The flies that had settled upon it buzzed about in agitation as he leaned in for a closer look.

It appeared to be a wild pig and it glared at him with baleful eyes through the cloud of insects. He fought back an odd compulsion to talk to it. It seemed to be a messenger of Death himself. Surely the Four Horsemen of the Apocalypse had been loosed upon the land. They had seen pestilence, famine, war and death. Newman recalled that apocalypse in the original Greek meant 'revelation' and he wondered what exactly was being revealed. As he stared at the head he tried to keep his mind from wandering to thoughts of Sophia, but without success.

"This too shall pass," he said to the head, his mind turning over the beginnings of a plan.

Auld was awake and restarting the fire by the time he returned. They had a hearty breakfast of scrambled eggs, ham and bacon, although the meal did not sit as well with Newman as dinner had the night before. A few hours later and far to the south they turned off of the highway onto a narrow road that led due west toward the mountains. After passing through a small town, the asphalt of the road slowly transformed to packed earth as it began to ascend the first of the foothills. Sophia slept in the back seat all morning, but after they broke for lunch she stayed awake, staring out the window at the scenery. The familiar red hills with their scattering of small dark bushes had grown into mountains of red rock scattered with bushes and small evergreens.

"We're in God's country now," Newman observed.

"You mean the part of the country he didn't nuke into oblivion?" asked Hyle.

Newman smiled. It was exactly the type of comment he had expected.

"You know, Hyle, you don't have to believe in the biblical God to appreciate nature and realize that you're a part of something much bigger," Newman said. He made sure to focus his attention on Hyle rather than his intended audience in the back seat. "How much do you know about Buddhism?"

"I know some of the basic tenants of Buddhism and Taoism," replied Hyle, "but I wouldn't say I'm all that knowledgeable."

"Really? Where did you learn about those?" Newman had expected some sort of smart answer about priests in yellow robes chanting *om*, so Hyle's reply caught him off guard. Already he was straying from his script.

"There are several books comparing quantum physics to eastern mysticism," Hyle explained. "Capra's *Tao of Physics* is probably the best known of the ones I read, although there are others. Why did you want to know?"

"You've made it clear that you don't share any monotheistic belief, but there are eastern philosophies that can be spiritual without being religious," Newman answered.

"So you've given up on converting me to Christianity but you're willing to settle for Buddhism?" Hyle laughed at the prospect.

"Actually I think this discussion is targeted at me," Sophia said. "And I'm interested to hear what he has to say."

Newman was thankful that Hyle's eyes were on the road and Sophia was behind him and unable to see the shade of red that must have accompanied the burning in his cheeks. He thought he had been fairly subtle by striking up the conversation with Hyle instead of Sophia, but he had underestimated how perceptive she could be. Rather than bother to deny it, Newman decided to accept the opening and move on.

"I'm no expert either," Newman confessed, "but you can get a pretty good idea of the basis for Buddhism from the story of the Buddha. Like Socrates and Jesus, the Buddha didn't write down his own teachings, so there are many variations, and the details of his life are also disputed, but there is agreement on the major points. His name was Siddhartha Gautama and he was born somewhere around 560 BC in northern India or Nepal. He was a prince in a small kingdom and lived a lavish life, provided with everything he could want and sheltered from the pain and suffering of the world outside the palace. There's a legend that his father was so protective that the royal gardener was instructed to remove all the withering roses before Siddhartha could see them. One day, Siddhartha rode outside the palace walls and saw an old man. When his driver explained that everyone becomes old, Siddhartha became curious and went for more rides outside the palace. On subsequent trips he saw a beggar, a corpse and an ascetic. These depressed him so much that he made his so-called 'great departure' and fled the palace life to become an ascetic himself to try to overcome old age and death."

"That probably didn't work out so well for him," Hyle guessed.

"No, it didn't," Newman confirmed. "He studied for years under several teachers and even tried extreme deprivation, nearly starving himself to death. The story goes that he realized that this wasn't the way he sought and, after accepting some food, he discovered what's called the Middle Way—a path in between indulging in material pleasures and the abstinence of asceticism. He sat down under a tree and vowed not to get back up until he had found enlightenment, which he achieved after forty nine days of meditation. From that time forward he was known as the Buddha."

"So Buddha is a title?" Hyle asked.

"More or less," Newman said. "It's usually translated as the Enlightened One, but I think the literal translation is actually better. Technically it means Awakened One."

"Why is that better?" asked Sophia.

"Because that's the whole point of Buddhism," Newman explained. "Enlightenment isn't some extremely complex thing that only a very few could ever hope to attain. According to the Buddha, if you open your eyes to a few simple truths you'd be well on your way, but that's the problem—most of us don't open our eyes." Newman paused for a moment to think of the best way to illustrate his point. "Do you know what nirvana is?"

"Isn't that the Buddhist version of heaven?" asked Hyle.

"Perfect," said Newman. "That's the common answer I was looking for. It's both correct and completely wrong. Nirvana is like heaven in that it's an escape from the material world and all the suffering that goes with it, but it's different because unlike the Judeo-Christian Heaven it's not a separate place or transcendent realm."

"Is it more like what Augustine and Avicenna believed about achieving a unity with the Divine Intellect rather than an immortal soul going to Heaven?" asked Sophia.

"Somewhat," Newman allowed, "but nirvana is a state that can be achieved by people during their lifetime as it was by the Buddha. In fact, people can even achieve enlightenment but choose not to enter a state of nirvana so that they can pass their wisdom on to others. Such a person is called a bodhisattva."

"I like that idea," Sophia interjected, "that someone would turn around after finding their way to enlightenment to help others to get there too."

"Wonderful," Hyle said. "If you achieve enlightenment, you can come back and show us the way."

"Absolutely," Sophia promised. "But it would probably help to let Newman finish telling us about Buddhism first." Newman laughed.

"There are two concepts that form the foundation for the Buddhist view of things," he continued. "The first is *dukkha* which is often translated as suffering. Originally the word *dukkha* probably referred to a bad axel on an ox cart—something that would be a continual annoyance. *Dukkha* doesn't have to mean extreme suffering. It can just be a discontent, a chafing, a constant dissatisfaction with life. The other concept is *Tanha*, which means desire. Literally it means thirst, but it can mean any kind of wanting—not just extremes of lust or greed, but also more subtle desires like wanting to live, wanting to be enlightened or even wanting to not want anything. These are incorporated in the Four Noble Truths. Life is suffering. The cause of suffering is desire. Suffering ends when desire ends. Desire ends by following the teachings of the Buddha."

"That's no fair," Hyle objected. "It sounded really easy until you got to the last one." Newman laughed again.

"Actually, the Buddha's wisdom is often distilled into the Eightfold Noble Path. The eight principles are right view, right intention, right speech, right action, right livelihood, right effort, right mindfulness, and right meditation. In this case right isn't a moral judgment—it just means proper or appropriate."

"Appropriate for what?" asked Sophia.

"Appropriate to help you to reduce desire and suffering and put you on a path toward enlightenment," answered Newman. "Sometimes they're described in three groups. Right view and right intention put you in the appropriate frame of mind. Right view means seeing the world as it is, not just as it appears to be. I'll come back to this one in a minute. Right intention means having the intention to decrease desire and cause no harm. The second group guides your actions in the world. Right speech and action mean speaking and acting truthfully in a way that doesn't cause harm. Right livelihood is a similar idea, extended to your choice of profession. The third group focuses on mental mastery. Right effort means making an effort to improve yourself. Right mindfulness means being aware of your own mind and mental states, but without having desire. And of course right meditation means meditating, which is a skill one can improve upon over time with practice, clearing and strengthening the mind with progress."

"Everything you explained makes sense," said Sophia, "but I still don't think I really understand the point."

"That may be because I haven't explained right view yet," Newman replied. "I didn't tell you what you're trying to see with that right view. What you're trying to see is reality. Not what we perceive and think of, but the reality behind all that. You're probably in a position to understand this better than the average person because of your background in philosophy, Sophia. What most people think of as reality is actually just a construction of our minds. Think about the observation of William James that consciousness focuses attention on certain things and filters out others. Think about all of Kant's categories of understanding. Our mind arranges things in time and space. It groups things into categories, sets expectations, draws boundaries. All of this is artificial. None of it is reality."

"So what is reality then?" Hyle interrupted. "Just emptiness? And you're supposed to find that by meditating?"

"No, that's a caricature of Buddhism that misses the point," Newman answered. There are three marks of reality in Buddhist philosophy. The first is suffering, which we already discussed. The second is *anicca* which means impermanence. Everything is compounded and changing. Everything we perceive is made up of parts which have grown or come together or been assembled and will, over time, change and come back apart again. Nothing is permanent. What we think of as discrete objects—whether they're flowers or buildings or planets or people—are just temporary arrangements of smaller components. We freeze these temporary arrangements into patterns and assign meaning to them, except we make the mistake of thinking that these frozen forms are the real world."

"It's sort of like Plato in reverse," realized Sophia, pausing to cough and catch her breath before continuing. "Plato believed that we needed to see past the illusion of the material world to the world of eternal forms. It sounds like Buddhism wants us to see past the illusion of the material world to see that things are even less permanent than they appear. We need to move away from the idea of forms instead of toward it."

"You mean to tell me that this mountain isn't real?" Hyle asked, pointing out the window.

"Yes," Newman replied. "Your mind perceives it as something permanent and separate because that's how the mind naturally works. It draws boundaries. It calls something earth and something else sky and draws a line between them. It grants existence to the things within those lines, and that's the illusion that the Buddha awakened from." From his expression, Newman could tell that Hyle was not convinced by this explanation. "Let me give you an example, Hyle. Have you ever been to a football game?"

"Yes, a few times."

"A football game is a *thing* by our typical understanding. It exists in a specific place and time. It can be observed. It matches certain criteria we expect and use to classify it. If you look closely though, there really is no football game. There's a stadium, there's a field of grass, there are spectators and players and a ball. At the end of the game they all go their separate ways. Some of the people who were the football game will later be a family or a company or a traffic jam."

"That's reminiscent of Heraclitus," observed Sophia.

"'You can't step in the same river twice,'" Newman quoted. "Yes, I think the Buddha would have had a lot to talk about with Heraclitus. Of course he might have had even more to talk about with Hume. Sophia, do you remember that you told us that Hume didn't believe we could observe a self any more than we could observe causality?"

"Yes," she replied. "He argued that we're nothing more than a collection of sensations. It was a similar argument to that of Bishop Berkeley—if you were to strip away all our sensations, ideas and memories, there would be nothing left."

"The third mark of reality is called *anatta*, which means no-self," Newman explained. "It's not so much a complete denial of the idea of self as it is an attempt to look at things from a perspective where the self is irrelevant. If all the so-called things we observe in the world are illusory, including other people, we ourselves must be part of the same illusion. Buddhists sometimes describes the self as a wave on the water. Not that different from your analogy of consciousness as ripples on a pond, Hyle."

"What would the Buddha have had to say to Descartes?" Hyle wondered aloud.

"Remember the flying man scenario, Hyle?" responded Sophia. "If you were suspended in absolute darkness from birth with no way to sense any part of your body, would you even have a concept of self? Avicenna thought you would, but I'm not so convinced. Just like Wittgenstein argued that language gains meaning only through use and interaction, I could see making the same argument about the concept of the self."

"Are you familiar with the African concept of *ubuntu?*" asked Newman.

"I have heard of it, but no, not really," said Sophia. Hyle shook his head.

"*Ubuntu* is a philosophy of community, but one of the aspects is that nobody can exist in isolation. We're only people in relation to other people. We need to belong to have identity."

"That's what I thought you were going to say the third mark of reality was," Hyle said. "Some form of unity or connectedness. That was a theme in the *Tao of Physics*—that according to Buddhism, Taoism and Hinduism, reality is all united somehow."

"I hadn't thought of it that way," said Newman, "but I suppose that's what makes eastern mysticism mystical. Those three philosophies not only share the general idea about reality that all is one, but they also share the idea that even though it's a simple truth, it's nonetheless difficult for most people to see. There's a Hindu saying that Atman is Brahman. Brahman is the transcendent reality which is the divine ground and source of all. Even the gods of Hindu belief originate from Brahman. Atman is the true self or the soul, so to say that Atman is Brahman is to say that all individuals are part of the universal whole. In both Hindu and Buddhist philosophy, the world as we perceive it is illusion and enlightenment comes from being able to see reality as it is—which is to say unified—not broken into separate objects the way we habitually perceive it."

"What about Taoism?" asked Sophia.

"The Tao simply means the Way," Newman explained. "The Tao is the way of nature, the natural rhythm and pattern and order of things, and we get ourselves in trouble by going against the Tao and trying to manipulate the world to fit our expectations and desires. The Tao is the fundamental essence of the universe, and yet Lao Tsu, the founder of Taoism, said that once you try to describe the Tao in words you have already failed. That idea of a unified reality that's hidden from us and which can only be discovered through a personal journey to enlightenment does seem to be unique to eastern traditions."

"Maybe, but the idea that truth or reality can only be suggested in allegory and metaphor was also held by Al-Farabi," Sophia noted. "And the idea that all is one unified reality isn't uniquely eastern. Remember Parmenides? 'That which it is possible to think is identical with that which can be.' Or Spinoza? Or the One of Plotinus or Geist of Hegel? And of course there's Schopenhauer telling us that we only appear as separate beings in the phenomenal world but are all one in the noumenal. The difference I see is that the eastern traditions focus more on mysticism while the western approach is more philosophical."

"What exactly do you mean by mystical?" Hyle asked. "To me mystical seems to be a synonym for illogical and obscure—like asking about the sound of one hand clapping. Maybe there isn't really some great truth hiding behind a veil of illusions. Maybe that's the reason it's so hard to find and nobody can put it into words."

"Even science is often looking for a truth that's hard to see," noted Sophia.

"And although it's different for each religious tradition," Newman explained, "they all have some truth to be discovered. The orthodox way is through scripture, doctrine and teaching, but mysticism is an approach where the seeker tries to find a direct connection to the truth. Mystic traditions may make use of teachers or doctrine to some degree, but they're only to help the seeker find their own way in the end. Mysticism is a very personal experience. There's an eastern saying that a finger is required to point to the moon, but having seen the moon, the finger is no longer required," Newman continued. "Think about it this way Hyle—think about those optical illusions where you can see things two different ways—like the candlestick and the two faces."

"Or the profile that can be a young woman or an old woman," Sophia added.

"Or a line drawing of a cube," Newman continued, "which can look like the corner is coming out of the page toward you or projecting back into the page away from you depending on how you imagine it. In all these cases, someone can help describe what they see and help you to see what you didn't see before, but when you do finally see it, it'll be a very personal connection. The idea is that the truth transcends what we can express through words or logic—it has to be experienced directly. There's a famous koan where a student asks a Zen master whether a dog has Buddha-nature. Yes and no are both inappropriate answers. The master answers *mu*, which means negative, as in the absence of an answer or something neither here nor there. That's the purpose of koans, like the one about the sound of one hand clapping. They demonstrate that words and logic are not the way to enlightenment. People can help point the way, but if you succeed it'll be only through your own persistence and willingness to bend your mind or open it appropriately in order to achieve your own enlightenment."

"That's counter to the whole point of science though," Hyle objected. "That's why I don't see the connection between quantum physics and eastern mysticism. Science is supposed to be based on principles that are generally accepted and can be independently verified. It's about as far from mystical as you can get."

"How many people can independently verify quantum physics though, Hyle?" objected Sophia. "Most people don't have particle accelerators in their backyards."

"True, but those types of observations are translated into mathematical equations that people can verify."

"I couldn't," Newman pointed out. "Could you?" Hyle considered this, realizing that he could not, but Sophia spoke before he was able to respond.

"Regardless," she said, "the equations are just a way of trying to describe something. They're not the thing itself. I could understand the equation that describes gravity without needing to have the first clue about how gravity works. With quantum physics and relativity it seems that the ideas and the mathematics came first and the observation that linked them to reality only came later."

Winded, Sophia stopped to draw a few deep breaths. Newman shot Hyle a significant look, but before he could respond, Sophia continued her argument.

"You've said yourself Hyle that we live in a Newtonian world in terms of what we can experience. Since quantum physics is beyond what we can experience, maybe it does fall into the realm of the mystical. And, similar to Buddhist, Hindu and Taoist philosophy, quantum physics is supposed to give us one unified explanation for the universe, isn't it?"

"Yes," Hyle confirmed. "Quantum physics may be the key that allows us to someday unite all the different forces in physics into one theory. Unified field theory has been progressing ever since James Clerk Maxwell united electricity and magnetism."

"What's left to unite?" asked Newman.

"There are actually several forces left," Hyle replied. "Even though it's not a force per se, Einstein unified time with space in his relativity theory. He was able to explain electromagnetism as a part of special relativity, but unable to unify it with gravity. Quantum electrodynamics managed to unify special relativity and electromagnetism, but also doesn't cover gravity, so gravity and electromagnetism are two of the forces remaining to be unified. The other two forces are the weak force and the strong force."

"We've discussed electromagnetism and gravity," said Sophia. "But what are the strong and weak forces? You've never mentioned those.

"The weak force is a nuclear force in atoms that's associated with radiation," Hyle explained. "The strong force is what holds subatomic particles together. There's a theory that unites the weak force with electromagnetic force at extreme temperatures—for example the conditions of the Big Bang—into something called the electroweak force. There were physicists working on a Grand Unification Theory which would have united electromagnetism with the weak and strong forces. Figuring out how to add gravity to that would result in what people call a Theory of Everything. You may have heard of people working on string theory, M-theory, supersymmetry? These are all attempts at unification."

"Is it fair to say that, since Newton, physics has been shifting from emphasis on solid bodies and particles to a focus on fields and energy?" Sophia asked. "It seems that science keeps breaking things down into smaller and smaller particles, and as it does forces become more and more important."

"I suppose you could make that generalization," Hyle replied after considering the idea, "but it's not quite that simple. Forces are explained in terms of particles and the line between energy and matter has been blurred. The interaction of subatomic particles is a whole field by itself."

"What exactly are subatomic particles?" asked Newman. "Last I knew we had atoms that were made up of electrons flying around a nucleus made out of protons and neutrons, so where do subatomic particles fit in?"

"It's complicated," Hyle warned. "There are literally scores of subatomic particles, but they break down into two different groups. There are particles that compose matter and there are particles that are called force carriers. Starting with the matter particles, there's one family of matter particles called hadrons. Maybe you've heard of the Large Hadron Collider in Switzerland? It was the world's largest particle accelerator, recently constructed to study subatomic particles. Hadrons are made up of subatomic particles called quarks."

"You've mentioned quarks before," Newman interjected, "and I had heard of them even before that."

"I'm not surprised," Hyle replied. "Quarks seem to have made it into the popular culture. But did you know that there are actually six types of quarks?"

Newman shook his head.

"There are up and down, top and bottom, strange and charm quarks," Hyle said. "The names don't really signify anything except a way to tell them apart. Quarks make up the two types of hadrons—mesons which are very unstable, and baryons, which are stable. Protons and neutrons are baryons that are each composed of a combination of three up and down quarks, held together by the strong force. The up quarks have a positive two-thirds charge and the down quarks have a negative one-third charge, so in a proton two up quarks combine with one down quark for a net charge of plus one. In a neutron two down quarks cancel out the charge of one up quark for a net charge of zero. And in addition to having a charge, each quark has a property that's designated by the color red, blue or green. Each baryon has one quark of each color. The strong force is sometimes called the color force for that reason. One of the interesting characteristics of the strong force is that it doesn't decrease over distance, which is why baryons are so stable."

"Is this all going to be on the final exam?" asked Sophia.

"You don't really need all this detail," Hyle confessed with a laugh. "But I wanted to at least give you a feel for the complexity of particle physics, because putting it all together into one unified theory is the big challenge."

"Okay," she said. "So there are six types of quarks, and three colors. Up and down quarks in different combinations—including one of each color—make up protons and neutrons, which are collectively called baryons and make up the nucleus of atoms. Got it. Please continue."

"Well done," Hyle said. "The other type of matter particle is the lepton. Electrons, muons and tau particles along with their neutrally charged counterparts the electron neutrino, muon neutrino and tau neutrino round out the matter particles. Each matter particle theoretically has a mirror image antimatter particle that could combine to annihilate the corresponding matter particle in a reaction that would generate a lot of energy. Anti-electrons—called positrons—have been detected, but antimatter doesn't survive very long in our world full of matter. That's a very quick and simplified survey of matter particles. With me so far?"

"I think so," Sophia answered. Newman nodded slowly.

"Good," Hyle said. "Because the other set of subatomic particles aren't really traditional particles at all. Remember how light can be both a wave and a particle? Energy and matter are interchangeable according to Einstein, so either description can be valid. The wave form of light is the electromagnetic force and the particle form is the photon. The photon is called a force carrier since it's a particle that transfers energy. Similarly there is a force carrier for the strong force that holds quarks together. It's called a gluon because it glues the quarks together. There's supposed to be a particle for gravitational force called a graviton too, although it has yet to be demonstrated."

"That sounds much simpler than the matter particles," observed Newman.

"That's partly because I only told you about the basic force carriers," Hyle said, "but mostly because I haven't tried to explain how they work yet. Although there's a corresponding area of physics called quantum chromodynamics that studies the strong force, the most advanced area of research around force carriers is quantum electrodynamics—QED for short—which studies electromagnetism. One of the founders of QED, Richard Feynman, invented a graphical way to represent the interaction of particles through force carriers. These Feynman diagrams always have three lines intersecting in some interaction. Travel up the page along the y-axis represents passage through time while travel from left to right across the page indicates motion across space. For example, a line representing an electron comes in at one angle and a new line leaves at a different angle from the intersection where the electron changes momentum it gives off a photon. A squiggly arrow representing the photon leads off in the third direction. Of course, each of these lines can arrive at a new intersection representing a new interaction and the diagrams can get pretty complex. One of the really weird properties of these Feynman diagrams is that you can interpret the same diagram different ways. In the example I just gave, the line representing the electron leaving the intersection in a new direction could also be interpreted as a positron coming into the intersection and annihilating the electron to emit the photon. Both interpretations are equally valid mathematically."

"Why is that weird?" asked Sophia.

"Remember that the y-axis represents time. For the positron to be entering the intersection in place of an electron leaving, the positron would have to be travelling backwards in time. That's called retrocausality—but before you get too excited—that's because it changes the causality of the equation, not because it does anything to alter cause and effect."

"That's not all that strange," Sophia said.

"There are also virtual particles," Hyle continued. "There are some situations where the best explanation is a particle which requires too much energy to exist as a stable particle. But because of quantum uncertainty, they can be explained by a virtual particle which can come into existence only for a short duration of time before it's reabsorbed by another particle, thus transferring energy.

"And there's the EPR experiment you told us about before," Sophia reminded him, "where the spin of one quark isn't determined until the other quark is observed, no matter how far apart they are. I think I can see the connection to eastern mysticism. According to quantum physics, the material world is a sort of illusion where all matter is actually energy and someday when that energy is fully understood everything will be explained by one unified theory."

"I don't know," Hyle said. "I still think physics is just an explanation of nature and mysticism is purposely illogical and obscure."

Newman turned in his seat and shot Hyle a look of pure disbelief.

"Really, Hyle?" he asked. "According to quantum physics things exist as both waves and particles at the same time, cats aren't alive or dead until you look at them, particles can move forward and backward in time and communicate information instantly across the universe, and you think that asking about the sound of one hand clapping is obscure and illogical?"

Hyle thought about this for a minute and answered, "Mu."

CHAPTER EIGHTY-FOUR

ZEBULON

Sophia was the first to spot their destination. They were descending along a road which hugged the edge of a mountain. As they curved around to the west, the view outside the downhill window changed from distant mountains to wide valley to desert. The land below was flat and featureless and red as far as the eye could see, with one exception. A single mountain stood like a lonely sentinel with a few faithful hills nestled at its feet. The mountain was striking enough, but what caught Sophia's eye lay just to the south of the foothills. A vast array of tiny objects sparkled in the light. It was impossible to make out what it was, but it was clearly not natural. She thought at first that it might be a town, but a few miles farther south, along a barely discernable thread of road she saw something that looked much more like a small town.

A few hours later, following Auld west again through the barren landscape along a narrow strip of road, they entered the small town Sophia had seen from the mountains. It was hard to imagine what people would do out here. Hyle suggested that there might be a mine in the mountain or an oil field nearby. The village was a loose collection of several dozen buildings, but there was a distinct center where the buildings were clustered closer together. There was nothing to mark the edge of town, but they were able to surmise the name of the settlement from a few of the signs as they passed through the town center. One on a small white building read Megiddo General Supply, and a chalk board outside Michael's Bad Judgment Diner claimed the best food in Megiddo, but "best" had been crossed out and the word "only" had been written over it. An old pickup truck, painted white wherever the metal was not rusted away, sported a bumper sticker that read, "Megiddo, AZ isn't the end of the world... but you can see it from here." There was no sign of life anywhere in town and even here, in the middle of nowhere, the windows had been smashed. Newman scowled but said nothing as he surveyed the town. They did not bother to stop.

The barely-paved road continued on to some unknown destination in the west, but Auld turned into a space between two buildings, following a trail that ran north toward the mountain. Scrub brush grew here and there, but for the most part the land was flat and barren. They followed Auld for several miles, the dark figure of rider and motorcycle almost lost from view beyond the cloud of dust he kicked up. Behind them the small town was obscured beyond their own dust cloud. It was like driving in an orange fog. Hyle kept his eye on the ruts of the dirt road and paced Auld closely enough to keep sight of him, but back far enough to avoid the worst of what he kicked up. Several miles out of town, Auld paused for a moment and abruptly turned left, leaving the trail to cross the hard-packed earth. As the orange powder settled, a spectacular view materialized before the travelers.

The two ruts led straight on toward the mountain, into the low point between two foothills. Now that they were closer, the foothills looked like they might qualify as small mountains themselves, but they were dwarfed by the true mountain that rose up between them in the distance. It was not the typical mountain of granite covered with pine trees or snow capped peaks. Nor was it a solid block of stone. Instead it was composed of countless boulders, from small to gargantuan, looking more like some rockpile of the gods than a mountain. The rock was of the same Martian hue as the earth they had just crossed and the powder that now caked the hood of their car. Not a single tree or scrub bush grew on its surface. The two foothills were smaller versions of the mountain, roughly equal to each other in height, and the road led to the center of the valley they formed. A massive concrete wall filled the gap. Several stories high, it was a cross between a castle rampart and a modern dam. Where the road met the wall was the dark shape of a rounded door in the same medieval style they had seen in Asher. There was no question. They had arrived at Zebulon.

More fantastic than the mountain and the walled city below it was the assemblage outside the gates. Many thousands of vehicles were scattered around the plain at the base of the hills. Shelters and modes of transportation in every size and shape imaginable filled the space in both directions, as far as the eye could see, leaving only the road and a narrow strip on either side of it unpopulated. Motorcycles, cars, pickup trucks and minivans, shared the vast flatland with a colorful swarm of tents from pup tents to large cabin tents, make-shift lean-tos, pop-up campers and Winnebagos, all clustered around the foothills. Turning off the road to follow Auld, they skirted around the edge of the campground city, pointing out to each other some of the more interesting sights. They passed more than one tractor trailer that was being used as living quarters, and in the distance, close to the wall, what appeared to be a circus tent. There was a city bus supporting a huge tarp fastened all along one side and an ancient school bus that had been painted bright blue with giant white daisies. And everywhere there were people.

"I haven't seen so many people out in the open since we left Asher," observed Newman.

"I feel like I'm arriving half a century too late for Woodstock," Hyle replied.

As they circled the mountain, the campsites began to thin out and Auld picked an area a few dozen paces away from an original VW bug and a pup tent. A young couple sat on the ground leaning against the shady side of the car and watched as Auld unpacked. Hyle and Newman emerged to help him, and as soon as they approached, Auld left them with instructions for setting up camp and making sure Sophia was settled while he rode off to look for medical assistance.

Through trial and error the two men figured out how to set up the tent. They unfurled the sleeping bag and helped Sophia to lie down inside. It was not much later that Auld returned with a rider—a young Indian man who looked like he had long ago forgotten the meaning of the word sleep. He crouched down at the entrance of the tent, pulled the flap back and gently woke Sophia. The other three watched from behind as he asked her some questions, examined her arms and head and finally took her temperature with an old glass thermometer that he sterilized in the flame of a butane lighter. His bedside manner was apparently good. He said something to Sophia, laid his hand on her head in a parting gesture and left her with a solemn smile on her face.

He took a few steps away from the tent so that he could speak in private to the men.

"It's definitely radiation poisoning," he told them. "A severe case. I told her that it'll be her strength that gets her through."

"What can we do?" asked Hyle.

"You should keep her away from people who are sick. Her immune system is compromised, so infection is her biggest threat right now. She has a low grade fever, so if you can find someone with antibiotics that would help, but they're very hard to come by out here."

"What are her chances?" Newman asked. The young doctor hesitated.

"It's hard to say. There are many variables."

"Doctors make that type of prediction all the time," Hyle said. "Give us your best guess." The doctor sighed.

"Ten percent? If she doesn't catch something. She has a very bad case. There's nothing else to be done for it. You can give her nutritious food and rest, but she'll either turn the corner or she won't."

There was a difficult silence until Auld offered to give the doctor a ride back.

"No, thank you. I'll walk. I have some places to check nearby. Good luck."

"You said we were going to find help here," Newman complained once they were alone again.

"As much as anywhere," replied Auld. "Do not give up yet. Tomorrow morning we will go out and look for antibiotics and maybe we will find another doctor for a second opinion."

Auld passed out some food and they ate a flavorless meal in silence as the light faded.

The next morning Hyle and Newman were awakened by a tapping on the roof of the car. A man's face peered inside the passenger window. He rapped on the roof again.

"Hey in there," he said with a southern drawl. "Come on out. I need to talk to you."

Hyle studied the man as he tried to blink the sleep out of his eyes and force them to focus. There was something odd about his appearance. He was average looking—a little on the short and heavy side, middle aged and balding. It took Hyle a moment to figure out that it was his attire that seemed out of place. He was wearing a suit and tie. Curious, Hyle obliged, zipping the door open and extracting himself from the car.

The first thing Hyle noticed was that there were two larger than average men standing a respectful distance away. One was tall and muscular with a shaved head and a single gold earring. The other was only slightly above average height but built like a bear. He sported a crew cut and a boxer's nose which had been flattened and twisted to one side of his face. Both wore dark suits and sunglasses and looked almost comically stereotypical, although Hyle could not decide whether they were going for government agent or mafia thug.

"What's this all about?" asked Hyle. Newman heard the concern in his voice and decided to get out of the car himself.

"Allow me to introduce myself," the stranger said, extending a hand. "I'm Zach Goldman, Mayor of Lower Zebulon. I've just come to welcome you to town and discuss your land use fees."

"Land use fees?" Hyle repeated in disbelief. He looked around the barren landscape. "We're in the middle of a desert."

"Well if that's all you care about, you can find yourself another nice piece of desert about five miles west of here."

"Are you trying to tell us that you charge people to camp in the middle of this wasteland?" asked Newman from the other side of the car.

"I charge people to camp out here on *my* land and participate in this community," the mayor corrected. "Now, would you like to negotiate a fee or will you be moving along?"

"I don't suppose you have any sort of proof that this is actually your land?" Hyle challenged.

"If you'd like you can speak to my lawyers, Smith and Wesson," he said, nodding to his two enforcers and laughing at his own joke.

"Let me handle this," Auld said. Newman jumped. The voice was right next to him but there had been no sound to signal Auld's approach. "Let us go talk over there." Auld pointed out into the desert.

"I got nothing to say that can't be said right here," the mayor replied.

"I do not wish to speak here. We will come to our agreement over there." And with that Auld walked several dozen paces away from the campsite. The mayor looked annoyed and watched him walk away, clearly debating what to do. Ultimately he decided to follow Auld and nodded to his two bodyguards to accompany him. Newman and Hyle watched from beyond earshot.

The negotiations started with the bear taking up a position behind Auld and frisking him while Auld held his arms out. After the search the man kept his position behind Auld. The tall man stood behind the mayor and off to one side. Auld and the mayor talked for a few minutes, both looking very serious and shaking their heads frequently. The conversation seemed to take a turn for the worse when the bear, who was still standing behind Auld, pulled out a pistol and leveled it at the back of his head.

"This doesn't look good," Newman observed.

Just as Newman finished speaking, Auld blurred into motion. He stepped backwards, grabbing the gun in both hands and spinning, using the gun arm as a lever and sweeping his leg around behind him. Before anyone could react, he occupied the space where the enforcer had been, holding his gun, and the enforcer lay prostrate on the ground with Auld's foot planted firmly on the side of his face. The mayor leapt back and took a few more shuffling steps away while the tall bodyguard froze with one hand inside his suit jacket. Never taking his eyes off the pistol now aimed at his head, the tall man slowly and deliberately pulled his hand out and tossed his gun into the dirt. Auld said something to him and waved his pistol. In response, the man reached around to the small of his back and threw another gun onto the ground beside the first. Another wave of the pistol produced a knife from a sheath around his ankle. After one final signal from the pistol he sat down cross-legged on the ground, glaring at Auld all the way down.

Satisfied that the bodyguard was no longer a threat, Auld turned his attention to the mayor. They talked briefly. The mayor did most of the speaking, gesturing frantically and shaking his head. Auld said little. After a minute of this lopsided exchange Auld ended the conversation by aiming the gun at the mayor's face. The mayor was suddenly inspired to find a hold-out gun in his breast pocket, contributing his small derringer to the pile of arms. Auld collected all the weapons, said a few more words, and turned his back on the mayor and his thugs to walk back to the campsite. Hyle and Newman watched the three other men dust themselves off and walk away briskly.

"That was amazing," Hyle said as Auld approached.

"Until they come back for us in the middle of the night," Newman said. "Or send a bunch of their friends."

"They will not do that," Auld replied.

"How do you know that?" demanded Newman.

"Because they understand the consequences if they do," Auld replied in a tone that closed the discussion.

A crowd was gathered in the distance and Newman headed toward it to see what was going on. They had agreed to split up, with Auld on his motorcycle searching the far side of the camper city while he searched the near side. Hyle was staying with Sophia. As he approached, Newman could make out a man in the center of the crowd standing on something that raised him several feet higher than his audience. At the edge of the crowd he could hear the speaker's voice but could not make out his words.

"Excuse me," Newman said quietly to a woman nearby. "What's this all about? Who is this?"

"I don't know his real name, but we call him Father Brimstone," she replied. "He's telling us to repent because the world is about to end."

"How can you tell what he's saying?"

"I can't today, but that's what he says every time he talks," the woman explained. "He used to just preach on Sundays, but this week it's been every day. It's not as crazy as it sounds though. He quotes parts of the Bible that match up pretty well with things that are happening now."

"I see, thanks," Newman said. He was interested to hear the sermon, and guessed at some of the things the preacher might be saying, but reminded himself of the purpose that had brought him here. "You wouldn't happen to know a doctor or where I could get some antibiotics?"

The woman said that she knew a very good doctor but had no idea where she was at the moment. Newman reprised a conversation he had been having all morning. He explained Sophia's situation and got sympathy but little else in return.

"You should try to get her in to see the Prophet," suggested an elderly man who had been listening to the conversation. "He has the power to heal people."

"I heard that he's not letting people inside anymore though," the woman said.

This too was part of the conversation Newman had been through before. He thanked the man and woman for their suggestions and continued skirting around the edge of the crowd. The next few hours brought him no more success, but they did bring him closer to one goal. After leaving the assembly he had stopped wandering randomly and moved in one general direction. Although he had found no antibiotics and no new information, Newman had found his way to the front gate of Zebulon. Like the doors of the gate of Asher, there was a human-sized door set into one of the massive doors of banded wood that sealed the road. In front of this small door a few dozen people waited in line. Newman took his place at the end. A clean shaven young man in neat clothing turned back from the door with an older woman, possibly his mother, complaining and gesturing angrily as they walked away. One by one people were turned away from the door and the line moved forward. Some spoke for only a few seconds and some argued for many minutes, but in the end they all turned away disappointed.

When it was Newman's turn he approached the square window in the door and the face it framed.

"Bread line's closed for the day," the man said from inside. Newman could almost hear the words "move along" and wondered at the man's indifference.

"That's not what I'm here for," replied Newman. "I want to see the Prophet."

The doorman actually laughed at this, but it was a humorless laugh.

"You and just about everyone else out there," he answered. "The Prophet's not seeing anyone this week."

"Why? What's so special about this week?"

"He's busy preparing for the big ceremony on the solstice. He's not letting anyone in until it's over."

"But I have a friend who's very sick," Newman protested. "I can't wait that long."

"I'm sorry," the man said, "but my instructions are clear. Nobody comes in until after the ceremony."

"Maybe the Prophet would make an exception in our case," Newman tried. "I'm one of the people chosen for Asher and was the Proctor for the Third Canton."

"If that's true then you know that once you leave you can't come back," answered the doorman.

"I didn't go back. I came to Zebulon," Newman pointed out, but the man shook his head, clearly unimpressed by the distinction. "I'm travelling with two others—a woman who was in training to become a proctor and another man. The Prophet has had people on the lookout for us since we left Maine." Newman was still not convinced that this was true, but it seemed to spark an uncertain memory with the doorman.

"Wait here a second," he said, pulling his face back. The window closed and a murmur rippled through the line behind Newman. He decided not to turn around. The voices behind him were becoming an angry buzz by the time the window opened again.

"Have a seat somewhere. Someone's going to check," the face in the door told him.

Newman obliged and sat down off to one side of the door with his back against the concrete wall. Time passed and he watched the line dwindle to a handful of people. A boy turned away from the door and approached him.

"That man said to tell you that you'll have to come back next week," the boy said, pointing back toward the door. Newman considered going back to argue, or getting back in line, but realized that it would do no good. The sun was far to the west behind the familiar brownish haze. It was near the horizon by the time Newman made it back to camp. He was surprised to find Hyle and Sophia sitting in front of the tent across from a young couple, engaged in conversation. There was something different about Sophia, but he was unable to identify it before he was distracted by conversation.

"You must be Newman," the young woman said as he walked into camp. "I'm Storm and this is my fiancé Bobby. We've been hearing all about your adventures." She had a Celtic triskelion tattooed on her ankle, and next to a large crystal pendant, Newman noticed that the edge of another tattoo—evidently the wing tip of a fairy or an angel—peeking up from below the wide neck line of her tee shirt.

"Did you find anything?" asked Hyle.

"No," Newman said, recounting the highlights of his search. "I even tried to get in to see the Prophet, but evidently he's not letting anyone in right now."

"The Prophet?" Hyle repeated. "What did you do that for?" Newman hesitated.

"He's supposed to be a faith healer," he answered, bracing himself for Hyle's reaction.

"You don't believe in that, do you?" Hyle responded. It was not a question.

"He is though," Bobby interjected. "I know a guy who went in with a real bad infection on his leg and came out a couple days later completely cured." Storm nodded vehemently in agreement.

"A lot of people believe in faith healing," Newman answered. "But you have to have faith. That's why it's called faith healing. If you don't believe, it doesn't work so well. Weren't we just talking about something like this a few nights ago?"

Hyle was about to object, but he caught something in the way Newman emphasized his last point. He thought back to their discussion about the placebo effect and realized that Newman hoped faith healing might have some benefit for Sophia. He was not sure if Newman believed in it or not, but that was beside the point.

"Why wouldn't they let you in?" asked Sophia.

"The Prophet's preparing for some big ceremony for the solstice," Newman explained. "I even told the gate guard that we—" He stopped to choose his words carefully in front of the two strangers. "—had travelled all the way from Maine."

"I wouldn't have expected the Union of Faith to be celebrating the solstice," Hyle said. "Isn't that kind of pagan?"

"You're joking, right?" asked Storm.

Newman laughed. He knew what she was going to say. He had been hearing variations of it all afternoon.

"No," Hyle answered. "I don't see why they're making such a big deal of the solstice unless they're trying to avoid favoring Christmas or Hanukkah."

"This isn't just any solstice," Bobby explained. "It's twelve twenty-one twelve. It's the end of the Mayan calendar. That's the day the Mayans believed that the world would end. The Long Count calendar is a cycle that's over five thousand years long and the zero date was set three thousand years ago. After tomorrow that calendar runs out."

"Except some people don't think the world will be destroyed," Storm added quickly. "Some people believe that it'll be the beginning of the fifth age, which will be an age of enlightenment where humanity will evolve into a new level of consciousness."

"And some people believe earth will collide with a mysterious planet, get sucked into a black hole or have its poles reversed by a solar flare," Hyle added. "I remember all the disaster hype that started a few years ago."

"I like Storm's version better," Sophia said. She started to say something else, but stopped and tipped her head. "I hear a motorcycle," she said.

As she turned her head to listen for the motorcycle, Newman realized for the first time what had changed about her appearance.

"Where did you get that?" he asked, looking at her head, which had been wrapped in a lightweight burgundy scarf.

"Storm's been helping me with my hair. She used to be a hair stylist," Sophia answered. "Do you like it?"

Newman nodded appreciatively. When her long hair had been exposed the bald patches were increasingly noticeable. Now the scarf covered most of her head, Sophia looked healthier than she had since leaving the storm shelter. Only her face showed the effort she was investing in the conversation.

A cloud of red dust preceded Auld's motorcycle into the camp.

"And this is Nicolas Auld," Hyle said to their guests as Auld approached. "Any luck?" he asked Auld.

"A little, but don't let me interrupt."

"It's okay," Hyle said. "We were just learning about how the world is going to be destroyed in a couple days."

"Bobby and Storm were telling us about the Mayan calendar," Sophia corrected.

"It's interesting to talk about," Hyle conceded, "but do people really believe it?"

"Oh yes," answered Storm. "A few weeks ago about five hundred people left here in a big caravan to go down to Mexico."

"Izapa," Bobby interjected, "where the Mayan Long Count calendar was discovered. They wanted to be there for sunrise on the solstice."

"We would have gone with them but we got here after they had already left," Storm explained. "It would have been cool to be there. Whatever's going to happen at sunrise on the solstice is probably going to happen there."

"But we're still going to be in the dark here," added Bobby. "Izapa is about an hour east of here, so we'll still be an hour away from sunrise when the big event happens. That's why me and Storm are planning to stay up all night and watch the stars."

"Stars?" Hyle echoed, looking up at the brown smog. "We haven't even been able to see the moon for the last four months, let alone stars."

"Who knows what we'll be able to see before tomorrow night is over? This is more than a once in a lifetime event and we'll be watching," Bobby replied following Hyle's gaze. "Aw, damn. Sorry, I've gotta boogie. It's almost sunset."

"Why, what happens at sunset?" asked Newman.

"That's when I meditate—sunrise and sunset."

"Transcendental Meditation," Storm explained. "Bobby knows all about the different paths to enlightenment and such. He was just switching from Scientology to Baha'i when we met. He was in such a crisis. Then we checked out the Union of Faith. That's how we found out about this place, even though we weren't invited to go."

"Yeah, so when these guys blew me off I decided to go check out TM," Bobby concluded. "I took a one week course during the summer, and I'm glad I did. I think those cats are really onto something. They kind of take the best bits from Hinduism and a bit of Buddhism and whatnot and blend it all together in a way that makes sense. I was trying to get Storm into it, but you know, she's Storm, and then the war happened."

"I'm just not into that kind of stuff," Storm said apologetically. "It's cool and all, but I guess I'd just rather find my own way. Besides, Bobby shares all the best bits with me. And it really does help him. I can tell the days that he forgot to meditate because he seems so unbalanced. It wasn't cheap, but I think it was money well spent."

"It better be. Too late to get my money back now," Bobby laughed. "But now I really got to go. I can't afford to miss any sessions since I only have another day and a half to get it right."

Storm and Bobby said goodbye to everyone and then returned to their campsite by the VW bug.

"I didn't realize there was a deadline for enlightenment," Hyle said once they were safely out of earshot.

"Human beings are always casting about for something to believe in," observed Auld. Sophia detected that familiar undercurrent of hidden meaning. "It's sad that people always seem to miss the fact that they are the ones who give things meaning," he continued. "Which reminds me, I did manage to find a few things for you, Sophia." He dug into a black leather satchel as he stepped toward her and held up something small between his thumb and forefinger. "First this. It is one day of antibiotics. Take it now."

He handed the pill to Sophia and she swallowed it with an involuntary grimace at the aftertaste.

"Second is this," Auld said, and produced a large black book with a plain cover and small white letters on the spine."

"*Annals of Parapsychology*, volume 7," Sophia read aloud, puzzled until she heard her own words. "Is this—" Auld nodded.

"Yes," he answered. "It is the last article by Anderson Poimen before he disappeared and resurfaced as the Prophet."

"Where did you find something like that out here in the wilderness?" Hyle exclaimed.

"You are not the only ones here interested in the origins of Zendik," Auld explained. "Finally I got you this," he said to Sophia, and he pulled out an apple and handed it to her. "It is not much, but a nice change from canned food and dried rations."

The men had a meal of canned food and dried rations and discussed the end of the world prophecy. Everyone in the makeshift settlement was anticipating some event at sunrise two days hence, but Newman and Auld had heard many variations on the theme. Most people were aware that they were approaching the end of the Mayan calendar and also that the Prophet had planned a sunrise service for that date. Opinions varied about whether the two events were linked in some sort of cosmological way or whether the Prophet had scheduled the service in reaction to the inevitable public interest in the Mayan prophecy. Auld said that Zendik had evidently commented on the Mayan doomsday prophecy in a sermon several months earlier saying that he believed that it would mark the dawning of a new era and the creation of a kingdom of heaven on earth. Newman had not heard of any such beliefs during his time with the Union of Faith, but agreed that the idea of a heaven on earth was consistent with their teachings.

While the men talked through the last remnants of daylight, Sophia read the article from *Annals of Parapsychology* with great interest and ate absently from her apple.

CHAPTER EIGHTY-FIVE

WHAT DREAMS MAY COME

In the morning, Sophia awoke tired and disoriented. She had fleeting memories of a dream so surreal that it took a while to convince herself that she really was awake and recall where she was. When she reached over her head to fumble for the zipper on the door of the tent, she was surprised at how heavy her arm felt. There were footsteps outside the tent and a buzz of familiar voices. She felt a cold hand on her forehead and heard Auld's voice from a distance.

"She is burning up," he said. "Go back to sleep, Sophia. Save your strength."

When Sophia awoke again she was being helped to sit up. Hyle was on one side and Newman on the other. Auld had her swallow a pill and some water.

The third time Sophia woke up her head felt clearer and her arms were not as heavy. She pushed aside the tent flap and crawled out into the daylight. Newman and Hyle were sitting by the dormant fire pit talking.

"Sophia," Newman said when he saw her emerge. "You should rest. What do you need? We can bring it to you."

"No," Sophia replied. "I'm too sore to sleep anymore. But it's cold out here. I wouldn't mind a blanket."

She tried to stand up, but her legs refused to support her weight. Newman hurried over to help her up and walked her over to the car next to the fire pit. He checked her forehead with his hand as Hyle appeared from behind the car and draped a survival blanket around her. The two men peppered her with questions. Was she feeling better? Yes. Did she want something to eat? No. Was she warm enough? Getting there. Sophia looked at the sun, which was low in the sky. She could not remember whether it was east or west.

"Is it afternoon?" she asked. "And where is Auld?"

"Yes," Hyle answered. "You've been sleeping all day. We've been taking turns napping too. Auld is off on some secret mission. All he would tell us was to get some rest.

"Did he take that article? I hope you got a chance to read it first." Both men shook their heads.

"No, he was gone first thing in the morning," Newman said.

"He's been coming and going all day," Hyle added. "It was just luck that he happened to be here when you first woke up with that fever."

"Why? What was the article about?" asked Newman.

Overcome by a wave of fatigue, Sophia leaned back against one of the wheels of the car and fought the urge to close her eyes.

"I didn't understand it completely," she confessed. "It presented his theory called 'collective solipsism' which, as near as I could figure, says that everyone creates their own reality, but also that there's some higher level of reality that's created by the interaction of each individual reality. It was full of references to studies where belief or prayer was shown to have some measureable effect on outcomes. It also had lots of calculations about the power of different affirmational beliefs against each other and against confutational belief."

"Sounds like a bunch of New Age malarkey," said Hyle, "but at least it helps explain why he decided to start up his own cult. If he thinks that prayer can have a real effect on the world it makes perfect sense."

"It sounds like a pretty scientific paper to me," Newman remarked. "How can you be so quick to dismiss it?"

"Just because it sounds scientific doesn't mean it is," Hyle replied. "People dress things up as science all the time to make it look more credible. Look at intelligent design. But eventually real science will sort out the fact from the fantasy. The so-called experiments he references probably can't be duplicated. Just like Sophia's psychic ability with the tarot cards. If something is true, science will be able to demonstrate it to be true using reproducible experiments."

"Zener cards," Sophia corrected. "And do you still believe that about science after everything we've discussed?"

"Yes—wait. What do you mean everything we have discussed?"

"Do you want the chronological list?" Sophia asked. She tried to scowl at Hyle but was too tired to put much emotion into it.

"Sure," answered Hyle. He almost added, "Knock yourself out," but thought the better of it.

"In my opinion there's still a viable rivalry between empiricism and rationalism," Sophia replied, "but without even getting into that, there's also a long history of the uncertainty of knowledge. You could start with Heraclitus and his claim that everything is in constant flux. You can't step in the same river twice. From there go to Timon who called logic into question by noting that every logical deduction was based on assumptions, leading to an infinite regress."

"Those arguments are too general to be meaningful and a few thousand years before the birth of science," Hyle countered.

"Fair enough," Sophia agreed. "In that case, start with Descartes and all his observations that our senses are untrustworthy sources of information. Then go to Bishop Berkeley and his argument that when you strip away all the attributes from a physical object, there's nothing left. The so-called real world is made up only of perceptions rather than things that exist apart from our perceptions. Next you have Hume who applies that same argument to the concept of a 'self' and even calls cause and effect into question. Remember his argument that the future isn't obligated to repeat the past? What could be more fundamental to science than cause and effect? Then there's Kant, who points out that there must be some innate framework upon which we arrange our perceptions for the world to even make sense to us at all, with the implication that this framework also helps shape how we see the world."

"There are some problems with that idea though," Hyle interjected.

"Wait, I'm not done yet," said Sophia. "You can have your turn in a minute. After Kant there's Nietzsche who didn't believe that there was any absolute truth at all. Finally you have three modern thinkers—Wittgenstein, Gödel and Kuhn—each showing in their area of study that our ability to discover the truth is shifting and difficult to nail down at best and may even be destined to be incomplete."

"Now are you done?" asked Hyle when Sophia paused for a moment.

"Yes," she said. "Your turn."

"If your point is only that there will always be uncertainty in science, I agree," Hyle conceded. "Science never proves things conclusively, but the longer it fails to disprove them, the more likely they are to be true, even if the odds never get to one hundred percent."

"But you think that science is getting closer to the truth?" asked Sophia.

"Sure, just look at the constant advances in technology. I buy Kuhn's argument that science can involve major changes in thinking, but I don't buy the radical interpretation that one paradigm is no better than another. Science is like doing a jigsaw puzzle. You can put together chunks of the puzzle because they form a clear picture even if you don't yet know where they fit into the whole puzzle. Once you see where a chunk fits you might have to remove a few wrong pieces to put the chunk where it belongs. That's analogous to a new paradigm raising some new questions even though it solves old ones. The point is that you wouldn't remove a huge chunk of the puzzle that makes sense to replace it with a smaller or less certain piece. You'd only make the change if it made more sense in solving the puzzle."

"So the new paradigm must subsume the old one," Sophia summarized. "Sort of like Hegel."

"Yes," Hyle agreed. "I suppose you could call the old paradigm the thesis and the anomalies which call it into question the antithesis. Even if it's not perfect, the new paradigm would have to address both sufficiently to be considered a synthesis."

"So if your model for science is a jigsaw puzzle, does that mean that you believe that science is closing in on a final solution?"

"I do," answered Hyle. "Look at the unification of forces. It may be that the puzzle is missing a few pieces that we'll never be able to fill in, to account for Gödel, quantum uncertainty and the like, but at some point we'll have all the big chunks of the puzzle connected and we'll start filling in the individual pieces."

"Isn't that a little egotistical though, Hyle?" asked Sophia. "Hegel thought philosophy was wrapping up in his time, but there are a couple centuries' worth of philosophers who would probably disagree."

"Ego has no bearing on whether something's right or wrong," Hyle observed. "I'm just going on what remains to be done. We seem to be well on the way to unifying the four remaining forces. If that's done successfully there will still be a lot of science to be done, but I'm not sure where any major new paradigm shifts would come from."

"Hyle, you once argued that religion had a track record of changing to protect itself from the advances of science," Newman pointed out. "Now look at the track record of science. One of the characteristics of a paradigm shift is that scientists don't see it coming. Look at what scientists believed a thousand years ago. We find most of what they believed then to be ridiculous by today's standards. It's said that knowledge is increasing exponentially. If that's true, what are the chances that our current theories won't look equally ridiculous a few thousand years in the future?"

"A fair point," Hyle allowed. "You know the Arthur C. Clarke quote about any sufficiently advanced technology being indistinguishable from magic? I suspect that a thousand years in the future our technology will be that far beyond what we can imagine today. Who knows? Ten thousand years in the future we may be energy beings teleporting from one galaxy to another. Nonetheless, it seems that we're getting close to placing the last big chunks of the jigsaw puzzle where they belong." Newman shook his head doubtfully.

"Given what you've told us so far about modern physics—where light can be a wave and a particle at the same time, where cats can be both alive and dead until they're observed, where one particle at one end of the galaxy can instantaneously determine the spin of a particle at the other end of the galaxy—I'd say we're ready for another paradigm shift any time."

"What if a jigsaw puzzle isn't the right analogy?" asked Sophia. "When you do a jigsaw puzzle you're working with a finite and predetermined set of pieces to create a picture bit by bit. Your point, Hyle, is that the rules of science demand that you must be making progress toward a more complete picture. But who says we have to be working with puzzle pieces? What if it's more like creating a mural or a tapestry? Normal science is coloring in the images and adding the details to the existing picture and a paradigm shift is adding a whole new scene that changes the meaning or the context of the original picture."

"The problem with the tapestry analogy is that science is trying to make a picture that matches the reality that we observe," Hyle said. "That's why I picked a jigsaw puzzle. You're talking about an act of pure creation that no longer has to correlate with reality."

"But what if the picture *is* reality?" Sophia countered. Her mind moved rapidly across a range of topics and she tried to keep pace with the concept that was emerging. The pieces of her own puzzle were starting to fall into place. "Why do we believe modern physics? Because we can create logically consistent mathematical formulae that correlate with what we observe," she said, answering her own question. "But why should nature correlate to mathematics? We have no better explanation for that than Pythagoras did. We still give mathematics the same sort of mystical reverence that the Pythagoreans did, but we don't stop to question the connection. What if it's all in here?" Sophia asked, tapping a finger to the side of her head.

"Isn't that essentially what Kant argued?" Newman suggested. "That we interpret the world through a logical framework that pre-exists in our minds?"

"But we've already demonstrated that Kant was wrong," objected Hyle. "The concept of time being absolute and the straight Euclidean geometry of space have been replaced by curved non-Euclidean geometry and relativistic space-time."

"Kant's argument doesn't depend on a specific model of space and time," Sophia said. "The main point is that we need some type of framework. Our experience of space and time doesn't really change, even if our model of the world does. You could conceive of even more radical explanations for space and time, but they wouldn't change our experience."

"Are there more radical explanations of space and time?" asked Newman.

"Sure," said Sophia. "There are still problems of infinity to be answered like what came before the beginning of time or what is beyond the edge of the universe."

"Curved space-time helps address that," Hyle explained. "Imagine that we lived in two dimensions, but on a globe. You could travel in a straight line forever without ever leaving the surface of the globe. Curved space-time may work the same way for three dimensions. And supposedly time was created in the Big Bang."

"Of course, there's also the idea that time doesn't really exist at all," Sophia responded. "If you think about it, the past exists only as memories and the future exists only as expectations. Therefore past and future exist only in our thoughts. The only thing that can really be said to exist is the present. But even the present has problems. It has its own version of quantum indeterminacy. As soon as you try to measure or mark the present, it's gone—like trying to determine the position of an electron."

"And how does that help defend Kant?" asked Hyle.

"I don't know that it does," Sophia answered, gathering her thoughts. "I think I got sidetracked. I wasn't trying to defend Kant. In fact, along with time and space, maybe you could throw out all his other categories of understanding along with the idea that we're trying to make sense of an external world. Maybe mathematics correlates to what we observe because mathematics and our experiences come from the same place. Maybe it's our conceptions—not some external reality—that create our experiences."

"Does that mean that the earth really was flat a thousand years ago, and that half the people in loony bins really are Elvis Presley or Jesus just because they think they are?" Hyle argued.

"Let's come back to those questions," Sophia said. "I'm exploring a new paradigm here. Work with me. Why does mathematics correlate with nature? Math is an internally consistent logical construct that can exist entirely in the absence of the material world."

"Can it though?" Hyle asked. "At the most basic level math is based on the concept of integers and counting. Without nature, what would there be to count? In the absence of discrete items in nature to count, would we even have a concept of numbers? You can make the same argument for science. Science is based on observation first, and then induction of general rules from observed patterns."

"A good question," Sophia agreed, "but think back to our discussion about Buddhism. Where does the idea of discrete objects in nature come from if not from our minds? The distinctions between mountains and sky or football games or people don't come from nature. They come from us. Maybe the rules of science and the laws of nature do too. Did it ever strike you as odd that nature is symmetrical? Maxwell decided that nature should be symmetrical and that electricity should be able to produce magnetism. Then, lo and behold, he goes out and demonstrates that it's true. Same with de Broglie. He decides that nature should be symmetrical and that if electromagnetic waves can be described as matter particles, that matter should be able to be described as waves. And again, nature accommodates this desire for symmetry. Why?"

"Maybe nature is just symmetrical... by nature," Hyle suggested.

"Don't you see though?" Sophia protested. "In both cases it's a human desire for symmetry that seems to precede the discovery of symmetry in nature. What about the thought experiments of scientists like Galileo and Einstein? They're not progressing science by observation and induction of general principles. These are people making things up in their own minds. The only difference between thought experiments and philosophy, or even acts of pure imagination, is that the thought experiments must conform to your rules of science, Hyle. They must add to the tapestry without substantially undoing any part that's already been created."

"And thought experiments must ultimately be able to be tested empirically," Hyle pointed out.

"The key word is 'ultimately,'" noted Sophia. "If the thought experiments helped expand our concept of nature and our concepts are what determine the structure of nature, then of course they'd ultimately be confirmed by experimentation."

"Wait, are you saying that the real world is just something that we make up?" Hyle asked.

"Maybe," replied Sophia. "But not just something we make up. Something we make up according to some very specific rules."

"Do you realize how crazy that sounds?"

Sophia ignored Hyle's question.

"Does it strike you as odd at all that light should be the only thing that's not relative?" Sophia asked.

"No," replied Hyle. "Why is that odd?"

"Light also happens to be our main means of experiencing the world," Sophia observed. "Sight is the primary mode of perception. In fact, it's so primary it's fundamentally associated with knowledge."

"It was God's first act of creation," Newman pointed out. "'Let there be light.' We call knowledge enlightenment, shed light on a subject."

"Apollo was associated with both light and knowledge," added Sophia. "And the fire of Prometheus, in the days before electricity, was a symbol of both light and knowledge."

"So light's symbolic of knowledge," Hyle agreed. "Maybe that's because evolution selected for vision since light is the quickest way to convey information from a distance. What does that have to do with relativity?"

"Maybe it's not the speed of light that's constant," answered Sophia. "Maybe it's the speed of perception. Maybe it's human consciousness that's the constant in the universe. Hyle, you said that when the four remaining forces in physics were unified, most of the major puzzle pieces would be in place. But what if there's a fifth major force? What if the last thing to be unified is human consciousness itself?"

"But human consciousness isn't a force in physics," Hyle objected.

"Schrödinger's cat might disagree with you, Hyle," Newman said. "Determining whether something is alive or dead seems to me to be a fairly important force."

"That's just—" Hyle stopped himself before saying that it was only a thought experiment.

"If matter and energy are interchangeable at the quantum level," Sophia continued, "then maybe it won't take us ten thousand years to become energy beings. Maybe in a sense we already are but we just don't know it yet."

"Now you're making all those people who are waiting for the earth to be destroyed tomorrow look sane," Hyle retorted. "If you're claiming that reality is nothing but a mental construct, why can't I just believe that I'm Superman and fly out of here?"

"Could you believe that you're Superman?" asked Sophia.

"That's not the point," Hyle objected.

"Actually, that's entirely the point," countered Newman.

"I understand the objection though," Sophia allowed. "Clearly reality conforms to certain rules. We can't just imagine anything we want. In fact, it doesn't appear that as individuals we can change reality at all."

"Yes, exactly," agreed Hyle. "If you want to argue that reality is just a creation of the human mind, you need to be able to explain why we can't just imagine things differently and have them become different. If you can't explain that, then the normal view that reality is independent of what we think seems like a better explanation of things."

"Would you say that the English language is a creation of the human mind?" asked Sophia.

"Of course," answered Hyle.

"Can you change it however you want?"

"Not however I want," Hyle conceded, "but I can make up my own sentences. I can even coin new words."

"All according to a set of rules though," Sophia pointed out. "If you venture too far outside the rules nobody would understand you and your new use of the language would go nowhere. You'd just be jabbering. You'd be discounted like the guy who believes he's Elvis or Jesus. Do you remember the realists and nominalists, Hyle?"

"I think so. You mean the talk we had back in Asher?"

"Yes," Newman confirmed. "I remember that the realists believed that words had an inherent reality of their own, especially universals. That was how they explained how everyone could have the same understanding of a word like red even when it described something that had never been experienced before."

"Yes, I remember that," Hyle said with a laugh. "I remember thinking how incredibly stupid an idea that was."

"Stupid like the idea that the sun moved around the earth?" Sophia suggested.

"Exactly," Hyle agreed.

"Meaning that it was a perfectly reasonable idea for the knowledge people had at the time," said Sophia. "And that it only seems foolish through the lens of the knowledge we have in the modern age. Much like our current ideas will seem foolish to people a thousand years in the future. What if the material world is our version of realism, Hyle?"

"I don't even understand what you're asking."

"What if the material world is like a language? We think that physical objects have their own independent reality just like the realists thought that universal words had their own independent reality. We laugh at the ideas of the realists now, but will people laugh at our idea of the material world a thousand years in the future? Maybe what we call the physical world is just a way for us to communicate with each other just like language is. We teach children language. Do we also teach them physical reality? We point to pictures of discrete objects. We teach them about object permanence. It takes children years to develop a solid sense of what we call reality. Maybe it's not as natural as we think. Maybe what we call reality exists only by mutual agreement the same way language does. Nobody has the power to change it individually, but collectively we give it meaning."

"That might solve the problem of free will too, Hyle," Newman realized aloud. "Remember when you said that, because of cause and effect, in order for us to have free will we'd all have to be prime movers, existing outside the laws of nature? If we collectively create the laws of nature, that would be exactly the case."

"Before you get too excited, Newman, where does God fit in to this scheme?" Hyle asked. "Would this mean we really did create God in our own image?"

"I suppose it would," Newman allowed, thinking through the consequences as he spoke. "But it would also mean that He is real."

"Along with the flat earth, the geocentric solar system, Zeus and Thor," Hyle noted.

"Except that those ideas have been supplanted by new ones," argued Sophia. "Sort of like old words like 'forsooth' that aren't used anymore. As our tapestry of knowledge grows, we need to write out old parts of it to make room for parts that no longer fit."

"I understand the idea that knowledge progresses," replied Hyle. "That's the foundation of science after all. But how do you explain the fact that many of the old ideas, like the flat earth and the geocentric universe, were written out largely due to observations that didn't agree with the common belief of the day? The round earth and heliocentric solar system would have had to be there already before anybody imagined them."

"The ancient Greeks proposed both theories, and Aristotle believed the earth to be spherical," Sophia said, "although he argued for a geocentric model. But, maybe, like Schrödinger's cat or James' pragmatism, the nature of reality wasn't determined until it was convincingly demonstrated. And maybe it was determined from some other area of thought."

"What's that supposed to mean?" asked Hyle.

"I don't know exactly," Sophia confessed. "Remember Leibniz's best of all possible worlds? His idea was that even God was limited by some rules of possibility. Maybe the same idea applies here. Maybe the earth had to be round and the solar system heliocentric to avoid logical conflicts with ideas that already existed."

Hyle shrugged, unimpressed.

"It seems that not just science, but all of human history, has moved in paradigms," continued Sophia. "Do you remember the quote you liked from Auguste Comte?"

"You mean the one about how civilization goes from an animistic and religious stage to metaphysics and then to science?"

"Yes. There's another way to look at that," Sophia suggested. "In the first age of history, people worshipped nature and spirits and pantheons of deities. As you pointed out, this gave us little control over our environment, so in the second age of history, power became centralized. The idea of a privileged earth in a geocentric solar system fit well with the idea of the central authority of the monotheistic Church and the sovereignty of monarchs in a feudal state. In the third segment of history, all of those ideas were challenged by the idea of individualism—Copernicus argues that earth is just one of many planets, Luther champions the individual relationship with God, Locke questions the supremacy of monarchs over their subjects, and the empiricists emphasize the observations of the individual over the teachings of authority. Finally, at the beginning of the twentieth century, we have the rise of relativism and uncertainty. Nietzsche proclaims that God is dead, meaning not just the biblical God, but the idea of Absolute Truth. Freud and Marx do the same work on psychology and economics. Einstein demonstrates space-time relativity, quantum physics adds indeterminacy, and we find that even mathematics and language can't bring us certainty."

"I think that just shows the significant effect that science has on other types of thinking," Hyle replied.

"Maybe so," allowed Sophia. "But maybe it's the other way around. Maybe our view of reality has been evolving across all fields of thought, and what scientists 'objectively' observe is much more a product of the times than they realize."

"What about God then?" Hyle asked, returning to his original question. "If so many people believe in some version of God, then according to this theory, he must exist. Not only that, he'd be dependent upon our belief for his existence. I suppose you could argue that this is why organized religions have been so opposed to science—God would have a vested interest in keeping us ignorant of our own power. And what about Satan? Or maybe I should use the name Lucifer in deference to my roommate's old girlfriend, because in the battle to ultimately defeat God, the best tool may be our enlightenment through science and philosophy."

"I think it depends upon which idea of God you mean," Sophia suggested. "If you mean the classical idea of God as a discrete entity, maybe that is a human creation, and I'd agree with your analysis. On the other hand, theology already seems to be moving toward a broader concept of God, and I think there's a way to have a concept of God that's not in conflict with science and philosophy."

"How would that work?" asked Newman.

"It's a little complicated," Sophia replied, pausing to gather her thoughts. "Remember that mathematics is incomplete by definition according to Gödel's theorem?" Newman nodded. "And also remember that an incomplete language can be understood by a higher level meta-language?" He nodded again. "If our mutual construction of reality correlates to mathematics, there may be parts of it which can only be understood at a higher level than we're able to comprehend."

"Are you suggesting that God is just some higher level meta-language?" asked Hyle. "I could almost go along with that definition of God."

"I'm saying that there may be things that will always be beyond our understanding," replied Sophia. "Things that exist outside the natural world we've created for ourselves. That's your definition of supernatural Hyle—that which exists outside the laws of nature."

"But seen from that higher level, all humanity could be understood as a single entity," added Newman. "Like that description of the ant colony that's seen as a single entity by the ant eater."

"Or Heidegger's concept of the One or the They," Sophia replied. "It's a singular force that influences and defines us, while at the same time we help to create and define it through our participation."

"That also seems to fit with Tillich's concept of symbols and his view of God as the ground of being," Newman noted. "We're all participants in being, but as a whole—as a state—it's beyond our comprehension, eternal and unknowable."

"I suppose that's true, Newman," agreed Sophia. "In that view, Hegel ends up being pretty close to the mark. We're all part of Geist, creating and discovering reality and building toward the ultimate goal of self-realization."

"Sophia, I seem to remember you calling Hegel arrogant for thinking that he had brought philosophy to its logical conclusion," Hyle said. "Now it seems that you're trying to do the same thing for philosophy, science and religion, all at the same time."

"I'm not really trying to do anything but stay conscious," Sophia said with a weak smile. "And I think I'm about to give up on that for now."

She pulled the survival blanket tight around her neck, leaned back against the wheel of the car and closed her eyes. A million ideas and possibilities scratched at the back of Sophia's mind, but she was too tired to think any further on them. Within minutes she was asleep.

The sun hovered just above the horizon when Auld finally returned to camp. He looked at Sophia, curled up beside the car under a silver emergency blanket and oblivious to the sounds of the motorcycle. Hyle emerged from inside the car and Newman leaned against the front wheel, where he had been resting fitfully.

"Get some sleep," Auld told the men. "I will wake you in a few hours."

"Why? What are we doing in a few hours," Hyle asked.

"Sophia's getting worse," Newman interjected.

"I know. Did she eat?"

"A little bit," answered Newman. "Not much."

"She will be okay, one way or another," said Auld.

"What does that mean—one way or another?" Newman demanded.

"We will bring her to see Zendik tonight. For now, go to sleep."

"I thought he wasn't seeing anyone for the next few days," said Newman.

"He is not, but he will see us. We are going to break in." Auld grinned broadly after delivering this news and laughed at the reaction of the two men.

"I heard that the Prophet actually lives in a fortified complex underground, inside the mountain," Newman objected, "even if we could get over the walls."

"If he built this place in anticipation of some final battle, that's probably true," Hyle noted. "I don't think we have much chance of getting in."

"There is a hidden cave on the other side of the mountain that leads to the compound. Even Zendik does not know about this," replied Auld.

"How do you know about it then?" Hyle asked.

"I have been busy doing research today."

"What about the guards?"

"We will have to avoid them, or they will try to shoot us." Before Hyle could voice a protest, Auld added, "If we do nothing, she will die."

"Sophia's in no shape to be mountain climbing though," Newman pointed out. "Especially not at night. Or spelunking for that matter."

"We will help her," Auld replied. "Now, get some rest."

CHAPTER EIGHTY-SIX

THE APOCALYPSE

Shadows of twilight spread across the desert as the trio set out for the far side of the mountain, following the motorcycle taillight around the edge of the makeshift city until the campsites began to thin out. Auld stopped his motorcycle and shut off the engine, preparing to abandon it and go on foot in order to eliminate the risk that the lights, or even the heat signature of the engine, might alert a sentry. He would walk ahead of the car, picking out a path, using a shielded flashlight only as necessary.

Sophia stirred in the back seat. "I like this song," she mumbled.

All across Lower Zebulon people had collected in groups to await the coming of some significant event with the dawn. A huge bonfire blazed in the distance, surrounded by a crowd that was visible only as an amorphous shadow blocking the base of the flames. With the engine of the motorcycle silenced, the notes of a guitar rose clearly above the murmur of faraway conversation. A low voice joined the guitar. The first few words were too quiet to make out, but then the voice soared into a plaintive wail and Newman caught the words "Heaven" and "Hell," and then, in the next line, as expected, "blue skies" and "pain."

"Pink Floyd," he said. "One of my favorites too."

Sophia muttered something incoherent. It did not sound as if it were in response to Newman. Meanwhile, Auld pulled a few items from his saddlebags and the car rolled forward slowly, staying close behind him as he set out for the far side of the mountain. The journey was long and slow. Barely enough moonlight penetrated the cloud layer to be able to make out the terrain. Hyle spoke little in favor of concentrating on Auld's outline ahead of them and most of the distance was covered in silence. By Hyle's estimation they had traveled roughly half the night before Auld finally stopped. They woke Newman and shifted Sophia to the front seat in his place.

"How is she going to be able to climb that?" Newman asked in a voice somewhere between a whisper and a yawn. As he spoke his eyes scanned upwards, trying to find the top of the mountain ahead of them. It was perceptible only as a black emptiness against the lesser blackness of the dimly illuminated sky.

"With this," Auld replied, and held out an armful of tangled ropes. "Help me get this on her."

Sophia became more alert as they worked the ropes around her legs and shoulders and waved Auld and Newman away, tugging on the ropes to do it herself.

"I'm not an invalid, you know," she said. "I can get dressed myself."

Despite her protests, Sophia was still not fully aware of what was going on and did not understand how the harness was meant to work, so Newman humored her while quietly working around her, undoing her mistakes while her attention was focused elsewhere. Once the ropes were in place, Auld asked her to sit still. Newman took her hands and held them together on her lap for a moment. They burned between his palms.

He placed his hand across her forehead and tried to convince himself that it was the cold desert air that made her fever seem so much worse.

"Here, take this," said Auld, thrusting something into his hand.

Newman reached out even as his eyes focused through the darkness to identify the object. His hand touched cold metal and pulled back reflexively. The gun fell to the ground.

"They will be trying to kill us," Auld said quietly.

"We've already had this conversation," Newman replied. "I will not carry a gun."

Auld gave a suit-yourself shrug, retrieved the gun and inspected it before handing it to Hyle. Hyle tucked it into the back of his belt. With considerable effort and a little assistance, Auld approached Sophia backwards, crouched down to slide his arms into the harness and then stood back up, hoisting her off the car seat and into the air. Her shoes dangled several feet off the ground. Although she had lost weight over the last week, Sophia was still a considerable burden. After a few staggering steps, Auld found his stride and headed for the mountain. Hyle and Newman fell in behind him.

Dirt alternated with patches of bare stone to form the ground beneath their feet, but the core of the mountain was often so covered with boulders that this surface could not be found. A cottage-sized boulder stood as a landmark at the base of the slope and they circled around it, picking their way between smaller rocks to begin the ascent. Most of the way the grade was shallow enough to allow them to walk, although occasionally they were forced to use their hands to navigate difficult footing over boulder fields and steeper inclines. Auld demonstrated an aptitude for picking a good path, and even encumbered by his passenger and the burden of blazing the trail, Hyle and Newman had difficulty keeping up. Sophia slipped in and out of consciousness, sometimes mumbling things that no one was able to understand.

After a few hours of climbing, their pace had slowed considerably. Auld stumbled more frequently. On one steep grade loose rocks gave way beneath his feet. He pitched forward, splaying his arms and legs to look for a purchase, but was unable to keep from sliding. Rubble clattered down the path as he, with Sophia strapped to his back, slid back down, stopping only after colliding with Newman and knocking him off balance into a pile on top of them. Without a word, Auld struggled to his feet and started back up the slope.

Not long afterwards, the mountain rose up in a wall of cracked stone too steep to ascend. They picked their way along the base of this cliff face, losing a bit of altitude as they traveled, eventually encountering a spiky, cactus-like bush that blocked the narrow ledge. It was the only sign of life they had seen on the mountain. Just before reaching the bush Auld stepped sideways and disappeared into a crack in the rock face. The white glow of a flashlight emerged from the opening. Following closely behind, Newman could see that they had entered a fissure leading down sharply into the heart of the mountain. Two layers of rock met here. One solid layer formed the ground of the cave. The layer above it had split, creating a gap that was widest at their feet and narrowed above them, tapering to a point somewhere in the darkness above their heads. Although Newman was not claustrophobic, at eye level the walls were close enough to awaken some primeval fear in the depths of his subconscious. Suddenly the flashlight ranked among the most significant technological achievements of the human race.

The cleft descended steadily at an angle sharp enough that Sophia's heels sometimes scuffed against the stone. In the steepest stretches the best that Newman and Hyle could do was a controlled skid with their arms braced against the walls to keep their balance. The pitch down was steeper than the path up the mountain, and the way was relatively straight and clear, so what had taken several hours to climb, they were able to descend in a fraction of the time. When the fissure finally terminated in a small cave, they were nearly back to ground level. Several passages led out of the cave and Auld swept his light across each one before picking a tunnel. A few minutes later they emerged into another cave with more passages. This time Auld bypassed some larger openings for a passage small enough that it required him to crawl on hands and knees, the two other men stooping behind him. A moment later they stood upright again in an enormous cavern.

Before Auld covered the flashlight with his hand, allowing only a narrow beam to escape between his fingers, they caught a glimpse of supplies surrounding them in all directions. Rows of high shelves stacked with boxes filled the center of the cavern and crates, pallets of shrink wrapped boxes and fifty five gallon drums clustered around the edges. The floor of the cavern had been leveled with concrete. They were able to move quickly and silently through aisles and yet it took them a considerable time to reach the other end of the cavern. Although it bore some resemblance to a huge warehouse or discount store, the distance was better measured in units of city blocks.

After several city blocks Auld stopped momentarily and directed their attention to a light and the sound of voices nearby. At the end of the aisle he signaled for Hyle and Newman to stay where they were and then disappeared around corner. There was the clatter of a small object on concrete, a muffled thud, an interrupted exclamation of surprise and the sound of a brief struggle, and then Auld reappeared at the end of the aisle to wave them forward, Sophia still resting peacefully on his back. A wide corridor led out of the cavern. The square opening was clearly man-made and the tracks of double tires marked the floor. Also on the floor were two men in guard uniforms. Newman was relieved to see that they were still breathing.

A flight of stairs a short distance into the corridor brought them up to a hallway. Oil lamps held by wall sconces provided the minimum amount of light needed, and combined with the hewn stone walls, gave the impression of a medieval castle. Watching the flickering orange light of the flames on the red rock, Hyle got the unshakable impression that they had descended into Hell. They traveled quickly along the hallway. Passing a section where the walls were smooth concrete and the stone beneath their feet gave way to wooden planks that echoed hollowly as they crossed, Hyle realized that the mountain was shot through with narrow chasms like the one they had descended. Auld guided them through a network of corridors and doorways, occasionally backtracking to let guard patrols pass. Newman and Hyle quickly became disoriented, but Auld seemed to know exactly where he was going in the labyrinth.

Eventually their path was blocked by a pair of guards stationed at a large and ornately carved wooden door. They stood back to the door, one on either side, watching along what appeared to be a larger perpendicular corridor. As Hyle and Newman waited for Auld, who seemed to be deep in thought contemplating a strategy, a bell rang in the distance. The two guards had a brief conversation. It was too far away to overhear their words, but their tone was unmistakably one of surprise and disbelief. One guard broke off the discussion with a shrug and hurried off down the hall. The other guard followed. Auld hastened to the door with the other two men close behind. He inserted a couple metal sticks into the keyhole with one hand, pressed the thumb latch with the other and swung the door inward, waving Hyle and Newman inside.

«« »»

Sophia awoke to find herself sitting in an armchair, facing a broad mahogany desk, its graceful curves representing a time long past when people cared more about craftsmanship and aesthetics. The door directly behind the desk and ones in the wall on either side gave Sophia an eerie sense of déjà vu. She had been having strange dreams interspersed with equally strange bits of reality and was not yet entirely convinced that she was awake. Images of being carried up a mountain had the vague sense of being real. The cloud of crows that had covered everything in shadow before retreating to reveal a blue sky felt like a dream. Pictures of a dark underground warehouse were too fragmentary to classify. Sophia realized that she had no idea whether it was day or night, how she had gotten here or even where here was. A fire burned somewhere behind her. The smell of wood smoke hung in the air and light danced in time to the hiss and crackle of the burning wood. It cast the shadows of three figures on the wall ahead of her, stretched such that their heads ran back along the ceiling. Sophia wanted to turn her head to see who it was, but she was too weak. She was relieved to hear a familiar voice.

"What now?" whispered Newman.

She saw another chair in the room. It was a large wingback armchair with floral upholstery, set off at one corner of the desk and angled slightly to face the seat behind it, symmetrical to Sophia's own chair. She looked at the arm of her chair and fixated on a rose, admiring the detail and shading of the petals. As she stared, the picture resolved into singular threads. She could see each individual color, the places where they crossed and the empty space in between, and wondered that the small bits could come together to make such an image. Further still, she could see the fine hairs bristling out from the sides of each thread and the twist of the smaller strands of fiber that composed them. Beyond the limits of her vision Sophia imagined looking deeper, down to a level where the molecules arranged to form the fibers and where atoms formed the molecules. Somewhere down there electrons winked in and out of physical existence and quarks were held together with a force that never weakened.

"We wait," replied Auld. "Not long."

There was more conversation, but the voices faded—or perhaps the voices continued and she faded—Sophia was not sure. Hearing her three companions had convinced her that she was awake and yet time moved strangely the way it did in dreams. She was not sure whether it was seconds or hours later that the door behind the desk opened, but she recognized the robed figure the instant he stepped into the room. The Prophet. He was as ageless in person as he was in photographs and his appearance was a study in contradictions. His hair was thick and carefully styled, giving it a youthful touch that offset an almost unnatural whiteness. In a similar way the tan of his face offset the crows feet around his eyes—eyes of an intelligent and piercing deep blue. Sophia was reminded of Delacroix as the eyes locked on her.

"Welcome, Newman," he said. "I am Asha Zendik." His eyes shifted. "Hyle, Sophia, welcome." He nodded at them in greeting, his hands tucked into the opposite sleeves of his cassock like a monk. The gold and crimson trim of his white robe flashed in the firelight. "You seem to have picked up a fourth," Zendik said, his eyes shifting again to Auld. "By what name do you call yourself?"

The odd wording of the question only confirmed what Sophia already knew. Zendik recognized Auld. She could hear this in his voice the same way she could tell when Auld played his games with wording. Something else was similar about their voices. They both spoke with an accent. Although it was difficult to place—Sophia guessed native dialects from Irish to Indian, and ultimately wondered if it might be an affectation—Zendik's accent gave his speech that same enchanting musical quality that made it a pleasure to listen to and made everything he said seem more meaningful. Sophia was sure that Zendik was aware of this effect and cultivated it. She felt her eyelids closing and did nothing to stop them, allowing herself instead to slip into the rhythm of his voice.

"Auld. Nicolas Auld," Zendik repeated after Auld introduced himself. "Good old Nick, of course, of course," he continued, as if just remembering a long forgotten friend. "How did you find your way in here?"

"There is a cleft that leads to the caves behind your warehouse," Auld answered, briefly flashing his characteristic grin.

"A tunnel? How careless of me to have overlooked that. And what about the guards?"

"They seem to have just been called away by something urgent."

"I see. Lucky timing for you," Zendik observed. "Nonetheless, I'm glad you are here. I'm sure you have many questions."

Everything Sophia heard had the ring of half truth to it. She got the odd sense that Auld and Zendik were staging a performance for their benefit, or playing some secret word game with rules only they understood.

"How do you know our names for starters?" Hyle demanded.

"Names are very important," replied Zendik. "I make it my business to know them. Did you know that in the days of old people believed that if you knew a person's true name, you could control their soul?"

"Is that what you believe?"

"No," Zendik answered with a patronizing laugh that made Hyle bristle. "But it is closer to the truth than you might think."

"Yes, we know. We've read your theories," Hyle retorted.

"I hope it was the paper in *Annals of Parapsychology*. That was the most recent and complete set of ideas I published," said Zendik, looking briefly at Auld as he said this before addressing Hyle again. "It is clear from your tone what you think of my theories, Hyle. But then, answer this question—why are you here?"

From force of habit, Hyle's mouth opened, but no sound came out. He had expected Zendik to deny his past. Instead, he acknowledged it and turned the tables with his question. There were two reasons he could think of and he was hesitant to admit to either. Zendik laughed.

"You travelled all the way across the country for this meeting and now you have nothing to say? Then let me try," Zendik offered. "You want to know whether I orchestrated a global nuclear war and maybe engineered a plague as well. If I confess to these atrocities, you plan to exact revenge on behalf of the human race. You even brought a gun along with you just for such an occasion."

"No," Newman interrupted. "We came to see if you could help Sophia. Auld brought the guns. They were only in case we needed to defend ourselves. Right, Hyle?"

Still Hyle said nothing. He could feel the weight of the pistol against the small of his back and tried to block it from his thoughts.

"I know you believe that, Newman, but Hyle is driven by different motives," said Zendik. He shifted his gaze back to Hyle. "There are only two things holding him back from shooting me on the spot. He is almost sure that I'm responsible for the recent holocaust, but he can't quite figure out a motive, and like any good scientist or juror he wants to be sure beyond the shadow of a doubt, before passing judgment and performing the execution. Isn't that so, Hyle?"

Hyle fought to keep himself from trembling, unsure whether it was from awe at the accuracy of Zendik's assessment or anger from being laid open so casually. This goal had been a fantasy for so long, perhaps it was just a rush of adrenaline as the idea of killing Zendik moved from harmless theory to actual possibility.

"I can see why people call you the Prophet," he allowed. "But you mentioned two reasons."

"The second reason is right there," answered Zendik, nodding toward Sophia's chair. Hyle's eyes were drawn there involuntarily. She was slumped into the corner, head resting against one of the wings of the backrest. He had never seen her look so pale and fragile. In the flickering light he could not tell if she was resting or unconscious or—

"She is beyond the help of medicine," Zendik continued. "You don't believe in anything else, but you also don't want to admit that you are out of options. There is some part of you—some little spark deep inside you that you keep suppressed—which still hopes for a miracle. Isn't that true, Hyle?"

Hyle nodded slowly.

"I will address both your uncertainties," continued Zendik. "But let me talk not only to Hyle the scientist, but also to that part of you that still holds out hope for miracles, because I myself started with science, but ended up with miracles. My research in psychology exposed me to some remarkable studies on the brain—not just as an amazing organ on a purely biological basis. I learned about yogis who can slow and stop their heart. I read studies demonstrating that the power of prayer can decrease crime and increase the chance of conception for women who wanted children. In my own research I started to see patterns that made me think that there was more than just standard biology going on. I became very interested in parapsychology and designed a number of studies for various psychic abilities. What I found was a tiny shift in the numbers—small, but enough to convince me that there was something there."

"Then why didn't you do a more thorough study for a respectable journal?" asked Hyle. "I'm sure you know that small trends can be shown to be significant by looking at a larger sample size. Why not just expand your study and convince the scientific world instead of abandoning science and starting a cult?"

"The numbers were not only small—they were frustratingly irreproducible," Zendik explained. "In fact, the more controlled and scientific the study, generally the harder it was to find a statistical difference between the results against just random chance. It almost seemed as if the design of the experiment subtly influenced the outcome such that the more skeptical and unbiased the design, the less there was a chance of finding something."

"There could be a real obvious explanation for that," Hyle suggested.

Sophia mumbled something that sounded like "too many goats," but nobody seemed to hear her.

"Yes, there could be. But there could also be a less obvious one. I began to think about this observation and the power of prayer and belief. Was it possible that belief was responsible for this slight shift in the numbers? What if we could unlock this power somehow? What if we could tip things in our favor, ever so slightly, but consistently in everything we did? Natural selection and evolution is supposed to work on this type of slight and constant pressure. What if we could do that with belief every day? I began to have flashes of insight, scraps of illumination, glimpses of something much greater than anything we currently understand. Have you ever had a dream where you composed some wonderful song or poem or created some brilliant invention, but then woke up with only pieces of the idea? This happened to me, but I was awake."

"That sounds almost like divine revelation," observed Newman.

"Perhaps," allowed Zendik, although he seemed to leave a lot unsaid. "But I still had more questions than answers. If belief could change the odds ever so slightly, why was it limited to almost negligible effects? Why couldn't we just wish ourselves to be richer, healthier, stronger? Or wish the world to be a more perfect place?"

"You mean create Heaven on earth?" Newman asked, remembering the discussions at his first Union of Faith meetings.

"Exactly! Why not?" replied Zendik. "Inertia. That's what I realized. The ancients thought that motion was the natural state of objects in the heavens and stillness was the natural state here on earth. It was Newton who showed that inertia keeps objects in their current state—whether moving or not moving—until acted upon by an outside force. It is the same for reality. Things don't change unless they're acted upon by an outside force. That force is our belief. Sometimes the belief of just a single person can be strong enough to create a radical change, like pushing on a huge boulder that's teetering on the edge of a cliff. Sometimes the strong belief of a large group of people is insufficient, like a huge boulder resting on flat ground. Most of the time our belief has a small and almost trivial effect."

"But what creates the inertia?" asked Newman.

"Other thought and belief. And it has always been harder to create than to destroy.

Therein lies the answer to Hyle's question about why I didn't try to do a more acceptable scientific study. The very attempt would have been doomed to failure because most people would not believe it could work."

"Why not isolate a bunch of believers and then do the experiment?" asked Hyle. "If you think skepticism is somehow dampening your psychic effects, remove it from the equation."

"Isolate them where? We all share the same universe and the same reality."

"So conveniently there's no way to prove whether this power is real or not—" Hyle stopped himself as he realized the implications of what he was about to say. "—unless the skeptics themselves are eliminated."

"Now you begin to understand the difficult decision I had to make," said Zendik.

"Decision?" Hyle exclaimed. "The decision wasn't yours to make. Just because you have some crazy idea—"

The mounting tirade was silenced by the simple gesture of Zendik's upraised hand.

"Is it your decision to make to shoot me in order to avenge the human race or to protect them from whatever you think I have planned for the future? If not you, then who? Do you not feel compelled to act on knowledge that you know to be important and which you may be alone in knowing? If you would kill one person for such a vague concept as justice, would you not sacrifice a small group of people for the benefit of all?"

"We're not talking about a small group. We're talking about hundreds of millions of people. Maybe billions."

"Certainly billions," confirmed Zendik with no trace of emotion, "but only a few generations in the ongoing history of the human race, such as it is. Those lives would have ended anyway. Think a hundred years into the future, or a thousand, and those lives become an increasingly small fraction. The human race was on the wrong track." Zendik's eyes moved between Hyle and Newman, searching for understanding in their faces. "What's a few more years or decades of chasing after a bigger house or nicer car, or fighting wars over lines and colors on a map? Those lives had already been sacrificed to the false gods of technology and materialism. In trade for that is the possibility of creating a Heaven on earth, perfect and eternal."

"Who are you to think that you have the power to make that decision?" Hyle demanded.

"Who am I that you think I have already done so?" countered Zendik.

"Your followers call you the Prophet," Hyle said, "but many of them believe you're more than that. Do you claim to speak for God, or do you believe that you actually are God?"

Zendik swept the wide sleeves of his robe aside with a circular motion of his arms.

"There is much more in this universe than meets the eye, Hyle, yet I have never claimed to be anything more than what you see." He circled his fingers back to point at his chest. "I am who I am. People may choose to believe what they will."

"How would we know, Hyle?" interjected Newman. He seemed suddenly unnerved, casting sideways glances at the Prophet and taking an involuntary step backwards. "Revelation isn't always accompanied by a blinding flash of light and clap of thunder, or a heavenly choir of angels. Prophets sometimes get their revelation indirectly, and Jesus never claimed to be the Son of God. Maybe it's not something that we can know. Or dismiss."

Hyle shook his head in disbelief, clearly unwilling to even entertain the idea.

"Regardless, do you expect me to believe that destroying technology and humanism and sending us back to the Stone Age will somehow allow us to create Heaven on earth just by wishing it to be so?" Hyle asked. He looked back and forth between Zendik and Newman, no longer sure who he was addressing.

"Those who choose to believe have the power to create," replied Zendik. "The war was just the catalyst to set things in motion. The evidence is all around you already. Have you noticed a stronger connection with nature and with other people since the war? Have you had an increasing sense of déjà vu or dreams that seem to have more bearing on reality? The more people believe, the more those tiny numbers that separate belief from random chance grow. The wider that margin grows, the more people believe. We are beginning to see miracles. We are rapidly approaching a critical mass."

"That's why you planned a ceremony for this morning," Newman realized aloud. "Everyone's been speculating about a new age coming with the end of the Mayan calendar. You're tapping into that belief. It's a self-fulfilling prophecy."

The Prophet nodded, but before he could respond, Hyle spoke.

"According to your theory, if belief creates reality and people believe that you're responsible for miracles, what kind of power would that give you? Could that belief create God? Maybe you think it already has." Hyle glanced over at Newman. Playing along, trying to get into Zendik's head, the comprehension took him by surprise. Hyle suddenly understood the full breadth of Zendik's vision—a brilliantly crafted, logically consistent and self-supporting delusion that could tolerate no alternative views. "That's why you staged your own death," he concluded. "You had to bury your scientific work so that nobody else could put all the pieces together. If word got out that this was just some big psychology experiment, nobody would put their faith in you and the whole thing would collapse."

"Like the placebo effect," noted Newman.

"Now you understand my interest in you," the Prophet acknowledged, eyes darting back and forth between Hyle and Newman. "Even before the war I was having dreams about important travelers who would turn up in one of my cities. When you arrived in Asher I was aware of it, hoping that Delacroix would succeed in his task of integrating you into that community, but knowing that you were destined to journey here, destined to make the decision which now faces you. You understand my secret and the power it holds. Things are fragile now. We are at a tipping point. Join me. Help me create a paradise on earth. It is within our reach." Enhanced by his lilting accent Zendik's words were charming, as hypnotizing as ripples shining on the water, but beneath the surface sharks circled.

"We didn't come here to join you," Hyle replied, unfazed by the threat he inferred.

"Why not?" Newman interjected. "He's talking about helping to create a perfect world. Why wouldn't you want to be a part of that?"

"First of all, I liked the world the way it was, imperfections and all. Second, I understand this whole concept of manipulating reality, but that doesn't mean I believe it."

"Hyle, remember the prophecy from Asher about the three travelers? Magister Delacroix was afraid that you two would leave together and you'd meet a third traveler. I was hoping to prevent that prophecy from coming true, but now it's clear that I'm the third traveler. If the Prophet foresaw this months ago, what else has he seen that we don't yet understand?"

"Fine," said Hyle, "believe in the prophecy if you like, but how can you condone killing millions of innocent people? Have you forgotten about that?"

"Maybe it was God's will," Newman suggested.

"Then maybe I don't like God's will."

"Maybe all these events are necessary to bring humanity into a new era," insisted Newman. "Open your mind to the possibility, Hyle. There's much more going on here than we can explain otherwise." He paused and looked over at the armchair. "I wish Sophia were better. She'd convince you. She understood this whole theory of collective solipsism better than any of us, and she was having exactly the precognitive dreams we were just talking about."

With an expression of slowly growing comprehension, the Prophet shifted his attention to Sophia, as if noticing her for the first time, slumped and pale in the armchair, and then to Auld, whose shining eyes and broad grin seemed to anticipate a punch line about to be revealed, and his look of comprehension changed to one of betrayal. Perhaps feeling the focus of intention upon her, Sophia spoke.

"Pay no attention," she said, her eyes still closed and words slurring together, "to the man behind the curtain."

Newman and Hyle were so intent on Sophia that they failed to notice the Prophet's expression shift one more time to one of panic. Unobserved, he rummaged around behind the stacks of books on his desk, opening a brass bound wooden chest, and withdrawing a small pistol. The crack of the gunshot shook the room, rattling glass in the curio cabinets before giving way to a ponderous silence. A dark hole ringed with crimson appeared in the shirt over Sophia's abdomen.

《《《 》》》

Until the moment Zendik entered the room, Sophia had been losing her struggle to remain conscious. His presence was just intriguing enough to tip the balance in her favor a little longer, but she was unable to focus on his words. Instead, she found herself captivated by his accent and the beautiful way it shaped each syllable, stringing one after another into words, and words into sentences. Too weak to open her eyes, she pictured the arm of her chair where fibers twisted into threads, woven together to form a rose.

No longer able to hold on, Sophia felt the world slipping away. She knew that she was dying, but the realization bothered her far less than she had expected. Her mind fractured. Instead of fading into darkness, she entered a strange state between consciousness and dreaming where sensations, memories and imagination ran in parallel, mixing freely, her conscious mind flitting in and out among them, observing, analyzing, commenting, and then disappearing, only to appear somewhere else. It was very much like lucid dreaming, she realized in a burst of conscious thought, retaining some ability to think but no longer able to control the direction—or directions—that her thoughts took.

The sequence of her life streamed by. Even as it did, her mind noted the cliché with amusement, and then became annoyed with itself for wasting precious time on such a trivial analysis. Yet another fraction of her mind observed this self-conscious exchange with amusement. As Sophia listened to Zendik discuss the importance of names, scattered scenes from her childhood played in the background, blending together with the perspective of adult hindsight to create a parable about the indomitability of the individual spirit against the pressures of society. This gave way to memories of her bright college years, when every idea was fresh and important and the answers to all life's questions seemed to be just around the corner.

She felt a twinge of regret, for years past, lives lost, and the destruction of the school, but in this flood of reminiscence time moved too quickly for mourning. She saw herself at the ad agency next, rising through the ranks with an instinct for what people—her clients and their clientele—wanted to hear. A word popped into her head, and in her imagination she heard it in a scolding German accent. *Bestand* the accusing voice said. You gave up on your quest to understand people, it seemed to tell her in that single word. You chose to treat them as means to an end and in so doing, you also gave up on yourself.

Had she wasted her life? What was the point? It was a natural thing to wonder at the end of the story. Back in Asher she had not considered herself to be one of those people who needed to be saved from greed and materialism. Those things had never been her motivations. Success had come naturally, almost accidentally, but had she perhaps allowed it to lull her into complacency? Had she let herself fall into just that type of life the world expected her to lead? The discussions with Newman and Hyle had rekindled her passion for philosophy, but had she been using it just a as a mental escape?

Even as she considered the complexity of the rose, the complexity of her own life, and in parallel lost herself in the subtle tones of the Prophet's voice, a third fragment of her mind still managed to follow the conversation between Hyle and the Prophet. Without hearing discrete words, she not only absorbed the meaning of the dialog, but also understood the thoughts and emotions of the speakers, as if their raw intentions radiated through the room, directly into her mind. Zendik was explaining why he was unable to demonstrate his theory in a controlled experiment, and there was a subtle desperation in his effort to penetrate the fortress of Hyle's skepticism. Sophia identified the problem immediately. From one corner of her mind she tried to explain to Hyle the sheep-goat effect. She saw Helena, sitting cross-legged on her futon, smiling, but could not tell if Hyle had heard what she said.

"You have a philosophy for every occasion," he said, rounding on her, "but do you actually believe anything for yourself?"

The question took her by surprise before she realized that, like Helena, this was just a memory. It had been invoked by her reflections on the purpose of her life, and she recalled John Dewey's theory of the spectatorial view of philosophy. She was always in the bleachers. Always analyzing, drawing parallels—just like now. Never on the field. Never in the game. But what did that mean? What did it take to jump down onto the field?

Zendik was talking about flashes of insight and inspiration, and Sophia's mind jumped to the bonfire at midnight. *Weave a circle round him thrice and close your eyes with holy dread, for he on honey-dew hath fed and drunk the milk of Paradise.* No less than Augustine and Al-Farabi had rejected the idea of a separate heaven in favor of something more like Buddhist enlightenment. Was that what Zendik had glimpsed? She pictured shadows on the cave wall. It was a beautiful metaphor, but could she really bring herself to believe that nothing physical was real? Religion told her yes. Science told her no. After two and a half millennia, philosophy seemed to throw up its hands in despair.

An epistemological debate erupted in Sophia's mind, touched off by William James whispering to her in the voice of pragmatism and fueled by visions of her discussions with Newman and Hyle. Given two unprovable alternatives, which one would give her life more meaning? She recalled Pascal's Wager. It skewed the balance, yet choosing between two uncertainties was not sufficient. Kierkegaard wanted her to take the leap of faith, but Nietzsche warned her that God was dead. Maybe there is no conflict, Spinoza argued, since the material and rational are just two ways of looking at the same thing. The path up the mountain is the path down the mountain, Heraclitus agreed. But Descartes seemed to slice this unity apart, separating empiricism from rationalism so thoroughly that they could never be reconciled, leaving Locke and Leibniz to quarrel about which side was real and which illusion. Just as the success of Newton and modern science seemed to win the day for empiricism, Berkeley called into question the very concept of a material world, only to be outdone by Hume, who concluded that fundamental ideas like cause and effect and even the concept of the self were nothing more than convenient habits of the mind. Kant's attempted compromise based on innate categories of understanding was undermined by relativity, which demonstrated that time and space, two of Kant's most fundamental categories, were not such solid ground after all. Everything led to uncertainty. Analytical philosophy, undertaken by Russell and his colleagues to ground math and science, the hallowed ground of empiricism, on a logical foundation, had instead called the sanctity of logic into question. Gödel had demonstrated its limits using logic against itself. Were we nothing more than biological machines, sophisticated computers, destined to be limited in our own self-knowledge?

To believe this would not only cede the possibility of ultimate knowledge, but the possibility of free will as well. Quantum physics and relativity opened a strange new world of science, but offered nothing to break the deadlock. Kuhn argued that science moved in paradigms, and Sophia wondered if that was not true of all human thought. She thought of Hegel's *zeitgeist* and her own argument about the great eras of human understanding. Thesis, antithesis, and synthesis. Was it possible that everything could be resolved in a new paradigm?

To have free will we would all need to be prime movers, she heard Hyle argue. I'd say we're ready for a paradigm shift any time, Newman replied, when light is a wave and a particle and cats can be alive and dead. What if all the divisions were artificial? Mind and body, rationalism and empiricism, science and religion, Apollo and Dionysus, God and Satan, free will and determinism, synthetic and analytical, wave and particle, even alive and dead—what if they were all illusory? Do we create our own reality? Do we participate in the symbols that we create? Atman is Brahman.

As the philosophical debate neared its apotheosis, Sophia felt Zendik's attention suddenly shift to her. Newman had just said something about precognitive dreaming. As if she and Zendik shared the same splintered mind, she sensed that he was suddenly aware of her thoughts, and she felt his concern swell into panic and then into rage. She was so close to understanding that she experienced her own twinge of panic that her dawning insight would be lost in the distraction.

"Pay no attention to the man behind the curtain," she said to the Zendik in her head, even as she reached for the curtain to pull it aside.

She realized, with the highest virtue of detached disinterest, that she had been shot, severing any last connection she had with her body. She felt weightless, limitless, aware of every sound and sight, every thought and motion in the room, sensing everything from all directions at once and yet unconcerned even as Zendik raised his pistol a second time.

The material world is part of our language, Sophia realized, but it is no more inherently real than the universals of the realists. The limits of our language are the limits of our world, but a limited language can be fully understood in the context of a higher level meta-language. Geist coming to know itself through the individual human experience. Man creating God in his own image, the imperfect demiurge of an imperfect world. Consciousness as the final force of physics. She stared into the space between the two faces, looking for the candlestick. And then, in a burst of light, she *understood*.

«« »»

As soon as he realized that Sophia had been shot, something primal took over inside Hyle. Without fully understanding what he was doing, he grabbed the gun from the small of his back, swung it around and fired. Zendik looked down at his chest, then across the room, his eyes filled with surprise and pain—pain not from the physical wound, which spread slowly in a rough circle of crimson across his chest, but instead a torment of loss and despair, of watching things unravel and spin away, just out of his reach, like an artist watching the labor of his life tossed casually into the fire, the curling edges of the canvas enfolded in flame, the images blistering and peeling as he looks on. Swaying, his gun arm dropping momentarily, Zendik gathered himself, focusing his will, hurling his entire essence into a single word, as if this one syllable could change the path of history and reforge all of creation.

"No," he gasped, leveling the pistol again, his sapphire eyes locked on the oblivious Sophia, at once addressing her and the universe. He squeezed the trigger.

In the space between the gunshots Auld, grinning like a madman on fire, crossed the center of the room in a single stride and launched himself across the desk, one hand reaching for something at his belt, the other outstretched to seize the Prophet by his head and shoulders. An explosion shook the room, shattering glass, blowing Hyle and Newman off their feet, sending Sophia's chair somersaulting backwards, the intensity of its force obliterating any memory of gunfire and all that came before. A blinding white flash of light burned retinas, the thunder of the explosion deadened eardrums, and the acrid odor of smoke choked mouths and nostrils leaving intact only the sense of touch.

Newman lifted his head experimentally. The pressure against the back of his skull disappeared. With the impression that he had succeeded in moving, he rolled over and pushed himself up to hands and knees. Coughing the smoke from his lungs, his mouth performed the action of calling for his companions, but he could hear nothing beyond the static hiss of white noise. He crawled forward, sweeping the floor ahead with one hand, pushing aside debris, until he came to a wall. Bracing against it, Newman pulled himself up to a standing position and balanced carefully on his feet, only then realizing that elevation was useless without the benefit of sight and slumping back down against the wall.

After a similar experience Hyle, blinded and deafened, feeling his way across the floor, stopped when suddenly his hand failed to find anything at all. Carefully he leaned forward, moving his hand down and in toward his body until his wrist caught on the jagged end of a broken floorboard. He explored the edge of the hole, just inches ahead of the hand that bore his weight, feeling as far in both directions as he could manage without moving his legs. He was just beginning to believe that he could discriminate the motion of his hands against the black opening when he felt a hand on his shoulder, pulling him backwards, and sensed more than heard a voice speaking into his ear.

As their senses recovered, Newman and Hyle found themselves standing in what remained of the Prophet's office. A haze filled the room, the individual particles catching the firelight and drifting aimlessly, slowly yielding to gravity. With the exception of the glass in the cabinet doors and a few pictures that had been knocked down, the walls were remarkably intact. All but extinguished by the blast, the fire on the hearth was struggling to come back, flames growing and casting an increasing light across the room, assisted by small patches of flames from burning books and papers scattered around the floor. The desk was missing, and the floor had been blown away where it, and the Prophet, had stood.

"He must have dropped a grenade," Hyle guessed, barely able to hear his own voice as he yelled. "The desk probably saved us."

There was no sign of Zendik or of Auld. Newman edged toward the hole, called out and, hearing nothing, dropped a skeleton key into the darkness. No sound of impact returned. Standing by the door, Sophia watched as their shadows danced on the far wall in the light of the fire behind them, waiting for them to finish their investigation.

"They're gone," she said. "Come. It's time to leave."

She seemed to be stable on her feet Hyle noticed, and he attributed this partly to adrenaline and partly to good fortune because, judging from the position of the bloodstain-ringed hole in her shirt, the gunshot wound had actually grazed her side.

Outside, two guards in dark gray military uniforms took position, one providing cover from a short distance away down the corridor while the other, cradling an assault rifle against his shoulder with one hand, reached for the door handle with the other. Caught off guard, he leapt backwards when the door opened and swung his weapon around. Stepping calmly through the threshold and ignoring the guard's command to stop, Sophia closed the gap between them and placed her palm gently on the end of the rifle.

"It's over. Put your weapons down," she said, pushing the barrel aside.

Realizing he had been suppressing the thought that he might never hear Sophia's voice again, Newman appreciated for the first time how beautiful it sounded. Sophia spoke with confidence, as if their compliance was a foregone conclusion, and amazingly it worked. Abandoning protocol, both guards approached the doorway, weapons lowered and backs turned to the trio. Once they had entered the room, Sophia led Newman and Hyle quickly down the corridor, rounding the corner before shouting erupted from the Prophet's chamber. As the complex came alive with the sound of yelling and clanging bells, they retraced their steps, rapidly navigating through the maze of hallways to the stairwell and down to the warehouse without encountering anyone. The two men followed Sophia, Hyle marveling at their good fortune and at the fact that Sophia seemed to share Auld's uncanny sense of direction, Newman trying to scratch at something that was tickling the back of his mind. He was sure that there was something different about Sophia other than her regained vitality, but in the haste of fleeing the compound and the poor flickering lamplight he was unable to put his finger on it before they entered the darkness of the warehouse.

Taking them each by the hand, Sophia led Hyle and Newman across the pitch black warehouse and back up through the series of caves and tunnels to the surface. Outside the world was on the verge of a new day. The sun had not yet appeared, but light issued from a narrow band of purple along the distant horizon, dim yet sufficient to send them blinking out of the darkness. A spotted owl, perched on the spiny bush at the mouth of the chasm regarded them warily as they emerged. Spreading its wings, it dropped into flight down the side of the mountain and disappeared into the shadows.

"It's almost sunrise," observed Newman in a reverent whisper.

"Twilight," Sophia amended. "The time between light and darkness. Or darkness and light.

Hyle began to say something, but she hushed him.

"Just watch," she said, taking his hand. She reached out to Newman on the other side and took his hand too.

The earth seemed to hold its breath as the purple band of light widened and brightened and the top of the sun broke over the distant mountains. Even behind the veil of smog it was a majestic event, the giant circle of red ascending with surprising speed, clearing the horizon only minutes after first appearing. Each awed by the sunrise in their own way, the three travelers watched in silence, Sophia still staring, mesmerized as the gap between the sun and horizon grew. Shaking free of the spell but not yet willing to break the silence, the two men looked on as the panorama slowly transformed. The rust colored fog around the sun thinned, dissipating as if melted by the sunlight.

As the haze retreated to reveal an expanding arc of pale blue sky, they stood there watching, hand in hand—Hyle, Newman, and between them Sophia Xiao, her long auburn hair shimmering in the brilliant morning sun.

Made in the USA
Middletown, DE
26 March 2019